To A Wonderful
Husband.
Happy Birthday
All my love
Pamela
xxx
March 1985

DREAM WEST

DREAM WEST

David Nevin

NEW ENGLISH LIBRARY

First published in the United States of America by
G. P. Putnam's Sons in 1983

First published in Great Britain in 1984 by
New English Library, Mill Road, Dunton Green,
Sevenoaks, Kent.
Editorial office: 47 Bedford Square, London WC1B 3DP.

Printed in Great Britain by
St Edmundsbury Press, Bury St Edmunds, Suffolk.

British Library Cataloguing in Publication Data

Nevin, David
Dream West.
I. Title
813′.54[F] PS3564.E853

ISBN 0 450 06078 0

ACKNOWLEDGMENTS

Dream West is a novel but readers will see immediately that it is firmly grounded on the facts of John Charles and Jessie Benton Frémont's vivid lives and on the history of the United States in the mid–Nineteenth Century. The book has been more than eight years in preparation and I owe much for the help I have received.

The largest debt is to my talented wife, Luciana Colla Nevin, who took part in every phase of the book but the actual writing. She shouldered much of the research burden and she worked with me day by day on concept, character, scene development and meaning. She served as first reader and her comments were an integral part of the passage toward final copy. She typed manuscript several times with a critical eye for inconsistencies and missteps. She was always willing and never complained and her perceptions, criticisms and insights are ingrained in the book.

For several years we were privileged to hold a research desk at the Library of Congress which we manned together. A desk and a stack pass in that magnificent institution give one the world. Many people there were kind to us, but year in and year out Bruce Martin, Research Facilities Officer, made possible the fullest use of the resources.

Other institutions also gave us much kindly assistance. Paul Janiczek of the U.S. Naval Observatory in Washington, D.C., helped us grasp the relationship of stars and mapping as practiced by Frémont and Nicollet. Perry Fisher and Elizabeth Miller made possible several months of study in the Columbia Historical Society's collections on early Washington, D.C. Virginia Renner made us welcome at the Huntington Library at San Marino, California, where everyone we met seemed eager to help us use the Frémont Collection. Ruth M. Christensen and Glenna Schroeder opened the Frémont Collection at the Southwest Museum in Los Angeles. At the Bancroft Library at the University of California at Berkekey, the main repository of Frémont papers, Robert Becker and other staff members helped us through both the Frémont and extensive early California collections. Professor Donald Jackson, editor with Mary Lee Spence of *The Expeditions of*

John Charles Frémont, which the University of Illinois Press is issuing, graciously advised me on the problems in following Frémont's expedition routes. James R. Bentley searched the collections of the Filson Club in Louisville.

Finally, I owe special thanks to Frank Tortorich of Jackson, California, historian of the Eldorado National Forest, for different and most exciting research into the High Sierra in the dead of winter. At some 10,000 feet, with the cold a palpable and malevolent force, he and I strapped on snowshoes and started across the same vast, open snowfields that Frémont and his men had traveled so painfully a century before. Tortorich proved to be a talented guide to the flora and fauna of the High Sierra and to the nature of life in snow so deep that it bears little relation to the ground beneath it. Those unforgettable days were essential to my feeling for the inner meaning of all Frémont's challenges to the mountains in winter.

D.N.

For Luciana

CONTENTS

PART ONE

15

PRAIRIE

THEY PASSED INTO A SHALLOW DRAW with saddle leather creaking, and were letting the horses drink when an antelope with high pronged horns burst from a wild-cherry copse. Not ten yards away it stopped and stood motionless, gazing at them with eager curiosity, its head thrust forward, its round black eyes brazen and bright. The frozen moment, the animal tight as a quivering spring, struck Frémont like a vision. He saw a vein throbbing in its white neck and he felt his own heart in cadence. Then the antelope sprang sideways and was off, sailing over the prairie like a low-flying bird.

"We'll see buffler soon," Louison Freniere said. "Antelope are always bold when buffler are about. Beyond that ridge, I wouldn't doubt."

Buffalo. Ahead the ground rose in a steady sweep to a long dominating ridge a half-mile distant. Frémont stared at it; his pulse had not slowed and he smiled.

Both men were well mounted and each led a fresh horse already saddled for the chase. They passed a prairie-dog village where hundreds of the little yellow animals stood yelping at them, their short tails jerking with each cry. A gray owl with white-ringed eyes gazed imperturbably at Frémont from a borrowed mound. It looked strangely calm.

"Yes," Louie said, almost to himself, "I can feel 'em." He glanced at Frémont. "You'll be on your own then, Charlie. Pick you a cow and hold to her—you've got to run that horse like you was running on your own two legs. Never mind the breaks and draws and them damned prairie-dog holes. Think you can cut yourself loose like that?"

"I'm ready," Frémont said. He took a deep breath. Ever since St. Louis, all the way up the Missouri to Fort Pierre on the fur company steamboat and out across the wide open country of the Dakota Sioux, he had been waiting for his first sight of the legendary herds that blackened the land. Buffalo—Freniere and the others on the expedition seemed to think of nothing but that thundering sport and princely food of the plains. It was dangerous—the galloping horse was half blind in the dust, and if you fell, likely you'd be trampled or gored—but the danger was half the fun.

"Hell," Freniere said, "you ain't *never* ready for buffler till you come up on 'em." He was half-coaching, half-challenging. "You've got to *run,* understand? Horse is faster, sure, but a buffler can run all day, run the best horse right into the ground. Slap leather once and there goes your chance."

On the first day out Freniere, himself a magnificent horseman, had caught Frémont grabbing for the big Spanish horn on his saddle and he never let him forget it. But Frémont had learned a lot in ten days. Now Louie was sitting slouched in his saddle, throwing quick glances at Frémont and talking in bursts.

"Horse is no fool, you know. And he don't really give a damn if you get a buffler or not—*he* ain't going to eat none of it. He'll take you up and give you your shot, but he's sure as hell got to know you really want to go. It ain't no time to tuck your butt."

"Tuck my butt?" Frémont said, suddenly nettled. "The day you see me tuck my butt, you can have my gold watch and pistols." He wondered if he sounded hollow.

"Well, you ain't never gone after buffler before," the hunter replied. He grinned, wolfish and keen, and Frémont saw that he was nervous, too.

It was coming on noon and the sun was high in a white sky. Light burned over the ridge and pressed down against Frémont's eyes until they ached. He tugged his hat brim low; he could see mile after mile of endless, unmarked prairie, rolling like a troubled sea. High overhead an eagle circled on motionless wings, a speck in the vaulting sky. It was a land to set a man free. . . .

They were halfway up the long slope. Grass grew in tufts and clumps, gray-green and stunted but strong enough to keep a horse going forever. Little puffs of dust rose under the horses' hooves and blew instantly away. The dry air made the wind feel cool, but a trickle of sweat formed under one of Frémont's arms and ran down his side. Louie, staring ahead, had lapsed into silence. His brass-bound rifle lay across the pommel of his saddle and unconsciously the web of his hand fitted itself to the hammer, ready to draw it down on cock.

Louie was about Frémont's age, maybe twenty-five, a lean, tall man, dark face burned darker by the open, long black hair falling to his shoulders. Once Frémont had asked him why he didn't cut it. "What," he said, "and break the hearts of half the girls in St. Louis? It's right purty, Charlie, when it's combed out, and there's no shortage of belles who want to comb it." He was wearing blue homespun trousers over rough boots and a buckskin smock belted at the waist. It was nearly black with age and grease and was molded to his shape. Most of the fringed whangs that might once have shed water in the rain were gone.

It was nothing like the gorgeous suit Freniere had worn the day Frémont joined the expedition in St. Louis. That suit was of buckskin too, but clean, soft as glove leather, worked until it was almost white. Its whangs were all intact, rippling a full six inches, and the shirt and matching moccasins were brilliant with red-dyed porcupine quills and the beadwork of the northern Sioux. Some patient woman far up the Cheyenne River had made it—and doubtless given Freniere her heart as well. . . .

17

It had been sunny and warm in St. Louis on that day in early May. They had been lounging in front of Pierre Chouteau's American Fur Company, where the expedition was outfitting. These warehouses of gray stone had supplied the western fur trade for three decades, but now the compound just off the levee was quiet. The men had assembled for a final muster and Frémont, who had arrived so late from Washington he'd nearly missed the expedition, was getting acquainted.

"They got buffler in the Smoky Mountains, Lieutenant?" Louie had asked. Frémont had been on two surveying expeditions into the western Carolinas and considered himself a woodsman. But no, no buffalo.

"I figured not," Freniere had said. "Well, you got a treat in store for you, I'll say that. Buffler is the biggest, fastest, god*damnedest* animal in the whole world, bar absolutely none. I'll put it up against elephants in India for wonder and Spanish bull for power—"

"Grizzly is the baddest," a swarthy man named Martineau had said.

"That's right, and buffler is the best. He's like a king, d'ye see, he's a challenge: it takes a *man* to ride him down and stop him. 'Course they're easy enough to kill by creeping up on 'em, but hell, that's like sleeping with a woman in a bundling bed—it ain't near the fun it might be."

"God almighty, yes," the heavyset Bladon had said with an explosive laugh. He had a kinky black beard. "I spent a night in one of them years ago. Give me the stone ache for a week."

"And eating," Freniere had said, ignoring Bladon, "why you just ain't et till you've had buffler roasted on a prairie fire, a few chips tossed on the coals for seasoning. Fat cow makes beef taste like putty."

"God's truth, Lieutenant," Martineau had said. "Buffler will spoil any other meat in the world for you."

The office door had opened then and Mr. Nicollet came out. Frémont had reported to him upon arrival the night before. Nicollet was a Frenchman who had come to America eight years before, in 1832, to explore the frontier; he'd been much taken by Frémont's own French heritage and his command of the language. St. Louis, though American for nearly four decades, still felt itself a French city, and most of the men on the expedition were *voyageurs* from the old French fur trade on the northern lakes, as accustomed to the canoe as the saddle.

"Gentlemen," Nicollet had said, smiling, and the men had fallen silent. The astronomer was in his early fifties and his hair was iron gray, though still thick. Frémont thought his eyes looked tired. His manner was gentle and the men had started to call him Papa Joe.

"All's ready, then," he'd said in a voice that sounded short of breath. "There'll be nineteen of us and we'll draw our livestock at Fort Pierre. The *Antelope* starts up the Missouri at dawn and every man had better be aboard. You're free tonight to wind up your business here—just make sure you don't wind yourselves so tight you miss the boat."

Louie had winked at Frémont.

"Any of you who haven't met Mr. Frémont should do so," Nicollet went on. "John Charles Frémont, Second Lieutenant, Corps of Topographical Engineers, United States Army. As you know, the expedition is under the auspices of the Army, which is reimbursing the American Fur Company for costs. Mr. Frémont is the Army's official representative. He'll serve as second-in-command and will assist me in the scientific side of the expedition."

He paused, looking from face to face. "Bear in mind that the whole purpose—the *only* purpose—of this venture is to map the great stretch of terrain lying between the headwaters of the Missouri and the Mississippi. We'll take six months, all told: here to Fort Pierre and across to Fort Snelling on the upper Mississippi, and we'll be back in late October—well, say early November. Now, let me say again that there never has been a map made anywhere in America—or, I venture to say, anywhere in the world—of the quality and the particularity which we will achieve, nor one which employs the scientific methods we will use. So I'm counting on every one to do whatever may be necessary to make this achievement possible."

He had nodded to a dour man with searching black eyes. "You know Mr. Provost—he'll serve as camp conductor and will be responsible for keeping us moving in good order day by day." Hearing the name, Frémont had glanced quickly at Provost, who returned the look without expression. Etienne Provost was a famous name on the frontier. Frémont judged him to be about Nicollet's age, but he looked harder. He was a mountain man and had trapped with Jim Bridger and ridden with Jedediah Smith; he had fought at Pierre's Hole and year by year he'd brought his beaver down to the great rendezvous on the Siskadee. . . .

"And our friend Louison Freniere," Nicollet said with a smile, glancing at the man in the glorious buckskins, "has signed on as a hunter and will keep us in meat."

"We won't have no food problems, Papa Joe," one of the men called. "Buffler sees Freniere in his fancy suit and he'll drop dead of shock."

Freniere grinned and lifted the rifle he carried. "Never you fear, boys. If the suit don't get 'em, my old Hawken will." Made there in St. Louis with an octagonal barrel of soft rolled iron, brass-bound to a cherrywood half-stock, muzzle-loaded and fired with the new-style caps that were putting flintlocks out of business, the Hawken was as fine a rifle as you could buy in the world. It had cost a full forty dollars and all the way from St. Louis across the great northern prairie, Frémont noticed that the hunter watched over it as he might have a woman. Nicollet had instructed Frémont to spend his days with Louie and learn the feel of the land, and Freniere had promised to make him a hunter as well.

Now, as the two horsemen neared the crest of the long, dominating ridge, Freniere's hand still rested on the Hawken's well-blued hammer, Since challenging Frémont he had ridden in absorbed silence, his hat pulled low, ignoring the immensity of land around them. He reined up and dismounted, glancing ahead at the glare-struck sky, and dropped a slender rawhide loop over his horse's head.

"Don't never pay to top a ridge like you owned it," he said quietly. "Never know who's watching beyond. We'll walk up for a peep and see what we see."

At the crest he crouched and then flattened and crawled forward.

Frémont followed, elbows grinding in white dust, the smell of sun-warmed sage astringent in the air. A stinging gnat lighted on his face and he flicked it away. Louie stopped moving and together they looked down into a vast bowl of open country. It dwindled to blue haze in the distance and in between it was rolling and broken, tawny-colored and gray-green with bunch grass and sage, and there were dark patches on it like timber where timber didn't belong.

"What'd I tell you?" Freniere said softly. The patches were buffalo grazing, fifty or seventy to a herd, and there must have been fifty herds. He nudged him and jerked his head and Frémont looked to the left. There, just below the crest, much closer than the others, was a herd of nearly a hundred. A huge old bull was in command. The wind was blowing across the animals and no man scent reached them. They were moving slowly to the right, feeding as they went, making a constant grunting noise that Frémont realized he'd been hearing since he first looked. A pair of gray wolves skulked behind them, hungry and disconsolate. The old bull, though unalarmed, was watching the wolves. Frémont realized his hands were trembling slightly.

"Boys'll be happy tonight," Louie muttered. They had found no game but antelope and the men were grumbling. They hobbled the two horses they had ridden all morning and took their fresh mounts. Frémont's runner was a big bay with white stockings, an intelligent, good-natured beast named Barney who worked without complaint. The girth was loose and Frémont cinched it tight, bracing with his knee. He checked the cap on his stubby plains rifle and examined the .50-caliber pistol he carried in his belt.

Louie swung to the left so that they topped the ridge behind the herd and started toward it. Frémont seized a breath. His lungs were not working quite right. The old bull saw them against the sky and threw up his head and bellowed. The herd lurched into a sudden gallop and the bull turned to meet the horsemen, head down, snorting and pawing the ground.

"Hi-yah!" Freniere yelled and his horse leaped away and Barney tilted into a gallop as if he were spring-loaded. The bull was not at all intimidated but when the last of the herd passed him, spreading and moving faster, he turned and followed, bellowing threateningly. The horses separated and Frémont forgot about Louie, for he had fixed on a cow. He gave Barney his head, reins high and spurs hard in his ribs. The cow could hear the horse behind her and she stretched into a dead run, but Barney had fixed on her too, and he was closing the distance.

Thunder filled the air, the horse's hooves on the hard ground, the herd drumming in full gallop, cows bawling in anger and fear. Dimly Frémont heard the bull's rumbling bellow and a calf's piercing squall and his own loud voice. The cow galloped head down, throwing up clots of dirt, and dust clouds blotted out the other animals and stung his eyes. The horse was gaining and Frémont crouched forward, part of its flexing motion, reins in his left hand, rifle in his right, shouting encouragement. Another cow, a calf at her flank, blundered out of the dust on their left and Barney shied to the right as the strange cow reared backwards. Then Barney loosed a new surge of speed and closed with the cow, just behind her right shoulder, just where he belonged.

So close, she was stunning. Frémont had never seen an animal as awesome. Her hump was as high as his waist as he sat his horse. Her shaggy hair was matted, tawny-colored on her forequarters tapering off to black-brown on her rump, winter hair coming off in ragged clumps. Her little horns were polished hooks, her eyes shot with blood, her mouth open, tongue out, streamers of foam whipping behind her.

Staring at the great brute size of her, the horse matching stride for stride, the wind crashing in his ears, his own voice howling and wordless, he knew now what they meant by the sheer joy of the buffalo run. She cut sideways into a small draw, seeking its brushy cover, and Barney turned hard behind her. They crashed through low brush and Frémont heard it cracking under the horse. He felt Barney shift and twist as if he were dancing and he caught a glimpse of hole-pocked ground beneath him, but his mind hardly registered its meaning. The cow glanced over her shoulder, her bloody eyes glaring. Her big head rolled and she hooked a horn at the horse's chest. In mid-stride Barney sprang sideways. Frémont lurched against the animal's neck and his left foot lost the stirrup. The rifle slipped and he clutched it frantically against Barney's wet flank and regained his grip. Cursing, he grabbed the saddle horn with his rein hand and that snapped the horse's head back and checked him and threw Frémont forward again. He loosed the reins, fumbled his foot back into the stirrup, found his seat and rammed spurs into Barney's ribs.

They closed again and Frémont dropped the reins and brought the rifle to his shoulder. He half-stood in the stirrups and the horse, confused by the signals, checked again. Before Frémont could fire he was thrown forward and he grabbed up the reins. Sweat ran in his eyes and blinded him, but his hands were full of reins and rifle and in a moment he forgot the burning. The big horse felt him take control and burst forward. The cow hooked at him and canted off in a new direction and Barney cut after her and closed again. Now, holding the reins in his left hand, clasping the horse with his knees, Frémont rested the rifle on his left forearm and fired at two-foot range. Two hundred grains of powder exploded and drove a slug the size of his thumb into the cow's side. She grunted but her stride didn't break. Frémont stared at her. It was like an apparition. He had hit her a killing stroke and she wasn't going to fall—she wasn't even going to stop running.

He knew he never could get powder and slug down the muzzle on the gallop—never mind the easy way Freniere had described the trick—and he thrust the rifle into its boot and drew his pistol, thumbing back the hammer.

The pistol was his weapon. He was in good control, reins in his left hand, crowding Barney against the cow, pistol aimed across his left elbow, drawing a killing bead—when the horse dropped out from under him and he pitched forward, flying, falling. He heard Barney grunt as its chest struck the ground, and he threw up his left arm and landed on his face, sliding and rolling. The pistol fired and flew out of his hand. He lay there a moment, ears ringing, eyes closed on darkness, oddly conscious of a bitter yet clean grassy odor, and then he lifted his head and saw his cow disappear in the brilliant sunlight, her stride still unbroken. A half-dozen cows thundered by, hooves pelting his face with dirt, and a young spike bull leaped directly over him, a sudden dark bulk overhead and gone, showing no interest in attacking him.

Then the herd was past and he was conscious of the quiet; he heard hoofbeats drumming down, fading in the distance. Gingerly he moved his arms and shoulders and felt his neck and decided nothing was broken. He was still half-stunned and thought he might vomit. Then he discovered the source of the odor. He had landed in wet buffalo dung; it was in his hair and smeared on his face. He wiped it from around his eyes. Barney struggled to his feet and stood heaving for breath by the grass-filled little gully that had thrown him.

He heard hooves and turned to see Louie riding up with a look of concern. It occurred to Frémont that he was lucky to be alive. He wiped his face. This damned dung was all over him. He had a savage headache, but the ringing in his ears faded and he became aware of a new noise. The hunter was sitting his horse and laughing out loud. Sudden rage filled him. Missed his cow, fell off his horse like a damned fool—

"Goddamnit!" he said, glaring at Freniere, his fists balling unconsciously. His throat was raw.

Freniere's smile faded and he took on a wary, thoughtful look. He waited a moment and then said softly, "You been bathing in shit for some reason, Charlie?"

Frémont looked at Louie, and then he began to laugh.

"Life's little blessings,"he said. "It broke my fall."

The hunter nodded and his smile returned. "You get a shot off?"

"Might as well have thrown a stone. She took that slug and never slowed down. I couldn't believe it." He ran his hands along Barney's legs. There were tender spots, but not the real pain that would mean broken bones. The horse was streaked with lather. His muscles were quivering. Frémont loosened the saddle and girth and pulled bunches of dry grass and began scrubbing him down, drying him and working his muscles. Barney sighed and gave several little snorts.

"Ran off her ribs, I expect," Freniere said. "If you don't hit 'em in the lungs or the spine, you won't get 'em. It's funny, the buffler's so big and that vital spot so small. Did you aim on that spot, like I told you?"

"Aim? I was lucky to get a shot off."

"Never knew a man to get a buffler first try. I run seven cows before I brought one down."

Seven? Suddenly Frémont felt good. By God, he had run the buffalo and it was true, there was nothing else like it on earth. And this land was full of them and he would run another tomorrow and the next day and the next, and damned if it would take *him* seven runs before he stopped one!

He let Barney graze a few minutes and then he tightened the girth and they rode together to Freniere's kill. The two wolves were making a cautious approach. Freniere rushed them and they whirled and ran, their brushes tucked. They stopped a little way off, sat on their haunches and watched.

The cow lay on her side, blood still dribbling from her mouth. Gouts of it stained the ground around her. Grunting, Frémont helped Freniere roll her onto her chest, hindquarters cramped beneath her, forelegs spread and cradling her head. She looked as if she were asleep. She was huge. The top of her hump was level with his shoulder even when she was flat.

Freniere drew the long butcher knife he carried in a scabbard at the small of his back and sliced out her tongue with a steady, sawing stroke. Leaning against her rough hair, he made a long incision down her spine and laid the skin to one side like a table to hold his cuts. He began to butcher, explaining as he went along. He took the boss, that little hump on the back of her neck, and then the hump itself and what he called the hump ribs, which Frémont saw was a sort of extended vertebrae that supported the hump. He took the fleece—a rich strand of ungrained flesh between the spine and the ribs that was covered with a three-inch layer of fat. He laid the pieces carefully on the folded skin.

"Oh," he said, straightening his back, "but this is a fat 'un. That fleece fat there'll make your face shine with gladness."

He unhooked a tin cup from his belt, lifted the massive head, rested it on his shoulder and cut the throat. Foaming blood poured out and he thrust the cup into the stream. When it was full he held it up, took a swallow and shoved it at Frémont.

"Drink that, Charlie," he said. "It'll make you a true son of the plains."

Frémont took the cup without hesitation. Of course he would vomit, but better to fail trying than to fail for not trying. On the first swallow he began to gag, but then he realized that it was not so bad. It tasted like warm milk, fresh and very rich. His stomach held and he emptied the cup and handed it to Freniere.

"Not the best drink I've ever had," he said evenly, "but not the worst, either."

Freniere gazed at him with a look of open delight. "*Hi-yah!*" he whooped, and fetched Frémont an openhanded clap on the shoulder that staggered him. "You're all right, Charlie! You're not just a star-gazer. You're going to make a first-class buffler man yet!"

The camp was in deep shadow when Freniere and the Lieutenant came in. Etienne Provost, crouched on his haunches mending a pack strap, watched Frémont unsaddle the white-socked bay, moving stiffly, favoring his left shoulder. The big horse went down on his knees and rolled, shivering with pleasure, scrubbing his sweaty back while Frémont studied him critically, hands on his hips; his hair and jacket were caked with cowflap. Provost smiled to himself and spat. Took himself a little fall. Well, wouldn't be the last time.

"That one yours?" He gestured with the buckle toward the great raw carcass bulking on the meat cart, where Boucher and Peters were already at work.

Frémont looked at him—one quick, alert glance, measuring; then he shook his head. "No," he said simply. "She's Louie's. I missed."

Provost chuckled. "I wouldn't wonder."

"—*This* time." The Lieutenant held up one forefinger, and again there was that intense flash in his eyes; hot, almost defiant. Didn't like to miss, then; that was a good sign. Handsome young feller—looked too fine-spun for the wilderness. 'Course you never knew. Have to see how he salted down.

Frémont had the horse up now, and was rubbing him down. Small man, but quick and wiry; stronger than he looked. Nicollet said he was a good learner, accurate with all that star-gazing folderol they sat up messing with half the night, but that didn't prove nothing. Have to see how he did when the coffee and tobacco ran out, and his boots wore through, and the weather turned savage.

"Look as if you been wrassling one," he said in quiet amusement, and someone over by the fire laughed.

Frémont grinned then. "Yeah," he murmured, "I got into it with both hands." He'd finished hobbling the bay, and he walked away quickly toward the little knoll where Nicollet had set up the instrument tent.

"Now don't you sell Charlie short," Louie called. "You boys should have seen him take off after that cow—like he by God planned to *ride* her . . ."

Several of the men standing around the fire had turned to Freniere, listening.

"I told him wouldn't be no time to be tucking his butt—"

"That's for sure," Peters said, "and then some!"

"Got him a little hot, that did. But I want to tell *you,* old Charlie didn't let any grass grow under that horse of his."

"That so, Louie?" Provost said.

Freniere turned and faced him. "Shining gospel. He took his chances. He missed his cow, sure—but it wasn't for lack of trying."

Provost grunted, and ran his eyes over the camp. The spring-fed stream winding down a fissure in the prairie was small enough to step across in places but above, where he'd sited the main camp, it had widened into a shallow pool. The small bar oaks and ashes growing beside it had a stunted look. Later in the year it would be bone dry. The carts were disposed in a rough half-circle beside the pool, their shafts atrail; only a few had been unloaded. Boucher had hung an iron pot from a tripod over the fire and was fixing racks of buffalo ribs on sticks. The dry wood burned with little smoke and collapsed into ruddy coals; Martineau judiciously added buffalo chips to flavor the meat.

Provost sighed, set the strap aside and settled back into his saddle pads. He'd already posted guards: Terrien was with the horses, and he could see Menard above the camp, scanning the horizon for movement against the light. The Yankton Sioux were friendly, but with Indians you couldn't never be sure; not with good horses in camp and night coming on. Peters was bringing wood for the fire, and on the flat below Dixon, the expedition's guide, was working on a horse that had gone lame, cradling the hoof on his knee, digging at something jammed in that tender place between frog and buttress, while Zindel held the animal's head. Sour, silent old Bill Dixon, keeping busy, trying not to think about Mr. John Barleycorn. . . .

Well, every soul had its demon, as Papa Joe said. Provost studied the knoll again; Nicollet was seated on a box writing in his journal, using the tailgate of the equipment cart as a desk; Frémont was standing beside him talking, one foot cocked on the spoke of a wheel. A movement on the rim of the hill behind Frémont caught his eye then—a wolf that ducked instantly from sight. Provost chuckled. Empty. He'd heard a fancy Virginia gentleman once. "I say, nothing but barren, lifeless spaces. Everywhere you look." Damn fool—the whole land was humming with life! A million creeping, gliding, soaring things. But you had to know *how* to look, that was all. . . .

"Aaaiii, festin!" Boucher sang from the big fire. "Come on in, now!"—and there was a quick movement toward him from all points. A pale sliver of moon had appeared in the eastern sky; the west was still bright. The odor of cooking meat was overpowering. Martineau was cracking bones with a small ax and thumbing out rolls of marrow—trapper's butter—which Boucher kept stirring into the iron pot. The soup bubbled viscously, marrow and molten fat and blood from the butchering, bound with pepper, its aroma swirling on the light wind.

"If it tastes as good as it smells," Frémont said, "we're in for one hell of a treat."

"Tastes better than that, Charlie!" Freniere told him, and Boucher laughed.

All of them were around the fire now, throwing down their apishamores for couches, gazing at the racks of roasting meat, their eyes glinting; there was an air of contained excitement, like men gathering in a tavern. The meat crackled richly, and droplets of fat made tiny yellow flares in the coals, which now glowed deep red. Bread was rising in a Dutch oven, and a big coffeepot nestled at the edge of the coals. Later on the luxury of bread and coffee would be only a memory, but now the expedition was young.

"Ribs are ready," Boucher announced.

Provost cut close to the bone and with the first mouthful, dense and gamy and rich, it all came flooding back—his wild young manhood and the first glorious years on the plains, the buffalo in vast surging seas and the dust whirling against the sun in a golden storm.

"Look at Charlie!" Freniere bawled across the fire. "Afraid there won't be enough to go round. . . . Didn't I tell you buffler'll make prime beef taste like putty?"

The sky was darkening and a single star appeared high overhead. A wolf drawn by the smell howled suddenly, hung close, and one of the men laughed. After that came yelps and snarls, and Provost knew coyotes had got up the spunk to join their braver cousins.

Peters fetched more wood, and the fire blazed high. The men ate rapidly with their hands, faces flushed in the firelight and wet with grease. They were ribbing each other, calling back and forth, roaring with laughter. Martineau, late to the feast, slid the crackling meat skewered on his ramrod onto his plate. Someone called to him and he turned, laughing; the ramrod in his hand bumped Bladon's stick where meat was roasting. The stick fell and the meat dropped into the coals.

"Look out, Goddamnit!" Above his kinky black beard Bladon's pale face went instantly dark. "Clumsy bastard!"

"Sorry," Martineau said, "I was—"

"Sorry don't cut it," Bladon answered, his eyes bright. He slipped the point of his big knife under the edge of Martineau's plate and flipped it upside down into the fire.

"Now wait a minute, mister . . ." Martineau dropped the ramrod and his hands came up. "You got no call—"

"Call? I'll call you, sonny!" Bladon was on his feet like a cat, the knife weaving freely at his hip.

"All right," Provost said from across the fire.

Martineau broke backward, his eyes on the knife. Bladon paused an instant, then came on in a rush, the knife held very low, and Provost saw Frémont, sitting next to Louie, set down his plate and stick out one booted foot. Bladon tripped over it and went sprawling, rolled over and came up facing Frémont, his eyes wild. The Lieutenant was on his feet now.

"You want some, soldier boy?" Bladon hissed. "All right, then!" He took a quick running step—and stopped. Frémont's hand had gone to the butt of his pistol and rested there; his eyes were black as onyx in the flickering dance of the fire. Aside from that one swift gesture he had not moved.

"Just didn't get my big clumsy feet out of the way in time. Did I?" he said easily, and then smiled; but there was a hard, forbidding edge in his voice. Bladon glared at him, confused.

"Put up that knife, Bladon," Provost told him in the tone that had stopped a hundred fights from Natchez to the Devil's Tower. "I won't have a man cut over no damned piece of meat."

Bladon turned toward him then, his face stamped with that deep, curious excitement. "Shee-it, Mr. Provost, I don't need no knife." He dropped the weapon on his plate with a clatter and in the same motion, wheeling, his fist came sailing up from the ground like a stone on the end of his arm and smashed into the side of Martineau's head. Martineau fell face down as if his feet had been snatched from under him, and Bladon started forward.

"No boots, either," Provost said; he was standing now, too. "You've settled it—that's enough." He stared at Bladon, studying him. One of Nicollet's demon souls. Killed a couple of men in knife fights down the Santa Fe Trail. "You're a troublesome man, Bladon," he said. "We got no room for that kind of trouble here. Now you watch your step, hear?"

To his surprise Bladon grinned; Provost saw he was all relaxed now, the way you might feel after you'd had yourself a woman three-four times running.

"Right, Mr. Provost," he answered readily. "You're the boss." Martineau was sitting up, shaking his head dumbly, and Bladon extended a hand. "Come on, Marty—no hard feelings, eh? What the hell: you done me a turn and I done you one." Confused, Martineau put out his hand and Bladon lifted him easily to his feet. "Boucher, let ol' Marty have that piece of tongue you promised me. No hard feelings, eh?" And he took his place by the fire, looking pleased, and started to tear at his ash-coated meat, though the glance he shot at Frémont was uneasy and sullen.

The camp's happiness flowed over the brief trouble like balm. Provost sent two men to relieve Terrien and Menard, who came in whooping with anticipation. They ate slab after slab of the rich, grained meat, mopping their plates with steaming bread. And in the dark beyond the circle of carts the wolves and coyotes whined and yipped. When the fire flared up, their eyes flashed like gold pieces, savagely near.

Then came coffee strong enough to float a nail, and sugar sifted on bread dipped in buffalo grease. The men broke out rough shag tobacco and pipes they fired with glowing coals. The scent of tobacco blended with the roasting meat and they lay back on their elbows, cradling their tin cups, belching and joking, jubilant with the gorging. And Provost watched them somberly, his old eyes narrowed against the smoke; the quarrel, and the torrent of memories the buffalo meat had raised, had darkened his mood.

Nicollet had gone back to his seat at the tailgate of his cart; the tallow-candle lantern flickered bravely against the night. At the fire Menard and Freniere were talking about the buffalo and the miracle of their inestimable numbers, millions on millions of them drumming and rumbling across the endless plains, so you could hunt them for their hides and flesh to the very end of time. . . .

"Waugh!" Provost said suddenly. Their words had just reached him. "Wasn't that way with the beaver. There was millions of them, too, and we killed them off. We trapped them streams dry."

He lit his pipe with quick, nervous puffs as their faces turned to him. "Hell, there wasn't never more than six hundred of us all through the Snake and the Siskadee, and Bear Valley, too. We figured the beaver would last forever. We couldn't believe no different. But the time come when you'd bait your traps with prime castoreum and set 'em out, and day by day you'd come back and find 'em empty. Them beaver was gone."

He wanted to talk now, needed to, his voice hoarse and low, and the men lay in the dark, smoking and listening.

"You want to know what happened to the fur trade? We killed it, that's what. And by'n'by we was coming down to rendezvous with a handful of plews, no more'n a single horse could pack. Just about every one of us ended up in the partisan's debt, just for powder and lead and a little foofaraw for your woman and whiskey for the pain in your knees."

He stopped and belched, and just when the silence would have forced someone to speak, he added ruminatively, "You get the rheumatiz, you know, setting your traps knee-deep in water running right out of the snowpack. Makes a man's legs ache like a poison tooth. Man needed a little whiskey . . ."

Peters said: "The beaver'll come back, won't they?"

"Maybe. But it don't matter none. Folks won't be wearing beaver hats no more. *Silk hats.* Can you believe that? Don't seem like a flimsy piece of cloth would make a hat a man would want to wear, but then you can't tell about city folk no ways—they don't think like real people."

They pondered that, the sky dark and the fire barbaric and leaping, the men's faces red.

The rendezvous swept into his memory again. All the trappers coming in with their pelts and the partisans out from St. Louis with pack trains heavy-laden with supplies and hawks bells and rings and mirrors and bright cloth and vermilion by the pound and tobacco to see a man through the year. And whiskey. Whiskey, by God. Horse races and card games and the Indian hand game on which a man could lose everything, lose his beaver and his horses and his woman—and if he *really* cut the fool and didn't want to live, even his piece. And roaring drunk all the while, drinking whiskey until he was blind and puking. The Indians came and with them their women and a man could take him a wife or trade in a wife for a new one or just take a woman, using her hard and back in an hour for more, such a pressure of seed had he built up in that cold year in the mountains. . . .

"And in eighteen and thirty-two—let's see, that's eight long years gone now—that year we was at Pierre's Hole and we heard that the Gros Ventres was coming on the prod. Now them is Blackfoot, you know, and there was never a meaner, tougher Indian than a Blackfoot. When they torture a man they keep him alive for hours, screaming every minute, and their women busting their nuts with every scream. So we rode out to meet 'em, and they sent out a war chief to parley, making a delay, you know. Big strapping fellow in a scarlet cloak, give him by the damned British for sure, and he was carrying the peace pipe like he wanted to smoke, the damned, cheating . . . and Antoine Godin rode out to meet him, with a Flathead. Blackfoot had killed Godin's daddy the year before over on Big Lost River, and you know Flatheads all hate Blackfoots. So this war chief reins up and puts out his hand and Godin shakes it and hangs on and says, 'Shoot,' and by God but that Flathead shoots. And Godin pulls him close and they lift his scalp quicker'n you can say it and ride back waving the bloody scalp lock and that blood-red cloak. And then the fighting begun."

"What happened, Mr. Provost?" Menard asked.

"At Pierre's Hole?" Provost said irritably. "Why, fought all day, that's what. And finally they run. We lost some men and the Flatheads lost some—they're fighting men, them Flatheads—but the Gros Ventres lost a plenty more and they ain't forgot it to this day."

Frémont was watching him intently, scowling; and the aversion in the younger man's face stung him all at once.

"You think that ain't right, don't you? Godin shaking that Indian's hand? Well, you got a lot to learn, young feller. You going to get by on the frontier, you'd better learn right quick how hard things can get."

But the Lieutenant didn't look away; after a moment he nodded. "That's true, Mr. Provost," he said quietly. "I've still got a lot to learn."

"Bet your boots," Provost answered, but hollowly. The soldier had taken it well. He felt morose, and cross with himself for flaring up like that. I'm getting old, he thought sourly; old and cantankerous. Like Gabe Bridger.

"Hell, it don't matter," he said in vague conciliation. "It's all dead and buried now. . . . When we whipped them Gros Ventres that day we felt like kings. But there wasn't no rendezvous this year and I don't believe there'll ever be another."

Abruptly he threw the dregs of his cup onto the blackened coals. There was a sharp hiss. He rapped his pipe hard on his boot heel and the gray dottle fell to the ground.

"Man was free in the mountains," he said. "Lived like he wanted, did what he wanted, killed if he had to. It was hard, but you was alive, d'you understand?"

He sighed and belched again. "Well, no use crying. No white folks out there and none going. Ain't no *reason* to go. Most beautiful country God ever wrought, but you can't eat that."

There was a long pause and Louis Zindel spoke.

"But lots of folks are ready to go west, no?" He was a small man with a round, merry face and a sunny personality. He had been an artilleryman in the Prussian Army.

"Not a one that I know about."

"The farmers back in Ohio—they lose their farms when the banks close, and they say Oregon is the place to be."

"She-it! Ain't nothing in Oregon but the Hudson's Bay Company, the damned grabbing British. Them and a handful of Yanks gone there to farm."

"In Ohio they talked about the Oregon Trail as if it's the road to the promised land."

"Trail? What's the matter with you? There *ain't* no Oregon Trail, least nothing a stranger could follow. I know what you're talking about—the route that runs up the Platte to Fort Laramie and on to South Pass, sure, but it's just a general route, it's not a trail. What d'you think—that it's a *road?* With a stagecoach running every day and the driver blowing his bugle polite as you please?"

"Well, but how did those caravans get to the rendezvous?" Frémont asked suddenly.

"Went up the Missouri by keelboat," Louie said, "dragged foot by foot against the current. Hardest work in the world. Boucher manned them tow lines some, didn't you, Boucher?"

Boucher grunted. Slowly he raised a massive arm and flexed the bicep.

"There's nothing there, with the fur trade gone," Provost repeated gloomily. "Or go to California and see how the Mexican'll deal with you—he'll show you the inside of his dungeons, that's what. And the same in Sante Fe—they like the trade caravan that goes down every year, but that's all."

"Damned right," Bladon said. "I walked a team down that trail five years in a row. They're glad enough to get the goods, but it don't pay to make no missteps around them Mex soldiers."

"Nah," Provost concluded, "nothing left. A few trading posts like Fort Laramie. But God almighty, there's hardly a white man between Kansas

Landing and Laramie, and damned few who even know the way. Just me and Ol' Gabe and the like, who've followed the beaver. Some Ohio farmer was to set out on his own, he'd be lost in three days, vulture bait in ten. Hell, if a man wants to farm, he's got his family, his stock—why, there's never been a *wagon* gone through those mountains, don't you understand? Never. Ol' Gabe guided that missionary party out to Oregon three, four years ago—that doctor fellow, Whitman—and all they had was pack mules and they ate most of them and damned glad to have 'em. Huh-uh. Oregon Trail, my ass . . ."

"There'll be one someday," Frémont said from across the fire. "Someday soon."

"How do you come by that?" Provost demanded, irritated all over again. "Why shoot, son, you've never even laid eyes on that country."

"Not yet. But there's going to be a wagon trail to Oregon because there *has* to be one."

Provost snorted. "You'll never live to see it."

"Bet I do, Mr. Provost. My gold watch against that fancy silver bridle of yours."

"Fair enough!" Louie crowed, and slapped his greasy hands against his thighs. "I'll hold the stakes."

"Hell's bells, you won't live long enough either, Louie," Provost told him, and the circle of men laughed in chorus.

"Yes he will. We all will," Frémont said softly. He grinned at Provost then—that quick, defiant smile—then got to his feet and hurried up to the knoll where Nicollet was already setting out the instruments.

The moon was high now, sharing the sky with a million million stars. Provost smoothed out his apishamore, rolled himself deftly in one blanket and worked himself comfortable, dozing and waking, watching Frémont and Papa Joe working on the sightings, their heads together in the lantern's flicker. Feisty young feller, had to give him that. No bag of wind, either—meant what he said. Pretty slick, tripping up Bladon like that; then the move to his pistol. No fear in him at all. Maybe—just maybe—he'd be the one to break trail through that Godforsaken country, you never knew. At least he wasn't no Washington dandy come along for the ride. . . .

STARSIGHTS

DAY BY DAY FRÉMONT RODE across the great open land, logging its contours, and often he found himself riding with Provost or following their guide, William Dixon, on his long probes ahead. Provost was never as garrulous as he had been that night by the fire, but he smilingly allowed Frémont's eager curiosity about the whole untouched West to fire his memory. Dixon, a thin, dark man, was engaged in a losing battle with whiskey. He brought none into the field, but he often rode in silence, his system sweating out its residues, his eyes full with longing. He was a fine guide; he knew the ground and, to Frémont's surprise, he perceived it quite differently from Louis Freniere.

Louie saw the country in an immediate way, in terms of its occupants, whether game or men; saw cover, habitat, sign. Dixon saw terrain as a relief map in his head. He studied it as a sheet of open country running hundreds of miles in all directions, populated by roaming buffalo herds and nomadic Indian encampments, in a fluid, always changing mass. He watched the patterns in the rise and fall of prairie shapes and understood the systems by which creeks fed streams and streams fed rivers. He grasped the tilt of the land, the long westward rise that led ultimately to the Rocky Mountains. Day by day Dixon rode ahead, searching for the route that avoided a second and third crossing as the stream looped, looking for strong grass, avoiding the sage that gave so little nourishment. Carefully he placed them on the terrain's anchor points—important streams, crucial changes of river direction, high places visible from a distance—so that each could be pegged to the map Nicollet was planning. Like all prairie travelers, Dixon relied on natural landmarks—the red pipestone quarry, the mound shaped like a coiled snake, Medicine Knoll, where the young Sioux engaged in medicine rites had foiled the Rees who crept upon him through the night, the boulders that lay like a broken war club, the chalk cliffs. And Frémont, excited by this broad view, open as the country itself, blazed everything into his mind.

They left the James River, crossed to the watershed of the Cheyenne and were moving north toward Devil's Lake when they encountered Wahanantan's band of Yankton Sioux. The Indians were camped in a poplar grove in a big bend of river, pausing on their move to the regular fall buffalo surround. Dixon knew Wahanantan well and after a visit returned to say that the Indians would receive the entire expedition the next day with a feast.

"Now you'll see something, Charlie!" Freniere said, popping his hands together.

The white men rode into the poplar grove escorted by thirty horsemen. The Indians' faces were painted and they wore dressy feathers in their hair and fur robes draped gracefully over bare shoulders. Frémont looked eagerly about the camp. Some two hundred tall lodges were pitched in relative order among the trees, covered with talismanic designs in vermilion and blue, ocher and black, their lower flaps now tied open for ventilation. A lance leaned against one lodge. A war shield hung below it, and with a start Frémont saw streamers of human hair ending in tufts of dry skin attached to the lance. Ahead Wahanantan's lodge stood separately, its fine skins scraped almost white.

Wahanantan was tall and he wore his gray-streaked hair cast to the left. His leggings and tunic were richly worked and his buffalo coat told the story of his wars. Proper to the occasion, he held a pipe and a war club. A small group of princelings was about him; one, a young man of the chief's height who wore a bear-claw necklace and a single eagle feather in his hair, stood with such an air of authority that Frémont marked him as Wahanantan's successor. As if he recognized Frémont's corresponding position, the young man caught his eye and smiled, the hard face suddenly warm.

Wahanantan spoke in a graceful, oratorical way, Dixon translating, and Nicollet answered with equal flourishes and then ordered trade goods opened as presents. The Indians crowded close, murmuring in surprise and pleasure as criers announced each item, rapping on upright posts with heavy sticks for emphasis. Looking glasses, scissors, knives, tortoiseshell combs, vermilion, fishhooks, ribbon, tobacco—the people laughed and clapped hands to mouths and called raucous jokes to each other, and Frémont felt his own perspective suddenly widening as he watched the excitement that simple civilized artifacts could produce on the high plains . . .

A feast was being prepared and the Indians milled about, staring at the white men with friendly curiosity. Louie nudged Frémont. "Nicest people on earth when they're feeling hospitable," he said quietly. "Meet them tomorrow and they might show you another side." The men were stalwart and muscular, and the women were pretty. One he noticed in particular, a young woman with a brightly worked buckskin blouse cut in a deep V that revealed her breasts deliciously when she moved her arms in a certain way. She saw Frémont watching her and smiled and her smile made her pretty as a prairie flower. She walked right up to him, her round hips rolling under her buckskin skirt and said something in a voice that was brash and musical. She was looking directly at him. Louie grinned.

"Name's Watermelon," Freniere said. "Fits her figure, huh? She's taken with your handsome face, Charlie. Give her man a present—a knife, maybe—and she's all yours. Later, you know, when the feasting's done."

Frémont shot a startled look at the hunter. The girl smelled fragrant as a meadow, and he wanted to press his fingers into the buckskin swelling on her hips.

"Don't mistake her," Louie said. "She ain't selling you nothing. Woman here likes a man, she just naturally wants to try him. The present is just for her man's dignity—that's the custom."

Desire rose in Frémont until it compressed his heart and he had trouble breathing. The offer was so unexpected!—he realized that his hands were trembling. But he saw Louie grinning at him with St. Louis eyes. Any other way, yes—but not rutting in the grass, pants down and senses blind and every man in the party hot and interested. The girl was watching his face and her smile faded until she seemed plain.

The men were ranging themselves in a circle with Wahanantan and his principal warriors. Frémont found himself sitting beside the man with the bear-claw necklace. "Name's Fiery Tail," Louie had said earlier. "Sioux go off and fast and have visions when they choose their names, you know. He probably seen a comet that night. Good name, though; he'll burn up an enemy, all right. He's the young war chief." Frémont had chuckled, but now there was nothing amusing about him. His arms and legs were scarred with self-inflicted mourning slashes for family losses, perhaps to the smallpox epidemic. His chest was a mass of scars, evidence that he had sought the worst of the testing sun dance, and his heavy shoulder was raked with parallel slashes that could have been inflicted by the bear claws that now adorned his throat.

Gravely the circle of men passed a pipe of red stone, a reed stem hung with feathers and totems neatly fitted to the bowl. The mixture of tobacco and *shongsasha,* the bark of the red willow, was harsh and wild. The women served horn dishes filled with a rich meat stew. Louie winked at Frémont and barked softly like a puppy but Frémont ignored him. Afterward Wahanantan led them to an open meadow beyond the trees, which had taken on a hard green look in the early afternoon sun. The grass was strong and there were dusty patches of goldenrod. Purple aster was brilliant among the trees and children wandered among blackberry brambles, their mouths streaked with juice. Wahanantan arranged the white men with a few of his chiefs as an audience, and the games began. There were wrestling matches with very heavy falls, lacrosse played with studied roughness, horsemanship that beggared Freniere's best. It was an easy, happy afternoon, the Indians cheering over the falls and betting on every turn, the winners exultant, the losers shouting for another chance. What a warm, happy people, Frémont thought—why did white men consider them dour?

The trouble began innocently enough; the white men wanted to reciprocate, give a show of their own. Frémont saw old Provost talking earnestly to Nicollet, and when Nicollet nodded, he gestured to Zindel. The little Prussian cannoneer was an expert in rockets, which was why Nicollet had engaged him: rockets with small explosive heads, while hardly devastating weapons, would be impressive enough to turn the odds should the party find itself under serious attack. Zindel moved his cart into the center of the field and began opening boxes while the Indians watched; Frémont saw that they were puzzled but pleased by the novelty.

"Rockets make a grand show," Louie said.

"And it never hurts to let 'em know what we've got," Provost added.

They watched Zindel fit the rocket bodies, without their explosive heads, to long staffs which he thrust into the ground. Zindel had distinctly bowed legs which the Indians found irresistibly funny. Freniere often ragged him—the only gunner on earth, Louie would say, who could serve his piece from the front: pass the ball between his knees and never feel the breeze. Now the young warriors imitated him, bowing their own legs and hobbling about, laughing and pointing. Zindel's sunny face was glowing; he wasn't at all offended.

When he was ready he doffed his hat and bowed low to Wahanantan and lighted the rockets. They gouted flame and roared and soared off on tails of fire, like birds from heaven or hell. The Indians were stunned. Children screamed and women ran among the lodges. The men stood fast with their eyes wide and their faces strained, staring after the dramatic birds. Even Wahanantan had an irresolute look.

Their mood changed as quickly as glass shatters. The younger men were plainly angry; suddenly Frémont was uneasy. Then Fiery Tail raised a commanding hand and the others fell silent. Tossing his head, his arm sweeping toward the white men, he spoke in a tense, compressed tone and Frémont saw Wahanantan nod. Fiery Tail wheeled and hurried away, five other braves following. Frémont understood. The Indians had offered a pipe and a feast and had shown their skills and their sports; the white men had responded with a show of power.

Dixon tried to speak to Wahanantan, but the tall chief held up a dismissing hand. "They got a damned burr up their tails," Provost said slowly.

"I don't like it," Dixon said, returning to the group of white men.

Provost scowled at him. "Take it easy," he said. "They ain't going to make real trouble."

In five minutes there was a stir. The waiting crowd parted and Fiery Tail led the five warriors onto the field in single file. Their faces were freshly painted and they wore crests of war-eagle feathers on their heads. They carried powerful bows of ashwood bound with rawhide that had been wrapped wet. Fiery Tail was singing loudly, a chanting, discordant song. The white men stirred at sight of the weapons, but Louie said softly to Frémont, "He's singing a hunting song, not a war song. That's a good sign. But he's dangerous."

At a distance several men braced a heavy post upright and attached a life-size figure of straw in an old buckskin blouse, a gourd for a head. At Fiery Tail's signal the men fitted arrows to their bows and fired. But the arrows were not aimed at the figure: they flew in a high, lofting arc. As the arrow left the bow each man reached for another and another and another, firing so rapidly that the sixth arrow was off before the first had reached the top of its arc and started down. The arrows were speeding streaks in the sky, almost invisible and yet a living presence, thirty-six sticks that followed the same trajectory and fell to earth to stand bristling within a ten-foot circle.

"Beautiful," Frémont breathed to Louie. "They've *recreated* Zindel's rocket. D'you see?" But the hunter only gave him a cold stare.

Fiery Tail stepped back and leaned imperturbably on his bow while the five warriors notched arrows and loosed them at the dummy on the upright post. Frémont would not have imagined that the arrows could reach the figure, which was just in comfortable pistol range, and certainly not that they could be accurate. But they lifted on a slightly rising trajectory and dropped like bullets toward the target. Four pierced the dummy and the fifth narrowly missed. Now, speed-shooting as before, each man pulled arrow after arrow from his quiver, fitting, drawing, shooting, fitting another. Most of the arrows pierced the straw-filled body, but none touched the gourd.

"You've just seen what makes 'em so dangerous," Freniere said from the side of his mouth. "Once you fire they can get off a handful of arrows while you're reloading, every one of 'em a bull's eye."

Now Fiery Tail stepped forward, walking like a young stallion. He faced the white men with a cold, insolent look and when his roving gaze reached Frémont it stopped and locked there, and Frémont understood the taunt. Then he put two fingers over his shoulder, plucked an arrow from his otter-skin quiver, notched it, and fired with hardly a glance—and it went high. It struck the post above the dummy's gourd head and quivered there.

"Ha!" Zindel exclaimed, and laughed. But the other men didn't speak and no one smiled.

Turning that cold look on Zindel, who seemed suddenly abashed, Fiery Tail fired again. The arrow flew on the same trajectory and struck the post at the same height, an inch from the first arrow. All right, Frémont thought, no error. Fiery Tail fitted another arrow, drew and fired—and this one split the shaft of the first. This was what the watching Indians had been awaiting. They laughed and yelled, grunting in loud approval. And in the midst of the shouts, the big man's hand snaked over his shoulder for another arrow and this time he drew the bow back until it seemed certain to break, his great bicep drawn full behind him, bear claws buried in the rise of scarred shoulder against neck, and when he loosed the bow the arrow flew flat as a bullet and smacked through the center of the gourd, pinning the figure's head like a nail. Then, while the Indians shouted to each other, Fiery Tail looked at Frémont, as if he had been singled out, and walked off the field to stand by Wahanantan, his arms folded.

The demonstration, so forceful and elegant, stirred Nicollet's wonder, but Provost reacted differently.

"We'd better answer that, boys," he said without consulting Papa Joe. "Freniere, you and Martineau shoot. Zindel, Broussard, Peters, Bladon, load and keep the pieces moving up. I want you to blow that damned gourd off of there."

It took seven shots, the arrow in the gourd splintered by a bullet, the gourd jerking from the blows before it shattered.

"All right," Provost said. But Frémont saw that again it had been the wrong note. The Indians were watching somberly. They had challenged, but with élan and skill. The whites had responded like savages, blowing apart a target that was within easy rifle range. With pistols it would have been more sporting—and a memory ticked deep in his mind. He saw Fiery Tail watching him and he thought of the game that he and Bradcliff had played in the Carolina mountains. You had to be good—and quick—but it was effective. And he had practiced it, done it two dozen times only—what? a year ago, no more. Why not? He drew the pistol he carried in his belt and checked the cap.

"Let me try something," he said.

Provost looked at him dubiously, eyeing the pistol. "Don't try it unless you know you can do it."

"I can do it," Frémont said. He felt calm and easy. He tucked the pistol under his left arm and opened his notebook and from the back took a quarto sheet, twice folded. He unfolded it.

"Give me four awls," he said. Everyone carried an awl, the slender pointed shaft that served as a primary tool, from nail to drill to toothpick. "And Louie," he said to Freniere, "be a good fellow and get my other pistol from the saddle pocket."

The Indians saw that something new was afoot and they were quiet again, watching. Frémont walked to the post and stripped away the remains of the figure. He snatched out the stump of the broken shaft that had pierced the gourd and spread the paper where the gourd had been, pinning it to the post with the awls. He took a half-burned stick from a fire, knocked off the coals and with the charred end drew several black lines across the top of the paper. Toward the bottom he drew a half-circle and around it black curls. Hair on top and beard below, it amounted to a face without features, though he knew that this would not be evident to the watchers. He thought of Bladon's black beard and his paper-white face. The Indians were silent and the little knot of white men had not moved.

Deliberately he walked back to the marksman's position and stood easily, a pistol in each hand. He stared at the Indians. Wahanantan stood a little apart from the others, his face cold and remote. Frémont waited until Fiery Tail's eyes met his, and then he turned with his pistol up and brought it down, slow and steady. He fired and immediately swapped pistols, hand to hand, and fired again. Now there were two holes in the paper below the hair mark—eyes. A few of the Indians began to grin but most looked puzzled and, as a result, irritated. Frémont held both pistols by the muzzles in his left hand, a finger between them, and poured powder in each. He rammed patched balls and fitted new caps, working smoothly and quickly, his hands quite steady, and brought the pistols up and fired again. Two more holes, centered and below the eye holes, one above the other this time. Again he reloaded, drew down and fired both pistols. Two more holes appeared, one at each side of the lowest hole—a wide mouth under a nose. Now everyone understood and there were grunts and exclamations of approval. The Indians were grinning and nudging each other. He glanced at the white men behind him. Their faces were blank with surprise.

Again, quick and steady, he reloaded. The Indians were moving toward him but they paused when he raised the pistol again. He sought out Fiery Tail and when he had the big warrior's eyes he grinned deliberately and bowed. Then, very quickly, he pulled the piece down and fired.

Another hole appeared squarely between the empty, staring eyes. The lethal message was entirely clear but deftly done and the Indians shouted approval.

Beyond him he heard Provost grunt in relief. "Purty fair," the mountain man said. "Purty damned fair."

Fiery Tail came striding out of the crowd, the others making way for him. He came straight to Frémont and a broad smile cracked his rough face. Up close he towered a half-foot over him as he clapped a heavy hand on his shoulder, laughing and speaking in Sioux.

And Louie, now very elated, murmured in Frémont's ear, "Says you're his brother. Says you're blood Sioux under your ugly white face."

Frémont clapped his own hand on the big man's shoulder and said loudly, smiling, "You're pretty good yourself, my friend—for a redskin."

Fiery Tail grasped his meaning before Louie could translate, and laughed aloud and turned, his arm holding Frémont's shoulders, and gave an oration of obvious praise, to which the Indians responded with approving grunts and yells. And then there was nothing for it but to smoke another pipe and have another round of the stew—which really was delicious, Frémont thought, if you could only rid your mind of the image of the yellow puppy mewing and wagging its tail as the stone hammer fell.

It was late and very dark, but in the starlight Frémont could see tears leaking from Nicollet's right eye.

"Let me finish, Papa Joe," he said.

The old man was stubborn. He wiped his eye with a dirty handkerchief and bent quickly to the instrument.

"You know I can do it," Frémont said.

"I know," Nicollet answered. "Mark."

Frémont raised the candle lantern and read the instrument's pointers. It was a small brass telescope that slid on a vertical brass ring which in turn moved on a horizontal ring. It measured the angles between stars.

Nicollet always took the first readings. They gave true time, which showed how much their London chronometer was off; thereafter they would time each starsight to the chronometer but in the final calculations would include the instrument's variance. These were the crucial readings. The accuracy of all that followed depended on them.

When the time sights were done, Nicollet sat on a camp stool and pressed his palms against his eyelids. In the starlight his face looked haggard, full of hollows.

"You'll have to finish tonight, Charles," he said. "Maybe you're right—I should leave the sightings to you for a few days. I see well enough, you understand—it's these miserable tears."

Frémont was tired too, but he was young. The stars that they needed to fix their place precisely—the key to Nicollet's radical concept of mapmaking in the wilderness—often came late. Night after night he and Nicollet were up while the men slept. Sometimes they dozed for an hour or two and then dragged themselves awake for the next sighting. Nicollet had developed a shallow but persistent cough—when they bathed in a stream one day, Frémont had been startled at how thin his arms and legs had become.

Now it was well past midnight and the camp was still. Peters was with the remuda and Louie had the camp watch; Frémont saw him moving beyond the carts, the Hawken cradled Indian fashion in one arm. An owl sounded, melancholy and introspective. Frémont turned the little telescope northward.

"I've looked at the North Star almost every clear night since I was fifteen," Nicollet said, his good spirits returning. "It never fails—which is more than can be said for most men."

Frémont adjusted the eyepiece. The star circling over the Pole flashed and glittered, its movement plainly visible. He centered it, working quickly but precisely.

"Mark," he said, and held the lantern to the instrument. He called the figures and Nicollet entered them in the logbook. He sighted the North Star fifteen separate times and then reversed the instrument, found the bright star of Capricorn in the southern sky and made fifteen more readings. It was good work, soothing and steady in the cooling, quiet night. The well-made instrument moved exactly on its bearings, the light squared crisply in the lens, and he managed a nearly identical interval between each sighting. When averaged, these readings would give a rough position immediately; when they were refined in the intricate calculations to be made for the final map, they would give the latitude of this night's camp in degrees, minutes and seconds north of the equator.

Afterwards, Frémont's eyes ached. He sat quietly, pressing away the pain with his fingers. There was something deeply stirring about the linking of his own human precision to those dancing lights millions of miles away. He stood on a meridian, a single line that stretched between the earth's poles, and by his instrument, his eye, his intellect, he anchored himself precisely to that line. It put him in control—as if the universe were tamed to his command. He smiled at that; just the same, he liked the feeling of power using the stars gave him.

"Thirty readings, north and south," Nicollet said in his scratchy voice. "Now, that is exactitude. And exactitude is what makes *our* map unique."

They had run north along the Cheyenne after leaving Wahanantan's camp, clear to Devil's Lake. In the field, Nicollet and Frémont rode well apart, ranging the country in broad zigzags, making rough sketch maps of how the land lay, the streams interrelated, the hills were thrown. In their daily notebooks they entered the flora and fauna they encountered, the weather, the nature of the soil. They measured the altitude with barometers that were accurate to within a few feet, and at night they sighted the stars that fixed them so that every feature would appear on the map exactly where it was. What Dixon perceived of the land in a rough, intuitive way, they were refining to a scientifically accurate picture on paper that anyone could read.

Until now, not a single map of the ground west of the Mississippi had been based on exact positions taken from starsights. What passed for maps were small and casual, with squiggly lines for rivers and arbitrary marks for mountains; generalized descriptions in sketch form, vague and ambiguous, based on memories, estimates and myths picked up from trappers and Indians. No mapmaker had actually seen the ground he mapped, no one had established the relationship of each point to the whole.

"No wonder frontiersmen laugh at other maps. They're off hundreds of miles when they aren't altogether imaginary. Even Captain Bonneville's map is useless—the one in Washington Irving's book." Nicollet broke off, coughing, the dirty handkerchief pressed to his mouth, and shook his head crossly. The very idea of Bonneville exasperated him. "No positions, few details, nothing fixed. He doesn't even have altitudes—he must not have known how to use the barometer, though Humboldt demonstrated its use thirty years ago. Well, all right, he was a line soldier on leave to trade in furs—his mapping was only incidental. When I told Provost about Bonneville, he laughed so hard I feared for him—said Bonneville didn't even know how to find furs, let alone make a map." He shook his head. "*Bon Dieu,* it's a disgrace to call that thing a map. Just wait until they see ours. They won't believe such precision is possible!"

Frémont smiled. His eyes had stopped hurting. There was an hour before the next reading and he settled back. He liked to listen to Nicollet's ruminations in the small of the night. Papa Joe often amazed him. Frémont knew it was why Joel Poinsett had named him Nicollet's assistant.

Poinsett was Secretary of War, as well as a power in Charleston, Frémont's home. It had been his great good fortune that Poinsett had spotted him early and, after Frémont's father died and left him penniless, had sponsored his education at Charleston College. God knew he was grateful. When Poinsett took over the War Department in Van Buren's cabinet, he had created a new and separate Corps of Topographical Engineers to handle the Army's mapping and named Frémont one of its thirty-six commissioned officers. Two months after Frémont arrived in Washington, Poinsett had called him in to explain his assignment to Nicollet.

"I thought I'd tell you myself." He was slight and urbane, with a gentle face. "It's just the sort of thing I'd have liked at your age." Frémont had listened intently, thrilled by his prospects. Nicollet, too, had caught the Secretary's interest. A ranking French astronomer, he had applied the latest mathematical theories to stock speculation in France and had been quite successful—for a while.

"Then, of course, it all blew up," Poinsett said with a smile. "Business isn't very scientific, which any businessman could have told him. It ruined him, so naturally he came to America. Now understand, he hadn't a penny—he came here determined to follow the explorations of the upper Mississippi that Marquette and Joliet started two centuries ago. A certain gall, don't you think?—but by God, he did it. The French in St. Louis seem to have welcomed him royally. They say he plays the violin like an angel, which probably helped—St. Louis is pretty crude, for all its cosmopolitan pretensions."

Poinsett paused and then added casually, "That's one of the reasons I thought of you; he has English, but he's much more comfortable in French."

Frémont's father had been a French émigré, his mother a high-spirited Virginia girl of good family, who had fled an earlier, anguished marriage in Richmond; they had spoken French at home because, as his father would say, it was the language of love—he could still remember the smile that brought from his mother in those days, when her hair was still black and her face unlined—before the darker days to follow. . . .

In St. Louis, Chouteau's people adopted Nicollet. They let him travel on their packets and live at their trading posts. And with a canoe and a couple of Indian guides, he'd managed to fix once and for all the sources of the Mississippi River.

"A stunning achievement," Poinsett went on. "You see, Schoolcraft was right in identifying Lake Itasca as the source—but what Nicollet did was grasp the lake as a whole, locate it precisely and demonstrate how the entire system worked. And all by himself! Well, I heard about it just as we started the Topographical branch, so I called him in and asked what else he'd like to do. He didn't hesitate an instant—said he wanted to map the area between the upper Mississippi and the Missouri. He had brilliant ideas—and he made such a case for it that I told him, 'Do it, Mr. Nicollet, do it!' "

Now, miles from the muddy Missouri, moving steadily toward the upper Mississippi, they were doing it. The watch was changing in the silent camp. Louie awakened Bladon and the black-bearded man sat in his blankets grumbling in a low, angry voice. Frémont heard a wolf howl in the distance.

Nicollet stretched and coughed and pressed the back of his hand to his lips. "We'll amaze them," he said, picking up his thought, "—that is, if we're successful. God knows there's plenty still to be done." He sighed again. "That's the problem. This is the great chance. If we muff it, there won't be another."

"We won't muff it," Frémont replied in surprise.

"No, no," Nicollet said hastily, "of course not. I shouldn't have put it that way. But time is pressing—feel that little coolness in the air?—and there's so very much to be done. Well, we'll just have to keep after it . . ."

"But we *are* well along."

"Not nearly enough. But agreed, I don't intend to fail." Nicollet slapped the notebook against his knee. "I've had enough of failure."

Frémont laughed. "Here we are on a most successful tour and you talk of—"

"Because I know failure, do you understand?" Nicollet's voice was suddenly darker, harsher, the voice of a younger man. "I have tried it and I do not like it." Frémont saw he was aroused. "You should save your laughter for when you've had some experience. Then you'll find that failure has no friends and is not at all amusing. Failure opens your doors to enemies. It encourages trash to attack, *it brings out vermin.*"

The force of his pain angered Frémont, but it was an anger directed not at Nicollet but at those who had hurt him. In a confused way—he loved the older man at the same time that he was stung by his rebuke—he wanted to defend him as he might have defended his own father. By now he knew the story well. Nicollet's fellow scientists had blackballed him from the Academy of Science, had revenged themselves and driven him from the country; but they were the very men who had expected to share his profits when his market theories seemed to be working, before everything collapsed.

"Maybe you could turn it all around," he said. He was full of the idea, hot and enthusiastic. "Why not? When the map is finished, every scientist in America—every statesman—will be talking about it. You have important friends—let them help. Let Mr. Poinsett speak to the ambassador." Nicollet's face had changed. Frémont had a sudden sense of what he might have looked like when he was facing his critics. "I know Mr. Poinsett would, he'd be glad to. Let him *force* your acceptance into the Academy, by God! Serve them right. After this, no one would dare deny you . . ."

But Nicollet only shook his head. "No," he said, his voice quite calm, "I've been through all that. It's tempting, but the trouble was that I always *wanted* it; that's what made me so vulnerable. I wanted the Academy—prestige, honor, position. And because I wanted, they could crush me. Well, I learned: who wants nothing cannot be hurt. If your work goes well, no one can deny that. If I ask for nothing, I can be refused nothing."

"Yes, but my God—"

"Charles, I've been through the fire—and after that a man is different. Tempered or destroyed or maybe both—but different. You'll see—everyone faces the fire, sooner or later, and no one is the same afterward. You will see."

He stopped. Frémont found nothing to say. He heard the wolf cry, farther away. Nicollet looked around the camp and at the sky and then in a perfectly relaxed voice said, "I'm a scientist, not a political man. And the Academy is all politics. They talk of science and pure knowledge, but they really want just what every human being wants—power, authority, position, the right to bend others to one's will. It's merely a different arena. And what you find in the long run is that power doesn't really mean much."

He stretched slowly. "That's the lesson of the stars," he said, smiling sadly. "The stars are monuments to our unimportance. Every time I look in the telescope I realize how minute we are, how short our time, how little attention the universe pays us. Teaches humility."

Frémont said, "Do you know, it seems to have just the opposite effect on me. The stars make me feel . . . well—part of it all, at one with it . . . stronger and bigger than life. Odd, isn't it?"

"Not really—but then, you like power yourself. You like to take charge, to assert yourself—as you did that day in Wahanantan's camp."

It was the first reference Nicollet had made to the pistoleering exploit. "Well," Frémont said uncertainly, "there's something about this country that makes me want to *do* things, big things. I don't know . . . it's so grand, so free, that you feel as if you could do—oh, exciting deeds."

"Well, what is as exciting as control, authority, imposing one's will, placing one's mark—in short, power. Isn't that so?"

"I hadn't thought of it quite that way."

"Then think of it. It's important. You're a hungry young man, I'd say, even if you haven't identified all your hungers. The time will come when you'll find power far more alluring than women." He paused, looking very seriously at Frémont. "And when that time comes, I urge you to remember that power is precisely as dangerous as it is desirable, in exact ratio."

He's burned out, Frémont thought suddenly. He's tired and weak. He felt a sense of his own strength. Of course he wanted to act, to take charge of things. Of his destiny. It was as if it were written in some golden book that he must strike a mark on the face of the world—some blazing, imperishable triumph that would erase the dark shadow that had lain across his heart's core ever since he could remember. . . .

"I'll remember that," he said. "But who knows what will happen?"

"Who indeed?" Nicollet echoed, as if his interest had already faded. "Only the stars are certain. Only the stars. . . . That is one of the few comforts of my life. Come now: Andromeda has joined us. We can finish for this evening."

The sky had changed. A slender moon was up, its horns sharply defined, its light faint on the ground. Frémont readied the sextant which he would use to measure the angle of distance between two stars. He fixed the *alpha* star of Andromeda square in the eyepiece and turned the thumbscrew until in the instrument the star seemed to approach the moon. As they drew near each other a cone of light extended from one to the other and then they joined.

"Mark," he said, and Nicollet entered the figures. The cone of light distorted the reading; it was a matter of experience to know when the contact was clean and Frémont had found this disturbing at first. He took another observation on the bright star and when he had a dozen they would average to something reasonably precise. He turned to the western sky for the *alpha* star of Cygnus, the constellation of the Swan, and took another twelve fixes, and then turned back to the east for another until, all told, he had a dozen readings each on six separate stars. His eyes ached and his hands were trembling, but the figures were solid. They would give the most difficult of positions, longitude—their distance within a hundred feet or so from zero degrees at Greenwich, England, on the other side of the world.

Nicollet turned to him then. "You have become expert, Charles, a master," he said quietly. "A buffler man of the sextant, as Louison might put it!"

Afterwards Frémont rested, and thought how much he had learned from both men, the hunter and the star-gazer, while Papa Joe fitted the sextant into its velvet-lined case. Nothing moved in the camp. Bladon was on watch, sitting motionless with his rifle; for a moment Frémont wondered if he had fallen asleep, but then the blocky figure's head turned. The wolf was quiet now; perhaps it had found solace or had simply passed out of hearing.

A star shot a brilliant arc across the sky, and he tracked it absently. He was thinking about the buffalo—the brute size of it, the tearing rush in pursuit, racing reckless and ardent under this high canopy of sky. He was at home here—as much a part of this measureless, splendid expanse as Louie, or old Provost. . . .

He had found his vocation, and his life. After all the false starts, the headlong restlessness that had led to his expulsion from college not three months before graduation, that had flung him into the arms of Cecilia. Above all, the mortification of that anguished secret he had held deep within him ever since he'd been old enough to feel anything, that had gnawed at him like the fox hidden under the Spartan boy's cloak, that could still burn like a coal in his heart's core—

He thrust the memory away sharply, turned again to the stars. He wondered idly what had happened to that farmer he had met on the steamboat going down the Ohio. Bound for Oregon. The land of promise.

Papa Joe was too tired. This was no land for tired, embittered old men. Immense, brilliant country, sky like a cathedral vault, empty and awaiting him. Awaiting this expedition that would nail it down, fix its contours for all time. It was like destiny unfolding—the open land, the beckoning of pure space itself. And drifting toward sleep he saw himself on Barney, a tiny figure loping surely on a vast plain that ran into blazing light, westward under the great sky. . . .

COMMAND

"BOYS DON'T LIKE IT, Lieutenant," Provost said. "Feel that air—it won't be warm again. Time's running. We should have been at Renville's two weeks gone."

"We'll get there," Frémont said. "Put some tobacco in their pipes and they'll feel better."

"Sure, but there's a hell of a long way to go after Renville's. Don't forget, we ain't fixed for winter—no furs, no snowshoes, not enough blankets. Light capotes don't block real cold, you know."

"Oh, we'll be gone by winter."

"We'd better be." The mountain man turned in his saddle. "What's wrong with Papa Joe, anyhow? Way I understood it, he'd already covered the ground east of here, between the Couteau and the Mississippi. But he keeps us turning up one stream and down the next like an otter. Like he plans to explore all winter."

"Well," Frémont said, "a map like this one is never really finished."

But Provost had touched his own deep concern. Nicollet had changed. His intensity was not abating. In fact, Nicollet's earlier travels *had* covered the ground from here on. They could stop now and the map would be complete. But Nicollet seemed reluctant to end it. Day by day he delayed, refining details of terrain, unearthing new questions to be answered. He was getting . . . obsessive. Instinctively Frémont shied from the word. Of course, every added detail would improve the ultimate map—but they had immense detail already. . . .

"Skinny and ragged as scarecrows," Provost was saying, nettled and uneasy. He and Frémont were riding together, out of earshot of the others. "And sour as vinegar—hell, who feels like laughing when his pipe's empty and his guts are running?"

The old trapper was right, Frémont knew. Sunlight warmed his shoulders as he rode, but the air was cool and winy, and it carried a warning: the world was turning and they were far from home. Joe Renville's fur-trading post at Lac qui Parle would have new clothes to replace their tatters, blankets, powder, lead—and most important, tobacco. Everything was worse when the tobacco ran out. The coffee had gone first, and then the sugar and then the flour; for weeks they'd eaten nothing but fresh-killed meat and most of the men had the runs. The camaraderie around the fire was gone, the yarns and gibes and laughter. There had been two serious fights, the worse one between Bladon and Peters. Peters had emerged with a broken nose which Nicollet had set and taped, but he had been in almost constant pain since.

"They're rusty and mean," Provost went on. "It was all I could do to keep Peters from going for his rifle. If he'd picked it up, Bladon would have killed him before he could turn around."

"Bladon's a sorry devil," Frémont said.

"He's trouble, all right. Looking for it. What's worse, he's hard on horseflesh, hard on equipment. Hasn't got no sense for what's right."

Over the last three nights the weather had made everything worse: rain gusting on a hard north wind. They had used the tents, though no sensible man liked to sleep in a tent in Indian country. Twice the wind had blown the tents down, the men scrambling out cursing and shouting, their blankets drenched. Once the wind had reached under their fire shelter and blasted the coals into the downpour and it was hours before they had fire again. Their eyes were bloodshot and heavy from loss of sleep.

They had come great distances. From Devil's Lake they had crossed to the Red River of the North and then swung south into the Couteau des Prairies, that broad plateau that divides the watersheds of the Missouri and the Mississippi. From here they would turn eastward for the Minnesota at Renville's. Then they would be in forest country and they would go down the Minnesota in birch canoes to the Mississippi, where Fort Snelling stood sentinel on its bluff. Finally, running ahead of winter, wet paddles flashing in the sunlight before the storms of winter, they would sweep down the father of waters, south toward home, clear to Prairie du Chien and a waiting steamboat. . . .

Camp was plain that night, efficient as always but quickly done. Boucher set stringy antelope on roasting sticks and when the horses were cared for in the remuda below the camp the men spread their blankets on the grass to dry out the last of the storm's dampness. They ate quickly, in nearly total silence. A flight of eleven swans flew up the lake, white wings beating silently against white wings in the water; and the men watched them, but no one spoke. Dusk came earlier now, but before night fell most of the men were asleep. Provost had taken the first watch; Frémont saw his bearlike figure moving easily about the camp, rifle in the crook of his arm, making a last perimeter check before full darkness came. If Indians in search of horses were tracking them, tonight would be the time: weather clear, ground dry, men exhausted. They had passed several more Yankton Sioux encampments and the Indians had been friendly enough, though Frémont had noticed some of the younger men studying their horses.

The stars began to blaze in the darkening sky as Frémont and Nicollet readied the instruments. A cool wind, not hard but persistent, flowed from the north. It made Frémont think of nights in the North Carolina mountains when pumpkins were ripe and corn shocks stood in ghostly rows in little fields. He raised the hood of his capote and put his back to the current of air. Nicollet held the candle lantern close to the star tables in *The British Nautical Almanac.* Frémont studied him in the dim candlelight. The lines in his face were deeper. His cough had hung on, and Frémont noticed that he usually set his supper plate aside unfinished. Tonight, however, he appeared refreshed—there was a curious energy in him and his eyes seemed bright as he planned the starsights. For three nights running there had been no stars and they had estimated their positions. Tonight's sights must be especially precise.

"This should finish up the plateau, shouldn't it?" Frémont ventured.

"Almost."

"Then we can move on to Renville's."

"In due time." Nicollet sounded irritated now.

"But we're already overdue," Frémont said. "Provost says an early winter could catch us."

"*Quelle folie!* I know this country, Charles. We've got plenty of time and countless things still to do. Men like to complain. But when we stock up at Renville's, they'll be happy again. Provost is acting like an old woman."

"The thing is, he knows you've already covered the ground."

"Of course," Nicollet said impatiently, "and since he knows nothing about maps, he assumes that's all there is to it. *Précision,* Charles! That's why we are here. What was done two years ago has to be made consistent with what we're doing *now.* You see that, surely?"

"I suppose," Frémont answered uncertainly.

Nicollet had the instruments set up. "Enough of that. The stars await us."

The sightings were crisp and strong, as good as any Frémont had made. They worked in silent absorption, the camp quiet, the men dark lumps in their blankets. Provost awakened the next watch and Martineau got up, shaking his head, and presently Frémont saw him among the carts, a tall, thin man whose movements were oddly graceful. Frémont and Nicollet napped for ninety minutes, awaiting the moon, and forced themselves awake to find it high, looking chill and infinitely far away, burning out the light stardust. It was well after one o'clock when Frémont saw Martineau moving silently among the sleepers. Martineau crouched to awaken Zindel and Bladon and in a minute Frémont saw Zindel going toward the remuda. Bladon had not moved, and Martineau came back. He shook the burly man's shoulder.

"Goddamnit!" Bladon flung off Martineau's hand and sat up. "I'm awake. Get your filthy hands off me!"

Martineau recoiled, stepping back.

"Then get up, damnit," he told him angrily. "It's your watch and I done *woke* you up already."

"I'm up, you son of a bitch," Bladon said. "Get the hell away from me!"

"You watch your tongue, mister." Martineau's voice was shaking and Frémont saw his rifle come up. "I've had my fill of—"

"That's enough, Martineau," Frémont said. "He's up—go ahead and turn in."

"All right, Lieutenant," Martineau answered, "but I ain't going to take his shit forever." He moved off, his narrow back rigid, and Frémont saw Bladon roll onto his knees and heave himself upright.

"Worthless man," Nicollet muttered softly. "I had a feeling when I hired him but I ignored it. That's usually a mistake."

Bladon urinated at the edge of camp. He came back with his rifle loose in his hand and took a piece of meat from the pan left warming on the coals. With a grunt he settled under a tree to eat it, his rifle on his lap. Frémont finished the last of the starsights and began packing the instruments. His body ached. Then, surprised, he saw Nicollet open his journal and prepare his pen.

"Papa Joe," he said, "aren't you finished?"

"I've just had the most engaging thought," Nicollet said. He looked up, his eyes bright. "You remember the inconsistency in the flow of that stream we crossed—what? was it day before yesterday? I think I've solved it."

"For God's sake, Papa Joe—you've got to get some sleep!"

"Actually, I'm not in the least tired—you know, the stimulus of an idea."

Frémont was shaking his head. "You're going to destroy yourself."

"Yes, yes, Charles. You remind me of my old *maman*. 'You go to bed *immediately,* Joseph!' " He smiled, but the rebuke was plain. "I'll go to sleep soon enough, my boy. Soon enough. You really don't have to tuck me in."

When Frémont rolled in his blankets Nicollet was still sitting on the instrument box, writing intently by the flickering light of the candle stub. Frémont watched him for a moment and then he was instantly asleep.

He awakened before dawn, suddenly disturbed. The stars were paling and there was a gray note in the east. The men were stirring. In a few minutes Provost would be routing them out, shouting, *"Lève! Lève!"* Now there was the peaceful moment before the call, the blankets warm, the morning air cold on his face. But something felt wrong. Looking around, he saw Nicollet—*Nicollet was still up.* The old man sat on the instrument box, a rifle over his knees, his head sagging under the hood of his capote.

The sight filled Frémont with alarm. He threw back his blankets and pulled on his boots. He bent over Nicollet.

"Papa Joe?"

Nicollet looked up. His eyes were puffed and his face was like dirty paper. He gestured with his head.

Bladon sat leaning against a tree where Frémont had seen him last. He was asleep, his head fallen to one side, his hat awry. His rifle had slipped from his hand.

Nicollet raised his hand. "Heard him snoring. What was I to do? Awaken him? If he slept once, he'd sleep again." His voice was so low Frémont had trouble hearing him. "Animal," the astronomer said indistinctly. "I'd rather take the watch than dirty myself dealing with him." His head sagged again. "Wait till morning—let the men see . . . what *canaille* he is. Wake them all up, Charles. Let them see . . ."

"Wake them, hell!" Frémont said. You couldn't shame a man like Bladon. Papa Joe should know that. He'd flash that slow, evil grin, and in the end he'd feel clever; he'd feel he'd put one over. "Never mind them. He's got some answering to do."

Zindel was coming in from the remuda and Frémont saw Louie sitting up in his blankets. Frémont checked the caps on his pistols and slipped them back in his belt. He leaned over Bladon, lifted his rifle and kicked him hard in the ribs. He wanted Bladon *up,* on his feet; he hadn't thought beyond that.

The blow knocked Bladon away from the tree. He fell on his side with a loud grunt. Suddenly he wrapped his arms around his head and gave a loud, horrified squeal.

"He thinks you're going to scalp him, Charlie," Freniere called. Someone laughed.

Bladon rolled onto his knees, recovering. His head turned quickly to the laughter. Then he looked at Frémont. His hat was off and his hair tangled. His face was white in the dawn light and his hand went unconsciously to his beard.

"What the fuck is going on?" he asked ominously. "Did you just up and kick me?"

"You were asleep on guard duty. You're under arrest."

"Just a Goddamned minute, mister. I wasn't asleep—I been wide awake."

"You were snoring like a pig. The whole Dakota tribe could have walked in here and lifted our hair." A plan was taking shape in his mind; meanwhile it was important that the men understand the situation quickly. "Mr. Nicollet stood your whole watch. Look at him—he'd rather take the watch than deal with a man who would sleep on duty." He saw the men look at Nicollet.

"You son of a bitch," Bladon said. "I ought to kill you."

"Don't you threaten me, damn you. Get up!"

Bladon lunged to his feet. He gasped and pressed his left hand to his ribs.

"I believe you busted him in," Freniere said. To the others he added, enjoying the moment: "Lieutenant kicked the shit out of him."

"Shut up, Louie," Frémont said. He was tight as a bow string but he made his voice formal. "This is a matter of military discipline."

Red blotches spread over Bladon's face. "Military?—shit on that! Who the fuck do you think you are?" His hand flexed near his big knife. He had a bunched, coiled look, and for a moment Frémont thought that he would draw. He was intensely conscious of the near pistol snugged in his own waistband, but this time he didn't let his hand move.

The moment passed. He said smoothly. "You're in a lot of trouble, Bladon. As military commander—"

"Fuck that noise," Bladon said. "I ain't no soldier boy." A cunning look came on his face. "What the hell are you talking about? This ain't the Army—you ain't got no guardhouse. You're on your own out here, sonny boy."

"You signed on a military expedition," Frémont said. "That puts you under military orders." He knew this would come as news to the men. They were all awake now.

Bladon gave Frémont an insolent grin. "Come on, Lieutenant," he said. "Settle down. You're green and I think I'll let you get away with this. I ought to cut your belly—but shit, you just got a case of greenhorn nerves, making such a fuss. You see any Indians? Anyone lose their hair? No harm done." He spat and his voice went hard. "See what I mean? You can stick that soldier-boy talk right up your ass—and without no squad of riflemen, what do you aim to do about it?"

"I don't aim to do it—I'm doing it," Frémont said. "I'm convening a court-martial, myself as president, Mr. Nicollet as associate. I charge you with dereliction of duty. I'll testify that I found you asleep at your post. Mr. Nicollet will testify that you slept three hours and that he heard you snoring. Then I'll find you guilty and assess the penalty."

Bladon stared at him, uncertain again. The men listened in stony silence. Frémont couldn't read their faces. Provost had a calm, distant look. He understood discipline: he hadn't survived all those years in the mountains without it. Zindel was a soldier. Boucher watched with a troubled expression, as if he didn't quite comprehend. Louie's arms were folded.

"You may consider all that as accomplished," Frémont said. Then he rolled the dice. "You have been tried and found guilty. The penalty is dismissal from the expedition, or five lashes."

The bluster went out of Bladon and Frémont saw something deadly in his face. "Ain't *nobody* going to flog me," he said.

"I'll have you spread-eagled over a cart and your back scored faster than you can say your name," Frémont said. "You have three minutes to decide. Get out and I'll give you an escort to Renville's. Your pay will stop today. Or peel your shirt and take your lashes and that'll clear the books."

He paused. There wasn't a sound. Dawn had broken cleanly; the eastern sky was bright. A fish splashed in the pool. The same eleven swans flew over the water in the opposite direction, but none of the men looked up.

"Take your choice," Frémont said. "Two minutes."

"You're bluffing, Lieutenant," Bladon said. He was trembling. "You're big-talking like a kid."

"Zindel," Frémont said, "bring up an empty cart and set it hind end to." His eyes roved over the men and settled on Boucher. "You've got a good arm. Double a pack strap and make sure you don't hit him with the buckle end."

No one moved. Frémont had shifted the ground, and they were involved now. Boucher looked uncertainly at Provost.

Slowly Provost nodded. Like a judge pronouncing sentence, he said: "Son of a bitch slept on guard."

"Say, listen," Bladon cried, half-turning toward the others. "He's crazy! We never signed up for no Army show. Shit, you fellows better—"

"You bastard," Martineau said. "Cursed me when I woke you. Everybody's dog-tired. But it was *you* went to sleep." He spat on the ground. "I wouldn't piss on you if you was on fire."

"Boucher," Frémont said. "Get the strap."

Boucher unbuckled a pack. He doubled the strap and slapped it hard against his hand. It made a loud cracking noise. Zindel seized a cart by the shafts and pushed it forward.

Bladon's eyes flashed. He was crouched and all at once he looked crazy, mouth open, spittle running into his beard. His hand quivered an inch from the elkhorn haft of his knife. Frémont had never seen a man look like this. It set loose something wild in him, something that ran like quicksilver, and he realized that the control of it was an acute pleasure.

"I'm warning you, Bladon," he said. "Move on me and I'll kill you." He did not touch his pistols. "And then I'll give you a decent burial."

The animal passed out of Bladon. Abruptly he closed his mouth and straightened. "I'll go," he said slowly. "Ain't nobody going to flog me, not never. But I'll see you again, mister."

Frémont nodded. "Whenever you like," he said. "Now get yourself gone." He turned to the men. "All right, boys—let's stir up the fire and get some breakfast roasting."

To Nicollet, who had not moved or spoken, he said quietly: "Can you ride, Papa Joe? I don't want them sitting around talking about this."

"I can ride," Nicollet said.

The air was cold. Not just crisp and chill. *Cold.* Frémont wakened shivering under both blankets and read the thermometer: eighteen degrees. The figure alarmed him. They were camped in a deep forest of maples and lindens. Above him dark limbs rose against the pale sky; they were almost bare. Winter was at hand—and now they were very late.

Shaking his head, Frémont went down toward the pool to wash. His feet scuffed a few dry leaves and the noise made him uneasy. His eye roved from trunk to trunk, awaiting the anomalous shape or the clatter of birds that would mean an intruder. He was at home in the woods—but to his surprise, he already missed the open prairie. Ahead he saw Provost squatting at the pool, his heavy body braced against the tree. Provost looked up with a peculiarly stern expression.

"Ice," he said. "Look at that. Half an inch." He rapped it with his knuckle, making a hollow sound. "Ain't good," he added slowly.

"No, it's not," Frémont said.

They had come far, but plainly not far enough. They had reached Renville's at last and rested and replenished their supplies. Bladon had been there and gone; a surly bastard, old Joe Renville had said. Three canoes were awaiting them, tightly lashed and well pitched, built of birch to their order and charged to the fur-company account. William Dixon had separated there; he'd set out for Fort Pierre, hoping to beat the winter over the prairie. Renville had taken their stock at barely twenty cents on the dollar paid at Fort Pierre and they had started down the milky Minnesota in the three canoes. Now they were only thirty miles from Fort Snelling and the Mississippi, but there was another hundred and fifty miles on the father of waters to Prairie du Chien, where they'd be lucky to find a steamboat—

and already there was half an inch of ice on the pool and the air was biting cold.

"Something's wrong with Papa Joe, Lieutenant," Provost said. "He ain't turning loose."

That was true, too. Point by point they had examined the river and its contributing streams, starsights at night, sunshots at noon, compass shots on every turn, checking, positioning, sketching, analyzing the volume of water in each side stream and its fall. It was meticulous work, beautiful work—it was almost as if Nicollet dreaded seeing it end.

After a moment Provost said, "It don't matter no more about the map, you know. Whether he needs the information or whether he don't. We've run out of time."

"Well, hold on, now," Frémont said.

"Winter's making up for real now," Provost said. "Any day now this bright weather will break and snow'll come—and *real* cold. River'll lock up and there'll be a foot or two of snow, and we'll walk out. That's dangerous."

"Well, Papa Joe thinks—"

"He don't know this country. He spent one winter here and it was a mild 'un and late. He don't have no idea of what weather can be here when it turns mean." He stared at Frémont. "Anyway, don't he act like he's stopped thinking?"

The question irritated Frémont for its very accuracy. "That's ridiculous."

But Provost held his stare, solid as a stone block. "Boys don't think so," he answered. "They don't intend to walk out. Moccasins are thin and their boots are broken. No real winter gear. No pack animals. They'd be in starving time afore they got clear—I'll tell you the fact, they're thinking on getting out and letting Papa Joe come or stay, just as he likes."

"Well, hold on," Frémont said.

Provost added deliberately, "Same goes for you, Lieutenant."

The raw threat angered Frémont. "You watch yourself, Mr. Provost," he said sharply. But he knew all too well that Nicollet's attitude *was* strange—his fascination with picayune details, his casual confidence that the weather would hold. Papa Joe was evading reality. It wouldn't do.

Frémont's sharp reply had startled Provost. His brows came down against his eyes and he growled like a bear.

"No, *you* see here—"

But Frémont cut him off. This was no time to quarrel with Provost. And there was no reason to. "Never mind that," he said. "I think you're right." The decision had come, crisp and clear, formed in an instant and acted upon. "I'll tell Mr. Nicollet that we're going straight out now—you get the men started."

"Think he'll listen?"

"I won't leave him much choice. Get the men ready."

A slow, rare smile spread on Provost's face. He nodded. "I'll do that," he said. Frémont turned toward the camp and when he glanced back the mountain man was still standing by the pool, watching him.

The coffeepot was boiling, and he filled a cup and went to the instrument tent. He was still conscious of the oddly respectful look Provost had given him. Nicollet was coughing, and in a moment he came out in camp moccasins, staggering a little, boots in his hand, galluses hanging down around his waist. One of his boots had torn at the crease near the toe. He sat down heavily on the instrument case, still coughing.

Frémont draped a blanket around his shoulders. When Nicollet had the spasm under control, Frémont gave him the cup. He held it in both hands and sighed. Standing, looking down at his leader, he thought that morning was the cruelest time to inspect an old man—Nicollet looked destroyed.

"Cold this morning," Frémont said. "There's a half-inch of ice."

Nicollet glanced up at the clear sky. "Sun'll warm it up," he said casually. Then, peering at Frémont, he added, "Well, we're near the end. Just details now. There's a creek below here that puzzles me. Carries too much water for the land it's supposed to drain. Maybe it runs farther—or perhaps there's a second tributary . . ."

"That's a minor detail to risk getting trapped in winter."

"We won't get caught."

"Provost says real snow can come any day now. The only question is when the first blizzard hits."

"Oh, Provost—I know this country, *mon gars*."

"You don't know it that well—you've spent one mild winter here. And it came late."

Nicollet's eyebrows went up. "So you've been talking to him, have you?" There was a glitter in his eyes. A thin rime of sweat stood on his forehead despite the cold. Frémont touched him with the back of his fingers. The skin was hot. He was running a fever. Perhaps he'd been feverish for days. He had never really recovered from the night he'd taken Bladon's watch. He even coughed in his sleep now.

"You're ill, Papa Joe," Frémont said quietly.

Nicollet cast him an angry look. "No, no," he said. "it's just the coffee. Makes me sweat." Then, as if to mollify him, "All right, we can move on. Just a squint at the creek, nothing elaborate, then on to Fort Snelling. But we do have a problem going down the Mississippi from there. We simply *must* work our way down the west bank carefully and rechart it. Two weeks—well, say three."

He *is* ill, Frémont thought. To talk of weeks now was madness.

"No," he said. "That means getting caught for sure. Too much risk. We're going to have to move. And move quickly."

Nicollet looked up, surprised—and noticed the bustle in the camp. The men were trotting as they bundled the gear and moved it down to the canoes.

"What's going on?" he asked ominously.

"I told Provost to get things together." Frémont made his voice matter-of-fact. "We can make Snelling by nightfall if we push it. We'll spend a day there and start downriver the next. I intend to get you out before the rivers lock."

"No! You're talking like a fool. You'll jeopardize everything."

"No, we won't. The map is complete now—at worst we'll lose a few refinements."

Nicollet blinked at him. "But it's the *refinements* that make the difference! That's the polish, the *précision*—I don't have to tell you that."

"But the alternative is to get frozen in—cache the instruments and walk out. Suppose we lost the data? What then? I just can't take that risk."

"*You* can't?" Nicollet flushed. "And just how does it become your responsibility?"

"Well, sir," Frémont said carefully, "I'm responsible to you. And then, I'm also responsible to Mr. Poinsett. This is a military expedition, after all—"

"By God, sir," Nicollet cried, suddenly very angry, "do you think you can deal with me as you dealt with Bladon? You are speaking to—" He caught his breath and burst into a paroxysm of coughing.

The question struck Frémont like a blow. He stared at Nicollet in consternation; he realized again how much he cared for the old man—there was a sudden sharp memory of his own father just before he'd died, much younger but with the same ravaged quality he now saw on Nicollet's face. Impulsively he dropped to a knee and took the astronomer's hand.

"Oh, Papa Joe," he said softly, "you know better than that—surely you do. But you must realize—"

"Realize!" Nicollet said. "I realize you're a damned insubordinate puppy! . . . Provost!" he called, and had another fit of coughing.

"Don't, Papa Joe," Frémont said quickly. He heard the change in his voice, the softness gone. "Don't try it. He's going to go, we're all going—and so are you. Don't force the issue."

Nicollet stared at him suspiciously. "Why are you siding with them? They're ignorant. Decent men but ignorant. They've never understood what I'm doing, but I thought you did. But you don't care either, do you?" Sweat ran down his face. Before Frémont could protest, he was pleading: "Charles, don't do this to me! Can't you see—the map must be flawless. This is my last chance! There'll never be another. I'm old, I admit it, I'm old. The world is still before *you,* but I—and I can recoup, do you understand?"

Frémont rose on a wave of anger. "So that's it," he said. That's what this mad wandering in the wilderness was all about. "You're as hungry for your lost honors as ever. All that sanctimonious talk—"

"For God's sake, don't be naive." Nicollet threw down the empty cup. "I gave you excellent advice, all very true—but don't expect me to live up to every high-minded idea I voice."

Frémont glared at him, torn between contempt and that oddly forceful affection. He couldn't reconcile the old man's raw ambition now surfacing so dangerously with the wisdom he'd shown so often—did the astronomer take him for a fool?—and yet he had a feeling that some complexity was escaping him.

"This is my last chance," Nicollet repeated in a quieter tone. "Everything depends on this map. There'll be more expeditions, bigger ones. Poinsett said as much—the whole western country cries out for real exploration, real mapping. And who's to do it? I am, we are—that's why every position we take is crucial! What we produce must be perfect—and everything else will follow. Try not to be obtuse."

The answer outraged Frémont. He glared at Nicollet, seeing the feverish eyes, the crumpled face, the galluses hanging limply at his side. Such excellence turned in on itself!

"You're ill," he said brutally. "You're half out of your head and you're not making sense. It's you who's running out of time. The rest of us can get out, no matter what the weather does. *You're* the one who won't make it—you're the one we'll have to bury in the snow. And by God, sir, I won't let that happen!"

The camp was broken, the men were ready; only the instrument tent remained. Provost approached them.

"Later!" Frémont called in a tone that stopped Provost as if he'd struck a wall. Without a word he turned and rejoined the men.

Nicollet seemed not to have noticed him. He was gazing up at Frémont, his face twisted. "Dear God, but youth is cruel—understands nothing, takes everything. Wait until you're old, my boy, and everything dwindles down to a single chance and some arrogant young man butts *you* aside."

Frémont gazed at him, appalled. It wasn't true, it was the other way around: age was selfish and single-minded. He winced at the old man's anguish and started to deny the charge—but he knew that he had won and he felt pleased. He felt newly calm and in control, ready to be generous.

He knelt again and put a hand on Nicollet's knee. "No one is butting you, Papa Joe," he said gently. "You're not losing anything. The map will succeed just *because* we are getting out. With all the data intact. Can't you see that?"

Nicollet's head had sunk forward as if in surrender. Sadness seemed to interlay Frémont's triumph—well, enough of that; he was moving them out and there was nothing more to it.

The astronomer looked up and Frémont, startled, saw he wasn't at all broken.

"Very well," Nicollet said coldly. "Then *you* will have to do it. What we must have is a thorough reconnaissance of the western bank from the entrance of the Minnesota to Prairie du Chien. Now, you say I'm too ill, too old—"

"I didn't say too old."

"Too old, that's what you meant! Then you must do it. We will go on to Snelling, and there you will take the grand canoe and five men—all strong, all young. You will work the western bank: every turn charted, every entering stream pinpointed by sightings. If snow catches you, hole up until you can travel again. If the river freezes, walk. I will wait for you at Prairie du Chien."

"All right," Frémont said.

"Not 'all right'!" Nicollet said fiercely. "Rather, 'Yes sir!' I am not asking, I'm *ordering*—since this seems to be a day for orders. I'm detailing that part of the expedition to *you*—and I will hold you responsible for it. Remember that, Lieutenant!"

It was as if Nicollet had regained himself. The cough rattled in his chest but he suppressed it. Frémont realized that the old man felt badly used and was retaliating—and suddenly he knew that should he fail, the older man would roast him. But he would not fail. Even if the ice caught him, he would get out. He liked the idea—a small command executing a last, vital mission.

"Yes sir," he said, "without fail."

GATEWAY

FRÉMONT JUMPED OFF THE STEAMBOAT onto the St. Louis levee, and the queen city of the upper Mississippi Valley unfolded before him like a magic carpet. He whacked Louie on the shoulder. "Look at that!" he cried.

It was stunning—the noise, the people, the excitement, the *city*. They had come down the Mississippi to Prairie du Chien, but that was a town, nothing at all like this; there they had found that Nicollet had gone on and they had followed. Frémont felt as if he had been forever in the wilderness. The most mundane things had a delightful air of freshness; wherever they looked there was something to catch the eye.

St. Louis was big: it had a brewery, a tannery, a foundry, an ironworks, a yard that could haul the biggest steamboats for repairs. It had a four-story hospital, and a new courthouse going up to accommodate its contentious lawyers. Its hotels were the envy of the West and there were more newspapers than a man could find time to read. Ten steamboats landed every day. There were saddlers, gunsmiths, bootmakers, wainwrights, apothecaries, mercantile emporiums. Limestone warehouses still stank of furs at wharves along the river, with boat chandlers, rivermen's hostels and taverns shouldering among them. From the floodplain the city climbed swiftly to a commanding height, where the streets widened and the buildings were finer, made of hewn stone and brick, their triple-sashed windows framed in white. Sixteen thousand people lived in St. Louis, and it seemed to Frémont that all of them were out on its streets in the warm winter sunshine.

"Ain't it a joy?" Louie said. They stopped for a bowl of gumbo and had three, so luxurious was it to their trail-worn palates. A clock on the cathedral tower turned to eleven and bells cast in Normandy tolled the hours. A boy burst from a printshop with a sheaf of newspapers. Frémont saw the red twist of a barber pole and marked it for later. Iron wagon wheels rumbled on coblestones, a whip cracked overhead, a fight boiled out of a tavern and they stopped to bet on its outcome. A man in a fine frock coat nailed legal papers to a post, and a constable with a silver star eyed them coldly, marking their faces. The odor of beer drifted from a tavern where a man was telling jokes in brogue to bursts of laughter. A slender woman approached, hooped skirts swaying, and they stepped carefully aside to give her passage. She looked at Frémont, her lips red, her cheek smooth, a flash of blue eye quickly lowered. Oh, the city! The people and the impact of their numbers, the power of their laughter and their quick movements, the sight of a woman, her waist so small you could put your hands around it and pick her up and swing her about, and then lay her down—

"We were too long on the trail, Louie," Frémont cried, but even as he spoke he had a sudden flashing image of that high sun-shot prairie, the sky running unbroken to the ends of the world, and he felt a longing that was as sharp as the odor of horsemint crushed underfoot.

Louie had turned to watch the woman. "I'll go along with that," he said. "I'm ready to *howl.*" He threw up his arms and for a moment Frémont thought that he would loose a joyous bellow, but he seemed to think better of it. He was ready for action, which meant the Green Tree Tavern, where every right-thinking riverman and trapper and plainsman went when he came to town. Hard on the riverfront, it offered all a man could want—good food and liquor, the merry rattle of dice mixed with the murmur of stud-poker players. You'd see your friends and you'd get the news: who's in town, and who's come and gone, and who's dead—and who did the killing.

And women. Freniere cut a glance at him, his grin going sly. "They got willing women in this town," he said. "You ain't had a woman till you've had a St. Louis woman. Hoo-*eee*! They love to dance and they love to drink and my, oh my, but they love to love." He was laughing. "Ain't no taming 'em and ain't no stopping 'em. St. Louis woman gets aholt of you, she'll turn you every *which* way but loose!"

Mischievously he studied Frémont. "Come on, Charlie," he said. "That's what you need—it'll take some of the starch out of you."

Frémont laughed, and shook his head. His blood ran hot at the thought, but his mind had already tracked the evening through to its cheerless end. He hungered for a woman, true enough, he knew he was incomplete without one—but what he sought would never be found in any whorehouse. With a stealthy throb of regret he thought all at once of Cecilia: her great luminous eyes, the way her hair fell in a glistening black rope of braid along her throat. "Ah, Jean—*c'est ton destin de rechercher le bout des choses* . . ." Her voice surprisingly rich for such a young girl, the Creole intonation singsong and dreamy . . .

To search out the end of things. She'd sensed that in him more than understood it. He'd fallen wildly in love with her—for months he could think only of her lithe, sensual grace. Ah, the obsessions of fifteen. . . . He'd been expelled from Charleston College because of that white-hot first passion, to the consternation of old Dr. Roberton and his mother's furious dismay.

"The chance of your life, and you've thrown it away—for *nothing*!" Her lovely soft face forbidding and severe. "You and I, already hanging by a thread, so—*vulnerable* . . . we of all people can never afford this sort of thing, John. Never! Do you understand me? Do you?"

In his anguish he'd bitten off the obvious reply and left the room, wandered half the night through the palmetto woods and swamp, weeping and raging. He had been forced still again to swallow his rage at what they had endured. Yes, it could lead to shame, to public disgrace—he knew *that* well enough. All right. He could put Cecilia behind him, he would harden his heart for his mother's sake. But it was what he *was*: it was the fierce, impulsive urging of the heart—and the heart never lied, he knew that with every beat of his young blood . . . He would live with the live coal lodged in his belly. But he would follow his own star, his *own* sense of honor—and by God, they would accept him for what he was. . . .

"I'll pass for tonight, Louie," he said softly now. "There's too much to see."

They went on to Judge La Place's where Nicollet was staying, and Frémont reported on his survey between Fort Snelling and Prairie du Chien. He'd mapped the entire west bank, as he'd known he would. Snow had caught them on the fourth day, and the river had frozen over below Lake Pepin, but the six of them walked into Prairie du Chien in good order, proud as punch and twice as cocky. Papa Joe, pleased with his summary, told him that Missouri's senior senator, the famous Thomas Hart Benton, of whom Frémont had heard Poinsett speak so enthusiastically, was giving a reception later that afternoon; Nicollet planned to attend and he wanted his protégé to accompany him.

There was plenty of time first for a round at the Green Tree, and he and Louie went down into the narrow, oddly angled streets along the river. Here were many of the old French houses of palisaded logs set upright and daubed with mud, a veranda across the narrow front. Frémont could smell the wind coming off the river. Now the buildings were on stone pilings and stairs led up to their porches. Women watched at the windows, giggling and peeping out. One flung up the sash and cried to them: *"Vous me trouvez charmante, hein?"*

Louie doffed his battered hat. *"Bientôt, chérie!"* he called.

The door of the next house popped open with a bang. A big man in a fancy shirt, an apron around his waist, had snatched a smaller man onto the porch. The man seemed dazed. His hat fell off. His hair was mouse-colored and shot with gray. Just then the bartender stepped back and gave him a savage kick that sent him sprawling headfirst down the steps.

"Now hold up! Stop everything!" the man squalled incongruously, and suddenly Frémont recognized him.

"My God," he said, "that's Mr. Beasley . . ."

"Friend of yours?" Louie asked in surprise.

"He was on the steamer coming out from Cincinnati." Of course, on the *Louisville Queen,* a sallow little man with a wife who looked ill, on his way from an Ohio Valley farm to settle in the West. He'd had his hands full keeping his daughter's chastity intact—indeed, she'd almost surrendered it to Frémont in a lounge chair on the hurricane deck one night. He had just made the breathtaking discovery that she was wearing nothing under her voluminous gown when her father had come up braying like a goat, and sent her packing . . . and then, holding Frémont, had talked to him for over an hour, rhapsodizing the dream of going west. "Out to Oregon, b'God, for a new start. I tell you, young feller, the Ohio Valley's done for. It's all in the hands of the moneymen, them rapacious devils. No place left for an honest farmer working the soil. I tell you, ain't no greater story in all mankind than when Jesus Christ went into the temple and whipped the moneylenders. Lashed 'em! Scattered their coin!"

He'd paused to spit a gout of tobacco juice over the railing at the dark water below. "Only He didn't whip 'em hard enough. Seems like they've prospered ever since. Well, the Oregon country is the answer—they say the corn tassles out over a man's head and land is free for the taking. Now, I ain't never seen no land of milk and honey—but Oregon's the place, son. I'm on my way!"

Now the farmer picked himself up from the street and ran back up the steps, yelling, "Oh no you don't, you ugly sin-loving devil! I'm taking my daughter out of there!"

The bartender punched Beasley, driving him back down the steps with quick, light blows, punishing but not finishing him. Beasley's eyes were glazed; his mouth was bloody. With a mean half-smile, the bartender caught his shirtfront and cocked his fist like a mallet—and then Frémont had stiff-armed him in the chest. He grunted and stepped back. Beasley fell to his knees.

"That's enough of that," Frémont said.

"Who the hell are you?" the bartender demanded.

"You want to find out?"

The door flew open and a girl ran out, her round face red and angry.

"Ellie, get the hell back inside," the bartender said.

"You shut up, Harry! He's my paw and I'm telling him to get out of here and leave me alone!"

"You heard the lady," Frémont said. Ellie didn't look much different than she had that night on the steamer. He'd ached all the next day, but Beasley had never taken his eye off the girl. Frémont was relieved that she didn't recognize him.

"Ellie," Beasley staggered to his feet, "come out of there. That's a damned whorehouse. Ellie, *you are selling your body!* Come out of there, come home . . ."

"We ain't got no home and you know it! You can't take care of me. Look what you done to Maw."

"I didn't—"

"Paw, you done ruined everything you touched, but I ain't going to let you ruin me."

"Honey, please, that ain't so. You know I tried."

She stared at him, and her anger faded. "Oh Paw, for God's sake, go on away, won't you? You done killed Maw—just leave me alone."

"Ellie . . ."

"Don't you see—this is something I can *do,* Paw."

"You can do other things."

"I don't know what. And anyway—" she grinned, a sudden bittersweet flash that made her pretty again "—at least I've had some experience at this."

And she was gone, the door slammed behind her. Beasley started to cry. Then he saw Frémont and recognized him.

"What are you doing here?" he asked feebly.

"Come on, Mr. Beasley. You need a drink."

The Green Tree was dark inside. It was warm and smelled of meat and pickles and beer. Frémont saw a horseshoe bar of scarred mahogany with its brass rail gleaming. Two barmaids who might have been twins looked up, expressionless, and he heard a piano playing somewhere. A game was on, cards slapping down and men laughing, and someone waved to Louie, who held up a demurring hand. As they maneuvered Beasley to a table, Frémont saw on the wall above them a huge painting of Jackson at New Orleans, American gunners looking over their black barrels at Packenham's troops marching in close order, British red coats so soon to be scattered and dying. Not that there was much truth in the big, varnished panorama. The militia had cowered behind their cotton bales, pinned there by officers with drawn pistols, forced to take the chance against the sure thing. So much for art.

A waiter brought a whiskey bottle and three small glasses. Frémont filled the glasses but didn't touch his own. Beasley bolted the drink and held another in his hand, cradling it, warming on its presence.

"Oh, my God," he said. "My own daughter in a bawdyhouse. I tell you, this benighted country's been the ruination of me. I never should have left the Ohio Valley." He drank again and Freniere refilled his glass.

"But then, I was ruint there, too. They took my farm at the sale, you know. Took it all. Left me just enough for a wagon and mules . . ." He looked up. "Well, I'da made it, too. I know I would. That's a fact. I don't give up too easy." He glared at Frémont. "I'm a tough old boot. I'da made it."

"What happened?"

Beasley looked at him in surprise. "Well, hell, there ain't no way to *go* to Oregon." He emptied the glass and Freniere shrugged and refilled it again.

"*Ain't* no Oregon Trail! Folks laughed in my face when I asked about it. Ain't no way to the promised land. That's all a lie. Don't nobody go. Trail ain't even a trail."

"It's a trapper's route," Louie said. "Ain't like a wagon trail, with ruts you can follow. Such as it is, it covers two thousand miles of empty country, plains, mountains—"

"It ain't worth nothing if you can't follow it."

"That's for sure." Louie glanced at Frémont. "Remember old Provost?"

Beasley grasped Frémont's forearm as if it was suddenly important to make everything clear. "Seen then I couldn't go on—well, I couldn't go back, neither. Didn't know *what* the hell to do. We camped in that marsh south of town, and after a while I had to sell off the stock. Found me work, but then Sarey come down with the fever."

He emptied his glass again. "Well, directly she went to shaking with chills and next thing you know she'd be burning up. I done everything I could to keep her alive—wrapped her in wet cloths trying to break the fever. And then Ellie threw a fit and said I'd killed her maw. Wasn't true, God knows it wasn't true . . ."

He began to cry then—short, hiccuping sobs. "End of the road, boys."

Tears streamed down his face and into his pale mustache. "I'm through."

"No, you're not," Frémont said, in pity.

"Ruint!" Beasley cried loudly. He looked up, his eyes fierce. "That Oregon talk is a dream. False as the devil's tongue. It lures a man like honey lures a fly—and it kills him."

Frémont stared at him, appalled and angered. This shouldn't happen to any man, let alone a hardworking Ohio farmer. How could that great, sun-drenched sweep of prairie turn into a man's disaster?

"Thomas Hart Benton," Nicollet said, "is chairman of the Military Affairs Committee of the Senate. I don't suppose I need point out how important that makes him to us?"

"To us?" Frémont echoed. He was still thinking of Beasley; he couldn't shake off his sense of the man's terrible anguish.

"Yes, to us!" It was late afternoon and they were walking to Joshua Brant's home, where Senator Benton was holding open house. Brant had married Benton's cousin; Benton made his headquarters there when he was in the city. "Senator Benton has his finger on the Army's budget. If he approves an expedition, that pretty well assures it; if he disapproves, that is certain to kill it." He slipped his arm through Frémont's. "Benton is a great enthusiast of western exploration. He is essential to us, my boy. Essential."

When Frémont had seen Nicollet that morning he had thought him rested and improved, but now he was not so sure. He seemed fretful and tense. They walked slowly, past homes of stone and brick, the flowerbeds mulched for winter, the gazebos forlornly empty. Listening to him, Frémont realized that Nicollet was disturbed by the prospect of seeing Benton.

Everyone knew of Benton, of course; many assumed that eventually he would be President. Mr. Poinsett admired him extravagantly; he himself had represented South Carolina in the Senate and served in the diplomatic corps. He knew everyone. But he thought Benton the greatest of the lot, for his service to Andrew Jackson alone.

"The country was headed for another revolution if the general hadn't come along when he did, Charles. It was Tom Benton who carried Jackson's battles in the Senate—and it's there that the great issues are settled. When it comes to the test, Tom Benton's a great man."

Benton was one of four giants in the Senate—and the other three usually were lined up against him. Henry Clay of Kentucky might outmaneuver him; the golden-tongued Daniel Webster of Massachusetts might soar over him in debate; the implacable John C. Calhoun of South Carolina could string out logic in strands as fine as spiderwebbing; but none was Benton's equal in tenacity, will and force of personality. So it was no surprise, as Poinsett had declared, that when Martin Van Buren succeeded Jackson four years ago, people assumed that Benton ultimately would succeed Van Buren.

Yet Nicollet clearly had quite a different view.

"Politician. Beware of all politicians, Charles. American politics are barbarous, really. Men abuse each other in the vilest terms—the crowd seems to expect it. And now we have that old bumpkin Harrison, who spent his life on the frontier and shows it. You can see why we especially need Benton's backing now."

"Sir?"

"The Democrats are out, Charles. Joel Poinsett will be replaced in March. How will a new administration view our work? Better to have a powerful friend in the Senate, eh?"

"And he *is* a friend?"

"We must make him one—if we can. He's—well, so damned egocentric, so certain that he knows everything, you can never be sure if he's even listening to you." Nicollet was plainly nervous. "He's used to bowling men over—that's why they fear him, I suppose."

"He killed someone, didn't he?" Frémont asked.

"Twenty years ago. People still talk about it. He and a young lawyer named Charles Lucas had some silly quarrel and met on Bloody Island. Lucas was wounded and he pinked Benton. That would have ended it, I suppose, but for the boy's father, the old judge."

Nicollet sighed. Man's intransigence pained him. "Judge Lucas hated Benton—he's a vitriolic old devil to this day—and he spread stories. Benton took them as having come from young Lucas, declared himself unsatisfied by the last meeting—which was his right—and demanded another. And shot Lucas dead that time. Old Lucas has called it murder ever since, which of course it wasn't—Lucas had a pistol too. But people felt that Benton forced the fight unnecessarily."

"What does Benton say?"

"*Grand Dieu!* Who would ask him? Really, Charles."

"I just wondered."

"Wonder no more, then. They say he never discusses it and never responds to the judge's aspersions. Ignores him. That takes a kind of courage too, one must admit."

Frémont could see the setting sun striking the far bank of the Mississippi below them. The river itself was in shadow and had a cold look—soon it would freeze here, too. He shivered suddenly. The meeting with Beasley had given an undercurrent to the day, like the river running dark against the glowing bank.

A dignified black man met them at Joshua Brant's door and took their coats. Congenial sounds came from within: men talking, a woman's laugh, a ladle clinking against a punch bowl. They stepped into a large drawing room where candles already were lighted. The windows were high and the walls covered with a light French wallpaper that set off the dark floors of polished walnut, left bare in the St. Louis fashion.

Frémont recognized Benton immediately. The Senator was a big man in his late fifties, wearing a black frock coat of the old cut and a white silk stock tied in a flowing bow. He had taken a commanding position before the fireplace, where he stood with his head thrown back, looking down a massive wedge of nose at an admiring circle. He seemed to radiate power. When Nicollet presented Frémont and Benton's slightly bulbous eyes turned on him, he understood all that Nicollet had been saying; without qualification Benton was as forceful a man as he had ever met.

He took a glass of pale wine from a passing tray. The circle of men shifted readily to admit him and Nicollet; they were plainly in attendance: deferential, reluctant to disagree, quick to laugh at Benton's sallies. Pierre Chouteau was there in a splendid velvet coat. An old trapper boss named McCaffrey wore a white fringed buckskin jacket and reminded Frémont a little of Provost. Two men were planters, one a judge. A steamboat captain named Bingham wore pilot's trousers, a chart of the Mississippi actually woven into the fabric, and there was a stern-looking wagonmaster from the Sante Fe trade. A legislator named Caldwell seemed uneasy in the company and paid slavish attention to Benton.

"Can we look for better times, Senator?" Captain Bingham asked. "My boat's been tied up more'n she's run, the last three years."

"Don't doubt it a bit," Benton said. "The whole country's been reeling since Thirty-seven. I predicted the crash far in advance."

"They shoulda listened to you," Caldwell said.

"Now, don't misunderstand me," Benton said. "When General Jackson took the national treasury away from the private bankers, he never did a greater thing. Those rascals controlled our economy—which meant they controlled the nation. More powerful than the Congress *or* the President, by God—until they met a man brave enough to take 'em on—and strong enough to whip 'em."

"Played hell with the money, though," Chouteau said.

"Reclaiming money from the central bankers didn't cause that, Pierre," Benton countered reprovingly. "It was what he did with the funds. Jackson thought spreading the money around in state banks would keep power from getting centralized in any one place. I tried to tell him the state banks would lend it right out and that would heat the economy red hot—and sooner or later it would bust. Well, the general understood power better than he did money. He went ahead, and it busted like an egg, just as I said it would. And my friends, that's why Van Buren lost the election."

" 'Twas great while it lasted, though," said a factory owner whose name Frémont had missed. "I'd never a'got my factory without those easy loans."

Chouteau gave him a sour look. "Everybody got those damned loans, and most of 'em couldn't repay. You could see the crash coming a mile off." Men like Chouteau would always see it coming, Frémont thought; men like Beasley never would.

"Well," Benton said, reclaiming the floor, "you gentlemen know my position—hard money, a gold-based coinage, and you wouldn't have these problems. When the value of money fluctuates, that's fatal for the little man."

"They don't call you Old Bullion for nothing, now do they, Senator?" Caldwell said admiringly. Frémont saw a pleased look cross Benton's face at the use of his famous nickname.

"Well," said Chouteau, "it's been hard on the Mississippi Valley. I'll tell you, Tom, *mon vieux,* we're drying up like a backwater pond."

The wine tray passed again and Nicollet took a fresh glass with a little sigh of appreciation. Several latecomers had joined the circle around Benton. Across the room, a man with pointed mustaches came to the end of a droll story and three women rewarded him with peals of laughter. Frémont heard Chouteau saying that it just seemed as though there was nothing left in the West—and suddenly it was like listening to Provost again in the dark around the campfire with the smell of roasting buffalo heavy on the air.

"Looks to me like we're gonna let a whole empire slip away from us," Chouteau said.

"Never," Benton told him, his voice harsh. "That would be a crime."

But in the next breath the Senator had to admit that whatever was to take men west in the future, it wouldn't be fur. They all agreed; the mighty fur trade that had poured through St. Louis was gone. Frémont remembered old Provost on Astor's people—greedy, conniving souls with packs full of shiny gewgaws and whiskey, the better to bilk the Indians. All to take the beaver, and no thought of anything else. Old John Jacob Astor had come out of New York to found Astoria on the mouth of the Columbia for his American Fur Company, but then he'd lost it to the British in the War of 1812, leaving the Hudson's Bay Company in control of the Oregon fur country. But it was American trappers who had taken hold in the Rocky Mountains. Astor's people merged with the Chouteau interests in St. Louis, and ultimately Pierre Chouteau, his hands now tightly gripping the lapels of his fine velvet jacket, had succeeded to control—but control of what?

It was over, Chouteau was saying gloomily. Benton was nodding, a hard, compressed look on his face. It was awesome to think of half a continent where a few intrepid white men had roamed for forty years now abandoned with hardly a mark of their passage, as untouched by civilization as it had been at the start. Just a handful of trading posts, Fort Laramie and Fort Bridger and Bent's Fort, and even they were fading now. The beaver were gone, the trade was dead. There was a sharp edge in Chouteau's voice, his knuckles white against the black velvet, and it struck Frémont that this margrave of a once-mighty empire was a frightened man.

There was a little silence, like a memorial. Glancing into the second room, Frémont saw a girl move suddenly into view. She was followed by three young cavalry officers from Jefferson Barracks, dragoons with bright yellow stripes down the sides of their blue trousers. For an instant Frémont had a notion that she was fleeing them—and needed rescue—but then she resumed conversation with them. He stared at her. She was extremely pretty—no, she wasn't, it was more than that, she was *beautiful.* A strong, fine nose, uncommonly large hazel eyes—it was her eyes that made her beautiful. She wore her shining dark brown hair shorter than usual, gathered with graceful looseness at the back of her elegant head. Eighteen, perhaps. Or twenty. Or sixteen. It was hard to tell—and it didn't matter at all. She was wearing a pink gown, candy-striped, with a rose sash, and the color set off the translucent pink and white of her skin, glowing and so alive, filled with a kind of light.

One of the officers struck Frémont especially, a tall, handsome fellow with a grand yellow mustache who had a way of leaning forward with easy grace when he spoke to her, as if he were lifting a mount over a difficult hurdle. Frémont took an instant dislike to him and wished he had worn his own uniform. It was a foolish impulse, of course; he wasn't in St. Louis with troops and it wouldn't have been appropriate, but still—then a shadow that suggested acute boredom crossed the girl's face as the tall officer said something he must have meant to be witty, and Frémont felt a flash of elation. Her eyes were roving over the confident subaltern's shoulder as he talked on—they met Frémont's and stopped.

The contact held, prolonged itself. Her eyes remained openly locked to his. He stared back, heedless, knowing it was rude, that he should wrench his gaze away from this remarkably candid girl—but he didn't care. He was making a fool of himself; in a moment she would be offended . . . and then she *smiled.* He had never seen such a smile. Bright as a prairie sky, the bond between them so strong it was as if he could feel her hand warm in his. A girl of spirit, of infinite spirit and charm. And there was sand there, too—he knew it without question. He thought all at once: *the very girl for me*—and could have laughed out loud. For another crackling instant they held each other and then, with the faintest nod that assured him that something real had happened, she turned back to the three officers. She was smiling still, but it seemed to Frémont nothing at all like the smile that she had given him. He was filled with a strange and headlong excitement. He must find a way to—

Nicollet had nudged him. "*Attendez,* Charles," he murmured in warning, and with a physical effort Frémont forced himself to return to the conversation. They were still discussing the bitter termination of westward movement. Benton had an engaged, aggressive look now. For two hundred years Americans had pushed west—over the Appalachians ridge by ridge and into the Ohio Valley, settlers sufficient to bring Kentucky and Tennessee into the Union before the turn of the century. Then Missouri, Arkansas newly entered, talk of Iowa next—but there, poised on the edge of the great western grasslands, the advance had stalled.

Nor was it only Missouri that wanted expansion west and the growth that followed in its wake. The *nation* wanted it, Benton was saying authoritatively, the more so since the crash. Ruined farmers and men whose jobs had vanished were looking west, seeking new land, new opportunities. But nothing had happened. The bitter irony of the failing fur trade was that white men were pulling *out* of what should have been the greatest empire the world had ever known.

Benton glared down his long nose. "The problem, gentlemen, is that until now this country's advance has been made by individuals—mountain men, then pioneer settlers, men willing to clear eighty acres and plant a stand of corn and wait for civilization to catch up."

Nicollet was nodding, his lips pursed.

"But no individual can press on alone into grasslands. Everything is different there—without trees for building, without the abundant rainfall of forest country, how can he possibly make his eighty acres succeed?"

Frémont, watching the other men nodding glumly, felt a surge of impatience. The girl was still talking to the officers; once she laughed, a heedless, merry laugh over the sound of voices.

"Those first pioneers have carried us on their backs for two hundred years. Now we must find new ways. For our time." Benton might have been on the Senate floor. "I say we must act. We must explore this empire. Learn how to *use* it. We must have more information than even the wisest trapper can give us—with all due respect, Mr. McCaffrey."

The man in buckskin smiled suddenly, looking wintry and pleased. "Fact, Senator," he said. Frémont glanced at Nicollet, but his mentor showed no disposition to speak.

"Yes," Benton said now, in full voice, "we have to find a way to open the great West. I foresee a day when it will be teeming with settlers, when the white canvas of immigrant wagons will sail on those prairies like ships on a busy sea. I see an empire, gentlemen, that stetches to the Pacific—yes, and reaches beyond, across the vast Pacific to China—"

"Oh, for God's sake," Frémont heard himself say impatiently, "why do we talk of China when a man can't get to *Oregon* to save his very life?"

Thomas Hart Benton had been enjoying himself, standing with his back to a warming fire, the center of attention. He was resting from the campaign—eleven hundred miles in the saddle, crossing and recrossing Missouri. Not bad for a man of fifty-eight. His own seat in the Senate wasn't up this year; he'd done it all in support of Van Buren's feckless hopes for reelection, and Missouri's people hadn't let him down. They'd held for the Democrats even when the cause was hopeless and their hearts weren't in it. Did it for him, God bless 'em.

He enjoyed this kind of talk, relaxed, the campaign over, surrounded by old friends—enjoyed it the more, too, because he could attend it with a quarter of his mind. They were good men, but their perspective was a view of the world as seen through a crack. Still, when a man had shinnied to the top of the pole, could he expect those below to share his view?

Actually, he was thinking about the shambles he'd find when he went back to Washington. The men here were puling about the crash, but they should see the bread lines in New York and Baltimore. When he had offered warning, fatuous little Van Buren had smiled and actually said to him, "Your friends think you're a little exalted in the head on that subject." Benton had bowed without a word, thinking, *You will feel the thunderbolt, my old friend.* No tears for Van Buren—he'd had his turn. Let him go home to Kinderhook and raise apples. Benton was at peace. It would be a tonic to be in the opposition for a change. Why, it would be like a vacation after the Jackson years.

And it would free him for his real interest, which was opening the West, doing something about Oregon. Outrageous that the blasted British should still be there, making their footless claims to the whole kit and caboodle.

Chouteau had surprised him just now; he sounded like an old woman. Of course the trade was dying, and that's what it deserved. Forty years they'd had, and they'd done nothing but strip out furs and money, greedy as hogs. Hadn't raised a building or brought in a single settler. No, what was needed was a whole new approach that would open things up! This nation hadn't grown by waiting, and that wasn't Tom Benton's way, either!

He'd been rolling along on his favorite theme when this young chap Nicollet had brought along had broken in on him, rudely enough. Anger flared in him; he stared hard at the younger man, seeing him clearly for the first time, trying to remember his name. *Frémont*: that was it.

"Now, you mind your manners, young feller," McCaffrey was saying. "You happen to be talking to Senator Benton."

"I'm fully aware of that, sir," Frémont answered evenly, though his eyes flashed once.

"Charles," Nicollet rebuked him, "I *beg* you to remember—"

"I simply want to speak the truth . . ."

"Senator," the astronomer was saying nervously now, "I very much regret—my assistant is a—"

"—a most precipitate young man," Benton finished for him, his voice heavy with irony. He fastened Frémont with his eyes. "But go on. You have something further to offer, do you?"

"I've just come from a man who's been broken by the Oregon myth, as surely as if he'd been shot down in the street! We ramble along as if it were some remote academic problem out there in the distance—but it isn't in the distance for this man. He's ruined *now*."

Frémont. Army officer, wasn't he? Yes. Abert's section. Strong-looking young fellow. Good eyes. Mustard in him, apparently. Of course he could be just another one of these young hotheads trying to make an impression with a lot of blow and bluster. But watching him Benton didn't think so; there was more to him than that.

Frémont was talking about some farmer he'd met named Beasley. "It's a terrible waste, Senator. A man's life destroyed—and it didn't have to happen at all! There doesn't *need* to be any mystery about the western territory."

"So you say, sir," Benton replied with a grunt.

"I say so because it's true, sir! There's no reason for the Oregon Trail to be almost unknown, when there's such a hunger to use it. There's a way. There *are* solutions—and here we stand gabbling about it like a flock of geese . . ."

"Charles!" Nicollet repeated sharply. "*Prends garde . . .*"

"Not many men have compared me to a goose," Benton said softly in the sudden, taut silence. "At least, not very often. Do you make that comparison, sir?"

"I misspoke, sir." Frémont recovered himself quickly. "I beg you to accept my apologies. But with all respect, I must stand on my point: there *is* a ready solution."

"And what may that be, pray?" He summoned his most formidable stare, and the young man flushed; but he held Benton's gaze.

"Sir, we have just returned from an extensive examination of open country."

"I'm quite familiar with Monsieur Nicollet's work."

"And the map we'll produce from it will open that territory."

"Ah, well," Benton muttered, "maps . . ." He was suddenly bored, and curiously disappointed. There was something in the man that had caught his attention, seemed to promise more than this. "We have too many maps. They do more harm than good. Just generalized descriptions in sketchy charts. Usually they're wrong; sometimes they lie; none are practical. I thought—" He broke off, coming to decision: enough of this. "Very well, sir. I accept your apology."

But Frémont said quickly: "Those were not scientific maps, Senator. There's a huge difference."

Benton's interest stirred again. Could there be something truly new here?

"Do you really know what you're talking about?" he asked sharply.

"Yes, sir, I do."

"What do you know about the far West—the sweep to the Rocky Mountains and on to the Pacific?"

"Not much, sir, but—"

"A wise admission, Mr. Frémont. None of the rest of us knows much either. The whole western half of the continent is a mystery. It's an empire—rich, beautiful, inhabited only by small nomadic tribes, a handful of human beings on land that could support millions—and we know nothing about it."

"But science strips away mysteries," Frémont said.

"Do not preach to me, sir!" The iron was back in his voice. "You are confident to a fault—the confidence of ignorance, I shouldn't doubt." He gave Frémont a scathing look and saw him swallow.

"Now, you look at immense problems and say you have solutions. Just like that!" He snapped his big fingers. "The fact is that there has *been* no exploration of the American West worthy of the word." It was one of his favorite themes: they'd heard it before, but let them hear it again. He raised a blunt finger and fixed his eye on Frémont.

"Lewis and Clark were magnificent," he said. "Gave us our first sense of the range of the continent. But obviously they produced a very general picture. Zebulon Pike did the same for the headwaters of the Arkansas until the Spanish collared him. Now, Lewis and Clark went out in Eighteen-and-ought-four and Pike in Ought-six. And there hasn't been a really sound expedition since."

"Well, there was Long," Frémont said.

"Long was a disaster, sir! Long and his fanciful wanderings in that six-oared skiff of his. Long should have stayed at home—that's how he could best have served his country!"

A small silence grew before Benton continued. "Now," he said, as if there had been no interruption, "the greatest explorer of them all was never officially considered an explorer. A trapper, Jedediah Smith."

He saw Frémont nodding. The lad knew Jed Smith's work. Good.

"In Twenty-six he set out with nineteen men on a walk that took two years. Crossed the Sierra Nevadas into California and gave us our first view of that glorious province. Wintered up in Oregon with those rapscallions of the Hudson's Bay Company. He grasped the meaning of South Pass—and of the whole western picture, for that matter. He was as good a man as I ever knew."

"That's a fact," McCaffrey said. "Toted a Bible in his saddle pocket and said a service every day. I rode with him in Twenty-nine, and he wasn't afraid of nothing. You'd never have a better man to lead you."

"Exactly," Benton said. "But in terms of exploration, he was charting out fur grounds, and he didn't talk much about what he found. I often spoke with him. He understood the West better than any man alive. But he put nothing on paper save his journals—and when Comanches killed him down on the Cimarron in Thirty-one, all he knew went under with him.

"You've studied his journals, have you?" He shot the question suddenly, and Frémont blinked.

"No sir," Frémont said, looking a lot less assured. Benton grinned to himself: wanted to paddle in white water, did he?

"You'd do well to. Jed Smith was the best, always excepting Lewis and Clark, who are nonpareil. And the worst? Stephen H. Long was that man, sir. It was he who saddled us with the idea that everything from Missouri to the Rocky Mountains is a barren wasteland. I knew that popinjay before he published his useless map. Printed 'Great American Desert' over the entire plains area. Printed it—the gall of the man! Now, that map lied, in fact if not by intent. Said the plains were *uninhabitable by an agricultural people*—those were his very words! You've seen the land, Mr. McCaffrey—is it desert?"

" 'Deed not," McCaffrey said. "Supports buffalo by the million."

"Exactly. If it'll produce grass, it'll produce grain—it is no *desert*! My suspicion is that Long had never seen prairie before and that he was homesick to boot." He saw Frémont smile as if he knew the feeling. "But unfortunately, the acceptance of this ridiculous notion in the East has helped block any organized westward movement."

He paused and decided to bring Frémont to heel. "A few minutes ago you seemed to suggest that I should be able to remedy the situation with a finger snap, if only I had the wit to recognize the need. It may interest you to know that it was my bill—in Eighteen-twenty-three, a bit before your time—that opened the Santa Fe Trail. And my Oregon bill, to do the same for the Oregon Trail, was first introduced in Twenty-five. It's been reintroduced in every Congress since. You didn't know that, I expect?"

Frémont shook his head. His face went red. But he held Benton's gaze.

"And the *reason* that bill fails in each session is that too many members are persuaded that this so-called 'desert' will always block the movement west. Now, I intend to start that movement. You have solutions, do you? Explain them, sir."

Frémont had collected himself again. He answered smoothly: "Perhaps I should defer to Mr. Nicollet—"

"I'm addressing you, sir! It was you who objected to our gabble."

The shaft registered, but Frémont didn't appear shaken. "Any man can follow the map we're making. Anyone at all. Because it shows exactly what's there. If the map says a certain stream enters thirty miles from another, that is exactly what he'll find on the ground."

"Thirty miles?" Benton was surprised. That *was* new. "That precise? Bonneville's map, the one Washington Irving published, appeared on a duodecimo page."

Frémont smiled now. "A map that can be published on a book's page can't have real detail. Ours is immensely detailed—by starsights, longitude and latitude, compass readings, and terrain sketches. It's a whole different order of mapping, Senator."

Benton was fascinated. He gazed at Frémont a long time without speaking, and this time Frémont held his tongue. Yes, an interesting young man, and strong. There *was* mustard in him. Benton had pressed him a bit and Frémont had taken it without undue concern. The lad was a plunger, too—made his move and didn't back away. Benton liked a man who was willing to act. The fellow was naive, of course, and he'd put his foot in it at the start, but Benton had spoken out of turn on occasion himself. Cared a bit overmuch about that farmer, too—the man sounded like a damned fool and fools deserved what they got—but sentimentality in the young wasn't a fatal flaw.

And this map talk—*damned* interesting. Odd that he'd never drawn such understanding from Nicollet. The Frenchman struck him as fussy, not fatuous exactly, but not a man to whom one would give a great deal of attention. But Frémont had made it all vivid somehow. There was a vigor in him, a quality of force. Benton understood the force that ran in some men. It was a rare quality, much rarer than high intelligence or great beauty, and for a person so endowed the only limits were those of circumstance. His mind was flying ahead. The United States was destiny's child, bastion of democratic freedom against the absolutism of Europe, and the western empire lay fallow and waiting. There would be room for good men.

"You have an ardent supporter," he said to Nicollet.

"Youth is precipitate, Senator," Nicollet answered uneasily.

"But is he correct?"

"Oh yes. We'll be months in preparation but when we're finished the map will be precisely as he says."

"You'll do all this in Washington?"

"We leave within the week."

"I'd like to see this epic as it takes shape," Benton said. "Perhaps a visit to your workrooms would not be amiss?"

"It would be our honor, Senator."

Benton nodded and turned so as to present his back to Frémont and spoke to someone else: the goose remark still lay between them—let the young man dwell on that. But as he talked to others he turned the images of the map in his mind. Jessie would enjoy this, he thought. Suddenly he could hardly wait to tell her about it. She would cock her lovely head and her eyes would brighten and she would ask clever questions. She would see what he saw—and she might see more, too. She always did. She had a way of reaching beyond him, in some dimension he lacked; some quality of human warmth, a kind of gentle sympathy, though there was nothing docile about her, thank God. Old turkey cocks who held the nation's power gathered around her laughing like boys and solicited her opinions. She would be interested in this matter of the map.

He looked around the room for her—yes, there she was, talking to three young dragoons. He watched, amused, as she handled the youths the way she did the statesmen at home, but then it struck him that she seemed rather too practiced. That skinny cretin with the mustache, bobbing like a chicken, looked positively unhinged.

"Jessie," he called, interrupting what someone was saying to him, "I think your mother needs assistance. Do go to her at once, won't you, child?"

"Oh, at once, Mr. T!" she responded with a bright smile, and he grinned despite himself. Years ago, Nathaniel Macon, that grand old Democrat from North Carolina, had chided him for his dogmatic bombast. "Old Toller Tom," Macon had declaimed, "tolling the bell against every bad idea like a universal conscience. Rest yourself occasionally, for God's sake—and rest the rest of us!" The phrase had delighted Jessie and ever since, when she was in high spirits, she called him Mr. Toller or Mr. T. Now she dropped him a little curtsy that might well have been ironic, nodded to the three crestfallen dragoons and moved toward the doorway.

Frémont, feeling buoyant now, confident about his encounter with Benton—it had been tricky there for a moment, like crossing a bad stream on a log that starts to turn—was moving toward the girl when the Sentor called to her. Of course! His daughter. He could see the resemblance immediately; it explained some of her sophisticated assurance, too. Jessie: what a delightful name. He couldn't imagine her with any other. Her intelligence and grace and lack of pretense made it exactly right. But now it was too late to reach her . . .

He stopped, staring after her in dismay. She moved easily, nodding to someone, responding to another's greeting, her neck slender and strong. At the door she turned, her hand lightly on the frame, and looked back—and found him. She'd sought him out! And she smiled at him, directly at him, as appealing as anything he had ever seen, yet with no trace of the coquette. His hand was raised, he wanted to call to her, and then with a last gay flash she was gone.

The room seemed empty after that; he was pleased when Papa Joe thought it time to leave. Outside, however, he realized that his mentor was angry.

"Whatever did you mean, talking to him that way?" There was no moon, and they walked slowly in the cold. "I *told* you how important he is to us."

"Well, I apologized," Frémont said. "I think he accepted—"

"I mean—telling him all that."

"Why not? He seemed interested."

"Charles, you have a great deal to learn. That's not at all how things are done! They have to be brought along carefully, one delicate step after another. *Finesse, mésure*! You're not butchering buffalo carcasses with Freniere. You showed a disturbing lack of subtlety. Besides, he knew everything you told him—I explained it to him months ago."

Nicollet was breathing hard and he stumbled on a curb. Frémont caught his elbow. "Well," he said, "it didn't hurt him to hear it again, then."

"I'm afraid you've compromised us—didn't you hear his irony?"

"When?"

"That I had such an ardent advocate."

"Oh, that—I thought he rather liked me. And I like him."

"One doesn't like or dislike a man like Benton. One courts him. It's quite different."

"Well, I *liked* him," Frémont repeated. "Did you see the girl?"

"What girl?"

"The one he called Jessie. Isn't she beautiful?"

"I don't know. Yes, I suppose so. I'm afraid you've lost sight of—"

"I intend to marry her," Frémont said.

Nicollet stopped dead. *"Pour l'amour de bon Dieu!"*

"Well, why not?" Frémont demanded. The girl had taken hold of him completely. He had never seen such a girl—certainly he had never in his life felt as he did right now. Not even with Cecilia had he known such a sense of pure elation, of joyous certainty. Not remotely.

"Are you out of your mind?" Nicollet said. He started to walk again. "She's Benton's favorite daughter. Hostess at his open houses. She is his closest confidante—everyone in Washington knows her. Don't talk rot, Charles—she is the apple of his eye! The *important* thing is not to jeopardize the work of years . . ."

Frémont walked dutifully beside the irascible old man, not really listening. Of course, maybe he wouldn't care for her when he actually met her. She might turn out to be an empty-headed little flirt, or one of those toffee-nosed Washington creatures, preoccupied with nothing more than ball gowns and gold braid . . .

But he knew better. He knew better, deep in his very bones.

DREAMS

"YOU WERE RIGHT, MR. T," Jessie said as she set the heavy tray on his desk. She kept her voice entirely casual. It was well before daybreak and they were in Benton's third-floor study in the big house on C Street that stood at the foot of Capitol Hill. A stillness lay over the house and over Washington; a solitary carriage passed, rolling toward the Hill. It was her favorite time of the day when she was at home, had been for years; it was when they worked together.

"About the school, I mean," she said. She saw his surprise and glanced down at the coffee she was pouring. "You know," she added carelessly, "sending me there and all."

Benton looked pleased. The school was a sore point between them. He was sitting at his long desk and one of the wide casement windows behind him was slightly ajar; she heard the crackle in the fireplace and felt the room warming. His astral lamp with its base full of sperm oil cast an easy light against the polished silver coffeepot. Half smiling, he took the cup and asked, "How did you come to that conclusion?"

"Well, not lightly." She gave him her radiant morning smile. "To decide that I was wrong—oh, certainly not lightly!"

They had come back from St. Louis after the campaign and she'd returned immediately to Miss English's Female Seminary in Georgetown. This time the school had seemed more than ever like a prison. Coming home for an occasional weekend was like parole—pleasant but tinged with the knowledge that she would have to return.

From the beginning, the idea of going to a formal school had struck her as a terrible humiliation. She had grown up in the classic tradition, with tutors, and what she'd liked so much about it was that her father himself had been her chief tutor. On fair days he would take her along to the Senate and leave her in the Library of Congress, that book-lined room just off the chamber with its stone balcony overlooking the mall. She had studied Audubon's prints and John White's sketches of the first Virginia settlements and plates from the Louvre and comparisons of the French Revolution with its American model and histories of Rome and the debates from which the American nation grew—and afterwards, walking home at noon, Mr. Toller would put it all in perspective. Since the nuns in St. Louis had perfected her French, the Library let her sit *ex officio* on its purchase committee and have a say on the French works it should own. . . .

"Now," she offered, "you understand I'm not saying that Miss English isn't an old biddy, because she is, and the girls are just as vapid as I've always said. But I've learned some useful things—well, for one, that I really was at fault in the ridiculous affair that sent me there in the first place. Now, *that's* a change, don't you think?"

He was gazing at her—a bit ruefully, she thought. Two years ago it had been the most incredible drama; now she saw its melodramatic side. This foolish young congressman from Rhode Island or somewhere had spoken to the Senator about her. Asked for her hand! She had barely known him—when her father had first approached her with thunder in his face, she couldn't even place the man. He had come several times to their open houses and doubtless she had charmed him a bit. That was her duty, after all, to circulate and put people at their ease, and she did it well. The most important people in Washington seemed to take pleasure in her company. That was why she had so resented her father's sudden perception of her as a child. But perhaps he had been right, for it had never occurred to her that the congressman would think—let alone that he would speak to Papa . . .

And so she had been banished. There had been tears and foot stamping—well, she had not gone easily into exile. But she remembered his pale, angry face, too; there had been nothing funny there. In her final protest after a night spent choking on tears, she had cut her heavy braids close to her head—the scissors tearing loud in her ears—and laid them on his desk. But it had not been for nothing. She was a fighter: she had lacked weapons, not will. Indeed, that was what had made it worthwhile—when he saw those severed braids, he knew that the fight had been real.

Now she giggled. "I was awful, wasn't I?"

"You said I was a bully."

"No! I couldn't have."

"Yes. I remember it well. You said, 'No wonder they call you a bully.' " He still looked hurt.

She laughed. "Well, I was distraught. I suppose I encouraged that man precisely because I didn't understand his overtures. I've learned *that* much at Miss English's."

She was watching his face covertly. So much was at stake here; so very, very much . . .

"That's really what the school is about," she said in an offhand way. "The same lesson in a hundred different forms. Miss English would never admit it, but it's what every point turns on." In fact, there had been some pleasure in the lesson. At school dances she found she'd learned it rather well, so well that Miss English had spoken to her, which in turn had taught her a little about circumspection. But the boys at those dances—they were so callow! Now she shrugged. "It's artificial. But then society *is* artificial, isn't it?"

"Of course—that's what keeps us in bounds."

"At first I thought I was supposed to learn manners, but after all, I'd learned them from Mama, whose manners are better than Miss English's will ever be." She saw him nod; he put family ahead of everything and everyone. "But once I understood what really was afoot it wasn't uninteresting. I've learned my lessons well enough, I think." She grinned suddenly, neatly sidestepping the danger she had opened. "Well enough that, painful as it is to admit, you were right."

"It's a good school that encourages real propriety," he said with a sententiousness that made her mouth tighten. She was silent, wondering if she had misplayed a card, but he turned easily to the business at hand, as if what she had said was of no consequence.

"Now, about the dinner tonight," he said. "There'll be a dozen. You arrange the table, if you will, and I'd like you to act as hostess. Your mother is poorly again. She'll take supper in her room."

Jessie felt a flush of familiar pleasure at this and consciously set her own aims aside for the moment. More and more frequently her mother was too ill to assume a burden that Jessie knew she found distasteful even when well. The result was a vacuum that Jessie was happy to fill. Her sister Eliza, who was two years older, had no taste for the role, but Jessie reveled in it. It made her Mr. T's social partner in public as she was his intellectual partner in the privacy of his study.

"Now, you'll want the guest list," he said, and she took a small pad. "I've invited—" He broke off to drink from his cup and sighed with pleasure. "Ah, that's good," he said. "Do you know that coffee never tastes as good as on these mornings when you're here to pour it?"

He waggled the cup at her. "I wonder what facts explain that," he said. He was parodying himself, which meant that his mood was excellent. Senator Benton's fame for his pursuit of the facts was well founded. He knew more than most men through sheer hard work, much of it done at this desk. He had an insatiable appetite for information. That was the fundament of his power; his great personal force was his own, but what gave it authority in the public arena was the base of knowledge on which it rested.

"Now," he said, smiling, "could the time of day make the difference? Surely the loving hand that pours it couldn't flavor it?"

"Oh, Mr. T," she said, laughing, "they should hear you on the Senate floor—suggesting an extraphysical cause for a subjective phenomenon. Whatever would they think?"

"Shocked to the core," he said genially. He was ponderous as a bear, she thought, when he tried to be funny. It was a side that he reserved almost exclusively for her.

"It'll be our secret," he said, "like so many things we've talked over in this study, eh?"

They smiled like old conspirators. She was his favorite, she had always known that, though he tried to hide it from the other children; and she returned his love with a wholehearted fervor. Years ago, when she could barely carry the tray, she had formed the habit of rising when he did, a bit before five o'clock, making coffee and slipping into his study. Here he shaped his ideas into arguments he would fire across the Senate floor like missiles. She became his audience and he began talking out ideas; at first she listened and then she wrote them down and then made suggestions; and the time came when she could pick out a point he had missed—and what a look of respect he would give her then! . . .

"Anyway," he said, setting down his cup, "the dinner. It's for a British visitor named Sir Roger Dunston. He's Joel Poinsett's guest—I'm really doing this as a gesture to Joel. Sir Roger represents the British diplomatic service in some inscrutable fashion. Another Englishman on tour of America—as if that patronizing scoundrel Dickens didn't do enough damage! Better put him on your right. There's no Lady Dunston—at least not with him—so put Mrs. Poinsett on my right and Joel on your left. After that, seat 'em as you like.

"Then the Crittendens. John's to be Attorney General in the new administration—did you know that?" Crittenden was the junior senator from Kentucky, a Whig like Clay but a close friend of theirs. She knew that he would be the only Whig there.

"Attorney General!" Jessie exclaimed. "How wonderful. Won't Maria be happy?" She was very fond of Maria Crittenden, who was rather like a perfect older sister.

"She'll make a charming cabinet wife," her father said. "Then I've invited the Linns, of course, and Henry Dodge." Linn was the junior senator from Missouri and Dodge represented Iowa Territory; both men shared Papa's passionate desire to see the country move westward.

"And finally, Nicollet, and that bright young assistant of his—Frémont."

Her pencil didn't waver as she wrote the names, and her face didn't change. She felt that her father was watching her; she did not look up.

Papa seemed to have taken a most fortunate liking to Lieutenant Frémont. He had visited the map room at the Coastal Survey Building a number of times. One night Frémont had come to dinner and on impulse Papa had invited him to a musicale at the school a week later. When she had seen him standing with her father in Miss English's reception room, she had felt the same smile coming, the same rush of blood as at that first meeting in St. Louis, and she had floated across the room to be presented. She had seen him twice since at her father's open houses, and once they had danced. . . . Well, now she must decide what to wear.

And oh, God bless wild, far-away Oregon!

"Have you been back to the map room?" she asked now in a perfectly even voice.

"Yes, and it's fascinating. Odd how much the sheer unfolding of it attracts me. Do you know how they do it?" She shook her head. "Well, first they take each day's raw figures and reduce them to absolutely precise positions through astronomical tables and mathematical computations—it's all well over my head, I can tell you. Then they consult their sketch maps and their notes from the field and pencil in a rough outline on big sheets they've unrolled on these long tables. then they refine, checking and erasing and resketching until they decide it's absolutely right—and then they ink it in." He was as enthusiastic as he had been the first time he mentioned it, on the steamboat returning from St. Louis. "It's the exactitude, Jessie! Once you understand how to read the lines, you really can see the country in your mind's eye—the steep hill, the stream turning and running off in a new direction. It's a new land, being born. Yes! I think they're right—I could get on a horse myself and follow that map across open country."

"Monsieur Nicollet must be a genius," she observed.

"Yes, it's his concept, I'm sure. But actually, I seem to get more from Frémont. That young fellow has given me an education in mapping. Offhand, I'd say he's the one who brings Nicollet's abilities into focus—there's a certain authority about him."

She busied herself with the sugar tongs. She could think of *no* answer to this that would not be dangerous.

He said, "Did I tell you I talked with the next President the other night? President Van Buren gave a small dinner for him at the White House."

"What's he like? General Harrison?"

"He's a genial, rather charming old fellow. Doesn't know much, which is why the Whigs chose him. And decent, though that's more than you can say for his backers. In the middle of the dinner he said to me, 'Now Benton, don't be putting your harpoon into *me*. If things happen you don't like, why put it right into Webster or Clay, but spare me!' Quite disarmed me, I must say."

She laughed appreciatively. "Someone at school saw him riding alone in Rock Creek Park practicing elocution."

"The new President perceives himself a classicist—Webster is telling it all over town that he keeps cutting references to Roman proconsuls from the speech, and Harrison keeps putting new ones in. I'm beginning to like Old Tippecanoe already!"

"It may all be to the good, don't you think?"

"Who knows? That's not the usual result of losing an election."

"Oh, I understand there's a cost in losing, here and at the local level too, but I meant"—she hesitated—"well, I wonder if the Democrats weren't too successful for too long."

"That's a rather shrewd observation."

"I mean—everything seemed frozen, as if there were no way to respond to change or to new challenges. Like those species that lose the capacity to deal with change and die out."

"Think the Democrats are a dying species, do you?" he said with a grin.

"Of course not, but just the same, maybe breaking up the old pattern, painful as it is now, will free everyone to move off in new directions. Didn't you say you think the chances for the Oregon bill are better than ever? Maybe it's really a time of golden opportunities." He was gazing at her, smiling affectionately. "Do you think that's foolish?" she asked.

"No, my darling girl. That's what I've been thinking, too. I suppose that's why I feel so cheerful about the change—my, I do like the way that pretty mind of yours works. You know, you have an intuitive sense for what's real."

In the midst of her pleasure, she realized she would never have a better opportunity.

"That's what I like so much about being here," she said. "It's *real* here. At the school . . . oh, the school is a hothouse. And I'm not much of a hothouse flower."

"A very pretty one, though."

She made a mouth at him. "I care about the real things in the world. The things you deal with all the time, Papa. I grant you Miss English's training is valuable, though really I got most of my social graces from Mama—now, you stop grinning! Didn't you just tell me I'm to be your hostess tonight?"

"Touché," he said, looking at her with amusement.

"Well, Papa, going back and forth is like going from the real world to an artificial one. It seems even more so after being in Missouri with you for the campaign. Sometimes I feel as if I'm a painting on someone's wall. There's more real world in ten minutes in this study than in a whole week at school. Real ideas scare Miss English—once I said in class that Calhoun's threat in Thirty-two to take South Carolina out of the union was the greatest peril to the nation since the Constitution was written—"

"That's exactly right!" Mr. T boomed in his Senate-chamber voice. "And that dog isn't dead yet, what's more."

"But Miss English tutted me down. Half her students are from the South, you see—and she steered us right back to the importance of serving a proper tea." He frowned; she knew how deeply he cared about issues. "Oh Papa, don't you think I've learned my lessons? I want to live in the world again! I'm so tired of fluff."

His face was thoughtful. He was listening, taking her seriously, and she made her final move.

"And admit it," she said in her most reasonable voice, "You miss me too, don't you?"

"Of course—"

"No, I mean I'm useful to you. I help you in real ways—our conversations, the secretarial—well, you've always said I was your best sounding board and that I had worthwhile ideas, too. That's true, isn't it—you weren't just flattering me?"

"No, Jessie, that's true. And I do miss your help."

Softly she said, "Let me come home, Papa. I need to feel useful. Everyone who's intelligent does."

"Well . . ."

"I haven't asked you in a long time. But living in cotton batting bothers me more and more. Let me come home and work with you mornings, the way we always have. Won't you?"

There was a long silence. It was the most crucial appeal of her young life, and she knew it. She had been as subtly persuasive as she knew how. She composed herself and waited.

"Maybe"—he hesitated—"maybe when the next term ends—"

"The term is ending now, Papa," she said, too quickly.

"Is it indeed?" He came suddenly alert. "Do I scent some artful scheme here?"

"Oh Papa, you know me better than that."

"I know you just that well, missie."

"But . . ." A chasm had opened before her. "But you said—"

"Don't rush me, Jessie," he said; but he was smiling. "I'll have to talk to your mother."

"Oh, Mr. T," she cried and she was up and around his desk, feeling his reassuring bulk, his arms closing powerfully around her. "You're so good." He would decide—her mother wouldn't care, and anyway she could persuade her mother. It was settled—she was coming home!

She was still flushed with happiness and anticipation late that afternoon when she started to dress. Everything was ready—the kitchen on schedule, the table laid, silver freshly polished, hothouse flowers in vases. She chose the candy-stripe gown with the rose sash she had worn in St. Louis that afternoon. It matched her mood and it was provocative—or would he notice?

She had just tied the sash and tucked away a last errant strand of hair when she heard the distinctive rap of the brass knocker on the front door. She hurried downstairs. Dodson was admitting Lieutenant Charles Frémont. He looked up with a flash of sheer pleasure at the sight of her. He was fifteen minutes early and she knew it was not by accident. She led him into a small parlor just off the entrance and they stood chatting, ever so slightly self-conscious. It was the first time they had been alone.

All her impressions were confirmed and strengthened. He was so handsome with his fine aquiline nose and strong jaw, his eyes a startling blue against that wind-darkened face. There was an alert, open interest in the way he looked at her which excited her. He had such a sense of promise about him! A quick authority, an assured competence. *You could rely on him.* That was it. He was mature, but he didn't make her feel precocious, as so many older men did. He simply saw her as a woman—and that made her a woman; she felt the last vestiges of childhood slipping away.

A pause came in their talk and then, watching her with a quiet, pleased smile, his hands clasped behind him, he said directly: "You look charming, if I may say so." He hesitated a fraction only. "Lovely, of course—but exciting, too."

"Do I?"

"Oh yes. That's the dress you wore in St. Louis."

She had hoped he would notice but now, unaccountably, she blushed.

"I think you wore it tonight for me," he said in that decisive way of his.

She was startled and said without thinking, "Yes. I did."

"Did I tell you that you had a profound impact on me that afternoon, Miss Benton?" He had *not* told her, of course, not in so many words. "Well, you did—do you know what I said to Mr. Nicollet?" She knew he was speaking on impulse too. "I told him that you were the girl for me." He was watching her face. "I made up my mind on the spot. Papa Joe was shocked. Do I shock you, too?"

Her heart lurching, smiling at him in pure delight, she shook her head. It was the most direct, the most beautiful thing she had ever heard.

"I put you on notice, *mademoiselle.* I am serious."

He was very intent, with a quality that drew her in and shook her so that her breath caught and then, though his face had not changed and he had not moved, she knew that he was going to kiss her.

She swayed toward him—and then reason restrained her. She stepped back, but at the same time she smiled and said like a promise: "I take notice, *mon Lieutenant.*"

The knocker sounded; other guests were arriving. She turned and saw her father at the door to the parlor watching her. She had no idea how long he might have been standing there.

The British visitor, Frémont decided, was very tired or ill, or perhaps both. There was something contentious about him that was all the more noticeable in Senator Benton's gracious dining room. He sat to Jessie's right at the end of the long oval table. He was Benton's age, a fussy, dyspeptic-looking fellow with mottled skin that had once been freckled. He laughed abruptly, showing his big yellow teeth, and held the table for a time with an amusing description of his travels in America. By steamboat and canal, railroad and stagecoach, on horseback and by shank's mare he'd journeyed; he complimented them on the extraordinary variety of the country despite its cruel distances, but it was plain that he found it rude, gross, and exhausting. It made Frémont think of Mrs. Trollope's venomous book and Dickens' distempers. And yet there was a certain aggressive intensity about Sir Roger Dunston, too; it struck him that the man wanted something though he couldn't imagine what.

At first Frémont had been simply dazzled by the august company—a ranking leader of the Senate, the outgoing Secretary of War, the next Attorney General of the United States. He was here himself, of course, only as a courtesy to Papa Joe. Nicollet sat directly across the table talking to Senator Linn and coughing delicately into his napkin. He'd had two quick glasses of wine and his face was slightly flushed.

A tall black man Jessie called Dodson was serving from a sideboard that gleamed in the candlelight cast from crystal wall sconces. A long silver tray down the center of the table held condiments and, at each end, silver candelabra. Frémont saw that Dodson remained alert to Jessie as he worked, taking his cue from her signal, responding to a dropped spoon, an empty glass. Jessie seemed completely at ease and engaged in animated, attentive conversation with Sir Roger as if to blunt his waspish asides; Frémont saw she was running the dinner as old Provost had run the camp.

She had a self-possessed authority that he certainly didn't feel in this exalted group; it tended to make more remote what had happened between them. The encounter had disconcerted him—he had nearly lost control, and she had perceived that and forestalled any consequences—but it had revealed his feelings accurately. She fired that unbraked, impetuous quality in him; this girl was like no one else he had ever known and seeing her here in these elegant surroundings heightened his tumultuous feelings, at once conflicting, of desire and distance. Her obvious ease contrasted sharply with his awe of the company, and in a sudden, disconsolate twinge he wondered if a woman so poised could remain interested in him for long. Then, remembering the joyful ardor in her eyes, that faint but unmistakable sway of her slender body toward his, he drove away the thought.

His annoyance with the British visitor deepened when he saw a slyly malicious smile flicker across the man's face at Senator Benton's mention of an American aristocracy. Benton was saying that although the Democrats were on their way out, the people would never give up the changes in American life Andrew Jackson had wrought. It should be remembered that the nation's founders—the men who had managed its revolution and formed its government—were American landed gentry, not unlike the British aristocracy; but an entirely new money crowd had seized control with the rise in manufacturing power early in the century and was returning Americans to a kind of economic bondage as real as the old political one.

"An aristocracy of the *Almanach de Dollar*?" Sir Roger blandly inquired.

"Precisely that, sir."

It was this baneful aristocracy of the dollar that Jackson had crushed in what the Senator called the second great American period. Jackson, he declared, was the true liberal, the true democrat.

"And the changes he brought about are profound. And popular. We ended imprisonment for debt, for example—how in God's name is a man to get *out* of debt if he's locked away in prison? We ended limiting the vote to property holders—now every free man has the vote—"

"But no woman has," Maria Crittenden said from her place beside Frémont. He saw Jessie cast her a look of sparkling admiration.

"Now, Maria," her husband said indulgently.

"Well, my dear," Benton smiled, "that'll come. We've laid the groundwork for it. And for public education, too—let every man's child learn to read, eh? And last year President Van Buren ordered the workday on federal projects reduced to ten hours—now you'll see workers pressing business to follow suit. That's the nut of it: it's a new world we've entered. In America, Sir Roger, the principle of *demos krateo* has prevailed."

The faulty Greek startled Frémont, though he saw that it made Benton's point. Then the Englishman coughed violently. He put his napkin to his face and suddenly Frémont realized he was fighting down laughter. His eyes glinted over the napkin, contemptuous.

Frémont glanced apprehensively at Benton, but the Senator appeared unruffled, though his unbuttoned cordiality was gone. He said quietly: "I find the phrase useful. The fact is that democracy is the government of the future, sir. In due time the absolutism of Europe's monarchies—including your own, if I may say so—will rock before popular demand for the democratic form. Yes, I think it appropriate to honor its Greek roots—even when it amuses."

Sir Roger seemed not at all abashed. But Frémont saw that Jessie had a watchful expression now that made her look older and rather commanding, and again he felt a disturbing sense of distance from her. Then she caught his eye and gave him such a look of open pleasure it swept away all his doubts.

"She *is* charming, isn't she?"

Frémont started, half alarmed, half delighted to share these feelings that were consuming him, and looked at Mrs. Crittenden closely for the first time. She was a warm, attractive woman, her fresh skin belying her graying hair. She seemed to radiate energy. "You display remarkably good taste, Lieutenant," she said softly, and immediately he liked her.

Suddenly everything seemed right again. Frémont was very glad he'd restrained himself when he returned to Washington. It hadn't been easy. His natural impulse had been to seek Jessie out the day after he saw her, and certainly after he knew she was back in Washington. But he had waited—and this uncharacteristic restraint had made him aware of just how much promise he had seen in her eyes that day. And so he'd approached his courtship with the same careful attention that he and Nicollet were giving the map.

He'd had some assistance, too—fortuitous if not divine. Papa Joe had asked Colonel Abert, the Topographical Engineers commandant, to continue Frémont's assignment to the expedition, and now was teaching him how to translate the field data into the minute, infinitely refined lines on the map. Day after day Nicollet sat on a high stool wrapped in a heavy sweater, coughing, his eyes hot, and directed him. Eventually Senator Benton had come to the map room—as Frémont knew he would—and on his second or third visit he'd invited him to dinner.

He saw Jessie nod to Dodson, who removed the main course and put small dessert plates before them. He brought fresh glasses and filled them with a light wine.

Sir Roger was interrogating them now about Texas, five years a republic and desperate to enter the Union—would that admission come to pass? And then immediately he answered his own question. "I should think not," he said. "The northern abolitionists will never consent to more slave territory, eh?" Then, before anyone could respond, he added with an explosive laugh: "We in Britain find it passing odd that a country born in the commitment to life, liberty and the pursuit of happiness should still tolerate slavery!"

Frémont sighed. They didn't need a tactless Englishman to ruin the evening—slavery talk could do that all by itself.

"Sir Roger," Benton said with slow displeasure, "I don't enjoy talking about slavery. Here or in your colonies. But I will say that this is not a slave household. Dodson, here, is a freedman in my employ. I hold no slaves, though it's legal to do so in Missouri—and in the District of Columbia. Personally, I abhor the institution—and furthermore I see it as deadly dangerous."

Talking in a measured way that brooked no interruptions, Benton lamented how that hateful issue had come to dominate American public life over the last twenty years. Every question seemed finally to turn not on its own merits but on its effect for or against slavery. In the North, the abolition movement grew stronger every year. And in the South—

"Why," Benton said, "when I was a boy in Tennessee, everyone recognized slavery as an evil that ultimately must be brought to an end." Frémont's own boyhood in South Carolina, where southerners like Henry Laurens had opposed slavery, had reflected the same attitude. "But now," Benton went on, "sensible men will tell you with a straight face that slavery is a blessing—on the one hand it Christianizes and civilizes black Africans, and on the other it allows white men to create a perfect society in the Greek mold." With a sour smile he added, "But if you've spent any time in the South, I'm sure you've found that the perfection of man is no more advanced there than anywhere else."

But even to make such a statement in the South these days, Frémont knew, would be to court a challenge. He had a sudden vivid recollection of the night in Charleston when Jack Dillingham had slapped him—*slapped* him, he could feel the tingle in his cheek still, see the horror in Jack's eyes because Jack feared he was going to be killed—and it all had blown up from nothing more than Frémont's saying that he thought slavery as economically inefficient as it was morally repugnant. Fortunately, his common sense had overtaken him and he'd settled it by giving Jack a good thrashing. But there had been two clear results: most of his early friendships had withered, and he'd decided he couldn't spend the rest of his life in a South Carolina turned inbred and narrow, unwilling to face a clear moral right. His sense of justice, his own need for space, forbade it.

"One other thing," Benton said with a grim look at Sir Roger. "No one should take the question lightly. This division of North and South into ever more adamant groups represents the greatest of all threats to the Union."

"Do you really think your democratic Union could shatter?" Sir Roger asked. Frémont caught an odd eagerness in his voice too, as if he scented opportunity.

"Tell him, Joel," Benton said shortly.

"Well, of course, Roger," Mr. Poinsett said. His testy, irritated tone was quite unusual for him, and Frémont remembered that the Englishman was his house guest. "It's already been threatened. South Carolina started a secession movement nine years ago. President Jackson saw the danger—he wouldn't have it and he mobilized troops. He named me his special representative in Charleston, and it was quite a trick to persuade the firebrands there that secession would mean war." Poinsett glanced down the table. "You remember those days, Charles."

"A very unhappy time, sir."

"Tom was right," Maria Crittenden said abruptly in a no-nonsense voice, "slavery talk makes bad table talk. Sir Roger, you mentioned Texas—what do you think of its prospects?"

"I think, madam, that Texas will come to its senses and remain an independent republic," the Briton said.

"Well, hear, hear," Linn said, startled by this undiplomatic bluntness. But Frémont felt this wasn't the Briton's real interest—he had a sudden impression that they were being baited.

Benton said he believed Sir Roger mistaken to expect the situation to hold—Texans were Americans, Tennesseans and Missourians mostly, who had gone there as colonists in the '20s and staged a legitimate revolution in the '30s. Sir Roger countered that the Mexicans had never accepted that revolution; they continued to talk about reclaiming Texas.

This roused Henry Dodge at last. The representative of Iowa Territory was an indefatigable trencherman who had not said a word. "That got settled at San Jacinto. After the slaughter at the Alamo, Sam Houston lured the Mexicans east and whupped 'em good. I'd say they'll stay whupped."

"Exactly!" Sir Roger had reversed his ground with a triumphant smirk. "There's no reason for Texas to hide under American skirts except for its financial needs, and they're easily enough rectified. Just as its protection from Mexico is easily enough guaranteed."

Benton said with alert interest: "Britain would accept that role, you're saying?"

"It might. 'Twould be our preference that Texas remain independent."

"Yes—you'd like to check American growth, I'd wager."

"We see no advantage in an ever expanding United States." He had shocked them with that, but as if he hadn't noticed, he went right on. "Aren't you big enough? God knows, it's hard enough getting about in your country now."

Nicollet stared at him with perfect French disdain for such distasteful Saxon crudity. Mr. Poinsett was studying his plate. Frémont saw Jessie give her father a deliberately quizzical look, her eyebrows raised.

"With a little help from us," Sir Roger continued, "Texas can take care of itself. Actually, Mexico might like that quite well—an independent neighbor to the north, a buffer between it and the United States. You're not very popular in Mexico, you know."

"Perhaps Mexico would be so pleased," Benton said with a quick, hard smile, "that it would invite you into California. That has occurred to Whitehall, doubtless?"

"California!" Was the diplomat startled by the sudden turn? Frémont couldn't tell. "We have no designs on California, Senator. None whatsoever. That is solid Mexican territory."

"In fact, it is not solid at all," Benton replied. The conversation had become a debate between the two men. "You must know that the Mexican hold on it is tenuous at the very least—indeed, California scarcely *has* a government. And the Bay of San Francisco, I'm told, is one of the world's great natural harbors."

"I know nothing of that," Sir Roger said shortly.

"Then you should inquire at the Admiralty, sir. The Royal Navy has made a careful examination of that superb bay. The fact that Mexico doesn't use it makes it no less valuable."

"Are you suggesting an American interest in California, Senator Benton?"

"Ah, Sir Roger, I am expressing an American antipathy to a *British* interest. Our interest in the far West is to the north. Oregon, sir. I expect you know a bit more about Oregon?"

Sir Roger gave a wintry smile. "That we do, sir. Oregon is British territory."

There was a subtle change in the man now. His voice had lost that desultory, faintly derisive note, and suddenly it struck Frémont that Sir Roger had come at last to the purpose he had intended from the start. With a stunning sense of his own inexperience, Frémont realized that what had just dawned on him was well understood by the others: they were quiet, leaving the conversation a colloquy between host and guest of honor. Jessie's expression was merely attentive and poised.

"Not so fast, sir," Benton said sharply. "It is *not* British territory. It is jointly held under treaty by the United States and Great Britain. Equal rights, sir. By force of discovery."

Sir Roger waved his hand. "Oh, I know the treaty—only too well. And doubtless some adjudication will have to be worked out. But as a practical matter, Britain holds Oregon. By occupying it, sir."

Benton shrugged. "By an accident of the fur trade."

"I would not call it accidental. At any rate, there's plenty for all. Britain has no interest in the land south of the Columbia River. I think that will prove to be the ultimate boundary between our nations."

"You're an optimist, Sir Roger. The Columbia Valley is central to our claim. There is growing sentiment here for claiming *all* the coast—right up to Russian Alaska, to Fifty-four-forty."

"Now, I say—that *is* unrealistic."

"Perhaps. But the situation is pressing. The Russians are moving. They already have outposts in California—I suppose you're aware of that?"

Frémont saw that Nicollet's interest was fully engaged now. The old Frenchman listened intently, eyes shifting from one adversary to the other. Frémont had the excited sense of being privy to the collision of huge forces, the shaping of great events.

"We are watching the Russians," Sir Roger said.

"The fact is that the west coast is a vacuum. The Mexican presence in California is manifestly weak. And the presence of both the United States and Britain in Oregon is so feeble as to invite outside attention. No wonder the Russians are reaching—the czars have always been empire-minded." Benton smiled, and Frémont saw he was trying to ease the tension. "They yearn to escape from that perennial icehouse of theirs, eh?"

The Briton made a dismissing gesture. "They're of little moment. They've barely recovered from the Napoleonic wars. No, we anticipate no difficulty in holding Oregon—clear, as I say, to our outpost on the Columbia."

Benton frowned. "That is dangerous thinking," he said slowly. "It interferes directly with our own valid aspirations. Remember, sir, that while Britain thinks of global empire, America sees its destiny in an empire that sweeps across its own continent."

"Until, that is, it encounters British territory," Sir Roger countered firmly. "There it must stop."

Benton stared at him. When he spoke Frémont heard a harsh new note in his voice. "The United States will not accept limitation to the Columbia.

May I remind you that any treaty that replaces the faulty treaty now in effect between us would have to be ratified by the Senate? And the Senate will follow my lead on this subject. That is a fact that Whitehall would do well to remember."

The Briton gave a sardonic smirk. "Whitehall knows your name full well—though I wouldn't have thought the Senate so monolithic on any subject."

"Senators recognize my strength on western matters," Benton answered gravely. "I might say I come to it on high authority—that of Thomas Jefferson himself. I remember seeing him on the day before Christmas of Eighteen-twenty-four. We sat by the fire in his study at Monticello and talked all afternoon about the West." His voice had softened; Benton clearly revered the memory of Jefferson. "Do you know that when Talleyrand signed over Mr. Jefferson's Louisiana Purchase, Livingston asked him what he considered its western extent. And Talleyrand replied: 'You have purchased an empire, gentlemen; make of it what you will.' "

"That's all very well for Talleyrand—"

Benton raised a hand. "Please do not interrupt me, sir," he said in the formidable, forbidding tone Frémont remembered from St. Louis; the Englishman fell silent, his face reddening. "Mr. Jefferson discussed his dream of the West that afternoon—his attempts to explore it, his conviction that our American destiny lay there. Our manifest destiny, sir! And he encouraged me to take up the western mission. It was a laying on of hands, sir—*this nation will move westward*."

The dessert plates were gone and Dodson had poured a richly fortified port. But no one had touched his glass and no one ventured to interrupt the two men. Jessie's watchful look had not relaxed.

"Now," Benton continued, "this is *our* empire. We will never accept the Columbia as boundary. It denies us a port on the Pacific. And that denies us equal standing in trade with the Orient. There are two great ports on the western coast—San Francisco Bay and Puget Sound. The bay is not open to us, but the sound is. And let me assure you that we will have it."

Suddenly the Briton's irritation boiled into anger. "It is politic, sir, to talk of what you *hope* to achieve rather than what you *will have*!"

Benton glared at him. "As to what is politic, let us talk of Fifty-four-forty—press us and you will find our radical elements demanding we go all the way to Russian territory. Britain could end with no position whatever on the western coast."

"A ridiculous statement, if I may say so! Her Majesty's government can defend its positions—the Royal Navy would find your statement vastly amusing."

"Sir Roger, the United States has fought two major wars in its history. Both were with Britain. We doubt neither the British capacity to provoke nor our own to deal with that provocation." His voice now actually alarmed Frémont. "I don't suppose you had the honor to be with General Packenham on that fatal day in Eighteen-fifteen when he met Andrew Jackson at New Orleans?"

"I did not, sir. I was with Wellington at Waterloo that year! We settled the Corsican's hash once and for all. We had bigger fish to fry."

"But you did not fry *us*. Nor would you, over Oregon."

"By God, sir!" the Englishman cried. "Do you dare—" His finger shot out angrily and struck his full wineglass. It flew over with a tinkling clatter and the wine gushed thickly over the white linen. There was a moment of absolute silence. Sir Roger stared at the purple flood and then looked up with a different expression, as if surprised to find himself at a quiet dinner party in Washington.

He looked at Jessie. "My dear," he said, "I *am* sorry."

At once she gave him a brilliant smile and put her hand on his arm. "Look upon it as a harbinger of good, Sir Roger," she said. "May we spill nothing but wine over Oregon."

"Well said, very well said," Poinsett exclaimed in relief, giving the Briton a disapproving look, and Maria Crittenden softly applauded. Jessie's remark had broken the tension; there was a sudden babel of talk and movement. Frémont realized with surprise that she had been awaiting an opportunity to change the talk's direction.

The Englishman raised the fresh glass that Dodson had deftly supplied. "Our gallant young hostess has given us the proper tack. Wise men recognize wise counsel, eh?"

Then, turning the glass stem in his fingers, he said almost diffidently, "Still, you know, the matter won't go away. Eventually our countries will have to deal with it. If I may ask without renewing passions, I still wonder why you feel so confident of American possession."

It was graceful, if not quite an apology, and Benton responded immediately. "Because of our settlers, sir," he said. His voice was easy and correct, but Frémont heard no warmth in it. "You mention control by occupancy, but who are your occupants? A handful of Hudson's Bay Company men pursuing a trade that even now is dying. Where are the people with whom you might populate Oregon, Sir Roger?"

Frémont realized Nicollet's eyes were on him—a quick, almost conspiratorial glance. The Briton's lips moved, as if he was searching for an answer.

"But the United States is filled with people hungry to go to Oregon," Benton said. "Good yeoman farmers, sir, skilled at clearing the forest and turning it into farmland. They are ready, eager to come by the thousands. To be followed by those artisans and merchants who make thriving communities."

"You paint a handsome picture, but in fact your settlers are *not* going west, are they?" He gazed at Benton, his restraint of a few minutes before forgotten. "They don't go west because they can't. The land they must cross is impassable—desert, sir."

"That is a fallacy."

"Fallacy? Your own explorers so report it, Senator. Your maps so describe it."

"You have accepted the prevalent misinformation," Benton said calmly. "Men who've actually covered that ground know it's grassland—"

"Oh, come come, Senator, that sounds very much like piffle, if you'll forgive my bluntness. It'll take half a century for you to settle Oregon in serious numbers." He was enjoying himself again. "Suppose you tell me—if you can—how you expect to overcome these natural barriers."

"Why, I will," Benton said. He was rising to the challenge like a buffalo bull, and again there wasn't a sound in the room. "I'd like you to carry this message back to Whitehall: we will never be driven from the Columbia River Valley—and we will never surrender our rights to Puget Sound.

"And for earnest on that promise, I tell you this: I intend to commission Mr. Nicollet to map the Oregon Trail and open it to emigrant wagon travel. I intend to *flood* Oregon with settlers, sir!"

There it was. Frémont shot a quick glance at Nicollet, who was staring wide-eyed at the Senator. For weeks Papa Joe had been talking about his hopes for another expedition to map the upper Missouri, but had been hesitant to broach the project. What Benton now proposed without an instant's warning was bigger, more exciting, more significant by far. With the United States Senate behind it, with the whole nation awaiting its outcome, such an expedition would guarantee any explorer's career.

Now the Briton had found no answer, and the Senator turned away from him with a telling indifference. "I've been thinking about this," he said to the rest of the table, "since seeing the incredible detail in Mr. Nicollet's new map. We want a full expedition—let's lay to rest once and for all that myth of the high plains as desert. Let's tie down the trail, mile by mile, with a report that gives the western traveler all his answers—water, grass, availability of game, attitude of the tribes along the route. Mile by mile."

He turned to Poinsett. "We'll do it through the Topo Engineers. Would thirty thousand cover the costs, Joel?"

Poinsett glanced at Nicollet, who nodded vigorously.

"Well, John," Benton said to Crittenden, "will the Whigs in Congress go that far with me?"

"You won't have any trouble with that, Tom."

"Very well," Benton said, slapping his hands together. Frémont saw Jessie looking at her father with amused admiration. He wondered suddenly if Benton had staged the entire scene to give the Englishman his message in the most dramatic terms.

"So, Mr. Nicollet," the Senator said, "this isn't the most orthodox way to offer a man a commission, I'll admit. But what about it—is what I want feasible? Can you give it to me?"

Nicollet's face was scarlet. He looked ready to burst. *"Oui, oui, bien sûr!"* he cried, excitement slurring his words. "I assure you, sir, we'll give you a map anyone can follow to Oregon. We'll analyze terrain, plant incidence and specimens too, of course—rainfall, crop potential, obstacles to travel—everything that the latest scientific—" He seized an incautious deep breath—and his voice exploded in a spasm of coughing.

The congestion boiled up in his thin chest and shook him like a rag doll; in the moment of the table's troubled attention, before Mrs. Linn put an arm around him and reached for a glass of water, Frémont saw Nicollet for what he was—a very sick, infirm old man. It was heartbreaking. Papa Joe. Frémont read a desperate appeal in his eyes; the old scientist's hand fluttered toward him. He'll spoil it all, Frémont thought—he'll never get any better, he can't do it, they can all see that. And then, like a bursting light, came the thought: *But I can do it.* Ambition ignited and spread like flame in pitchy wood. *I can lead that expedition!* He looked around the table. Everyone was staring at Nicollet except Benton. The Senator was looking straight at Frémont, and their eyes met. All at once Frémont realized that the older man knew exactly what he was thinking. And though Benton made no sign, Frémont was sure he saw concurrence in those cool, pragmatic eyes.

Nicollet's cough subsided into an exhausted wheeze. Mrs. Linn, cradling him, held the glass to his lips. Again he made that fluttering, suppliant gesture.

"Certainly, Senator," Frémont said clearly, "we will open the way to Oregon. For the nation. We can give you everything that is needed. I guarantee it."

"Jessie," Frémont said urgently, "I must see you—"

"Must?"

"You know I must. This changes everything. Oregon—it means I may be leaving soon."

"Leaving!" She held up her hand as if to stop him, and without thought he took it in his.

"Of course. Oh, it's the chance of a lifetime, a hundred lifetimes! It's *my* chance. Didn't you hear him? He's magnificent. . . . Jessie, we *must* see each other."

"Yes," she said then, as if overcoming something. "We must."

As they had risen from the table she had slipped into the adjoining drawing room, and he had followed her. Over her shoulder he could see the guests in the outer hall—Nicollet wrapping a white silk muffler about his throat, Benton helping Mrs. Poinsett into a dark fur coat. He saw Benton turn, glance into the drawing room, and then come directly toward them.

"Your father," he murmured.

She dropped her hand and without turning whispered quickly, "Maria Crittenden will invite you to tea. Then we'll—"

"Jessie," Benton said, "our guests are leaving."

"Of course, Papa. I'll see them out."

She moved with a quick, graceful swing of her skirts, and her father stepped aside to let her pass. There was an intent expression on Benton's face and with a surge of delight Frémont realized that the Senator wanted to talk about the expedition right now. There was so much to be worked out, and time was—

"Mr. Frémont, your attentions to my daughter are to cease at once."

"Sir?" he said, stunned.

"You are quite obvious, sir, and I won't have it. She is an impressionable girl, much too young—she is only sixteen."

Frémont was struggling for balance. Impulsively he said, "Almost seventeen."

"*Sixteen,* sir!" Benton said with sudden ferocity. "You are not to see her beyond chance social encounters. *Chance* encounters. I will so instruct her. Do you understand—you are not to see her."

"Senator," Frémont answered stiffly, "you must know that my intentions are entirely honorable—"

"You *have* no intentions, sir!" Benton leaned forward, and suddenly he seemed measurably larger and filled with palpable menace; and Frémont knew again why he was so widely feared. "You will *stay away from her.* Defy me and I will break you." His lips were flat against his teeth and the words came as if under pressure. "I have broken far better men than you—stronger men, wiser men. Do not try me, sir."

Frémont felt as if he were being whipped backward down a muddy slope; he could hardly breathe. The old shadow had slid stealthily over his heart.

"Do not threaten me, Senator," he stammered in angry consternation.

"I *do* threaten you, sir! I give you fair warning."

Benton swung around and left the drawing room. In a moment Frémont saw him in genial conversation with Poinsett and the Englishman as they prepared to leave. Suddenly he felt naive and foolish. He had been reveling in high company, firing his ambition, dreaming of a brilliant future, and the older man had cut him down in mid-flight. Ordering him off like a puppy or some scapegrace drummer! Suppressed anger now burned through his shock and he realized that his hands were trembling. But even mortified, enraged, he knew that nothing had changed. If anything, his feeling for Jessie was stronger. He saw her now, laughing as she bade people good night. She was holding Maria Crittenden's hand as she spoke to the Linns, and then he saw her whisper to Maria. He was certain that she was the one woman in the world who could fill all the empty reaches of his heart. Yes, it was *she* who mattered, and Old Bullion could go to the devil!

He walked out of the drawing room very erect, still pale with anger but in full control of himself.

LOVERS

SHE HAD A BREATHLESS SENSE of her own disobedience, at once jubilant and frightening. Her father had told her that she was not to see Frémont—and here she was standing with him in the little gazebo behind the Crittendens' house. Frémont had put both hands on her waist and was holding her, looking into her eyes. Tall evergreens screened the gazebo; it was just cold enough so that their breath frosted lightly in the air—and then he kissed her and plunged her into something stunningly new. She had thought his kiss would be tender, graceful, romantic; but instead it swept her like fire. Heat flared red behind her closed lids. Her mouth opened; his arms went around her and instinctively she moved against him—and felt him harden against her belly. *Oh my God!* She snatched herself away and was across the gazebo, the back of her hand against her mouth. She stared at him solemnly for a moment, and then she came back and put her arms around his neck again and drew his mouth down to hers. "You'll have to stop us," she whispered. "I can't." But she knew that he would.

"Oh, Jessie," he said into her hair, "I was so afraid."

"So was I."

"Not of your father," he said quickly. "Of you."

She leaned back. "Of me?"

"That you wouldn't see me again. After what he said."

On the morning after the dinner when she had gone to her father's study he'd told her she could leave the school for good. And while she was planning delightedly to pick up her clothes and books, he had added almost casually that he preferred she not see Lieutenant Frémont again beyond chance social encounters.

It was straight political technique which she recognized immediately: give the good news and while the flush of pleasure is still on, tack on the bad. Like an amendment. A rider to a bill. To protest the latter would be to risk the former. Smooth. But this time Papa had outsmarted himself. He hadn't asked for her promise. That would have seemed a weakness—it would have opened discussion, given her a position, perhaps led to bargaining. He had issued a request in the manner of a monarch by divine right, and so the possibility of her disobedience had never arisen. It had left her nothing to say—but it also meant she had made no commitment. Three days later Maria Crittenden had invited them both to tea. Jessie had gone early to explain matters. Maria's face had turned wary.

"And what do you intend to do?" she had asked.

"Why, see him, of course!"

Slowly Maria had nodded, beginning to smile. "That's the girl," she had said. When Charles came she'd given them tea, and after a suitable interval sent them out to inspect the gazebo.

Now, still in his arms, Jessie said: "I never had a moment's doubt after that first afternoon in St. Louis. You were so—compelling. . . . I knew you were going to speak to me, and then I saw you talking to Papa. Quarreling, I could tell immediately—but you were holding your own. All along I had the strangest conviction that you would."

"I did put my foot in it." Charles was smiling. "But it was because it matters so."

"I know he likes you. It's us together he doesn't like."

"Well, I'll speak to him," he said. "Directly. And get it straightened out. It's the best way."

She stared at him, struck between terror and joy, and after a moment terror won out.

"Oh, no, Charles," she murmured. "No, no. You mustn't! He would be—" Suddenly she had an overwhelming sense of danger. "He would be *furious*."

"Jessie, I love you."

She nodded vigorously, "Oh, I love you, too."

"Then I will speak to your father," he said, smiling and looking very determined.

She peered carefully at his face. She couldn't have stood it if he had been frightened—she might even have stopped loving him—but the fact that he wasn't only increased her fear. Unspeakable dangers lay ahead, and she felt her throat tighten.

"No really, Charles, you mustn't—not yet. I understand him, the way nobody else does. You must promise." She was still in turmoil from the kiss, dazed and confused. There was a force in him like her father's, like her own, something that was wildly precipitate and aroused the same quality in her. She felt giddy and happy and in great peril. She had to hold his ardor in check.

"We'll see each other. We can meet here, Maria will let us . . . oh, Charles, just give it a little time, won't you?"

Quizzically he gazed at her, smiling; then he nodded and kissed her again.

For a while Charles seemed content to luxuriate in the pleasure he found in her and the open joy she took in him. At home she resumed the old relationship with her father, appearing early with coffee, settling into her chair, slipping into the subjects of the day. But now everything seemed altered. She had a growing sense of betrayal, meeting with him each morning as if nothing had changed. The betrayal wasn't in her disobedience, which she deemed simply reasonable, but in the lie implicit in hiding the most important thing in her life, in letting him believe that it was still he and not a strange young man who occupied the center of her world. Wasn't it a lie not to sing her lover's praises, not to let her father know how bright the days had become, not to remark on the change when everything *was* different?

She didn't love her dear old Mr. Toller less. She had just moved into a whole new order—the difference in the lighthouse lantern before and after the mirrors are in place. Could he possibly understand how she felt? Had he ever kissed her mother as Charles kissed her—had her mother felt that delirious, enraptured rush? She couldn't imagine her mother transported, and it wasn't just the temptation to believe herself unique. Maria had felt it, Jessie was sure of that; Maria was alive and vivid and joyous. And of course Papa brought those qualities to the public arena . . . but to love? To her mother? Six children, herself the product of their union, and she couldn't believe it; even in the act of love they would be—well, restrained. . . .

So how could he understand if she were to end this morning charade, exorcise her sense of betrayal and tell him? Not understanding, he would be implacable. She knew. If he even dreamed of what she was feeling he would pack her off—to Grandmother McDowell's plantation in the Shenandoah Valley, probably, there to be watched and cosseted and urged to be sensible. Sensible! And she would have to go. He controlled her life, he had a tyrant's power. And God alone knew what horrible fate he could contrive for Charles—a precise survey of the North Pole, or soil conditions on Tierra del Fuego. . . . Well, if one lacks strength in dealing with tyrants, surely one must use guile.

And if you loved the tyrant? And knew you were betraying him? And yet couldn't help yourself?

Mr. T seemed entirely oblivious of his daughter's turmoil. While everything had changed for her, she could see no difference at all in the blend of affection and authority with which he greeted her each morning. He was enjoying his new freedom to devote his time to the western movement. He had introduced the bill to appropriate thirty thousand dollars for a major expedition to map the Oregon Trail. He seemed to assume Nicollet would lead this expedition, and neither he nor Jessie mentioned the old astronomer's health—or the capable young Army officer who was Nicollet's assistant. Benton was confident that "the group," as he called his fellow westerners, would ensure the bill's passage with ease.

William Henry Harrison was inaugurated on a cold, brilliant day and Senator Benton took his whole family to stand on the Capitol steps and hear a speech of an hour and forty minutes that was studded with proconsuls. "So much for Mr. Webster," Jessie murmured to her father with a smile. But the truth was that politics seemed rather remote to her these days. For her seventeenth birthday Charles gave her a tiny gold locket on which a J and a C were lovingly entwined, but of course she could show it only to Maria, wear it only when she saw Charles. Maria had agreed to let them continue meeting in the gazebo, though she had given them a clear warning.

"I suppose if a kiss gets stolen I won't know anything about it—but I want your solemn promise that nothing more than that transpires."

"Maria!" Jessie had cried, scandalized and delighted.

"You're a grown woman, dear." Maria had turned to Charles. "Have I your word of honor, Lieutenant?"

"You do, ma'am." Jessie had thought it all rather droll, but Charles had looked alarmingly impatient.

The gazebo time was best. Afternoons they sat there talking away hours that flew like birds. She asked him endless questions, because she was interested and because she liked to watch his face when he was serious; he looked even more handsome when he was serious. He told her so many stories of the men on the expedition, especially Provost and Louie Freniere, that she felt as though she knew them too. Her questions grew increasingly thoughtful, and she soon knew much more about the rigors of going west in virgin country, the perils of the exploration to come, than did her father, which made her mornings with him no easier.

Charles talked of his ambitions with an enthusiasm that excited her. He was so open—so vital. She had a sense of limitless horizons unfolding before her, like the Great Plains themselves. He told her about Nicollet's failing health, and that morning on the Minnesota when he'd had to take command.

"You were wonderful," she said.

"Not wonderful at all—I hated to do it. But I know it saved his life. He's never mentioned it—we just don't talk about his health."

"It's getting worse, isn't it?"

"That's the problem. I owe him so much."

"Well, it seems simple enough to me," she said. "If he can lead the expedition, very well—you'd be glad to remain his assistant, wouldn't you?"

"Of course. But I don't believe he can. It'll be a much more arduous journey this time."

"In that case, there's no issue. You must do it. Anyone else would be a disaster—no one else knows how to apply his techniques. Isn't that right?"

He smiled ruefully. "I wish it were that easy. It's not clear that Papa Joe knows he's failing—or that he would admit it if he did. And then, there's your father. It's funny, you know—at the dinner, I had the strongest feeling, as if he wanted me to take over—as though it were my destiny . . ." He broke off and his voice changed. "And then, that tongue-lashing—out of nowhere! I'm damned if I know where that leaves me."

The fierce temper she'd already sensed but could only guess at came boiling up; she could see it in his face. He'd told her only a little of the encounter, but she knew her father.

"Warned me off like scum. And the worst part of it is, I haven't faced him on it yet."

The clash between the two men—the encounter past and the greater one to come—still frightened her. "Charles," she pleaded. She took his hand. "You promised . . ."

He sighed, jaw tight, and then nodded. "All right," he said tersely.

"It has nothing to do with the expedition anyway," she said.

"Well, of course it does! Who conceived it? We sit here talking as if there's no problem, and all the while . . . Jessie, really, I've got to speak to him—we've *got* to get this settled!"

She shook her head and her hand tightened on his. "Not yet. Please, Charles, not yet." Again he nodded, but somberly and reluctantly; she knew that now he was warning her.

For her, this time of waiting seemed delightful agony. She lived in a tumult of emotions. The very sight of a uniform stirred her, the sound of his name in casual talk rang in her innermost being; she wrote extravagant love notes which she carefully destroyed—indeed, he was so much in her mind she sometimes felt exhausted. She was moved for the first time in her life to share confidences with her older sister Eliza, while her little brothers and sisters were allowed to hover like four delighted magpies at the edge of the conspiracy.

They saw each other here and there, but under such rigid restraints that she longed for the sweet relief of the gazebo, where his strong hands catching her at the waist set off such wild sensations. At Benton's open houses they behaved with stifling circumspection; parties at other homes were unexpectedly dull if Charles wasn't there—and unendurably tense if he was. Dancing with insipidly flirtatious young men was miserable, but dancing with him was worse, constrained as she was to deny the stronger music of her heart.

When the day was mild, spring hinting its approach, she would dragoon her sisters into a promenade along Pennsylvania Avenue; and Frémont would slip away from the map room in hopes of meeting them. These encounters were by chance, of course—and chance encounters were within Papa's prohibition. So they would stroll, carefully apart, and the girls would fall back, giggling, and she and Charles would talk of a thousand things, so intoxicated with each other that the very cobbles of the avenue itself seemed to echo their joy. On the best days they would meet—by accident of course—on the neat walks of crushed gravel around the White House where the Marine Band played, amused that their secret whispers were covered by a storm of martial music.

Afterwards they would turn eagerly down the broad brick sidewalks past the great market at Fifteenth Street, where farmers' teams jostled for position and the President came at dawn to do his own shopping. They would admire the wooden Indian princess outside Queen's Tavern, and the new bonnets in the milliner's, and at Pishy Thompson's bookstore Charles once bought her a slender volume of Shakespeare's sonnets from a sidewalk stall. They would stroll past Gadsby's, the hotel where so many of the capital's figures lived, carefully circumspect in case one of the Senator's friends might see them. Carriages and hacks, horsemen and women riding sidesaddle, clattered along the cobbled streets; bootblacks called, "A penny a shine!"—a Marylander with a barrow stood in the gutter crying: "Live crabs—freshly deviled," in a raw country accent. Once Frémont stopped at a flower stall and bought her a gardenia that she carried in both hands, feeling like a bride.

"Oh Jessie," Eliza warned one day, holding her sister's arm and gazing at them both. "You're transparant as glass. If Papa sees you he'll know everything! I ran into Harriet Bodisco—she's very grand now, married to the ambassador, and do you know what she said? 'Invite me to the wedding, won't you?' Imagine!"

". . . It's all so confusing," Jessie burst out later to Maria Crittenden. "Everything is changing. Now I'm always upset!" She heard her voice rise and smiled quickly to counter the impression. After all, she really was supremely happy. Wasn't she? Maria gave her a warm, indulgent smile.

"It's confusing at home, too," she went on. "When I talk to Mr. T, I feel so badly. He's always been—"

"The center of things?"

"Yes. The center of things."

"Well, that couldn't go on forever," Maria said gently, and for some reason Jessie felt herself blush.

"But it's more than that, too," she said. "I feel like—like a cheat. I've always been able to talk with him, and now I can't. It's like a betrayal."

"Oh Jessie, it is not. Don't be silly."

"It's awful! Here I am in love and I can't say a word about it."

"How serious are you? Really?"

"It's like being on a great swing, rushing through the air—"

"His kisses are heavenly, are they?"

Jessie gazed at Maria, slightly shocked, and then smiled. "Yes; in fact, that's rather an understatement."

"Of course," Maria said carefully, "kisses are thin gruel in the long run."

"Oh, it's more than that—he's everything I've ever wanted, or dreamed of. He *cares* about things—the way I do. He's going to *do* things in the world, great things—and he needs me."

"Are you sure?"

"Utterly sure. He wants to make a mark, a real *mark* on our time, you know, and so do I. We fit together—he's brilliant, but I have good ideas too, and in some ways I'm . . . well, not necessarily deeper, but I think more—or at least differently—about some things. More reflective, I guess. I do see things he doesn't see. Sometimes I surprise him with how much I care. How much I know. Charles is so *committed*—to me, to the West, to the country. And that's what I want, too. To be committed—with Charles and through him. Committed to *life*!"

"Given your sex, that's how it'll have to be, won't it?" Maria said.

"Mr. T always says that a few people shape events, while most people are shaped by them. Well, Charles is one of the shapers. I know he is—and so am I. The plain fact is that we belong together, and certainly we can do far more together than either of us can do alone. And then, I'll never be even remotely bored with Charles."

"How do you know that?"

"I just do, that's all."

"Good girl," Maria said, and embraced her suddenly.

Later that same night, President Harrison died. The petitioners, the damned favor-seekers had nibbled him to death, John Crittenden muttered next day. He was pale and Jessie saw that he was deeply shocked. It had been very quick, he told them. A morning shower had drenched the President as he returned from marketing on foot; and in his exhausted state, pneumonia had taken hold. John Tyler of Virginia was President. Mr. T said Tyler was an ass—but a harmless one, which was a blessing. Charles told her later Papa Joe Nicollet was worried that the Oregon expeditiion might be jeopardized, but Jessie knew better.

The city went into mourning, its people subdued, its buildings swathed in crepe. An immense cortege, bands and caissons and black horses, Harrison's white horse riderless, boots reversed in the stirrups, would march from the White House down Pennsylvania Avenue to the Capitol. That meant it would pass the Coastal Survey Building where The Map was in progress. Lieutenant Frémont sent an invitation to the Benton household: perhaps the ladies would enjoy viewing the historic event from the map-room windows? Jessie's Grandmother McDowell promptly accepted and brought several friends, with Jessie in attendance. All that afternoon as the funeral drums tolled and the old women watched and pondered the nature of mortality, the young lovers sat by a fire at the rear and imagined—softly—their own bright future.

But in the weeks that followed tension marred their joy as that future seemed less certain and began to press them. The kisses in the gazebo were newly burning. They would lock together in sweet, urgent agony and then tear apart, trembling, full of undefined pain and frustration.

"Oh, my God," Charles groaned, "this is ridiculous! Here we are, stealing kisses like—like . . . I'm not a child, Jessie!"

She felt her own quick anger. "And you think I am?"

"No, but we're *acting* like children. I have to resolve this absurd situation—resolve it now."

She was drawn tight as a wire, filled with wild desire and wilder fear, and she snapped much more sharply than she intended: "No! You're always after me about this!"

He stared at her, her blue eyes wide, his face hardening in a way that she hadn't seen before.

"Jessie" he said, his voice tight, "I am a serious suitor. I'm a man of my word, and I don't by God quail before anybody—and that includes your father. Especially your father!"

He had been able to contain his resentment over Senator Benton's rough treatment of him, she thought, because he knew that he would win. He was going to take her from her father. She was caught between two forces, torn, and while this gave her great satisfaction, she nevertheless felt the need to defend Mr. T.

"My father is only looking out for my interests," she said crossly.

"Is he indeed!" He paused, glaring at her. "Why, that's outrageous! Your interests? What have *interests* to do with our love, our life together? This isn't politics, it's our future!" He whirled and stepped to the other side of the gazebo and turned back on her, moving with quick, alarming authority. "Is this a game? Are you telling me you don't give the same importance to us that I do?"

"Oh, how dare you!" she cried. "Here I am—in love with you, devoted to him, and both of you act like idiots! I can't talk to him, and now I can't talk to you. All you can think of is your stupid pride. *You* feel badly! How the devil do you think I feel!" She was more furious than she could ever remember being. "But no, you don't think about that. You drive me crazy with wanting you, and you don't care. You don't think of anybody but yourself!"

He stared at her in outraged amazement. "*I*—what about you? I've held off going to him only because you wanted it." Then, surprisingly, he beat back his temper. "The only question is: do you love me?"

"Well, of course I do! That's what we're talking about!"

"Good," he said. "I love you, too. That's all that matters." He raised his hand theatrically. "Do you realize what's happened? We've just survived our first quarrel."

She began to laugh, and suddenly tears streamed down her face and she choked, sobbing and laughing, and her arms went out to him without reserve.

"But even so," she heard him murmur, his voice muffled in her hair, "we can't go on like this, Jessie."

And holding him fiercely, trembling, she knew he was right.

Thomas Hart Benton stood at his study window, looking down on the street that fronted his house. A nanny walked past, shepherding three small children. It was almost ten in the morning and the air at the open window was still cool. Jessie was coming at ten—she had made a formal appointment, her face set in that strained, withdrawn look he'd noticed lately. *A formal appointment*! For herself and that Frémont fellow. Obviously they wanted him to reverse himself—just like that—and let the fellow call on her. And just how had all that come about? Had Jessie actually been seeing him? He scowled down at the street.

It was very disturbing. The odd formality of the request, the look on her face—why didn't she just speak up? It had been nearly three weeks since she had last come to the study at dawn. He hadn't asked her why she had stopped, but he'd missed her. She was punishing him, then. Or did she hope to strike some sort of bargain with him, force him to make terms? No, that was ridiculous.

She had spoiled him since she'd been home from school. She seemed more acute and authoritative, quicker, more stimulating; the school had given her a fine polish. He flexed his fingers, warming away a subtle pain in the joints; arthritis, he supposed.

Maybe he should let Frémont call. Occasionally. Well chaperoned, of course. She *was* rather grown up, turning into a lovely young woman; and in due time she'd be attracting real suitors. Eventually someone—not for a while, but eventually someone would come along with solid qualities of character and intellect—well, he'd see. Her mother could guide her. Elizabeth understood these things. Elizabeth had listened to Benton's proposals for six years before she'd made up her mind. Her sense of propriety was superb . . .

He stood blocky and square, legs apart, arms crossed, watching a pair of dun-colored dogs idle on the street and thinking about his wife. He had been thirty-three that year of 1815, staff officer to General Jackson, and preparing to leave Tennessee and settle in St. Louis. He had gone to visit James McDowell at his plantation, Cherry Grove, in Virginia and met his daughter. Elizabeth was twenty-one and there had been a remote, ethereal quality about her that had drawn him—gentle, pretty, with a manner that bespoke the Virginia gentry, her family lines as good as any in America—and he had proposed marriage. She had shaken her head, smiling, refusing him. Graceful as a princess.

But he had been back the next year, and each year thereafter, to propose again. She didn't like military men, she told him. Or Democrats. Or men with red hair, and his had auburn tints in those days. But in 1821, when he was about to take his seat in the Senate, she accepted. Her tart old Aunt Sally had sniffed and said that a Senate seat seemed to have improved him; but he understood Elizabeth. She was twenty-seven and he was thirty-nine; he'd given her time to find that the romantic dash of those Virginia blades couldn't stand up against his solidity. And she had made a fine wife—six handsome children, a gracefully run household—an ornament in every respect. Her health was poor and she loathed Washington and politics, no escaping that; but she had been steady, she understood what was important. It was the solid things that mattered. Worth, duty, dignity, propriety.

And honor. Standards. What else protected a man from temptation? Abruptly there lurched into memory his one catastrophic failure, a lapse of honor now more than forty years old. He never denied that memory or avoided it. Suffering its painful details again and again was his penance and his reminder that evil dwelt in every man and hell was a flaming pool awaiting those who slipped. At times it seemed impossible that he, Thomas Hart Benton, had actually *stolen money* . . .

But he had—and from the purses of his friends. Seventeen and enrolled at great cost to his widowed mother in the University of North Carolina at Chapel Hill, living in student quarters, he had rifled his friends' pockets—and been caught with their money. Temptation. Surrender. Exposure and disgrace. The punishment was a fiery stripe that cut to his soul. Denounced before the student body, expelled and sent home. And the next day still another student had called him out of his own house and made him admit to yet another theft. The jeering contempt in that boy, the cold iron of his mother's face, the stunned, disbelieving look on his baby brother Jesse's. There are crossroads in life marked with letters of fire, and a man can choose: he can yield to the evil in his heart and slip down the greased slopes of temptation to his utter ruin—or he can take such a grip on himself that nothing can ever shake him from the path of righteousness. And he had sworn two oaths that day: he would never yield again to that worm of evil; and so armored, he would never permit anyone to humiliate him. Let any man try and he must pay with his life . . . or take Thomas Hart Benton's life to save his own.

Standing there in his well-appointed study on the third floor of his handsome brick home—he could see the White House in the distance—he waited for the reassuring rush of anger that went with the memory. Oddly, it didn't come. By God, he was right because he made a *point* to be, and let no man . . . But then, righteousness wasn't always rightness. He shook his head: Jessie had unsettled him with her absence, and this formal request. Had Charles Lucas died there on Bloody Island with Benton's bullet in his heart because that schoolboy had demanded the money in front of his mother? They had fired at ten paces, a killing range, a fool's range, a man couldn't miss, but Lucas' bullet somehow *had* missed, and his had struck solid and square. The instant he heard its thump, striking home, heard the man's cry, he had known that Lucas was dead. For what? A foolish quarrel. They had already met once and hurt each other and that should have settled it. His face had shown none of his feelings then, nor had he admitted them later. Doubts and regrets would have been a different humiliation. But Lucas was dead at twenty-five, and what was the sense in it?

And Andrew Jackson . . . It was God's wisdom and none of his own that he hadn't killed him that time and changed the course of history. Well, it wasn't his fault—the general had attacked *him* in the lobby of the City Hotel in Nashville and he had defended himself. That's all. But what had that been over but fancied humiliation? Did it really matter that Jackson had served as second to Billy Carroll when Carroll wounded his own brother Jesse in a duel? Why had he taken the incident so personally and made such public threats?

Jackson had walked in on him in the City Hotel with a whip in his hand, big John Coffee just behind him. He could remember it as if it were today, Jackson crying: "Now defend yourself, you damned rascal!" and raising the whip. He had reached for his pistol but before he could touch it Jackson had dropped the whip and drawn his own and Benton had stared into a black muzzle hole that looked big enough to hold a man's head, knowing that he was as close to dying as he ever wanted to be. He still remembered the cold ferocity in Jackson's eyes. Jackson had pressed the barrel hard against his chest and walked him backward across the lobby; and then Jesse's bullets had struck Jackson, whose pistol fired as he fell, its powder burning Benton's coat. Benton had drawn then and fired as Jackson went down and missed, thank God, and Colonel Coffee had come up over Jackson's body gripping one of those knives that fellow Jim Bowie later made famous—and then the room had been full of shooting, slashing figures and Benton had been knocked tumbling down a flight of stairs with five cuts on his face and arms. But he had been up in time to see the terrifying whiteness of Jackson's long, noble face through the powder smoke as they carried him out on a mattress soaked through with his blood.

Jackson had dropped a sword cane in the melee and that afternoon Benton had broken it exultantly in the square—but his later thought, to which he returned again and again, was his true thought. If Jesse's bullets had gone a little differently, if Jackson hadn't had such amazing stamina, who would have saved the nation when it so desperately needed saving?

A decade later Tennessee had sent Jackson to the Senate and he had taken a desk near Benton's seat. Both of the men had awaited an opening and when it came Benton had put out his hand and Jackson had taken it and the awful breach was healed. Jackson had been young then, much younger than Benton was now. This came with a little shock—he had always thought of the general as *old*. Years later, one of Jesse's bullets had worked its way to the surface in Jackson's body and a surgeon had removed it. Jackson had sent it to Benton with a note saying that it was, after all, his property. And Benton had returned it. It was the general's, he'd said, by right of adverse possession, what with his having kept it about his person all these years. Well, they could laugh about it by then, but . . .

Now, standing by his window in the year of 1841, Benton felt genuinely out of patience with himself. "No, by God," he said aloud, "a pox on doubts." A man set standards and lived by them, and if fate cast a die with a single spot, so be it. That was the lesson of the university. He felt the anger flaring up, welcome, fortifying, reassuring. He had done damned well. He had mastered the books—valued them the more, perhaps, for their cost in lonely labor. And he'd done more with his knowledge than most men. It had guided him through endless pitfalls. Let no man cross him or touch his honor or violate his family. . . .

The French clock on the mantel began to chime ten, and he turned abruptly away from the window as the door opened and his daughter walked in—with Lieutenant Frémont behind her. She was formally dressed, he saw with surprise, wearing a locket that he had never seen: Frémont was in a neat, plain suit. Neither was smiling. She looked . . . different, somehow. She came clear to his desk and leaned against it, and there was a moment's silence.

"Senator Benton," Frémont said, and cleared his throat.

"We are married, Papa," Jessie said in a small, steady voice.

He stared at her, confused. "What do you mean?"

"I mean we were married. Charles and I. Father Van Horseigh married us. But—"

"Married?" There was a loud rushing in his ears that made his own voice sound faint. "You say *married*? You and this—this *fellow*?"

He looked at Frémont, who was standing to the right by the wall of books, and at this moment the young man gave an unfortunate smile. It struck Benton like a blow—sniggering, full of secrets, lecherous—and the red haze that had been crowding the edge of his vision covered him so darkly that he could hardly see the room. And then, laid with stunning clarity against the haze, he saw an image of bodies locked together, hair loosed across a pillow, her innocent face tight with passion—

"God damn you!" he said, staring at Frémont, his tongue thick. *"Violated!"* He stepped forward in one quick motion and caught up the heavy silver candlestick on his desk, reversing it and knocking out the candle.

"I'll kill you, you rotten bastard," he said in a voice he hardly heard.

He saw the younger man's feet shift and his hands come up; there was no fear in his face. *Good,* he thought, or maybe said, all lost in the roaring in his mind, *he'll fight.* The candlestick in his hand came back in a mighty swing and then Jessie had leaped in front of him and caught his arm with her weight so that for a moment he lifted her clear of the floor. She had her hands on the candlestick; dimly he heard her shouting:

"Papa, for God's sake, we didn't—what is the *matter* with you? We didn't consummate it! Don't—"

He stopped, staring at her; she snatched the candlestick out of his hand and held it behind her.

"You didn't—consummate? You—" Then, the mists clearing, he thrust instantly to the heart of the matter. "Then you are not married."

Her face was white and drawn and she still held the candlestick behind her, but she saw his drift immediately.

"Oh no, you don't," she said. "We *are* married. Legally. Forever."

"No—not if you haven't . . ." A spark of hope flared in him. He was trying to make sense of this, still badly shaken by his own burst of blind rage. There was a brackish taste in his mouth and he cleared his throat with a sudden rasp and didn't look at Frémont. He had been ready to kill the man in his own house, in front of his child. He couldn't remember when he had so lost control. He shook his head and seized hold of himself: this insane joke had to be set right.

"What on earth have you done?" he asked, managing an even tone. "Where—I mean who—"

"Maria," Jessie said quickly. "Maria helped us, she asked Father Van Horseigh—"

"A Catholic," he muttered.

She gave him a venomous look. "All the Protestants are *afraid* of you!" When he didn't answer she said, "So . . . well, we had a parlor at Gadsby's and Maria brought flowers, and we said our vows." She paused and then as if divining his thought, added: "It wasn't playacting, Papa. We had all the proper documents and everyone signed them and they're registered. We're married."

"When was all this? Yesterday?"

"No. It was"—she hesitated—"nearly three weeks ago."

So that's why she had stopped coming! The revelation seemed an added enormity. "And you hadn't the courage to face me," he said, and her shamed look told him that he was right.

But she hadn't consummated it—in three weeks! She was a child, she didn't *want* to be married. Some grain of caution—she was awaiting rescue, that was it.

"Three weeks—why did you wait?"

"Because we didn't want to—to start that way. In secret. Without you knowing. We wanted you to—oh Papa, *please,* we've always wanted you to approve. We love each other so much, and from the first you never would let us! I couldn't even *talk* to you . . ."

She was pleading. She had reverted—his little girl pleading for his favor. The sound infuriated him. She had spelled it all out: they weren't playacting. This vapid girl—so well-trained, so intelligent, so bereft of the slightest sense!

He heard his voice going thick as he ground out, "You stupid . . . stupid child!" She paled as if he had hit her. And then Frémont interrupted.

"Jessie."

"Yes?" She turned on him the same trusting, compliant expression that until now she had reserved for her father, and the look cut Benton to the heart.

"You can't persuade him, sweetheart," Frémont said in a low, level voice. "He thinks you're afraid of him."

"I am afraid, Charles. A little."

"No, you're not. We were married in good faith. We came to tell your father in good faith. That's the plain fact. He'll just have to accept it."

The sound of the man's voice frayed Benton's control. The interruption had broken the tension and he saw strength returning to his daughter's face. The arrogance of the remark flashed over him. *Have* to accept? He turned on Frémont and now the man's maturity struck him, a full-grown man counseling his child, controlling her. "How old are you?"

"Twenty-eight."

Eleven years. Benton stared at him. "What kind of a man are you to prey on children?"

"Jessie's not a child, Senator," Frémont said evenly. "I think you know that. I didn't marry a child."

"You seduced a *child*!"

"There has been no seduction, sir."

"You seduced her heart, you damned scoundrel!" Benton's big fists balled and he took a sudden step. Frémont was pale, but he didn't give way.

"Sir, I love your daughter," he said steadily. Two small red spots appeared high on his cheeks, and his aquiline nose seemed thinner than ever, but he gave no other sign of agitation. "I know this is shocking to you. But I promise you, I'll care for her, I'll cherish—"

"Spare me your cheap sentiments, sir! You have violated my family."

Frémont's eyes flashed hotly, he took a step forward—then got himself in control. "You're trying to sully this," he said slowly. "I think you're doing it on purpose. As a tactic." Benton saw Jessie look quickly at Frémont, a surprised, almost calculating expression on her face.

"Your daughter deserves better than that," Frémont said. "I don't think she's easily taken advantage of."

"You know my daughter better than I?"

"She is my wife."

The utter outrageousness of the remark struck Benton like a slap in the face.

"You are a contemptible coward," he said. "You are not worthy to say her name." His voice was big and raw, ringing the way it did in the Senate. "Stole her, but was afraid to ask. Married her, but afraid to face her father. Waited for *her* to come forward—"

"That is not true, sir. My not speaking to you was Jessie's wish—I honored it."

The aware, almost skeptical look was still on Jessie's face, and Benton turned to her abruptly. "Don't you see what you've got yourself into? Marriage is serious—and here you're ready to throw yourself away on this jackanapes. You who have such talent, do you intend to spend your life with a poltroon? This is not the way things are done, Jessie. You know better than this—you have standards, a sense of propriety." His voice was filled with contempt. "A decent man wouldn't—he hasn't a shred of honor in him."

From the edge of his eyes he saw Frémont move, and for a wild moment he hoped the man would attack him.

"Charles," Jessie said, both plea and command in her tone.

Again the Lieutenant checked himself. Benton didn't deign him a glance—he rushed on before Jessie could speak. "Everything you know tells you that's so. Everybody you know would confirm it. Oh, child, I promise you, when this romantic notion left you—and it would soon enough—you would be appalled at what you'd done."

"What I *have* done, Papa," she said firmly. She paused, studying him. "I believe Charles is right," she said. "You are trying to drive a wedge between us; and if he is without honor, then so am I. It's as he says—he wanted to tell you from the first, but I wouldn't let him. It was my duty to tell you—and yes, I was afraid, and he agreed to wait until I was ready. Does that make you proud, that I was afraid?"

"A decent man would have come at the beginning. I told him—"

"You told us both!—and I wouldn't let him come to you after that. I knew you'd do something terrible. You'd have sent me away, wouldn't you?"

"Of course. I'd have saved you from yourself—from making a shameful, cowardly mistake. I still will."

"No, you will not."

"This silly business will be annulled," he declared. "You're not really married, you see."

Her face was so cold and forbidding that he was startled. "Try that and you will never see me again."

". . . My duty," he said, but he was shaken. "You're an irresponsible girl."

"You *are* arrogant," she said wonderingly. The childlike quality he had seen was gone—that devil's support had put the iron back into her. "I never believed that before, but they're right. You haven't thought of us once—only of yourself, your pride. The incomparable Benton pride."

"I'm thinking of *you*," he said quickly, but he was too late.

"No—else you'd see what this has done to us. What did we want that was so dishonorable? Just what anyone wants. To be taken seriously. To court each other naturally, to fall in love."

She paused, glaring at him. "*We* should be ashamed? *You* should be ashamed! God—can't you understand? This is the most wonderful thing that's ever happened to me. I should be shouting for joy, I should have had a glorious wedding . . ." She began to cry, but she hurried on as tears streamed down her face. "But no, I have to arrange for my own wedding, no family, no friends—and now I'm standing here having to justify myself to the man who knows me best and should be most of all on my side. Shameful! Cowardly! Not to have done it, *that* would have been shameful and cowardly—to run from life, to run from our very hearts' desire for fear of what Papa would say, how Papa would act! No, this is all your doing, this trouble—*you* imposed secrecy on us out of your blind pride. You didn't care what we suffered—"

"Oh, yes," the hard rasp was back in his voice, "such impetuous love, so heedless, so unique that it just couldn't wait—what kind of love ignores decent propriety? That's not love—that's carnality, that's base lust—"

"Papa! Think about it a moment. We couldn't wait just because you *did* make it so secret. We're not fools, we'd have consulted, we'd have worked something out. It was that awful furtive secrecy you imposed—that's what made it all impossible! Don't you understand? There comes a time when you have to act. Going on the way we were would have destroyed us. And I wouldn't forsake what Charles and I have—I wouldn't let it be destroyed. Can't you see that?"

"Destroys so easily, does it?"

She looked at him in surprise. "Love is strong as iron and fragile as glass. Don't you know that, Papa?"

He felt an odd tremor. He had never had such a thought.

"You're too young to know about love," he said shortly.

"No, I'm not too young. That's the trouble—I'm not a child. And do you know why? Because *you* forced me to grow up. You wouldn't let me be a child: you wanted a confidante, a hostess, a secretary. You didn't want to play jacks—you wanted to talk politics. All right, I was glad to be used—but let's not forget that you used me. And when the moment comes that's inconvenient for you—when a man appears and I fall in love with him, oh my!—then you want me to be a child again. Papa's little girl. And if you could drive the man away, then you'd have me right back here listening to you scheme."

She stared at him, leaning against his desk, and said in a flat, clear voice, "Well, you can't have it both ways. You *made* me grow up and now you'll just have to live with it."

She had staggered him. She was speaking from weakness, justifying herself, but she was turning the truth on him too, adroit and clever, and with a surge of love and pride and something very close to fear, he saw himself in her; his force, transmuted. And fury rose in him again. Half-child, half-adult, honestly in love. All right, he would grant her that. And who gets this priceless gift? A mountebank, a rake, a handsome slickster who—but wait.

Why does he choose *her*? Why Senator Benton's daughter? The old suspicion fell across him like a worn cloak, comfortable on his shoulders.

"You're a hungry man, aren't you?" he said to Frémont, who still stood by the bookcase. "Let me tell you something. Everyone who comes to Washington wants something. The difference is that most of them won't go to such lengths to get it."

"Goddamnit, Senator—" Frémont began, but Jessie cut him off instantly.

"Papa, that's awful!" she said. "Has it been so long since you were in love that you can't remember how you felt?"

"I was never in love," he said sharply. "I mean—"

He glanced at her. He meant, not like this, abandoned, indecent—but he didn't want to explore that and he wheeled on Frémont.

"I know your kind of man," he said. "You ride on the coattails of better men. And now your patrons are losing power. Joel Poinsett brought you here, but he's out. He can't take care of you. And Nicollet—he taught you your trade, he shared a great command with you, put you into the highest circles. And now he's going to die. So who'll carry you—who's to grease your way now?"

Frémont's eyes flashed at him again; his face was like new iron in a forge.

Benton threw out his arms, smiling an ugly smile. "Why, the perfect solution. Marry! Tie yourself to one of the most powerful men in America. Force your way into the family of the *one* senator who can further your particular ambitions. You're a user, sir! You used Poinsett, you used Nicollet—and now you are using this child."

He paused, leaning forward, his big fists doubled, and said in a voice furry with menace, "But God damn you, you'll never use *me*."

The red spots on Frémont's cheeks were brighter and a thin white line ran down the ridge of his nose. He shook his head slowly, doggedly, beating down his fury.

"That's outrageous, Senator. But it won't work. It's not true and you know it. I refuse to take your bait. I don't want you or your name or your help. All I want is your daughter—and she wants me."

But this was Benton's game. He focused the attack. "Don't try to turn the issue. I know what you want. There's a great expedition coming—by God, I *saw* your ambition. You sat at my table and watched your mentor in a death tremor—and all you could think of was pushing him aside and seizing the plum for yourself!"

He saw the man flush and knew he had hit him.

"You're crazy to lead it, aren't you? You, the most junior officer in the Army!" He laughed, jeering and raucous. "Think those West Pointers will decide that you, a nobody with no real military background, should lead the most important expedition west since Lewis and Clark? Rubbish! You're desperate for a new patron and you elected me to the post. All you had to do was worm your sneak-thief way into my daughter's heart—right?"

Frémont's fists had tightened, and Benton saw him open them, consciously controlling himself. He started to speak and then shook his head.

"Answer me, damn you!"

"Senator, if I never had to lay my eyes on you again, I'd like that more than you can imagine. But your daughter loves you. That's why we're here. No other reason." Exasperated, Frémont added, "Good God, if I were trying to use you—" He stopped, shaking his head again. "Do you think me foolish enough to imagine that *this* would be the way to curry favor with you? I don't want one damn thing on earth from you! I got along fine before I ever heard of you—and when Jessie and I walk out of here, we'll do every bit as well."

And then, before Benton could respond, the anger that the Lieutenant had been throttling burst out, and in an entirely different tone he cried: "And as for your expedition, you can take it and go to hell!"

"Wait a minute, Charles," Jessie said, and in her sharp, clear voice Benton heard her returning the strength that Frémont had given her. "Don't be rash."

"Look, I want to be friends with him. I know how much it matters to you, believe me. But I will not crawl!"

"You don't have to crawl," she said. "Just don't be foolish about the expedition."

"No, that's out. I want no part of it—and that's all there is to it." He said to Benton, "After what's been said here today, it's out of the question. Please consider any interest I may have shown as formally withdrawn."

Benton was startled by the force of the man. He meant it, clearly. He studied Frémont, feeling that somehow he had miscalculated, but before the thought could lodge firmly, Jessie was speaking.

"Oh Papa, what idiocy is this? You've dreamed of such an expedition for twenty years—and along comes a man who knows what you want done, who knows how to lead it as no one else does, who wants nothing more than to serve your dream—and you spit in his face. Charles doesn't need you—you need him!"

She was standing very straight, pressed against a corner of his desk, and there was something hard and measured in her, a quality he had never seen before.

"Let some West Pointer take command and what will you have? Just what you've had all along. More reports on the 'desert.' More lamentations on the impossibility of settlement. Another setback. Don't you see *anything*? Charles is the best thing that ever happened to you—because he can *do* what you can only dream of . . ."

She was like a perfect stranger in his study. He had the stunning sense that she was capable of destroying him. "You think you're so strong, you're so proud of your power. But all you really can do is talk. Talk, talk, talk in that great blathering chamber of yours. But who's going to get on a horse and lead a column of men across wild country and *prove* what has to be proved? You're not. No—you're going to talk—and hope for a vague somebody to make your dreams come true."

Her voice dropped to a lower register. It had a steady, implacable note he found devastating. "Where is your wisdom, Papa, that you're willing to throw us away? I repeat it. Don't you see—we don't need you; you need us!

We're young but you're old. You're going to die—and we'll be here living, loving, bearing children."

He was struggling for words to stop her but she was on him like a great bird, wings buffeting him until his ears rang. "And long before that, you'll be old. You'll be weak and ill and then you won't talk about power. Oh no. Then you'll look to us, you'll want warmth and comfort and reassurance. And we'll give it to you because we love you—but not because you can demand it.

"The old need the young—it's not the other way around. Don't you ever think about these things?"

She fell silent, looking at him, but now he could find no answer. And in a moment, her voice growing still harder, she said, "All my life I've had such respect for you. Thought you could never be wrong. And now you're like a madman throwing away all that's precious in a fever of rage and pride." Again she paused and then said slowly, contemptuously, "You're the greatest fool of all."

"Jessie," Frémont said with sudden urgency, "not too far, now. Leave him some room. You'll only hurt yourself more."

She gave Frémont a look that Benton recognized instantly. It was the same look she had given him so many times over this very desk, but magnified tenfold, a hundredfold.

"It's all right," she said. "He can survive the truth. But first he has to see it."

They were in league against him. As if he already were old and they were deciding his fate. They had seized his floor—the man had stolen his *place.* His own girl—

"Oh Jessie," he cried, pain constricting his throat so that his voice didn't sound like him at all, "something has happened here, something evil—this stranger has stolen you, he's taken my baby—"

He stopped, hearing what he was saying.

There was a moment of silence and then she said in a low, awed voice, "My God, you're—you're actually jealous!"

The word was like a physical blow and at the same instant he saw dawning comprehension on Frémont's face. He tried to answer her but her strong young voice beat him down.

"Dear God yes, jealous of your own daughter! No wonder you're so tyrannical. So mean. You want to keep me for yourself, don't you? You can't stand it that I *love another man*!"

The roaring was back in his ears, red haze crowding his vision, the room heaving like a ship on a thundering sea, and desperately he gathered all his strength, his force and authority and position, and hurled it at her like a lightning bolt.

"Go to your room!" he shouted at her. "Go to your room this instant and stay there. This insane 'marriage' will be annulled this afternoon." He wheeled on Frémont, pointing at the door. "And you, sir, get yourself out of this house and never come near it. I'll horsewhip you in the street if I ever see you again!"

But neither she nor Frémont moved. His bolt was like a penny rocket, dying in the instant of its flash. Then, almost smiling, her eyes glistening and triumphant, his daughter stepped close to Frémont and put her arm through his; and Benton felt a wave of fear.

"This is my husband," she said in a voice that sounded to him like a funeral bell. "And I say to him as Ruth said." They were looking into each other's eyes and it was almost as if Benton weren't there. *"Whither thou goest, I will go; and where thou lodgest, I will lodge; thy people shall be my people and thy God my God. . . ."*

In the silence that followed, staring at their eager, confident faces, Benton felt suddenly beaten, his body heavy and slack. He wanted to sit down—desperately he wanted to sit down. Instead he made a noise that might have been a word, and turned and went slowly to his window. He pushed the glass farther ajar, needing air, and leaned against the frame, looking down at the street. The dun-colored dogs were gone. A man was loading a wagon.

Tears started in his eyes, blurring the scene below. He *had* wanted to keep her. She had found the awful little kernel of his need and shown it to him. Wanted to keep her company, her bright interest, her clever mind, their glowing mornings; wanted to remain the center of her attention, wanted to keep her his little girl. Not for her sake—face it, damn you, for your own sake. Keep her as a toy, a joy, a brightness against age. He wouldn't believe it, no—he raised both hands, fists doubled, staring down at the street—and he knew that it was true.

She was so—so *alive*—and the most surprising thought came: Elizabeth had never looked at him as this girl had looked at her man. Never. Nor he at Elizabeth. He had a sudden terrifying image of himself drifting palely through life like a wraith—and thrust it violently away. What had he learned at the university?—that temptation was always there, self-serving, urging you to take what you wanted. Was it his daughter's aliveness that he wanted? He had used her, she had flung it in his face, and she was right. It was as if she knew more than he, she the child so suddenly grown. As if their roles had changed, just as she had said.

All at once he was afraid, knowing that he could lose her, and he fought the impulse to turn to her. When had she grown up, and he too blind to see it? When she met Frémont? In the last hour? Didn't matter—she was grown now, she had battered him with the evidence.

His mind veered to Frémont. Older than she, accomplished, ambitious—what did he want? He felt a spark of his old anger, weak as the last ember in a dying fire. But why shouldn't the fellow want her, when he had seen the woman where her own father could see only the girl? And if she was grown, if she could give this man a look her father hadn't known was possible, could he say she was wrong? It was too late; everything too late, too much said, too much gone by. He still suspected that the man was a mountebank, an opportunist, but he had to give her her choice. And he could be wrong: those jeering classmates, young Lucas' cry, Jackson's face pale as paper against that bloody mattress—his use of his own daughter.

He could be wrong.

They had not moved; they were standing there watching him, waiting. With all the strength he had left, he managed the smallest of smiles.

"I guess we'd better tell your mother," he said.

PART TWO

SCOUT

"HAS MR. NICOLLET RECOVERED from his disappointment?" Jessie asked.

Charles shook his head. "He'll never forgive me."

"But it's not your fault—he's the one who's ill."

"He won't admit that. He can't."

She wished she hadn't asked. She was sitting beside him on the deep sofa, very conscious of her bare skin under nightgown and robe, and this wasn't at all the mood she wanted to strike. She put the after-dinner coffee tray aside and turned toward him. Fire in the brick fireplace gave the room its only light.

They were living in the guest suite of the Benton family home on C Street—a small bedroom, this cozy corner sitting room with yellow wallpaper that seemed to glow on sunny afternoons. She hadn't thought much before she married about where they would live—the need to confront her father had been all-consuming. When finally they had faced him down, they had gone to the drawing room where her sisters' delight in her news had made her feel that some sanity had returned to the world. And then Mr. T had reappeared in the doorway, his face ashen.

"You will live here," he had said. "You and—Lieutenant Frémont. Your mother is preparing the guest suite."

Charles had started to speak, but she had clamped her hand on his arm.

"Do you mean it, Papa?" she had whispered.

He had seemed terrifyingly distant. "It is the only reasonable thing," he had said. "Mr. Frémont will be off on expeditions and you should be here."

And now the time when Charles would be leaving was growing swiftly near. Her hand tightened on her husband's and he stirred against her on the couch. Her breath quickened. His head rested on her shoulder. Gently he kissed her cheek, his lips soft and warm. His other hand moved along her side until it held her breast lightly; she felt it swelling as if to fill his hand.

Of course he'd resisted the idea of moving into her father's house, but she had finally managed to persuade him. They'd gone off to Baltimore for a week and on their return he had talked alone with Mr. T; the two men had emerged from the study looking civil if not exactly congenial. A few days later she had got up well before dawn and gone to the study herself with the coffee tray. She had found her father sitting motionless at his desk, neither reading nor writing; she had a sudden impression that he had been waiting for her, that perhaps he had been waiting for days.

"Am I forgiven, then?" he'd asked softly, surprising her so that she rattled the cups in their saucers. He'd spoken casually enough, but she knew him very well—she had the sense that everything might rest on her answer.

"There's nothing *to* forgive," she'd answered.

"Do you believe that?"

She poured the coffee with a steady hand. "All of that is best put behind us now." Then, lest that seem too cold—he had after all opened his house to them, accepted the marriage with grim good grace—she smiled and offered, "I *am* sorry for some of the things I said."

His lidded gray eyes rose to hers. "But not all of them?"

She turned and faced him then, her hands folded. She knew better than to laugh, though she wanted to—for half a dozen reasons. There it was. He would always be the politician, maneuvering, pressing instinctually for specious advantage. Even with her. Even now. Her formidable, calculating, troubled Mr. T. Why had she thought *troubled*? Because he was: guilty and troubled and frightened. He had always been. Like everyone else . . .

"No," she said gently but firmly. "Not all of them, Papa. And now drink your coffee before it gets cold."

Now, his lips moving against her throat, Charles was saying in a husky voice: "Want to talk about the expedition, do you?"

He was teasing her—he loved the effect that he had on her. And so did she. Four months of marriage hadn't dulled in the slightest the feelings he roused; it was as if he had awakened something unsuspected, some intensity until now quiescent, and he never tired of stirring her. She struggled to keep her head, controlling the onset of passion, prolonging the pleasure.

"I don't like to think of Monsieur Nicollet angry," she said.

"Well, the Senator's helping on that."

Charles had become fond of her father. Of course Papa hadn't apologized that day the two of them talked, but Charles had told her later that Mr. T had said, "Well, sir, if I still believed all I said in the heat of anger, I wouldn't have asked you to live in my house." She lifted the hand that now clasped hers and slowly bit the ends of his fingers.

He sighed and stirred against her. His voice was calm, but his words dragged as if voicing them was an effort. "Papa Joe still has the report on our expedition to write, and that takes all his strength. The Senator's promised him that the report will be printed and widely circulated—that's very important to him now."

She left it at that. Recalling that brutal scene would have changed his mood, and she wanted him just as he was. But she admired the masterful way that Charles had carried it off.

The group had gathered in Mr. T's study, Senators Linn and Dodge and Frank Blair of the *Globe* and the others. And Mr. Nicollet and Charles. She had given them port in her mother's long-stemmed glasses and they had circled warily about the only question left: who would command the expedition? The room had crackled with tension. Mr. T had suggested that perhaps Nicollet was too indisposed to lead; Nicollet assured him tartly that it was nothing more than a bronchial irritation that soon would pass.

Mr. T then praised at length Nicollet's early work as evidence of his indomitable nature. Nicollet was not a man who would ever give up—so they, as sponsors, were obliged to question his own assessment of his health. Then, just as she had known he would, he tossed the ball straight at Charles. She had no idea if her husband was prepared.

"Your young assistant knows you best," Mr. T said. "Let's hear what he thinks."

But before Charles could respond, Nicollet said in a flat voice, "There's hardly any need for that, is there? It's perfectly obvious my 'young assistant' wants the command for himself."

Anger shot through her, but of course she saw at once what Nicollet was doing; he was a fighter and she knew how her father admired a fighter.

But Charles, undisturbed, said simply, "That's not the point, Papa Joe. It's yours to lead, if you can. But you're too ill to go into the field again."

"Ambition, gentlemen," Nicollet said, his voice thin and cruel. "You see ambition at work. Not a very attractive trait in the young, is it?" What a wretched old man he's become, she thought, and he'd seemed so sweet. "With all respect, Senator—Madame Frémont—what we have here is a youngster seeking to ride a mere bronchial irritation into a lifelong career!"

There was a short, embarrassed silence. Charles said then in a clear, firm voice that was utterly new to her: "Senator, during those last days on the Minnesota, with winter fast approaching, the rivers already freezing over, the men and horses hungry and exhausted, Mr. Nicollet—" he broke off, went on more gently, "Mr. Nicollet's health broke down. All the hard-won achievements of the expedition—to say nothing of the lives of the men—were in danger."

"They were not!" Nicollet broke in fiercely. "They were *not* in danger!"

"It was necessary for me to assume command and bring Mr. Nicollet out."

There was a murmur of surprise. Jessie glanced at Mr. T, whose pale eyes were wide. Even he hadn't known about that.

Desperately Nicollet cried, "That's a vicious remark, Charles! Vicious and untrue! You were impatient, I humored you. *C'est tout, c'est incontestablement tout!*" He was losing his English in his agitation. *"Un malentendu . . ."*

But even then there was a deep reluctance in Charles' voice—she could hear it—as he said: "Provost was ready to force you that morning. You remember."

"I remember nothing! Untutored woodsmen ignorant of the importance of science—"

"I count Provost as a friend," Mr. T said sharply.

"Senator, you value experience, you know the worth of wisdom—I appeal to you—"

"Papa Joe," Charles said in a tone no one could ignore, "We'd have buried you on the Minnesota if I hadn't brought you out when I did. You know it. That was a year ago, and you haven't recovered yet. You'll—" He stopped, bit off the words.

Then—most surprisingly—Nicollet turned to Charles and said entirely in French, so softly she could hardly hear, "And so, what has changed? They denied me the Academy—which I'd earned. You deny me this. Didn't I tell you? Men don't change, hungry men don't change."

Charles looked shaken at that. She couldn't understand it at all, and later he just shook his head when she asked; but when the meeting ended he went immediately to Nicollet. The older man turned away from him and she, still angry at Nicollet, called to Charles; but without replying he followed Nicollet downstairs. Watching from the little bulls'-eye window at the landing, she saw Nicollet stumble on the stone steps. Charles caught him, held him upright. They talked a minute, the straight figure and the stooped one silhouetted against the western light, and then Nicollet turned suddenly and pressed his face into the small of Charles's shoulder. She watched her husband's strong arm holding the old man; then Charles hailed a passing hack and they rode away together.

Now, his voice a whisper in her ear, her husband said, "He couldn't possibly do the Oregon Trail. There's no way round it, as Louie would say. Oregon is for the young and the bold."

"Like you," she murmured.

"Yes. Like me. It's just a fact of life, that's all. . . . Let's leave it now, darling. It's done."

He bit her earlobe very gently and she felt him unbuttoning her robe. Then his breath caught, he turned her firmly against him, and she knew he was through playing. The fire that he roused in her flamed; urgently she turned her mouth to his.

"But I want Provost," Frémont said to Pierre Chouteau. He had gone to the American Fur Company compound on the riverfront the moment he arrived in St. Louis; it was already June 1842. The company was supplying the expedition on credit against Army vouchers, and Chouteau had their equipment ready with a roster of men for Frémont to interview. But the guide—always the commander's most important man—was lacking.

"I can't let him go," Chouteau answered.

"But I *need* him—badly."

"I can't help that." Chouteau had opened a general trading post at Westport with Provost in charge. He was sure that town would remain the gateway as the line of settlements moved westward, the departure point for the trails to Santa Fe and Oregon. Soon the Kansas country itself would be organized as a territory.

"We'll find you someone, Lieutenant, don't worry."

"Just *someone* won't do," Frémont flared. "Who I really need is Bridger or Fitzpatrick, a man of that caliber."

"Of course. But they've both been out a year or more. No telling when they'll show up."

Frémont knew Senator Benton and the Army alike would rest easier knowing Jim Bridger or Thomas Fitzpatrick or Etienne Provost was riding with him. Fitzpatrick was called Broken Hand among the Indians, or White Hair; a rifle had blown its breech once as he fired, leaving his hand a bent claw; his hair had gone white in a day and a night, while he hid among rocks as fifty Blackfoot searched all around him; he'd listened to them discussing the tortures they planned for him. Old Gabe, as his friends called Bridger, had gone out with Ashley in Eighteen-and-twenty-two and there was nobody left who went back any further. At the Battle of Pierre's Hole, Provost had been right behind Bridger when a Gros Ventre's arrow had caught Bridger full between the shoulders; they'd pulled out the shaft, but he had carried the head in his back for years.

Meanwhile, here he was without a guide—the man whose skills and judgment meant life or death to any expedition, who *was* the expedition. Not a good sign at all . . .

They had planned it in two stages: this year they would explore as far as the Rocky Mountains; next year they would continue from the Rockies to the mouth of the Columbia. Frémont intended to reach Westport by steamboat and strike across Kansas, swing north to the Platte and Fort Laramie, the trappers' post far up on the high plains. After resupplying there, they would go on to the Sweetwater and then to its head at South Pass, the great entryway to the Rocky Mountains. South Pass was a vast swale in the mountains—so wide, Provost had told him, that you couldn't be sure you were there until you found the streams running west. All this was to be accomplished in five hard months.

At last Chouteau snapped his fingers. "I've got it," he said, "Andrew Drips. An old fur man—used to lead our caravans back when Bridger and Fitzpatrick were running the Rocky Mountain Fur Company. He'll be around Westport—Provost can find him."

"Why not let him run your operation there and I'll take Provost?"

"Like hell!" The fur trader colored slightly. "What I mean is, Colonel Drips is—ah, better suited to the trail than to running a mercantile operation. That's all."

"You don't make me feel very confident, Pierre."

"No, he's all right. Get him away from those Westport taverns and he'll do just fine."

Frémont started to ask Chouteau if *he* would ride to South Pass with Drips and then thought better of it. Right now he wished he had some of Jessie's flair for tact and persuasion.

Drips. An ominous name. He remembered Dixon on the Minnesota, dour and withdrawn, bound in the alcoholic's incessant preoccupation with drink. Well, he'd have to take Drips if he couldn't find anyone else, but it was a dismaying start for the most important western expedition in two decades. He decided to sit on his decision until he reached Westport. Maybe Provost knew of someone else.

The other preparations progressed smoothly enough. He chose most of his men, and would complete his complement at Westport, where Freniere was awaiting him. Louie had come down from Fort Pierre by steamboat; his message said he was raring to go. For camp conductor, the straw boss who would see to the camp's daily operations, Frémont chose Clement Lambert, whose quiet ability impressed him. "I'll give you a good camp," Lambert said in French, "everybody doing his work, stock strong, gear up to snuff—just that, no more." Unconsciously he ran his tongue into the place of a missing front tooth. "It's good we understand that from the start."

Frémont had left Washington in early May. He'd gone first to New York to purchase equipment—two sextants, a circle, a fine two-day London chronometer, barometers and thermometers, a daguerreotype apparatus with twenty-five polished plates, and an inflatable rubber boat made by Horace H. Day of New Brunswick, New Jersey, who complained that Charles Goodyear with his vulcanization patents was trying to drive him out of business. Frémont suffered Mr. Day in silence, wondering if the boat really would work; but it held its air in a remarkable way, skin so taut that you could drum on it.

In St. Louis he stayed with Joshua Brant and his family. His place at the Brants' dinner table, he calculated rather nicely, was four and a half feet, give or take an inch or two, from the spot where he first had seen Jessie talking to those three young dragoons. He missed her bitterly. She completed what he had not known was incomplete, filled what he only dimly had understood was empty; he felt he'd had the most blazing luck to have found her. Her face rushed wildly to his mind, urgent with some new idea, intelligence shining in her eyes, a characteristic tendril of hair floating free as she talked. She was pregnant: she had told him a month before he left, made him promise that he would be home before the baby came, assured him solemnly that it would be a boy—and he'd laughed in easy delight. He didn't care, boy or girl, just so she was safe.

They had come down the polished stairs together, their arms around each other, on that last morning. The whole family had been waiting to see him off. Even the Senator had bear-hugged him. The idea that Old Bullion might someday hug Frémont in affection would have been unthinkable on that day they'd confronted him in his study, but once the old man had seen Jessie's happiness, he welcomed him as vigorously as he'd attacked him. Benton's warmth had soon broken down his own reserve; to his surprise, he realized that the Senator had become more father than father-in-law.

And now the expedition was taking shape. Provost had most of their livestock ready at Westport. Eight carts Frémont had ordered from a St. Louis wainwright were delivered; Lambert methodically tested each wheel; a spoke that moved here would fall out on the dry prairie. Frémont rechecked all his instruments against the known coordinates of St. Louis.

He decided he was too busy to ride out to Jefferson Barracks, headquarters of the Western Department, United States Army. A courtesy call might have been appropriate, but he'd had enough of the Army before he left Washington. Picky auditors had hounded him for the way he'd handled the Nicollet expedition accounts. Three new complaints—masquerading as queries—had reached him just as he was leaving Washington to take command of his own expedition. It was the West Point mentality; Academy graduates resented his having entered the Army by appointment. Political appointment, they called it; but what other sort was there? Frémont had been on two railroad and land surveys in the Carolinas under the capable Captain Williams before coming to Washington, and was considerably more experienced than most of his fellow second lieutenants, but that had made no difference to them. His appointment by the Secretary himself to Nicollet's Minnesota expedition had raised hackles in the Topographical Engineers, he knew; doubtless his current command at Senator Benton's request had provoked an even stronger reaction. Well. So much for the petty, carping minds of West Point. He had important work to do . . .

The *Rowena* went shuddering up the boiling yellow Missouri, past farms and villages. Halfway to Westport it stopped at Franklin, now a quiet town faded from its brawling days as trailhead for Santa Fe. Frémont was on the hurricane deck idly watching a boy trying to drive four balky cows aboard when a man came to the top of the levee. He was lean and hard, dressed in homespun and a blue flannel shirt, carrying a well-oiled Hawken in a fringed Indian boot in one hand and a carpetbag in the other. There was an air of authority in the way his glance swept the boat; it made Frémont think of how Louie approached a new ridge, as he watched him stride lightly down the levee and jump aboard the *Rowena*. He was wearing moccasins brightly worked with beads.

Several local passengers sought out Frémont to ask him about his plans for the trail and whether he thought it would increase the value of their land. He took them for farmers, though a fat man with a tooth mounted in gold on his watch chain was admittedly a banker. They saw a high promise in western migration. The first large settler party ever had gone west the year before, headed by Johnny Bidwell of Platte County and a fellow named Bartleson. Now another big party had passed through no more than two weeks ago.

"This second bunch, I sold 'em some mules," one man said.

"How did they look?" he asked the mule seller.

"Able. More'n a hundred men, I reckon, and several families. Eighteen Conestogas and *mucho* stock. Good weapons. And Dr. Elijah White, he seemed like a sound man."

"You gotta hand it to them missionaries," the fat man said. "It takes a brave soul to carry the word of God into the wilderness."

"Or a Goddamn fool," Tessier hooted. "He's going to need more than a pillar of fire to show him the way beyond South Pass."

Dr. White had gone west originally with the fur-trade caravans bound for rendezvous, as had Marcus Whitman and another preacher named Jason Lee. Whitman had become a legend himself when he doped Jim Bridger with laudanum and whiskey at rendezvous and cut that arrowhead out of his back. Provost himself had helped hold Bridger down. "Old Gabe was biting on a stick, but I'm telling you, he grunted right smart when that knife tickled his chine."

The man Frémont had noticed boarding came on deck and walked directly to him. Up close he gave the same impression of great ability and force. His eyes were a pale, bluish gray, very steady; a dun-colored mustache drooped around his mouth.

"Name's Carson," he said without preamble. "Christopher. Folks call me Kit. I've knowed Clement Lambert some years. Me and him was in the mountains once. He says you're in need of a guide to the western country. I know that country pretty good—I'm headed there now. I believe I could take you anywhere you're of a mind to go."

The name meant nothing to Frémont, and he had listened closely to many a story about Joe Meek, Hugh Glass, Old Bill Williams, Joseph Reddeford Walker and the others. But no fireside tales had dwelt on this Christopher Carson or Kit or however he liked to be known. For that matter, he wasn't any grizzled veteran—the man couldn't be more than three or four years older than he was, maybe thirty-two or thirty-three.

"You're going out anyway, you say?"

"Going back; I live at Taos, up above Santa Fe. Been working out of Bent's Fort for some time now—I'm hunter for them."

Hunter for Bent's Fort: that would be no small matter. William Bent's massive Indian trading post stood on the banks of the Arkansas near where that river emerged from the mountains and began its long descent across the high plains. The man who could keep it in meat would have to know the country.

Frémont described their route quickly. "You know South Pass, do you?"

" 'Deed I do. Been through it enough times."

He sounded like a Missouri countryman. "Where are you from originally?"

"Right out of Franklin. I run off from the saddlery where I was apprenticed. That was—let's see—sixteen years ago. Later I heard old Mr. Workman posted a reward of one cent for my return." He smiled, relaxed but not familiar. "Reckon that was a fair statement of my worth at the time. But I've learned a thing or two since."

He was economical with words as he sketched in his background, answered some questions: he'd gone down the Santa Fe Trail a runaway, in Taos a couple of lean years, went to California on the Old Spanish Trail with Ewing Young in Eighteen-and-thirty—Frémont's eyes widened at that—pursued the beaver through the Rockies, trapped with Bridger for a time, led parties out of Taos—run the Rockies north and south, east and west—

"You've worked with Bridger?"

"Sure have. I been out in that country about half my life. Truth is, a man don't survive if he don't acquire a feel for land pretty damn quick. I been in my share of scrapes. Shot me some Indians and been shot at aplenty, but I've talked my way out of more tight places than I've fought out of. Indians—well, there's a hell of a lot of mean ones out there, but I've lived with the Arapahoes, and again with the Cheyennes. Got marriage relatives in both—my Cheyenne name means Little Chief. Honorary name, you know; they give it to me after I went after some stolen horses and took care of them who stole 'em. Only reason I'm here now is my little 'Rapaho daughter—I brought her to Franklin to put her in school. First time I've been back since I run off. Place sure has changed." He shook his head dolefully, grinning. "Even the folks has changed. No one knew me, 'cept for a couple of old aunties and my sister."

Frémont gazed across the yellow water, drumming his fingers on the wooden railing. The man looked able enough, spoke well, but still . . .

"I can't afford to pick the wrong man," he said bluntly. "Too much is at stake."

"I can understand that." Carson seemed about to say more and then closed his mouth firmly.

"I've had Andrew Drips recommended to me."

"If Colonel Drips is going, I'll just ride on down the trail and not trouble you no more."

That meshed. Frémont decided to try a shot.

"Well, Mr. Carson, I'll be frank with you. This is a very important mission. There are a lot of men in Washington with high expectations for it. I really need someone like Bridger or Fitzpatrick."

"They's both good men," Carson said, unruffled. "You couldn't do better. I'd advise you to get them."

"Neither's available—they're in the mountains now, and no one seems to know when they're coming back."

"That's a fact. I run into Gabe Bridger on his way out."

Carson had a glint in his eye. The return shot irritated Frémont and at the same time it crystallized what disturbed him.

"Look, these men are well known. If you're so skilled in the mountains, why haven't I ever heard of you?"

Carson's jaw set, his eyes turned flat and cold. "Because, likely as not," he said slowly, "you ain't spent enough time around the mountains your ownself. You ain't been to Bent's Fort or Fort Laramie neither, I reckon, or you wouldn't ask a question like that. Matter of fact, I'd guess you ain't never been west of Westport."

He spat cleanly over the side while Frémont watched him in silence. He could feel the anger in the man, and the iron.

"Tell you what, Cap'n. You're so chock-full of doubts about me, I'll just leave you to your soul-searching."

"Well, hold on," Frémont said mildly. He could see that the man was more resentful than sullen, and it pleased him.

"But I'll ask you one little favor," Carson added. "When you get to Fort Laramie or wherever you're going, you get aholt of old Gabe and ask him about me. Or Fitzpatrick—ask Fitzpatrick. Ask Sublette or Etienne Provost or Charlie Bent, ask—"

"Think Provost would vouch for you?"

"He'd better," Carson came back hotly. "Ask him about the time I pulled a Blackfoot off'n his back—old Provost, his hair has felt a touch loose ever since."

"Tell you what," Frémont said, feeling suddenly relieved. "Provost is at Westport."

"Is that so? Well, then. You ask him."

"Let's both talk to him. Fair enough?"

"Why, that'll be fine as frog's hair, Cap'n."

They shook on that. The hand Frémont grasped was harder than his own; the sense of certainty he'd felt about this man from the first—and that he'd learned to trust implicitly—had deepened. . . . Called himself Kit—but he was no parlor kitten, that was for sure.

TRAIL

THEY RODE THROUGH the Kansas River bottomlands, passing small farms and oak groves where cattle grazed. At ten in the morning they left the trees and saw the prairie before them like a rolling green sea, the sky huge and brilliant. Its sheer *openness* struck Frémont—familiar, exciting, liberating—miles and miles of grassland bare to the eye, the arching sky so vast that he had a sudden impression of the world itself, he striding on great legs across the turning globe. On a far hill smoke boiled up from a grass fire; he could see a line of red at its base. A group of horsemen moved in the distance, Kansas Indians heading for the river, and a light breeze carried the odor of sun-warmed grass and prairie roses.

Frémont touched spurs to the big bay he rode, loped ahead and turned off to let the column pass in review: seventeen horsemen, himself included; eight carts, each drawn by a pair of mules, and a following herd. Freniere and Carson were in the lead, riding slightly apart, each with his rifle across the pommel. Provost had done more than vouch for Carson—he'd bored into Frémont with those hooded black eyes of his and told him he was more than a bit lucky to get him, he didn't need to look no farther. That had been good enough for him. Carson and Louie were totally different in appearance and yet, Frémont thought, quite similar; they would be very hard to surprise. Just behind them was François Tessier on a horse that was too small for him. He was loud, aggressive, with a big beaked nose which he seemed to emphasize by the way he stood with his head thrust forward when he talked. He jerked his mount as he passed and Frémont decided to switch him to a cart. Louis Menard, whose skinny frame belied his strength, rode at a much easier gait; his long legs seemed to circle the horse's belly.

Lambert rode alongside the carts. He was talking to Raphael Proue, a heavy, jolly man Louie had brought down from Fort Pierre. Freniere and Proue had been friends since boyhood and Frémont had the impression that Louie did the thinking for both of them. Lambert said something over his shoulder to Ben Cadotte on the next wagon and Proue turned to hear Cadotte's reply. Honoré Ayot followed Cadotte; the men called him Honey as a play on his name and for his willingness to endure savage stings in order to take wild honey from the tree. His face had a lumpy, stung look that apparently was permanent.

Several wagons back Frémont saw his little cartographer, Karl Preuss, riding with Dan Simonds. Preuss detested horses; only half facetiously he had told Frémont in Washington that he would come only if he could ride a cart—and after seeing him on a horse, Frémont had readily agreed. Preuss was German; he spoke in heavily accented English and had trouble concealing his contempt for things American. Simonds, who rarely spoke, had a limited command of German from his mother, which endeared him to Preuss; as they passed, Frémont saw that Preuss was talking, his round wire-framed glasses glinting in the sun, while Simonds nodded patiently. As he loped to his place at the end of the column, Frémont felt so happy that he'd have whooped if he hadn't been commander: a good horse under him, his troops behind him, the whole world open before him.

They ran west along the Kansas, its wooded hills off to the right, making thirty miles a day or more. The men settled down: camp made two hours before sunset, stock hobbled, water drawn, fires started, guards posted as darkness fell and the men lounging, smoking their dank pipes, ready to sleep when starlight was bright. At the ford of the Kansas, where the way turned north toward the Platte, they found the river swift with spring runoff. Delighted, Frémont ordered the rubber boat unpacked and put a man at its bellows. They watched in surprise as the boat snapped itself open, swelling and puffing.

"Looks like buffler guts after a day in the sun," Carson said sourly; he felt any sensible man would fell a few trees and make a raft. On the last trip ferrying supplies across they overloaded the boat and it turned over; everyone plunged into the violent yellow water to recover the gear and Carson emerged shaking his head in disgust. But neither a dousing nor an irritated guide could quell Frémont's high spirits. They were modern men making a modern map that would hurry the future; you could spend half a day building a raft or inflate a boat in half an hour; you could sketch for an hour or let Daguerre's marvelous *camera obscura* make the picture in a few minutes. Let Carson learn that the world was changing.

Frémont liked Carson; he often rode with him, talking about the country or Kit's experiences. Carson was Scotch-Irish, a man of cool temperament and good judgment; he seemed to have been everywhere and to know everyone in the mountains. He had wintered up on the Green River in a hut covered with snow, dealt with a grizzly that sounded to Frémont like a monster out of *Beowulf*, tracked an Indian horse thief for four days and then, as both their horses collapsed, killed him with a snap shot at a hundred-fifty yards. Once he'd been caught in the open by a Sioux war party, all the trappers off their horses, knives out, cutting the horses' throats and pulling them down as bulwarks against arrow and lead.

"Later it hurts you that you done that"—he looked at Frémont as if he wondered if the commander could understand—"horse looks at you like he can't believe what you done to him so unexpected, the smell of his hot blood all over. But at the time you can't wait to get him down and get behind him. . . ." That started him thinking about horses. "The only real friend a man's got, but sure as hell we'll use 'em—bleed him in starving time, open a vein above his hoof and then cook the blood, and if things don't improve damned quick, kill him and eat all of him. . . ."

Frémont rode along listening intently, absorbing the lore of staying alive.

At night Carson used his saddle for a pillow and arranged it as a barricade. He wore camp moccasins when he slept, put a cocked pistol on the saddle and wrapped his rifle in the blanket with him where it would be dry and ready. Except when he crawled forward for a coal to light his pipe, he stayed back from the fire—away from its light, Frémont noticed.

"I never figured what kind of weapon an arrow could be," Carson said, scraping beans from his tin plate, "till the night one came out of the dark without a sound and hit Jules Garmetz in the back." He paused to pull his pipe alive. "Him and me was after beaver and it was cold and he was up against the fire warming himself when it come. Blackfoot arrow. Knocked him into the fire and he flung himself out on his back and that broke the arrow off and then there wasn't no way of saving him. Died afore morn with that arrow stub inside of him, and don't you think I rode cautious, slipping out of that country?"

The men were listening uneasily. La Pierre looked alarmed; Louie winked at Frémont. Frémont wondered if Carson were inflating his stories a touch; certainly he was reveling in his audience. "Arrow won't pull out, you know. You can push it on through and then break off the head and pull the shaft *back* out again, or you can wait till your blood softens up the thongs that bind head to shaft, and then *sometimes* you can pull off the shaft and leave the head inside of you. Stings right smart while you're trying to get the shaft loose, though. That's what they done for old Gabe, and he carried that head around three, four years before that missionary fellow cut it out of him." He looked around, blandly imparting information. "Some Indians dip their arrowheads in shit," he said. "That's bad. Indian shit is poison. Likely it all is, but you *know* Indians' is . . ."

They ran northwest, the ground steadily rising, crossed the Little Vermilion and the Black Vermilion and came to the Big Blue. Frémont heard it before he saw it, a hundred-twenty feet of bright water tumbling over a rocky bed, and it looked so fine that the men rode their horses right into it. They were entering the country of the Pawnees, who were much more dangerous than the Kansas; ahead were the Oglala Sioux. Limestone outcroppings appeared and now there was prairie sage with leaves that glittered silver in the wind, mixed with the wild roses and the amorpha's purple blossoms. When they crossed the low hills that ran along the Platte, Frémont saw nearly a mile of water with heavy timbered islands interwoven with channels that shone in the afternoon sun like a woman's golden braids. The Pawnees called it the Nebraska, meaning flat or shallow, and in places it was just a skim of water over quicksand. It was brown, and the water gritted on his teeth.

"You'll shit dirt for a week," Louie assured him, "but it scours out your innards. It's a regular health cure, Charlie!"

Night by night Frémont and Preuss read the stars, the contacts bold and crisp in the lens. The old sense of joy—and power—surged again in him. He felt half god, half artist as he gathered the imaginary starlines. Complex, interwoven, they lay tangled across galaxies, but he could touch them as a harpist touched his strings, and they made him part of the order of the universe.

Once Carson asked questions about the night's work, but Frémont was absorbed and Preuss answered with his usual querulousness and Carson didn't ask again. Preuss lacked Frémont's sense for the stars but he had that German precision with instruments, and he was superb in recording the day's terrain in the sketchbook. The daguerreotype apparatus didn't work very well and Frémont relied on Preuss' strong sketches of landmarks which would illustrate the report. They collected plants and pressed them in blotting paper for botanical identification and Preuss made watercolors of the more important ones. Once when they stopped early Carson rode in with some alarm, having come back from far ahead.

"Stopped to paint flowers, eh?" he said, face expressionless.

"That's right, Kit," Frémont said, and grinned at him.

Carson stuck his tongue in his cheek. "I see— Yours to command, Cap'n," and he rode off again.

Probably he *didn't* see, but he would eventually; Frémont meanwhile was busy filling his notebooks with observations on weather, geology, plants, game, soil samples that he took in glass vials; all grist for the report that would open this western country to any inquiring eye.

It was all a pleasure to Frémont, action fueled on red meat, deep sleep on hard ground and up at first light, shaking out the stiffness, strong coffee sending him bounding into the saddle ready for another day. He liked command just as he had known he would, and found it no more difficult than he had imagined. He heard a buoyant, crisp authority in his voice when he started them in the morning and stopped them at night, and though he left the details to Lambert, he expected—and got—a report morning and evening.

Moving up the Platte past Brady's Island and Grand Island toward the great fork, they came at last to buffalo country. This time Frémont fired precisely at that point where the long hair stopped, and his cow fell with the report. Looking around in elation he felt a wicked delight when he saw Carson's horse go down and Kit hit the ground like a flour sack and come staggering to his feet. Carson's big buckskin scrambled up and ran off in a panic of hysteria. Louie followed it at a dead gallop, careening through the vast dangerous herd in a display of horsemanship that left the men gaping, and eventually returned with the buckskin following docilely on his rope.

Proue was the camp clown, bumptious and happy-go-lucky for all his massive bulk.

"Hey, Honey," he yelled at Ayot, who was storing cooking gear in a cart, "you didn't piss in this coffee, did you?"

Ayot's lumpy face darkened. "No, I didn't."

"Can you prove it?"

The men started to laugh. "I want *coffee,* I don't want your stale piss."

Ayot picked up the big coffeepot. "I'll give you some hot coffee where it'll do you the most good."

Proue scrambled up. "Fuck you will," he said. He seized a piece of firewood. "I'll beat your Goddamn brains out. You're the worst cook on the Great Plains. You know that?"

He was amused but not altogether joking. Frémont said nothing; best not to intervene when the weapons weren't deadly. He saw that Lambert had reached the same conclusion.

Carson, laughing, shouted at Ayot, "You waste good coffee on that pisshead, I'll beat your brains out my ownself."

Proue whirled on him. "You want some of it too?"

"Don't hit me, Raffie!" Carson squealed in a quavering falsetto.

Ayot set down the pot, picked up an empty skillet and hit Proue on the head from behind. It made a noise like a gong and Proue fell to his knees, half-stunned. Tears of laughter ran down Carson's cheeks and Frémont saw that even somber little La Pierre was amused.

"All right," he said. "That was a nice little show. Now let's saddle up and move out."

Up the Platte they rode on rising ground, the elevation near three thousand feet at the river's great fork. Bare gravel patches were more frequent, vegetation thinner. Cactus appeared among the purple amorpha. Huge sunflowers were in bloom, with that tasty rootstock the Dakota Sioux called the apple of the prairie. At the great fork they crossed the South Platte, its water never more than twenty inches deep, and continued along the north branch. Late one day they saw a line of horsemen well ahead. Pawnee, maybe even Sioux. Rifles came up, loads were checked, caps set. But the riders came straight on, and in his glasses Frémont saw they were white men.

"Trappers, do you reckon?" he asked, handing Carson the glasses.

"I'll be damned," Carson said, squinting. "It's old Gabe."

"Bridger?"

"Yep. Escorting some traders, I do believe."

Bridger came forward slowly, an old rifle balanced on his pommel, wary until he saw Carson. He was a tall, strong-looking man a little more than forty. His face had an oddly square shape and it was deeply lined; he didn't look as if he would smile easily. When he heard where they were bound he said, "Then I've got news for you. Bad news."

The two parties camped together and Bridger joined them for supper. When he had his pipe lit and his hand around a tin cup of coffee well sweetened from their sugar store, he said, "The message is, the Oglala Sioux are running wild in the Sweetwater Valley. They'll kill anything that moves there." It came like a dash of ice water in Frémont's face; the expedition would follow the Sweetwater to South Pass.

Bridger said it had started the year before, when Henry Fraeb got himself killed down on Little Snake Creek. Fraeb was an old trapper leader and he'd had thirty men out for buffalo hides when three hundred Sioux hit him.

Right away Fraeb and his boys had killed their horses and forted behind the carcasses. They'd fought all day and Fraeb and three others were killed. But so were ten of the Indians.

"Sioux been brooding over their dead all winter long. And now they're ready to raise some hell and count coup."

Frémont was filled with dismay. They'd been jogging along peacefully, and suddenly here was a full-scale Indian war. There hadn't been a hint of it—he wondered if the troops at Fort Leavenworth had been alerted. Then he realized that Bridger had come out of the mountains through South Pass.

"Did you lose anyone getting through?" he asked.

Bridger looked surprised. " 'Course not. Went a hundred miles out of our way to avoid 'em. We slipped past afore they knowed we was there."

"You didn't see them?"

"Why, hell no. The whole point is *not* to see 'em."

"Then how in hell do you know about it?" Bridger's manner had got under his skin.

"Sioux chief I know." Bridger turned to Carson. "Remember old Great Belly? Well, he was up to Lodgepole, had all his wives with him. Got him a new one, by the way, sweet-looking little piece. Anyway, me and him smoked awhile. Says the young men got bad hearts this winter. You know how he is, butter wouldn't melt in his mouth, says he's the whites' finest friend but there's just no controlling the young men. Says they've been making medicine, held themselves the biggest damned sun dance he ever saw. Swear they're going to kill them some whites to make up for what old Fraeb done to them."

"Great Belly would know," Carson said.

Frémont's alarm was turning to anger. These mountain men were supposed to be mean as grizzlies, every one of them—and now they seemed to be throwing up their hands on the word of a single Indian. Looking around the fire, he saw Tessier with his beak nose thrust out, looking worried; there was a warning tightening in Dan Simonds' face, and even Freniere looked grave. Most of his men were settlement men, not Indian fighters; this kind of talk was dangerous.

"How serious is it, really?" he asked, voice sharper than he intended.

"Well, I don't know," Bridger said, giving Frémont a sardonic, derisive glance. "However serious you count your life, I reckon. Any man goes up the Sweetwater just now probably ain't going to live very long."

That frightened the men; he could see it in their faces, hear it in their silence as they stared at Bridger. The situation was running away from him. "Oh, come on," he said, "that's a bit of an exaggeration, isn't it?"

Bridger gave him a small, cold smile, his first. " 'Course," he said, "you may be a better fighting man than most—I hear tell you're fairly handy with a pistol—but when it comes to a small party facing fifteen hundred—*waugh!*"

Fifteen hundred.

"Mother of God," someone said in a low, strangled voice, and there was a babble in French. Frémont heard Ayot say clearly, "That ain't no kind of life for old Honey," and he saw Proue watching Louie for a cue. Carson, who had been so confident about Indians on the *Rowena,* was muttering: "Them kind of odds do make a man a mite cautious, don't they?"

Quite angry, Frémont said, "Well, I don't know if they do or not. Why don't we wait till we get to Laramie and see what the situation is before we start tucking our butts."

There was a long silence and then Bridger stood up. "You must have looked awhile to find this company, Kit," he said. Coldly he nodded to Frémont. "Obliged for the supper."

"Don't mention it," Frémont snapped. "Maybe I can do you a good turn some time."

Indian fear had driven the joy out of them. They rode apart in the day and were quiet at night and Frémont didn't hear much laughter. Then, on the afternoon of the fifth day, they topped a rise and saw Fort Laramie below. The fort stood like a monument alone on a grassy plain where the Laramie River joined the Platte, its heavy adobe walls fifteen feet high and topped with a palisade of pointed logs. A blockhouse surmounted the main gate and two towering bastions at opposite corners commanded all four walls. Laramie was an old fur-trade fort, built on a great crossroads of Indian buffalo trails that had been old when the first white men crossed the Atlantic. The fort meant civilization after the wilderness: food, drink, news, perhaps women—he could feel the excitement in the men—and for him, decision. The smell of absinthe crushed under the horses' hooves filled the hot, sunny air, and on a rock to one side a rattlesnake four feet long and thick as a man's arm rattled with lazy menace. It wasn't a good omen; Frémont lifted his reins and the party moved on.

They made camp below the fort, and while the men washed in the Laramie, Frémont watched La Pierre rub liniment into the forelegs of two horses that had gone lame. He would replace his worn stock here, but he thought these horses could be saved. La Pierre worked steadily with easy hands; horses were always calm around him.

Several clerks greeted them at the fort's entrance, a sally port fifteen feet deep that caught a continual breeze. Their *bourgeois,* Mr. Papin, was off visiting the Miniconjou Sioux, who were still peaceful. He'd return the next day; meanwhile the situation in the Sweetwater Valley remained unchanged.

Then what of Dr. White's party of emigrants and missionaries? *Oui,* they had gone on—but with Tom Fitzpatrick as guide. Old Broken Hand had come out of the mountains just behind Bridger, reported a man who'd lost most of his nose in a knife fight. He also had counseled waiting. But Dr. White had insisted that since his party was going all the way to Oregon, delay now meant they'd certainly be trapped in snow, and finally Fitzpatrick had agreed to lead them through the Indian country. Unconsciously the man's hand went to his ruined nose. Fitz had figured it fifty-fifty that he could talk his way past the Sioux without having to fight; If Laramie had a priest, the clerk said, he'd have had a mass said for the emigrants right then and there, black Protestants though they were . . .

When Frémont walked into the big open square, he found Preuss talking in German to an angry magpie perched in a willow-wood cage. The bird shrilled at him and Preuss laughed so hard that he had to take off his spectacles and wipe his eyes. Carson was lounging with some visiting trappers across the way; most of the men were already lined up at the rude bar in the mess hall.

The square was formed by the fort's buildings which leaned against the walls, their roofs serving as promenade and parapet. Sixteen men lived here, most with Indian wives and dark-eyed children. Small boys were playing, scrambling up on the big square fur press, used for baling beaver and flattening buffalo robes, where an older boy was trying to throw them off. King of the Hill: the same game in every land. Frémont smiled. Dogs barked around the children, ringing hammer blows came from a smithy, and he heard what he took for violin playing until he realized that it was an Indian singing. The fort was full of Indians, peaceful Brulé Sioux who had come in to trade, Carson said; they sat around talking, laughing, smoking, the women as loud as the men, both sexes painted with vermilion and dressed in odd mixtures of leather and cotton garments made back in Massachusetts. He had a hundred questions for Carson, but his guide remained deep in a conversation that seemed to exclude Frémont. Then the smell of fresh bread drifted across the compound, and behind it the sharp ringing of a dinner bell.

Papin, a deceptively soft-looking man, returned at sunset. The Oglala Sioux lived in fairly small bands, thirty to seventy lodges, he explained to Frémont. The tribe deplored war unless the provocation was real; war always risked retribution. But there was no controlling the young men—no Indian tribe operated on the basis of the discipline that white men assumed was fundamental to an orderly society—and when the signs were right they galloped off to the attack. This year they were hopping mad. It wasn't just the Fraeb fight—everything had gone wrong. There was a drought and buffalo were scarce, always a bad omen. The price of fur was down, but the Indians saw the market collapse as just a trader's trick. Their war was aimed primarily at other Indians—there was only a handful of white men in the whole country—but unfortunately they regarded those few whites as friends of their enemies, which was always the trader's dilemma.

So they were out there, all right, sore as bulls in rutting time. How many? Were they split into groups or coalesced into a mass? Were they here or there or somewhere else?

"Then what chance do you give Dr. White's party?" Frémont asked.

"Well," Papin said slowly, "old Broken Hand's got a way with Indians. They respect him, they know he's a fighter. And there's more than a hundred in White's party. Now, no matter how strong they feel, Indians know damned well that a hundred rifles well forted and led by a man as cool as Fitzpatrick—well, there's going to be plenty of dead redskins. They'll think a long time about that kind of cost."

He paused, knocking a thumbnail pensively against his glass. "That's the difference," he said. "They don't know Kit like they know Broken Hand.

And then, what have you got—twenty rifles? Twenty-five? An Indian sees that as sporting odds.

"And Lieutenant . . ." He paused again, this time for effect, and a startlingly cruel expression flickered over his soft, round face. "They aren't very nice. You ever see a man with his privates cut off and stuffed in his mouth? Pecker hanging out like he was sucking on it? Or a man tied down and screaming while a little fire is built under his head so the brains boil slowly until his skull pops? You really don't want to let 'em get aholt of you when they're in a fighting mood."

It was late when he left Papin. He went into the courtyard and on impulse climbed onto the western parapet. The sun was gone and the sky was dimming; below it the Laramie Mountains, dark with cedar and pine, were sinking into night. They looked lonely, mysterious, threatening. And beyond these mountains miles and miles of harsh open land sweeping up to the great Rockies—rough, broken terrain with countless ambush spots—and the horsemen, long files of them appearing and disappearing among the rocks, gliding silent as the night itself. That bastard Papin and his filthy torture tales, Carson's image of the arrow coming out of the night without a whisper of warning . . .

He was alone; it seemed to him he had never felt so uniquely alone.

The men didn't want to go, not one of them, not the bravest of them. Even Carson the knowledgeable, the strong—he didn't want to go. The men of the fort thought he was a fool even to consider pressing on; the legendary Bridger agreed; the only man anyone thought could get through—Fitzpatrick—had already gone. He pressed his fist against his teeth. The sky was purple black, the hills dark, cruel lumps. He thought of Jessie, safe in their suite, comfortable.

No whining! The risk of all their lives. It all came down on him. There was no one to share or advise or commiserate. He had been gamboling over the prairie like a fool, delighting in the charade of command. Now it was here. This was what command meant. He remembered old Major Lamprey back in Charleston one night long ago, very drunk, his pale eyes empty with remorse. "There's moments you don't know *which* way to move, son—when either way could be the mortal wrong one. Lead to disaster. All I could think was that time was running through my fingers and I didn't know where Danielson's people were . . . It's not knowing—if you could only know the facts when you need to—!"

Frémont put his hands on the parapet of logs in front of him, gripped them hard. There was something wrong with his breathing; he couldn't seem to get any air into—

Stop it. He gripped the rough-hewn wood until his knuckles ached. Do it or don't do it. Simple alternatives: stay or go. Nothing else. Well, suppose he waited. But for how long? How would he know when the danger was past? By then there'd be a new danger; there always was. By then some windbag politician or the War Department would be having some of their pretty little second thoughts—they might even cancel the expedition altogether. Good God, if a man stopped for every danger he'd *never* move! Was he to be denied the very trail he'd been ordered to map for a great river of emigrants to come? White's party had already gone ahead. Was the Army afraid to follow? What would the West Pointers say about that? And by God, they'd be right. For that matter, if White was in danger, it was his duty to follow immediately. Of course, White had Fitzpatrick—but was there only one man in the world who could deal with Indians? Papin said they would respect a hundred rifles; well, maybe they'd have to learn what a toll twenty-six rifles could take when they were well placed and well fought. Danger was woven in the very fiber of this country; you did what you came out to do, took the risks, paid the price if you had to. Otherwise, you stayed home, sang hymns and read the papers.

He slapped his fist into his palm and bounded lightly down the stairs. At the bottom, standing as if they'd been watching him, he saw La Pierre and Ayot and Tessier, the last with his nose held in place with white plaster from a fistfight the night before.

"How's the buckskin, La Pierre?" he asked easily, reading trouble in their faces. They weren't soldiers, after all; he couldn't order them to go.

La Pierre's eyes had a hollow look. "Carson just made his will," he blurted out.

"His *will*?"

"Yes sir," Ayot said. "Told us chapter and verse who's to get his property if'n he croaks."

"*Carson,* Cap'n," La Pierre said. He was trembling. "Old Kit knows this country. He knows these damn Indians. If *he* thinks—"

"Shut up, La Pierre," Frémont said sharply. "Somebody'll put a cork in your mouth."

He met Carson by the fur press. A full moon had risen, its light glaring across the open ground.

"What the hell is this about your making a will?"

"Well—if you're so damned set on going even when it makes sense to wait, that's how it better be."

"Couldn't you just *write* it out?"

"Talking will is the custom here," Carson said shortly. Frémont remembered then that Carson couldn't write; he had signed the articles with a mark. "Scrap of paper gets lost, but if you talk out your intentions before men you trust, word of it'll get back." He grinned bleakly. "What's the matter—it funk out the Frenchies?"

"Goddamn right it did! And you the guide! They figure if you're scared to death, what chance have *they* got?"

The moonlight gave Carson's face a savage look. "Cap'n," he said in a low voice Frémont had never heard him use before, "I don't take kindly to nobody questioning my courage. I'll be obliged if you don't do that again."

"Then what in hell is the matter with you?"

"Your trouble is, you got caution and fear all mixed up. Now, I am cautious as hell—that's why I'm not gone under ten years ago. I don't take no risks that I don't *have* to take. Personally, I don't see no reason to rush on—not for any fool map. Same ground's going to be there two weeks from now. Or two hundred years."

"That's got nothing to do with it. They need that trail mapped *now,* we've been told to do it *now,* the whole damned country's waiting for it and we're going to give it to them—and that's all there is to it!"

"That so?" Carson said in a cold, hard tone. He spat on the ground, plainly angry. "Then, shit—let's go. I'm ready when you are."

He turned and walked away across the square. Frémont stared hotly after him. Why the devil had he thought Carson such a gutsy fellow? Turned out that when the chips were down—ah, to hell with him. They were *going,* that was the point. The decision was made. The quick, light feeling he'd had on the parapet returned; he went to rap on the cook's door and make arrangements for the morning.

He awakened before dawn. The sour taste of fear was gone now. He rousted the men out.

"Let's go," he said, popping his hands together. "Breakfast at the fort. Coffee's getting cold!"

He led them there, turning to chivvy the slowpokes. The cook was awaiting them with a platter in each hand, buffalo steaks heaped on one and crisp bacon slabs on the other. His wife hurried in with a steaming coffeepot and another Indian woman brought platters of fried eggs, potatoes, and flapjacks stacked so high they trembled when she set them down.

"Well, Jesus H," Tessier said loudly, "this is eating!" He shot a glance at Proue, who looked away at once and poured honey onto a tower of flapjacks. Across the table Frémont saw Lambert holding a coffee cup and watching him with a knowing grin, his tongue thrust into the gap of his missing tooth.

He was waiting for them by the fur press as they straggled out. Dan Simonds was industriously mining a molar with his awl. The men belched and laughed; the sun burst over the walls and a mockingbird's lovely song came garlanding down from the flagpole. There would never be a better time.

"Hey Cap'n," Tessier called, "that wasn't the last breakfast before the hangin', was it?"

"Why hell no," Frémont said. He stepped up on the press and looked at them. "I wanted you boys to set out for South Pass on a full stomach."

He saw their faces tighten and there was a distinct silence. Carson stood at the ready, arms folded, face unreadable. Freniere and Proue looked unconcerned; Preuss was watching the men with an amused expression. But it was the quiet Dan Simonds who spoke.

"They say it's bad out there. They're talking it all over the fort."

"Yes, I know," Frémont said, easy in the confidence he felt this morning. "But don't believe all you hear. Nobody really knows. Some Indians have made some threats, that's all. We don't know how many or how serious they are, or if they're even there. Maybe they've already gone off hunting. Meanwhile, we've got work to do."

"If it's all so easy," Ayot said sourly, "how come Carson made his will?"

"You know," Frémont said, "I asked him about that. He said you fellows looked so nervous he figured a loud fart would set off a stampede. He was scared he might get trampled. But I told him you were lovers, not quitters."

A couple of them grinned at that, but Carson's expression didn't change.

"I don't know as I hired on to fight Indians," Simonds said.

"What *did* you hire on for, Dan? To drive a cart? Hell, man, the way you're talking you belong behind a plow looking up a mule's ass. It's late in the day to start wishing you were walking a furrow back in Missouri.

"And you, Menard," he said, turning. "You think those Indians don't fall down dead when you give 'em a galena pill? Think they're magicians, think you can't see 'em coming—do you believe that crap?

"Old Tessier, now—I expect he's scared the Indian'll bend that pretty new nose Lambert made him."

They were loosening a little.

"Now listen—when I signed you on, did you think we were going to a Sunday barbecue? I told you we were heading for rough country, and we're not turning back the minute we hit a little mud.

"Anyway, I don't believe there's that much danger." He saw Carson's eyebrows go up and plunged on. "They won't attack when they find out we're neither traders nor trappers. But to make sure, we've got extra powder and lead, we'll fort up properly at night, we'll mount extra guards—I promise you, we'll never camp where we can't defend. Now, any Indians attack us and a lot of 'em'll be dead. You ask Kit—Indians like killing a whole lot better than they like dying. If they think you're ready, they think twice about jumping you. Isn't that right, Kit?"

He had to know right now whether Carson would support him. After a second, Carson nodded. "Right as rain, Cap'n."

But he still didn't have them. He could see it in their faces. Then La Pierre said in a high, squeaky voice, "Fuck that, Cap'n! I don't want to go!" He stopped, swallowing.

"You scared, La Pierre?" Frémont asked. The man nodded dumbly.

"Come on up here." He gestured and La Pierre climbed onto the fur press. He caught his arm and made a show of peering behind him. "Boys, do I see some feathers starting back here?"

La Pierre flushed. It was a pity: La Pierre belonged in a stable, not in the field; he should have seen that at the beginning; but it was too late now. Now, hating himself, he had to use him.

"We're going to worry about you, alone here in the fort with no one to protect you," he said. He pointed at a covey of chickens scratching its way toward them. "First time that rooster over there gets a good look at you he'll be mounting you, and next thing you know you'll be laying eggs."

The men were grinning. They needed a place to lay their anxiety.

"Hey, La Pierre—you in the egg business now?" someone shouted.

La Pierre flushed again. Frémont could see the hurt in his eyes. "Cap'n, I only—" he began plaintively, but Frémont cut him off.

"No," he said, "too late to change your mind. They'll be calling you Chicken La Pierre from one end of the Missouri to the other, but there's no help for it—'cause the rest of us are going to South Pass right now!

"All right!" He turned to the others. "I'm going. Kit's going." He looked at Freniere. "Louie, I've never known you to back down from anything."

Freniere looked indignant. "What do you mean? Me and Raffie was ready yesterday. Hell yes, we're going."

"Preuss?" Frémont said. The owlish little cartographer, so often querulous, now said easily, "Oh, of course." And then to Simonds, "Come on, Dan—we go together."

Clement Lambert raised both hands over his head as if stretching. "Why hell, Cap'n," he said in a lazy voice, "let's saddle up—I've always wanted to see South Pass, anyway. . . ."

An owl was talking and there was another in the distance. Two owls: Carson listened very carefully. The column had come far up the Sweetwater, the altitude near six thousand feet, the nights cool and clear. There had been plenty of sign but no attack. Carson had waited each night for the blurred, stealthy rustle he had heard so often. But nothing came. Now two owls were talking. He eased the Hawken's hammer back on full cock and waited, on his knees, head low, watching for movement against the sky. If you kept low enough, a man could hardly move on you without showing head against sky. There was a sudden flutter and a small shrill squeal. Owl got him a mouse. He'd seen Indians come into camp on all fours under wolf heads, clicking two buffalo bones together to sound like snapping teeth as the dogs circled them, but it would take one smart Indian to imitate the death of a mouse. He eased the hammer down on half-cock.

He heard his name called softly and saw Frémont coming out from the camp, moving half crouched, moccasins making no noise. Jesus—seemed the Cap'n never slept. He had just been putting away the instruments when Carson went on watch. Now, two hours later, he was up again, prowling, checking the guards. He'd been this careful ever since they left Laramie. Carson couldn't criticize a thing. They'd moved well, making good time, nicely bunched, with pickets flung out on all four quarters. Where the Sweetwater entered the Platte they had cached their supplies in the ground, hidden the carts in a willow thicket and gone on with pack animals. Frémont saw potential ambush spots almost as readily as he did, and often they rode together to investigate them. The distrust he'd felt about the Cap'n after the brush with Gabe and the row that night at Laramie had vanished. Frémont still had Preuss painting those damn wildflowers and he took as many starsights as ever, but every camp he chose would have been easy to defend. He divided the whole party into three groups and each man stood one watch every night. That put eight on duty through the night, placed after dark where an intruder wouldn't expect them. By God, he was clever—hell of a lot more clever than Carson had realized. He'd learned his lessons well. Old Provost made a mighty good teacher. He'd said you could count on Charlie when things began to pinch, and he was dead right. Even the Frenchies had performed well—they'd gotten their confidence from the Cap'n.

Frémont knelt beside him and spoke in a low voice. "Nice and quiet."

Carson nodded. "They ain't out there tonight."

"We're close to South Pass now—another two, three days."

Carson was still surprised they'd had no trouble. Oh, the sign had been clear enough. Beaten-down places by the river where horsemen had stopped to drink, camps with blackened fire rings, the horse dung still holding a little moisture. They'd seen two or three bands, wary because they were small, and once Carson had cornered a Sioux alone up a canyon, sort of a standoff, each man ready to fight if it came to that. They had talked awhile, but the Indian didn't know anything.

"Signs just shifted for 'em, I think," Carson said. "Indians are like that. You'll never meet a better fighting man than a plains Indian on a swift pony when he's in the right mood and figures the signs are with him. But that mood can change fast. He has a bad dream or a favored horse comes up lame or a leader gets hit—why, he figures that's a message. My hunch this time is that the buffler are gone. You've seen how poor the grass is—the herds have moved on down around the Smoky Hill by now. A Sioux gets uncomfortable when the buffler ain't right—like if that pole star wasn't up there in place, you'd get pretty edgy."

"I would at that," Frémont answered, and Carson could tell he was grinning.

They were silent awhile, listening, watching.

"You were right," Carson said. "To come out from Laramie. And I was wrong."

"Yes. But not because we weren't attacked."

"No? Why then?"

"Because we had work to do, Kit. Important work. You have to do your work. You know that. You never let danger stop you from trapping."

"Fact. Beaver won't wait," Carson said. "You go after 'em when the pelts are fine or you can forget it." He sighed. "Truth is, all these star readings and scribbling notes and all didn't seem worth the gamble."

Frémont hesitated and then said, "It is, though. It is. I suppose I've never really explained enough." As he talked then, Carson noticed that he kept his eyes trained outward, into the dark, watching. He'd traveled many a night himself by the stars when it was too dangerous to move in the day—but Frémont talked of time so precise that you could measure it in fractions of an instant, stars that Carson had never heard of. He'd heard of Greenwich Mean Time, but never known that you could measure against it and thus place this particular bend of the Sweetwater so anyone in the world could come here and make camp in the same place—well, that was some different from maps drawn in the dirt. It was—it was opening up a whole *continent.* Listening to the Cap'n's quiet, tired voice, Carson all at once felt mortified. He was glad darkness hid his face. He'd been riding along for weeks sneering at something he hadn't even understood.

Frémont glanced at him and turned back to look at the distance. "How about a hundred wagon trains?" he said suddenly. "How about a thousand? How about a time when you can never be out of sight of a wagon, from Westport to Oregon? And Oregon as full as Missouri, and way stations every few miles between . . ."

The idea was awesome. "God almighty, Cap'n," he burst out, "that'll *ruin* this country!"

Frémont made no response and Carson wondered if he had offended him. Then Frémont said in a low voice, maybe sad, maybe just tired, Carson couldn't tell. "Likely it will, Kit. But that's the way it'll go."

It was bigger than he had thought. Much bigger. Listening to Frémont's low, even voice, he realized how little of the world he really knew, for all his travels. There were great forces moving, vast as the Rockies, as the thundering, limitless sky above South Pass, and he knew nothing about them. Nothing at all. And Charlie was part of them. Back at Laramie, he'd made that decision all by hisself, jammed it down their throats, got 'em up, made 'em go, and then kept 'em moving and confident. And the way he'd run things, they'd have handled the Indians had there been an attack; they'd have made things hot for 'em. Now by God, you had to hand that to him—that's the way Ewing Young had been. Some could cut it, some couldn't. And you never knew which ones.

Frémont yawned. "I'm going to sleep a little," he said.

"Cap'n," Carson said abruptly, "I'd like to say that when you go out next year, I'd be mighty proud to ride with you if'n you think I could be of service."

Frémont paused—then reached out and clapped him once on the shoulder. Carson saw that he was smiling. "I'll count on that, Kit," he said.

RAPIDS

THE RUBBER BOAT UNFOLDED, grunting and puffing as though alive while Menard worked the bellows. Finally it hardened to its full twenty feet and they floated it in the shallows. Frémont looked downstream. The river narrowed abruptly and entered a canyon. There was a swollen smoothness to the water that stirred anticipation, apprehension—both appealing; it might be very fast. Here the Platte cut through three broad ridges. Below the third ridge was an island—Goat Island—where they had camped on the way out. They had crossed all three ridges on horseback, plotting the river's position. Now, on their return, their mission accomplished, South Pass well behind them, Frémont intended to run those deep channels in the rubber boat.

It was dawn and he was eager to be away. He felt the river drawing him. They would breakfast at Goat Island; it was twelve miles away and on this water they should be there in an hour. Carson, continuing overland with the larger party, would reach Goat Island by nightfall—but by then Frémont himself would be far downstream. He planned to run clear to Fort Laramie by water.

"Let's go," he said. The men were loading supplies—food, weapons, axes, the instruments. The register with all the readings, the daily log and the book of field sketches were wrapped in oilcloth and stowed in a wooden box. There were reports of falls, though no one really knew. But his own readings showed that the ground dropped three hundred feet in the next twelve miles—likely there would be rapids. Preuss put his spectacles in a small wooden case which he buttoned into a pocket. He climbed into the boat and sat in the center, both arms around his big sketchbook, which he had bound in a rubber sheet and tied with cord.

"Take me, Cap'n," said Tessier, whose pride in his new nose had greatly improved his personality, though Frémont thought the nose as big as ever. "I'm an old boatman."

"Hell you are."

"Goddamn right. Give me a good canoe and a basswood paddle and I'll go to hell and back and never get m' feet wet. This sausage boat can't be all that different. Hell, Cap'n, I was five years trapping in the Canadian lake country."

"All right." Quickly he chose the others: Freniere, always ready for a lark; the strong, steady Lambert; Menard; Descoteaux, also a laker, a pock-marked man with long arms. Tessier and Descoteaux would take the pivot spot in the bow; Frémont would be in the stern with Louie; six paddles would see them through. Carson stood to one side, thumbs hooked in his belt, watching. He still doesn't like the boat, Frémont thought.

"When you get to Goat Island tonight, Kit," he said, "look for a piece of paper speared on a twig. If you don't see it, wait for us to catch up." He paused, grinning. "What's the matter?"

"You tip over in there and who's going to drag you out?"

"Oh hell's fire, Kit—worst that can happen is you get drowned!"

Carson kicked at a rock. "That's hungry water. You lose all that scribbling and what'll you do?"

"We're not going to lose anything. It'll be a Nantucket sleigh ride! I want to get home . . ." Frémont laughed again, and looked downstream at the sleek, swift water. He was feeling strong and confident, had felt that way ever since that first sight of the Rocky Mountains ten days before. They had spotted them from seventy miles away and stopped, staring at the great rising mass, white-crowned in places though it was August. Frémont had never seen anything like them—they were not at all like the tightly folded, smoky Appalachians. They were so—so *huge,* as if some great explosion had bulged the earth itself into the sky. Immediately he had decided to climb to their very tops.

They had come through South Pass, the taste of great triumph strong. Beyond, Frémont had chosen a small party and started up what he judged to be the highest peak. The climb would be the perfect cap for the report, a symbol of elation and daring at the end of the long journey across the plains. For the man who had never seen such mountains, the potential settler who would be Frémont's most important reader, what could be more reassuring than the fact that the explorer had immediately taken on the highest? But he knew that was just talk—he really was climbing because it was so strange and wonderful and awesome. They had climbed for two days and it had not, after all, proved so difficult. Preuss had fallen on an ice field and slid four hundred feet until a boulder stopped him, but otherwise there had been no mishaps, and Preuss had been so pleased his spectacles hadn't broken that he ignored his bruises. At the summit, panting and exuberant, Frémont had jammed a ramrod into a crevice and flown the expedition's flag. Frémont's Peak. Well, why not? Who had a better right?

And now they were going to run the river. He grinned and gave Carson a little salute. "Don't *worry* so, Kit! Your hair'll turn gray . . ."

"That rubber boat'll be the death of you yet, Charlie."

"See you boys at Laramie," Louie bawled and pushed the boat off the bank. Instantly they fell down toward the opening canyon and when the boat struck the smooth water it surged ahead like a runaway carriage crowding the horses. Sheer stone walls mounted above them. Frémont heard a roaring beyond a turn.

"Steady on, Cap'n," Tessier called. "Just keep her straight." He and Descoteaux were using their bow paddles as guides; at this speed paddling was superfluous. At the turn a sheer stone wall faced them. Water boiled against it and then poured to the right, slipping smoothly down a short, steep incline. He saw the danger when Tessier did: the bow would stall in the churning water for a moment, the stern would come around and they'd pitch down that incline backwards.

"Dig! Dig!" Tessier yelled as he and Descoteaux strained the bow around. The boat lurched suddenly down the incline. At the bottom it checked in a pool, turned half around, straightened, shot around another bend and another, confronted a recent rock fall and bumped over it. Jagged rocks beat against Frémont's knees through the boat's cloth bottom, but the fabric held. The canyon opened into a grove of cottonwoods and closed as suddenly into another narrow chasm. Ahead a boulder the size of a small cabin had compressed the stream to a channel narrower than the boat. They all saw the danger at once and backed their paddles hard, but the boat shot into the opening like a cork jammed into a bottle. It wedged in with a jolt that threw them forward.

Shouting in French, Lambert and Menard thrust their paddles against the stone, trying to lever the boat through. It lurched forward and stopped again. Sheets of icy spray flying off the boulder drenched them. Water lifted the stern and with a squeal of wet rubber the boat slipped free and lunged forward. Frémont was sure it had been torn, but the air chambers were drum tight. He was still checking the boat when it struck another rock, shuddered, slipped off, fell through a sluice amid sheets of spray, and popped out of the canyon. Suddenly they were on a broad plain. The river immediately widened and slowed, all its violence gone. In the intense quiet Frémont heard a killdeer's loud whistle. They paddled to a willow grove and beached the boat. The sand was full of mica which glittered in the sun.

"Let's not wait for Goat Island," Frémont said. "Let's make some breakfast." He lay on the sand, the sun drying his clothes. That had been some ride—rougher than he had expected. The sun felt good after the chill and the tension. Much rougher—but still, they had come through without mishap. The smell of roasting meat brought him up, ravenous. As he chewed the hot buffalo strips the violent canyon began to seem remote. The men were ribbing Tessier for letting them get caught in that chute. The next ridge, perhaps two miles distant, looked larger than the one passed. But that didn't necessarily make it more difficult. Certainly Old Buffler Guts had proved itself—that narrow passage would have made kindling of any wooden boat.

When they reached the next ridge they landed and climbed until they could see the cut of the channel zigzagging away. The beginning of it looked mild enough . . . and the alternative was to carry all their supplies as well as the boat on their backs over miles of rough country.

"Let's run it, boys," Frémont said. "You with me?"

"You're the Cap'n," Louie boomed.

It started easily, the water deep and smooth—and then became immediately formidable. The channel was narrower, the pace faster, the turns more violent. Because the ground above was rising swiftly they seemed to be sinking into the earth. It was growing darker. Glancing at Freniere, Frémont saw that a set, strained expression had replaced his grin. No one spoke.

They heard a roar ahead. "Hold her back, boys," Frémont called. "Let's see what we're getting into." Back-paddling, they eased around a turn and saw another bend dead ahead. They negotiated through more bends, the roar ever louder, before they rounded a sharp point of broken rock and saw an appalling sight. Straight as a knife stroke and almost as narrow, the river ran at least a quarter-mile; the surface was white and foamy. Spray rose in clouds where the water beat against black rocks that stood like sentinels. There was an eddy to one side. They pulled into it and Frémont climbed onto a boulder for a better view, his heart beating furiously.

The stone walls were almost sheer, rising a full five hundred feet above them; they were in a fissure, as deep as the mountain had seemed high, buried in the earth with the rock almost meeting overhead. The sky was a ribbon of brilliant blue, the light below soft and shadowy. Small white birds skittered from rock to rock and splash marks made black streaks that quickly dried to gray. Far above them whole logs hung from points of stone, high-water marks. When Frémont lowered himself to the boat he had to shout against the men's ears to make himself heard over the river's deep, sullen roar.

Preuss thought that he could walk on a ledge overhead but after a hundred yards it ended and he returned. He tied the chronometer bag around his neck and took his place in the center of the boat on his knees, holding his sketchbook wrapped in oilcloth. They attached their longest line to the stern. Lambert and Freniere climbed on to the ledge; they would try to lower the boat to the next eddy and then follow along on slabs of rock.

Immediately water boiled over the stern and Frémont looked back to see the rope dragging the two men across the ledge. They scrambled desperately for footholds, were snatched off the rock. The boat hurtled forward, Tessier and Descoteaux in the bow digging deep, shunting them this way and that to avoid the great black rocks. Spray drenched them, half-blinded them. Frémont felt the boat collide with a boulder, bounce off, fall down a deep slope, collide again, half turn and hurtle on. Far behind he saw the two men, their heads black dots in the water.

When the river turned at last it created a shallow eddy and they paddled into it. Frémont roped himself and waded into the icy water, gasping, his teeth clenched. Louie came first and was thrown into the eddy, but Lambert missed it. He had a dazed look and was choking. Frémont leaped and caught him, wrapped his legs around his waist while Tessier and Menard hauled them both back.

It seemed even darker. Now the rock blocked the sky almost completely, and the river was louder. Frémont coiled the line and stowed it: there was no climbing out from here and no going back; they would have to chance it together, all of them in the boat. For a moment, listening to that ominous roar, he felt a thrill of fear run cold into his belly. The power—the incredible power that had flung the boat around like a wood chip . . . yet they had ridden it this far, ridden that power, beaten it. At once a wild determination took hold of him. They'd come this far, and Goddamnit, they'd make it the rest of the way.

"I told you we'd have some fun," he shouted. "Now let's *run* this son-of-a-bitch!"

Only Freniere managed a cheerful look, good old Louie, but that was enough, and they pushed out into the current, all of them on their knees, paddles digging hard as the boat hurtled down the roaring river. They shot through a narrow sluice, snubbed into a pool below, spun around and rushed on backwards. Shouting, Frémont and Louie used their paddles as brakes while the bowmen clawed the boat around. They crashed over a small falls without spilling, made one turn, and another and still another, and suddenly there was more light, the walls were not so high, and all of them realized at the same instant that they were going to make it.

"Hi-yah!" Freniere yelled. Tessier started a French boatman's song and they picked up its rhythmic chant, paddles flashing, spray a blinding silver haze, their hearts soaring. The boat shivered, flopped over another higher, hidden falls they hadn't seen, plunged bow-down into the pool below, snubbed against a rock—and the stern lifted. It seemed quite slow to Frémont; he watched the boat fly up and over, saw the water and the sky, and then the boat crashed upside down and he was under the dark water, paralyzed with cold, his mind still filled with the sight of the sky. He smashed against a deep rock and instantly understood his danger, cradling his head in his arms. His head broke the surface, he flung the water from his eyes, struck another rock with his back, managed to turn and fend off the next one, and found himself in an eddy. He felt gravel under his feet and clung to a rock. His head hurt, and his left shoulder; but nothing was broken; his whole body seemed to work—yes, by God, he was alive!

He dragged himself out of the rip, half-stunned, blinded by spray, and looked around wildly. Freniere was bear-hugging the butt of a cottonwood jammed between two boulders. Menard—it looked like Menard—was sweeping on downstream, his arms flailing in the white water. Lambert had hold of Tessier by the belt and was hauling him out of the current by main strength. Near them little Preuss rose up in a tangle of flotsam, still clutching the bundled sketchbook, his hair plastered slick against his round head. Descoteaux was on his hands and knees in the shallows, wagging and wagging his head like a dog and vomiting water in great gouts.

"All right?" Frémont roared at Tessier, who was feeling various parts of his body as though it were some priceless china figurine. Tessier gazed back at him, nodding somberly. Menard, clinging to a rock downstream, waved feebly. They were all right. All of them, alive, all whole. His men. It was miraculous—

"Aber die Kartesberechnungen!" Preuss was crying, his eyes wide and

black without his glasses, pointing wildly at something. *"Die Urkunden! . . ."*

The records.

The boat was lying in an eddy fifty feet downstream, crushed and half-deflated. Frémont ran to it, the water dragging hard against his thighs. It was upside down, twisted grotesquely; air was still escaping from a small tear in one of the pockets even as he gripped it. Everything that had been in it was gone. Everything. He straightened, looking around frantically. The wooden box in which he'd packed the register, the field sketchbook, the daily log—all the expedition's findings, all the figures on which the map depended—was bobbing against a rock, filled with water, its top torn off. It was empty.

"Mein Gott," Preuss was saying, standing near him. "Our work, all the calculations—and they were so perfect, so complete . . ."

The map. It wasn't possible. Staring up at the canyon walls, Frémont felt as though a fatal artery in his body had been opened. He was dizzy and wondered vaguely if he had a concussion. All of it lost—all because of a momentary impulse to race on back, hurry home in triumph. What was he going to tell them back in Washington? What in God's sweet name would he tell *her*? What would she think of him?

Preuss was still talking incoherently, half in English, half in German, wringing his hands. Freniere was out in the channel, his head under water, groping around for something.

"Shut up, Preuss," Frémont told him. Maybe they could find them. Maybe they'd floated, they were waterproofed—surely there was air in the package, the current was fast—

He called them all together, started them down both sides of the river, driving them, moving from rock to rock, pulling trees and snagged branches apart, searching. When they reached bare wall, they swam until they crashed into boulders, and again crawled out. After a time the chasm widened, the walls no longer sheer. They found an ax, a saddlebag filled with jerky, three blanket rolls caught in the thickets. They hunted until their hands were raw and their faces were white with cold, until they never wanted to see white water—or any water—again. And finally, a good two miles downstream, Frémont heard Lambert shouting, screaming, from the other side, saw him holding the dripping package in one hand, waving with the other. He recognized it instantly and waved back, then sat down suddenly on a wet black rock.

Louie splashed over and sat down beside him. "Found 'em, eh? Jesus, you are one lucky son."

He burst out laughing then, he couldn't stop himself. He said: "I'm always lucky. Always was."

"Well, *I* ain't." Louie shook his head, looking desolate; he was bleeding over one eye. "Lost m'Hawken," he said. "Couldn't find it nowhere. It's gone." Frémont saw tears in his eyes.

"I'll get you another one, Louie," he said. "That's a promise."

"Won't be the same."

"Nothing's ever the same."

"Damn-fool stunt," Tessier said, holding his left arm; all his happy bluster was gone. "Could have got ourselves killed. One by one, or all together."

"It wasn't the smartest move we ever made," Freniere agreed. He lay down on the rock with his eyes shut, then opened them and grinned. "But it sure was a daisy-cutter while it lasted, wasn't it?"

Jessie awakened—she must have been asleep after all—to see Charles standing over the bed, holding the baby. A tiny fist thrust out of the pink blanket, and he smiled; the uncommon tension with which he'd been studying the child vanished. She knew he was afraid he would drop the tiny bundle that rested so securely in his strong hands. She sank into the bed, feeling exhaustion drain from her body. It was *over*—the worry, the waiting, the pain. She had done it. Done it well. She felt so satisfied, so whole and proud. Never mind that other women had babies—*she* had had *this* baby, that's what mattered. It was a gift only she could give, to him, to herself; a perfect, unique gift. She peered up at his face: did he understand that? could he? could any man?

He had arrived four days before her labor started. She'd been unbearably distended, and she saw that he'd never imagined what she would be like. For just an instant he'd found her grotesque—she'd seen it written on his face—and then he'd treated her as if she might collapse at any moment, when in fact she'd been fine for nine months.

Alarm flickered. Was he disappointed by a girl? She had promised him a boy—she'd been so utterly sure. Why had she been so sure? Wishful thinking—all men wanted their firstborn to be a boy, she was certain of that. She had always known that if her sister Eliza had been a boy her relationship with her own father would have been entirely different. But she had never wanted to be a boy herself—she liked being a girl, and so would her daughter. . . . It seemed to her that some time had passed, but he was still there, still gazing into the pink blanket, his wind-roughened face flooded with wonder.

"She's our daughter, Charles," she said, her voice sounding far away. Then she blurted, "I promised you a boy."

"You promised me a baby, sweetheart," he said, "and you've given us the most beautiful baby in the world."

"You don't mind . . ."

"Darling Jessie," he said, "*this* is our baby—no other one would do at all. She's exactly right." He paused. "Do you know, she looks like you? That makes her perfect."

She smiled. "She looks like a baby," she said practically, feeling content.

He handed their little girl to a nurse and turned away from her bed. In a minute he was back again. He had something in his hands; when he unfolded it she saw that it was the flag he had taken on the expedition, the eagle in the upper corner clutching the Indian peace pipe on a field of blue.

"This flew from the top of the highest peak of the Rocky Mountains," he said. "I brought it home for you." She knew he had been saving it for this moment. He spread it over the bed. "It's yours," he said. "You've climbed the very highest mountain of all."

Looking at him, she touched the rough fabric with her hands and drew it against her cheek.

He was standing at the window staring into the street when she came into the study; he did not turn around. He was wearing the buckskin blouse Louie Freniere had given him, which surprised her—then she realized he'd put it on as a talisman, something to get him in a reminiscent mood, perhaps; but it didn't seem to have done much good. The writing table was littered with half-filled sheets of paper, the writing crossed out or trailing off into slashes and abbreviations. One page held a maze of doodles: a mustachioed face whose eyes and nose and mouth were round black holes, a configuration of stars that looked like Orion with his belt and sword. When she looked up he was dabbing at his nose with his handkerchief, and she saw it was stained red.

"The nosebleeds again?" she asked.

"Yes. Isn't it strange? The minute I sit down and try to write that damned thing . . ."

She said lightly: "I thought a little tea might stir the creative juices."

"It'll take a good deal more than tea." He turned then, his face tight and strained. "It's no good, Jessie. I just can't get it right."

"Of course you can, dear—when you talk about it at dinner parties it's all so real. I feel as if I were right there riding beside you."

"I'm going about it all wrong. It's a military report, that's all it is."

"Oh, but it's so much more than that!"

He ignored her. "It's a military expedition, and I've been trying to make it into some kind of grand adventure."

"Well it *was,* Charles."

He glanced up at her—that alert, boyish look. "Well, sure it was—I'm not running it down, Jessie. But you know what I mean."

"No, I don't. You said—"

"Those fishy-eyed West Pointers—can't you just see them waiting to pounce on it? 'This snotty young Frémont: who the blazes does he think he is, Cortez?' " He laughed mirthlessly, shook his head. "No, it better be a straight action report—short, direct, no frills. Where I went, what I did. Plain and simple. After all, the map is what really counts."

"That's not what you've been saying."

"Well then, I was wrong," he came back irascibly. "I suppose I can be wrong, can't I?"

She bit off the instinctive reply, said gently, "If you just wrote it down the way you've told it to me, nights . . . It's a wonderful story. Wonderful."

"I can't, Jessie. I've tried—it all turns stiff and highfalutin. Look—see for yourself."

He snatched up several sheets and thrust them at her irritably. It was true; it wasn't Charles at all, there wasn't any life, any fire in it—it sounded like some pompous, dull old man. She stared at the last page, thinking quickly; said, "Why don't you tell it to me, just the way you've been doing? And let *me* write it down."

He frowned at her. "Dictate it, you mean?"

"Well, yes . . . or just talk it out."

"Won't work. With you in the room."

"Why not? I'm in the room when you're telling about it."

"I'll wander off the subject."

"We can fix that later." She paused, added softly: "It wouldn't hurt to try, darling. What have we got to lose?"

The first minutes were stiff and halting. Then he got caught up in it again, as she knew he would—was on his feet, pacing around the room like a caged panther, his fine blue eyes flashing, the words coming faster and faster. And writing for her life, the pen scratching across the page, she saw it all—Kit Carson's hat brim flaring up in front as he rode hard, Preuss bent over his sketchbox humming a Volkslied, the Sioux warrior watching from the top of the canyon wall like a gaunt bronze statue; and everywhere the vast gray-white sky rolling away over the open prairie like a continent unfolding for all time . . . She felt a breath-caught excitement deeper than anything she had ever known before.

The next morning they began again, and soon they had an effective routine. He would talk for an hour or so while she took notes. When she didn't understand or was curious, she asked questions that caused him to see an event entirely freshly or to remember a telling detail in all its vividness. The story became increasingly alive for her; as she worked it through her mind she felt as if she had truly been there, riding with him, eating buffalo steak in the snapping red glare of the campfire, bathing in the pewter-dull water of the Platte . . . It came to her that she wasn't simply refining dictation, she was *writing.* It assumed an easy, unobtrusive order under her hand, the sentences balanced and tight, the images bright, phrases that were clean and graphic coming readily to mind as she needed them. She had been writing for her father for years, but Charles had had adventures old Toller Tom never dreamt of. She knew too that she was making a fundamental contribution to the report, and she knew the result was good. It was a pleasure to read—she was sure of it—without sacrificing either factual accuracy or the tone that would be acceptable in an Army document.

And she enjoyed the work in a way she had not realized was possible. As if for the first time a deeper part of her had been released. There was so much that was enjoyable now: she had a charming husband and a beautiful child; in a year she had moved from a precocious girl to a mature, whole woman, accepted at last in the adult society that, she now realized, had only indulged her in the past; her husband had come safely home, and official and unofficial Washington was highly impressed with him.

The vital map was also taking definite shape on Preuss' tables and attracting excited attention in the Capital. Their social schedule grew positively exhausting. The next expedition was already being planned—it would carry Charles all the way to Oregon—and everyone wanted to talk about it.

Lily, who had been a perfect infant at six weeks, became a terror at three months. Night after night she awakened with colic and Jessie was up for hours soothing her back to sleep. But this new experience of writing was of a different order, comparable only to the feeling she had had when the newborn child first seized her nipple. The words poured out of her mind and her heart with a force she'd never felt before.

"What's this business about the bumblebee?" he said quizzically one day, looking up from her draft. "I never said that. Did I?"

"Yes, you did," she said. "At dinner the other night." When he was on top of that mountain, a bumblebee blown aloft on rising air currents had landed on the knee of one of the men. He'd made a pretty thing of it at the table for the children; the humble bumblebee that had gone exploring, on its way to Oregon to make honey for the settlers.

"It was true, wasn't it?" she asked.

"Of course it was true, but it doesn't belong in a report."

"Why not? I thought it was interesting."

"Well, a bee above fourteen thousand feet—that must be unusual. It isn't that it's wrong—but Jessie, I never *dictated* that . . . you're just adding things in. Aren't you?"

She gazed at him. He had run the risks, the terrible risks—it was his expedition and his report. In her new creative joy, was she trying to reap without the work of sowing? Truth was, he couldn't write this well. She wasn't stealing anything—was she? Taking away from him what was rightfully his alone?

In the silence he got up and began to pace as he did while dictating and presently he resumed the account. Her head started to ache as she wrote—she'd been up most of the night with the baby and wondered if she was taking the grippe—and a bit later she realized she'd lost the thread of what she was saying.

"I'm sorry, darling," she broke in, "I've missed something, apparently. Let's go over this again, can we?"

"Of course." His good humor had returned. She thought how handsome he looked in the new uniform he'd bought at Marchand's; the tunic collar was unbuttoned. "Where are you?"

"You said the rubber boat was nearly crushed between these rocks, and you were worried that it might have been damaged . . ."

"Yes—it's amazing what strains that rubber fabric can stand." He laughed, shaking his head, remembering. "Louie said, 'If we'd only had this ugly old black sausage on the Minnesota, Cap'n.' "

". . . and then you looked for a way out of the canyon, and gave it up . . ."

"*Wasn't* any way out—those walls were four, five hundred feet high, dropping sheer . . . there was nothing for it then but to keep on paddling, run the gauntlet. What a merry-go-round that was, Jessie! What a sleigh ride."

She was watching him with growing consternation. "And then you hit these second rapids and the boat tipped over, and you hit your head on a rock, and you got ashore and made sure everyone was all right—"

"Lord, we were lucky—it was a miracle! Not even a broken arm in the whole bunch, not even little Preuss. I tell you, he had the most comical expression on his face, rising up out of that tangle of driftwood! I tell you, it was—" Something in her expression stopped him then; he glanced at the notebook, at her again. "Didn't you get that, Jess? any of that?"

"Yes. I got it." She folded her hands over the pen quill. "What I haven't got is *why* you did it."

"I told you, there wasn't any way to walk out, the walls—"

"—I meant, why you decided to run the river in the first place."

He frowned at her, said with irritation: "Why, it was part of my job, Jessie. I was ordered to explore the river, and I was doing it. Can't you see that?"

"But you didn't take any readings in the canyon, you couldn't have if you'd wanted to . . ."

"Look," he said hotly, "there's no substitute for a field survey—these are decisions you've got to make on the ground. How can you judge something like this? You've never even been in the field!"

"Field survey," she cried, "—you very nearly got yourselves drowned! What can justify that? If you wanted the—the adventure of it, why in God's name didn't you send the records around with Carson?"

The word stung him. "It had nothing to do with adventure! I planned to be out of Laramie long before Carson ever got there—and I was! Speed was of the—"

But she was angry too. "And so to save one day on a five-month expedition, you jeopardized it all—to say nothing of your own life!"

"Who are you to question what I did? In country like that, you've got to run a few risks—"

"But not when there's no need! When you can lose the fruit of all that work, run all that danger! Not to mention the trust people have placed in you. . . ." Her voice was shaking now, she couldn't control it. "When Nicollet put the expedition in danger, you called him to his senses and brought them all out. Now you've done the same thing! In fact it's worse: at least Papa Joe did it out of obsessive professional zeal—*you* were willing to throw it all away because of a childish lark."

"All right," he nearly shouted, "maybe I shouldn't have done it! But it worked out all right—"

"Yes, because you were lucky!"

"I'm always lucky, I'm a lucky man."

"Oh! And God has told you so, I suppose? And you're always going to be lucky. Admit it—if you hadn't found the records, the map would have been wiped out."

"But we *did* find it," he said between his teeth.

"That's no answer! I may not be able to tell off Gabe Bridger or climb the Rocky Mountains, but I sure as fate know a piece of pure folly when it's staring me in the face! That may have been the luckiest thing you ever did, Charles Frémont, but it certainly wasn't the brightest . . ."

He looked at her then—a troubled, angry glance that faded away to simple chagrin. There was a tense little silence. Then he put his head down. "That's what Louie said," he murmured ruefully.

"You're right," he said, and watching him she knew how hard it was for him to get that out. "It was—unnecessary. An unnecessary risk. I thought I could get away with it. I knew better. I had no business trying . . ."

He was looking at her, his handsome face open and contrite and appealing. Impulsively she rose and ran to him, ran into his arms.

"Oh, Charles," she said. "I love you so . . ."

"Dear, dear Jessie. I make you put up with a lot, don't I?"

"No," she said. "But if you did, it would be worth it."

She put her cheek against his shoulder, partly to hide her face, for she had just had the most astonishing notion. All her life she'd been dominated by her clever, all-knowing papa, however she had manipulated him in small ways. Then she had married an assured, accomplished man eleven years her senior and she had transferred that unblinking adoration—no other word for it, really—to him without a thought. Now there had been a certain pleasure catching him in an outright error. It set her free, it removed the subordinate feeling she'd had all her life and never even noticed. It was as if she had matured in a single stroke. She loved him all the more now—vulnerable, capable of error, first trying to squeeze out of admitting it—human in other words . . . he was not a paragon at all but rather a very good man. She felt she had moved to another plane of love altogether.

She tightened her arm around him, pressed her lips against his throat. "Oh Charles," she repeated, "I do love you so."

He put both hands on her shoulders and gently disengaged her. "Sit down, Jessie," he said. "I want to tell you something."

His hands were in his pockets and he leaned against the window frame. "You might as well know how I am," he said in a flat voice. She wondered if she had done real damage.

"Truth is, I don't always think a great deal about what I do. If it seems a good thing to do, likely I'll do it. Lots of situations, you know, don't give you much time to think. If you're going to do it, you've got to move fast. Or the chance vanishes. That's how I am—I get a feeling about it and I move."

"Even if it's in the wrong direction, darling," she murmured, and smiled.

"But remember there's another side to it: if you do something and it fails, then that's a new situation and you have to decide what to do *then*. At that point, obviously you'd just as soon you'd done it differently, but it doesn't pay to look back at your mistakes. Dwell on them. You can get to questioning everything you do—and you wind up doing nothing."

He paused and his voice changed a little. "Once, years ago, I climbed a little mountain in South Carolina. I was about nine, I guess. And then I couldn't see how to get down. I was still there, scared to move, when it got dark." She could see the child crouched on a high ledge. "Spent the night there, cold and hungry, and the worst of it was when I realized how stupid it had been. Sooner or later I'd have to try, and the only way to do it was to take it one step at a time and work it out in progress. Sure enough, in the morning I was down in an hour. Got home in time for breakfast. Then Mother gave me a hiding."

He dropped into a chair across the table from her. "You see, the way to do things is to *do* them. Not much point in explaining them later—they're already done. And no point in apologies. You've done what you thought best. If it was wrong, let it be judged. I'm always willing to stand on that."

She said, "Well, I don't see anything wrong with apologies."

"But what's an apology except a plea to set aside judgment once a failure is evident—a plea to be excused from the consequences? But you can't be excused. Forgiven, maybe, but not excused. An act is real, so its consequences are real. The fact is, we define ourselves by what we do."

"Instead of what we might wish or intend?"

"Exactly. Or so I see it. I'm willing to act. If I'm wrong, I'm willing to bear the consequences."

She nodded, understanding him, accepting him. Loving him utterly. It had been quite a morning: everything had been at risk; everything was enriched.

"As for the river," he leaned back in the chair and looked straight at her, "doubtless it wasn't my wisest move. Maybe I learned something from it. Maybe not. Now let's just say it in a simple paragraph—we encountered rapids, the boat turned over, we lost a bit of gear. That's all we did lose, after all."

Slowly she shook her head. She saw the consistency of him—going when other men held back, forcing those frightened men out of Fort Laramie, climbing the mountain, running the river. He defined himself: he was what he was.

"No," she said, "let's capitalize on it. It's a marvelous story. Let's take it straight: offer no alternatives, raise no questions. No apologies. No regrets. Let it be the most natural thing in the world."

Which, she thought, given everything, was just what it was.

"Are you sure?" he was saying. "I wouldn't do it that way."

She watched him a moment; then she made up her mind.

"Charles," she said steadily, "—with the book—the report, do you feel I'm taking over—in the writing, I mean . . . usurping something that's yours?"

He didn't answer; without looking at her, he nodded. "Maybe I do," he said.

"But you like it, don't you? What we've done?"

He nodded again.

"And you think it's good?"

"You know I do. Only . . ."

"Look," she said. "Let me tell you how I see it. I've an ability here, a very exciting ability, a kind of gift I didn't even know I had. And it's useful. It's my contribution. It doesn't take from you, diminish you in any way—it complements what *you've* achieved. I think you ought to use what I can do, but if you don't want to accept it . . . well, I'm willing to take it down word for word, like any secretary."

That wasn't true, actually—she wasn't willing just to copy dictation, and he'd be a fool to want that. Why didn't she say what she felt? Now was the time.

"Don't you understand?" she said. "It reads well because it's full of love. Why do you think you make me see it as clearly as if I had been there? Because you *did* these marvelous things. Because I *see* you there. Because I love you, that's why. And seeing it that way gives it the quality of—of—life—that's why it's good, Charles . . . So tell me, don't you want me to help?"

She waited then, holding her breath. There was a glittering intensity to the moment; so young in marriage, they had come to a turning point. Everything would be different if he yielded now to smallness.

Then he smiled, that smile she found so dazzling. "You're a very intelligent woman," he said. "You're right—you have a special gift, you do give it something that I can't. Let's keep on." He paused. "You know, Mrs. Frémont, we may do pretty well together."

"Oh, I'm so glad!" she said. "And I'll take the bee out—that bumblebee. Probably you're right . . ."

"No, leave him in." He kissed her tenderly on the lips. "He'll be our own private honey-maker."

GREAT DIVIDE

When Jessie saw Louison Freniere open the Brants' gate and come up the walkway with a loose and easy stride, a rifle in one hand, she decided to ask him. It was May 1843, pleasant in St. Louis but not yet warm, and the Second Expedition would be leaving soon.

"How do, Miz Jessie," Freniere said, bounding up the steps. She was sitting at a small table on the porch; Lily was in her playpen.

"Hello, Louie."

"Cap'n home?"

"He's inside, talking to Papa."

"Come to show him m'new Hawken." He held the rifle in both hands. "Ever see anything prettier? Cap'n got it for me."

Well-oiled and gleaming, the weapon had a lethal quality that she knew would be comforting where they were going.

"Like the decorations?" he asked. A scene was carved in the stock, a horseman firing on a buffalo. "Found me a wood carver down t' the Green Tree—kept him in whiskey and meals a day and a night while he done that."

The buffalo had a rather porcine look, but she admired it extravagantly. " 'Course," he said, looking pleased, "this feller hadn't never actually *seen* a buffler."

Lily was gazing at his fancy buckskin outfit with round eyes. "Sit down and keep us company, Louie," Jessie said. She closed the leather case which contained the Second Expedition's roster and supply lists. This time she had taken charge of the paperwork, signing her husband's name to vouchers in her own clear hand. Soon her part would be ending. The men would go out to South Pass again and from there they would track the Oregon Trail through the dangerous Blackfoot country to the Snake River and down the Columbia to Fort Vancouver, the Hudson's Bay post. A fearsome journey, but this time at least she felt more a part of it.

She personally had signed on every man but Carson, who would come up from Taos and meet Charles at Laramie. As she had read aloud the agreement to serve and witnessed each man's signature or mark, she had learned a good deal about them. Now she felt she could follow the expedition's progress in her mind's eye. She intended to wait in St. Louis this time; and already she could taste the loneliness. Her father would be in Missouri through the summer campaign, but by early fall he too would be gone.

"Tell me, Louie," she said, "why do you think Carson made his will at Fort Laramie?"

"That nettled the Cap'n pretty good." He grinned. "But you ain't really asking me about last time, are you?"

She flushed. "Really, Louison, I'm quite grown up. I want to know."

"Yes ma'am." He looked abashed. "All right. There's danger. But it don't have to happen and probably won't. Now, last year there was special trouble—took a lot of nerve for the Cap'n to push 'em out of that fort. But this time it'll probably be calm. And we have around forty men this year—that's as big as most war parties. Wouldn't be honest to pretend there's *no* danger, but we can handle it—don't you worry none."

When the door opened and her husband came out with her father, Freniere jumped up in obvious relief. He showed them the carving; she saw Charles' eyes flash with pleasure when he looked at the buffalo.

"Let me see that," Mr. T said. He snapped the rifle to his shoulder, sighting steadily down the barrel.

"Why, Senator," Freniere said, "you look like you're pretty good with a piece."

Her father's head swiveled slowly, the rifle still at his shoulder. "You thought I wasn't?"

"Well, I'd heard you talked folks to death," Freniere said. "Didn't figure you'd need no gun. Back there with them Washington pork eaters."

Mr. T lowered the weapon and laughed. "You young scamp," he said. "I haven't forgotten how. Have you fired it yet?"

"Cut a dollar in two at a hundred yards, Senator—sideways," Freniere said, and skipped off down the steps.

Lily was holding up her arms to her grandfather, and he sat down with her astride his thigh. She was his first grandchild. She reached for his watch chain and he detached it from the watch and gave it to her. She kicked her legs, letting the chain spill through her fat fingers.

"Oh, one other thing," Mr. T said to Charles as he jounced Lily on his knee. "You should keep an ear cocked for news of California. Burton Foster's boy went out with Bidwell's party two years ago, and Burt's been hearing some surprising things."

Jessie felt resentful. They were heaping too much on him: since you're going to Oregon, why not look into California? But Charles was watching her father with intense interest and she had to confess she was intrigued, too. California was a land of mystery. Exotic. Eldorado. Once she had studied Spanish colonial policy for her father, and she knew that Spain had actually arrested foreign visitors to its colonies. Since Mexico had thrown off Spanish rule in 1821, nothing had changed much. To this day very little was known about the Pacific province. A sailor named Richard Henry Dana had written an excellent book she'd badgered her father into reading; *Two Years Before the Mast* was a seaman's odyssey, but it was full of new information on California. A few American traders had settled there, marrying into California families; a few trappers had gotten through. Joseph Reddeford Walker had led a party there, and so had Ewing Young. When she'd learned that Carson had ridden with Young, her confidence in him had risen sharply.

"Burt says Bidwell's party was well received," Mr. T went on. "His boy's taken up a thousand acres on the Sacramento River, virgin land, no trouble at all. He had to become a Mexican citizen, and that meant becoming a Catholic, but Burt says he wasn't anything before. . . . A couple of surprising things. He says some four hundred colonists are there already—form quite a little community, most of 'em outside the settled areas. Burt says the Mexicans welcomed them at first. Now they're having second thoughts. But the government'll have a time getting rid of 'em now."

"A little like Texas, then."

"That's exactly what I'm wondering." Lily dropped the chain and the Senator leaned over to retrieve it. "The Mexicans welcomed young Austin and his colony at first, too—then when the colony grew, they didn't like it. And we had our Texas Revolution."

"What was the other surprising thing, Papa?" Jessie asked.

"Well, Burt says this fellow Sutter has built a regular empire there. Got a huge grant, herds and crops and so on. Even built a fort. In fact, he's been made a government official of some sort. Has his own army and acts like a king."

"Do you believe that, Senator?" Charles asked.

"I don't know—it hardly sounds credible, but there must be something to it. Maybe Burt's boy is overimpressed. But still . . ."

"Sutter?" Jessie asked. "I thought he was a charlatan."

She remembered the name. Some of the Senator's constituents had complained about him. Sutter was a Swiss who claimed to be of noble origin and said he'd served as a captain in the Swiss Guard of King Charles X of France. He'd come to St. Louis, set up a trading expedition to Santa Fe and then—so his partners claimed—had run off with the venture's proceeds.

"Of course, his partners were no better than he," Mr. T was saying, "and who knows if their version is true? But if Sutter made anything in Santa Fe, he lost it all in the Westport dry-goods venture. Next thing we knew, he'd gone west—to the fur rendezvous with Chouteau's people and from there to California. His partners wanted me to make an international claim. And our ambassador at Bern reported that far from being a nobleman, this Sutter was a failed merchant from some little Swiss town who'd skipped out just ahead of debtor's prison. Think of that—a failure all his life and now he has an empire! If he does. But I'll bet he owes everyone in California—he must have done it all on credit."

"A new recruit came today," Jessie interrupted. "Said you'd remember him from the time with Papa Joe Nicollet. Zindel—"

"Of course. Our rocketeer. And a first-class gunner." Charles had that look of sudden enthusiasm. "You know, now I've got a gunner, maybe I should take along a gun. A twelve-pounder—that mountain howitzer. Nice little brass piece, caisson, two mules."

"Well, Charles . . ." Jessie saw her father frown, and knew he was going to object.

"I wish I'd had a gun that day at Laramie," Charles said. "The boys would have felt a lot better with a twelve-pounder and fifty rounds of canister, and I would've too—not many Indians are going to attack against a howitzer, no matter how many there are."

"You'll be going to the mouth of the Columbia, Charles," The Senator was saying cautiously. "British are there. A cannon carries certain implications . . ."

But the idea of a howitzer and a man who could use it—suddenly her mind was crowded with the image of hordes of Indians attacking at a dead gallop, shrieking and scalping; and the fear she had been suppressing burst into the open.

Slicing across her father's voice, giving him a sharp, warning look, she said quickly: "What a wonderful idea! It'll give you protection—oh, I'll feel so much better about everything if you have a cannon." She was talking to keep her father silent. "Isn't it providential that Zindel should turn up just now? I told him to come back this afternoon—we'll sign him right on."

She cut her eyes at her father. He was watching her warily, but his hands were folded in his lap, and with relief she realized that he was not going to object further. As if feeling the brief tension, Lily began to cry.

As Frémont took the sentry's smart salute at Jefferson Barracks and watched the flag snapping in the morning breeze, he was glad he'd decided to wear his dress uniform. He'd ridden out to Headquarters, Western Department, United States Army, to arrange for arms for the expedition, and he felt immediately the crisp, polished, businesslike air. It was dauntingly military. Long barracks of gray limestone with full galleries faced the parade ground. He could hear the mutter of rifle practice in the distance. A punishment squad wheeled in close-order drill and a whitewash crew was busy on stonework and tree trunks that already looked impeccable. It was the most imporant post in the West, and it looked it. He dismounted and handed his reins to a trooper who, with punctilious élan, led his horse behind the low headquarters building that looked down the length of the parade ground.

Doubtless the post reflected the personality of the department commander, Colonel Stephen Watts Kearny. He was an old-line frontier officer famous for his iron discipline, which men accepted—and some even liked—because it was applied evenly. The rules were clear: transgression meant punishment. No excuses, no exceptions. Any man could live with that, Benton had said approvingly. The Senator had known Kearny for years, admired him and made sure his career prospered; a senior officer could have no friend quite like the chairman of the Senate Military Affairs Committee.

When Frémont was ushered into Kearny's spartan office, the commandant took his salute with a gesture and shook hands perfunctorily across his desk. He was about fifty; lean, unsmiling, a man used to authority. Silver eagles gleamed on his epaulets. The national colors were at one side, a regimental pennant at the other. Behind him, Frémont noticed, a window of many panes threw light in a visitor's eyes and left his own in shadow.

Kearny took the requisition and ran down it quickly. "Pro forma, I'm sure," he said, reaching for a pen. Then he stopped. "A *howitzer*?" His eyes rested on Frémont's, glinting—an expression he couldn't read.

"Sir, my orders are to connect the survey I made last year to South Pass with the Pacific coastal survey made by Commander Wilkes of the Navy. That will take me to the bar at the mouth of the Columbia, which means passing through a good deal of hazardous country."

"It takes a skilled artilleryman to handle these pieces. I understood that your expedition is composed of civilians."

Frémont could hear an undercurrent of distaste in Kearny's voice at the use of the word. He explained Zindel's military background.

"But even if the man *is* competent," Kearny said distantly, "a howitzer wouldn't be of much use against Indians. They don't fight that way—they function as light infantry, or light cavalry at its lightest. Speed, surprise, stealth—you won't find them fighting from breastworks and you're not likely to have anything to bombard. The piece plus equipage weighs twelve hundred pounds; you'd do better to take an extra twelve hundred pounds of beans."

Frémont contained his irritation. The colonel was used to riding into hostile country with two hundred well-trained dragoons at his back; he should try it with a handful of men who could always decide they'd had enough and were going home.

"Sir," he said politely, "Ashley took out a piece in Twenty-six and found it effective. Lewis and Clark had a gun—"

"A one-pounder."

"Yes sir, but they used it effectively. Fraeb was forted and fought all day; doubtless he'd have been glad for a chance to lay some canister among the Indians as they charged. I understand that most combat is in small groups, but at Laramie last year the Sioux were said to have massed a thousand or more."

"I thought that was loose talk."

"Nobody at Laramie thought so. My men were pretty uneasy. If I may say so, sir, I'm taking a relatively small party through known hostile tribes. The gun would be most useful as a morale factor for my men. They'd have welcomed it at Laramie, certainly."

Kearny didn't answer immediately. He drummed his fingers on his desk. Outside a private was polishing the brass evening gun by the flagpole; it was a six-pounder and it looked as if it were made of gold. "How soon do you depart?" Kearny asked.

"In nine days, sir."

"That's very short notice." It was hard to see Kearny's face in the light. "Tell me, what class are you, Lieutenant? thirty-seven or -eight?"

Frémont flushed. He was sure the colonel already knew the answer to his question. "I haven't the honor to be a graduate of West Point, sir," he said stiffly. He sketched in his background: the Carolina survey work under

Captain Williams, the tour with Nicollet, his own expedition the previous year; in military terms it had an inadequate ring.

Kearny nodded. "I asked because of your obvious ignorance of Army procedures. A request like this should have been made weeks ago, to your own superiors in Washington."

"Sir," Frémont said, "I explained that I only just learned I'll have a gunner."

"Prudence dictates that if a gun is necessary, then a gunner should have been sought; and if it isn't, then the chance presence of a gunner hardly makes it so."

It dawned on Frémont that the man intended to refuse him and he felt a spurt of real anger. "Sir," he said, "I hope that you won't deny me the weapon. I've thought it over very carefully, I've talked it over at length with Senator Benton—"

He broke off then. That was enough, he didn't want to sound insubordinate. Sometimes it's good to be cautious, Jessie had said.

"Very well, Lieutenant," Kearney said in a frosty, ominous tone. "I will authorize the howitzer on the grounds that a field commander should be able to choose his own weapons—within reason. And the howitzer is just barely within reason. But I will tell you that I don't like your implication. I have known and admired Senator Benton for many years, but I do not look to him for military direction. And I don't believe he intimated to you that I do."

It was a sharp reprimand and Frémont colored. Still, he suspected that the decision had been going against him until he invoked the Senator's name.

"Thank you for your decision, sir," he said, anchoring the important point quickly, and made a nice apology for any misunderstanding. Rather ungraciously, Kearny nodded his acceptance and stood up. The colonel made no move to shake hands, nor did he offer even conventional good wishes for the long and arduous journey that lay ahead.

Frémont rode out at a hard gallop, delighted that he didn't have to serve under Stephen Watts Kearny.

Charles had been gone only a couple of weeks and already Jessie felt lonely. Lily was fretting over a new tooth, Mr. T was downstate renewing political ties, the rest of the family seemed out of sorts; in the yard the pale gray locust blossoms were falling to the ground. Charles was still in camp outside Westport, making his final preparations. The last of his men, Baptiste DeRosier, had been delayed in St. Louis and was riding overland to meet him; she had written a last and determinedly cheerful letter to go with DeRosier. At the very earliest it would be January before Charles returned. The months seemed to stretch emptily ahead.

She dressed and went out for a walk, her feet crushing the fallen blossoms. The day was warmer than she had expected; deep summer was approaching. She turned along the river and watched the Westport packet depart with hoots and thrashing paddles. It was going upriver: if she were aboard, she would be with him in three days. She wished now that she had gone along to Westport for those final weeks. In a wagon yard an emigrant train was making up. A woman about her age sat on a wagon's tailgate nursing an infant and Jessie stopped to talk. They were going up the Platte, the woman said; her father spoke of Oregon, but she was sure that they could find suitable land someplace short of that awful distance. The baby didn't take to traveling. She didn't mention a husband.

Jessie said suddenly, "Oh, I wish I were going with you," and tears came to her eyes.

Distressed, the woman put out her hand. "Whyn't you come along?" she said. "Pap would make a place for you in the wagon. I know he would."

Jessie shook her head wordlessly, smiling. Tears would never do—she had months and months to go. As Louie said, they were forty strong this time, and they had the brass gun, whose very sound was likely to discourage hostile Indians. She took hold of herself, thanked the young woman and wished her well.

At home, dropped on her sewing basket, was an official letter addressed to her husband from Topographical Engineers headquarters in Washington. It gave her an uneasy feeling as she ripped it open. It was from the commandant himself, the placid Colonel Abert, but he had been anything but placid as he composed this. The St. Louis Armory, which had issued Charles the gun on Colonel Kearny's orders, had passed the requisition on to Washington. It seemed that the simple matter of a small brass cannon, its bark designed to deter Indians, had reverberated through the War Department with the roar of all Napoleon's artillery.

Now, sir, Colonel Abert wrote angrily, *what authority had you to make any such requisition?* My, Jessie thought, he *was* in a pet. Her eye hurried on to what she saw immediately was the key paragraph:

The object was a peaceable expedition to gather scientific knowledge. If there is reason to believe that the condition of the country will not admit of safe management of such an expedition—and of course will not admit of the only object for the accomplishment of which the expedition was planned—you will immediately desist in its further prosecution and report to this office.

It was a stunning turn. *Report to this office*—in effect, if Charles admitted that danger existed, he was to be recalled. But that made no sense; the perils of Blackfoot country were well known. Other concerns were afoot here. Professional jealousy, perhaps? She knew that Charles' success with the First Expedition had aroused antagonism among the corps' West Point officers. Had they seen a chance to use this issue to replace Charles with one of their own, and gone to work on their colonel?

She reread the letter, searching out its nuances. There was such insistence that the expedition's only purpose was mapping and exploration. But what else?—why stress that point? She pictured Colonel Abert writing urgently at his desk. He was more Washington man than military man; the only thing likely to disturb him was something political. She remembered Mr. T's reaction to the first mention of the gun and now, reflecting on it, she could sort out the political objections. How would the British react to an American contingent arriving at Fort Vancouver with a cannon? Could they blow such an incident into a diplomatic crisis for their own purposes? For that matter, someone might suspect that Charles —representing the western group—intended to provoke a crisis in order to force his own government's hand in the Oregon negotiations with the British.

Something Maria Crittenden had said to her once popped into her head. "The Army'll always be leery of Charles, you know. You might as well get used to it. He's a wild card—more answerable to your father than to his commanding officer. You see, they can never be sure whether he's pursuing their interests or the Senator's."

"Aren't they the same?" Jessie had said, only half-seriously.

"Don't be ridiculous," Maria had snapped. "Do you for one minute imagine the Army's primary interest is opening the West?" Then in a gentler tone she had added, "Remember, dear, any organization fears what it can't control."

Of course. Sitting with the letter in her lap, Jessie was relieved. It was just politics. The cannon had stirred some alarm which had descended on Colonel Abert, and his letter was no more than the frantic effort of a little man to establish a record that would clear his own skirts: Whatever you may be up to, Lieutenant Frémont, it's none of my doing, as this directive proves. . . . It wasn't really important.

But then she saw the letter's immediate threat. Washington knew Charles' schedule. Probably a second copy was on its way to Westport—perhaps on the very packet she had watched depart. At the least, the letter would deprive him of the gun and send him defenseless into the most dangerous country in the West. Or it would delay him as he awaited a reply to *his* response. The time left to get his men through the mountains before snow immobilized them would be disastrously narrowed.

In an instant she decided: she wasn't going to let pusillanimous political fears endanger his expedition. She ran out the back door to the stables and found Clarkson polishing the Brants' carriage.

"Go to DeRosier's house," she told him. "If he hasn't gone, have him come to me this instant!"

She was on the porch when DeRosier's horse swung around the corner. He was a capable-looking man and he hurried up the walkway.

"Can you leave for Westport immediately?" she asked. "I have a most important message for the captain." She paused. "Riding overland, you'll beat the packet, won't you?"

"Yes'm. River loops and winds."

"Good. Good."

She hurried to her desk and scrawled, *Darling husband—there are very important reasons for you to leave at once. No time to explain—I beg you, leave within the hour. Trust and go. I love you—J.*

She folded it, sealed it,wrote his name across it. "Give him both letters," she said, "But tell him I said to read *this* one first."

Ten days later there was an answer. It contained a single line in Charles' hand: *My darling—I trust and* go.

Then she sat down and wrote a careful, diplomatic letter to Colonel Abert explaining why he would not be hearing from Charles at this time. No blame should attach to Lieutenant Frémont, she said, for it was *she* who had sent him on before he could receive the letter. What the colonel perhaps had no way of realizing was the crucial significance of a cannon with the warlike tribes to the west of Fort Laramie. . . .

That night she slept with the assurance that she had made her second contribution to her husband's career. She was using her gift of love.

On the late August afternoon when Frémont led his column over South Pass the air was so clear he felt he could see a thousand miles. It was like riding across the top of the world under the glistening sky, a soaring bridge between what he knew and what he had come to learn. From here the Oregon Trail wound through incalculable mountains until it came down to the lower Columbia; sometimes it followed Indian trails but in most places there weren't even signs that men had passed. The sun leached turpentine from the sage; its odor filled the air.

The men were hard, burned down to bone and sinew by the Prairie crossing from Westport. Carson had come up from Taos to meet them, and Frémont had chosen as camp conductor for the Second Expedition the famous mountain man, Tom Fitzpatrick, old Broken Hand. There was something authoritative in the way he lifted his crippled claw when he gave an order that made men want to obey him. Often Frémont left him in command of the main column and with Carson, Freniere, Preuss and a few others rode out to examine the country in detail. Preuss hated to leave Menard's cart; he complained in his heavy accent, and Frémont enjoyed watching Carson try to control his irritation. Raffie Proue bedeviled Preuss with practical jokes, but oddly, the little German took them so well that the two men had become fast friends.

At the end of the line of carts came the cheerful gunner, Zindel, on the two-mule limber that drew their howitzer. Following was a rear guard led by Tessier. Well ahead of the column, sweeping for game but keeping an eye cocked for Blackfoot sign, Freniere rode with a swarthy young man named Alexis Godey whom Carson had brought up from Taos. Godey wore his blue-black hair to his shoulders, and his eager intensity appealed to Frémont; Louie was breaking him in as hunter.

They were good men, superbly qualified for this business of path-marking. Frémont realized he was riding the crest of a national dream: his timing was perfect, fate and his own ability had given him the coachman's box, and the future seemed to have no limits. More than nine hundred emigrants were moving west this year in hundreds of wagons. Some were already ahead, camped in the rich valleys of the Green and the Bear, fattening their stock after the hard prairie crossing. This year's pioneers were the advance guard; behind them a flood of Americans waited for him to show the way, to map the trail. The startling public reaction to his first report—the newspaper stories, the letters, the prominent men who sought him out—all underscored the importance of the mission.

And his next report would give them still more, for this country was full of marvels Jessie would bring to life in that exciting way she had with words. He rode along thinking of her; there was a richness to what they were together that he had never anticipated . . . Trust me and go, she had said, and he had moved the men out of Westport within an hour. Probably the cannon was the problem, some Army sensibilities ruffled, or perhaps they had sent some new instructions not at all attuned to Benton's aims. But it didn't matter—she had put him safely out of reach. No official recall could reach him now.

The column passed a seeping spring; its rivulet was running west; they had breakfasted on Atlantic waters and they would sleep tonight on Pacific tributaries. The trickle joined another and became a feeder creek to the Little Sandy up ahead, which in turn fed the Green River. They stopped at a willow grove by a small pool, and Proue found a bush heavy with ripe huckleberries. Soon the men were stuffing the sweet fruit in their mouths.

"That's bear food, y'damned fools," Fitzpatrick yelled in exasperation. "Close up or you'll come round a bush and say howdy to a grizzly. Or a Blackfoot, one . . ."

A long cloud had been building near the summit; it lowered, darkened, emptied sudden rain. The men crouched in their slickers, water spilling from the broad brims of their hats. In five minutes the sun reappeared; in fifteen the air was dry. Now it had a cool, winy quality, and Frémont knew that it would be chill before morning. They started downslope into light timber and forded the creek, the iron tires of the carts grinding against sand. The creek was larger, already carrying away the shower's runoff. That local rain cloud strung along the summit would water much of the nation: four great rivers began here and wound off to distant seas. The Sweetwater, which they had just left, became the Platte; a bit to the north was the Yellowstone, which became the Missouri; near it rose the Snake, which became the Columbia; and the Green, which they now approached, ran along the western edge of the Rockies, became the Colorado and swept across the desert to the Gulf of California.

And maybe there was one more—the mysterious, glorious Buenaventura, which no one had ever seen. It was said to drain the Rocky Mountain snowpack right into San Francisco Bay—a westbound equivalent of the mighty Missouri! The Spanish had searched for it fruitlessly, Lewis and Clark had looked for it on Jefferson's specific instructions—but just the same, trappers promised that it was there, over the next rise or the next ten more, but surely out there. Mapmakers included it or omitted it on whim; but then, you couldn't trust their maps anyway.

"I don't believe there's any such river," Carson said. They'd been talking about the Buenaventura all day. The trail led definitely downslope now amid clumps of light timber. Frémont reckoned it four hours till sunset, two till camp. He saw Louie and Godey watering their horses at a pool; two five-point bucks were lashed to the horses' pack saddles. Godey was prone, drinking, upstream to the horses, his hair fallen in the water.

"Fact is," Carson went on, sounding stubborn, "I never met a man who's actually seen it. If a river runs from the Rockies clear to the Pacific, I say *someone's* going to see it."

Good old plain-spoken Kit: seeing's believing. But it was the very grandeur of the idea that appealed to Frémont—a great river waiting to be found, a water route that would amount to a Northwest Passage opening trade to the Orient right across the girth of the continent, with a single short portage across the Continental Divide. What a discovery that would be—what a plum for his next report!

Anyway, like most simple views, Carson's was too easy. This country had never been studied systematically; its travelers had sought fur, not information. Kit had one good point, though: if the Buenaventura entered San Francisco Bay, it had to cut the Sierra Nevada.

"And that's the damnedest set of mountains you *ever* saw," Carson said. "High as the Rockies, stone towers and cliffs and snowpack God knows how deep. Believe me, the Sierra Nevada are *some* mountains."

"But rivers do cut gorges," Frémont insisted. "And if there isn't a Buenaventura, then we've got a real geographical puzzle. Look, we're talking about draining all the Rockies west of the Divide, plus the east slope of the Sierras—the Colorado and the Columbia certainly can't drain it all. So where does the water go?"

"Say, Cap'n"—the scout turned in his saddle—"you got more on your mind than just getting to the Columbia, ain't you?"

Frémont grunted. The whole West lay before him, full of possibilities: the land untouched, the British on the Columbia living on borrowed time, California a mysterious province of sunshine and roses in which an itinerant Swiss bankrupt could create an empire, trade with the Orient stretching beyond. . . . Where *did* all that water go? There was no room for myths on his map—he wanted to *know.*

"You plan to map the whole damned country, then?"

"Not in detail . . . but after we've finished the route to Oregon, there's not much point in coming back the same way, is there?"

"Well, wouldn't be nothing wrong with finding a good place to winter. Build up the stock and rest the men. Start back at first crack of spring."

"What's the matter with you, Kit? Why lie around when we could be doing something new? We'll swing south from the Columbia; then we won't have to wait for spring. Maybe we'll find the Buenaventura—maybe we'll paddle right into San Francisco Bay!"

'Uh-huh. Like the Platte Canyon run, I suppose."

He glanced at Carson, and the two men laughed ruefully. "No—no rapids this time . . . I want to see these Sierras. I don't want a map that leaves anything up in the air."

His tone had sharpened and Carson said, "Well, no call to get fussed up. I ain't backing off, only I like to know where I'm headed."

"Where you're headed—hell, Kit, half the fun is finding out! You'd be making saddles back in Franklin right now if you didn't feel that way."

Day by day the country grew rougher, the canyons more precipitous, the rivers more violent. The map was his first duty, of course. Fitzpatrick and Carson knew the way, though now and again they had to puzzle out the next step. Frémont followed them, overruling them occasionally to choose an alternative route that he judged would be easier for emigrant travel. His real concern was to get down on paper exactly what they showed him. The familiar details filled his notebooks—starsights, barometer readings, compass headings, angles of entry and declivity, quality of grass, quantity of game and careful narratives of each day's march to match the sketches that flowed from Preuss' pen.

Of the Buenaventura there was no sign, but they came to the huge salt lake that Gabe Bridger had found in 1824; Gabe had tasted the water and cried: "Hell, boys, we are on the shores of the Pacific!" Frémont sent the main body on to Fort Hall to resupply, and set out along the lake with a captain's guard. Preuss fell off his horse the first day and claimed it was the horse's fault: it was an Indian pony, hence unreliable.

"Preuss," said Carson, "you'd fall off a rocking horse." Godey nearly strangled with laughter and Preuss's face went dark; he got back on the horse and stayed on.

The great lake did look like an ocean. Frémont boiled five gallons of its water down to fourteen pints of pure white crystal. He knew it had no outlet; Ashley's men had circumnavigated it in canoes two years after Bridger found it. Yet the Bear River fed it: why didn't it overflow? There were stories of vast whirlpools draining its center, and the men had very serious faces when Frémont ordered the rubber boat inflated. He heard Louie say quietly, "Shit, Godey, he won't get us in no trouble. He's up on things like that." In fact, though, a storm arose, the boat's panels parted, and they barely made it back to shore. Lying exhausted on the sand, he thought about the disappearing water. Much evaporated into the dry air—the Bridgers of the world couldn't imagine the volume of water that could move as gas—but could that be the whole answer?

Supplies were scarce at Fort Hall, the easternmost of the Hudson's Bay posts. Gladly Frémont took what could be spared and led his party over ground that became steadily wilder and more barren. At last they came to the high rim of the great canyon of the Snake River and stood looking at the ribbon of water flowing seven thousand feet below.

"Told you I'd show you some country, didn't I?" Carson said with as much pride as if he'd chiseled the gorge himself.

It was magnificent, no denying that, but somehow Frémont found it unsatisfying, too, cruel and violent, gloomy conifer forests stretching off to the north, sere bush country running to the south. It was Louie who put his feeling into words.

"It's a privilege to see what God can make when He puts His mind to it. But as for me, I'll take the high plains when the buffler run—one of them days where you feel like you can see a hundred miles. Know what I mean, Cap'n?"

The brutal canyons finally defeated their carts. No settler wagons had come so far; prodigious work remained to make this a real road. Only the cannon and its limber remained on wheels; the men would never leave that gun. When they came to a gorge where they had to lower it on ropes, Billy Rasmussen exclaimed in dismay, "We'll never get it down that." He was a skinny youth who readily saw obstacles; Frémont would have paid him off at Bent's Fort but for his undeniable talent with tools.

"Shut up, Billy," Zindel said. "Gun goes anywhere." Zindel supervised the descent, putting ten men on a rope behind the gun, and even then they lost it twice and the limber's shaft was smashed. They killed a mule for food that night—there had been no game for a week—while Rasmussen shaped a new shaft with a drawknife. As Frémont studied the route up the far wall, Fitzpatrick drawled, "We got fifty more canyons like this one up ahead, Cap'n." But no one thought of leaving the gun: it was their reassurance, though there had been no cause to fire it; at night they dragged it in among the campfires, slapping its brass hulk familiarly.

Still, Frémont saw no reason to appear at the headquarters post of His British Majesty's Hudson's Bay Company with a cannon in train; that might be tempting fate. They left the Snake, cut across to the Walla Walla, followed it down to the Columbia where that river hurtles through the Cascade Mountains. Here his men would rest the stock while with Preuss, Godey, and Freniere he ran downriver by canoe to Fort Vancouver.

"This is the way to travel," said Preuss. "Maybe we paddle home around the Horn and to hell with the horses, eh?"

A sawmill was whining as they reached Vancouver; Frémont found the sound as sweet as violins. They turned a bend and there, on a hill, was an imposing fort with walls of twenty-foot vertical timbers. It overlooked a small settlement at the water's edge. A British bark lay at anchor, unloading supplies onto a lighter. As the canoes ground ashore a tall man with a shock of white hair hurried down from the fort.

"John C. Frémont, United States Army," Frémont said formally, extending his hand.

"John McLoughlin." The man had a broad smile and Frémont liked him immediately. "Welcome, Lieutenant—we heard you were coming."

An imposing Scotsman of about sixty, Dr. McLoughlin was famous across the West for his generosity and his temper. Frémont knew he had trained as a physician at Edinburgh before coming out to run Britain's western fur trade.

Fort Vancouver was huge—ten times the size of Laramie—but it was the people and the movement, the very noise of the place that excited him. A tame bear on a chain, a smith's hammer ringing, carpenters and wainwrights at work, a corral full of milling ponies, hand trucks trundling supplies from the bark into commodious warehouses, children playing blindman's buff—it was almost a miniature St. Louis.

McLoughlin gave him a dinner he was likely to dream of after that stretch of mule-meat stew; later over coffee, they talked. Frémont was pleased that the Scot did not view him as an enemy; no American—trapper, missionary, settler—ever had been denied his assistance. Jed Smith had wintered here on one of those great ranging treks Benton so admired, and he and McLoughlin had become such friends that Smith refused thereafter to trap in territory the Hudson's Bay Company had staked out.

When Frémont asked what McLoughlin heard of California, the older man smiled. "Given American suspicions of our intentions there," he said, "I suppose I should have news aplenty. But I must tell you those suspicions are overdrawn. Our real interest lies to the north—in Puget Sound, which is a magnificent harbor. That's why we want the Columbia as a dividing line. You'll notice I've built my fort on the north bank and persuaded you few Americans to hold to the south bank."

"I have to doubt you'll hold that dividing line on the Columbia, if I may say so without abusing your hospitality."

To Frémont's surprise, McLoughlin chuckled. "So do I," he said. "If the United States cares enough to blaze the Oregon Trail, then settlers are sure to travel it. And settlers in number will make this country their own."

"That is Senator Benton's view," Frémont said cautiously.

"He's a wise man. As a friendly warning to the Senator, though, you might want to convey the idea that it would be most dangerous to try to push us past the Forty-ninth Parallel—to deny us rights on Puget Sound. That would mean certain war. But as to the Columbia country . . . well, let me say I'm an Oregon man. This is my home. I'd always supposed I would die a Briton, but I may be an American before that time comes."

"We'd be the richer for it," Frémont answered.

The talk curled back to California. McLoughlin knew Sutter well; the Swiss had spent a month at Fort Vancouver on his way to California four years before.

"We were all quite taken with him. Clever, witty, told marvelous tales of court life—we invited him to stay for a year as our guest. But he was in a great hurry."

When Frémont suggested that Sutter's background might not be entirely as represented, McLoughlin smiled. "Ah well, he'd hardly be the first man whose origins improved as he moved west. If he's playing a role, who's to say it isn't the one to which he was destined all along?" He gave Frémont a shrewd look. "You're thinking of going there, perhaps? California?"

"Not unless I find the Buenaventura and float right on into San Francisco Bay."

"Ah," McLoughlin said, looking pleased, "the Buenaventura—now there *is* a quest! If it does exist, I can tell you where you'll find it." He drew a crooked line on a tablet representing the Columbia. "Now the Cascades eventually run into the Sierra Nevada and the Sierra runs . . . oh, nearly to Baja California." He sketched in the mountains and drew a valley between them and a rough coastline. "On this side, the west, the Sacramento feeds into San Francisco Bay, right? On the east, there's some of the meanest country you'll ever want to see. If it exists, the Buenaventura has to be there, somewhere in the same latitude as the bay. That's the area still left untraveled.

"Do you see?" His finger stabbed at the rough map, red hair bristling on the back of his hand. "Run down the eastern slope of those mountains and you'll cut the Buenaventura—or you'll disprove it forever. But I promise you: you'll never see harder country. Never."

It was the god*damnedest* country he'd ever had the mispleasure of traveling, Carson thought. Seemed like all the rock was flint; it broke down the horses and it was pure hell for a man in parfleche-sole moccasins. Rock everywhere; now, you'd expect rock to turn loose a little water, but when they did come on any, like as not it was salty. You could see salt encrusted on the rank grass growing around it, could see the stock curl their lips when they tried it. Armadillos had been pissing in it, Bill Ingalls said. Good sweet grass was rare and the horses were looking poor. Their shoes came loose and all the nails were used up and all the metal that could be made into nails; so they often went lame and then the rider walked—and pretty soon he was limping, too.

The canyons were contrary, one after another laid across their path more'n a thousand feet deep—work down one side, slow, checking the animals, the wheels of that damned gun locked, old Zindel scared shitless someone would let it go bouncing all the way to the bottom, turn it into a ball of brass junk. Which might have been a good move; there'd been a time he'd thought Godey was going to do just that; Alex was hotheaded, you had to watch him. They'd popped it just once, at Klamath Lake, when Indians had raised signal smokes all around them but refused to show themselves, a right unfriendly thing to do. Cap'n laid a shell amongst the smokes, and did they leave in a hurry! If the Klamaths were fixing to attack, they changed their minds right smart. But who knows about an Indian?

It was hungry time. They were still a way from eating their moccasins, but country with bad water and little grass just naturally didn't produce much game. Day after day he and Louie and Alex had ranged ahead, riding in a cold wind from the winter desert that made a man feel like his eyeballs had dried forever; at night he dreamed of herds of fat Sierra mule deer, but in the day he never saw 'em, and what you couldn't see you couldn't shoot.

Frémont had come back from Vancouver all full of piss and vinegar and started them south along the eastern flank of the Cascades. They'd celebrated Christmas with a drink of brandy, butt-up against the Sierra Nevada. Those mighty mountains reared right out of the desert, so near they blocked the sun by midafternoon; they looked raw and dangerous, the saddles choked with snow, the peaks wind-whipped and icy; they made a man feel the size of an ant.

It was hard to believe that on their far side lay the Sacramento, where the sun always shone and the living was sweet. Gardenland country it was, with honeybees and orchards full of fruit and pastures full of beef. Folks said the Californios were lazy, but Carson had formed the opinion they were just plain sensible. They worked as hard as necessary in a spot the Creator seemed to have designed especially for good living, and the rest of the time they played—rodeos, horse races, turkey shoots, bear hunts, and at night, with wine flowing and lanterns lit, *fandangos* and *bailes*, where the guitars played and the pretty girls spun their skirts in the air . . .

The colder and tougher this country got, the hungrier the men got, the more he liked to tell 'em about Californy. He was bullshitting them a little, but it wasn't all lies and he could get their saliva running like a spring freshet. And the women: he'd discovered the hombres couldn't watch all their women *all* the time—well, the plain fact was that a man had to guard against his natural tendencies in California lest he wear himself down to a nub.

That was the other side of the mountains; this side fascinated the Cap'n. He rode for miles without taking his eyes off 'em. Carson remembered his own first breathtaking view of the Tetons, the first year out with Bridger, but they were nothing to this. Cap'n was in hog heaven. He had never known a man who relished new country more. Frémont didn't care if the trail was hard and the food was short. If they were going someplace new, someplace interesting—and if it was new it *was* interesting to Charlie—nothing else mattered. He was still mapping every step of the trail, writing away in his notebook. The men felt easy with him. He might lead you into trouble, no denying that, but likely enough he'd lead you back out, too.

Like now—compared to where they'd been, the river where they were camped was like a gift. Grass sweet and strong and the river full of the fattest trout a man would ever want to see. The Washoes hereabouts threw the fish up on the bank the way buffler cows dropped calves. They called the river the Truckee, but in gratitude for its bounty, Frémont said he was going to name it the Salmon Trout River. Twenty, maybe thirty pounds they weighed, with two red stripes under their mouths that made them look for all the world like their throats was cut. The boys were wild for them and the horses were looking better hour by hour. But in the distance he could see the desert and the sheer mountain flanks running south. Hard country—and many a mile between water holes. He reckoned they had five hundred miles to go before it would get much better. Stock up on them fish, boys.

He saw the Cap'n coming down from the instrument tent and got up to meet him. Claybank was filleting the salmon, and Menard was laying the strips on drying racks over cedar smudge fires. After it had dried, that smoky fish would be good for months. Carson could see from Frémont's step that he was restless, and sure enough, they started downriver to go look at the remuda where old Fitz was salving stone bruises on the poor horses' legs. He saw the little German on a rock, sketching the mountains, his sore ass presumably forgotten. Preuss had ridden a thousand miles since he'd claimed he wasn't used to a horse.

"You were right, Kit," Frémont said to him, without any palaver. "The Buenaventura doesn't exist." They were beyond the last place where it might have been. "We're right on a parallel with San Francisco Bay." Carson was startled; involuntarily he glanced up at the vast heights of snow towering over them: California had never seemed farther away.

"God, but it would have been something to have found that river!" Frémont looked cast down as a kid sent to bed without his supper.

"Have you figured out where all the water goes?"

"I think so."

This whole stretch between the Rockies and the Sierra Nevada was a basin without outside drainage, except for the Colorado and the Columbia. The Great Basin, Charlie called it; a very rare occurrence anywhere in the world, for such a huge area not to drain to the sea. Carson would never had thought of it by himself; that so often happened when he talked to Frémont—it was a sensation he enjoyed. He had found himself a leader.

"You remember all that grass standing through the ice at Klamath Lake? We missed the lake—that was a marsh. This country's full of sinks that may become marshes or even lakes when the melt is running. And what's left, what doesn't evaporate, just sinks down to the water table."

"Well, there's no shortage of sinks in this country," Carson said. Ahead he saw Fitz bent over, rubbing down a big black gelding's left foreleg.

"My theory's right," Frémont said, "and by God, I'm going to say so. I'm going to spell it right out on the map itself."

"That'll be something important, will it?"

"Not to settlers, but for professional geographers it'll be the most exciting conceptual finding of the expedition." Charlie slapped his hands together in sudden enthusiasm, revealing himself in a way that Carson rarely saw. "Yes sir," he said, "a real piece of geographic work. We've disproved the Buenaventura and we've solved one of the central terrain problems of the West. I'll tell you, Kit—if they thought the First Report was something, this one'll knock them over!"

"There you go," Carson said, feeling oddly touched, as if he had been trusted with a confidence. He looked off across the desert into which all that water vanished. "*Now* all we got to do is figure out how to get this pee-riceless information back to Missouri without starving to death."

SIERRA

Morning blazed on the Sierra Nevada. Frémont watched the snow at the heights turn from red to apricot to glowing white. The bare stone spires slowly bled from warm tawny to cold gray, illusion fading into hard rock.

"I'll show you boys where we are," he said to his subalterns, who were warming themselves at a small fire before the instrument tent. In a notebook he sketched the Columbia, the mountains, a rough coastline showing San Francisco Bay. He drew a line for the Sacramento, an X for Sutter's Fort, another for the river on which they were camped, another X for their position.

Louie reached for the map. "Only a half-inch from Sutter's Fort?" he said in surprise. "How far's that in miles?"

"Less than a hundred," Frémont said. "Hard to believe that it's summertime so close, isn't it? Right, Kit? You're always talking about the Sacramento country—fat beef, fresh fruit, luscious girls. Land of plenty, eh?"

There was a short silence. They were all staring at him.

"God almighty," Godey said after a moment, "he wants us to go *over.*"

Frémont saw quick amusement in Preuss' face. The other men turned to look at the mountains. Fourteen thousand feet, sharp as an ax on edge, snow against rock far above where any tree could live.

"Jesus, Cap'n," Freniere said in a whisper, *"up there?"*

"I'll tell you, Louie," Frémont said gently, "it's a lot like the first time you drink a cup of buffalo blood—it looks harder than it is."

Freniere grinned faintly. "Hell you say," he said, but he had recovered himself.

Carson had a suspicious, irritated look. "You been planning this all along?"

Frémont smiled and shook his head. Had he? Not really. But he remembered Benton's speculations: there *was* a hunger at home for information on California. If he'd found the Buenaventura—but he hadn't. If he'd met trappers or Indians who knew the Sacramento—but the truth was, he hardly knew more today than when he'd left St. Louis. Yes, disproving the

Buenaventura was a feat of sorts and his Great Basin idea was an important geographic concept, but one was a negative discovery and the other scientific esoterica. Neither led the way to fame and fortune . . .

"No," he said, "but I didn't expect to find myself with supplies short, stock run down, game not worth a damn, and a thousand miles to go before it gets any better. I wouldn't mind going over to Sutter's for new supplies and fresh stock. I wouldn't mind seeing California, either."

"Me neither," Tessier said, to Frémont's surprise. "I like the idea! Hell, yes—I'm ready."

"That's 'cause you don't know nothin' about it, sonny," Fitzpatrick told him crossly. "Surer'n shit stinks, no one's ever done it that I heard of. Hard enough to cross in summer. *Nobody* would do it in winter. No reason to."

"But we've got reason," Frémont said. "Anyway, you've wintered in the mountains. You too, Kit."

"That's different," Carson answered carefully. "You set up on a good beaver stream. You can move on snowshoes, set your traps and all. But you don't venture none up on the high ground."

Fitzpatrick gestured impatiently with the bad hand. "You understand, Cap'n," he said, "a man can get around on snowshoes. That's not the problem. It's the horses. The weight, the supplies and equipment. You put a horse in twenty feet of snow and watch that sumbitch flounder. And the weather—*one* storm drops as much snow as the lowlands get all winter. Wind comes through the passes like a tornado. Blow a man right off the mountain. I mean it! Churns up the snow till everything is white—you can't see the sky and you can't see the ground. I been caught in that a time or two—mountains ain't anything to be taken lightly, I promise you that."

"Well, I don't intend to get caught up there. We'll find the right pass, wait for the right day—come on, Tom, you're not telling me you couldn't *get* across, are you?"

"I'll make it," Fitzpatrick declared after a pause. "I don't know about the horses."

"Well, hell, they won't have any choice but to come along."

Carson laughed. "Might as well saddle up, Tom. When the Cap'n decides to go, ain't nothin' going to hold him."

"Anyway," said Godey, his grin restored, "if the girls are as panting hot as Kit's been saying, that's reason enough for me."

"Hell yes," Tessier said. "I've got a yearnin' to see this here promised land . . ."

The going turned out to be harder by far than anything they'd encountered. For two weeks they wandered in a labyrinth of stony ground, narrow passages, chasms and blind canyons, hunting for routes into the mountains—a usable pass. Game continued scarce, food supplies shrank. The stock was wearing badly and a sourness settled over the men; even Proue had little to say. The Sierra seemed to get bigger but no closer; daily the mountains became more awesome.

When a group of Washoe Indians in rabbit-fur tunics came into camp from netting rabbits on the sandhills below, Frémont traded with them for snowshoes and dried vegetables. He was determined to find a guide. Their leader smiled when he understood Frémont's intentions. Impossible to cross the mountains in winter, he said, making quick, sharp gestures to indicate how the snow and ice would block them. His friendly expression was belied by shrewd and watchful eyes; he looked at the circle of listening white men with an expression that was half-mocking, half-compassionate. He knew of white men living beyond the mountains; one of his tribe had crossed over in summer and visited what must have been Sutter's Fort from the rude sketch he scratched in the dirt. He shouted something in a hoarse voice, and a well-muscled fellow with intelligent eyes came into the ring of firelight.

Carson christened the youth Mélo; the word seemed to mean friend and the Indians used it constantly. Mélo and his leader chuckled over the white men's plans until Frémont opened his pack and shook out a length of scarlet cloth as bright as a cardinal's feathers. In the awed silence that followed, Mélo slowly touched the cloth, but when Frémont pointed toward the mountains, he withdrew his hand as if burned. Frémont took out a Hudson's Bay Company blanket, brilliant green wool smooth as a baby's cheek, with its four black points representing the four beaver pelts it was worth in trade. He let Mélo drape it over his shoulders. The man's lust to possess that soft warmth was almost obscene. Frémont gave the blanket a threatening tug and gestured toward the peaks again. This time, after a long hesitation, Mélo nodded. When the older man protested, the youth turned on him with sudden force and said something that silenced him.

In the morning Mélo lashed the cloth and the blanket into a tight roll that he slung across his back. Godey readied a horse for him and Mélo sprang up on one side and fell off the other.

"This sumbitch is going to be my favorite redskin, Cap'n," Godey cried in delight. "Imagine an Indian who can't ride!"

Mélo gave Godey a sharp look—they were about the same age—and an hour later had made himself an adequate horseman. He led them up the canyon, turned at a cleft rock and climbed onto a ridge, skirted the head of another canyon, ran four miles up a small stream and climbed out again, always moving toward the mountains. His command of terrain reassured the men, who made endless jokes at his expense.

"You boys go easy," Frémont cautioned. "We wouldn't want him to say the hell with it and go home."

"We'll cinch a rope around his neck if he tries that," Carson said darkly.

The way became steadily rougher and steeper. The nights were colder now; ice falls appeared in the streams and finding open grass became almost impossible. They had to bring up the horses one by one and attach long hauling ropes to the gun. Rocks tore the men's moccasins and bloodied the horses' legs. Frémont prided himself on the toughness of his feet, but soon they were badly stone-bruised and he was favoring his left heel.

The men were glum; their anger began to focus on the gun and on Zindel. Sometimes they spent most of the day hoisting the piece and its limber up sheer rock chasms, sweating even in the cold. Their diet was thin and they had to rest longer after each hoist. Frémont noticed that they no longer slapped the brass barrel and called it pet names. They called it that fucker, and they didn't look at it except when they had to help move it. Like a luxury grown too expensive, it had become a burden and a reproach.

On the third time in a single morning that the gun's wheels wedged in a chasm too narrow to admit them, Zindel threw quick hitches around the barrel. When the men above lifted, one of the hitches slipped and the piece fell on Bill Ingalls' foot.

"Fuck you and your no-good fucking gun to hell!" Ingalls screamed. He leaped at Zindel, reaching for the gunner's throat. Zindel danced quickly around the limber and turned with a wooden mallet in his hand. Instantly Ingalls' butcher knife flashed.

"Hold it!" Frémont shouted, his voice like a whip. "Put up that knife, Ingalls! You, Zindel—drop that hammer before someone sticks it up your ass." He'd broken their momentum and before they could react he added loudly: "That gun has gone as far as it's going. We're leaving it right here."

"And good riddance," Tessier muttered, panting. "Frigging brass monster . . ."

Zindel had a crestfallen look as he watched them trundle gun and limber beneath the draping skirts of a huge fir. The men were quiet now, neither sad nor glad; they had come to hate the gun, but abandoning it was a defeat that left them naked. The mountain loomed ahead; already it had turned back their gun. Frémont had a sudden image of Colonel Stephen Watts Kearny sitting straight and humorless at his desk, his office arranged so that the light struck a visitor's eyes. There would be trouble over this. Well then, let it come. The hell with it.

But leaving the gun made travel no easier. They moved mostly on foot, leading the horses up passages that would have baffled mountain goats. They climbed into the snow belt, found ice underlying loose snow and pressed on; the snow was six inches, a foot, a foot and a half; the horses whinnied and balked, their breath frosting and their haunches quivering. Mélo led them unerringly forward; Frémont realized that not once had he seen the young Indian smile. He kept the blanket rolled and lashed over his shoulder, refusing to risk soiling it. At last he brought them into a valley that broadened suddenly. At its head was a sharp preliminary ridge; beyond that, Frémont could see the vast central chain, magnificent and unnerving. They rounded a turn and saw steam rising from a hot spring and a field of bright grass which meant life for the weakening horses.

The next day, plowing through snow three and four feet deep, they reached the last intervening ridge. The gigantic main chain was still ten miles away, across a rough, undulating valley; it looked as barren and unforgiving as a prison wall. The altitude here was seven thousand feet; the mountains reared another seven thousand into the brilliant air. Immense trees marched upwards and stopped at the point where trees no longer could live. And far above soared towers of stone and ice, jagged as lightning strokes, rounded as river rocks, smooth with shining snow, shaggy with glittering, broken ice. Frémont gazed at it, glad the others could not see his face. This was what he intended to conquer.

Straight ahead was a rounded peak that looked like a bear's back. To its right was a cleft and to the right of that a pinnacle that seemed sharp as a blade. Frémont saw Mélo gesture toward the cleft.

"That'll be our pass," Carson said, and added, "he says here is where the real snow begins." The Indian stood with his rolled blanket gripped under his arm; he was feeling the material absently, as if to assure himself that the prize was really worth being in this fearful place.

They started that afternoon and the horses were immediately in trouble. The snow was deep in a way that Frémont had never encountered; what elsewhere would be the most violent of blizzards here seemed normal; it was as if the ground below had vanished. Men on snowshoes broke a path but the horses plunged through. They whinnied and reared in panic, feeling nothing solid beneath them. Within a hundred yards the column was stopped, the lead horses mired to their bellies, quivering and blowing, eyes rolling, the men cursing in dismay. Frémont led the way back to the preliminary ridge where wind had scoured away the snow.

Their fires were blazing when two Washoes walked into camp on snowshoes made of bark stretched on willow frames. They came lightly across the snow, kicked off the shoes, and entered with pine nuts in outstretched hands, symbolic of their pacific intent. One was about fifty, lean and sinewy, gray streaks in his hair. He was a man of authority; Frémont heard a crackle in his voice when he shot a question at Mélo.

Mélo answered at some length, gesturing toward the peaks, until the older man interrupted him. He said something sharp and Mélo bristled and spoke angrily, pointing at Frémont and Carson. Shaking his head, the Washoe turned peremptorily to Frémont; he had an outraged look. Frémont had no trouble following the old man's harangue, as Carson threw out phrases. Nor did the men. Frémont could see their awed, alarmed comprehension; Tessier was rubbing the bridge of his nose as if it pained him, staring over his hand at the Indian. Proue was standing next to Louie, his mouth slack.

The heights were impassable, the old man was saying, his companion nodding in doleful confirmation; snow piled on snow, rock stacked on rock, ice growing on ice; wind that swept everything before it, ice sheets on which an eagle couldn't find purchase, cliffs that dropped away farther than a man could see. It would be utterly impossible with horses: with his hands he showed them the horses' feet walking on ice, slipping, flying from under them, the horses plunging off cliffs, the men slipping after them. He showed them snow that buried great trees, avalanches that broke without warning, slopes shiny with ice, snow glare that would blind them. They were dead men.

When he was done, the white men sat in stony silence. He turned on Mélo and said something swift and brutal, a startling quality of contempt in his voice as he pointed at the blanket Mélo still hugged. Mélo looked down, refusing to meet his eyes. Then, in the silence the old man gestured to his companion and they both tied on their snowshoes and were gone, light as night birds, slipping down the mountain toward warmth and sanity.

The first sun of the following morning turned the snowy heights crimson and put a softening glow on the cold rock. Frémont was reading the thermometer—a bitter eighteen degrees—when he heard Carson say in a loud, alarmed voice, "Where's that Goddamned Indian?"

Godey burst out of the woods from the direction of the latrine. "The son of a bitch is gone," he yelled. "I seen his tracks beyond the shithole."

Fled—deserted—left them to face the worst of the mountain alone! The men were shouting to one another. Frémont had a moment of rage so intense that it took his breath. That piece—of—shit! Worthless, lying—

"Let's us track him down, Cap'n." Godey looked wild, eyes pale green against his dark face. Imperiously he flung back his long hair. "Me and Kit and Louie—we'll find that son of a bitch or leave him dead in the snow, one."

Frémont saw Louie checking the Hawken's load. Things were going out of control. He collected himself. "No," he said, "you won't find him. He'll be out of the snow and leaving no tracks on stone by now. He knows the ground. He's gone."

"Never trust an Indian," Carson said.

"Cheat you every time!" Godey's voice was still high.

Preuss cleared his throat and said in a pedantic way, "Of course, from his viewpoint his actions do make sense."

Frémont saw that Preuss was right and it made him even angrier. Carson said: "Why, you contrary little bastard."

Preuss looked surprised and hurt. "That's not at all appropriate," he said. "I only meant that we tend to ignore the cultural differences between us and the Indian." His voice took on a lecturing tone. "We assume the Indian shares our values and that when he violates them he must be without honor. But from *his*—"

"To break his word—that's all right?" A tic quivered in Fitzpatrick's furrowed cheek.

"He thinks we're mad to cross in winter. So why should he risk his life for us?"

Godey was beside himself. "You fat-faced sucker," he cried, "if you love him so much why the fuck didn't you go with him?"

"That is a non sequitur," Preuss said. He was stuttering. "If you're so tough, why are you afraid to cross *without* him?"

Godey roared, "Don't you call *me* yellow, you four-eyed Dutchman! I ain't scared of nothing," and lunged at Preuss with his fist cocked. Frémont jumped forward. His shoulder hit Godey before the blow landed, and knocked him sprawling.

"Both of you—that's enough!" he said. "Mr. Preuss is entitled to his opinions. Even if they *are* stupid." Preuss started to answer and Frémont snapped, "Be silent, Karl!"

He looked around the circle of men. "Let's get ourselves together here," he said briskly. He gestured toward the notch in the mountains. "There's the pass—we can't miss it. Truth is, the Indian wouldn't have been much help anyway. He's never been up here with snow on the ground. That's why he got scared and ran off. Now, it may worry hell out of him to be someplace where things look different—but new ground is *our* business."

They were still alarmed and unsure. He gave brisk orders: Fitzpatrick and a half-dozen men to take the horses back to the hot spring with its bright grass; the others to start building sledges and snowshoes under Rasmussen's direction. He saw the slender carpenter's face flush with pleasure. "And Kit and I will scout the valley and find a camp on the far side." He paused, then added easily, "When we're set we'll pick a good day and skip over the mountains and down to Sutter's. What's ten, fifteen miles?" They were still uncertain; he grinned as if he were enjoying himself. "Let's snap shit!" he said, popping his hands together. "Let's move!"

He and Carson tied on snowshoes and stepped off into a stunning new world—the world of truly deep snow. This snow wasn't just a cover as in the East—it was a presence. From five to twenty feet and more in depth, it assumed shapes of its own that had nothing to do with the shape of the land lying forgotten beneath it. The *shush shush shush* of rawhide against snow accented the quiet. Wind sighed in the tops of trees. White firs, lodgepole pines, mountain hemlocks with graceful nodding tips stood in groves separated by expanses of smooth white. He passed small trees which were in fact the tops of trees of medium size; the disproportion startled him. He was walking at treetop level! Separated from the hidden ground, not a moving thing in sight, not a living creature; a gripping sense of loneliness seized him, and he spoke to Carson to hear his own voice, to hear Carson's voice in answer. Then a chickadee fluttered in a white fir, its thin whistle like a lonely flash against the sighing conifers. He saw the gouged tracks of a snowshoe rabbit and the delicate prints of a fox that was circling the rabbit, but the game animals—the hoofed game—long had vanished, deserting these dangerous heights which now he and his men—and their horses and mules—must cross. Ten terrible miles lay before them. He walked on, shaken by the prospect, beating down his fears.

Mélo had said the real snow began here. This was what Fitzpatrick had warned of—snow that drove hoofed animals away, snow that defeated horses. It would be different when they reached the great heights. There the slopes were too steep and the rocks too sharp to hold deep snow. You could break a path for a horse along a steep hogback as far as the ridge lasted. It was in the swales, in this wide and relatively flat valley that yet was in the high snow country—there the trouble came.

Up ahead he saw a dark smear which proved to be a sheltered hillside facing south, where the snow had melted down to show grass spears. Good: horses would paw down to grass if they could see it. To the left he saw an irregular shape; it was a ridge, but after a few feet it disappeared. There were other ridges, but none offered real help in getting the horses across the valley and into position to force the pass. The men would have to build a road—make heavy mauls and beat down the snow until it was compacted and hard enough to bear the animals' weight.

They began at first light. Frémont took the lead, standing with spread legs, lifting the maul and driving it straight down between his feet. Lift, drop, lift, drop—the pain started in the hips and worked up through the shoulders until a man wanted to scream and fall down and try to dream that he was anywhere else in the world. They took turns and they learned to hate those mauls as a man can hate a woman in a ruined marriage; Frémont could see it in their faces, in their reluctance as they took the wooden handles and positioned themselves and started the brutal rhythm. As they worked they watched a storm build on the far side of the mountains. Clouds rolled up from the west full of sea moisture and poised on the summit, black and full, sending snow flying over in glittering streamers that flashed in the sun and evaporated. On the fourth day when they were nearly across, the storm burst over and rolled down the eastern flank to envelop them. They struggled to keep fires alive in the holes they had melted by firing entire trees. In the morning they found their road filled in, their work destroyed.

They started again, retracing their route with the awful mauls. The food ran down. The peas from Fort Vancouver, the dried fish, the pine nuts purchased from the Washoes were all exhausted. They were living on mule meat now, and most of them had diarrhea. They would hurry off, bent over and holding their guts, and then stop, bare themselves, and gush hot liquid that stained the snow. When they came back they lurched, breathing hard, looking somehow shamed. Their turns on the mauls were shorter and often they fell when they were relieved. Ice matted their beards, their skin tore easily, their lips cracked and bled, the blood freezing unnoticed. At night Frémont lay awake and listened to his men moan in their sleep. But in the morning they got up, ate some mule meat, drank warm water—they were always thirsty, pouring water from their bowels—and picked up the mauls again. And the great chain of mountains reared before them, looking ever higher and more dangerous as they neared its base.

Darkness was falling on the streets of St. Louis. Jessie stood by a window watching a man hurry up the walkway to the house opposite. A light snow had fallen, and he left dark tracks on the walk. She dropped the curtain.

"Lay another place," she said to Sally, who was setting the table.

"Yes'm," Sally said. She was a freedwoman and had a round, intelligent face with a ready smile. "Someone coming?"

"Maybe Mr. Frémont is coming."

"No! Do you mean—have you heard something?"

"No," Jessie said. "I just don't want him to walk in and see us going ahead without him."

"Miz Jessie—" Sally began.

"Don't argue with me, Sally. Do as I say!"

She paced from the dining room to the living room and back. She felt wild and strange, had all day—another interminable day! Like all the days since Charles had left and her father had taken the family back to Washington. She had gone for a long walk and spent an hour perfecting her French and Spanish with the nuns who'd taught her as a child. She continued the study of exploration to which her father once had set her; now she was reading Von Humboldt and, in the original Spanish, both Fr. Junípero Serra's *Report to the Prefect on the Founding of California in 1769,* and the account of the old conquistador, Bernal Díaz, of the subjugation of Montezuma two hundred years earlier. History. The explorers and the kings. What had it meant for *their* women, waiting, wondering through the night hours? Oh, where *are* you, Charles?

"If he doesn't come for dinner," she said aloud, "we'll put a lamp in the library window. Better set the small table there, too." She glanced at Sally's face. "Don't look at me that way," she said sharply. "I *know* he's on his way. He wrote from Fort Hall in September and said he'd be at Vancouver in November. That's three months ago. He was coming back by the southern route, so winter wouldn't stop him. And three months is enough time—I have a feeling he's near, or that he—"

Three months. Tornadoes, flash floods, treacherous rock faces. Fever, pneumonia, Indians appearing like ghosts and vanishing again, waiting for the blinding rain, the windstorm, the nodding sentry . . .

Lily started to cry. The child had been playing with a rag doll. Now she ran into the dining room, holding up her arms. She wore black patent slippers that buttoned on her ankles; Jessie noticed that they were getting scuffed. She took the child in her arms. Lily was changing every day, leaps of amazing change that would never be repeated—and Charles was missing them all. He had missed her first step; soon he would miss her first word. She wondered if he really cared. He would say he did, of course, but did he really? Gone nine months; if he cared, would he have abandoned them—

She stopped, holding her breath, cold with shock. What an awful, stupid thought. He was out there somewhere in winter, cold, hungry, perhaps in danger—

"Oh, I *miss* him so," she whispered, and when Lily gravely patted her cheek, she wanted to cry.

"Miz Jessie," Sally said, "never mind telling me to hush 'cause I'm gonna say it anyway. It ain't good for you to be brooding like this. We all think about Cap'n Frémont, you naturally most of all, but to get to thinking he's coming any minute, that's—"

"It's all right, Sally," she said with a wan smile, stroking Lily's back. "I don't know when he's coming. But I know he will come—he *must* come. So we've *got* to set his place—don't you see?"

They were ready long before first light. They ate the last of the mule-meat stew and loaded their horses. They had left the Columbia with well over a hundred horses and mules; barely half had come this far; how many would reach California? No one spoke; the silence grew oppressive. Louie was standing near him; when he threw back his head to stare at the cliffs, Frémont thought he looked middle-aged. A red glow appeared in the east, and the peaks overhead caught an answering glow.

"God damn that fucking Indian!" Menard said abruptly.

The old chief's words, his tongue unknown but his meaning so clear, seemed to ring aloud. Snow on snow, rock on rock, ice—and now they were going up.

"We're going to prove that old bastard a liar," Frémont said in an even voice. "The sky's clear. Yonder's the pass in plain view. We'll be at the top by nightfall—and from there on, everything is downhill."

They were at the foot of an entering ridge that rose like a buttress at a right angle to the mountain's main chain and ran up to the pass. Once he'd got work on the road well started, Frémont and Carson had climbed the mountain that was rounded like a bear's back so they could look down on the route to the pass. It was steep and rough, but Frémont was sure it was possible. A gully with small trees partway up would make a camping place if necessary. But they wouldn't need to camp—they would make the summit in a day. Immediately beyond it he had seen a grove of gnarled whitebark pines and grass blown free of snow. They'd be all right when they reached the summit.

Moving light fell down the mountain. Chilblains throbbed in his heels and he flexed his right hand in the improvised mittens, trying to ease the ache in his knuckles.

"Let's go," he said.

He led the way, stamping great switchbacks up the broad foot of the ridge. It was getting hard to breathe. Relatively shallow because of the slope, the snow compacted readily. When they struck ice he swung his pickax with easy new skill. An hour later, with red sun at his back and the peaks above the color of ripe peaches, he could look across the valley to the place where Mélo had deserted them. He heard a clatter behind him, a curse, a startled neigh. As he turned, he had a sudden vivid image of men and horses winding black against peach-colored snow. Then the horse, hooves clattering, breath steaming, began to slide down the mountain.

"Heads up!" Carson shouted.

On the switchbacks below, men scrambled out of the way. The horse slid as if sitting, forelegs plowing snow, mane flying, looking incredulous and outraged. A murderous rock was ahead, but then the ground shifted and the horse slid off into a hollow and stopped in deep snow. Zindel scrambled up and seized its lead rope.

"He's all right," Zindel called. Frémont saw the horse snap at Zindel, who leaped backward. "Madder'n hell, though." But no one laughed.

Ahead the ridge narrowed suddenly to a razorback of broken rock which the wind had scoured free of snow. The climb, and the sound of voices calling, had loosened Frémont and he felt better. He had the men moving now; momentum itself was a tonic. He could see the pass, far above and to the left, a cut in the mountain wall. He cast a quick look at the sparkling sky. Sierra weather rode western winds in from the Pacific. It might be snowing just beyond the pass and they wouldn't know it until the clouds bulged over the crest and the snow was upon them. But what the hell, as long as the sky was clear—unconsciously his eye strayed again to the narrow cleft where the first clouds would appear. If they did.

At the razorback he took off his snowshoes and went nimbly over the rocks. The razorback extended to a bluff that rose in a facing cliff. The whole ridge struck him now as a great bridge that vaulted to the heights. It had eroded on both sides to form deep hollows that were choked with snow.

These hollows pressed hard against the mountain proper, whose walls formed tall cliffs. The ridge towered between them. The ridge's right side was impassable, a cliff that ran nearly to the crest, where it turned and joined the wall of the mountain itself. On the left, which opened to the pass, lay the rough and broken ground he had studied from the round mountain.

The bluff before him turned back toward the mountain on the left. Frémont led the way under its wall to a steep slope covered with red heather that rose sharply behind it. Stout whitebark pines guarded the top; beyond them the route on up the ridge looked clear. The horses could come up one at a time, supported on long ropes windlassed around the trees. He brought up the first, a big chestnut that blew anxiously when it saw the slope. The horse lunged and scrambled, dirt flying from under its hooves; when it stopped with its sides heaving, the rope attached to the packsaddle held it until it was ready to start again.

Afterward, breathing hard, he watched the next horse maneuvered up. The process took longer than he liked. The sun was already high. They wouldn't make the pass by nightfall. They would have to camp in the little wooded gully after all. He adjusted his black silk scarf over his eyes to ease the snow glare. A steady current of cold air moved down the mountain and he turned his back to it. A hard west wind would be blowing through the pass—he wondered if it was already sweeping snow clouds up the western slope. Ice crystals blew off the mountain's flanks, sparkling as they fell.

He left Carson and Fitzpatrick to bring the horses up and set out with Freniere. Ingalls and Godey followed, each leading three horses. The ridge ran smoothly upward, even but narrow. They were on the lip of the cliff that fell to the right; on the left a slope ranged from steep to impassable. There were ice patches here and there but little snow. In sheltered places where the sun warmed the rock, water filmed the ice. They avoided the water; wet moccasins meant frozen feet.

The wind grew stronger. Frémont wrapped his scarf tight around his face. His hat brim fluttered. Louie walked with his head down. Ingalls' horses were balking, trying to turn away from the wind. A sudden gust staggered Frémont; he lurched into Louie, bumping him toward the edge.

"Jesus, Charlie!" Freniere gasped, dropping to his knees.

Frémont heard Ingalls cursing the horses. The wind gusted, swirling and whipping, and kicked loose snow up the left slope into their faces. The wind died, reappeared, blew straight across the ridge from the left. The cold stung Frémont's eyes. They'd be suffering from frostbite soon if this kept up. He heard a clatter and turned quickly. One of Ingalls' horses, a speckled gray, was down on the ice. Ingalls dropped the other lead ropes and tugged at the gray, shouting for it to get up. Frémont could hear panic in his voice. The horse struggled for footing, its hooves rattling on rock. Its right hind leg went over the edge and it screamed, lunging forward, the heavy pack dragging it back.

"Git up!" Ingalls shrieked. He turned the rope around his wrist and pulled, trying to lift the animal, sliding down himself.

Frémont caught Ingalls by his collar, jerked him back. "Let him go!" he shouted. "Let go the rope!"

Ingalls dropped the rope as if it burned him and sprawled back against Frémont. The gray's other hind leg went off. It clung to the rock with its forelegs. It had a terrible look in its eyes. Then it screamed again and slid over the edge. Frémont dropped to his knees and peered over. He saw the horse tumbling below. It screamed once more, a high, humanlike sound that broke off in mid-cry. Frémont watched the tumbling body until it disappeared.

Shaken, he looked at Ingalls, who was on his knees and very pale. "Much obliged, Cap'n," the man said over the wind's noise.

Gusts whipped the horses' manes and tails. The wind seemed stronger. A shadow flitted past. He glanced up, saw a small, ragged cloud and looked quickly at the pass. A bank of heavy clouds was advancing rapidly.

Now it wouldn't be a matter of stopping short; now it would be all they could do to reach the gully and its lifesaving firewood. He told Freniere and Ingalls to take the remaining horses on to a narrow cleft he'd spotted in the rock. It was a bit before the gully and was sheltered, with a little grass. The horses below would have to climb up one by one in relays. He hurried down the mountain to explain his plan.

"Figured as much," Fitzpatrick said. "Damned wind's slowed us too. You, Rasmussen!" He gestured with his bad hand and the slender carpenter leaped up. "You take that bay there and start on up—Cap'n says the wind's a bitch, so watch yourself. Come back for another soon as you git him there. Move!"

The main cloud bank swept overhead and hid the sun. Something like blown sand stung Frémont's face. It was sleet—still very light, but sleet. He turned to Carson.

"Let's go up and set camp—we'll need it soon."

They reached a place where the ridge narrowed abruptly and saw that Rasmussen had stopped. He was on his knees, and the bay was pulling back, trying to turn tail to the wind.

"Kid's in trouble," Carson said. They slipped past the fractious horse. "Hyah!" Kit said sharply, seizing its halter. "Settle down, now."

Rasmussen's face was pale. "It's the wind, Cap'n! My God. I never *saw* wind like this . . ."

"Just take it slowly."

"Horse keeps fighting me. Pulling me off balance . . ." he glanced to the cliff edge and looked away. "I ain't no good on heights, Cap'n." His mouth quivered. "Don't know if I can cut it."

Being alone was what bothered Rasmussen. Frémont considered walking him up. Sleet whipped his face. It was getting late. Then he saw Zindel struggling up with two horses.

"Damnit!" he shouted. "Kit—go down and turn Zindel back. One horse to a man."

He seized the front of Rasmussen's coat and jerked him to his feet. "The hell you can't cut it," he said in a hard voice. "You get your ass up that slope or I'll kick it up there! You understand?"

Rasmussen nodded once, anger driving fear from his face.

The wind seemed much colder, its gusts stronger. Ahead he saw that the rise along the lip of the cliff ran into an even steeper upthrust no horse could climb. But there was a way around it to the left, and beyond a broad, open slope that led to the pass in the distance. Just around the sheer upthrust they found the sheltered cleft; it was quiet inside though the wind buffeted loudly. The horses weren't feeding; they needed water. Hell, they all needed water: his own mouth was dry. Dehydration. You could eat snow, but it burned the inside of your mouth and contained so little water that it only made your thirst worse. *They had to have a fire . . .*

The gully lay a half-mile farther on. Frémont and Carson worked around the edge of the mountain, passing among great boulders that had tumbled down from above.

"Should be right in here," Frémont said.

They came to a field of unbroken snow, a sixty-foot swale that dipped slightly. Beyond they could see the open slope that bore around the mountain to the pass. There was no sign of a gully.

"For God's sake!" Frémont cried. "Where *is* it?"

"*This* is it," Carson said "Snowstorm that filled up our road below done filled up our campsite, too."

Frémont stepped forward and sank into the snow—soft, new, too deep for horses. He stared at it, aghast. They would have to make their night in the cleft shelter.

"Dry camp," he said. No wood for fires, no food, no water.

"Worse than that, maybe," Carson said slowly. "This snow is built up pretty good—we go to beating down a road up here and the whole shebang may come down. Avalanche."

It was after dark before the last horse came in. The sleet was heavy as glass, but snow hadn't followed. They rigged a tarpaulin windbreak for the horses. Now and then hail struck the stone walls above them and rattled down. Frémont walked about, beating feeling into his hands and feet. The racketing wind made him think of the old Indian's voice—full of portent. That gray had gone over just as the old bastard had predicted. Avalanche up ahead, ready to slide. Rock on rock, snow on snow. The men were worn ragged, panting painfully in the thin air, shriveling up with dryness, thirst, their faces streaked with frostbite. Several had tried to eat snow despite Carson's warning. He remembered the old Washoe's contempt, his assurance. But hold on, by God—they were well up the mountain and that grove of pines was just beyond the pass. Firewood, shelter, grass—certainly this wind had scoured away the snow. It's an ill wind—the foolish phrase ran in his mind and he stopped himself. His head ached savagely.

A figure rose and lurched toward the entrance. It was Sammy Claybank, the Kentucky farm boy, their butcher.

"Where're you going, Sammy?"

"Just down the road."

Frémont seized his arm. "Don't you know where you are?"

Claybank jerked himself free. " 'Course I do. What's the matter with you, Cap'n—we're climbing this here mountain. But the thing is, my paw's barn is just a half-mile or so down the road—it's *warm* in that barn, Cap'n." In the pale light Frémont saw that he was weeping. "I screwed little Mary Morris in that barn, but that was long ago. Long ago." His voice trailed off and he let himself be turned around.

They got to talking after that. Frémont listened, his head hurting. They talked about spring on a Missouri farm, a swimming hole where the willows touched the water, about how when you cut a certain cactus water spurts out as if from a spigot, about digging a hole in a desert draw and getting an inch of water and knowing you would live another day. Someone talked about eating salt-cured ham and drinking water by the bucketful.

"You boys ain't suffering, are you?" Fitzpatrick asked. "Why, this ain't nothing." And as the wind whipped at his voice he was off on a string of yarns—the taste a dead Indian's carcass gave a certain spring, the time he *crawled* across eighty miles of desert after a bullet had smashed his leg, how the water was so scant down on the Cimarron Cut-Off that the oxen melted away to shadows, just ten sets of horns still plugging along, bound down to old Santa Fe . . .

"This bullshit gets any deeper," Carson said over the wind, "likely we'll all be drownded."

"You bastards think this is funny?" Menard cried suddenly. "This ain't funny. We're stuck on this mountain, iced in like flies on fucking flypaper and you're telling jokes—shit! You're crazy!"

Ingalls' thin voice sounded as if he had just been awakened. "Avalanche ahead—them goddamn cliffs behind—shit, we may never get outta this fix."

"Damn right," someone said, and several voices agreed.

"Let's get out of here."

"Away from this *wind*!"

"Cut out that talk!" Frémont told them sharply. "You'd never make it back down to the Truckee, anyway—it's ten times farther than we've got to go. We've got to get *through the pass*—and we will tomorrow! Now shut up and save your energy."

Carson said in brutal disgust: "You pissants should've stuck close to your mamas' skirts. Wait'll you've gone a week without food. Wait'll there are fifty Blackfoot skulking around outside knowing you gotta come out. Wait'll you're trying to ride home with an arrow up your ass and you got a hundred miles to go. That gray what Ingalls lost off the cliff—run down and ask him how *he's* doing tonight. Then tell me how you're hurting."

"You tell 'em, Kit," Proue said. His words rang loud as a shot and they realized that the wind had died. The silence was eerie.

"God damn," Louie said in mock awe, "when Kit gets pissed, even the wind stops to listen."

A wave of laughter burst over them; they were laughing like fools, wheezing and rocking. The wind had stopped.

And finally, finally dawn came.

The snow packed in the gully would never be harder than in the morning cold. Frémont stood on the edge, looking at that smooth, treacherous surface. It was only sixty feet across. He shivered, the cold seeping into his body.

"Wait for me," he said to the others.

He tied on snowshoes, looped a rope around his waist, gave the coil to Freniere to pay out, and stepped gingerly into the deep snow. Slowly, easily, he started across, tamping down lightly with each step, waiting for the shift under his feet, the sliding that would mean avalanche. Ahead was a rocky projection—the gully's far side. He reached the halfway point—the most dangerous place of all; moving slowly, steadily, tamping, smoothing, afraid to stop now, afraid to speak. He reached the rock, climbed onto solid ground, and looked back. He had left a smooth path in the snow a foot and a half wide, nearly a foot deep, and nothing had slipped. The sky was lightening and the clouds had a thin look; they were moving slowly, flowing east. He looked off to the left at the pass. The dawn sky there seemed white; perhaps it was clear sky. If the sun came out, the softening snow in this steep gully would never hold their passage.

He started back, easy steps, widening the path, snowshoes loud in the silence. Carson awaited him with two mauls. He took one and turned back to his work, tamping gently, steadily, Carson behind him. When they reached the other side, they worked their way back. Four men took up the mauls and he put the others to work gathering stone; he told them to look for wide, flat rocks. The men talked in whispers; the human voice can have odd effects on loose snow. When the surface was as hard as they could make it they set the stones in place to serve as paving. Blue sky was showing in the west, the clouds drifting on. Gently, gently they started the horses across, one man to an animal, talking to it, soothing it down, and the last horse had completed the passage when the clouds slid away and the sun fell on them, warm against their faces.

Blue sky, the pass in sight, the danger slipped—the men brightened in release from the hazardous crossing. Frémont studied the pass. It was some two miles away and a thousand feet higher, but the route to it seemed clear. They would cross a long, curving slope where the snow looked shallow enough for horses to walk.

"We'll make camp before noon, boys," he said jubilantly.

He put Tessier in the lead with three animals carrying meat and camp equipment; he wanted no delays when they reached the grove. But as Tessier started a big black gelding, Frémont saw how tightly the dry camp had drawn men and horses. The snow's icy crust supported the black's weight for several steps; then the horse broke through with a jolt. It took two or three more steps, regained its confidence and broke through again. It was off balance and it went down on one knee and scrambled up, blowing in fear. The sharp edge of the crust had cut its leg and Frémont saw blood flecks on the snow. Its ears went back and it snapped at Tessier.

"Hyah!" Tessier cried, "you son of a bitch!" His face was red and he cracked the lead rope hard across the horse's nose. The horse whinnied, backed into the mule behind it and instantly kicked the mule in the chest.

The mule reared, trumpeting in fury, hooves slashing the air, and Freniere jumped to its lead rope and dragged it away.

They would have to make a path. It would slow them, but it would be nothing like the pain of tamping deep snow. Frémont took the lead again, breaking the crust with a pickax. Louie and Carson were behind him, widening the path and stamping it down, and Godey and Proue followed with mauls. The shallow snow compressed against the ground and they made good time. The sun felt warm on Frémont's back. After a while he looked around and saw their trail curving around the mountain's flank.

A ledge leading under the rocky promontory was covered with thick green ice from a spring that seeped in better weather. Carson roped himself and began cutting a level path. Frémont was watching the ice chips fly when he felt the first breath of wind, treacherous as a whisper he didn't want to believe. Involuntarily he shook his head, but the wind strengthened and became a cold current flowing down the mountain. Oh no. Not now. The sun's warmth disappeared. The sky was clear, but ice crystals blew out of the pass in a sparkling cloud that showered down to the hollow below.

When the path along the ledge was finished, Frémont signaled to Fitzpatrick to start the horses. On the far side of the promontory the wind struck him so hard it staggered him. It was stronger than it had been the day before. Here it blew unimpeded. The whole equation had changed—this violent wind made the cold itself a greater danger than the cliffs of the day before. The others were waiting for him, backs to the wind, shirts or strips of blanket wrapped around their faces. He fitted his own scarf, his head pulled down so hard that an ache started in his shoulders, and put a double thickness of black silk over his eyes, which already had a grainy feeling from the glare. He had purchased the black silk in St. Louis for all the men to use against the prairie's glare in high summer; now it was saving them in the Sierra's snow.

No one spoke and at last Frémont gestured with his head toward the pass. Louie led off, each stroke of his ax loosing ice crystals that clattered far down the steepening slope. Frémont brought up the rear with a maul, working with his head down, lifting and dropping. His hands were cracked, the skin broken; they ached and burned. His breath was short with rage and chagrin. *This goddamned pitiless wind!* The sky had promised him everything, he had felt free as summer, it had seduced him like an innocent, like a child, had offered him the prize—and then taken it away with a laugh. Choking, he stopped, leaning on the maul handle; he looked around, the peak on the right, the bear-back mountain round and immense on his left, the vast valley behind him, he and all his men flyspecks on the immensity of the mountain, supplicants pretending to authority, mocked by a sky so innocently blue. He felt they'd worked an hour, but the pass seemed no closer. Had he miscalculated the distance? He turned back to the promontory, and saw that they had come barely a hundred yards—and realized he'd mistaken minutes for an hour. Careful, careful: despair, self-pity are the worst sins. Because they eat away at the will. He crept along, concentrating on his work.

The wind started tears that froze at the corners of his eyes. The air was so thin there was nothing to breathe; his heart pounded crazily. His breath condensed in the scarf and froze; he crushed the cloth with his hand and ice flakes fell down his neck. His hands were on fire. Then the burning disappeared and he found that he had trouble holding the maul. For a while he worked one-handed and put the other in the pocket of his capote. The pain came back and he switched hands. Something seemed wrong but he couldn't tell what. Lift, drop, lift, drop. He studied the pass ahead. They were going *down!* Louie, cutting blindly, had turned downhill. Looking back, Frémont saw a definite swerve in their path. He shouted. The wind blew the words away. Louie had already moved down onto steeper ground. Frémont dropped the maul and ran forward. His snowshoes tangled and he fell face down in the snow. Immediately he was conscious of a curious warmth. No! *Get up.* Now! He thrust himself up. His face was freezing, he knew. There was no feeling in his right cheek. He lurched forward, pushing Proue out of the way. Proue tumbled sideways in the snow and shouted something that the wind whipped away. He had to reach Louie—get his attention.

When he seized the pickax, Freniere fell to his hands and knees.

Frémont ignored him. He took a new bearing on the pass and swung the ax. It slipped in his hand and the flat struck his shin. Cold intensified the violent pain, but it was his carelessness that alarmed him. Dangerous. Man wouldn't live an hour up here with his blood leaking into the snow. Less. Calm, now. No panic! He licked his cracked lips. His tongue was dry. They had been thirty hours without water. He fell again, lifted himself on his ax, staggered. His feet felt wooden; anxiously he checked his mocassins, but they were still dry. He felt weak as a rag, which struck him as very surprising. He was always strong, always had been. . . . This damned mountain.

They could not stay here. Move on. Hurry. He was concentrating on hurrying when he decided that his ears were freezing. It was the first time he had thought of his ears. He wondered if he should slap them. He saw them shattering at the blow, falling in bits and pieces. He moved along, considering this image slyly, remotely. He could *see* himself crouching on the ice field. This damnable headache; the sun seemed to get much brighter. The wind roared so loudly he could hardly hear it and he decided to ignore it. It would have to take care of itself; his job was to get them into the pass and by God, *he would not fail*! The resolution was overwhelming—and instantly forgotten. The old bastard had told them—the wind would blow them off the mountain. Tried to blow Ingalls off Freeze them, grind them, abrade their flesh, bones bright in winter wind—he yawned. The act amazed him, then its implication frightened him.

He turned to check the others and saw them strung out two hundred feet behind him, plodding blindly along his cut. He looked at the pass for range instead of bearing and saw that it was quite close. But it looked odd and he realized that it was unexpectedly high. Weren't they coming up to it? He studied it, saw that just ahead the ground rose in a steep slope. The sun was overhead and the slope glittered. It was ice and they would have to cut their way up. As he moved closer the wind seemed to slacken; they were coming into the lee of the slope. He called a rest at its foot and they crouched there, backs to the wind, cold sun pouring over them. No one spoke. Can't stay too long. He waited, felt a delicious, treacherous lassitude and thrust himself up violently.

"Come on," he shouted. "Let's get the hell up there and get a fire going."

Still, the short rest had helped. Carson began chopping switchbacks up the ice slope. Frémont followed until he could look back over the trail. The glare was a white haze. Orange, yellow, scarlet streaks flashed deep in his eyes despite three layers of black silk. His eyes kept shutting against his will and he forced them open, straining to see. Half the horses were through the promontory; they were badly strung out and two groups seemed to have stopped. Something wrong. Then he saw three dark specks well off the trail on the downslope side. He locked his hands in a ball before his eyes and peered through his fingers. Yes, they were horses, motionless, tails to the wind, far off the trail. There was no sign of a man near them. Something really wrong.

He was shuffling down the trail at a trot, his snowshoes clattering, filled with foreboding. If horses were free, he was losing men back there. He stumbled and fell, taking a hard jolt, and got up without feeling a thing. He came to Tessier, whose three horses laden with mule meat and cooking gear were moving steadily in single file. Tessier raised a hand in weary greeting.

Well beyond, he saw the horses stopped on the trail. The wind seemed to blow him along; it matched his mood. By God, they hadn't come this far just to break down! He fell again, got up. A man was sitting on his heels with his head down, still holding the horses, which had half-turned from the wind. It was Menard. Frémont slapped him on the shoulder and he fell over. He lay on his side in the snow, not even trying to get up.

"What the hell you doing, Menard?"

Menard shaded his eyes, peering up at Frémont through black silk as if wondering who he was. "Gotta rest minute, Cap'n."

"Don't be a fool—come on, move!"

"Gonna rest," Menard said stubbornly. "I can't go on no more just at this time."

"God damn you, Menard," he roared. "You get up or I'll quirt you bloody!"

"Now listen," Menard said.

Frémont snatched the lead horse's rope from Menard's hand and slashed it across his face.

'Get up, God damn you," he said, and hit him twice more, enjoying it. "Get—on—your—*feet*!"

Menard rolled onto his knees, grunting with rage. He stood, tall and skinny, rocking unsteadily. Before he could speak, Frémont thrust the rope into his hand.

"Now move, you ugly, gutless son of a bitch," he said, "and don't stop till you're *up* that hill."

He felt capable of beating Menard to death with his fists on the spot; he could hardly breathe and he found the sensation alarming but he knew it was real. Then Menard jerked the lead rope and went lurching up the trail.

Preuss had stopped his horses just behind Menard's animals. His back was turned and he had his sketchbook out, his chapped fingers clamped around its fluttering pages. Frémont saw that there was nothing there but disconnected scratches.

"Grüss Gott, Cap'n," Preuss called pleasantly. He added something that the wind snatched away, and Frémont leaned closer to hear. "Think we should do a detail map of the pass itself. *In allen Einzelheiten.* Don't you think?"

With a start, Frémont realized he had forgotten the map.

"This sketch will get us oriented," Preuss shouted. "We'll need bearings from the pass proper, and so on." A tremor of cold shook him so violently he dropped his pencil. He stooped to retrieve it and fell headlong. Frémont caught him under the arms and helped him up. Preuss stood rocking in the wind, cursing softly in German; Frémont knew he was weeping behind the black silk wrapped over his glasses.

"You'll freeze if you don't move on," he said. "Now get going!" He stood so that he blocked the wind, gripped the little man by the shoulders. "But you're right. The map is important—*vielen Dank, Karlchen.*"

Frémont put his ear close to Preuss' lips and heard him say, "I would die up here if I didn't have the map, you know."

"You're not going to die!" Frémont shouted.

"No—but only because I have the map . . ."

The three horses off the trail were still standing just as he had seen them from above. When he was near he saw a man lying in a depression the size of his body, his face resting on both hands. It was Rasmussen. Frémont knelt beside him, turned him over, and saw that he was asleep, his eye cover pushed up. Frémont shook him insistently.

Rasmussen's eyes opened. His cheeks were streaked white with frostbite. He blinked and then, as if remembering where he was, looked alarmed.

"Horses got away from me, Cap'n," he said. He mumbled something more.

"Speak up, Billy!" Frémont said harshly. "Talk louder!"

"That old black stumbled and cut hisself, got spooked. Then they was all out in the snow—fussing and acting up. Kept getting away from me. Wore me out, running in snow . . ." His voice trailed away and Frémont shook him again."Then I fell down. Out of the wind it was warm. You know? So I rested a minute. Just resting." He looked furtively away from Frémont.

"You were asleep," Frémont shouted. "You'd have died here in an hour! Don't you know that?"

"Oh no, sir—"

"Come on, Billy—I'll help you get the horses together."

Rasmussen nodded but he didn't move. "Wore out, Cap'n," he muttered. "You think—" he paused, blinking. "Everything—anything can be done. That ain't true, Cap'n. Lots of folks can't—"

Frémont gripped the boy's shoulders hard. "That's right," he shouted. "Lots of folks stay home and never do a damn thing! But you're not like that, Billy. You're an explorer, a pathmaker—you're riding with Frémont! That *means* you can do it! You hear me?"

He shook him still again. "Come on, now!" he roared. He hauled Rasmussen up, half lifting him. The effort made great black spots appear before his eyes. They leaned against each other, gasping. One of the horses was down and couldn't get up. Frémont loosened its girth and the packsaddle fell to the ice. He kicked its ribs; reluctantly the horse stood. The two men tried to lift the heavy packsaddle. Frémont could see the strain on Rasmussen's face.

"Come on, Billy," he called sharply. "Got to do it. Now—*heave!*" The saddle went up and both men fell against the horse. When Frémont's vision cleared again he tightened the cinch and led the horses to the trail.

"Now look," he said. "Right up the trail and don't stop for anything! You'll be fine now. We're going through . . ." He clapped Rasmussen's shoulder.

The last horses were coming through the promontory as he approached. He and Fitzpatrick brought up the rear, leaning against the wind on a path now beaten solid. Carson had every horse in the pass when they started up the slope. At the crest Frémont paused alone to look back. He cupped his hands before his eyes, squinting through his fingers.

Sweet Christ, they'd done it! They had won! He could see their trail curving down to the gully and beyond that the cliff they had followed. He could see the razorback they had climbed, the great valley, the secondary ridge where Mélo had deserted them and the old warrior had consigned them to death. There was no sign of a living thing. Brilliantly etched in the sun, the snowfield panorama was magnificent and implacable and totally unforgiving; any rational man would say that it was quite impossible for men and horses and baggage.

They were going to make it. If every horse dropped in its tracks and they wound up barefoot and groping on their hands and knees, they were going through. Nothing was going to stop them. Nothing! He knew it, absolutely. He glared hard at the scene, as if he wanted to fix it forever, proof against the future; then he turned and went into the pass.

PART THREE

SACRAMENTO

THE STALLION did a quick little sidling dance and then reared, its hooves flashing in the strong, flat sunlight as if it heard band music; and the men lounging at the stable door laughed and nodded at one another.

"Hoo-eee!" Carson cried, and swept his new Mexican sombrero off his head. "Sixteen hands if he's an inch. Now *that* is one piece of prime horseflesh!"

"A perfectly gorgeous animal," Frémont said. "Magnificent."

John Sutter clapped his hands with pleasure. "He's yours, sir," he proclaimed. Frémont gazed at him in astonishment. "That's my wish, Lieutenant. Humor me! It's a long ride back to Missouri, and an intrepid commander like you should ride a proper mount." His shrewd gray-blue eyes were snapping. "We'll prepare vouchers against the United States Government for the stock and supplies we're furnishing your party—but *not* for this horse. Let him be a token of New Helvetia's delight in your unexpected visit."

The stallion shook its great head, its mane rippling richly in the breeze, and then looked straight at Frémont, its nostrils flaring.

"Knows his new master," Louie said. "See him?"

"I'm—I'm overwhelmed," Frémont said to Sutter. "I'm in your debt, sir."

"Nonsense!" Sutter, rotund, authoritative, called out in Spanish, and the Mexican boy led the big stallion up to Frémont. "Don't mention it. No more than a gesture of friendship between us."

"What you going to call him, Cap'n?" Kit asked.

Frémont patted the hard, quivering shoulder, passed his hand expertly over the great barrel of the ribs. "Sacramento," he said suddenly to Sutter. "In honor of your lush, hospitable valley—which has quite literally saved our lives!" Carson was staring at him quizzically, and with a grin he realized he himself sounded a good deal like Sutter: the man's grandiloquence was catching.

Still, it was true. They had spent two more weeks working their way down those terrible ridges from the pass, contending with more ice and slides and treacherous snowfields. By then men were falling more often, and taking even longer to get up again; Proue broke his wrist, and old Fitzpatrick's feet, badly frostbitten, had given out; they'd put him on a horse, and when that was impossible, had to carry him bodily, four of them, groaning and slipping, with Broken Hand angrily protesting every inch of the way. Billy Rasmussen collapsed completely, and Ingalls had gone right out of his head—they'd finally had to tie him up and lead him like a pack animal, moaning and drooling at the mouth, his eyes rolling.

By then most of the animals were dead, and they were down to a day's supply of mule meat. But he'd brought them through, as he'd known all along he would, without the loss of a man. And when they passed out of the snow into a land of running water and high grass and fields in violent orange bloom, it was truly like finding the gate to the Garden of Eden. Freniere killed a deer and some quail; the surviving horses tore at the bright grass in a frenzy of delight. The mountain brook that had led them down into this magical, verdant land had swelled into a stream hurrying past tilled fields and a cabin with windows of real glass, and after that a river that meandered gently through rich, grassy banks—and there all at once was Sutter's Fort, with its eighteen-foot walls of whitewashed adobe, its stables and storerooms tucked snugly against the inner walls, guns in corner bastions sweeping the surrounding country; Sutter's flag swirled against a brilliant sky, and guards waved to them from the gate.

And California! The fields ablaze with poppies and broom and lupine, bees buzzing, fat cattle resting contentedly under the great live oaks, whose leaves were as shiny and green as holly. What a lucky, opulent land! After the salt-caked moonscape of the Great Basin, the flint harshness of the Sierra, this newfound land *was* paradise . . .

Frémont had liked Sutter at once; he was about forty, with a long, rather pointed nose and quick, darting eyes. There was something magnetically attractive about him and his gallant European manner. He was a man of great style, of gestures that were both handsome and practical. This magnificent horse—Frémont was aware of the motives implicit in such a gift to the head of a U.S. Army-sponsored expedition, an officer who had the ear of Senator T. H. Benton; Sutter might well expect the United States to control California one fine day. He was quick-witted and a man of schemes—how else could he have assembled an empire on credit in less than five years?—but that the stallion was bread upon the waters made it no less handsome.

Sutter's duchy ran for miles and miles—he had shown it all to Frémont with an almost boyish pride. He had huge fields under cultivation and herds of horses and cattle in his pastures. His laborers were California Indians whom the missions had trained, and he had nearly twenty skilled white men working iron, wood and leather in basic manufactories he'd established in the fort. He had plans for a sawmill and a gristmill and even intended to establish a woolen industry.

Still, the fort reflected its owner. Frémont was soldier enough to know that its antique guns were of little account and that it would hardly withstand real attack. But then, no attack was in prospect—or at least none seemed to be. A big fort fitted Sutter's image of the boundless future, which he discussed with an appealing grandiosity. Perhaps his army was his measure—fifty young Indians wearing blue trousers, white shirts and red kerchiefs, whom he drilled regularly in the courtyard. They mounted guard, shouted "All's well," on the hour and fired an evening gun, but Frémont thought that it was lucky for them there was no one to fight.

The odor of roasting meat drifted on a breeze. He felt a sudden rush of hunger. He and the men were slowly filling out—Louie had lost that look of sudden aging—but they were always hungry. The tantalizing odor rose from a *barbacoa* pit where an old Indian was roasting a fat steer and a hog, dressing the meat with a pepper sauce as he turned it. A grand celebration was in preparation: Sutter had invited the foreign settlers in the area to a feast for Frémont and his party.

There were about four hundred foreigners in all of California, Sutter had told him, mostly Americans. They had drifted in over the years from God knew where—trappers, wanderers, seamen who had jumped ship. The Mexican government no longer jailed such visitors. Now it tolerated them—if not gladly. A few lived in the coastal settlements, but most had taken up land, usually as squatters. Perhaps fifty had located on the Sacramento. They counted on Sutter for supplies, and he in turn hired them when he needed their skills.

Now a man was tuning a fiddle and Indian workers were dragging long tables into the courtyard and setting out pitchers of wine and flagons of brandy. Sutter was inordinately proud of his own distillery; its spirits, along with what furs his men could find after the Hudson's Bay sweeps, hides and tallow, a little wheat, were the sources of his empire's income. Frémont had taken a polite sip. The brandy was rough but pleasing; from the tiny broken veins radiating across Sutter's face, he thought that his host found it a good deal more than that.

"Don Carlos Gutierrez sent word that he's riding over today," Sutter was saying; Frémont could hear a certain tension in his voice.

"He's a friend?"

"Friendly, yes." Sutter sighed. Obviously Don Carlos Gutierrez Medina, the nearest big California landholder, was a trial to him. Gutierrez' ranch, twenty miles away, had been the most distant from the coastal settlements until Sutter established his fort. At first Gutierrez had been very helpful—he had provided Sutter's foundation herd and many supplies—but lately he had been talking about payment.

"A small-minded man, really. He can't see there are grand things to be done here. Good God, there'll be plenty of time to settle debts when I'm fully established. Do they think a man can create a—a *kingdom* overnight, and still maintain a Bank of England credit rating?"

His face reddened and he shook his head. "He's just a back-country rancher, that's all—though he does have the governor's ear and a bit of influence." He gave Frémont a quick sidelong glance. "He'll be very surprised to see you."

"My position is clear. We entered California in legitimate distress." Frémont smiled. "I think our condition on arrival established that."

"Oh, quite, quite. I wish he'd chosen another day, that's all. He and the settlers don't get on well. He finds them rough and uncouth, and getting far too strong—suspects they'd like to seize the country. Some of them would, too, though Don Carlos overestimates their strength. On the other hand, *they* know very well he'd like to see them ejected from California. He'd get rid of all foreigners if he could. So would a lot of Californians, you understand."

Sutter smoothed his big mustache with his fingertips; the clear eyes belied his veined face. "That doesn't apply to me, of course," he added with characteristic loftiness. "I'm a unique figure. Independent. The settlers turn to me, the Californians admire me." He had become a citizen of California and hence of Mexico, and the governor was so taken with him that he'd been appointed magistrate on the Sacramento with full authority to hold court, punish transgressions. Frémont wondered if this distinction didn't match the pretensions of Sutter's army, but still, it was not unimpressive. Few settlers had bothered to become Mexican citizens; and now that the government was frowning on them, they felt vulnerable.

"Anyway, there aren't enough troops in California to trouble me," Sutter declared pugnaciously. "Let 'em try—and I'll give 'em a charge of grape and send 'em back to Monterey with their tails tucked!" Then he deflated as rapidly. "But you can see it's awkward. I'd never have invited Don Carlos and the settlers at the same time. Ah well, I'll pour enough brandy to keep them all in high spirits."

He hurried off to the kitchens. A group of riders came through the gate, some twenty settlers with a number of Indian wives who mingled with the fort's women. Frémont saw Tessier and Ingalls, who'd been visiting with the settlers for the past few days, hurrying across the courtyard toward him.

Carson was rubbing the gray's nose reflectively. "That Sutter thinks he's a regular gilded rooster, don't he?"

"I'm not so sure," Frémont answered. "he's a fancy talker, but he gets things done. Look around."

"Just the same, I'll bet what he is changes from day to day."

Tessier grabbed Frémont's hand, admired Sacramento, and then came directly to the point. "Ingalls and me, Cap'n, we'd like permission to leave the expedition here." So that was why Tessier had favored the mountain crossing. "Found me a piece of the sweetest land you ever seen."

Well, why not? he thought. They had served well—and they might be useful here in California someday.

"My two brothers and me got a farm in Missouri that's just big enough to support two. My brothers'll stake me long as I need, in return for my third."

"All right. How about you, Ingalls?"

"I aim to work on Tessier's place awhile. Ain't much for me back home. This is God's country, Cap'n. Seems like you stick a seed in the ground and next day it's a plant and the week after it's Jack's beanstalk! You know I'm partial to Texas, but the best of Texas ain't a patch on this."

Tessier led Frémont and Carson over to the settlers, proud as a schoolboy introducing his teacher. A tall fellow in greasy buckskins that clung to his legs, accentuating his height, came to meet them. He spun his foxskin cap abruptly so that the tail hung alongside his face.

"Ezekiel Merritt," he said, offering his hand, "late of Kentucky and points west. Mighty pleased to know you, Cap'n." He talked around a huge chew of tobacco; brown juice dribbled from both corners of his mouth and stained his black beard.

Carson pounced on a second man. "Big Fallon," he said, "you old Indian-humper, you! I didn't know you was in Californy."

A shambling man, solid enough to bow a horse's back, pushed off a hitching rail and shook Carson's hand. "Been out two, three years now, Kit," he said. "Come out for the beaver and found me some land and a woman—she-it, I'm going on becoming a respectable feller since you'n me drunk corn whiskey at rendezvous."

Fallon turned to Frémont. "Heard plenty about you, Cap'n," he said, winking ostentatiously at Carson, "and some of it good. How you come to be in California?"

"Flew over the mountains," Carson put in quickly.

"So I heard. No white man ever got over them mountains in winter. Truth is, takes a set of balls even to *decide* to go."

"That's a fact," Merritt said. He introduced some of the others. There was William Hargrave, a serious, sensible-looking man of about forty. Burly William Purvis, with eyes like raisins set deep in his fat face, shook hands but didn't smile. Joseph Chiles had led a party from Missouri the year before that left just ahead of Frémont. A couple of Boston men who'd jumped ship in San Francisco and several from the Bartleson party of 1841 came forward. John Bidwell, who had emerged as leader of that group, was now one of Sutter's managers. Frémont immediately felt at ease; they might have been talking at Laramie or even St. Louis.

"Mighty nice to have you here, Cap'n," Merritt said, "what with us all wondering how things are going to break."

Frémont saw Hargrave's face sharpen, and Fallon's.

"Break?" he asked cautiously.

"Seems like it can't go on like it is," Merritt said. "But it's been that way ever since I come, and I'm here six years. What I mean, nobody *runs* the place. Mexico don't pay it no mind. And the Californios don't like the Mexicans for sour apples."

"Californios or Mexicans—them bastards is all the same," Fallon said.

"Don't let a Californio hear you say that," Hargrave told him.

"Piss on 'em all," Purvis growled. His raisin eyes seemed to hide behind his cheeks. "Ain't none of 'em no good."

"When I got here," Merritt said, "the Californios had just throwed the Mexicans out. Right out on their asses. I figured we had us a full-scale revolution—but shit, nothing happened. After a while the Californios got to talking about how much money it was costing 'em to maintain the government, and year before last Mexico sent up a new governor."

"*And* his Goddamn army," Fallon added sourly.

"They're the problem, all right." Merritt nodded, the foxtail sweeping his cheek. "The governor ain't a bad sort but he brought a couple hundred soldiers, drug 'em right out of Mexican prisons, and he ain't got no money to pay 'em. They gotta rob to eat, that's the fact. Wouldn't surprise me none if the Californios up and threw them Mexes out all over again." He looked meaningfully at Frémont. "Too bad we don't have a good Missouri man to kick some asses around here. Old Tom Benton would know how to handle California. Or Colonel Kearny, hear?"

"Well, *somebody*'ll come along and take this place," Fallon said, "and what we want to watch out is that it ain't the stinking redcoats."

"Uncle Sam ain't gonna let that happen."

"That's just what the Californios are afraid of," Hargrave said sharply. "That's why they're talking about throwing *us* out."

"Bullshit," Purvis muttered. "There's more of us than they got soldiers. And we got rifles and we got knives, come to that."

Merritt said: "You wasn't here back in 'Forty when they seized Isaac Graham and forty, fifty others and sent 'em off to Mexico in irons. Scared the rest of us shitless. And it was the *Mexes,* not the Californios, who turned that around and let Graham and the others come back. Now there's talk that a new order done come up from Mexico City—from Santa Anna himself—to get rid of us."

"That's just what set Texas off, you know," Ingalls said. Frémont heard an eager note in his voice. "Back in Eighteen-and-thirty when Mexico seen how many Texas settlers there was, they said enough's enough. No more. The Texans figure next thing the Mexes would try to throw them out. And one thing led to another and then the revolution come and you know what happened—old Sam Houston whipped Santa Anna's ass."

"Sure," Fallon said, "these Californios have heard about Texas, too—that's why they want to throw us out. Now. They're scared we'll up and throw *them* out."

Purvis looked at Frémont. "When we heard you'd come over the mountains in the dead of winter, Cap'n, you being an Army officer and all, we figured maybe that was what you had in mind. Is it?"

Dangerous talk: maybe having to abandon that damned cannon had been a blessing in disguise. Frémont hardened his voice intentionally. "That's foolish conjecture, Mr. Purvis, and no truth in it."

"None, Lieutenant?"

"None at all. I warn you, I won't countenance that kind of talk."

Purvis measured him a moment, then walked away sullenly. Frémont saw Merritt studying him.

"Well," Merritt said at last, "ain't none of us got a crystal ball. Now, do we?"

The meeting—if that's what it was—broke up then, the guests drifting toward the liquor and the women.

"No wonder Big Fallon wants to settle down," Carson said. "I've never seen a place so pretty."

"I liked the tall fellow," Frémont said. He thought that Merritt presented himself as less than he was, which might make him Sutter's opposite.

"The others listen to him."

"I wouldn't want to turn my back on the one called Purvis," Louie said.

"He's a blowhard," Carson said in disgust.

"That's true. But he's mean, clear through."

Earthen plates were stacked by the *barbacoa* and an Indian was cutting slabs of juicy meat. The fiddler had been joined by a guitar and a fellow who rapped on a rawhide drum; they were practicing together softly. Menard was talking to Merritt, the two shaped so alike they might have been brothers. Preuss had sketched a map in the hard dirt, and Fallon with a stick was redrawing part of it. Godey was talking to the cooks, looking romantic and wild, hands moving as if giving instructions, the women laughing; one gave him such a look of languorous invitation that even at a distance Frémont felt its intensity.

Don Carlos Gutierrez Medina rode through the fort's gates on a black stallion fully the equal of Sutter's gift to Frémont. Half a dozen retainers followed him, including a slender youth who bore a sharp resemblance to Gutierrez. At sight of the gathered Americans he looked about in wary surprise, then dismounted with easy grace, an air of authority about him; he was of medium size and wore a small black beard. Frémont thought he would be a dangerous antagonist.

"United States *Army*?" he said, picking up the end of Sutter's introduction. He did not return Frémont's bow.

"I am an engineering officer," Frémont said evenly in passable Spanish, "leading an exploratory expedition of civilians. We came over the mountains to rest and resupply."

"*Ahora? In medio de* invierno? Astonishing—I've never heard of such a thing." His Spanish was rapid, liquid; Frémont struggled to keep up. "You mean with men? With *horses*?" His face had a tight, suspicious look. The number of Americans had clearly unsettled him. He was hot-tempered, proud, a man who acted before he thought. Like me, Frémont told himself with some amusement. Rather a lot like me . . .

Then Don Carlos smiled—a hard, forbidding smile. "You must have wanted to come badly. Very badly indeed. I wonder why."

While the other listened, Frémont briefly explained his mission, emphasizing the straits in which he'd found himself on the eastern slope of the Sierras.

"Still," Gutierrez said, "it was convenient, wasn't it?"

Frémont decided to turn the slur. "More than convenient, sir—it was a godsend to be able to come here to recuperate and reoutfit ourselves."

"Captain Sutter," Gutierrez said with a sudden baleful look, "you'll forgive me if I express some surprise. An American Army officer enters California under the most unusual circumstances—and where does he come? Straight to this mysterious—I will even say perfectly *unnecessary*—fort of yours, which has become the center for every ragtag foreigner in California! Do you think I am blind?"

"Don Carlos," Sutter said with surprising dignity, "I am here by right just as you are: a citizen, a holder of the governor's grant. You abuse my hospitality when you suggest that there is anything irregular in my position."

"The governor will be most interested—"

"The governor already knows," Sutter retorted. "I posted a report on Captain Frémont's arrival."

"*Bueno!* I am very relieved to hear that."

There was a muttering, a sullen undercurrent among the settlers. Gutierrez glared at them hotly, hands on his hips. He opened his mouth to speak.

"I am deeply sorry," Frémont said quickly in his best Spanish, "to be a cause of misunderstanding between two distinguished officers of the sovereign government of Mexico." The crowd was quiet again; the two antagonists were watching him—Don Carlos with haughty skepticism, Sutter with bumptious resentment. He smiled easily, threw out a hand to where the members of his party had mingled with the crowd. "Surely a handful of exhausted, half-starved, frostbitten *viajadores* (he chose the word "travelers" deliberately over "explorers")—if I'd had any idea our appearance in this great province would cause such—irritation, we would have never thrown ourselves on the mercy of your munificent hospitality."

There was a murmur of relief among the guests. Sutter's face wore a shrewd, tight smile now; even Gutierrez' retinue had relaxed. It *is* catching, Frémont thought, on the very edge of laughter; another month or two in this lush empire and I could turn into another Sutter, conjuring up visions of fiefdoms and private armies . . . But wouldn't Jessie be proud of me! The soft answer.

Sutter was, characteristically, first to recover. His manner changed instantly; he became the soul of easy, amiable grace. "Well said, Lieutenant, nobly said! Who could refuse asylum to brave and weary men?" And to Gutierrez, taking his arm courteously: "Come, my dear Don—what is there to bandy words about? We're old friends, you are my guest. The meat is done to a splendid turn, the wine is already flowing. Let's put aside this trivial misunderstanding . . ."

And after several cups of wine and a huge plate of beef, Gutierrez' temper improved vastly; Sutter had set a small table for the three of them where Indian women brought food in relays. One was the woman Frémont had seen smiling at Godey. She had a lithe, sensual body, her dark skin glowing against a white cotton shirt, and she gave him a glance that was brazenly inviting. His breath went suddenly short and he looked down at his plate. A settler's wife joined the musicians and sang in a brassy voice. Frémont saw Godey catch the lithe woman about the waist and swing her to the music; the cup in his left hand never spilled.

"May I compliment you on your hospitality, Captain Sutter," Frémont said, raising his cup. "It's been a good while since we've seen anything like this, and we're grateful."

"My pleasure, I'm sure. Hospitality is a California custom, is it not, Don Carlos?" Sutter was holding a pewter mug of brandy and had given a similar mug to the Californian, whose manner continued to mellow. Frémont had taken a ritual sip, but Sutter and Gutierrez drank steadily.

"We Californians are a supremely gracious people," Sutter said, gesturing with the mug. "For example, we have no hotels. There aren't any real towns beyond the coastal entrepots, you know—but even there, from San Diego to Yerba Buena, you won't find a hotel. A good Swiss innkeeper would starve in California. And why? Because wherever you go you'll find someone ready to take you home and give you a bed and a handsome dinner. Stay a week if you like, stay a month. You'll find that hospitality never wears thin in California.

"Or take horses. You can ride the length of the country from ranch to ranch—forty, fifty miles—and turn out your horse, catch up another, and go on. Sooner or later the horses will be returned. It works out—no one worries. And likely as not there'll be a party wherever you stop, eh, Don Carlos?"

"We do not demand an excuse to entertain, certainly," Gutierrez said, looking pleased. "We are a warm-blooded people."

"And an honest, natural people!" Sutter proclaimed. He cut a sudden sly glance at Frémont. "There's not a spoke-wheeled vehicle in all of California. They cut rounds from trees—like chopping carrots—for wheels. A Boston ship brought out a wagon once, but in the dry summer the wood shrank, the spokes fell out, the tires came off—ruined. Isn't that glorious?—a natural country, untarnished by man's complications."

"Spoken like a man who enjoys his own distillery!" Gutierrez said with a laugh. "And I share that pleasure. For your cellar alone, Captain, you are more than welcome in California." Sutter refilled Gutierrez' mug. Frémont covered his with his hand.

Gutierrez turned to him with convivial warmth. "You must forgive my sensitivity to foreign intervention," he said. "We Californios are very few in number—hardly more than fourteen thousand of us, men, women and children—with another twenty thousand thoroughly untrustworthy Indians in our employ. And you Americans seem eager to fill any empty space. Granted that our host here has won our hearts with his excellence. Still, pity though it may be, most newcomers—especially the Americans—are not of good class. Rude, grasping fellows. Woodsmen, drovers, bankrupts—even fugitives from justice." He waved a hand toward the tables. "Would you really want such men to determine your future?"

Frémont caught sight of Carson, laden knife in one hand, spinning some outrageous yarn, and Freniere slapping his knee, roaring with laughter.

"Such men *are* my future," he said quietly. "And I count myself lucky they are my friends."

"Ah, the American ideal." Don Carlos smiled his hard, arrogant smile. "Every man a king! No—it's a myth: the mass man wants whipping, harnessing, by God—one lash or another, or he'll soon yield to his own base desires and destroy himself. Now, I'll give Santa Anna that. The scoundrel." He paused while Sutter refilled his mug. "Santa Anna courts the masses until he's in office, and then he courts the aristocrats just as assiduously, my friend. Applies the lash and holds everyone in check. After that absurd debacle in Texas when Houston lured him into the creek at San Jacinto and he gave away the country, naturally the people threw him out. They'd have hung him at the time. But what did the paisanos do? When he came back they gave him their hearts all over again, and now they are happy to call him a dictator! And it is a dictator the masses need."

Gutierrez took a deep drink and patted his lips with a beautiful lace handkerchief. His eyes had a glazed look. Neither Frémont nor Sutter spoke.

"Of course, that is not to say that the dictator Santa Anna is what *California* needs. In fact, we threw the scoundrel out once and may well do so again." He glowered at them suddenly. "California is a land peculiarly favored by the gods—it should not rest in a dictator's hands."

"You are thinking of independence, then?" Frémont asked.

Gutierrez shot him a quick, dark glance. "I am a loyal servant of Mexico. That is, I would like to be. Perhaps one day, when conditions are changed, and we are stronger. When we can send—"

There was a violent commotion and the music stopped. People had gathered in a ring. Frémont heard shouts, and someone cursing in Spanish; he jumped to his feet and pushed his way into the melee. One of Gutierrez' men lay face down on the ground. Purvis had the slender California youth by the shirtfront. He hit the boy hard, sent him sprawling.

Gutierrez broke through the circle, his face wild with rage. *"Bruto!"* He struck Purvis full in the face with a black braided quirt, again. *"Canalla!"*

"Why, you greaser son of a bitch," Purvis said. He put his hand to his face where long red welts had appeared, reached for his knife.

In one motion Gutierrez drew a flintlock pistol. "Scum," he said in Spanish, "I will kill you for this!"

Sutter thrust himself between the two men. "Hold on," he cried, rounding sharply on Purvis. "You can't go around striking people in *my* fort—I'll have you in irons!" He shouted to his guard, and the brightly dressed Indian soldiers ran forward. They seized Purvis by the arms; he shook them off with a heave. Gutierrez' pistol came up. Merritt threw his arms around Purvis then and said something to him. Purvis stopped struggling and nodded. The Indians surrounded him.

"Hold him there!" Sutter said in an angry voice. "Don Carlos, my abject apologies. I assure you that this man will be disciplined. Severely!"

Visibly holding his temper, Gutierrez put his pistol away and took the boy's face gently in his hands.

"All right now?" he asked.

"Sí, sí," the boy said, embarrassed.

"Bueno," Gutierrez said. He turned to his men, lifted his hand. *"Vámonos!"* The Californians mounted and the black stallion capered a neat circle. Gutierrez gave Frémont and Sutter a stiff salute and led the way out through the gate in a clatter of hooves.

In an ominous voice Purvis said, "You're mighty fucking polite to them Goddamn greasers."

"You be silent! You've caused enough trouble with your big mouth." Purvis started to speak but Sutter shouted him down; he was white with fury. "—I don't give a damn how it started! You're at fault when you eat my meat and then strike one of my guests. How dare you come here and—good God! Don't you men understand any of the pressures that plague this province? It's a tinderbox!"

Merritt said, "Well, Cap'n Sutter, ain't none of us going to let them Californios abuse us no way. And that's just what was afoot. You didn't see what happened so you ain't much call to judge."

"You men are fools!" Sutter's voice was shrill; the brandy was talking. Frémont saw Merritt stiffen. "The real test of the next ten years will be how we can function *together*—all of us!—in damned dangerous times. How we can hold what we've got—all of us. To let some quarrel that flows out of a brandy keg jeopardize a future that—"

"I ain't no fool and don't you call me one," Purvis said as if he had just gotten his thoughts together, and added distinctly, "You fat four-flushing bastard."

Sutter paled. Frémont knew he carried a pistol beneath his coat. He saw him glance quickly around the fort. His soldiers were watching; their sergeant said something in a low voice, and they eased closer. Merritt caught the move and straightened, his long arms loose at his side, hands curled. Sutter's chief overseer, a New Orleans Frenchman with a slash scar on one cheek, appeared in the storeroom doorway with a shotgun.

"Holy shit," Carson said softly. "Here we go."

Frémont stepped in front of Sutter. "Captain, permit me a word if you will. I'm an outsider, a newcomer, yet I have a real interest in California." Merritt was watching him speculatively.

"Perhaps the problem here is that everyone is right," Frémont said. "Naturally these men don't want to be abused. Equally you don't want your guests affronted. I'd say the Californians acted naturally too—they felt outnumbered and when Purvis slapped that boy—he was Don Carlos' son, I take it?"

"That is correct," Sutter said. "Inexcusable breach." He glowered at Frémont, his face very red now. "It's all very well for you to nominate yourself as peacemaker—"

"I'll tell you my position," Frémont said firmly, giving Sutter a hard look. "I'm here with a party of well-armed, highly capable men—Americans, sir, who react badly to seeing other Americans roughed up. I'm an officer of my government—indeed, I have a duty to aid Americans wherever I find them."

Sutter started to interrupt, but Frémont put up his hand. "Do me the courtesy to hear me out," he said. It was a command, and Sutter fell silent. "Now Don Carlos has already challenged our presence here. Out of deference to you and to the situation, I took no offense. But I have *no* intention of letting our presence provoke more quarrels. Or lead to the further abuse of American citizens." He glanced around at Tessier and Ingalls. "Don't forget that two of my men have already joined these settlers. It's clear where our sympathies lie. So I warn you—if it should become necessary, my men and I will take a hand in this. I hope that will not prove the case."

There was a short silence. Frémont looked at Merritt and grinned. "All right!" he said. "Captain Sutter has given us one hell of a party. Let's forget this damned foolishness and go back to enjoying ourselves. Captain," he turned back to his host, "where are those musicians? My boys don't want to fight—they want to dance!"

"That's right," Louie called in a loud, merry voice. *"Hy-yi!* Let's hear us some music and drink us some grog."

"I'll go along with that," Fallon said.

The others were watching Merritt. "Fair enough," the tall man said at last. "All right, boys, Cap'n Sutter done give us a hell of a good party just like Cap'n Frémont says. He's about the only friend we got in this damned valley—I say we owe him and Cap'n Frémont three cheers. What say? *Hip, hip—"*

Three times Merritt led the cheer, the settlers and Frémont's men together, their anger fading into smiles. Sutter, mollified and flattered, grinned resignedly and signaled the musicians.

An hour later Frémont was watching Godey dance the lithe woman closer and closer to the stables with their inviting haylofts when Merritt appeared beside him. The tall man leaned quietly on a hitching rail. He spat a long, luxurious stream of tobacco juice that stood on the ground in dust-covered drops. Godey made another turn past the open door and this time he led the woman inside. Her strong body was pressed hip to hip to his and her arm was around him.

"That was a right smart piece of work you did, Cap'n," Merritt said. He bit the end off a tobacco plug and chewed contentedly before he said softly, "Think you might be around these parts for a spell?"

"Who knows, Mr. Merritt?" Frémont smiled. "Stranger things than that have happened. . . ."

GRAND DESIGNS

JESSIE AND CHARLES were greeting guests in the great reception room of the Indian Queen Hotel on Pennsylvania Avenue when she felt his hand touch her arm. Ever so gently he stroked the inside of her bare elbow, and she shivered.

"Captain Frémont," she murmured.

"Yours to command, ma'am."

He was so splendid in his blue uniform with its double row of gold buttons; there were the new captain's bars on his epaulets, a brevet promotion from the chief of staff himself, Major General Winfield Scott. She was wearing a gown of creamy satin with a pale rose sash and a low bodice from which her breasts swelled in becoming fashion—she had seen the rush of desire in Charles' face when she turned from her mirror that evening and presented herself with a little flourish. He still had that fine burnt look of the outdoors, his eyes like sapphires against his wind-roughened skin. He had been home since August of last year, but you could tell at a glance that he had ridden in from the West.

Their Report on the Second Expedition had made a great stir—Congress had combined it with the first Report and ordered ten thousand extra copies printed for public distribution. The newspapers were full of talk about Charles and the West and the brand-new vistas he had opened to that mysterious province on the Pacific. All Washington seemed to have read his reports; letters and invitations had poured in; and now the friends of westward expansion were honoring him with a formal dinner.

The Indian Queen's reception room was already crowded. Marble-buttressed fireplaces blazed at each end of the huge room, where paintings of Jackson at New Orleans and Washington at the Delaware stared down in gilt frames, and walnut furniture gleamed in the soft candlelight of girandoles and crystal chandeliers. Guests entered with eager faces, the men in formal dress or uniform, the women bright as flowers, their hair bound up with silver combs, diamonds and pearls at their throats, their voices gay as birds as they waved fans and made laughing little sallies at men more powerful than their husbands.

Washington society adored parties—most of all when a new administration was coming in. James K. Polk, the Democratic dark horse from Tennessee and an old friend of Mr. T's, had been elected President three months after Charles returned. (She tended to date everything by when Charles returned.) The excitement tonight was for Charles—and thus for her—it was her world after all, this scene she saw before her, and her heart quickened with a sense of great times just ahead for them, opportunities like precious gems for those who knew how to capture and polish them.

These men and women around her, seeing and being seen, their faces alive and alert to exploit every advantage—she knew them all too well. With a casual smile, a slight freezing of manner, a question left unanswered, a quip turned, they felt each other out, crystallized positions, accepted defeats, betrayed loyalties, forged alliances, made enemies. The world of power and maneuver. How alien, how essentially trivial it all must seem to Charles, after rapids and salt lakes and ice fields! And yet there was an undeniable excitement here, too; and she knew he felt it—even if it would never be his way . . .

Several girls who had been at Miss English's school so terribly long ago were here; she saw a man from the White House whose name she couldn't place, a new Associate Justice, five of her father's confreres from the Senate. Senator Dix of New York, of course, and Henry Dodge, and the old family friend, Francis Blair, who hoped that his Washington *Globe* would become the organ of the new Democratic administration as it had been for General Jackson's and Van Buren's. Mr. T knew Polk well enough to bet that Blair would be disappointed.

What a pity Mr. Nicollet was not here tonight. Poor Papa Joe—he had died alone and out of his head in a Washington hotel room while Charles was running down the Columbia. Charles had been genuinely saddened. . . . Her father was standing with his back to a fireplace, hands behind him elevating the tails of his frock coat, talking in his booming Senate voice. Her mother was ill again, but there was Eliza by the Federal mirror with her new husband William Carey Jones, a pale young attorney with limp yellow hair.

A waiter in a scarlet jacket bowed before her, champagne glasses steady on his silver tray. She liked the old Indian Queen—President Monroe's inaugural ball had been held in this room and John Tyler had taken the oath in the parlor upstairs after old General Harrison died. In the adjoining dining room, a butler with a peremptory voice was marshaling his forces as he gave a final check to gold-edged plates and crystal and hothouse camellias. Nearly a dozen waiters circulated through the crowd, turning their trays neatly to avoid collision. On a side table there was a large crystal bowl filled with a mahogany-colored punch that she knew was well laced with whiskey or gin.

There was a little stir at the door and James Buchanan of Pennsylvania came in. He would be Secretary of State in the new Polk administration and had already given up his Senate seat. He made straight for her.

"Jessie, my dear," he said, kissing her hand. "This is a bit better than being a bridesmaid, isn't it?"

She gave a little curtsy. "Much better, Mr. Secretary-designate."

He looked pained. "Don't I deserve better than that?'" he said. He was still holding her hand. His hair was graying and his face still wore that satisfied, oddly dull expression. The new President must intend to be his own Secretary of State; why else would he have chosen such an inconsequential man?

"Dear Mr. Buchanan," she said lightly, "of course you do! You averted disaster that day." She saw she had pleased him. Buchanan had been her escort when Count Bodisco had plucked Harriet Williams right out of Miss English's school and married her; as Russia's ambassador, Bodisco had chosen men of state for his groomsmen and Harriet her friends as bridesmaids. Jessie had tripped on her gown as they followed the little count and his tall bride down the aisle—she could still remember her horror as she started to fall—but Buchanan had steadied her so smoothly that no one had noticed.

A stranger was talking to Charles, a short person with a red face she had seen at the punch table earlier. He wore a rather moldy formal suit and looked like a newspaperman. She'd learned to spot them on sight.

"By God, sir," he said explosively. "A work of genius! We plan to run your every word in the *Star*—the Cincinnati *Star,* sir, read all over the great state of Ohio, if I may say so, a *bible* of information to all good Democrats."

Charles' name was better known in Ohio than the President-elect's, the man said; he wondered if he might interview him the next day—needed his views on the western movement. "The people of Ohio talk about nothing else, sir."

Charles looked uncomfortable. She had lost count of the writers who had called; newspapers in New York, Boston, Philadelphia and Baltimore were publishing the report at length.

A man with very thick eyeglasses peered nervously at Charles and asked if he would consider giving a lecture on California at Independence Hall. Before Charles could reply another fellow interrupted in stentorian tones.

"And may I add to that, sir, an invitation to be speaker of honor at the Athenaeum in New York City? The board has authorized me to deliver the invitation in person." The Philadelphian glared at him, his eyes bulging hugely behind his glasses. "At the Athenaeum"—the New Yorker might have been referring to a cathedral—"of course you will be the only speaker, whereas at Philadelphia I daresay you'll be sharing the platform—"

"Certainly not!" the Philadelphian retorted in high agitation.

"—with God *knows* whom."

George Bancroft came in, quick, graceful, elegant as always. Bancroft was one of her favorite visitors to the Benton house, for his remarkable learning and his witty and authoritative conversation. He would be Secretary of the Navy in the new administration, but she knew he would be a good deal more than that; it already was clear that Bancroft spoke for Polk in areas that went far beyond naval power. He came toward her, smiling, in his face a pleasurable awareness of the room's awareness of him—and then Mr. T had waylaid him and in another moment they were deep in conversation.

Colonel Abert, smiling genially, shook hands with Charles. Their uniforms were identical except for rank; the colonel had designed the uniforms himself when the Topographical Engineers achieved corps status.

"Congratulations, *Captain,*" Abert said, plainly seeing a brevet captaincy from the Chief himself as an honor eclipsing everything else. "Miss Jessie," he said to her, bowing. "Such a pleasure . . ." There had never been a word about the cannon, neither its requisition nor its loss. Perhaps he'd forgotten about it—or had he filed it away where all such rash and insubordinate acts are filed in the tireless, inexorable memories of colonels?

"Colonel," she said, "you and Charles are the most glamorous-looking men in Washington."

Abert, very pleased, explained his design problems at such length that she missed the name of the stout New York publisher who had just introduced himself to Charles. His house was printing a trade edition of the Report, bound in calfskin.

"There is of course great interest in the West," he said, "but also in you personally. That will increase, I'd judge, as the book circulates." He hesitated—she saw he was older than she'd thought—and then said somewhat cautiously, "I don't know if you realize what a flair you have for writing." The words struck her like a dash of water. She knew her expression was betraying her, but the man was watching Charles intently. "I'm never wrong about a talent such as yours. Well, almost never. It is, after all, my business. Your ability to combine information with sensitivity and colorful anecdotes in prose that's alive—well, it's quite remarkable, I must say. More than that." He was studying Charles shrewdly. "It would excite me in a professional writer; it astounds me in a professional soldier."

She didn't know where to look. This editor was fearfully perceptive. She felt obscurely afraid for Charles if the precise nature of the report's authorship were revealed—and yet there was a curious, covert excitement, almost a *desire* for it to be known. Was she being disloyal?

She started; Charles' hand had found hers. "Well," he was saying to the publisher easily, with that charming smile, "a tremendous amount of loving effort went into the writing—I can tell you that."

She squeezed his big hard hand, wanting to laugh out loud, to kiss him in front of all social Washington; she loved him more at that moment than she ever had.

They had left St. Louis by steamboat as soon as he'd returned. That had given them ten glorious days with nothing to do but make love and talk and fuss over Lily; and the fourteen months of his absence had rolled away, the tears with which she'd greeted him had turned to laughter. He was thinner; there were lines in his forehead and cheeks that hadn't been there before, more steel in his blue eyes now than sky. But his ardor was more compelling than ever.

In Washington they had rented workrooms and she'd returned to writing as naturally as though she'd never left it. This time she moved into the work without hesitation, drawing him out deftly, shaping the narrative, tightening and focusing, heightening what excited her, relying on her instincts as she followed the party through those forbidding mountains. The agony of the pass had horrified her—she had laughed in wild relief at the royal pretensions of Sutter. All was well that ended well, true . . . But there—again—was that impulsive decision to cross the Sierra—in the dead of winter. Yes, it was a thousand-mile trek eastward through wasteland to Laramie and Westport and yes, it *was* immensely important to make an on-the-spot appraisal in California; and yet . . . This time she'd confined herself to one long, direct gaze, and he'd given her that rueful, mischievous glance of his, and laughed, and then they'd both laughed together; but the stealthy concern had brushed her again. He was so brave, her Charles Frémont. But sometimes she feared for him.

The work had gone more favorably than before, the more so as Charles now took an almost proprietary pride in her literary skill.

"It's the way it is on the trail," he told her one morning. "Two good men are *three* times as effective as one because they complement each other. That's how we are together. I like that, darling."

That was what counted: together they were more than either could be apart. That they could not publicly admit her coauthorship didn't matter—it was, after all, a military report addressed to Charles' commanding officer, and it would retain that form even in a published edition.

"It's that intangible reality," the publisher was saying, "the force of emotion between the lines, that makes this book valuable. Without that unique capacity to make people see what you saw, take them bodily where you went, you wouldn't have a tenth of your audience." There was that speculative pause of his; and then he said, "With that quality—and if your audience is ready for your message—one book can make you famous overnight. Mark my words."

George Bancroft had freed himself from her father and approached them, and the publisher moved on. Bancroft was smaller than Charles, with bright eyes and great charm, though he tended to cut up anyone who disagreed with him, and often made enemies. Intellectual arrogance, Mr. T liked to say, was least forgivable in those with superior intellect, for they should know better. Superbly educated at Harvard and Göttingen, he had made himself famous with his *History of the United States,* which rang with the sentiments of Jacksonian democracy. Spokesman for the Democratic party, he had moved early to Polk's support, and now Polk was using him everywhere as minister-without-portfolio.

"A striking piece of work, Captain," he was saying to Charles enthusiastically. "I've just sent a copy to Humboldt in Paris."

She saw her husband's eyes widen; he held the great Prussian explorer in absolute reverence. "You do me honor, sir. But I'm afraid he'll find it trifling."

"To the contrary! He'll be delighted with it. I know him quite well—twenty years ago I went from Berlin to Paris with a letter from his brother, and he introduced me to the intellectual life of Paris. He's old now but still very hale—I saw him last year. It wouldn't surprise me at all if he arranged an invitation for you to speak at the Academy."

The Academy! Jessie instantly recalled Papa Joe's perennial hunger for its recognition. What irony if Charles should be—

"Jessie, darling! You look perfectly exquisite!" Maria Crittenden, stunning in a brilliant red velvet gown, embraced her. "And haven't we come a long way since you two were stealing kisses in my gazebo! George," she added, dropping the tiniest of curtsies to Bancroft's formal bow. He and her husband were enemies; Jessie could see the tall figure of John Crittenden, whom Kentucky had returned to the Senate, talking with her father across the room.

"Now confess, Jessie," Maria said, drawing her aside, "after all those years at the tail of your father's comet . . . how does it feel to be flashing across the sky yourself?'"

"Well," she said, "it's really Charles—"

"Oh, bosh! That's not at all true. Men rise or fall in direct relationship to the quality of their wives—and that's nowhere truer than in Washington. You know that!"

Jessie grinned. In fact, she did know that. And yes, she liked being a grown woman, standing by her successful husband. Yet it was a feeling confirmed not by outer acceptance but by what they *were,* what they had become. Something had happened to them both while Charles was away, though she had noticed the difference first of all in him.

He was older, tougher, more accustomed to command. He had always been sure of himself—a man when she had flirted with boys—but this was different. There was a quality of—well, of incontestable *authority* in him, a subtle intensification of what he had been. The story of his passage over the Sierras had emerged in bits and pieces as they watched the banks of the Ohio slip by, and it was only later she'd decided that the change had taken place there. He told her of standing on the last steps of ice at the crown of the pass looking back over the way they had come—that scene lodged permanently in her mind. He had accomplished something very few men in the long history of recorded exploration could have done, and he knew it.

Later still, she'd realized that her own experience had matched his in those anguished months from February to August when she'd set a plate at dinner every night and set a lighted lamp in the window, ignoring her family's alarm as she grew thinner each day. In early summer a report had drifted down the Oregon Trail from Fort Vancouver—trappers had talked to Indians who said a party led by a man with strange blue eyes had gone into the high snows and perished. The family couldn't hide it from her—she had sensed their knowledge and forced it out of them—but she had fiercely rejected the rumor, and settled down to wait. *He was coming back,* she had never doubted it, and as the Missouri sun burned away the months she had worn down to the bedrock of her own strength. The sun and the waiting had stripped away the girl and left the woman. Could Charles understand that?

As Maria moved off, Jessie heard Mr. Bancroft saying to Charles: "California is the key, of course. Fascinating place, absolutely full of promise. Tell me—that formidable mountain crossing. I've had some experience in the Alps. Striking across strange mountains in winter is no small matter. Must've been rather alarming to the men, even the old trappers."

"The alternatives were rather alarming too," Charles answered with a small smile.

"I daresay. Still . . . no threat of mutiny, eh?"

"No sir. My men don't mutiny."

"Any men will mutiny, given certain circumstances."

"Not *my* men." She saw her husband's face harden. "I won't permit that."

"Good." Bancroft nodded, as if something had been settled. "You'll go out again, then?"

"Just to the Rocky Mountains this time. A summer expedition."

"Well, splendid. Let's make time to sit down one day soon. I'd like to talk with you about California."

Without thinking, Jessie said, "Is Mr. Polk interested in California?"

A cool disapproval veiled Bancroft's face as he turned to her. Instantly she knew it had been a mistake. "My dear," he said, "there's so much for him to think about now that I doubt he'd have time for the West. I'm merely indulging an old historian's curiosity."

It was a reprimand, after which he nodded rather distantly and moved away, but it had been worth it—she had seen in his eyes that he was lying. And if the new President was interested in California, then he certainly was interested in the man who knew the most about it.

California . . .

The room was full now; the dinner marshal, a fat man with muttonchop whiskers who wore the gold sash of some obscure organization, bowed to them.

"If you and Madame Frémont will do us the honor, I will escort you to table," he said in a loud voice. Charles bowed and they followed toward the dining room. It all struck Jessie's sense of irony, but Charles was looking proud and pleased as a guardsman on parade.

"Oooh, Captain Frémont," she whispered, "I hope it won't all turn into a pumpkin at midnight."

He looked at her sharply and then grinned. " 'Long as you leave me just one of your slippers, I'll find you—don't you worry about that!"

She seized his arm; thinking of Bancroft's cold gray eyes she shivered.

There was a loud knock on the door.

"I suppose that'll be Simpson with more insoluble problems," Benton said irritably. Jessie glanced at Charles, at her father again. He looked exhausted and it struck her suddenly that he was getting old. He'll make Simpson pay for that knock, she thought. Simpson was the clerk of the Military Affairs Committee, which had been meeting almost daily.

The very idea of war seemed incredible, a bad joke. She and Charles had hurried back from a brief vacation in South Carolina to find the Capital in turmoil. Mexico had always said that for the United States to admit Texas would mean war, but no one had taken such bluster seriously.

"Why, Texas has been free for years," she had protested when they'd seen the glaring news one carefree, sunny morning on the Carolina beach. They'd helped Lily build a resplendent sand castle, then eaten a picnic lunch while Lily napped, awaiting the tide; and at last Charles had opened the newspaper. "I remember Sam Houston sitting right in our drawing room telling us about the hideous slaughter at the Alamo. That was nine years ago, for goodness sake! Why should they go to war *now*?"

"Because they believe they can win," Charles answered. "Retake Texas, drive out the settlers—how should I know? *You're* the political expert, not I."

The tide edged in, the tiny bastions crumbled while Lily frantically piled and plastered sand, and Charles read the reports out loud: the joint resolution to admit Texas had passed Congress; statehood had been formally offered; the Mexican ambassador had called for his passports, broken off diplomatic relations. And Charles was a soldier. As the last of the sand castle fell in, Lily began to cry: their first real holiday was over . . .

Of course it was serious, her father had told her when they reached home: the committee was voting war funds, the President was calling up volunteers.

"Come over this afternoon," he'd said. "I need to see you. Both of you. Right away."

The committee was running late, and they'd waited for him in his hideaway office. It was a small room, its vaulted ceiling supporting enormous weight, the molding on its creamy walls outlined in pale blue. A horsehair couch faced a cold fireplace; a stuffed leather chair stood by the open window and another in front of her father's desk. Mr. T had come in and was pouring Charles a glass of port when the knock sounded. But it wasn't Simpson: it was George Bancroft, a bit out of breath and less urbane than usual.

"Ah, I was afraid I'd missed you—there're new developments."

Her father said quickly: "Jessie and Captain Frémont are here; they returned last night."

She wondered whether she and Charles should leave, but Bancroft said with apparent pleasure, "Why, excellent." His harried look seemed oddly in contrast with the enthusiastic note in his voice; pouches had formed under his eyes since she had seen him last.

"We can take a stroll," Charles said.

"No, no, stay—by all means, stay."

Mr. T said, "What's up, George?"

"Two serious strokes." Bancroft took the chair by the window. "First, the British have secured tentative Mexican agreement to a treaty that would recognize Texas' independence, provided"—he paused for effect—"that Texas in return would refuse to join the United States."

She saw immediately the force of such a move. Mexico had never admitted the fact of Texan independence; twice it had made minor moves to recapture what it insisted on viewing as an errant Mexican province. The Texans had beaten off each attempt, but they lived in dread that Mexico would send a full army against them.

"The Mexicans would guarantee to leave Texas alone?" she asked.

"And the British would enforce it."

"Outrageous interference!" her father exclaimed. "But interesting, too. The Mexicans might just accept that, what's more—but the Texans wouldn't. They're good Americans, Missouri men, Tennessee men—they know where home is. I'd say the real question is, what is Britain up to?"

"Especially in light of the other news," Bancroft said. "They've just turned the President down flat on his Oregon proposal."

"By God! Just like that!"

"Just like that. The British minister didn't even bother to consult his government."

"Then he already had the authority to reject it," Mr. T said thoughtfully. "That must mean their position has hardened."

That *was* a serious turn. Polk had succeeded as a dark-horse candidate on his promise to admit Texas, come what might, and settle the Oregon question; and he had taken his election as a mandate. Now Texas was coming in and the President was nudging the British toward a compromise to end the tandem arrangement under which the two countries had been holding Oregon. His plan to extend the existing line between Canada and the United States along the Forty-ninth Parallel to the Pacific was reasonable enough, and the British had indicated privately it would be acceptable—which was just what Dr. McLoughlin had told Charles.

Bancroft's legs were crossed, one booted foot jiggling. "Now, Tom, why should there be such a turnaround at just this moment?"

"Because they don't like our expansion, by God. They can see we intend to be dominant on this continent and they're not having it. They haven't any legitimate interest in Oregon below the forty-ninth, you know that—the fur trade's gone and our settlers are tilting it toward us anyhow. They've got more than Oregon on their minds."

"Quite true," Bancroft murmured. "But we can't tell . . . we can't make out their intentions. If Mexico really intends to fight, then the British offer gains weight. We have information that the Mexicans have ordered fifteen thousand men onto the Rio Grande, and they'll still have ample reserves."

"Fifteen thousand!" Charles exclaimed. "That's twice the size of our whole army."

"That's right. General Scott testified this morning. There's a popular notion, you know, that we're much stronger than Mexico. That's true industrially, but not militarily. Our troops have seen no combat beyond occasional Indian squabbles; theirs have been fighting off and on for twenty years. They're well blooded."

"But they've been fighting their own people," Jessie said, "all those revolutions and counterrevolutions. That's not really war—"

"Yes," her father broke in, "and they'd find American troops a different sack of rattlesnakes. But that's not to say they aren't formidable."

"Yet they haven't retaken Texas," Charles said.

"Texas doesn't interest them much as real estate—it's Texas as symbol that makes the trouble. Their leaders rationalized Sam Houston's victory as Santa Anna's own personal defeat, something that had nothing to do with the nation. They could get away with claiming they could retake it any day, but that assertion won't hold water when Texas joins the United States. That's the problem."

Bancroft added, "Also, they believe their saber-rattling has kept us from admitting Texas until now."

"But that's certainly not true," Charles said.

"Of course not," Mr. T said. "Utter damned nonsense. Our failure to admit Texas long ago is all the result of our own miserable politics. Sectionalism kept 'em out—nothing but sectionalism. I tell you, it's a curse!"

"Oh, Tom, you overstate," Bancroft said, suddenly impatient.

"I do *not,* by God!" Mr. T said. Bancroft had irritated him. He leaped up and began pacing. "You're a historian—you should have the long view—"

"Papa," Jessie murmured. But he was in full cry, caught up in his overriding obsession.

"Less and less do we decide things on a national basis. The South protects slavery and fights the tariff, the North fights slavery and insists on the tariff for its factories. Why, the North—with your own precious Massachusetts in the lead, don't forget that—has kept Texas out for nine years, for no other reason than that it amounted to an extension of slave territory . . ."

"Nor is that such a despicable reason," Bancroft said quickly.

"It's the *wrong* reason!" Mr. T set his wineglass on the mantel with a click. "Of course slavery is a pernicious institution—you know my position on that—but to keep Texas out on that account alone is downright preposterous. I tell you, George, if each region continues to press only its own interests, this country can go up in smoke. Civil war, sir! It can destroy us."

"Oh, come come, Tom," Bancroft said impatiently. "North against South? I can't foresee that. Really!"

Jessie rolled her eyes at Charles, but he was not smiling.

"Still, Senator," Charles said, "since Texas was admitted in the end, perhaps sectionalism is on the wane." Jessie saw Bancroft's lips tighten again; the whole digression had vexed him.

"Rather it's that expansionism is on the rise," her father said, "and high time, too." She knew Mr. T actually believed that in pushing the country westward he was following God's will. A part of her agreed with him—certainly one *could* make the case that God had created the American democracy as a guidepost to the direction He intended mankind to take, and hence expanding the nation must further God's work. Perhaps . . .

Her father was rummaging on his desk. "Here," he said, "let me read you something."

But now she was as impatient as Bancroft. This was no time for perorations over Manifest Destiny. Bluntly she said, "So? is there to be war with Mexico or not?"

"We think not," Bancroft answered. "It's every bit as dangerous as your father says, but we still think we can settle it by negotiation."

"Provided old John Bull gives you time for that," her father said wryly.

"—But how does Great Britain fit into this?" she asked.

"California," Bancroft said slowly and succinctly. "That's how."

Jessie came all alert; she saw a muscle flex once in Charles' cheek. Forsythia blazed yellow in the April sunshine beyond Bancroft's shoulder.

"Why do you think the British are so interested in Texas?" he was saying, watching Charles. "We know they've always been hungry for California—and the fact is, the Texans have been talking about linking with California for years. They've already tried to seize New Mexico. Got their noses bloodied, but it shows their thinking."

He smoothed the hair at the side of his head in a rapid gesture. He was talking directly to Charles now. "If Britain sponsored Texas, assured it financially and protected it, then Texas would be free to grab *California*—as proxy, of course, for Britain. Or Britain could move directly on California and later combine it with Texas."

"And in that case," her father broke in, "if they held on to Oregon they'd have the entire west coast, clear down to Baja California. That, plus Texas, would give 'em the dominance on this continent they've always wanted. They've never forgiven us our revolution, damn them!" He aimed a thick finger at Bancroft. *"There's* your explanation for the shift on Oregon, by God—they want it all."

"Of course, that's only supposition," Jessie said cautiously.

"Sound supposition, though," Bancroft said. He was talking down to her; she heard his impatience. "This British meddling isn't new. There's been serious talk in London of supplying a European monarch to straighten out Mexico's problems." He began ticking off fingers. "We're told repeatedly that Britain has offered financial assistance in return for a lien on California. That Irish priest McNamara wants to put ten thousand Irish Catholics there—that would make it a British colony overnight. The Hudson's Bay Company's even offered to arm and supply Mexican armies in California."

He folded the last finger down. "They've been active all along, you see—the difference now is that they're involving themselves directly."

There was a short silence.

"I think it's plain," her father said slowly. "California is the real key to the conundrum."

Bancroft nodded. "The thinking is that we might be able to solve the problem with a substantial cash payment."

"Purchase peace, do you mean?" Charles demanded with an edge in his voice.

"No, no, we're not paying blackmail, nothing like that. We're offering to buy *territory.*" The United States was prepared to pay Mexico up to forty million dollars for California and New Mexico—if Mexico abandoned a claim on Texas which no longer made sense.

"We're going to *buy* California?" Jessie said aloud. It sounded incredible. Listening to Bancroft lay it out so casually, she was certain now that he wanted something of them. Of Charles. His face had that glossy, assured look and he was talking directly to Charles; her father was listening without expression, and she was sure he had heard it all before. "Will that work?" she asked.

"It didn't when General Jackson tried it," Mr. T said.

"Granted," Bancroft said, "but everything is different now. Surely Mexico understands that. Texas is lost to them. California is slipping away." To

Charles he said, "Didn't you imply the Californians were on the edge of revolt when you were there?"

"That last governor Mexico sent up enraged them, all right—I'd guess they've run him off by now. Or tried to."

"You see?—they can't handle California any more than they could Texas. Mexico's in constant chaos. Everyone is suspicious, every leader's a potential dictator, every president more worried about a coup than anything that might happen abroad."

He shook his head wearily. "Look, we're offering them a way out. They're desperate for money and it's in an honorable tradition: it's directly analogous to Jefferson's purchasing Louisiana from Napoleon—territory that's a liability to the other party but has real *value* to us."

"A fascinating idea, Mr. Secretary," Charles said; his eyes were snapping with interest. "Could you describe how that could be effected?"

"Yes." Bancroft stopped, lips pursed, and then said: "It's very, very delicate—you understand that any talk about this could blow it apart at their end?"

"They know that, George," Mr. T replied. "Jessie has heard more state secrets than you ever will."

"Doubtless," Bancroft said, his face very smooth. He didn't like that, Jessie thought. "At any rate, Herrera wants to negotiate. He's a moderate, sensible, quite an intelligent man. He understands that Texas is gone and California may follow. His problem is that to *say* so would destroy him politically. Mexico's having an election in four months, in August. Assuming that Herrera wins and that he can stave off a coup from the right, he says he wants to negotiate a sensible conclusion."

"And you think it'll work?" Charles pressed him.

"All I can say is, it would be in everyone's interest. It'll take some maneuvering, and there's a lot that could go wrong. But in the end I think we'll settle Texas and purchase California."

"That's a damned optimistic view, George," Mr. T told him.

"You think there'll be war, then?"

"Yes. Or stalemate. But I'm doubtful that Mexico can get itself together long enough to negotiate. That's why I think we'd better look lively in California."

Bancroft turned solemn. "Well," he said, circling her father's doubts, "certainly California *is* the paramount question." He hesitated, looking at Charles. "It's quite the ripe plum, isn't it? . . . And what's to happen to it if we *can't* purchase it? If the Californians do jettison Mexico, what then? Independence? If Texans had difficulty as an independent republic, imagine the Californians trying it. It would be a vacuum—and who would step in? Us? The British?"

He paused while her father unstopped the wine decanter, and then sat there, silent, twirling his glass. "Well, I can tell you this: the President *doesn't intend to lose California.* He's quite a remarkable man, you know—full of hidden depths that only become evident when you work with him."

"Hidden depths," Mr. T echoed him. Jessie knew that her father was amused: no sooner did a man become a cabinet officer than he developed a respect bordering on reverence for the President who had elevated him. Depth wasn't at all the word she would have chosen for the humorless, leaden Mr. Polk, with his downturned slash of a mouth.

"Yes, truly," Bancroft said. "Intelligent and strong. He's very hard to divert from a course. At dinner one night he told me he has three territorial goals for his administration: to admit Texas properly, settle the Oregon question—and make California an American possession."

"Take California?" Charles asked in amazement.

"Not *take,*" Bancroft said hastily. "The President has no thought of seizing. Certainly not. By purchase, he hopes—but ultimately, however it happens, California will fall into the American orbit. We have momentum. We have the settlers. And thanks to your brilliant work, Captain, they now have a route."

Mr. T said suddenly: "Or will the British seize it—under whatever pretext—while we're maneuvering toward it peacefully?"

She said nothing, nor did Charles, and Bancroft went on musingly: "Of course, if Mexico agrees to sell, well and good. Or if war should be forced upon us, then our Pacific squadron will seize California immediately. I've been given explicit instructions about that. But what about alternatives? The delicate in-between conditions? How can we position ourselves to fend off the British—and yet do nothing to jeopardize these immensely delicate negotiations?"

Bancroft sighed and leaned back, stretching out his legs. His lidded eyes rose again to Charles. "What's your view of the current situation in California, Captain?"

"Very much in accord with what you've been saying," Charles answered. "It's the most underdeveloped country I've ever seen. I got the impression that its government scarcely exists—if they *have* thrown off Mexican authority again, that's certainly left a vacuum. That's why Sutter could grow so quickly. In a power vacuum he's free to expand without restraints."

"What's Sutter like, by the way?"

"Kit Carson thinks he's a gilded rooster, but there's more to him than that. He has gall, daring, imagination—but his judgment's questionable, he's impractical, he can be arrogant."

"A dubious ally, then?"

"Ally isn't the right term, I'm afraid. But he's certainly potentially valuable. His loyalties are all to himself, but his interests are not those of Mexico or Britain. And he does function as a rallying point, a base for the foreign settlers."

"They're the key." Bancroft's fingers drummed on the chair arm. "Do you think they'll respond like the Texans? Act independently, as they did?"

"The settlers aren't that strong yet. But the ones I met were good frontiersmen. They can fight, I'm sure. They're very aware of what happened in Texas and they bluster a bit, but their real concern is that the Californios will throw them out."

"Would they fight that?"

"If they could get together."

"If they had a leader to rally round, eh? Too bad there's not a Sam Houston there to—" He broke off, smiling. "And your next expedition stops at the Rockies, you say?"

Charles gave him that quick, mischievous grin Jessie knew; she started, felt her face redden. What was the matter with her? Why hadn't she seen this unfolding—

"There's plenty to be done beyond the Rockies," Charles answered levelly, "but I've no orders."

"Ah well, orders," Bancroft said, waving a negligent hand. "What might be done?"

"The immediate need is to map a more direct route to California."

California again—she felt as if she had been hit physically. Struck in the face. How long this time? How many months, years—of waiting, wondering, fearing? And what lay underneath this easy speculation—what was Bancroft *not* saying?

"We'd need to mount a far different kind of expedition than we'd planned," she heard Charles saying. "Bigger. Cost more. I'd need sixty, seventy men to be effective. Carson again. Godey, Freniere. Tessier after we arrived."

"The settlers are the key to the whole thing," her father repeated. She saw that he knew just what Bancroft wanted—they were echoing each other. "But they're like a rudderless ship—strong but very likely to run aground. Now, you can talk to them, Charles—you've dealt with them already. And at the same time, you have the political sophistication to see things in a big frame."

"I might say," Bancroft said, "that the President was very impressed with the leadership you displayed in getting your men across the Sierras. Very impressed. They weren't soldiers under orders, after all—they were frontiersmen, men very like the settlers. I told the President it was my opinion that under a less aggressive, less—charismatic leader, they might well have mutinied. Or come all apart, simply collapsed."

Jessie listened to this in turmoil. She was a Washington woman, and ambition clashed with dismay like swords. They wanted him: her father, Bancroft, the President himself wanted Charles to go out and secure California! High stakes. Instantly she knew that if he could bring California into the American fold there would be no limit to his future—he could become a national figure of supreme importance, better known than the Secretary, better known than Old Bullion from Missouri. All at once she thought: *He could become President.*

But the risks!

Suddenly it struck her how exposed she and Charles were. They weren't at the White House receiving instructions. No Army officers were present; there would be no orders. Bancroft wasn't even connected with the Army—he was *Navy.* And what had he said? Nothing, really. No orders, no directives, no formal instructions. Did he speak for the President?—he hadn't exactly said so. Did Charles see this? A cold intuition told her that if something went wrong, Bancroft would have no memory of this conversation. It all would be some terrible mistake that a rash young captain had made. High stakes indeed. She looked at the sleek, impassive Secretary and wondered why she had ever thought she liked him. If the political wolves closed in, snapping, she and Charles would face them alone; and what could even her father do then?

As if reading her thought, Mr. T said heavily, "There are immense dangers, however. Even the *appearance* of an attempt on our part to seize the place could be fatal."

"Quite so," Bancroft said quickly. "It's touch-and-go getting this new Herrera government to negotiate, without precipitating a coup from the right. Any suggestion of duplicity—of armed seizure while we talked—would destroy the negotiations and probably the Herrera government as well. It might set off the very war we intend to avoid."

"And at the same time," her father said, "that's just what would bring the British in—it would be exactly the pretext they so obviously seek."

She gazed at her father in consternation. He and Bancroft were both looking at Charles inquiringly. They're singing a duet, she thought; cuing each other like music-hall characters. Did her own father intend to use them so? For a moment she felt a stunning rush of rage. Charles would carry the weight, face the dangers, take the risks; she would wait at home, cut off from him for months. And yet, the opportunity was literally overwhelming in its implications . . .

"One quick question," Charles said. "Did I understand you to say that in the event of war, the Navy *would* move?"

"Yes. This week I will send orders to Commodore Sloat of our Pacific squadron that in the event of proof positive of war—actual declaration and combat—between the U.S. and Mexico, he is to seize California. That'll be for strategic reasons, for a bargaining position—but above all to preempt a British move."

"And those orders would govern my actions as well, I assume."

"Yes, of course—but they depend first of all on the outbreak of a war which in fact we intend to avoid."

"So I would be operating in limbo—on the opposite side of the continent, months away from news or instructions " She saw something harsh and sardonic in his expression. "It *is* a rather difficult assignment."

"I wouldn't call it an *assignment* exactly . . ."

"Whatever you choose to call it then," Charles said flatly. She had a sudden vision of him on that icy, windswept ridge, staggering with exhaustion, whipping Menard, heartening little Preuss, dragging Billy Rasmussen to his feet.

"Well," he said to her father, "I'm willing to try. But the Secretary just said that it *wasn't* an assignment. I'd like to hear—from him—just what he does think it is."

"Why, I . . ." Bancroft began, and stopped.

"What are your expectations, sir?"

He'll back away, she thought instantly. She saw a flush stain Bancroft's face.

"I have no expectations, Captain. None has been voiced in this room." To her father, Bancroft said, "He oversteps, Tom."

"It's his neck on the chopping block," her father answered coolly.

"Just a moment, Mr. Secretary," Charles said in a tone that stopped Bancroft short. "I need no rebuke from you. Let me tell you something, sir. This won't be any lark. You're sitting here behind a desk. I will be out there with a small party, feeling my way between the settlers and Sutter's people and the Mexican authorities. I will be out there holding the croker sack, Mr. Bancroft. No one knows how long it'll take, or how it'll come out."

All at once with his left hand he covered one of hers, and to her utter surprise continued in the same voice without looking at her: "And *its's equally hard on my wife.* Do you understand that? She contributes precisely as I contribute. So what you ask of me, you ask of her."

In the silence that followed he turned to her and she saw that ardent fire flash for a moment in his eyes. "And what you take from me, you take from her." Then he turned back to Bancroft and she saw the same rocklike expression stamped across his face.

"So it's damned hard, Mr. Secretary. I'm willing to do it, but I want to hear some specifics and I want to hear them from you. There'll be no written orders, I take it?"

She was proud: Charles had seen where they were leading him. They want the luxury of indirection, of *non*commitment, wanted him to assume the entire burden, and he was astute enough to perceive, resolute enough to challenge. She studied her father's face; was he so willing to have his children draw the chestnuts all alone? She had a sudden, somber insight: she would never again feel about him quite as she had. Was that the meaning of growing up? Just then his eyes met hers; he cleared his throat.

"His point is valid, George. Give him an answer or I'll suggest that he not go."

"Very well," Bancroft said warily, as if he had been bested. "No orders beyond those existing. But when you expand your expedition, when you appear at Sutter's instead of Bent's Fort, there'll be no official surprise, no recriminations."

Charles said: "No queries or recalls?"

"None." Bancroft made a steeple of his fingers and rested his chin on them, gazing at Charles. "I think you know our—all right then—expectations. You can see the dangers in taking action—or in failing to take action, given certain circumstances. You must realize we can't instruct you because we can't foresee events—and because inevitably orders would become public and our abolitionist friends would use them as a club to beat us to death. They'd claim we were grabbing California as a southern state and *that* would blow the negotiations sky-high. Understood?"

Charles nodded. He was calm, but her own apprehension would not go away.

"And does what you say have the approval of the President?" Jessie asked flatly.

The Secretary hesitated.

"Tell him, George," her father said in a tone that permitted no equivocation. "Tell them both. They have a right to know."

Bancroft made an irritated gesture with one hand. "Very well. But I warn you that outside this room I will deny the entire conversation. Is that clear?"

When Charles nodded again, Bancroft repeated, "Very well. I do specifically speak for the President of the United States. In everything I have said here, I have spoken for him. He understands that you are going to California. He approves the mission." He glanced at her. "Yes, madam," he said, reading her expression, "it was planned before today, you are quite correct."

But they *had* made him say so! "One final point, Captain," Bancroft said. "Take no action which would precipitate war, nothing that would disturb the peace, but be advised that *the President does not intend to lose California.*"

There was a very long silence. Then Charles stirred and said, "I'll cross the Sierras before snow flies. Then we'll see."

"I'm sure you'll do your duty," Bancroft answered smoothly. "It will merely be up to you to *define* that duty."

He was humming some tune about far mountains calling; she'd heard trailmen singing it back in St. Louis. He was saddle-soaping his boots with industrious cheerfulness, working the leather deftly with his fingers. He'd never been a spit-and-polish soldier—he'd been almost indifferent about his uniforms—but on his trail boots he lavished all manner of care. It was amazing what hard wear good leather could stand, he liked to tell her, if you only treated it well, kept it supple and well greased.

"I can't say I like it very much," she said aloud. She'd admonished herself to be quiet, but his incessant humming nettled her. That restlessness had hold of him again—it was almost like a fever; she could feel it in his hand, see it in his glance, whenever he was going into the field; even his walk changed subtly.

"Can't like what, honey?"

"This *mission* or whatever you want to call it." She went on braiding her hair, which now reached below her waist again, with unthinking dexterity. "No orders, no government backing, not even contingency plans."

"Yes," He laughed, the boot in his hands, his eyes dancing in the soft, amber light of the whale-oil lamp. "Can't you hear old Kit?" His voice took on Carson's easy drawl, full of amused outrage: " 'You mean they want us to take over a country that ain't independent, from another country that don't run it, and hand it over to still another one that won't admit it—all without nobody knowing it's even been *done*?' "

"It's not all that humorous, Charles."

"Of course it is. Nothing to it if you're a Washington panjandrum: you just don't let the right hand know what the left hand's got in mind."

"Charles . . ." She let go her hair and went over to him, knelt beside him, and took the boot out of his hands. "I want you to promise me something."

"Well now, that depends, ma'am," he drawled.

"I'm serious. Please. Promise me you'll be—prudent."

His expression changed then; he took her hands. "It's not my style—"

"I know."

"—but I'll be careful. Take it slow and read sign. As Louie says."

"You've got to . . ." Now, here, in their bedroom in the night silence, the conversation in her father's office seemed even more menacing, bristling with snares and pitfalls. "This is much riskier than running the Platte or crossing the Sierra . . ."

"Well, I don't know about that."

"Well, I do! There it was only nature—here you've got *human* nature, Charles; people scheming for power, tricking, betraying each other . . . Promise me you won't do something rash, like that Sierra crossing."

He smiled at her impatiently. "Now don't go around on that. We've been all over that. If I hadn't seized the moment we'd have to wait till spring—we might never have got to California at all!"

She ran her fingers over the back of his hand. "I missed you—God, you *know* how I missed you . . . but Charles, I'd have waited *twenty* years rather than have them find you frozen to death on top of some damned mountain!"

"It worked out all right."

"Yes, but what if sometime it *doesn't* work out all right? sometime you're *not* lucky? Sometimes it's wiser to wait, Charles, to draw back, be cautious . . ."

His eyes were troubled now, searching her face. ". . . Don't you have confidence in me?" he asked softly.

"*Of course* I have confidence in you," she cried in distress. "That's just the point—you're the most wonderful man who ever lived! Only you've got this impetuous streak in you, this devil-may-care brave thing that sometimes makes you act before you think, and I'm afraid of it, Charles! You can undo everything in one rash impulse, *everything*! . . . And you can *do* anything, darling; you can scale the very highest peaks of all if you want to, there's nothing you can't achieve if you set your heart and mind to it. Do you know what I mean, Charles, what I'm saying?"

He gazed into her eyes deeply, and nodded. "Yes. I know that."

"It's one of those times when events are in flux, everything is wide open and waiting—these moments come along only once every few decades. This one is *ours,* Charles. I know it! Promise me, if something unforeseen and too risky comes up, you'll take a deep breath, and fold your hands, and tell yourself: *'The cautious seldom make mistakes.'* Will you?"

"Who said that—Bancroft?"

"*Please* be serious. It was Confucius. Just say it to yourself when there's some risky moment. As a charm. Like that arrowhead Louie carries in that little bag around his neck. Will you, Charles?"

"All right. I will. I promise." He rose and drew her to him then and kissed her; the clamor in her blood was suddenly overpowering—her very core was liquid and on fire; she would have fallen if he hadn't been holding her.

"Oh, Charles," she moaned, "it's for me, really, only for me. I can't live without you. I realize that now . . ."

"I know," he said. His breath was warm against her throat. "I can't live without you, either. But I'll come back to you, I always will, I know it. It's our destiny. . . . You're a glorious woman, Jessie. The loving, lovely woman for me . . ."

MONTEREY

By late August Frémont was at Bent's Fort on the edge of the Rockies, choosing the last of his sixty men. It was a big company, mostly strangers; he didn't let rough manners and a taste for whiskey stand against men who could ride and shoot. He had reclaimed the big California stallion, Sacramento, from pasture at Westport, stripped the surrounding country for first-class horses and mules, and made sure that every man was well armed with rifle and pistol. He himself was carrying one of Samuel Colt's remarkable new revolvers, as they were calling them. Ten of his ablest people were Delaware Indian scouts led by a square-faced chief named James Sagundai, who carried a war club with a knot on the end bigger than a big man's fist.

Carson hurried up from Taos and brought along a fellow named Dick Owens in whom he set great store. Tom Fitzpatrick was away, but in his place as camp conductor Frémont engaged another trapper captain of equal stature, Joseph Reddeford Walker. He felt immediately comfortable with Walker, who was nearly fifty, his black hair streaked with gray, a Tennessean who had made epic journeys. Like Jedediah Smith, he had been one of the first Americans to venture over the mountains into California; like Provost and Fitzpatrick and Bridger, he held a thousand trails etched mile by mile in his mind. He was overfond of his own middle name, a small vanity that tickled Carson, who called him Old Reddy.

"Reddy, hell," Walker would growl in return. "I'm more than ready to whup your butt, Kit." He liked Carson.

Preuss had found a steady job in Washington and his wife demanded he keep it; his place had been taken by a young artist named Edward Kern who looked promising. Alex Godey and Billy Rasmussen had joined at St. Louis.

Frémont had found Louie and Proue awaiting him on the landing at Westport, Proue square as a barrel, Freniere tall and slender in his beaded city suit, the Hawken with the buffalo scene carved on its stock cradled in his arm. He had stuck an eagle feather in his hatband and anchored it with a turn of thread; it made him look like a cavalier. With a huge grin, he'd confided that matrimony had done snuck up and caught him. "Made a new man outta him, Cap'n," Proue had said, "and half the girls in Fort Pierre, their noses went right out of joint. But I dried all their tears."

At Bent's Fort Frémont learned that the Texans had voted themseves into the Union on July Fourth. That was the signal for General Zachary Taylor's troops to enter Texas; they would march for the Rio Grande to protect territory now deemed American. The Mexicans had said the admission of Texas would mean war—but they'd also agreed to talk. Which would it be? There was no word on that, just that the Texans had staged one wild, hell-raising Fourth of July in celebration.

In three hard months Frémont cut a new, more direct route to California across the Great Basin, and camped on the eastern flank of the Sierra Nevada in late November. Here he decided to split his party. He would take fifteen men straight over the mountains to Sutter's, running ahead of the first real snow. Walker would take the other forty-five south, find a safe pass, and come up the western flank. It would be just as well to appear modestly at Sutter's; he could reveal his full strength when he chose.

The fort was quiet when Frémont and his small detachment arrived. Sutter's flag still flew, but there was no sign of his opéra-bouffe army. Sutter greeted him warmly enough, though Frémont saw a flicker of alarm in his eyes. There was no news from abroad. The Swiss entrepreneur hadn't even heard of Texas' admission into the Union or Mexico's threats of war; neither event seemed to interest him. As predicted, the Californios had in fact thrown out the governor Mexico had sent to rule them. Did that mean they were now independent? No, they still considered themselves Mexicans; they simply rejected Mexican authority. Yes, yes, Sutter agreed testily, it *was* confusing. He had changed considerably in the past eighteen months. His face was puffy and veined and he darted quick sidelong glances at Frémont.

"Look here," he said at last. "Why have you returned?"

"Still mapping; it's an endless procedure," Frémont answered casually.

"You can cause a lot of trouble, you know."

"You weren't concerned the last time."

"Things are different now. But since you're here, what do you intend to do?"

Frémont said he planned to winter here, rest, examine the Sierras in more detail, and start for Oregon in the spring.

"I suppose that's all right," Sutter said. "And with only fifteen men, they can hardly consider that provocative."

"Provocative?" Frémont caught him up sharply.

Sutter then poured out an incredible story. When the rebellion began, he had led a column of American settlers in support of the Mexican governor, *against* the rebelling Californians. But Micheltorena's position had soon collapsed and he had fled. Quite naturally the Californians felt that their old suspicions of Sutter and the settlers were confirmed. Frémont could hardly credit what he was hearing: Sutter, who had seemed so authoritative and politic, had chosen the wrong side when it was evident that he needn't have involved himself at all! And the settlers had made the same stupid mistake.

"Where does that leave you?" he asked.

"Oh, my position's unchanged. They've no hard feelings, you know—they understood I was only doing my duty as an officer of the government. Nothing personal at all." Nervously he nodded. "I'm still magistrate, still the governor's—the *new* governor's—representative in the Sacramento Valley. But my neighbor, Gutierrez—that scoundrel, you remember him?—he's trying to persuade General Castro, the new commandant, to seize my fort and install *him* as magistrate!" Sutter had a strained look now, his long nose as pointed as an awl. "He'll get nowhere, of course. I'm very close to General Castro. Very close. But still, it's not pleasant."

The next day Frémont waited in his camp by the river for the settlers; he thought it better that they come to him, and he was sure they would. Sutter sounded so querulous and indecisive—where was the commanding figure of the year before? More than ever, the settlers were the key, but how the devil had those idiots managed to put themselves on the losing side?

He didn't have long to wait. The following afternoon a half-dozen horsemen appeared, led by two men—one rider thin and angular, the other bulky as a bear: Ezekiel Merritt and Big Fallon. The rider behind them spurred forward. Tessier reined up with a clatter and cried, "Hot damn, Cap'n, but ain't you a sight for sore eyes!" He half-fell dismounting in his impatience, clasped Frémont's hand, seized Carson in a bear-hugging *abrazo,* while the others gathered around them. Tessier had bought the land he wanted; he and Ingalls were working a hundred-fifty head of good cattle already, Ingalls had found himself a woman . . .

Merritt approached with his hand out. "Mighty good to see you, Cap'n," he said. Brown juice was still leaking from the corner of his mouth. "I told 'em you'd be back. Didn't expect you this soon, though." Then his smile faded. "This all the boys you brung? Don't look like but a dozen or so."

"Oh," Frémont said easily, "I've enough to do what I came to do."

"And what's that, Cap'n?" Fallon asked. Purvis and William Hargrave joined them.

"Look around. Explore the territory. Find out what's going on."

"We thought maybe you come to help us out," Purvis said bluntly. He hadn't changed; his eyes were round as a bear's and as shiny.

Frémont ignored that. "I hear you boys got yourselves in a fix with the Californians. What in hell prompted you to back the Mexicans?"

"The Californios always talked about throwing us out, and that Mex governor never gave us no trouble." Merritt looked embarrassed. "We figured we'd be better off with him than with the Californios running things. And then Sutter—"

"Shit on Sutter," Purvis said.

"Well, we did get fooled on Sutter, I guess," Fallon admitted. "Thing is, Cap'n, he's a lot better merchant than he is a soldier, for all his soldier talk. He just ain't no kind of leader at all."

"That's the problem," Merritt said. "Seems like we can't never agree on nothing. What we need in the worst way is someone all the boys'll listen to—someone who can knock heads together."

"But it worked out," Frémont said. "You're still here . . ."

"Yeah," Hargrave said, "but for how long? The Californios are gonna come down on us like a duck on a june bug."

"Sutter says he's still in solid."

"Like hell," Fallon said. "You know what he's up to? He wants to sell his fort to 'em so they can put an army here and stop any more American settlers from coming in."

Frémont's head came up. "You sure of that, Fallon?"

"Hell yes, I'm sure! And old Vallejo over to Sonoma wants to take him up on it."

Frémont glanced questioningly at Merritt.

"Mariano Vallejo—big general, Cap'n. Used to be commandant of California troops and he's still got a regular arsenal over at Sonoma. In northern California what he says pretty well goes. Always claims he's a friend of the Americans, but I don't know—you see, Sutter's got so many debts out they could seize his fort anytime. He's trying to sell before the roof falls in."

Well, now—that changed everything. His uneasiness about Sutter had been right. He was no longer a force to work with; if anything, he was a threat to be circled warily. And if the Californians were serious about turning back American emigrants, they were more hostile than Frémont had expected. Could forcing trail-worn emigrants back into the deadly desert be construed as an act of war? Would it justify retaliatory measures by an American officer?

"That puts some pressure on you," he said. "If they stop new settlers, won't they come after you next?"

"They say those who've taken out Mex citizenship will be all right."

"Ah. And you've all done that?"

He saw their faces tighten.

"We're Americans, Cap'n, not Mexicans. And you gotta become a Catholic, kiss the Pope's ring and all. The little religion I got, I ain't about to give it away."

Frémont shifted ground again. "You hear about Texas? They voted themselves in—Texas is a state now."

This *was* news, all around; there was a sudden stir of excitement.

"God damn!" Ingalls shouted. He loosed a Texas yell and slapped Fallon on the back. "That's what we ought to do out here—just grab it and go. What I've been saying all along."

"How the hell would we do that?" Hargrave snapped.

Merritt was watching Frémont as he spoke. "There's seven, eight hundred of us now," he said. "More'll come this year, and if the Californios try to turn 'em back, that might just touch it off."

"We never been able to get together on nothing before," Fallon said morosely. "Wouldn't on this, neither."

"That's because there's nobody worth listening to," Merritt said. "Up till now, that is."

There was a long silence.

Purvis said: "We're looking right at you, Cap'n. We figured that's why you come back. If it ain't, then suppose you tell us straight out what you're doing in California."

Careful, now. You don't want to start something you can't stop. Remember what Jessie said. But Jesus Christ! A whole empire in the balance, hanging ripe in the tree—and these donkeys hemming and hawing and swapping insults.

"Well, I didn't come out here to lead a revolution." He gave them a severe look. "Do you take me for a common filibuster? Use your heads. If the United States intended to seize California it would've sent an army and a fleet, not an exploring party."

"Say, Fallon," Carson said, grinning widely, "you boys ain't asking us to *fight* your war for you, are you?"

"Don't give me no shit, Kit," Fallon rumbled. "This is real. This is a fight we could lose."

"That don't set too good, Cap'n Frémont," Hargrave said, "an American officer telling American folks its own government don't give a damn."

Frémont said: "It's your land. It's your future that's at stake. If you don't care enough about it to—"

"We do, Cap'n," Merritt said quickly, looking very serious. "If'n they push enough, we'll get together."

Frémont scuffed the dirt with the toe of his boot. "Well. If and when you do, Mr. Merritt, maybe we'll have something to talk about."

"Let's saddle up and go see the rest of California," Frémont said. He stood looking down at Carson, who lay with his head resting on his rolled apishamore.

The scout sat up suddenly. "Fifteen years ago, a fellow went around visiting and they tossed him in the calaboose, muy pronto."

"Wouldn't that make things interesting."

Carson studied him a moment and began to laugh. "You looking for a little excitement, Charlie?"

"Of course not, Kit," he snapped with mock severity. "You know me better than that. Of course, if any should happen to come our way . . ."

Well—why not ride right into Monterey, the capital of northern California? right into the lion's mouth? There'd be news at Monterey if it existed anywhere—and news seemed the only antidote to the quandary in which Frémont now found himself. Nothing had turned out the way he'd expected. Sutter was a spent force and the settlers were more vociferous than ever, begging him for the overt leadership he couldn't give without violating the President's injunction. He was frustrated, raw with impatience. It was now January 1846—the Mexican negotiations should have started five months before. Had they succeeded, or broken down? Either result would solve his problem—but suppose they were dragging on, were now at their most delicate, and he made a move that destroyed everything? *The cautious seldom make mistakes.* He smiled slowly, thinking of Jessie, missing her, wanting her. . . .

The trouble was that while he wasn't here to start a war, neither could he afford to wait while events caromed off on their own—they might carom into the wrong hands. If he could just find a way to weld the settlers into a cohesive body . . .

Head on down to the coast and see what happens—why not? Walker's party hadn't arrived yet, but that was all right. He'd leave Godey and four men to meet Walker and bring him along. He was fed up with sitting around, listening to Kit's tall tales. He wanted to see this country that he had come to shepherd into American orbit and fill with American settlers . . . Within the hour they were mounted and moving.

Riding in line, Frémont and Carson in the lead, Louie and Proue bringing up the tail, they came out of the Sierra foothills into rolling grass country marked with stands of live oak, cottonwood, tall pines, and dense clumps of madrone and manzanita. Wild horses galloped close to examine them, and glossy cattle spurted away spooky as deer when Frémont tried to approach them. That livestock would be worth a fortune anywhere else; here it was actually left untended.

The riders passed into settled country. Trails gave way to a road rutted by cart wheels. They crossed a crude bridge and began to see widely scattered houses of mud-colored adobe with red clay roofs. Some had orchards, vineyards and small gardens tucked behind their walls. Once Frémont saw a wheel lifting water from a creek, sending it through sluices to irrigate the fields. Still, seen from a rise, the ranchos made such occasional patches they only emphasized how little the land was used. A fertile, well-watered country that begged for settlers like those now moving into Kansas in ever greater numbers, pushing the frontier out to the very edge of the grasslands. The salt desert, those backbreaking canyons had balked them—so far. . . .

The road led into a mission that lay in ruins. Sutter had told him about them: eighty years earlier Catholic friars had established twenty-two missions, each a small empire with granaries, warehouses, corrals, and outbuildings surrounding a church with twin belfries and carved oak doors. Indians—acolytes, the friars had called them—had provided the labor for these agricultural utopias. But Church power had waned in Mexico after the revolution. A dozen years ago the missions were closed, their lands placed in the public domain. Sutter's Indians had come from these closed missions.

It was a revelation to ride among those vast crumbling structures. Roofs were gone and adobe walls were melting back to earth, ghosts of structures past. Only the church remained in use, its bells ready to summon the faithful to mass. What a profligate people, who could leave land as rich as any in the world to lie fallow and let a great institution's buildings collapse in the rain.

The few people they met appeared gracious. A man saluted them from a pear orchard, children clung to a wall and giggled as they passed, a woman drawing water from a well gave them a smile when they touched their hat brims. Horsemen wearing tight black suits with brilliant *serapes* and high-crowned hats eyed them—and their weapons—warily, murmured "*Buenos días, señores,*" and moved on. The lack of reaction to their passing made the men uneasy.

"There's an old saying with Apaches," Carson said. "When you *don't* see 'em is the time to watch your scalp. Reckon we're getting sucked in?"

"I don't think so," Frémont said. He had a plan ready. If soldiers appeared, Louie and Carson were to slip away and ride hard to find Walker. There was some risk in taking such a small party into what might prove to be enemy country, but they were well armed.

The winter rains had begun. The ocean was near—you could feel it; fog seeped over the hills carrying the smell of the sea. The clouds bellied low and stiff winds drove the rain under their coats. It seemed much colder than the forty-five degrees Frémont's thermometer showed. They rode with their heads pulled down, their rifles booted and covered.

Near Monterey they camped on a stream. Frémont and Carson rode alone into the queen city of northern California and found it a village with streets of sand. Frémont had supposed that because there were so few people in the interior there would be crowds here, but the streets were almost empty; their arrival created no stir. The Argentine pirate Bouchard had sacked the town in '18, and they said it had never recovered; not easy to replace things like forges and rifles and augers out here on this wild coast. But imagine a simple freebooter being able to humble a provincial capital that easily!

The rains passed; the sun sparkled on houses of plastered adobe that had been carefully whitewashed, their roofs glistening red tile. Here and there gates were ajar; inside Frémont could see lush central gardens. The town was built in a bowl that fell to a partly protected bay. A hard wind blew off the Pacific, kicking whitecaps against blue water; the two ships in the harbor had set second anchors. Both ships flew the Stars and Stripes—merchantmen out of Boston, he judged. At the foot of one of the streets he saw a long wharf and a customhouse.

On a hill overlooking bay and town was a *presidio* of yellow stone, the Mexican flag snapping overhead in the wind, soldiers in blue uniforms lounging outside its gates. Here was the seat of military authority for all of California, headquarters of the new *comandante,* General Castro, whose favor Sutter so ardently courted. Frémont studied it: this sleeping lion atop the hill, what would it do if he rode up with his lance and pricked its paw?

First, though, he would see Thomas O. Larkin, The American consul to California, who might have some news. Larkin was an American trader who had lived fourteen years in Monterey. Secretary of State Buchanan had been taken with the thoughtful clarity of his reports. He was a Boston man in his late forties with graying side whiskers and pursed lips. He received them in a home with floors of waxed red tile and furniture that was rudely made but well polished. He introduced his wife and children, who were the first born to an American woman in California's history; Mrs. Larkin poured tea for them.

"I hadn't expected an American officer." Larkin's voice was nasal and flat; he sounded slightly accusing. "May I ask your purpose in coming here?"

Frémont repeated his easy formula of an explorer in need of a wintering place, adding casually that he did hope for some news of the negotiations.

The consul flashed him a look that was at once wary and appraising. "Not a word." He waved a hand as if to dismiss the subject. "I'm sure that's a dead issue anyway."

Frémont let his surprise show.

"Well," Larkin said, "Washington's been trying to buy California for years. I never thought they had any chance of succeeding." He put down his cup and added, "I'm working on my own plan to persuade the Californians to bring the province under American protection."

"You are?" Frémont's head was spinning: just how many plans *were* there to take California?

"That's why your arrival is—well, not very opportune," Larkin said; he gave a very small smile. "No offense, of course, but it would be fatal for the Californians to scent force in your presence when I have virtually talked them into joining of their own accord."

"You surprise me, sir," Frémont said.

"Why? You do know that they have separated from Mexico? Well, then—they won't be able to stand on their own."

"Yes . . . I looked for a British warship in the bay."

"To be sure—that's a threat. But we'll move first. Unfortunately the Californians are so busy squabbling among themselves that it's hard to get their attention on real issues."

It seemed that California had in effect two competing rulers. One was the military commandant, General José Castro, in his yellow *presidio* on the hill, who controlled northern California. Ostensibly he was a Mexican Army officer and his men wore Mexican uniforms, but in fact they were all Californians and took no orders whatever from Mexico City. The other California power was the governor, a bombastic man named Pio Pico who controlled the south from Los Angeles. North and south were at each other's throats, always had been, probably always would be. Whatever Pico did, Castro disapproved, Thomas Larkin said, waving his pipe like a metronome; whatever Castro did, Pico challenged. When either armed to defend California, the other instantly assumed that the real purpose was an attack on him.

"You expect to rally them to us, despite their wrangling?" Frémont asked. It sounded wrong; if Larkin succeeded everything would be solved, but it sounded wrong.

"Yes, I do. General Castro can't commit himself immediately, but General Vallejo is on our side."

"At Sonoma? But he's the one who wants to buy Sutter's Fort to block further American immigration. . . . Do you mean to say he's on *our* side?"

Now it was Larkin's turn to show surprise. "Oh, you know about that, do you? I think it's more that Sutter wants to sell than that Vallejo wants to buy."

"The settlers are worried, though."

The consul's lips pursed into a prim line. "Pay no attention to them, Captain. They're ignorant men at best. Unfortunately, the Californians accept them as representative Americans, when in fact they're just common trash."

Frémont saw Carson's face go hard. Larkin was too much the Bostonian or too long away from home: half of Missouri was made up of men like Merritt.

"They're American citizens, Mr. Larkin," he said quietly. "And many of them are good men. Honest, dependable men. I would not call them trash."

The consul flushed. "Of course I was speaking in generalities."

"Not in general, not in particular . . ." He paused. "A majority of the Californians support your approach, do you think?"

"Well, a substantial group also wants Britain to form a protectorate. And another's interested in the French, for religious reasons. But I'm convinced we have the best chance."

The best chance! Chance wasn't at all what Frémont had in mind. He listened to Larkin with growing dismay. To dismiss Larkin's "common trash" was to abandon the strongest American card. To assume that partisan Californios would all agree to American rule struck Frémont as downright naive. More likely one group would break and turn to the British, and then the Royal Marines would deal with the rest. The situation was even more volatile than he had feared.

Two days later Larkin took Frémont to the *presidio.* General Castro had learned of Frémont's presence only that morning and wanted to see him. The general awaited them in an office that was draped in red velvet yet still seemed rather shabby. A pouter pigeon of a man, he wore a Mexican general's dark blue uniform whose gigantic scarlet lapels reached from breastbone to shoulder. He was very sure of himself. After some casual chat with Larkin he rounded suddenly on Frémont, plainly for effect, and demanded to know why he had come to California. Frémont quietly described his need for a winter refuge. He had decided in advance that if he were going to challenge the general, it would not be in his office.

Californians were well aware of the desirability of their rich province, and found the sight of armed foreigners offensive, Castro declared; on the other hand, they were a generous and compassionate people. Therefore Frémont and his men would be permitted to remain in California for the winter—but only in unsettled areas.

"I order you to withdraw immediately to the far interior. Go into the San Joaquin Valley, beyond the last settlements." He chuckled. "The hunting there should please your men—I understand they're wild as Indians."

"Not all *that* wild, *Señor General.*" Frémont smiled. Another gilded rooster. The woods were full of them out here. He remembered old Benton analyzing the loss of half North America by the French, his hooded eyes hard with cynical wisdom: "When you possess something of great value that others covet, you must be prepared to defend it."

Castro frowned, stood suddenly, dismissing them. "*Bueno.* All understood? Withdraw immediately to the interior. Avoid the coast and all settled areas. Permit me to warn you that the consequences of disobedience will be most serious. *Buenos días, señores.*"

Frémont rented a vacant ranch about twenty miles inland from Monterey as a bivouac for his men. He sent Carson to intercept Walker's group and a few days later met them at the ranch. They were spread through a large oak grove with a curious air of domesticity, he thought as he rode in; tents, cooking fires, meat smoking on racks, clothes drying on bushes, the remuda in the distance; it was like coming home.

"Big Fallon turned up a while back," Walker said. "Been years since I seen him. Had a long, skinny fellow named Merritt with him. Mouth full of tobacco—"

"He's going to swallow it one of these days."

"That's the one. They was some impressed with our boys. And Merritt asked me special to tell you they'd done some tall thinking on what you said."

Frémont waited a week, and then another week; each day the pressure grew. It was February. After six months, surely the lack of news from Mexico City meant that something had gone wrong. He could wait here forever with his men getting staler and more restless every day—and eventually they would see a company of Royal Marines coming down the road, and then the fat would be in the fire for good. He had to *do* something . . .

There was a stir at the edge of camp and Larkin rode in. Frémont went to greet him. "Do you bring me news?"

The consul gave him a sour look. "No news," he said, dismounting. In that instant Frémont knew he had waited long enough. He felt a sense of relief that was almost physical and gave Larkin a broad smile. "But there are disturbing rumors about you," Larkin continued as he gazed about the camp.

"Are there? I certainly hope they're favorable ones."

"Good God, Captain," the consul said. "It's true. You have so many!"

The men came up to measure the visitor. Frémont could see them through Larkin's Boston eyes: powerful men, full-bearded, trail-lean, faces burned dark, knives in their belts or their boots, pistol butts against their ribs; men you'd want on your side in a fight but wouldn't like to see hanging around your daughters. He hid a grin under his hand. Good thing Kit hadn't passed on that remark about common trash—he'd threatened his favorite scout with the old bastinado if he so much as hinted at it. Even Kern, the artist who'd mastered the instruments so well and turned out lovely watercolor studies, had a bronzed, swaggering look. Sagundai, the big Delaware chief, strolled past, his hair in braids, his face set in its usual malevolent expression.

"Lord," Larkin whispered, "who is *that*?"

The Indian heard him and whirled, threw up his war club with the terrible knot on its end, barked, *"Sagundai!"*—and bowed. Larken went pale.

"Chief of my Delaware scouts," Frémont said gravely. "One of the most dangerous men in North America."

"Really," Larkin said, "this is outrageous! I assured General Castro—oh, he isn't going to like this at all. Not at all!" He urged Frémont to withdraw immediately to the interior.

"I'm not going to run off," Frémont said. "We're not bothering anyone—and if we do, I daresay we can deal with it. My men have come a long way. They need to rest and have a little fun."

"Well, go as soon as you can," Larkin said uneasily. "And go inland—don't bring men like these down toward the coast."

"You've got a lot to learn about America, Consul. It's a big country."

Frémont waited another week. Californians from neighboring ranches came to visit. The boys enjoyed the attention. Contests sprang up, the Californios stunning the Americans with their horsemanship, the Americans reciprocating with plain and fancy shooting. The Americans threw a party with a feast and no shortage of liquor. The Californios brought their own music and came ready to dance.

It was a big night, the kind that loosens everyone up, spotted with occasional eruptions. Slats Abercrombie thought he had a firm understanding with a plump, big-breasted California girl, who at the last minute decided to go instead with Bushnell. Abercrombie hit Bushnell with a skewing iron and Bushnell laid his face open with a single stroke of his blade; Frémont got that broken up and Bushnell was ready to claim his prize when the girl's father, a dignified *viejo* with great white mustachios, turned up and shook out his horsewhip. It looked as if the war over California was going to start right there, until Carson and Proue bulled up between them and got them separated. About then Abercrombie figured out what had happened to him and went for his pistol—and all that saved *that* situation was Frémont's express order that there were to be no loaded handguns in camp. Bushnell swore he was going to cut some California throats before this night was over, and Walker got so mad he offered to turn both men loose if they'd guarantee to kill each other. All in all it was, as Carson observed ruefully next morning, some piss-cutter of a night.

All the same, it was a precarious state of affairs.

The men were full of the devil—too much time, too little to do. This infernal waiting! It was time to move. Somewhere, anywhere . . .

"Good," Walker said. "Where we heading?"

"Down toward the coast; down toward Monterey again," Frémont said. He saw Carson's slow grin. "Let's go see what we can see. Isn't that why the bear went over the mountain?"

Ten days later, after they had gone nearly to Monterey and then circled south, moving slowly and casually, stopping each night where they pleased, a Mexican officer followed by two dragoons swept into their camp at a canter, not bothering to slacken speed among men and horses. A mule with packsaddle half-unloaded jumped skittishly. The saddle slipped and the mule began to kick.

Carson bawled angrily: "Hyah! Slow them horses down!"

The officer reined roughly before Frémont's tent and dismounted. He was young and plump and wore a brilliant uniform with high black cavalry boots.

The men crowded around, staring. "Now, ain't he a beauty?" Bushnell murmured, loud enough to hear.

It helped, Frémont saw instantly, that General Castro had sent an arrogant young fool to deliver his reaction to their march through California. The general's message, which the lieutenant haughtily presented, noted that Frémont and his men had not followed instructions, and ordered them to depart California immediately or be expelled.

The young officer added his own embellishments. He advised them that to try the general's patience was to learn the mettle of the famous California lancers. Frémont would be lucky to avoid being hanged; and as for his men—the officer glanced about contemptuously—they would be running for the high mountains, each with a lancer's initials carved on his backside.

Frémont waited, giving the youth rope, watching his men get angry. He was angry himself, but very comfortable too, calm as always at the prospect of action, his decision made.

"That's enough, Lieutenant," he said finally. "Here is my answer to General Castro."

All right! He ripped the paper in two and dropped it on the ground. In formal Spanish he said, "I find your manners and your general's order unacceptable. I am an officer of the United States. My men and I have entered California peacefully, we have committed no offense, and we refuse to be singled out for arbitrary treatment."

The young officer looked as if his uniform had become suddenly too tight. He started to reply but Frémont cut him off.

"Tell General Castro that we'll stay just as long as we please and we'll go where we like. We will not be intimidated. Inform the general that any attempt to carry out his intemperate threats will have the most serious consequences."

He took a sudden step and the lieutenant involuntarily gave way. "Now go—before you find yourself in real trouble."

The officer mounted, checked his suddenly fractious horse, and called, "You will be punished for this!"

As the soldiers galloped off Louie said into the small silence, "I thought that fancy sumbitch was going to swallow his tongue there at the end."

Someone laughed, but several men looked uneasy. The sun was setting; a chill had come in the air.

"I don't much like getting orders from some popinjay in a cocked hat, whether he's a lieutenant or a general," Frémont said. He watched the men. They all had to be content. "Any of you boys trembling at the thought of a Mexican soldier?"

"Mex soldiers back in Taos sure ain't fighters," Carson answered easily. "Say they're lovers, but the women say, 'Unh-uh!' " The men were grinning now. "They're four-flushers, that's what they are."

"Tell you what," Frémont said. "It wouldn't surprise me if the idea of looking down sixty rifle barrels cools them right off. But just in case they want to try us, we'll move in the morning to that hill we spotted yesterday."

The Delaware scouts came in at first light: no one had approached in the night. Fifteen minutes later they were saddled up and moving.

Hawk's Peak was several hundred feet high. On three sides it was a difficult climb; the fourth—the mountain's front—was an easier slope, where a trail had been made by cattle driven up to graze. On ahead a level stone outcropping formed a ledge. The top of the hill flattened out for about sixty grassy acres, a third of it in timber. There was a good spring among the trees. The men started cutting logs for a rough breastworks; Frémont selected a slender sapling, had it stripped, tied on a flag—and up went the Stars and Stripes to a loud cheer. It was the first time American colors had flown over California soil.

"Looks good, don't it?" Carson said. "Looks like it belongs."

A little after noon Frémont saw a tower of dust rising far down the road. He focused his glasses: A column of troops in blue uniforms was riding at double time, lance tips upright and glittering in the sun, muskets in boots. He was conscious of a curious tightness under his ribs. At the end came a small artillery piece, a four-pounder, probably. The Californians had rallied more quickly and effectively than he'd expected. Whistling softly between his teeth, he thought of the brass cannon abandoned somewhere in the Sierra, and Zindel's sorrowful face. What a comfort it would be now. . . .

The men were watching. No one said anything. Quickly he put them to work improving the breastworks, Rasmussen and Godey trimming the logs and notching them so they locked together. He ordered a long trench dug behind it, and earth packed against the logs. If there was shelling he wanted his men to have somewhere to go.

While they worked he posted sentries on the back and sides of the flat top, and led Dick Owens to where the mountain fell off in sharply broken rock. Carson's faith in Owens had proved fully justified. A big man whose intelligent blue eyes rarely showed much expression, he and Carson had started a farm together outside Taos and he seemed as happy as Kit to have escaped its tedium. Owens hadn't spoken to Frémont more than a half-dozen times since they'd left Bent's Fort, but he always made sense and he was always ready. Frémont like him.

"Look, Dick," he said, "if they come at all, they'll come up that easy cowpath at the front. But if *I* was doing it, I'd come up here." He gestured to the field of rock below. "Steep as hell but it's passable, it's got good cover and I'd figure we wouldn't be watching it. I'd come up on foot, very quietly, gather under the lip here, and hit us all at once. Wouldn't you?"

"Yep," Owens said.

"All right. There's two crucial places. See way down yonder, beyond that dead tree—they can't get up without crossing that in the open. And the other, close here, that stretch of open rock. I want you to keep watch on the first place. I'll send Sandy Pinkham to you, and if you see 'em coming, send him back in a hurry. Then we'll nail 'em at the second place. Got that?"

"Yep."

With Louie, Frémont went back down the way they had come to look at the ridge formed by the stone outcropping. It was flat, and deeper than it looked from below. A patch of low cedar grew clear to the edge at one place. An open, fairly level bench stretched down to the woods.

Later in the afternoon a courier brought a letter from Larkin, who wrote stiffly that the country was in an uproar and that Castro was prepared to throw two hundred troops against him.

Frémont scrawled a quick answer. He was strengthening his position, he wrote, concluding: "If attacked we will fight to extremity and refuse quarter, trusting to our country to avenge our deaths." He smiled grimly as he signed the letter: he was sure that it would become public and it certainly should make his point.

When the sun was low he saw distant movement and soon made out a new column of lancers, sixty or so; from the direction of Salinas came a battery of artillery, three guns with limbers, escorted by thirty lancers. As dusk fell he could see cooking fires in the California camp. He had expected the Californians to make a small show, but the situation had become real now.

He told Sagundai to be sure that his men ate well and slept; there would be work later. The big Delaware grunted; he had a skinning knife and pistol in his belt, a dagger on his powder-horn strap, a rifle in his left hand, the war club in his right. Well before midnight he led the Delawares down the path. Watching from above, Frémont saw them cross the ledge and then the open place and vanish into the dark woods.

Two hours before dawn the men were up, cooking fires behind log shields casting a faint light. Frémont heard an owl hoot. It hooted twice more and, after a pause, once.

"That'll be Sagundai," Carson said. "Watch for him, boys."

The Indian came into camp like a ghost. He squatted beside Frémont, leaning on the club. Sagundai spoke in a patois of Spanish, broken English, Delaware, grunts, sighs, grimaces. Frémont never had any trouble understanding him. His face, mobile as rubber, lighted with menacing cheerfulness at the prospect of battle.

The Californians were forming up, ready to march, he said, maybe a hundred of them. It looked as if they intended to come right up the cowpath—at least, that's what they said. Frémont was startled.

"You could hear them?"

Sagundai gave him a pitying look. "*In* their camp. Long*side* them." He held his hands about four feet apart. He gestured at Crane, a skinny Delaware with a hatchet profile and a single gold tooth in the front of his mouth. It seemed that Crane had wanted to lift some hair, but Sagundai had told him no, not yet. Frémont nodded solemnly. Delighted with the attention, Crane smiled, the tooth bright in the firelight.

Frémont quickly sketched his plan. Twenty men down to the ledge to meet the Californios. Twenty more under Walker on the breastwork to cover a withdrawal if it came to that. Ten under Owens to guard the perimeters. Sagundai and his party in the woods on the south side of the trail, ready to attack from the flank.

He tapped his twenty and led them down the path, Sagundai and Crane following. He included Kern in this group; the artist was proving himself an effective assistant. The men spread along the ledge, flat and out of sight, and he stationed Freniere, Carson and Godey beside him in the cedar thicket. Pale light had broken. The air was chill and very still. The open stretch below was indistinct, the woods dark and mysterious. In his mind's eye Frémont saw the first horsemen appear, pause, then start across.

He still didn't believe the Californians wanted to come up that hill against sixty rifles; maybe they needed a sting to dissuade them. Louie would fire first at the lead horseman, then Carson at the next, then Godey—one, two, three: and he wanted to see three empty saddles. If three shots and three down didn't discourage them, then the rest of the men on the ledge would open up, and then the Delawares would hit them from the flank. But if the Californians wanted to retire after that first bite, Frémont wanted them free to go. He caught Sagundai's arm, holding him hard, scowling: understood? he was *not to attack* until he heard *general* firing. Sagundai nodded, grinning ferociously. Frémont watched him cross the open stretch at a run, Crane just behind him, and enter the woods. The light was growing; he studied the ground.

"Let 'em come halfway across," he said. "To that white rock, say." He paused, peering. "Can you be *sure* of the shot, Louie?"

"You want his left eye or his right?" He gave Frémont a wolfish smile, and an image of the high plains flashed into Frémont's mind, sunshot, the sky immense, and Louie crawling over the lip of a hill, the buffalo beyond. That was a hunter's look; he saw Freniere's fingers move delicately over the buffalo carving.

Silence. The birds were gone. The sky was brightening swiftly. The men were motionless. No one spoke. War with California—war with Mexico—could begin in the next half-hour. Would begin. Were negotiations still going on? Would this blow them sky-high? Was it all a disastrous, irretrievable mistake? *The cautious seldom make . . .*

Jessie's face tense and pleading in the lamplight. Well, he *had* been, goddamnit. For weeks, months. He'd waited and palavered, rejected Merritt's and Fallon's overtures, and eaten crow from that stuffed popinjay of a Castro; and now he'd had enough. Enough!

The cautious—

If it went well, he might be decorated; if it went badly he could be cashiered—if he were still alive to answer the charges. But what exactly did "well" mean? He passed his eyes over Louie's stubby, cheerful face, Kit's lean, sardonic features. Would this three-sided hill become another Alamo—would their mutilated corpses shock a nation into war, if nothing else already had? Did he have the right to consign these good men, these close and trusted friends, to death and maiming?

He set his teeth. The hell with it. They were here, the die was cast, events were in control now. *But if they mean to have a war, let it begin here.* Who had said that? Some other troubled captain, waiting behind a barricade for the storm to break—

The sky broke into full daylight. Feeling preternaturally calm but aware of his thudding pulse, that strangely heightened sense of awareness, of crystal clarity, he lay still, watching the opening in the dark woods.

Sunlight cracked in a low slant over the hill behind them and caught the tops of the trees below. An owl talked: three hoots, then two.

The Californians were coming.

A dozen horsemen trotted out of the woods. They paused, milling about, as the troop emerged. Then an officer raised his arm and started across. Frémont studied them through his glasses. The officer in the lead had heavy red mustachios that joined red whiskers on both sides. No face in all his life had ever looked so clear. The men following him were dragoons, lances set in saddle sockets, muskets in boots. They were moving very slowly.

"They don't like it," Carson said softly.

The red-whiskered officer turned and called something in a loud, confident voice. Frémont couldn't make out the words, though the sound boomed across the open place in the morning stillness. Several voices answered him as though in argument. They weren't real troops, he realized; they were militia, local ranchers hurriedly dressed in uniforms, and they were just beginning to feel the significance of this long ridge facing them. The officer spoke again, more loudly, drew his sword and turned resolutely forward. He was approaching the white rock.

"Take him and the rest'll run," Carson whispered, his voice like a pen scratching on parchment.

The officer was at the rock. In the corner of his eye Frémont saw Louie's finger slowly drawing up trigger slack. His hand was perfectly steady. The eagle feather in his hat quivered. The California troops had stopped. The officer was fifty feet ahead of them, moving alone.

"Hold it," Frémont murmured.

Just beyond the rock the Mexican looked back and saw his men stopped. He turned his horse and rode back to them. There was a long wrangle now, a jumble of voices; then all the horsemen began to turn.

"I'll be a son of a bitch," Carson breathed the words. "Lost their nerve."

The column of dragoons filed back into the woods, the red-whiskered officer now at their rear, his shoulders slumped.

"That feller'll never know how close he came to pushing up daisies," Louie said. He lowered the hammer on the Hawken. His hands were trembling faintly now.

It was over. Frémont waited until he saw Sagundai striding boldly across the open ground to report, but he knew the Californios were gone and wouldn't be back. A demonstration was one thing; riding into sixty rifles was another.

"Pulled foot!" Raffie Proue crowed. "Couldn't face the music."

"Now that," Kit declared, "is what *I* call a three-ring Mexican standoff!"

Everyone was talking now, pushing at one another and whooping in relief.

Frémont took a deep breath and passed a hand through his hair. "Put on the coffeepot, boys," he said. "We've earned a little refreshment."

The Californians stayed in their camp that day and were there the next morning. Frémont studied them from above, and from time to time Sagundai sent in a runner with the same report: nothing moving.

At midday Owens brought in visitors: Merritt and Big Fallon. They had climbed the back side of the mountain carrying white flags. Owens was looking pleased. "I told Fallon he was lucky I didn't part his hair just to teach him some manners."

Merritt gazed up at the American flag. "Now ain't that a beautiful sight," he said wistfully. "I got some of the boys down the hill, and I can get more damned quick. You want about fifty of us to back you up?"

"Why no," Frémont told him calmly. "I think we're about finished here. They're not coming." He looked around at his men and smiled. "We can't wait forever for 'em to get up their nerve. They had their chance to try us, right, boys? I think we're going to go on about our business."

"We'd sure be proud to help," Merritt said uncertainly.

"Help us? You'd better look to your own affairs, Mr. Merritt."

The settler's eyes were large; he gave Frémont a puzzled, wary look. "But it's *you* done spat in their faces."

"Oh, we just wanted everyone to know we're here."

"Well," Merritt said, nodding slowly, "*that* point is made, with bells. I tell you, things won't never be the same in California. Not never again."

PALE RIDER

IT WAS LATE APRIL and time to go. Time to put California and its interminable, maddening uncertainties behind him. Frémont and his party were at Peter Lassen's ranch far up the Sacramento, the last outpost on the way to wilderness. They had spent six weeks drifting through settled country, moving with a provocative indolence, giving the Californios every chance to engage; and nothing had changed. The people treated them with the same blend of courtesy and indifference. The settlers remained divided, no news arrived from abroad, and Larkin still saw Frémont as an acute embarrassment.

It hadn't worked, he thought savagely. All his effort had sunk unnoticed into this amazing California lethargy, the way a feather bed will absorb a bullet with scarcely a puff of dust. He remembered Bancroft's bland expectations, his own naive assurance that he could be the catalyst, the conqueror. Were they all a little amused—even the settlers, even the British—at this feckless explorer *cum* freelance unable to find a windmill to demolish?

Well, now and then events control. A man struggles to shape his destiny, and then events flow over him like a thundering buffalo herd—or ignore him like a trout under a shelf refusing the fly. He had done everything he could within the limit of his mandate, which he now suspected had been skewed from the start. His jaws ached these days; consciously he unclenched his teeth. He was short-tempered with frustration, and the men became more restless every day. It was time to go.

They would head north above the Sierras into the Klamath country, on up the western flank of the Cascades. They would link the new route across the Great Basin to the Oregon Trail and be home by fall. At least it would be real, an end to this spongy ambiguity of shadows and hints and faint promises. Home by fall. . . . He thought of Jessie, saw her coming down the Westport levee at a run, skirts caught in one hand, Lily dragging from the other, her hair coming unfastened—the image left him dizzy with longing. But what would she think of his failure, after the first rapture had passed?—nothing to show for a year and a half but some new map points, the talk of empire dying in their throats, the old Senator strangely quiet. . . . Was that any way to go home?

Northbound they went, out of April into early May, past the Forty-second Parallel and out of California proper; good sightings, accurate positions, Kern turning into a mapping craftsman, old patterns falling into place; the hard Klamath country upon them, stony ground breaking horses' hooves, rations thinning; trail life, comforting because it was real. But Frémont rode half-turned in his saddle, looking back on failure, willing a messenger to come galloping out of the silent woods. It *couldn't* end this way.

Late one afternoon they were camped in a grove on the north shore of Klamath Lake. Salmon were in good supply, roasting on spits, filleted and laid on drying racks. Sagundai stood suddenly. "Horses coming," he said, and melted into the trees. Carson jerked his head at Owens, nodded to Freniere; they followed, rifles on full cock. The eagle feather on Louie's hat bobbed as he ran.

Three horsemen appeared, slowed to a cautious walk. The man in the lead was Tessier.

Frémont felt a wave of joy as the bulky man, smiling broadly, jumped down, staggered and nearly fell. "We've come some good piece," he said. "There's an officer from Washington back a ways. Says he has dispatches for you." The courier had gotten as far as Tessier's place on his own; Tessier had agreed to guide him along Frémont's trail. "He's about wore out, so we rode on to catch you. Left Ingalls and a couple of the boys with him."

They had met Indians after leaving the messenger, Tessier said; Klamaths painted for war. "We put our pistols in their faces and went right through 'em, but they sure wasn't smiling none."

At dawn Frémont started back with a small detachment—Carson, Owens, Freniere, Proue, Godey, Bushnell, Sagundai and three Delawares, and Tessier's men. They traveled hard, alternating lope and walk, eating up miles. Carson took the point, watching for sign, but the Indians made no appearance. They camped forty-five miles down the trail in an open glade on the lake's south shore. An hour later Ingalls rode in. An officer with wiry red hair and travel-stained clothes was just behind him on a worn roan.

"Captain Frémont? By God, I'm glad to see you, sir," he said, dismounting wearily and arching his back. "Archibald Gillespie, Lieutenant, United States Marine Corps." The roan sighed and put his head down as Gillespie opened a saddlebag and extracted a packet tightly bound in oilskin. "I've brought these many a mile—and believe me, the last five hundred were the hardest."

The packet was surprisingly slender. Frémont unwrapped it and saw three letters. One bore his name in Jessie's clear young hand, another was from Benton. The third, very thin, he opened. It was from Secretary of State Buchanan; it simply introduced Gillespie, without reference to his position or rank, as an officer fully in Mr. Buchanan's confidence. Frémont turned the single sheet over, examined the envelope. Was this *all*? Were there no instructions for him? He stared at Gillespie's dusty, exhausted face. All that effort—for *this*! It wasn't possible . . .

He tore open his father-in-law's letter, which sprawled over several pages, characteristically. He could see the old man crouched heavily over his desk, the oil lamp glowing as he orated his way along on paper. *I trust you'll keep a weather eye peeled for old John Bull who, with all the tenacity of the breed, never relaxes his grip on anything he's once sunk his teeth into; and though I have no doubt your path will be a thorny one, I am supremely confident you will move forcefully at this most crucial moment in our history.*

That was all—but the message was unmistakable. He turned to Jessie's letter then, wondering if perhaps they'd left more explicit instructions to her. It was the first word from her in more than a year, and it hurt him to have to scan it so swiftly. She said at the outset she would leave politics to Mr. T, and then went on to let him know in a dozen ways that she held him at the glowing center of her life. Irritated, pleased, a touch apprehensive, he read quickly, searching for the signal he needed so badly. *Dearest, I know that when the time comes you will act as you must. You won't feel too constricted by the lack of official authorization. These are propitious times, with so very, very much at stake for the nation—and for you and me, too. I know you will not fail to see your opportunities as they arise, and act—but discreetly!—on them.*

It was dark. The horses bunched in the glade were grazing, with their tails to a chilly wind that blew off the lake. Gillespie was sitting by one of the fires now, breaking a slab of red salmon apart with a knife, talking about his journey. He was a voluble young fellow, quite handsome, his manner quick and energetic. He seemed as much at home here as he might aboard ship—he was ragging Tessier and Ingalls on very familiar terms. Frémont filled a tin plate with fish and signaled the visitor, who joined him by a small fire where they could talk.

"Do you have verbal orders for me?" Frémont asked.

"*Specific* orders? No, sir."

"Mr. Buchanan merely introduced you—said I could put confidence in you."

"And Senator Benton?"

"Acquainted me with the situation as of November—nothing more." Of course, that wasn't quite true: Benton had let him know that Secretary Bancroft's instructions of May still held in November, but that was precious little. Incredulous, he demanded: "You chased me all this way—just to deliver these letters?"

"Oh, no—to bring you back to California! You're needed there."

"Am I, now! I languished there for five solid months and nobody needed me. Has the situation changed in the last month?"

"The important thing," Gillespie said slowly, "is that the President *wants* you there."

"Yes—well, he wanted me there before. But none of the conditions he expected arose, and all of the limitations he imposed held. What in hell's to be gained by going back now?"

Gillespie's manner changed abruptly. The amiable redhead joking by the fire disappeared and Frémont saw why he'd been chosen for this mission; it was easy to imagine him circulating effectively in an embassy crowd. He hesitated, gathering his thoughts, and then began to talk in a crisp, economical fashion.

On the express orders of President Polk, he had sailed to Vera Cruz, crossed Mexico by coach to Mazatlán, and taken ship for California. He had memorized messages for Commodore Sloat at Mazatlán and for Consul Larkin, which he'd delivered verbally; both merely reiterated the President's unwavering interest in California.

"My instructions to you? Well . . . I was to acquaint you with the President's thinking."

The assignment had fallen to Gillespie because his Spanish was fluent and he had a background in both diplomacy and intelligence. He'd been directed to report to the White House in civilian clothes at nine o'clock one evening, and he'd spent an hour with the President. He had formed strong impressions of Polk—quiet but forceful, highly politic, indirect, given to obscure and ambiguous remarks that nonetheless served to make his meaning clear. Gillespie had deduced three central themes: the President intended to have California, he was confident he could negotiate its purchase—and he counted on Captain Frémont's presence there.

"But what's new about that?" The words burst out of Frémont. "It's exactly the fear of *upsetting* those damned negotiations that has tied my hands."

From an inner pocket Gillespie took a leather case, extracted a slender *cigarro* and offered one to Frémont.

"What's new is that the negotiations have failed."

Frémont stared at him. That *was* news! "Do you know that for a fact?"

"As surely as anyone can. And with the talks off, I'm certain the President's determination to forestall a British move on California will be the cornerstone of his policy." He read the doubt in Frémont's face and smiled slightly. "Look," he said, "let me roll it out for you, and then you'll decide."

After Herrera was reelected in August, Polk had asked for a new statement of the Mexican president's willingness to negotiate. That confirmation reached Washington in October and the President, elated, had appointed John Slidell of New Orleans as his negotiator: Gillespie had been dispatched directly to Mexico, and he was on hand when Slidell reached Mexico City. At the American legation Gillespie had encountered an old friend—a cynical fellow, too long in the diplomatic service, perhaps, and overfond of tequila, but useful nonetheless—who had kept him abreast of the disastrous developments that followed.

The wind off the lake was colder. Most of the men were asleep now, rolled in their blankets under the trees at the edge of the glade. Frémont stirred the fire. The firelight glinted redly on Gillespie's beard. His eyes were shining: obviously he relished political maneuver.

What Polk had not grasped was that Herrera's reelection hadn't meant much—he remained under enormous pressure from the right. When Slidell arrived a storm of protest erupted. The Mexican press screamed that Herrera was peddling the national patrimony to the hated *norteamericanos*. Generals talked about hanging him to lampposts in the Gran Plaza; and under this onslaught, Herrera had backed down. Refused to receive Slidell. Now, it still might have been patched up when things cooled, Gillespie said, except that one General Paredes, a cold-eyed zealot, issued a *pronunciamento* declaring that *he* was seizing the government. Coup. Revolution. Paredes led his troops against the capital, and when he entered Mexico City, Herrera and his ministers called a hansom cab and fled. There'd been talk that Paredes had to order bunting hung at rifle point, but it was hung, and after he promised to shoot anyone who disagreed with him, the Mexican Congress had quieted right down. Gillespie chuckled and threw the end of his *cigarro* into the fire.

"I was in the Gran Plaza that day," he said. "Never saw anything like it. Maybe the people really do hate Paredes, I don't know, but they were drunk on glory that day. A half-million of 'em, dancing, spearing flowers on soldiers' fixed bayonets—and Paredes appeared on a balcony of the Palacio Nacional and made a speech to curl your hair. Talked for an hour at the top of his lungs, shouting that now, by God, a man with eggs was in control, they'd retake Texas and roll the *gringos* all the way back to Louisiana. And the people roaring *'Viva Mexico!' 'Dios y Libertad!'* every time he took a breath. It wasn't very comfortable to be an American in that crowd, I can assure you. And the very next day he had an army on the march for the Rio Grande—with orders to engage our troops on contact. . . . Then I got my orders and cleared out."

Gillespie was shivering in the night chill. "So where does that leave us? Quite possibly already at war; but certainly the negotiations are dead. Paredes used them to destroy Herrera—there's no way he could resume them himself even if he wanted to, which he obviously doesn't. My guess is that President Polk has taken this damned badly. He felt he had a promise to talk—he'll take Paredes' action quite personally. And you know, Zachary Taylor's on the Rio Grande with troops. If Paredes' men take a run at us—and they're going to—we're at war."

He peered at Frémont, smiling a lazy smile. "That means both you and I belong in California. What do you say?"

"I expect so," Frémont said. He felt a vast relief. "How *are* things there?"

"Ridiculous." Gillespie laughed softly. A proclamation by General Castro, issued after Frémont had left, said that all noncitizens would be ejected and their lands seized. It was just what the settlers had feared, but had it brought them together? Of course not. Merritt had called a meeting and they'd talked all night and decided exactly nothing. One faction insisted Castro was just bluffing. Still, Frémont owed the settlers something, for Castro was reacting at least in part to his challenge. He held a legitimate position in defense of American citizens, and the hazard of damage to the negotiations was removed. Yes, circumstances had altered—

Frémont saw the way opening before him.

"Larkin told me about something else that isn't widely known," Gillespie said. "A big group of California leaders got together and swore support for General Paredes. Given the fellow's attitude toward *gringos,* that shows pretty clearly how friendly the Californios are likely to be.

"And one other thing. There's an American warship in San Francisco Bay. USS *Portsmouth*, Captain Montgomery."

Frémont started. "Occupying, do you mean?"

"No no. Entirely peaceful call. But she's here because Larkin sent a distress message when you were up on that hill. Sloat sent the Navy to your rescue, but when Montgomery arrived, all was quiet, so he announced himself on a goodwill visit."

"Then he'll be leaving—"

"No, he will *not,*" Gillespie said emphatically. "I talked to him and made sure of that."

Gillespie yawned, his jaws cracking. He was totally exhausted. He went off to spread his blankets. Frémont stirred the fire, and crouching close to the flames began to reread the letters, over and over. Yes, the messages were there, couched in metaphor and intimation. The time is now. England must not get a foothold in California. We must move forcefully—but discreetly!—and sweep into the vacuum. Propitious times, momentous times—my God, yes! The time was right. He knew it in the very marrow of his bones . . .

The sound was dense, mushy, wet—one blow, like a melon broken: a sound Carson's belly remembered before his mind had even recorded. He had rolled free of his blankets and was on his knees, wide awake, had swept up his rifle without thought.

There was movement, very swift, very stealthy, at the corner of his eye. Men running. Someone was getting to his feet near the fire's dead ashes, and he heard Frémont's voice call, "Who's there?"

"Redskins in camp!" Carson roared. "On your feet! *On your feet, now!*"

A shadow swept toward him out of the dense black of the firs, something flashed dully. Hand ax. Instantly he fired and the man grunted and crashed into a fir's drooping limbs. Carson threw himself to his left and rolled away. A whip flicked just above his head and he heard the arrow clatter through the low branches.

Then the whole camp erupted in shouts and gunfire—a crazy-quilt of fire-flashes and stumbling, cursing figures, horses whinnying wildly, the harsh stink of gunpowder. There was a gout of flame two feet long: someone had overloaded in panic in the dark.

"Mark your man!" he shouted. "Take—care!"

He drew his pistol and stepped around the tree trunk, saw Crane in his striped capote swinging his empty rifle at several lunging figures, flailing and flailing. Carson raised the pistol, realized he would hit the Delaware, and leaped to one side for a flank shot. Two arrows appeared like magic in Crane's chest; they sounded like blows of a fist. *Whump-thump.* Black liquid gushed from Crane's mouth. As he went down, the lead Klamath sprang over him, knife in hand—and then Sagundai came out of the blackness, the gnarled war club swinging, and drove him back. Carson fired and missed, fired again and the Klamath howled and danced away into the dark.

He turned, saw Frémont standing as if on parade, bringing the big revolver down and firing, firing again. There was a scuffle over on the far side of the camp. The Klamaths were shouting to each other now; Carson could hear the alarm in their voices. Had enough, he thought. All right. One of them gave a high, harsh cry and then they were gone, with that swift, rustling movement; and then no sound at all.

Frémont was looking around, the pistol by his ear. "Who's hit? Was that—?"

Carson grabbed him by the shoulders and dragged him down in a rush. The whipping patter came then, low overhead, as he knew it would, pine needles dipped and jostled; there was a flat slap when an arrow hit a tree trunk solidly.

"Down, Cap'n," he hissed. "Keep down. Arrows coming now." He crawled forward quickly on his elbows. "Dick!" he yelled. Dick—you see the bastards?"

"Yep," Owen called calmly. "That rock patch, there . . ." He was behind a fallen tree, lying deep in shadow. Carson watched him fire, then roll on his back to reload. Frémont, on his knees now, fired four rounds into the black-splotched tangle of rocks and there was a cry broken off quickly. That man sure is some curly wolf with a pistol, Carson thought in wonder. Someone fired high into the massed wall of the firs.

"Slow and steady, boys!" he called. "They won't rush us again. Find you a target and squeeze off. Don't burn up powder, but don't leave 'em free to fire them frigging *arrows* . . ."

In a moment a faint luminescence appeared, a pearly light that mingled with the gunsmoke, the smoke from the dying fire. Rocks, stumps, the points of the firs grew solid; the stars drained away. There was no sound now; nothing moved. The Klamaths had seen the first light and . . .

Carson stood up. "All right, boys," he said. "They've hightailed it."

"Who's hit?" Frémont repeated.

"Crane."

"He's dead," Tessier called.

The camp was a shambles—blankets thrown every which way, saddles kicked over. Bushnell was sitting on a log holding his shoulder and Godey was bent over him. Lucky, Carson thought; got out of it lucky. If it had been Sioux they'd have got every last horse. Us, too.

"Where's Louie?" Proue was saying tensely. "Where is he?"

Carson looked at him. "He was over there, by that boulder."

They ran over, stepping through a tangle of clothes and weapons and cooking pots, and stopped short.

Freniere had never moved. He lay as if asleep, the Hawken cradled in his arms, his apishamore rolled under his head for a pillow. The top of his head was slick with blood. The ax had split his forehead, driven his eyes apart. They were open and staring. Most of his hair was gone; his open scalp had stopped bleeding. Sons-of-bitching Indians . . .

"Oh, Louie. Louie . . ." Frémont was crouched beside him.

"He's gone," Carson said.

Proue fell on his knees. "Get up, Louie," he was saying in a singsong.

"Get up, now!" His voice was a reedy croak. "Stop funning, Louie . . ." He gripped Freniere's shoulder, shook it frantically. *"Louie!"* he shouted.

"He's dead, Raffie," Carson said.

Proue leaped to his feet, his face white and raging. "All right!" he cried. "Who was on guard?" He whipped his knife out of its sheath, glaring at the others, his free hand shaking. "Who was it? *I want to know!*"

Carson glanced at Frémont. The Captain was gazing at Proue, his face slack; he'd never seen that look on Frémont's face before.

". . . I never posted one," he said softly. The sheer anguish on his face was terrible. "I—it slipped my mind . . . ."

"No—guard!" Proue screamed. "You let them come in here and—what the fuck is the *matter* with you? You crazy, butchering—"

He rushed at Frémont, who was standing now with his hands hanging at his sides. Carson took two quick steps and left his feet, drove Proue away and down, rolling and rolling. He got a grip on the knife hand and then Raffie hit him in the face and broke away. But Dick was on Proue then, along with someone else, and they held him, raging and kicking.

"All right, now!" Carson told him harshly. "It's over! What's done is done. Now get yourself in hand, Raffie, or I swear I'll lash you to a mule!"

They got shakily to their feet. Owens had Proue's knife. Proue was glaring at Frémont, panting. Then the tears began to run down his face and his broad shoulders shook. He went quietly over to Louie and put a hand on the bearded cheek, drew down an eyelid with his thumb. He held it down, felt around and found a small stone and weighted it closed, and then closed the other. He began to wipe Freniere's face clean with his shirt sleeve.

Carson went over to Frémont, who was still standing by the dead fire, staring at Louie's body.

"He's right. I've left things to Reddy too long," Frémont said.

"Hell, it's my fault, much as anybody's," Carson told him. "I should have thought of it. It's this odd-lot makeup party, fouled up our routine."

"No." The Captain shook his head doggedly. "I was last man up. I got to worrying about the—" He broke off and clamped his arms around him hard, as though he were cold. "I court-martialed Bladon on the Minnesota. Found him guilty as charged. Now look at *me.*"

"It's all right, Charlie," Carson said. "It's one of those things."

"—How could I *forget?*" he cried softly, his eyes huge with that boundless anguish. "And *Louie* . . ."

Carson put his arm around him. "It's all right, Charlie."

"No." Frémont looked down at his feet, his shoulders shaking rhythmically. "No. It's not all right. It never will be."

He shrugged Carson's arm off after a moment, and kicked at the fire's ashes. When he turned around his face was like Sierra flint.

"All right," he called, his voice carrying hard in the dawn stillness. "We'll bury our dead. And then we'll saddle up and find those bastards. *We will find them!*"

Carson marked out two grave plots, side by side. Owens and Godey spaded around the perimeters, cutting the turf until they could lift the sod and set it carefully to one side; then they began to dig.

Gillespie was bent over the Klamath Carson had shot in the first moments, exclaiming in surprise: it was the same man who had offered him a fish and ferried him over the river the day before. He was wearing a bear-claw necklace interworked with fresh-water shells of many colors.

"Chief," Carson grunted. Of course; that was why the other Indians had lost heart—figured the medicine was bad. The Klamath's scalp was gone; Carson saw his hair, wet and bloody, hanging at Sagundai's waist. A small English half-ax that had come down from Fort Vancouver hung in the Delaware's belt. It was new and very shiny.

Proue dressed Freniere in a clean shirt and trousers. He fitted soft new moccasins on Louie's feet, wrapped the torn head in a white cloth. He laid the body on a clean blanket and picked up the Hawken. He looked at the buffalo carving, feeling it with his fingers.

"He loved this rifle," Proue said. "He was so damned proud of it."

"You—keep the piece, Raffie," Frémont offered thickly.

"It stays with Louie," Proue said. He checked the Hawken's load and fitted a fresh cap. It had blood on the muzzle, and he wiped it away. Then he laid it carefully on the crook of Freniere's arm. He adjusted the powder horn, the cap box, the pouch of lead balls.

Carson watched him in silence. "You ought to take the rifle, Raffie," he said at last. "He'd want you to have it—you know that."

"I want *him* to have it. Maybe he'll need it where he's going. Ain't no priest to give him last rites . . ."

Frémont tried to say something more and Proue rounded on him, rage glistening in his eyes. "You shut your mouth, Cap'n! How do you know he won't need it? You got any real idea where he's going? Do you? I won't send him *off* without his piece—understand?"

Proue laid a soft cloth over Freniere's face, drew the blanket around him and lashed the body with rope from a packsaddle. Sagundai and the two Delawares were sitting on their heels around Crane's body, singing a burial song that sounded like the requiem mass Louie wouldn't ever have.

Proue inspected the grave, moved the body close to it, knelt and looked around sharply. The other men dropped to one knee.

"Hail Mary, full of grace, blessed art thou and the fruit of thy womb," Proue said in a loud, full voice. He went on with other prayers—perhaps he had been an altar boy once. The words soared into the cathedrallike trees, wind sighing in the needles lonely and implacable, so far from home, so far from wife and brother, Louie already vanished, the lump clay body going under all alone, small comfort of the Hawken in his arms. Pray for the living, Carson thought. The dead are dead. But oh, Louie. All those trails . . . He could not bear to look at Frémont's face.

Proue said clearly, "Oh, heavenly Father, look out for him. He was a good man. Please look out for him, now." And then, very loud, as if he were shouting across the sunstruck high plains at a departing figure, horseman riding under the vast sky, tiny in the blazing light atop a final hill, disappearing down a final slope, "And Louie—*we won't never forget you!* . . ."

Proue climbed down into the grave and Frémont and Carson handed the body down to him. Dead, he seemed bigger than in life, heavier. Proue laid it gently in place and slowly sifted dirt over it until it was covered. He shoveled in more dirt, tamping it with his boots as the hole filled. A couple of feet from the top they set in a layer of heavy rock, six inches thick and fitted like paving blocks, certain to stop any digging animal. They packed in more dirt and then replaced the turf, the grass still growing. Three men on horses rode back and forth across the grave, obliterating it, and then Proue built a huge fire on it. When the fire burned down it would leave baked earth and permanent ashes, a decoy from what lay below. No animals would find Louie, no Indians would find his grave to open it and mutilate his body. It was the last thing they could do for him.

The camp was struck and they saddled up.

"Give me that Indian's ax," Proue said to Sagundai. The Delaware stared at him. "My debt," Proue said. "Mine! You've got your scalp. It is part of my debt."

Sagundai nodded then and handed it over.

Carson and Owens led. They knew where they were headed. The trail bent off around the lake. The Klamaths were lake Indians, salmon eaters. The column moved at a hard lope until they saw the village ahead, maybe thirty huts covered with thatch fires burning, fish drying in smoke, canoes upside down on racks.

Frémont's arm flew up and he charged.

"Charlie!" Carson cried in warning. He leaned forward and threw his horse into a hard gallop. People in the village were scattering; women caught up children and ran toward rushes and trees in the distance. The men ducked into the huts and emerged with bows and quivers of arrows that they slung over their backs. Everyone was shooting now, riding all-out. Frémont was far ahead of them on Sacramento, riding alone. Carson saw him rest his rifle on his left elbow and fire at full gallop. An Indian's head exploded, he cartwheeled backwards crazily. The others started to run. Frémont booted the rifle and drew his revolver. One of the Indians turned and fired three arrows with unbelievable speed. One whipped off Frémont's hat; Sacramento stumbled, went down; Frémont flew over his head, hit hard and rolled to his feet. He had lost the pistol. Carson saw him looking wildly on the ground.

He shouted, "Charlie, get down!"

The Klamath drew another arrow, fumbled it, notched it, and drew the bowstring to his cheek. No time. No time to fire. Carson was very close now, straining over the palomino's neck; he snapped the reins and threw the horse directly into the Indian. The man went down, the arrow flying wide. Then he was past, and glancing back he saw the Indian get to his knees as Sagundai thundered down on him, leaning from the saddle, and dashed out his brains with a single stroke of the terrible war club.

The men were spread out, their pieces banging, powder smoke bluing the air. The Indians had turned and rallied now; Carson drew up and fired. The man went down, arrow digging into the ground before him. They were in among the huts. He could hear women wailing, the high "Yip-yip-yip!" of the Klamaths. Eight or ten of them were down, and the rest were running toward their women. Carson rode down another warrior, clubbed him with the rifle. Two Delawares were taking scalps, their knives bright and quick as they made their four slashes, snatched away the bloody trophies.

Frémont, back on Sacramento, had found a pitch torch, was thrusting it under the eaves of the nearest hut. The hut exploded in flame and he moved to another, and another. Godey was kicking down the laden fish racks, dropping them into the fires. Frémont had reached the canoe racks now, thrust the torch under the bottommost one. The flame ate at the heavy pitch; black smoke curled from it, the pitch ignited, the canoe above caught fire. Frémont's face was black with pitch, his eyes wild. All of the huts were flaming and Carson, reloading in the saddle, could hear the women wailing in the distance.

Five warriors had just come out of the woods. They stopped, staring—and Carson saw that one of the Indians was wearing Freniere's hat, the eagle feather swinging in the breeze off the lake.

Proue shouted: "That son of a bitch is *mine!*" He was galloping after the running men, hanging low in the saddle. The Indians separated, fanning out, and Raffie swept down on the man with the hat.

"Cover him now!" Frémont roared, and Godey and Owens rode after him hard.

Proue leaped from his horse onto the Indian's back. They rolled in the dirt. The hat flew off and cartwheeled away. Carson saw a knife flash in the Klamath's hand, come up, plunge down. Proue twisted aside, caught the man's arm and turned. The Indian screamed and Carson knew Raffie had torn his arm from the socket. Proue spun him, caught him in a bear hug, lifted him high in both hands and brought him down hard. The man's back broke across Proue's knee with a flat, dry sound.

The Indian shrieked again terribly, and Proue caught the man's hair in his left hand and the shiny new English half-ax flashed in the sun. He chopped at the Indian's neck, two strokes, a third, and the head came loose.

Proue held it by the long braids and ran toward the Indian women. He whirled the head around and around, blood flying from the neck stump.

"You want him?" he screamed, weeping. "You want him? *Take* him, then!"

He ran closer to the women, Owens and Frémont behind him, the head whirling, and then he let it go. It flew in a long arc, braids trailing behind it, struck the ground with a noise like a smashed gourd and bounded crazily toward the wailing women who stumbled and fell getting out of its way.

Then the smoke swept low over them, hid them from view.

REBELLION

EZEKIEL MERRITT had just dipped the bucket down the well when they rode into the yard: Sam Hensley, Big Fallon, Brad Smith, Purvis, a few others. Hensley said he had bad news. He was a sensible, steady man, worked on Bill Hargrave's place, and wasn't at all excitable. That Mexican Army lieutenant, Ferdinand Arcé, was gathering horses around the valley. The gather itself was not alarming; from time to time General Castro sent out for remount animals and sooner or later the government paid for them. But when the officer had signed for a dozen horses, he'd told Hensley with an ugly laugh he'd see the horses again—with a lancer in every saddle. Told him they were going to drive all the settlers over the Sierras and into the deserts beyond.

"Gonna use our own horses against us," Fallon said.

"You sure about that, Sam?" Merritt said cautiously. "Your Spanish ain't none too good."

"Hell yes, I'm sure," Hensley said. Merritt had never seen him so agitated. "He spoke real slow, laughing all the while. And his flunkies grinning at me like they was thinking about stringing me up right then and there."

"We figured we'd better ride over to Captain Frémont's camp," Fallon said. "Maybe this kind of news'll stir him off his ass to do something, for a change."

Maybe, Merritt thought as they set out. Frémont was a hard man to figure. He was plenty tough, you could see that, and Tessier and Ingalls couldn't say enough about the way he took them over the Sierras; a gritty hombre with a camp full of fighting men—yet he didn't want to fight. Well, it wasn't lack of sand; he must have had his reasons. Merritt figured Frémont was waiting for something. But what?

"You talk to him first, Zekiel," Fallon said. "You get on with him pretty good. I mean, he come back for *some* reason. Try and figure out what's stalling him."

Merritt found Frémont sitting by himself in front of that little tent he had, pitched under a live oak. The Captain's beard was freshly trimmed and he looked as if he had just bathed. Quickly Merritt explained the new threat.

But Frémont only grinned. "So they're going to ride you down with your own horses. Now that adds insult to injury, doesn't it?"

"Guess it does."

"What do you intend to do about it?"

Merritt knew his face had gone hot red. Still, he said it: "Well, we thought maybe you—"

"Why me? They're your horses, aren't they?"

"I guess we don't know *what* the hell do to," Merritt blurted out. "They ain't really done nothing but threaten."

"You'd let a man stand in your yard and threaten you?"

"No sir. I'd tell him to put up or shut up."

"If his answer was to punch your head off, he'd have a good start, wouldn't he?" Before Merritt could answer, Frémont went on, "Tell me, if you got the settlers together, how many could you muster?"

"Seven, eight hundred, I reckon."

"Take half—could they hold off a California force?"

"Sure, if they pulled together. These Californios don't know nothing about fighting. They're the damnedest horsemen you ever saw, but they've never had to fight. They been living easy. But most of our boys been in the mountains."

"Look, Ezekiel," Frémont said in a more friendly way, "the reason you don't get together is that nothing has happened to *force* you together. You boys have been indulging yourselves—jawing because you really didn't have to do anything more."

Merritt nodded uncomfortably. Damnit, the man was right.

"Well, we both know that won't last, don't we? This situation's created a vacuum—and nature won't tolerate a vacuum. Something—someone—rushes into it. If that someone isn't you, then it'll be the Californios, driving you people out one by one. Or the British—if you can't handle this Mexican lieutenant, I don't suppose you'll want to face a company of Royal Marines, will you?"

"That's mighty fine talk, Cap'n," Merritt said, his face getting stiff. "Mighty smart. But the trouble is, don't none of us know what to do." It puzzled him that Frémont had such trouble understanding, and he took a new tack. "Once I heard Sam Houston talk down in Texas. Now, there was a man without doubts. He knew what to do and he made you want to do it. But me—hell, I'm full of doubts. The boys hear it in my voice. *I* hear it in my voice. And we're all the same—I ain't gonna follow them any more'n they're gonna follow me."

Suddenly he was so angry he couldn't control himself; he shot a great gout of tobacco juice at his feet. "But Goddamnit, you *do* know! That's why we keep coming to you. It ain't 'cause we got no guts—it's 'cause we don't know. And we can't get *you* to do a Goddamned thing!"

To his amazement Frémont looked downright pleased. "That's right. Not a thing . . . You want to know what I'd do if I *was* doing it, though? I'd go take my horses away from that pipsqueak, and pass the word to General

Castro to stay out of the valley if he didn't want to get his tail burned."

Leaning forward, Frémont gave him a lesson in organization. How many men did Arcé have? Hensley had counted fifteen. All right: scout them with care and catch them all in camp; decide just what you'll do and make sure everyone understands the plan; put your party in two groups, one to hold the soldiers, the other to one side to give you a crossfire if you need it; assign targets to each party so you won't find everyone aiming at the same man if shooting starts; then throw down on them . . . but remember, if they make a move and you hesitate, a good many of you will be dead before sundown.

"See what I mean?" Frémont said. "Keep surprise on your side, and it's not all that hard."

Before Merritt could answer he saw Fallon and the others approaching. They'd delegated him and then they couldn't wait—same old story.

"Well, Cap'n," Fallon said hopefully, "what do you say?"

"I say you boys have yourselves a pickle."

"What would you do about it?" Fallon said, glowering.

"If they were coming after me—only they're not—I'd take my horses away and send 'em home with their brushes tucked. I'd give 'em a large, clear message."

"Come on, then," Purvis told him. "Let's all go do it."

"They're not coming after me. They're coming after you."

"Well, God damn," Purvis said loudly, his eyes in that ugly squint. "Listen to the soldier boy talk." Merritt saw something menacing cross Frémont's face. "How come you joined the Army if you don't never want to fight? Maybe you *can't* fight. Is that it?"

There was total silence.

"Are you calling me a coward, Purvis?" Frémont said in a soft, level tone, almost a singsong. *"Are you?"*

Purvis' eyes broke away. He started to shout something, and Frémont's voice cut across his like a whip.

"I've had enough of your mouth, Purvis. You're all talk and no action."

"Wait a damn minute, mister! I'll show you—"

"Shut up!" Frémont said in a voice like steel. "The people to *fight* are right over those hills, but you don't care for that, do you? You're a fool, Purvis—you don't even know which end is up."

Purvis looked as if he was swallowing his tongue. It struck Merritt that he'd never liked the man and that for all of Purvis' talk, he'd never seen him in a real fight. Frémont was right—this was *their* fight, and if they wouldn't make it themselves, then they were all just so many bags of wind.

"I'm going to go take them horses away from that snotty little bastard," he heard himself say out loud. "You boys can come along or you can go hide in your outhouses." They were all staring at him; Frémont's face was still hard, but his eyes were burning now. Merritt looked around, pleased; maybe he *was* something of a leader after all. "But if you ain't coming, then keep your damned mouths shut about what happens after—just knuckle under, and light out when they grab your land."

He checked the cap on his old rifle and snugged his pistol in his belt. "Let's go, Fallon," he said. "Sam. Brad. You coming, Purvis, or ain't you?"

Hell, they were all coming, every man jack, Purvis too. He whipped his horse into a gallop. That was the trick: tell 'em you're going, don't give 'em no arguing room, make 'em shit or get off the pot. That's how old Sam would have done it. Hot damn, that's leadership!

It was the *waiting.* Stomping around wondering what in hell was going on in Washington, on the Rio Grande. Not knowing was worse than hearing the most disheartening news. How long could this eerie, infuriating limbo go on?

Frémont inventoried their gear and had their tools sharpened, their guns repaired, the animals reshod. He held a payday with silver coins from his camp chest and broke up two lovely brawls at the fort over brandy and women. Make-work; he was waiting. *Had* the war started? Not a word came from outside. Sutter continued to avoid him. Walker started back for Missouri; Frémont released his party after the old trapper captain reminded him politely but pointedly that they'd been gone for more than a year with no end in sight.

Well, it did bother him, Walker said, to leave the Cap'n in the hands of a greenhorn youngster like Carson. In fact, Kit retorted, the Cap'n's *real* worry was that old Reddy would get lost and starve to death trying to find the Oregon Trail, and then the Cap'n would have to explain the loss of a government saddle. They parted laughing, which was as good, Frémont thought, as waiting in silence, helpless as a newborn colt. Suppose that California lieutenant had his men divided, suppose an alert guard stopped Merritt as they approached, suppose the California troops were able to get to their horses, suppose they called Merritt's bluff . . .

Two days later Merritt rode in whooping and laughing like a boy. Frémont had never seen a man so changed, so suddenly charged with energy and promise. They'd done it! Months of wondering, waiting, doubting—and now they'd done it. On their own. The boys had schooled hard on just how they would do it. Merritt explained like a triumphant general: at dusk they'd ridden in and caught Lieutenant Arcé and his men squatting around their cookfires. Those soldiers like to broke their arms getting their hands over their heads and they said yes sir and no sir and thank you sir. So the boys took the horses and Merritt told Arcé to get on back to Monterey.

"We gave him a message," Merritt said with a braying laugh. "We told him, 'You tell Mama Castro to stay the hell out of the Sacramento Valley or we'll tie a knot in his tail.' We told him this was *our* valley, by God, and wasn't *nobody* gonna run us off."

They were still celebrating this blow for liberty when Sutter clattered into camp on a dappled gelding and sat his horse, glaring down at Merritt.

"Have you lost your mind?" he shouted. "To take property by force, to interfere with a government officer on official duty—do you know what you've done? . . . And you, sir," turning to Frémont, "you encouraged them! I know it. How dare you come into California as a guest—and encourage men to common horse theft!"

"Wasn't stealing," Merritt said in a wary voice.

"Then what was it?" Contempt spread over Sutter's face. "Do you mean to dignify yourself as revolutionaries? Ridiculous! The Californios will be back in company strength to hang the lot of you. I should put you in irons myself—" he broke off and added quickly, "But I won't." Then, as if to himself, "Still, I'll be reporting this—" Abruptly he wheeled and left at a gallop.

"Where does it leave *him*?—is what he's saying, I expect," Merritt said dryly and someone laughed, but the others were quiet now. Some of Merritt's ebullience had faded. "All the same," he said, "we'd better do some figuring."

Frémont saw that they were watching him, waiting. He spotted Purvis at the edge of the group: Purvis would serve.

"Mr. Purvis," Frémont said, "when I want you in my camp I'll invite you. Until then, stay out."

"Now you hold on," Purvis said truculently.

"Do you want satisfaction? Is that it?"

"What? Look, I didn't mean nothing the other day—"

"Get out." Frémont told him.

"Cap'n . . ." Purvis paused, swallowed and with great effort said, "Cap'n, I apologize—"

"That's enough! Get out or my men will put you out. Don't let me see you again until I call for you."

There was a silence. Then with a slight smile Merritt said: "Cap'n's the boss."

Owens stood in front of Purvis with his thumbs hooked in his belt. "Ain't you got someplace to go, feller?" he said.

The others turned to Frémont with almost palpable relief as Purvis caught up his horse. They knew the ground had shifted.

"Well," Frémont said expansively, "you boys have got something going. What next?"

Merritt hesitated. "See what they do, I reckon."

"Why do you think you got the best of Arcé so easily?"

"We surprised him."

"Right. You acted and he *re*acted. And he didn't have much to react with."

Merritt glanced at Fallon. "Yeah, I reckon."

"So now you're going to wait till they act so that *you* can react. Think you'll do any better than Arcé did?"

No one spoke. Their good humor of a few moments before had vanished.

"Sutter gave you your answer," Frémont said. "They'll be back in strength, looking to hang you for horse theft."

Tessier said, "We ain't horse thieves, Cap'n. You know that."

A murmur of approval rose and Ingalls called in a shrill voice: "Remember the Alamo!" It had a hollow sound.

"It's up to you," Frémont said. "Are you horse thieves or revolutionaries?" The word frightened them. "Look, the real question is whether you control the valley or they do. There are Californios out here, too—that high-flying Gutierrez and his friends. I'll tell you something. If you don't take control, they will—and they'll have a company of Castro's lancers backing them up."

"What do you want us to do?" Fallon asked.

"*I* don't want you to do anything. But I can point out a few realities. There are just two strong points in northern California. Sutter has one, and I don't think he'll be hard to handle. The other is Sonoma—General Vallejo and his arsenal. Whoever controls Sonoma and Sutter's Fort controls all of California north of Monterey."

"God almighty," Fallon said; he sounded awed. "You want us to take *Sonoma?*"

"*I* don't, no. I never said any such thing. But without it you may find yourselves dangling from oak limbs. If you held it, the local Californians wouldn't be able to get themselves together, and Castro would know he was facing something real."

"Maybe we'd better call a big meeting," Merritt said. "Get everyone together on this."

"Wonderful," Frémont told him. "Then you can talk about it for a month until the Californians ride in. On the other hand, if you got thirty, forty men together and took the place, the others would have to join."

Merritt was nodding. "I reckon we can get thirty men; think thirty would do it?"

"If you plan it right."

"How would you plan it?" Fallon said; his mouth twitched at the corner. "*If* you was doing it, I mean."

"Vallejo's got a handful of men at most, right?" Fallon nodded. "I'd go in at dawn, ten men to close on Vallejo's place, ten to grab the armory, ten in the square to take people as they come out and run 'em into the armory under guard. It could be done in a quarter-hour."

Joseph Chiles, a Missourian who'd tried to bring an entire sawmill to the Napa Valley and had to leave its parts rusting in the desert, spoke for the first time: "You're talking revolution, Captain."

"No, sir. I'm not. You men are talking it."

Chiles continued as if he hadn't heard. "We could seize Sonoma. You can hold Sutter's. The rest of the Americans here would probably come in. They wouldn't have any choice. We could take Yerba Buena, too, there on San Francisco Bay—it's smaller than Sonoma. Maybe we could even take Monterey. But what then? How would the United States government look at it?"

"That's right," William Ide said. He'd been a schoolmaster back in Vermont; Frémont could hear education and a certain native shrewdness in his voice. "Before I get into something like this, I want to know where it'll come out. Don't forget; the U.S. left Texas to sink or swim for ten years. I don't know as I'd want to try to stay afloat that long."

Here it was. The sticking place. He'd better watch his step now. How would old Benton handle this? He saw the cold gray eyes, heard again the sonorous, hard voice edged with cynicism: *"It's his head on the chopping block, George . . ."*

"Times are different now," he said carefully. "I think I can say the United States would look with favor on what you might do. Of course, it would depend on how Washington saw it—and that might depend on how *you* saw it. And handled it. What do you want, anyway? Plunder?"

"Damn it all," Merritt cried, "that's the point! We're not bandits."

"Then figure out what you are, and act accordingly."

"I'll tell you what we are," Ide said. He turned to the others. "Let's get this straight right now. You boys better be with me or I don't want any part of it. I say we're setting up a country of our own." His voice was pedantic, yet oddly full of passion. "A democracy, just like the good old U.S. of A. Every man gets a vote—even the Californios. Elections fair and square. Religious freedom. None of this damned tyranny the Californios have been practicing—where they can run you off your land on anybody's say-so."

Ide had swept far beyond the others' thinking. Frémont saw the corners of Tessier's mouth quirking: he was fighting back a grin. Merritt was looking at the ground and so was Fallon.

"We'll borrow the great Thomas Jefferson's words and ideas," Ide cried. "We'll issue proclamations setting everything out in the noble style of our forebears! Are we agreed?"

No one answered him. Finally Frémont said mildly: "Makes sense, Mr. Ide. But first you have to do it, don't you?"

"That's the fact," Merritt answered. "Hell yes, let's go do it." His voice was firm. He turned to Fallon. "Let's go to Hargrave's place and start rounding up the ones we can count on. We'll make a sketch map of Sonoma and work out a plan like we done before. Like the Cap'n says."

Godey said suddenly: "I'll go with you boys. I wouldn't mind a piece of that myself." Frémont heard a half-dozen voices agreeing: his men ready to go.

"Then come ahead," Tessier said. "The more the merrier."

"No," Frémont said crisply. "You're not going, Alex. None of you are."

"Why not?" Godey said, hands on his hips, still smiling but half-challenging. With a brace of pistols in his belt and his long, gleaming black hair he looked romantic and wild, a buccaneer fresh from the Spanish Main.

Merritt was watching. So were Chiles and Ide. Only Alex didn't understand what was at stake here. Being Alex, he never would.

"Because I said so." Goddamnit, he had brought it this far, held it all together, he'd fought down the almost overpowering need to move, act, force the issue until it had half-killed him; he was double-damned if he was going to let a couple of hotheads ruin everything now.

"That's an order, Mr. Godey." His voice was as hard as he could make it. "Don't cross me!"

Near him Kit stirred, and said: "All right, Alex. Simmer down, now. Cap'n's running it. Like always."

Godey's eyes glittered with sudden anger, but his voice was easy. "All right, Cap'n. But you're letting them have all the fun . . ."

The week that followed was excruciating. Sonoma was sixty miles away; it would take Merritt several days to round up his men and lay his plans. Frémont didn't want to know more than that—indeed, it was crucial that he not know. Whatever his murky mandate—as suggested by Benton, intimated by Bancroft, authorized, he hoped, by the President—it specifically did *not* include leading a settlers' revolt in California. Encourage it but not lead it. On the other hand, a failed revolt would ruin him. It would open the way to the British, squeeze out the United States. It would lose them California. He could not lead, as he longed to do with all his heart—and in the end it would be judged all his fault.

He wrote out his resignation from the United States Army, addressed it to Senator Benton and filed it in his camp desk. Benton would know what to do with it if things went wrong, which they still could even if Merritt succeeded. *Was* there a war, for God's sake, or wasn't there? That was the infuriating, maddening question. War between the United States and Mexico would justify all this and more; but if war was averted, Frémont could be simply an embarrassment his government would promptly disavow as an unprincipled adventurer. Another Aaron Burr. Jesus. His skin prickled at the thought. He had a constant headache and his temper turned hair-triggered.

Then Carson and Owens only made it worse. They asked him formally to let them lead a force of twenty men in support of the settlers. Merritt and some of the others were all right, but most of the settlers were flighty and likely to pull foot under pressure. "They can get theirselves killed mighty easy if things go wrong," Carson said. "They need some steady hands." Since Frémont had been thinking precisely this, Carson's words infuriated him. Kit continued to point out the obvious: "If the Californios roll over them, you know, they'll be on us next—catch us sitting here sucking our thumbs . . ."

"Now, that's enough of that, Kit!" Frémont said in a real rage, and Carson recoiled, his pale eyes narrow and hard.

"But—hell, ain't we in it already, Cap'n?"

"No, I tell you *no*! Now don't push me on this again . . ."

The nights were worst of all. He would lie awake for hours, staring up at the black hood of the tent roof, or pace back and forth along the riverbank, watching the stars in their slow, majestic sweep around Nicollet's beloved Polaris, thinking of Papa Joe, and Jessie, and dour old Provost, and then a cheery, ruddy face with merry eyes. . . .

Going north had been the crucial mistake. He never should have left. He should have stayed right here and kicked ass—Sutter's, the Californians', the settlers', it didn't matter whose—and instead he had hemmed and hawed around for six months. Playing Talleyrand at his own tinpot Congress of Vienna, temporizing, conniving; playing the oily politico. Then, balked and frustrated, he had slunk away like a rebuffed suitor; and when at last the dispatches had overtaken him he'd snatched at them as at a lover's reprieve—and given over responsibilities that were properly his, allowed himself to forget the simplest, most basic command functions and slept away the night, obsessed with destiny and dreams of glory. . . .

And Louie had died. He heard the buffler hooves again and again in his haunted nights, saw Louie laughing on the plains. Wasn't Freniere's death a grim metaphor for his whole course of action in California? Because Louie deserved better. He had cheated Louie, then—not of his life exactly, a man could lose his life a dozen different ways on the trail, in the mountains, in Indian country—but of his chance to fight for it. Crane had that chance: he'd died on his feet, doing battle. Louie had never even moved. A hundred times Frémont told himself that Louie never knew what hit him, but that was only a cheap, self-serving lie. Louie had awakened all right, he'd known what was happening, had felt the intolerable pain as the blade split his brain. He couldn't move, but he had known when the Indian took his hair, the awful helpless indignity as he spun away in blackness, hands motionless on the Hawken.

Captain Success. Gazing forlornly at the wheeling, dusty stars, he shivered. He'd taken them over the Sierra, his reports thrilled the nation, he'd talked to cabinet officers as equals and suavely promised to carry out his President's aims. He had been so assured, so confident. Of course death was always around the corner—but he had expected it to stay there. It wasn't that he had thought himself infallible—the point, he realized in an anguished flash of insight, was that neither had he thought himself fallible. Riding south from Klamath Lake, driving men and horses, feeling older, colder, he was aware as he had not been aware before that something rode behind him. It rode his trail, horseman in black with empty eyes, drawing closer with each turn of the road, each collision, each mistake, each mischance. Hard on his trail, waiting. . . .

Frémont sent Sagundai and his Delawares roving the country to watch for movement. Every day Carson, Owens and Godey led small probes in different directions. Gillespie was at San Francisco, drawing supplies from the USS *Portsmouth.* Frémont put Ned Kern in Sutter's Fort with orders to watch for any unusual action. Kern, intelligent and resourceful, had made himself steadily more useful, and Frémont now ranked him just below the three scouts in value to his mission. But Sutter seemed to have lost his military pretensions under his mountain of debt; he gave no sign of taking any hand in the high-stakes game now being played.

At last Merritt rode into camp, bone-weary, a bit subdued but very pleased. He was old in the ways of revolution now, nothing like the man who had found such exuberant triumph in freeing Arcé's horses. They had taken Sonoma at dawn with thirty-three men, and Vallejo had surrendered after they awakened him. They had seized the arsenal, which contained two hundred fifty muskets, a hundredweight of powder and several small field pieces. Vallejo had been gracious about it. He had offered his sword, which Merritt had refused, and then had opened his wine cellar to the conquerors.

"Some of the boys got drunk, but Fallon's been watching 'em close. We don't want nothing to mess it up because it's all legitimate, you see. Mr. Ide was fixed on that—well, Chiles too, and Doc Semple. None of us wanted to be mistook for thieves, you know." He shifted his quid, and his face brightened. "We started a new *country*—the Republic of California. Made up a flag on the spot, piece of white muslin with a red strip at the bottom from some lady's petticoat. Billy Todd squeezed up some pokeberry juice and painted a bear on it for a symbol. That bear flag's flying over Sonoma now—some of the boys are already calling themselves Bears! When I left, Mr. Ide was working on a proclamation—making it all right, you see, so that the world will know we're serious."

Merritt seemed a little dazed by what he'd done. He'd gone to Sonoma and become midwife to a new nation. There was something different about him that puzzled Frémont until he realized that Merritt's beard was clean and his tobacco plug was small. He spat less often and, perhaps because his mouth wasn't so full, talked with a certain crisp authority.

They had brought General Vallejo back with them. Frémont could see that Merritt was awed by his prisoner. "Once I was in Judge Tuttle's house back in Butler's Crossing, Kentucky—delivered a ham my paw had cured," Merritt said. "They had a real piano, and flowers in vases of glass that had been cut in little squares to catch the light in different colors. Real quality folks. Vallejo's place was like that. Made me feel funny, walking in without knocking." He supposed he would parole General Vallejo.

"So that he can raise the country against you?"

"Think he would?"

"Do you imagine he's tickled to be made a prisoner? He's worth a lot more to you in your hands than out. Take him up to the fort and lock him up."

"What do you reckon Sutter'll say?"

"We won't give him a chance to say much."

It was time to deal with Sutter. Frémont told Godey to take a dozen men to the fort, armed, and then he waited quietly in his camp. A few minutes later Sutter galloped in. As he awkwardly dismounted it struck Frémont that Sutter had gotten fat in the last month or two. He remembered his easy authority when they first had met; had Kit been right about him all along?

"That fool Merritt has just brought—"

"I sent him," Frémont said sharply. "I want those men held. Those are my orders."

"Orders? You forget yourself, Captain. This is my fort."

"No sir. No longer. You may retain ownership of the property, but I have taken control. You are to make no moves—none whatsoever—without my permission. My men will enforce that. Do you understand?"

Sutter's cheeks quivered, he started to rage; but he hadn't built his empire on indiscretion, and he calmed himself. "You are an arrogant, duplicitous man," he said slowly. "I welcomed you, trusted you, and you've abused that. You've plotted all this—that simple-minded Merritt would never have acted on his own. You're really just a stalking horse for your government, aren't you?"

Frémont didn't answer: let the man talk himself down.

"They've ruined it—you've ruined it," Sutter went on accusingly. His hands were trembling and he put them behind him. "We lived here peacefully until you came. We'd have continued to do so. The government never would have ejected these people—it wasn't strong enough. That was all just talk."

"Think you'd have fared better under the British, do you?" Frémont said.

"The British weren't coming! That's claptrap—the problem is American, not British!"

"Do you actually think you can reverse the flow of history, Captain Sutter? That you can play some cunnythumb Napoleon and ignore the tide? I'd have thought a man of your experience would have known better." He nodded once; he was wasting time. "At any rate, the decision has been made. There's a time to act—or be passed by; you've missed your time."

"I have not! I won't let you take my fort—"

"I've already taken it," Frémont said. Sutter was shaking his head frantically; he looked as if he might cry. "You're welcome to stay in the fort, of course, and tend to your business affairs. But you'll do so under Mr. Kern's direction, and I warn you: interfere just once and I'll run you downriver in your launch and you can go take your chances with the Californians."

"I guess we're in it now, ain't we?" Carson just had to ask Frémont.

"Almost."

Carson thought he was mighty short. When the Cap'n had pinched that thimblerigging Sutter down to size, he'd figured the wraps were off; but no, not yet. They were alone at the edge of camp and the Cap'n was staring down the long, dusty road that led to Sonoma. He didn't look at Carson. He was waiting for something, but Carson wasn't sure what.

Frémont had changed. He seemed older, harder, more remote. He was turned in, somehow, reluctant to share his thoughts. Carson wasn't sure he liked the new man the way he had the old. He'd been like this ever since the Klamath country. Carson knew what it was, all right. Couldn't forgive himself for old Louie's scalp. Well, it was bad. But hell, they'd all been at fault—he, Dick, Louie himself, come to that. Easy living down here in the fat land had softened them up.

Anyway, it didn't do no good to go around brooding on something like that day after day. It could eat away your fiber like quicklime. It had happened, it was over, forget it; that was the best way. But Charlie wasn't like that. He couldn't let go of things . . .

Three horsemen appeared on the long road, lifting a dust tower into the warm June sky. They were driving extra horses and looked as if they had ridden all night. When they dismounted their mounts stood head down, not moving, and Carson saw dust caked around the men's eyes and in their neck creases.

One of them, a blond man with his jaw swollen on one side as if he had a toothache, said he was Tim Stepwith from up on the Feather River. Merritt had sent him—the Californios were attacking in force under a capable officer named de la Torre. Merritt had sent Henry Ford out with some men to scout the California lancers.

"Merritt wants you to come on ahead with your boys," Stepwith said. He sighed and laid his palm gently to his jaw. "He said to tell you that nature—let's see; that nature won't tolerate a vacuum—said you'd know what he meant. Is that right, Cap'n?"

"Right as rain, mister. Right as rain!"

Carson could hardly believe the change that overtook Frémont. There was a brightness in his face and a tight smile that seemed to be holding back something much bigger. He turned to him like a kid out of school and said, "In answer to your eternal badgering, Kit: yes, we're in it!" Proue was coming up from the river with a mess of trout, and the Cap'n called with a laugh, "Forget 'em, Raffie—we've got better fish to fry!"

When they rode into Sonoma later the next afternoon, it made Carson think of Taos with its adobe houses and streets of beaten clay, the church bells tolling for vespers. He thought of Josefa, his pretty little wife, a woman and yet, at seventeen, still some of a girl; he could see her stepping across the square at Taos in answer to the bell, black *mantilla* drawn over her head, eyes cast down, rosary beads intertwining her fingers. The town seemed full of Bears, lean rangy men with long rifles, like Bent's Fort when the trappers were in; many had brought their families, and Carson saw tents and tarps stretched between trees. Women were tending fires and shrilling at children who darted in the way of their horses. The town's only *cantina* was barred; someone had some sense, he thought. He saw Californio families watching from their doorways; their faces were neutral, but they hadn't run away.

The armory was a one-story adobe building with heavy gates. Overhead flew the Bear Flag, a red flash fluttering in the evening sun. Carson didn't think much of the bear—it looked about like that awful buffalo someone had carved on Louie's piece. Inside they found Merritt and Fallon with a few others. Ide was writing at a table; Carson could hear his quill scratching. Fallon and Merritt were cut from the same cloth, he judged, but he didn't like Ide. He was like a tightfisted grain merchant who ran your account in his head every time he saw you and found you definitely in arrears.

Merritt was excited. The men with Ford had found the Californios, jumped them, killed a couple. "The war has commenced," he told Frémont in a tense voice that rose more than he meant it to. Henry Ford was young, twenty-two or -three, but very assured; Carson knew immediately from his report that he could trust his judgment. He said he'd taken twenty men out to scout and presently they'd come upon the bodies of Tom Cowie and a fellow named Fowler from way up the Sacramento.

"They'd been tied to trees and ripped open," he told Frémont. "They was both hanging there, half-standing, their guts spilled out on their feet. Looks like it took 'em a while to die. Cowie'd been trying to hold hisself together—his hands was all tangled in his own guts." He shook his head; hard streaks ran down from his mouth. "We liked ol' Tom a good deal."

The sight made his men crazy mad, and when they found about fifty lancers stopped for the night at Méndez' ranch, they went straight in to attack. Killed two of them for sure, wounded some more, and set the rest to running while their officer tried to stop them with his sword. That officer was a good man, Ford said; big fellow with red handlebar mustaches from ear to ear. Carson saw the flash of recognition on Frémont's face. The Californios had taken off toward the bay, but Ford thought they still could be caught.

The Cap'n was a totally changed man, brisk, enthusiastic—he was *happy*. He asked quick, basic questions: he was taking charge. Were scouts on ranging patrol? Merritt shook his head, taken aback. What about the local Californios? Merritt said he'd sent Chiles, Hargrave and a few of the steadier men to assure them that no one would molest them so long as they didn't gather together. "They're quiet," he said. "A lot of them weren't that happy with the old government, you know." How many settlers had rallied so far? Hundred and fifty, Merritt guessed, and more coming in every hour, many with their families.

It paid, Carson thought, to have a man with some military sense in command; you could tell Charlie gave them confidence. He rallied them in the square and in an hour had formed five companies. He would lead the largest, of about seventy men, which included Sagundai and the Delawares. Two companies of about forty each, Ford commanding one and Dick Owens the other, would ride flank on the main company. The Cap'n had taken a real shine to old flat-faced Dick. Frémont spread his own men through these combat companies to steady the others. Merritt sketched a map in the dirt. Three roads led westward and converged on Sausalito, a village on the north shore that looked across the bay to the peninsula. The Cap'n figured that de la Torre's men were headed there. They would march at dawn; he would lead the main unit down the center road, Ford would take the road to the left, Owens the one to the right.

"All set, gentlemen?" Frémont asked. "Remember the old military adage: 'Ride to the sound of the guns.' "

Ford had a puzzled look. "Come again, Cap'n?"

Frémont laughed. "If you hear shooting, come a-running."

Ford grinned back. "Surer'n shit, Cap'n."

These Bears, Carson decided next morning, fell way short as soldiers. They could ride and doubtless they could shoot, but they had a hell of a time getting themselves together. If he took any of them into the mountains to run a few traps, they'd have to shape up fast. Cap'n was remarkably patient. Frémont was openly the commander now, and everybody knew it and snapped to accordingly. He cut out a dozen or so Bears who were still drunk, helped Ford separate his crowd from Owens' company, caught twenty muttonheads still gorging at the roasting pits and drove them to their horses, waited while those who'd forgotten their rations went to get them, and made a short speech in which he didn't say anything earth-shaking but pulled them together and made them feel important. Daylight was an hour gone before they galloped westward.

The ride was long and hard; there were delays, false trails; gradually de la Torre's scent grew cold. Too late they rode into Sausalito and found that the Californios had commandeered boats, crossed the bay to the southern peninsula, and fled on toward Monterey. Carson himself was itching to smell a little powder burning, but the Cap'n seemed content. And why not; they held northern California, and the long spell of hesitation and waiting was over.

Frémont found a launch, and a dozen of them rowed across to spike the guns in an old Spanish fort that stood untended on the southern headland. It was late afternoon when they returned to the north shore. A cold, deep-water wind slanted off the Pacific, and they raised a lateen sail and ran across the wind's face. The setting sun poured molten gold between the dark headlands looming on each side, gold that flashed off the black, wind-chopped water and filled their eyes, light and wind and the driving boat lifting them with excitement.

"The golden gate to the east, d'you see, Kit?" Frémont cried, pointing. "That's what this is all about—the trade of the Orient is going to pour right through this golden funnel into all America. Whoever holds this bay holds the continent itself. And now we've got it—and by God, we'll never give it up!"

Sure, Carson could see it when Frémont put it that way; Charlie was filled with excitement, caught in the brilliant light, in the dream of this western empire, the wind and the future fresh in his face.

And then Frémont leaned close to him and said, "At least, that's the way it'll go if our country's willing to back us up." Carson looked into his eyes and for a moment it was as if the Cap'n's face had opened to reveal his heart; and like a whisper against the wind, he added, "If it isn't willing, then you and I may hang yet."

Frémont had given him a rakish, irrepressible grin, and Carson thought, damn, you have to love a man like that; and was instantly embarrassed. Then Frémont opened the notebook he kept for the next report and Carson saw him write in bold black letters: THE GOLDEN GATE. Old Charlie was one hell of a trailblazer, but he was a poet, too. Carson knew he would never meet anyone to match him the rest of his natural life.

BEAR FLAG

FRÉMONT RODE INTO MONTEREY with one hundred sixty fighting men and saw American warships anchored in line in the bay below. American flags flew over the customhouse and the yellow stone *presidio,* where he had gone hat in hand to call on General Castro. That lordly officer had fled to the south, where he was trying to raise a force of horsemen to face the Americans. After all the agonizing uncertainties, war had been declared. Gillespie, all spit-and-polish now, had ridden jubilantly to tell him: General Taylor had given battle on the Rio Grande and was pursuing the enemy into Mexico.

He wished Jessie could see him today, riding at the head of a column, the Stars and Stripes aloft, the interior of Northern California under his control. He thought of his uncertainty of the year before, his cautious probing. All was different today—what sheer satisfaction lay in demolishing all doubt in simple, straightforward action!

At the edge of town a midshipman in crisp white uniform saluted briskly: if Frémont would come directly to the quay, Commodore Stockton, USS *Congress*, would meet him there. The youngster mounted a horse and galloped down into the bowl of the harbor, and Frémont saw a small boat pull away from the quay. The column of horsemen passed among the familiar lime-washed houses, hooves scuffing sand. An old man drew a burro laden with firewood to one side and several women watched from shuttered windows, their faces expressionless. Frémont didn't really feel like a conqueror, nor did these quiet Californians seem to feel conquered. The battalion filed down to the quay, doubled before the customhouse and stopped, the men dismounting in line and loosening saddle girths. United States Marine guards in dress blues gaped at them. Out in the bay, beyond the line of American ships, lay a tall man-of-war. It was British, Frémont saw, the Union Jack fluttering from a yardarm. None too soon, he thought. Touch and go.

A gig stood out from one of the American vessels and came swiftly shoreward, oars beating like an insect's wing; an officer was standing by the coxswain in the stern. The coxswain laid the boat against a landing float, port oars presented smartly in a wetly gleaming row, starboard oars backing down.

The officer ran lightly up the ladder. He was about fifty, hair and side whiskers still dark, his face ruddy from much time on the quarterdeck, and he carried himself with brisk assurance. Impulsively Frémont saluted. The officer answered with a smile and put out his hand. There were three broad gold stripes on his sleeve.

"Robert Stockton," he said. Frémont had an immediate impression that this was a man on whom command rested easily.

"Damned fine-looking column, Captain," the commodore said. "I watched you in the glass."

He met Carson and Godey. The sight of Sagundai stopped him. Stockton grinned and reached for the scout's war club, hefted it, slapped it hard against his left palm.

"I expect that converts a man to your way of thinking in a hurry," he said. The Delaware chieftain grunted; Frémont could see he was amused. "Used it once or twice?"

"Once or twice." Sagundai regarded him with an impressive stare.

Stockton strolled on down the line and Tessier caught his eye.

"Can you use that piece, soldier?"

Tessier was startled but he lifted the old .50-caliber Ballard and said: "Reckon I can, Skipper."

"Hit a man at a hundred yards?"

"Shit—hit a *dollar* at a hundred yards."

"Not bad," Stockton said. "Dollars don't shoot back, though. Do they?" He winked and Tessier laughed. Nodding, Stockton said in a quarterdeck voice, "Very well, lad. Carry on."

The men liked the commodore. He walked the whole line and made every man feel recognized. He looked at weapons, asked good questions, and fired one quip after another without the slightest loss of his command manner.

"Fine men," he said when he'd seen them all. "Rough but damned fine. How's their discipline?"

"Adequate," Frémont said. "They're civilians—you have to tell them why you want them to do something. But I'd put them up against any troops in the world. Well—almost any."

"I've studied both your Reports, you know—plunged into the wilderness without turning a hair, now I admire that. By God, when you were going down that canyon in that inflatable boat, I felt as if I was right with you—that was something!"

"My wife wouldn't agree with you there, Commodore," Frémont answered ruefully.

"Oh, well . . . women!"

The wind was kicking up a light froth on the water. Frémont saw a small lugger running close-hauled, two men in the stern setting out trawl lines. He asked Stockton for news of the war. The commodore rested a foot on a big cleat and gave an impressive précis. Mexican cavalry had crossed the

Rio Grande onto Texas soil, ambushed a patrol and killed a dozen or so American dragoons. On that pretext, President Polk had sent a war message to Congress; by the time Congress could act, the fighting had already started. On May 9—the very day, Frémont realized with a start, he and Gillespie had met on Klamath Lake and wondered if war had begun—American troops had broken the Mexicans and driven them back across the Rio Grande. General Zachary Taylor's men had followed, seized the town of Matamoros and by now—in early July—they presumably were deep in the interior of northern Mexico.

Word of these events had triggered the Pacific Squadron's long-standing orders to seize California's ports, starting with Monterey and San Francisco Bay. Stockton himself had just arrived in the USS *Congress*, six months out of Norfolk via Cape Horn; he was now assuming command of the Pacific Squadron.

Frémont in turn described the Bear Flag Revolt and his formation of the California Battalion. "So," he concluded, "I'm holding the interior of northern California. I have two hundred thirty-four men under arms, and I can double that figure whenever I like."

"A damned fine piece of work, Captain!" Stockton said, and clapped him on the shoulder. Frémont felt a rush of relief; he realized he'd been awaiting the commodore's verdict.

"You've seen our British friend," Stockton continued, gesturing toward the tall man-of-war. "HMS *Collingwood*, eighty guns, Admiral Sir George Seymour. Arrived a week after we did. I understand Sir George told my predecessor that if he hadn't seen the American flag flying, he'd have hoisted his own. Yes, sir: that close!" He gave Frémont a glittering smile. "But the question is, what now? The Navy's orders are simply to hold the ports, but your operations pave the way for a hell of a lot more." He paused and then darted a sudden question: "What were your intentions if we hadn't come?"

"To seize Monterey, hold northern California for presentation to the United States, and then consider taking the rest of the province," Frémont said without hesitation.

Stockton laughed. "Fine!" he said. "Damned fine. Well, I don't see why we should stop with the ports when we can have it all. I say it's time we seized the rest of this lovely land and installed a government compatible with our own. By God, I intend to see that the Stars and Stripes fly over California forever! Can I count on you?"

"Absolutely, sir: we're at your command."

"Splendid!" Stockton said. "I'll swear in your men as an irregular unit, United States Forces." He gave Frémont a sly, friendly look. "How will you feel about serving in the Navy—will that offend your Army sensibilities?"

Frémont laughed. The fact was he'd never served with troops, as his own commander once had pointed out tartly, and he habitually ignored the Army's command structure. He was in California for . . . whom? Benton? Bancroft? his government? All of them, presumably, but least of all for the United States Army.

"It'll be my personal pleasure, sir," he said.

Frémont found the next few weeks a testament to the efficacy of action. Stockton's force and vigor justified all of Frémont's own impulses. It was wonderful to drive ahead with full authority; he was startled at how rapidly things went. He set up camp outside Monterey and Stockton rode out, made a powerful speech, and called on the troops to volunteer.

His excitement infected young Henry Ford. "Goddamn right, Skipper! We're in it this far, and I say let's go all the way." He turned to his company. "Am I right, boys?"

"Hell, yes," someone shouted, and then they all were cheering. "Let's give the Cap'n and the skipper a hurrah!" Ford bellowed. "Hip, hip . . ."

Frémont went back to Sonoma and swore in another hundred men. He garrisoned Sonoma, Sutter's Fort and San Francisco, as they were now calling Yerba Buena, and reported back to Stockton, ready for action. Intelligence poured in from the south. General Castro was in Los Angeles, the province's capital and its most populous area. He had papered over the north-south quarrel with Governor Pico and they'd raised a motley force of five hundred. But every report said that the Californios were pitifully short of gunpowder and lead. They had a few old field pieces that might blow up if fired. Northerners and southerners continued to squabble. It was a force, Frémont believed, that would collapse at the first real shock.

Stockton laid out their tactics. He would take his sailors and marines to San Pedro in the USS *Congress* and advance on Los Angeles. Frémont's irregulars would embark in the USS *Cyane*, seize San Diego, and then march north to join Stockton's men in taking Los Angeles. It was simple, neat, direct; Frémont was impressed.

The *Congress*' band played the California Battalion aboard. Frémont and Stockton made speeches from the quarterdeck, the *Cyane*'s seamen ran aloft to set her sails, and the ship fell away from the quay. She beat a double reach across the bay, heeling in the wind, and then nosed into the great Pacific swells that broke against the headland. Frémont had spent two years cruising South American waters as a mathematics instructor aboard the USS *Natchez* under Lieutenant David Farragut, and his sea legs returned almost immediately.

After a happy hour on the quarterdeck watching the California coast sink to the horizon, he went amidships, where he had the distinct pleasure of finding the redoubtable Kit Carson looking green and miserable. The scout swallowed desperately as the ship climbed and fell across the smooth rollers—and then bolted to the rail and threw up all he'd eaten for days. Instinctively Frémont leaped aside as the wind hurled vomit back into Carson's face and sprayed it across the deck. A bo'sun's mate with tattoos covering both arms loomed before Carson, roaring, "Puke to loo'ard, you asshole!" Kit nodded pitifully. The bo'sun snatched up a bucket of seawater, shoved it into Carson's hand and shouted, "Now swab up the Goddamn deck!" which the scout meekly did. Frémont couldn't remember a finer sight. Later, finding Kit crouched on the forepeak dry-heaving through a scupper, he took pity on him and brought him an apple from the galley to munch. Carson said only four words until they were across the bar at San Diego.

"How you faring, noble scout?" Frémont asked him. "Ready for a five-course dinner?"

"Puke to loo'ard, Cap'n," Carson whispered feebly.

Taking San Diego required nothing more than putting his men ashore; the people in the sunny little village on the bay seemed indifferent to them, if not exactly cordial. The battalion set a steady pace for Los Angeles then, and by the time Frémont could join forces with Stockton's marines, the war was over. The Californios had buried their old field pieces and gone home; Castro and Pico were on their way to Mexico. The Americans marched into Los Angeles with the *Congress*' band blaring "The World Turned Upside Down," and by nightfall the American flag flew over all of California.

The Angeleños stood around on street corners and watched their conquerors calmly; they weren't loyal to Mexico, nor did they seem distressed to find themselves about to become American citizens. Stockton made a handsome speech about a new day of justice and prosperity dawning, and declared that he would set up a democratic government and order local elections. The town's *alcalde* answered with considerable dignity that Angeleños and all Californians would judge the newcomers by their actions. If freedom and prosperity did indeed flourish, then the Americans would be welcome. The band played for two hours, and if there wasn't dancing in the streets, neither was there shooting.

Frémont thought it a magnificent culmination to what had started the day he'd shamed Merritt into taking back those requisitioned horses. He could hear Benton's booming voice: the Senator would be ecstatic—so would Bancroft and President Polk. California was theirs! Manifest or not, the United States had pursued its destiny across the continent from sea to shining sea: the empire was a glorious reality. . . .

Three days later Stockton gave Frémont and Carson dinner in his cabin on the *Congress*. Well-educated and better read, he talked easily, told good stories, and knew national politics. They might have been at Benton's table, and it made Frémont realize how much he missed educated company on the trail. Carson said little, though Frémont noticed he handled himself well, unobtrusively following his Captain's lead in choice of silver.

When the stewards left them alone with a pot of strong Navy coffee, Stockton described his plans for California's government. It would be an American territory with an appointed governor and elected local officers.

"I'll serve as governor for the time being," he said casually, "but frankly, California isn't my interest—the war is what I care about. As soon as things are running smoothly I'll take my ships and move on." He took a sip of his coffee, watching Frémont over the rim. "Then I'll name you governor."

Frémont stared at him. It was like a dream coming true before he had thought to dream it. The commodore intended to sail south, seize the Mexican port of Acapulco, and march on Mexico City from the rear. He spread charts on the table and traced the route with a stiff forefinger, the back of his hand covered with liver spots. With his own men and a heavy contingent from the California Battalion which he expected Frémont to raise, he estimated that he could march the two hundred miles in four to six weeks.

"Their rear is their fatal weakness," he said. "They see the threat as from the east—Vera Cruz, over there on the Gulf of Mexico—and in the north. That's where they've deployed their troops. There'll be no opposition—we'll blow open their back door and win this war in quick time, by God!"

Could Frémont sign up four hundred of the settlers, men who weren't averse to a little fun and the taste of glory? Of course, he said. *Governor!* he thought, stunned. Perfect: Benton with his power in Washington could have the appointment easily made permanent. And Jessie: she would come out when things settled down—she would be the First Lady of California!

Dimly he heard Stockton say that he wanted Carson to hurry a report on their conquest back to Washington.

"Let me be frank, gentlemen," Stockton said. "When you're far from home and a great opportunity demands that you sweep far beyond what your government visualized, it behooves you to report as rapidly as possible. Then it's best for your government to hear about it from *you.*" He hesitated, tapping a gold ring against his saucer. "Much better than to have the news coming from sources that may not understand quite what you're doing, eh?" He turned that guileful, infectious smile on Frémont and added: "I shouldn't be surprised if you'd prefer to have your activities on the Sacramento described by someone who understands all the realities you faced, eh?"

His words seized Frémont's attention like a dash of cold water. How Washington first perceived his support of the Bear Flag Rebellion would be crucial. Carson was just the man to carry the message, for he could go straight to Benton and make sure that old Toller Tom understood it thoroughly. Benton would know what to do—he would take Carson to Bancroft, perhaps to the President himself.

"Time is vital, Mr. Carson," Stockton was saying. "Could you make Washington in sixty days with a good escort?"

"That'll be hard traveling." Carson paused, calculating. "Sixty days—yes, I can do that."

"And back in sixty more with answering dispatches? A hundred and twenty days round trip?"

Carson's eyebrows went up but he said, "Yes, I reckon I can. It'll take *some* riding, but I'll make it."

"Damned fine!" Stockton said. "Doubtless I'll be gone by then and Captain Frémont will be governor, but a ship will wait here for your messages. Come by tomorrow and I'll have my dispatches and some verbal instructions."

Riding back to camp, Frémont fell to dreaming. Jessie and Lily would come out as soon as he could arrange it, around the Horn or across the Isthmus of Panama. There would be a governor's mansion, not unduly pretentious but suitable for state functions. They'd have a ranch on one of those grassy hills that ran down to the Pacific where you could see the surf's white curl for miles, where the sea wind was always cool and the sunshine bright. And what he and Jessie would do for this long-dormant province! With Benton commanding at the fountainhead of power in the East and Frémont controlling the West, there would be no end to the possibilities for California. Emigrants would pour across the mountains, agriculture would expand, trade would boom. Perhaps there were minerals, lead as in Missouri, or iron—or even gold. There would be so much to build—docks, highways, whole towns. California would complete the western empire—and he and Jessie would be here, reveling in it, making up for the years apart, running it the way it should be run . . .

He hardly heard when Carson said quietly, "You want to watch that feller, Cap'n."

"Stockton?" he said, surprised.

"Why, he's crazy as a cow on locoweed. That business about taking Acapulco and marching on Mexico City. He's aiming to cross two hundred miles of the damnedest ambush country in the world and surprise their capital? I know a feller back in Taos used to work the caravans on the Acapulco road—says it's one mountain after another, gorges, high running rivers—bandits hit the caravans all the time. Deadly damned country. He tries that and he's going to get a lot of good men killed. You can't trust a man with ideas like that, Cap'n. You want to look out for him."

Carson rode out with nineteen of Frémont's men and made good time. They drove a herd and changed mounts two and three times a day. When they came to hard desert they took the bad crossings at night to avoid the September sun, moving carefully from water hole to water hole; this kind of country didn't forgive a careless man. On beyond they struck grass country—buttes, table mesas, tiny creeks trickling in the low places. Monument rocks of red sandstone glowed in the sun—he knew he was near home when he saw those. It was Apache country and a man wanted to keep a bright watch, but Santa Fe wasn't much more than a hundred miles on and Taos a bit beyond that. He had decided that he'd spend a single night at home with Josefa and then he'd run the Sante Fe Trail to the Missouri frontier. He'd go on alone by steamboat, and he might improve on that sixty days yet. . . .

Dust cloud up ahead; horses, probably, and plenty of them. Apaches? It would be one hell of a big war party, but still . . . He signaled his men off the trail, crawled up a high rock, and focused the glasses the Cap'n had given him. The lead group rode into sight. White men. Good enough. The point scout had a familiar look. When he was nearer Carson saw it was Tom Fitzpatrick. Damn!—old Broken Hand, his hat pushed back on his shock of white hair. Carson spurred forward, watching old Tom snatch his piece from its boot, the riders with him fanning out at each side. Then Carson reined up with a yell, and what a hoorawing they gave each other . . .

Fitzpatrick had been in Taos. He'd seen Josefa and she was fine, said she missed Kit. He was guiding for old Kearny now; when the Mex war started Kearny had formed the Army of the West, marched out the Sante Fe Trail and taken New Mexico. There had been a little skirmishing, but most New Mexicans had welcomed the Americans. So Kit's home country was the newest territory of the United States, signed, sealed, and delivered. Their old friend Charley Bent was governor. Now, Fitzpatrick said, they were going on to California; Kearny intended to seize that too, set up a territorial government—

"Do tell!" Carson could hardly contain himself. It wasn't often you got a chance to throw a surprise on a canny old dog like Tom; he reared back in high good humor. "Why hell," he brayed, "it's done took! You boys might as well turn around and go on home."

"That so?" Fitzpatrick said. They heard riders approaching on the gallop. "You'd better tell that to General Kearny. Here he comes."

"You mean 'colonel,' don't you?" Carson asked.

"Not no more; it's *'general'* now."

Stephen Watts Kearny checked his big dragoon horse; a dollop of foam flew from the animal's mouth. "Kit Carson, General," Fitzpatrick said. "Coming from California."

Carson knew Kearny, but not well; he had guided him out of Fort Laramie once. The Army man hadn't changed much; he was a bit grayer, his long face as grim and unsmiling as ever. Somehow you always got the feeling that Kearny pitied you just for being a civilian. The man wasn't at all like Frémont—you'd never mistake him for a friend. Carson imagined Kearny slept at attention, dreaming of salutes and reviews.

"How do, General," he said politely. "It's been a while since Laramie."

"That it has," Kearny said, his voice dry and remote. "Come from California, you say?"

"Yes sir. I was just telling Tom here that he don't need to hurry—California's already in the fold."

"What the devil do you mean?" the general demanded sharply.

"We took it—lock, stock, and barrel!" He described the situation quickly, feeling good; here he was nearly home and the bearer of good tidings to boot. Half of what he knew in this world he'd learned from old Tom; it was fun to pass on the news, and he laid it on a little.

"Cap'n Frémont pulled off the whole thing," he said. "You should have seen him, Tom—he was a caution! About like the way he took us over the Sierras that time. 'Course, later we had a little help from the Navy, but hell, we had it well in hand before the sailor boys even showed up."

"Captain Frémont was on a mapping expedition," Kearny interrupted.

Carson had been talking to Fitzpatrick; now he looked at Kearny's pale face and realized the general was angry. Immediately he wished he'd put a bridle on his tongue. He saw Fitzpatrick's mouth quirking at a corner. Oh shit, he thought.

"Well, of course, we was mapping," he said, "but things went a little further than that."

Kearny asked a series of tart questions about the forces in California. Carson answered now in monosyllables. The general turned to an officer beside him. "Major, in light of this information, I think we'll send C and D

Companies back to Sante Fe, and push on with Company B. No need to subject the whole force to a desert crossing if the situation in California is in hand."

"Very well, sir," the officer said, and wheeled his horse away.

"Any trouble on the road?" Kearny asked Carson.

"No sir; we kept our eyes peeled."

The general studied him a moment. "Well, you never know. Mr. Fitzpatrick has not traveled this route. You'd better turn around and guide us through."

Carson was appalled. "General, I can give you some men who know the road. But I can't go back myself."

"Of course you can. I need you. I don't want your men, I want *you.*"

"Sir, Tom knows this country. Even if he ain't never rode this route, he can find his way—"

"I *know* Mr. Fitzpatrick can find his way. But you've just come over this route. You're our logical guide."

"General," Carson said desperately, "I've been gone more than a year. I'm only a hundred miles from home! I ain't seen my wife in a dog's age . . ."

Kearny's face softened a little. "Well, I can understand your feelings—"

"And anyway, sir, I'm carrying special dispatches from Cap'n Frémont and Commodore Stockton. I guaranteed I'd have 'em in Washington in sixty days. I'm going to spend a night at home and then head on east. It'll be hellish hard to make that time as it is—"

He broke off, startled by the altered expression on the general's face.

"You will guide me to California, Mr. Carson," Kearny said in a hard, frosty tone. "Mr. Fitzpatrick will carry your dispatches east. They'll be in responsible hands."

"No sir," Carson said. "I can't do that!"

"You *will* do that. That is an order, Scout. *Give me the dispatches.*" Kearny's face was suddenly white and taut. Carson felt a touch of fear, but fury overrode caution.

"Goddamnit, General," he cried, "I've got my orders and I'm gonna carry them out. I ain't in your command and I ain't gonna—"

"That's enough! We are at war, and I am in command here. You will see us through to California. If you prefer to do so in irons, I'll oblige you."

"General—"

"Be silent, Mr. Carson! It's well within my power to put you before a firing squad for refusing to obey a lawful order. Be warned, sir!"

Without giving Carson a chance to answer, Kearny wheeled his horse and galloped back toward his body of troops.

In the silence that followed, Carson turned to Fitzpatrick. "Well, God damn, Tom," he said. "Now what's all that for?"

"You sure have developed a big mouth, Kit," the guide said. "What you been doing in California—running for office?"

Carson gazed after Kearny in angry consternation. Irons! Goddamn Army and their fool ranks, each a bigger idiot than the last one. Except Charlie. Jesus Christ. He's never going to forgive me for this one. What do I do now?

In the cream-and-yellow dining room a round table laid for sixteen stood under a glittering chandelier. Candlelight spilled gently over heavy linen and polished silver; it flattered them all—in Mrs. Polk's smiling face Jessie caught a glimpse of the Tennessee belle the President had married. Secretary Bancroft was seated on Jessie's right, and on her left a garrulous old friend of the President's from Nashville, a Mr. Cushing she'd met only once before. Her father was across the table, between Mrs. Cushing and Maria Crittenden. A cold soup had just been served and the First Lady immediately lifted her spoon. She was chatting about a theatrical extravaganza she was sponsoring with a group of congressional wives. After a moment she tossed the conversational ball gently to her husband; he answered with a barely audible monosyllable and went on eating his soup. Jessie saw Mrs. Polk's lips tighten into a thin line that made her look surprisingly like Mr. Polk. She reclaimed the ball, carried it for a minute or two, and then asked the President if he didn't think Duilio Grossi, the baritone who'd been such a success in New York, would be a good choice.

"Indeed," he said, the rhythm of his spoon unbroken. Jessie glanced at Maria, who shot her eyes skyward expressively. Why was the President always so secretive and withdrawn, so enigmatic! The conversation, being general, had nowhere to go; the silence stretched like fraying rope. Jessie concentrated on her soup, watching the intricate presidential seal appear in the bowl. The hazards of dining at the White House.

All at once Polk laid down his spoon. "Oh, Sarah, how the devil would I know? All that braying in Italian—I never listen to 'em if I can avoid it." He stared at Secretary Buchanan, seated at Mrs. Polk's right. "Do you detect any quiet tremors under the surface, Jim? any little signals that indicate they *might* be willing to listen to reason?"

The war. Jessie arched her back and took a long breath. This ever more dangerous war that seemed so pointless, yet was embroiling them more deeply every day.

"I fear the word 'reason' is not in the Mexican lexicon, Mr. President," James Buchanan answered. "They run on passions, and counterpassions." Buchanan employed a secret agent who had some shadowy access to Mexico's ruling circles—the Secretary sometimes brought his confidential reports to Jessie for translation. Mr. T, whose Spanish was flawless, would read them aloud, and while the two men discussed their contents heatedly, she would reduce them to English. Buchanan said he distrusted his official translators, but Jessie suspected he enjoyed escaping the pressure of decisions over at State. Like his employer, he had been happiest on the Hill. With his head of silver hair and his good-looking, empty face, he seemed better cast as an actor in a storybook pageant than as the senior officer in the cabinet of the United States.

The key to Mexican thinking, Buchanan was saying smoothly, was that it couldn't be dignified as thought at all. Santa Anna, returned from exile, was simply outdoing the ousted General Paredes in bombastic promises to thrash the hated *norteamericanos;* the man apparently projected some sort of mystical grandeur which his people adored, and no matter how disastrous the war news, no one in Mexico City doubted that the Hero of Tampico would produce another miracle.

"And when he doesn't?" the President retorted sharply. "When all of northern Mexico is in General Taylor's hands? What then?"

Jessie saw Buchanan glance inquiringly at her father, who observed that nothing outside the Mexican capital seemed to have much meaning—or even reality—to the ruling class. Look at their cavalier dismissal of California, the Southwest—

"It's so tedious!" the President exclaimed with sudden heat; he was still looking at Buchanan. Mr. T, startled, was frowning at Polk, his mouth working. "All we wanted was to settle the Texas border and discuss some territorial acquisitions we'd have paid for handsomely. And they agreed to talk, they *promised* me—" The President shook his head, offended, his mouth a severe line, his beady eyes roaming restlessly around the table. "Does their attitude make any sense to you, Jessie? You've seen the material . . ."

She was caught badly off-balance—she hadn't realized the President knew of her part in the translations; he always knew more than you thought he did, in his terse, secretive way—and she was mortified at the way he had dismissed her father's view of the war, had turned to her instead of her father now. "I—I thought their attitude analogous to the Parisian view of France, Mr. President," she said rather lamely. "A patrician contempt for the provinces."

He nodded, glancing away again. He fell silent as the entrée was served, then burst out: "Probably Scott is right. We'll have to go into southern Mexico after all—attack Mexico City itself."

Mrs. Polk gave her husband a sharp, pained look—this clearly was not her idea of dinner conversation—but the President plunged on. Scott believed that Castle San Juan de Ulúa on the Gulf Coast could be reduced by bombardment; once established in Vera Cruz the Army could force its way up the Camino Nacional straight to the capital city, deep in the interior valley.

Invasion of the heart of Mexico: the idea chilled Jessie. She had danced with Captain Sam Ringgold at a White House ball when war had been declared; he was tall and had an eager, vivacious manner. The dashing Captain Ringgold and his flying artillery, his beautiful little cannon with their shiny brass barrels; and at the battle of Palo Alto his guns had saved the day—swab, load, ram, fire, swab again—a ballet, she had imagined it, the gunners dancing in their strange saraband of fire, the guns like stage toys . . .

And then a ball from a Mexican cannon had torn off Sam Ringgold's legs. They had hauled him twenty miles, lying on the bed of an unsprung cart, trying to get him to a Navy surgeon who hadn't been able to stop the bleeding. The Hero of Palo Alto, bleeding to death on the bed of an old cart. It was all she would ever need to understand war's uncaring savagery. Her cousin Preston McDowell had burst into the house only that afternoon in his spanking new blue uniform with its double row of gold buttons that accentuated his slender height, the single silver bar of rank on his fringed epaulets looking innocent and festive.

Dear Preston with his soft brown hair and skin that any girl might envy. For years their aunts had imagined they might marry, but she had always known better, and so had Preston. He was engaged now to Millie Townsend. And Charles had swooped into *her* life like a wild young falcon. . . . Once, during that tense, awful period when she was secretly meeting Charles for strolls along Pennsylvania Avenue, Preston had come upon them unexpectedly, laughing in delighted surprise, towering over Charles' sturdier, stronger figure as they shook hands; and afterward he had written her a wonderful letter urging her to go ahead—that special knowledge of a shared childhood in league against adult pressures had told him how deeply in love she was, how troubled. . . .

Her father was talking now, about the Castle of Chapultepec and how it would have to be stormed by bayonet, and then the city's gates blown open by cannon fire. Scott himself had testified before the Military Affairs Committee that he would need 15,000 men, very heavy losses could be expected in the mountain passes . . .

"Yes, yes," the President broke in impatiently, "I know—that's only *another* reason why I don't want to do it."

Why, he's—he's *bored,* Jessie thought in sudden alarm, he's actually . . . People just weren't bored with Mr. T—not because he was perennially interesting, but because his power was such that any signal he gave had its importance. For an instant she studied her father: he was as grand, as imperious as ever—but he was aging: his jowls looked heavier, his hair was thinning badly. Only last month in an anteroom just off the chamber she'd heard two young members mimicking his oratorical flourishes; they had been embarrassed at her appearance, even contrite. But there it was. His old allies were disappearing; he had lost two crucial votes this year. The Senate was changing, Washington was changing. So was Missouri, for that matter, with new people crowding in, the slavery men even more adamant, and Mr. T still matching them thrust for thrust, in defense of that Union he held dearer than his own life. . . . But imagine James K. Polk, who wasn't worthy to carry Tom Benton's cane, not even troubling to hide his boredom! Involuntarily she shivered.

Of course the President had shown a surprisingly tough-minded bargaining skill over Oregon; despite that British rebuff of the year before he'd got just what he wanted—the boundary extended straight along the Forty-ninth Parallel to Puget Sound, the British whisked out of the Columbia River country in one stroke. Even Papa had been impressed. Polk had shrewdly presented himself to the British as barely able to restrain the Fifty-Four-Forty-or-Fight crowd who wanted to seize the entire coast all the way north to Russian Alaska. It was a risky business, threatening war with England when war with Mexico already seemed imminent; but Polk had got away with it.

Sam Houston had been in town at the time; during dinner he'd observed,

"There's more to Polk than you see, Tom. Comes from all those Tennessee poker games—a man learns a thing or two about running a bluff."

"I give him that," Mr. T had rumbled, "a consummate bluff. But don't you forget that the *real* pressure on the British wasn't Polk and the hawks—it was those American settlers streaming down the Oregon Trail . . . and you know how *that* got opened!"

The President had turned now to Harriet Lane, signaling the end of general conversation. Mr. Cushing wanted to talk about the Report of Charles' Second Expedition and she chatted with him. The Report, at least, was unalloyed good news. The commercial edition combining both Reports had gone through several printings and half a dozen foreign translations. Geographers and botanists had praised it. The great Humboldt had been most generous—he had even commented on the arresting significance of that bumblebee on the mountaintop; she'd cried out with delight, reading that. She'd had a charming note from Lord Chichester, president of the Royal Geographic Society, about a lecture he'd given on the Report. Albert Gallatin, Jefferson's venerable Secretary of the Treasury who had done so much in Indian ethnology, had written her, and Daniel Webster had asked her to tea to talk to him about the Report—and then quite predictably had done all the talking himself. There now were so many articles about Charles she'd stopped clipping them.

Not that it had been all tea and crumpets. She had encountered an Engineering Corps officer and his wife at a reception and they had avoided her pointedly—cut her, really. She hated the thought that Charles' fellow officers were jealous of him; but Mr. T had told her dryly that West Pointers were famous for their dislike of outsiders—more especially if they'd distinguished themselves. In which case their toffee noses would be *really* out of joint, now that Mr. Polk had named Charles a lieutenant colonel! Not that they'd ever believe it, but the promotion was entirely unsolicited—neither she nor her father had approached the President. Nominally it was for the Report, though in all truth she thought it reflected what Charles was trying to do for the President in California.

As if he'd been reading her thoughts, Bancroft turned to her and said: "And what do you hear from your pathfinder, Jessie?"

She looked at him levelly for an instant. "Not very much, really."

He nodded. "Yes. The distances . . ."

"He's gone back into California. They were attacked by Indians in Oregon—he lost one of his most trusted friends. Louison Freniere. One of *our* closest friends," she amended, watching him.

He shook his head. "It's certainly wild country."

"Isn't it?" She made herself smile at him charmingly. "Wild and unpredictable. And now he's back in California. In the thick of things. But you know more about that than I do."

"I?" His brows rose. "I'm completely out of touch, my dear—I'm off to London next month, you know."

"I know." He'd been named the new ambassador to the Court of St. James—a diplomatic plum. Still, she'd been surprised—it wasn't a patch on the Navy Department; and Bancroft *had* dramatically advanced Polk's name at the '44 convention and broken the deadlock between Cass and Van Buren. Was he going to London willingly? she'd asked her father. Hardly, Mr. T had admonished her; *no one* willingly gives up power. The fact was, Bancroft had burned himself out as the President's man; he'd borne the brunt of too many battles. And he'd made a few mistakes—not fatal ones, but still . . . The President was using others for the difficult assignments now.

"At least there's nothing in Secretary Buchanan's 'Mexican dispatches' that indicates their determination to fight for California," she offered clearly now. "That's good news, don't you think?"

"Presumably." Bancroft's eyes seemed to be fastened on an object just beyond her left eyebrow. "Of course, getting a workable treaty will be the real problem."

—*Yes,* she thought, all at once bitter and raging, *you* don't have to snatch a rifle out of a saddle boot and ride against those lances! or heap dirt on the body of your best friend. . . . Ah, thank God—thank sweet God himself that whatever was *going* to take place in California would not involve the collision of massed armies!

But *seventeen months* away, and no word at all for five—

"In all truth California is a *fait accompli,* I should say. The Navy is there—I issued the orders to Sloat to seize the ports. General Kearny will invade as soon as he's subdued New Mexico, which shouldn't take very long. Any treaty will certainly have to embrace New Mexico and California."

He ran on smoothly about the necessity for a sound treaty, the need to legitimize the actions, and she listened with a dull, cold sensation in the pit of her stomach. Not one word about Charles. Not one! She remembered that afternoon in her father's hideaway office: if anything went wrong, Bancroft wouldn't be there to speak; they would stand in the dock by themselves—she and Charles. And now Bancroft was leaving Washington, sailing to the other side of the world, a million miles from the tangled cross-purposes of the war.

"*Charles* is in California now," she reminded him.

"Of course. And I'm sure he's making a valuable contribution. With the war on, of course, the Navy, the Army—I'm sure California is in good hands . . ."

His face was bland, smooth, impenetrable; he was looking at his wineglass, which he held by the stem. Was this *all* that talk in her father's office had meant? The secret directions, the wishes of the President, the needs of the nation—it meant no more than this? Seventeen months of separation, the pain and loneliness, the interminable, grinding worry, and the risk—no! She would *not* let him leave it like that.

"You sent him there," she said in a low voice.

He gave her the quick, searching look. "Not at all. He was going anyway. Of course, I encouraged him. But Colonel Frémont is a national hero as an explorer. He hardly needs encouragement in matters of exploration—"

"No," she said. She caught his forearm and squeezed it hard. "You sent him. *Look at me!*" Bancroft turned a startled face to her now; she said in a very low, very hard voice, "You sent him to *bring in* California—to make sure we got in. Into the valley. You said that you spoke for the President. I want you to admit that."

"Dear romantic Jessie." He glanced nervously toward the President.

Her father was staring at her from across the table with heavy alarm, his lips moving in silent warning. She dug her nails into Bancroft's arm so hard her fingers hurt. "Admit it, damn you," she whispered. *"To me!"*

Her looked at her again and then his eyes dropped. "If it comforts you." Urbanity flowed back into his face. "Nothing has changed. Don't be rash, my dear."

Then he turned away to the woman on his other side. On Jessie's left, Mr. Cushing resumed his story of old General Jackson and the Tennessee walking horse. It required only that she nod, and she listened quietly, avoiding her father's eyes, conscious of her heart like a cold stone in her chest.

Carson wasn't about to forgive that hard-assed old bastard with the long face and the new general's stars. He'd been one day's ride away from Josefa, after more than a year gone. And he'd been looking forward to this trip; he had a great curiosity about the East. Like everyone in Missouri, he knew Senator Tom Benton, but it would be mighty different to waltz straight in with a message Benton was aching to hear. Why, Benton might even have taken him to see the President. Wouldn't that have been something! Kit Carson, trapper, scout, all-around fighting man, shaking hands with the President of the United States. Put her there, Mr. Polk! Well, how do, Mr. Carson, here, have yourself a shot of Tennessee mash. Why, don't mind if I do, Mr. President, sir. God damn!

Fact was, the Cap'n and only the Cap'n had made it possible for the United States to take California, and that point ought to be clearly made. The minute that sly possum Stockton had started talking, Carson had caught his drift: it mattered *how* the folks at home saw what you'd done. Carson didn't care about Stockton's message, but he'd have liked to have turned up all the cards for old Tom Benton.

Charlie deserved as much. And the more Carson saw of Regular Army ways with Kearny, the more he appreciated the Cap'n's easy manner. Frémont wasn't Army—at least, he didn't act it. With Charlie you did things because they made sense; with the Army you did things because Kearny or one of his flunkies said so. Coming back across the desert most of the horses had died. That hadn't been necessary—Carson had brought his own horses across without loss—it all came from one man calling his decisions down the mountain and everyone obeying them, no matter what. Then when they'd reached the California frontier, Kearny had bought a replacement herd of wild horses. Broncs! Crazy as coots, snapping, bucking. It wore the troopers out just to get them saddled. In a couple of weeks the brutes would have settled down, but Kearny wasn't waiting—hell no, old Napoleon had ordered an attack at dawn.

It seemed California had flared up since Carson had left—*bravos* in Los Angeles had jumped the Bear Flag garrison there, whereupon the Californios had gotten themselves together to fight again and now they controlled most of the south. Carson figured this was far less serious than it sounded, since the Californios still had neither organization nor supplies. Stockton was at San Diego getting ready to march north and Frémont was hurrying the battalion south again from Sacramento; they'd pinch out this little uprising between them in no time.

Kearny had taken an odd pleasure in hearing about it, though. "Not as whipped as you'd thought, eh?" he had said with that frosty smile, and Carson had snapped that by Jesus, *he* wasn't the one who'd turned back two hundred dragoons and come on with only one hundred. Then, seeing the look on the general's face, he wished he'd kept *that* thought to himself along with all the others . . .

The attack order had come suddenly. Kearny had sent a routine message to Stockton and presently Cap'n Gillespie had arrived with four men to guide the dragoons in. The marine had passed a party of seventy-five California lancers camped a few miles away near the village of San Pasqual and proposed the attack, though the lancers were warned now. In the Rockies tactics like that would get a man killed. But this was the Army.

It would be hard to imagine a more miserable beginning. They were up long before dawn; the damp December cold cut to the bone. The new horses fought like she-bears with cubs and Carson figured they'd be hours getting started, but then he heard Kearny say, "Let us move to the attack." If there *was* a plan, Carson didn't hear of it. Cap'n Abraham Johnston's troop was taking the point. Johnston was an amiable, bookish man with an insatiable curiosity about Carson's life in the high mountains; Carson decided that on a morning like this he'd just as soon ride with a man he liked, and he mounted. They crossed the first long ridge with dawn breaking; he saw troops strung out far behind them. It looked as if half the men weren't mounted yet.

An order was passed up the line: advance at a trot. Johnston shouted something and threw his horse into a gallop. Trot, damnit, trot!—but the troopers were galloping away and Carson touched spurs to Oglala. The day was coming up now. He saw the California camp down a long slope; the lancers were slipping into their saddles as smoothly as men pulling on their boots. There were a lot of them, a hell of a lot of them. Their horses danced and milled under easy control. He found himself hoping they would break and run, but they didn't. They formed a steady line, lances upright, muskets in hand.

Goddamnit, the order had said *trot*. Carson glanced around—and sure enough, they were alone. What in hell was Kearny *doing*? With Gillespie's men, the Americans outnumbered the lancers two to one—and here they were, twenty men galloping in alone to attack four times their number. The day was brightening quickly; the sun would be up before long; beyond the lancers' camp he saw the village of San Pasqual stirring. The little troop came down the long slope, hooves loud on hard ground. The line of lancers raised their muskets. Carson looked back again, hoping to see more riders break the crest of the hill. He heard a shouted command in Spanish and the muskets went off in volley with an awful crash. He saw a bullet smash Johnston's forehead and then his own horse went down and he flew over its head. He got to his feet unhurt, but his rifle stock was shattered and he couldn't find his pistol. The dragoons who had survived the volley charged into the lancers with sabers drawn. A horse was down nearby, no sign of its rider, and Carson snatched the carbine from its saddle boot and ran for a pile of rocks. He aimed, fired, missed—damn! the sight had been knocked all askew. Two lancers were closing on a dragoon. Carson banged the sight straight against a rock but before he could reload one lancer feinted the trooper and the other came from behind and drove his lance into the man's kidney. The trooper fell without a sound. Carson stared. That lance was murderous. Seven feet of springy ash, another foot of sharp steel—you couldn't fight that with a three-foot saber if the lancer knew his business, and these troopers were professionals.

A bugle was piping and Carson saw little Ben Moore galloping down the long slope behind them at the head of his troop. More riders were strung out behind and at the crest he saw General Kearny flogging his big roan with the flat of his saber. Cap'n Moore's men crashed into the melee, which broke into individual combats. Several Americans were already down. The fighting was eerily quiet; against a hush he could hear hooves thudding, sabers cracking against lances, horses squealing, men cursing and grunting. Carson stayed low in the rocks, firing when he had a clear shot, the bent sight throwing his bullets wide.

Three lancers were circling Cap'n Moore like wolves. Moore was a practical joker, and had kept the camp lively with his ringing laughter. His horse looked wall-eyed crazy and was bucking. Even at a distance, his face had a white, desperate look, but he kept his saber ready. A lancer rode up behind him. Carson aimed for the man's chest and hit him in the arm; he dropped the lance. Moore parried the next thrust and lunged with his saber, but the Californio yanked his horse back, dodged the stroke and threw his horse against Moore's. The impact turned Moore, and the other lancer drove his blade straight into Moore's chest. Carson saw a fountain of brilliant blood gush from his mouth.

He was filled with raging disgust. Good God—sabers couldn't fight lances. Why didn't they withdraw, get themselves together, get the fight onto their own terms? What the holy hell was Kearny doing! Then Carson saw the general ride straight into the battle with his sword held high. Kearny had favored his horse in the desert and now it was repaying him. It was under superb control; Kearny was a masterful horseman. The man was a bastard, but you had to hand it to him—general officer riding into the fight with thunder in his face and his saber swinging. But it still was no match; only the horse saved Kearny's life. A lance ripped him from behind and another drove through his sword arm. His saber fell to the ground, but he still stayed in the fight, calling encouragement to his men, the big roan dancing out of the way of each charge.

All at once the Californios began to break off. They were pointing, and Carson turned to see the dragoons' two little field guns arriving at a gallop. But one of the guns didn't stop—the mustangs pulling it were running away, their eyes rolling white, teeth clamped on the bits. The gunners jumped off as the horses ran among the Californios. Carson stared open-mouthed: even a civilian knew you weren't supposed to abandon your guns. But the other gun was ready to fire, and that was enough for the Californios. With a loud yell they galloped off, taking the captured cannon with them. Some of them were wounded, but they all were able to ride away.

In the long silence that followed, Carson walked onto the field. He walked slowly, stumbling a little; he felt as if he had been horsewhipped in the square on Sunday afternoon with the whole town watching. More than a score of American soldiers were dead or dying, and nearly as many more lay wounded. He found Kearny on the ground, a trooper tightening a tourniquet on his arm. The man was brave, by God; his long face was as gray as his hair from the blood he'd lost, but he was entirely calm. Heartsore, Carson squatted beside him and volunteered to slip through the enemy lines to Stockton for help.

Carson felt sick and helpless, all hollowed out. "Godalmighty," he muttered, "I never thought I'd live to see American soldiers whupped like this."

Kearny stared up at him. "Weren't whipped. We won an important victory."

"We did?" Carson said dumbly.

"We drove the enemy from the field," Kearny said. His lips were white and twitching. "That is the correct military objective."

"They want to surrender, *mi capitán,*" Don Jesús Pico said. "The whole army of California—officers, caballeros, common soldiers who had thought only to defend their sacred land . . . all prostrate themselves at your feet, Señor—*Gobernador* Frémont." Pico's extravagant manner nevertheless concealed a thoughtful man. "They have come here to the Rancho Cahuenga because they knew you were here. They have come to surrender to you personally—not to the arrogant Comodoro Stockton nor to the loutish Bears. To you, señor, because you are an officer and a gentleman, because they trust you, they believe their fate is safe in your hands—"

"All *right.* Very well," Frémont said. He needed to think. With his force of Bears he was within twenty miles of Los Angeles, where Stockton had broken the California resistance in a sharp little skirmish the day before that had cost a man killed on each side. The whole thing had been over before Frémont's men could engage. The Californios had fled north and when they encountered Frémont they'd snatched at this opportunity to surrender. Pico, whom Frémont had sent to hear their proposal, said that they had the gun they'd taken from the Americans at San Pasqual. A formal capitulation appealed to Frémont—it meant a decisive ending—but obviously Stockton should receive it. He was senior, had done the fighting, and was no farther away than a half-day's ride.

"No," Pico said, his heavy face darkening. "They won't surrender to Comodoro Stockton. They'll just melt away and go home—and then nothing is really resolved. That'll be bad for you and bad for our people. Much better to have a clear-cut surrender that we can all live with afterwards. A capitulation, legally signed. But not with Stockton—they don't trust Stockton."

"But they trust me?" Frémont asked skeptically.

Pico shrugged. "They respect you. The story of how you saved me is known everywhere, Señor General. Your act of mercy has made you a great reputation."

Frémont enjoyed the ebullient Jesús—he knew that Pico's admiration for him really reflected his admiration for himself: Don Jesús Pico of San Luis Obispo, a member of Governor Pio Pico's large family, was an important man; saving him, therefore, conferred importance on his savior. Frémont had pardoned Pico after a Bear Flag court-martial had ordered him executed for various parole violations. The sentence was legal, so Frémont had needed an acceptable reason to overturn it. That reason had been provided by the tears and lamentations of the handsome Señora Pico and her nine children; they made such a scene in the plaza at San Luis Obispo that even the Bears had looked relieved when Frémont granted the pardon. The reprieve had made a devoted follower of Don Jesús. He was a big man, rough-spoken at times, very able and not at all servile, though he loved to use flattery as a tool. Frémont liked and trusted him.

"But the trouble is," Frémont said now, "*they're* dictating the terms."

"No, no, my friend. They want nothing but to go home in peace. They defended themselves in honor, and they were defeated. So be it. Now they are willing to resume life under a new flag, new rules and customs. It won't be easy, but they will accept it. They will be good citizens—especially if they are not humiliated now. And you want them to be good citizens, don't you?—you will be their governor."

"I expect them to be good citizens," Frémont said sharply. "I'll punish any who are not."

"Exactly my point, Señor Comandante," Pico said, smiling, a teacher commending a bright student. "Malcontents to the new order must be punished. Found and punished! *Cruelmente!*"

Frémont raised an eyebrow.

"*Sí, señor*—but they will be hard to find, no?" His voice dropped to a conspiratorial note. "Look—they are defeated. But not *beaten,* eh? There is a universe of difference. Treat them generously and they will confer their loyalty; humiliate them and they will seek revenge. Think how guerrillas would prosper here—it is natural terrain for them, do you not think?"

Frémont frowned. "The mountains would make it difficult. But we could deal with that in time."

"*Sí,* my point exactly," Pico said. "You would punish—but perhaps the wrong people, eh? Which would anger them further, gain them adherents—oh my!"

There certainly was nothing servile about Pico. Frémont felt a shaft of irritation. "Are you threatening?" he asked.

Pico raised both hands appealingly, smiling his warmest smile. "Oh, *mi General,* can the defeated threaten? No, *señor,* never! I am merely looking ahead—I want your reign to be as glorious as I know your generous nature will make it, unblemished by foolish contretemps—"

Frémont raised a hand to stop him. In fact, Don Jesús had a good point. Stockton soon would sail away, but he himself would have to stay and govern California, perhaps for years. He doubted the Californios would muster themselves for guerrilla warfare, but just the same, the task of bringing the province smoothly to even a part of its immense potential was formidable. It certainly would be easier if original citizens were content. And why not accept their capitulation? Why not be generous? It was an easy gesture that could pay countless dividends in the years ahead.

Still, when he rode up to the *alcalde*'s office in the plaza at Los Angeles two days later to present the signed Treaty of Cahuenga to Stockton, he was uneasy. The treaty required all Californians to lay down their arms and go home, exacted no penalties for their uprising, and gave them full citizens' rights under the Constitution of the United States. And indeed, the commodore's dark face flushed darker as he read over the parchment document.

"Why in the devil did you do this?" he asked. He pulled at his bristling black beard, his eyes sharp and challenging.

Frémont explained his reasoning; he knew he was making a good case. When he finished Stockton sat in silence, drumming his fingers on the table, staring across the plaza. At last he turned to Frémont with a smile from which all tension had vanished.

"Well, damned fine!" he said. "I think you're right, by God! I might have been harder on 'em myself, but you're the one who must govern them. And after all, they're Americans now."

The commodore talked for half an hour about the campaign just finished. When Frémont told him that he had recovered the gun Kearny had lost at San Pasqual, Stockton laughed aloud. He locked his hands behind his head, propped his feet on the table, and told Frémont with relish that he'd had to send two parties to rescue the dragoons. Kearny's defeat had been entirely unnecessary—if he'd kept his forces together, the Californians would never have dared to engage him. Kearny had limped into San Diego and added his handful of dragoons to Stockton's marines and sailors.

"Arrogant fellow, though," Stockton said. "You know he turned our messenger around?"

"No!—You don't mean Carson?"

"None other. Sent our dispatches on, but he forced Carson to disobey my orders. Threatened to shoot him."

"Shoot him!"

"Or put him in irons. Or so he told Gillespie. Perfectly outrageous."

Frémont had an instant of deep alarm. But then, Benton would know what to do on the basis of the letters alone. It would have been better to have had Carson there on hand to answer his questions, but Mr. T didn't really need guidance.

"At any rate," Stockton said, "I'm having Kearny recalled. Look at this—he wants to usurp command."

He tossed a letter from Kearny across the table. Rude and abrupt, it said that Kearny had express orders from the War Department to conquer California and establish a civil government; it demanded that Stockton hand over to him full control.

"I wrote him immediately," Stockton said with a grimace. "Told him that any orders he might have were nullified since we had conquered the province and established a civil government long before he arrived. He didn't conquer anything; he was soundly whipped and had to be rescued. Did you know he lost a third of his command at San Pasqual?"

"No, I didn't."

"I really don't like his attitude—I told him straight out that I was reporting his conduct to the President and requesting his immediate recall. I may ask the President to discipline him."

He dismissed Kearny with a wave of his hand and began to talk about his civil government. It was full of problems, but he was sure Frémont would find solutions. He himself would be busy preparing his ships for departure; he intended to turn things over permanently in a few days. He'd long since abandoned his original plan to go through the jungle to Mexico City.

"So," he said at last, slapping the table, "damned fine! We've done a fine piece of work here—presenting California to the United States as a stable, peaceful territory. The President will be delighted. I'll bet he wishes the rest of the war was running as smoothly as we've managed here." He stood up and put out his hand. "Congratulations, Governor! Hold to the long view. There's a magnificent future here for you. . . ."

DUEL

SOMETIMES FRÉMONT felt he had been born to be governor of California, so well did the rôle fit him. He liked the decisions, the long hours, the sense of moving swiftly and confidently among perilous problems. He had a gift for power, a talent for quick, decisive solutions. He took over the *alcalde*'s office on the plaza in Los Angeles with its carved desk and iron-strapped furniture, its plastered fireplace ringed with tiles in colors as vivid as his spirits. He frankly enjoyed the lines of people patiently waiting to see him, the heads turning, the polite bows. Nevertheless, he remained plainspoken and, despite Don Jesús Pico's urging, refused to use an honorific; and this image of himself as an unassuming man who yet wielded great power also gave him a quiet pleasure. Papa Joe Nicollet had been right: it was his first taste of real power—and he found it almost unbearably sweet. It was action—magnified, focused, more intense than anything he had experienced. And action always set him free and lifted his heart.

Stockton had gone to Monterey to equip for war in Mexican waters. None of the Bear Flag men had joined him, but he didn't seem to hold that against Frémont. He had turned things over in a gracious little ceremony, and problems that had been left untended for months fell on Frémont in a deluge. There were public officials to be reinstated or replaced, courts to be reopened, a land-title office to be established, banditry cases to be dealt with, public health tended to, and elections planned. His first ledger of executive documents filled; his clerks opened a second one. Men from all over the territory collected in his outer office. When he tired of talking with them, he mounted Sacramento and rode out to see at first hand how matters fared, stopping to listen to paisanos along the way. *El Gobernador a Caballo,* they called him—Governor on Horseback: he liked the ring of it.

He had a consuming dream to develop California's trade with the Orient. That trade would depend on a swift and economical link with the east coast. Merchants needed eastern manufactures to ship, and an easy route for return goods from the Orient. So, by God, a railroad must be thrown across the Rocky Mountains! The audacity of the idea, its sheer physical challenge, was breathtaking. Still, he thought it possible—and there was not an engineer in the world who knew these mountains as he did. He collected maps, called in Kit and Godey, pondered possible routes. It must be far enough to the south so it could operate year-round—but not so far south that it would feed into Texas and New Orleans, and thus give new strength to the slaveholding states. St. Louis was its logical eastern terminus; it should run down the Santa Fe Trail and then cross the mountains north of Taos. Somewhere in the headwaters of the Rio Grande they must find a pass that a railroad could penetrate. They should be planning now. Eastern railroads soon would reach St. Louis. He drafted a long report for Benton which he delayed sending, as no reliable courier service yet existed between California and Washington.

As the months had worn on he'd felt more and more out of touch. He needed guidance now, official guidance from Washington on territorial affairs, private guidance from Benton on plans for developing this fabulous province. He had heard nothing from the Senator or Jessie, or the whole United States Government for that matter, since he and Stockton had captured California. Carson would have been back by now—it was late Janaury 1847—if Kearny hadn't stopped him on the road; Kit was still furious at the way he'd been treated.

Frémont was finding that the costs of government were staggering, especially since he was forced to operate entirely on credit. During the hostilities he had requisitioned what he needed, but he could hardly finance a peacetime government on seizures alone. Yet credit was expensive in a country that had so little capital. As soon as Stockton left, Frémont signed a note for nearly twenty thousand dollars in order to realize fifteen thousand in gold and goods. He suspected that the thirty-percent premium would raise some eyebrows in Washington. What if Congress were to disapprove these debts and repudiate them—would he be held personally liable? Sometimes he awakened in the still of the night and thought about this. He waited daily for an overland messenger or a ship with dispatches.

Washington should not forget, he wrote Benton, that California was, after all, conquered territory. Its natives were waiting suspiciously for the true nature of life under the Americans to reveal itself. Pico arranged frequent meetings with influential native Californians. Frémont never forgot that the September uprising had begun here in Los Angeles, against Gillespie's garrison. He suspected that Gillespie's excessively military stance had been the source of the trouble. He would avoid such mistakes—he prided himself that he didn't think like a soldier—but that didn't make the danger any less real. Pico said that many young men were talking rebellion, and talk was prelude to action. Frémont seized the high ground—he warned that he would tolerate no seditious actions; he would hang anyone who perpetrated them, and thereafter would treat Californians as a conquered people rather than as new American citizens. So far the men of influence had kept the young firebrands under control. But of course it was to these same men that Frémont must look for financing; he could hardly count on their influence if he was confiscating their property. So he paid exorbitant premiums and trusted that Washington would understand the pressures he faced.

Still, problems were the consequence of power. The California promise had been fulfilled. He would make it all work out. Pico found a handsome house to serve as the governor's mansion, and Frémont spent a happy afternoon in its garden imagining Jessie there receiving guests. When she arrived, he would throw a huge Governor's Ball and invite everyone he liked—native Californians, Bears and mountain men—to meet their First Lady. They would dance and pledge the future when Jessie arrived.

And he found his ranch. Pico located it, a fine property within twenty miles of Los Angeles. It was just as he'd imagined it, sprawled over grassy rolling hills overlooking the ocean and stocked with fat cattle. The adobe house was appropriately modest, the orange and olive groves well pruned, and a small river ran through them. He spent a full day riding over every yard of it. Here a man could live with a growing family and prosper all his life. A cool sea wind sent waves scurrying through grass that reached to his stirrups, and he could see miles of curving beachline, the rolling surf brilliant in the sun. Don Jesús arranged an option to buy.

So went Governor Frémont's term until some three weeks after Stockton's departure, when there came a brief note from General Kearny asking Frémont to call at his quarters across the plaza. It occurred to Frémont that the general might just as well have called on the governor; but why stand on protocol? He sent an answering note saying he would come that afternoon.

Carson was sitting in the *antecámera,* in a chair tilted against the wall, whittling. "Gonna pay a call on Old Stone Face, eh?" He looked up with an enigmatic expression. "Well, remember what Fitz says: 'Keep a wall at your back, and both hands loose.' "

Frémont walked across the plaza thinking of his meeting with Kearny at Jefferson Barracks so long ago—the light shining in his eyes, the remark about West Point. But things had changed now. Several men bowed to him and he saw a woman pointing him out to her child. A food vendor offered him a *tortilla* filled with meat; he refused with a smile.

Stepping from the warm, lively plaza into Kearny's room was unpleasantly like returning to the Army. The walls were bare; it was furnished with a plain table and three straight chairs; a field desk that had come from Missouri on a mule's back was open on a bench. Kearny was standing at the table, his expression as austere as the room. His greeting was barely more than civil. Without further preamble he picked up some papers and read aloud:

"Should you conquer California you will establish temporary civil government therein. These troops and such as may be organized in California will be under your command.

"These are the President's orders to me. And it is now my duty to assume command." Kearny looked almost bored, and yet there was an intensity in the way he threw back his head and said, "I therefore give you the following orders: One: You are to cease acting as civil governor of California immediately. Two: You will bring all papers of state to this office. Three: In respect to the California Battalion, you will clear *all* actions with me as your commanding officer. Is that sufficiently clear?"

For a startled moment, Frémont did not react. He was conscious of the room's quiet; women were laughing outside on the plaza. Why, Kearny was trying to use him to further his old quarrel with Stockton. Like a small-time bully who is subservient around authority but overbearing on his own, Kearny thought he could pressure Frémont now that Stockton was gone. But he sensed at once the real danger this arrogant, inflexible commander would bring to the unstable new province.

Speaking more courteously and calmly than he felt, he pointed out that he had been in California for nearly two years, that he had functioned under Stockton's command for many months, and that he considered himself still bound by Stockton's orders. "May I suggest most respectfully, General, that it is the commodore to whom you should address yourself."

Kearny dismissed this with a wave of his hand. His quarrel with Stockton would be settled by the President, he said; it did not concern Frémont. He sighed and sat down heavily. "Sit down, Colonel, sit down." He began massaging the wounded arm with his left hand. "This isn't an uncommon situation, you know. Junior officers often arrive in advance and enjoy a certain freedom of authority. Which ends, of course, when their seniors arrive. Now, I have given you a direct order. I want your assurance that you will obey it."

Frémont didn't need an instant to consider. "Sir, I do not consider myself under your command; and I respectfully decline to follow your directives until so authorized by Commodore Stockton or until the issue of supreme command is clearly settled."

Kearny appeared to have expected the answer. He regarded Frémont calmly, tapping a finger on the table. At last he said, "Colonel, I'm going to give you a piece of advice. I'm older than you are and I have had much more experience. Senator Benton and I have been friends for years and I've been fond of Mrs. Frémont since she was a child." Frémont had a sudden uneasy feeling; there was an undertone of impatience in Kearny as if he were carrying out some self-imposed obligation. "Now, I will tell you that you have placed yourself in a very dangerous position. Defying the orders of your commanding officer is reckless and unbecoming. I urge you to reconsider. If you do, I will forget this conversation." He paused. "If you do not, you will ruin yourself."

"Sir, I do not believe that you *are* my commanding officer. Commodore Stockton is, and I am obeying his orders."

"You are an officer of the United States Army, Colonel. How can a naval officer be your commander?"

"By the special circumstances that brought me to California. I see nothing so unusual in that, General. How can a civilian be *your* commanding officer?"

"What do you mean?"

"The President of the United States, sir. He is commander in chief of the armed forces, and your superior."

Kearny stared at him coldly. "You are a very foolish young man."

"On the contrary, sir, it seems to me it's your position that's—that doesn't seem soundly based. After all, Commodore Stockton had a presidential directive to seize California and govern it, and that order preceded yours. He and I took California last fall and he installed the civil government which continues to this day. All this took place long before you arrived."

"That's a ridiculous assertion, Colonel," Kearny said coldly. "California was anything but conquered when I arrived. The real fighting took place afterwards."

"That was nothing more than a disorganized uprising, General, against an established government."

Kearny shook his head. "I don't accept that. But as I said, the issue of naval control doesn't concern you. What matters here is your refusal to obey orders in the chain of command." He paused, said slowly: "That, sir, is mutiny."

The ugly word hung between them, a warning. He heard one of the women outside call something and there was a burst of laughter. It was idiotic: he had never been part of Kearny's command. The man was simply trying to use him—his real aim was to discredit Stockton, it was plain as day. He cared nothing for the welfare or the future of the territory.

"I fail to see how it's mutiny if your own orders do not support the orders you give," Frémont said.

"I do not debate my orders with junior officers."

"The facts simply don't support you. Whenever California was conquered, the one clear point is that *you* didn't conquer it. You were soundly beaten in the field and you had to be bailed out."

Kearny's face turned pale and rocklike. His long nose seemed to attenuate. "Obviously you've been listening to your ignorant friend Carson. It's a foolish officer who relies on a civilian's report."

"For God's sake," Frémont snapped "—everyone knows what happened at San Pasqual! The Californians have never stopped talking about it—it's their chief argument for mounting another rebellion. And as for Carson—he's seen more combat than most career officers have even heard of; whatever else Kit may be, he is not ignorant . . ."

Kearny made no reply; his expression hadn't changed, but his eyes held a curious, expectant glint Frémont couldn't read. Careful, now. Caution, a time for caution. Wasn't it? *Remember your promise.* Beating down his anger he pointed out that he expected to be confirmed in office as soon as dispatches arrived from Washington. "For the present, sir, we have exactly what the President wanted—a stable situation, a smoothly operating territory. In my opinion it would be disastrous to change government in midstream—"

"You're no judge of what the President or anyone else wants!" Kearny broke in harshly. "You have no authority here. You don't even *belong* in California—you've far exceeded your orders."

"No, sir. I am carrying out my orders to the best of my ability."

"Your orders direct you only to the Rocky Mountains."

"They were amended verbally—at the highest level."

"Indeed? I haven't much use for verbal orders. They let a man claim whatever he likes."

"Not between gentlemen, sir! A man's word is his bond. I resent your implication." Frémont could hear his voice shake. "I can establish authority for what I've done."

"You are a very rash, very headstrong young man."

"You are entitled to your opinion, General."

There was a short silence. Then Kearny said: "Your trouble is that you don't really understand the Army. What you will find in due course is that the Army's greatness lies in its authority, its certainties." His voice had a dry, distant sound. He might have been lecturing at the Military Academy: the Army functioned so well because individuals subordinated their personal aims and opinions to the collective whole; that is why a body of troops multiplied the power of its individuals by a factor of ten. "Any commander is temporary; replace him and the body goes forward with power undiminished. But jeopardize the *concept* of command—allow junior officers to set their own course, allow soldiers to decide when or why they'll fight—and you destroy the very core of the Army. I will never permit that, and in due time you will discover that I am right. *No man* can be allowed to challenge the Army."

It was getting late. There was no longer any noise from the plaza; the room's bare walls were as ascetic as a monk's cell. Frémont felt intensely alone—Kearny had aligned himself squarely with the awesome power of the Army itself. For the first time it struck Frémont fully that in the absence of some confirming document from Benton, all his authority rested on Stockton—who was Navy and who had left California.

But there was no justice in Kearny's position. He, Frémont, had not come here as a soldier. He was no part of Kearny's command, not a junior officer moving in advance and now reluctant to give up authority. That twaddle about command—of course junior officers must obey in a command structure, any fool knew that. But Frémont wasn't in that structure, he had been asked to move *outside* it—God almighty, Bancroft hadn't come to him as an *Army* officer! At this point, the fact that he was in the Army at all was just an accident. No. Kearny might be able to muster the full power of the Army against him, but he could never do so with justice.

Frémont was about to offer something to this effect when Kearny said in a voice of compressed fury that completely denied his detachment of a moment before: "God, how I hate a man who *uses* the Army—takes from it and gives nothing back! You like its rank and prestige, you use it when you need it, but you give it no loyalty and you would throw it off when it isn't convenient—well, *it doesn't work that way!*"

"Sir, that is grossly unfair—"

"You know what you are, Frémont? You're an *amateur.*" His voice slurred with contempt, the very word an insult. "An amateur soldier and an opportunist."

"That is insulting, General!" Frémont said hotly.

"You don't belong among professionals. I knew you were an amateur the day you walked into my office at Jefferson Barracks and asked for that gun on short notice." He added in a low, curiously intense voice: "You came to California on your own, hoping to advance yourself."

"Sir, I have already explained that I came on the highest—"

"You may have rendered some useful service here, who knows? But it was lawless service—all of a piece with your stubborn, senseless refusal to obey your commanding officer."

"Sir, I am not—"

"Do not interrupt me!" Kearny shouted, a sudden dark flush surging into his face. "You are masquerading as an Army officer—in reality you are an adventurer, a freebooter of the lowest sort. You think to make your name, and that wealth and fame will follow—but you'll find—"

"No!"

Frémont had come to his feet, trembling, his hands clenched, stung by this chain of abuse, enraged beyond measure by that word *amateur*. Enough, enough! He would take no more insults from this cold-blooded, conniving incompetent. None!

"If there *are* questionable motives here, they are yours! You ought to be court-martialed for your tactics at San Pasqual: an ill-conceived cavalry charge in which you needlessly butchered almost half your command—and you call yourself a soldier! I took men up and over the highest mountains in the dead of winter, under conditions *you* wouldn't have endured for six hours—and I *led* them, Kearny, I did not threaten them with court-martials or firing squads. Don't you lecture me on soldiering, or leadership either! You're a fraud, and an old fool . . ."

"Colonel, I warn you—"

"That's your real fear, isn't it? San Pasqual, and all those good men who didn't have to die at all . . . and you think if you can gain control of this province, it'll be easier for you to sweep it all under the carpet. Oh, no! *You're* the one clutching at power, my friend—and you haven't even earned the right to it! Well, Stockton wouldn't have let you get away with that—and neither will I!"

"Colonel—"

"We'll see who comes out of this on top. We'll just see, by God!"

He spun on his heel and stormed out of the bare, sterile room, past the frightened gaze of a shaken aide-de-camp with slicked-back hair and a tiny box mustache.

Sally tapped insistently on the doorframe of the yellow sitting room. "Miz Jessie," she said, "gentleman name of Carson is downstairs." Sally looked excited.

"Kit Carson?"

"Yes'm. He come all the way from California, just got here this minute."

The name washed away Jessie's reserves like a dirt dam before a freshet. Charles had been gone twenty-three months and seventeen days and she had been calm and hopeful and uncomplaining—and now all that dissolved in a rush of fear. She ran down the broad staircase with her fingers pressed to her mouth.

Carson was in the drawing room looking out a window; he turned quickly when she came in; the wedge-shaped jaw and mobile mouth, the steady gray eyes. So solid. Charles' best friend—and honest; he wouldn't lie to her.

"Charles," she breathed. "Is he—"

"No ma'am," he said instantly, "he ain't hurt or nothing like that. He's fine."

She saw her agitation mirrored in his face. She took a deep breath, calming herself; she couldn't remember ever losing her composure like this.

"Oh, Mr. Carson," she said, laughing with sudden, sharp relief, "please forgive me. I'm not usually so fidgety."

"I'd be obliged if you'd call me Kit, ma'am."

"May I? I feel as if I've known you for years—all Charles has told me about you." She brushed a strand of hair back with the heel of her hand. "I'm so happy to meet you."

"Thank you, ma'am. Same here." He spoke like a Missouri countryman. He was wearing a plain worsted suit of the sort common in St. Louis. As she calmed, the first impression was reinforced—he was a little older than Charles, confident in the same way Charles was, lean and burned dark from the trail. The look of him brought the high sky of the West into the drawing room; unexpectedly there were tears in her eyes.

"Do sit down." She gestured to a chair. "Tell me all the news! Did Charles send you?"

"That's right. There's a little trouble, you see. He needs some help—more than he can rightly spell out in a letter." He took a packet wrapped in oilskin from an inner pocket. "He sent me on to do some explaining."

The packet was warm from his body. She started to unwrap it and then stopped and held it tightly in both hands. "Tell me," she said.

"Well, you know, everything was dandy for quite a spell, there. I never seen a man enjoy himself so much—he's just a natural-born governor. Works night and day taking care of one thing after another, and the folks out there love him. You ought to see them flock into his office with their problems." He paused, frowning at the portrait of Mr. T on the far wall, and she felt a tremor of apprehension.

"What's gone wrong?" she said.

"Well, then along come that high-handed General Kearny. The whole ruckus started when he asked the Colonel to go see him. Old Kearny, you know, he's mighty hard."

"I know."

"And a tiger for regulations. Don't want to hear nothing but silence—and damned little of that, if you know what I mean. I warned Charlie he was out to lift his scalp, and soon as he come back I seen he'd found out for himself."

She listened with mounting misgiving as Carson described this ridiculous trial of strength between Stockton and Kearny. To charge Charles with mutiny was obscene! *Of course* Charles had refused to knuckle under—it seemed to her that Kearny was trying to foment mutiny against the commodore. He would be removed and court-martialed; none of his actions had legal force.

"Well," Carson said, "that scared the gee-whiz out of all the locals who'd loaned the government money. So the Colonel, he told me to saddle up and burn up the trail getting back here. I made it in fifty-four days, but I expect a good deal has happened since I left."

"What does he want us to do?" She kept her voice steady.

He hesitated; she saw that he was looking for a tactful way to put matters. "Well, you see, he'd been counting on the Senator getting everything fixed back here, and then sending him some operating instructions so they'd be working together. And Kearny don't understand any of that. Hell, Kearny's no governor—he's a *general.* He ain't got the confidence of the Californios, he thinks they're some kind of renegade half-breeds, he's only going to stir hisself up a hornet's nest. That's why Charlie wouldn't hand the whole lash-up over to him."

She felt a sharp, premonitory tremor. "He refused to relinquish the governorship."

"That's the ticket, ma'am. Fat's in the fire. And so, when your letters finally come—well, they was nice and all, but he claimed they didn't give him the free rein he needed."

"I see." This was serious, then. Very serious. How far had it really gone? "His letters didn't seem to imply anything like that."

"Well, I was supposed to deliver 'em and explain some things that he felt was too—that shouldn't be put to paper." He told her about Kearny intercepting him. "I still think there was something fishy about that. Did Tom Fitzpatrick deliver the letters?"

"Why no—they came by regular packet mail from St. Louis."

"Damn! Beg your pardon, ma'am. But Tom promised me, and I gave him all the information . . ."

They talked for an hour. Carson had a blunt, canny approach to things that she liked, and before long she had a pretty clear idea of what had happened since they'd reached California. She could see why Charles trusted his judgment implicitly. She was puzzled by Kearny. He was an old family friend—the way his long stern face would break into easy warmth at the sight of her had always pleased her, and certainly he owed much of his military career to her father. But when Kit explained what had happened at San Pasqual, it all began to come clear. How incredibly unfair—that Charles, who had taken California, now should have to pay for the fact that a bumbling latecomer had bruised himself through his own carelessness.

If only Mr. T weren't back in Missouri! He would know just what to do.

She needed to study the letters now. Carson was stopping at the Indian Queen. She extracted his promise that he'd be back for dinner that night and went off to her yellow sitting room. She unwrapped the oilskin and first read the letter that Charles had addressed to her. His steady, slightly cramped hand raced over page after page. He told her about his high excitement at being governor, the authority and accomplishment, about the ranch, the mansion. First Lady of California, a governor's mansion, a welcoming ball; oh, Charles darling, what gifts you lay at my feet! But nothing could blur his love for her, his need for her sustaining presence; after nearly two years away from her, his heart overflowed with longing for her.

Missing him in the deepest reaches of her body, wanting him terribly, almost ungovernably, troubled by Carson's disquieting news, she began to cry, wiping her tears with a handkerchief, not trying to stop. Later, feeling better, she squared her shoulders, opened his letter to her father, and began a systematic study of it and of his earlier letters. Now she could see clearly what he had hoped for: assurances of official authorization with presidential recognition of his mission and his authority. She had an image of him reading the disappointing answers, searching for a hidden message. . . .

She thought of the cryptic note she'd sent him from St. Louis to hurry him off with the cannon before Colonel Abert's angry letter overtook him.

There never had been a chance of confirming Stockton's appointment of Charles—she had known that instantly; her father had dismissed the idea with a wave of his hand. It was much too early, he had said, adding, "That boy of ours will know what to do in the meantime. He can take care of himself."

The trouble was that the war had roared *past* California. It had become all-consuming, driving out every other consideration, growing worse and worse as General Scott landed at Vera Cruz. Regiments of volunteers had been raised from every state, and the awful casualty lists were posted on every courthouse in America. Everyone knew someone who had fallen in Mexico. Scott had taken Vera Cruz just as he had promised and had driven inland through the yellow-fever belt to the mountains. There, at a place of fortified precipices called Cerro Gordo, he had won the sort of victory that leaves a nation in tears.

Her cousin Preston had been there. He had taken twenty-five men up a mountain he called Atalaya, where Mexican artillery on the crest had been depressed to send down wave after wave of grape. You could hear it in the air, shrieking all around you. When they reached the top and dislodged the Mexican gunners, five of his men were still with him. Twelve were dead, his letter said, and he didn't see how the other eight could live.

Lt. Ellsworth was hit in the stomach. He was in fever, he scarcely recognized me. Tom Martindale (he has the Second Platoon) lost his left leg above the knee. He cried when he saw me. He's in love with a girl in Richmond—says she won't want him now. I told him a man lives in his heart, not his legs, but I couldn't look into his eyes. I felt so ashamed—I was alive and whole. *Tom hated me for it. He said he couldn't keep from screaming when they took the leg. They give them a piece of wood to bite on, you know. I don't think this war will ever end. We've beaten the Mexicans here, but they're waiting for us up the road. We will have to do it over again and again.*

Since Scott had gone into Vera Cruz the public had soured on the war. They had cheered Taylor's campaign in northern Mexico, but with his successes the threat to Texas had ended. Mexico's capacity to retaliate seemed effectively destroyed. Why did we have to go to its heart, beat down the gates of its capital? President Polk's determination to crush Mexico utterly struck Jessie as an obsession. The people no longer believed in the war. With each bloody victory the President's stock seemed to sink further. He desperately wanted the vindication of a second term, but Jessie knew he wouldn't get it; indeed, she doubted whether his own Democrats would nominate him again. Even Mr. T had broken with him—the two hardly spoke now.

This national discontent had uncorked the slavery bottle again. For a precious little while the national westering impulse had overridden the hatreds that slavery evoked; the nation had been united on acquiring Texas and opening the West. But now there was growing suspicion, especially in the Northeast, that the war was little more than a plot by a Tennessee President to add territory that would vote with the slavery block in Congress. Totting up the war's cost and its casualties, people who Jessie thought were quite sensible otherwise seemed to have no trouble seeing a conspiracy. She was so weary of sly insinuations about "real" motives in the West—even California, the capstone of her father's western policy, was being made to appear no more than an empire-building land grab rooted in the desire to extend slavery.

Slavery was tearing the party apart. Zachary Taylor, the homespun Whig general, seemed everyone's choice for President in the next election. Even Mr. T was under pressure in Missouri, which was why he was home campaigning right now, though his term had three years to run. The state was filling with proslavery men who recognized in their senior Senator an implacable enemy.

She shook her head. All these concerns inevitably impinged on each other, on California, on Charles. They meant that Charles would have to wait awhile to have his appointment made permanent—but in the meantime, there was certainly no reason for him to be humiliated! General Kearny needed to be put in his place. Charles had gone to California on the instructions of his government; Stockton had seen fit to make him governor, and she wasn't going to let a Johnny-come-lately who was afraid to challenge the Navy vent his anger on her husband. Even if he was a general—especially if he was a general! She would go straight to the President; a word from him would set the whole matter straight.

It was more than a week before she could get an appointment, and then she waited nearly three hours in the corridor outside the President's office with Carson. She sat very straight, her feet together, her hands in her lap. The waiting told on Kit. He had walked into the White House and sat down as if he were sure the chair would break. All his easy assurance was gone; he answered her in whispers, glancing around before he spoke.

"Cheer up, Kit," she said in a firm voice. "He's got to see us now—he can't get out of his office without our catching him."

He gave her a horrified look and she suppressed a frown; his nervousness was infecting her. She had nothing to be uneasy about. They had served the country well. Charles—and her father—had opened Oregon, let's not forget, and that had paved the way for Mr. Polk's negotiating coup against the British. And it was Charles who had made certain that California would wind up in American hands.

She was reminding herself of this when a presidential assistant appeared, a thin waspish man who looked at her disapprovingly and said, "Well, you may go in now. He's terribly busy today—see that you limit yourself to ten minutes. Or better, five."

The President was standing in front of his desk in his graceful office and he greeted her in a vague, remote way, his mind obviously still on other things. When she introduced Kit the President's eyebrows went up. He shook hands but glanced at her inquiringly; she heard Kit start to mumble something unintelligible.

Immediately she said: "I brought Mr. Carson because I thought he could best bring you up-to-date on California."

The President asked rather sharply: "Why do you think I need that?"

It was too abrupt, her voice had been too shrill. She added that she had come in the hope that the President would clarify the situation in California. "You see, Colonel Frémont has been serving as governor under Commodore Stockton's direct orders. But now the Commodore apparently has left California and General Kearny is asserting the right of command. It leaves Charles caught in the middle, don't you see?" She hoped that she had cast it in a reasonable way.

Polk gave her a cold stare. His face was formidable, which she hadn't noticed before: had it hardened under war's pressure? "It's not a matter of *asserting* command—General Kearny is *in* command," he said flatly. "I have directed that the senior military commander will head the civil government, while the naval commander will have authority over ports and commerce."

That was bad news. Very bad. For a moment her legs felt weak. "But *Charles* has been serving as governor," she said, faltering. "For the entire province."

"I understand. Stockton exceeded his authority in appointing him, but it's all right. I'm sure he carried out his duties well, Jessie. Now we've regularized the situation—routine procedure in occupied territory."

"May I sit down?" she asked, knowing that it would put him at a disadvantage. She needed a moment to think: it was all much worse than she had thought.

The President frowned. "Of course," he said. "Forgive me—I'm pressed for time." She sat on a white settee. He took a straight chair and nodded Carson to a seat.

"Mr. President," she said, "there's been some—conflict between Charles and General Kearny."

"Has there? I haven't heard of it. But I daresay they'll work it out."

"I have reason to think that they may be on a—on a collision course. If General Kearny now has been given the command, then Charles may get badly hurt for having done no more than his duty."

"Why would that be? If he's done his duty . . ."

"Mr. President, it would be a great help if you could make some expression on Charles's behalf. He has served you very well. It could make all the difference—I know you understand that."

"Well, I'm reluctant to interfere in matters of low-level command."

"But if he doesn't receive *some*—" She broke off in dismay. That wily Bancroft, off in London! She felt confused, buffeted—she had come to have Kearny disciplined, and here she found herself fighting to save Charles. Where was all the tact, the light persuasive grace—where were the clean, judicious turns of phrase she'd learned at Mr. T's knee? How had it all gone wrong? The ground had turned slippery, and she struggled for a foothold.

"Sir," she said, hearing the strain in her voice, "All I'm asking is an expression of satisfaction with Charles' performance of his duty—something that would make it clear General Kearny is not to vent his anger on Charles."

He looked at her with quick distaste. "I doubt that General Kearny would do any such thing—he's a most responsible officer."

"Mr. President, he's a wounded man—you must know that. He took terrible losses at San Pasqual—pointlessly, needlessly. He'll attack Charles to draw attention away from his own mistakes."

Dryly Polk said: "You've become a military tactician, I see." He rummaged on his desk for a report. "Yes, he lost twenty-two men at San Pasqual. Do you have any idea what our *daily* casualties are running in this war?"

"Yes sir, of course," she said, "but in this case he needn't have lost any! Mr. Carson was present at—"

"I don't think I need Mr. Carson's instruction on this." His voice had a metallic bite. Carson looked as if he had been hit in the face. Polk's lips were pressed into a tight white line. "Those are serious charges," he said. "I have no reason to believe they're true, and I certainly don't care to have one of my general officers casually impugned. You're young, Jessie, but you should know better than this."

"Mr. President," she said, near tears, "I'm afraid Charles is to be made a scapegoat, the victim of Kearny's quarrel with Commodore Stockton. They may have a valid quarrel, I don't know—but I do know that it has *nothing* to do with Charles . . ."

Plainly exasperated, Polk looked at the polished brass clock on his desk. "It's a routine matter. Military procedure will resolve it, Jessie."

His smug assurance enraged her. "It will not!" she cried. "You know better than that!" She saw his eyes widen at her impertinence but she rushed on. "Military procedure seeks victims. It'll crush him, through no fault of his own. Mr. President, please, a word from you can solve everything—please, you *owe* it to him, don't you see that?"

"Owe it?" he said in an ominous tone, glancing at Carson. But she was past warning now, half-sick with dread.

"You sent him there! He went at your bidding, he made sure that we got California—"

His voice cut across hers like a blade. "No, madam! I did *not* send him there. Do not dare to imply that our acquisition of California was anything other than the natural consequence of war!"

Too late she saw the peril. She had blundered into his own personal, political nightmare.

"Oh, Mr. President, I didn't mean—"

She had never seen Polk angry. She put a hand to her mouth and felt it shaking against her lips. She had made an irreparable, fatal mistake. A political child all her life, she understood the awful power of his office for the first time.

Harshly he said: "The Pacific Fleet had orders to seize California in the event of war. General Kearny marched on California as an act of war. Colonel Frémont's presence there—*on a mapping expedition*—had no real bearing on military affairs. Do you understand me, madam?"

"Yes sir, of course. I didn't mean to imply—" She broke off, desperately searching for a way to rescue the situation. "But he's served his country well, you must admit that."

"As every officer is expected to do in time of war." He pressed his hands against his desk's edge. "No, madam. I will instruct General Kearny that he is free to release Colonel Frémont whenever he no longer needs his services. That will resolve the matter."

"But Mr. President—"

"Do you understand?" He was cold as stone. "I tell you flatly there was no more to Colonel Frémont's expedition than geographical exploration. Nothing more." He stood up suddenly. "You have your answer. And you have quite overstayed your time. I bid you good day, madam."

"Upon my word, Señor *Gobernador,* with my own ears I heard him," Jesús Pico said. He was indignant, but also solicitous, Frémont thought; a friend who has learned you are terminally ill.

"You must see this," Pico said, jumping up. "I am in Monterey, you understand, walking on Calle Principal with Jaime Jaramillo, who has supplied corn to the battalion in the amount of four thousand dollars. Don Jaime tells me General Kearny is saying that Governor Frémont is illegal—not bona fide, you understand?"

"Well," Frémont said, "Don Jaime—"

"*Sí,* Señor Coronel." Pico held up his big hand. "Don Jaime I don't listen to. Chirp, chirp—a sparrow! But then we see General Kearny."

Pico broke into a stiff-legged demonstration of Kearny walking on a Monterey street. His round, amiable face froze into a glare and his hands shaped Kearny's long countenance. "With officers all around him, you understand." He was rocking his shoulders to show them marching as to a drum. "So Don Jaime stops him and asks him straight, what about the debts?

"So the general says, 'You want to know what Frémont's debts are worth?' He turns to an officer. 'Give me a quarter,' he says. The man says, 'I've got a half-dollar, General,' and Kearny says, 'No, that's too much. No debt of Frémont's is worth more than a quarter.'"

They were closing in on him.

Stockton had left California without further word to Frémont. Only later, through rumor, did Frémont learn that Stockton had not simply sailed off; he had been replaced by another commodore, Shubrick, whose own ships were now anchored in Monterey Bay. Frémont sent him a polite letter asking for supplies: no answer. Kearny was in Monterey.

A troopship arrived with a regiment commanded by a Colonel Richard Mason. The new soldiers were in the north while the California Battalion held the south. According to Gillespie, Kearny had told Stockton he wouldn't press the quarrel then because he lacked the troops to carry it out. Now he had the troops.

Californians flocked to Pico. Rumors arose on every side: Frémont's debts were to be repudiated, his orders countermanded. Anyone cooperating with him was subject to penalties. Frémont was to be arrested, tried, punished for mutiny. Young officers from the new regiment were saying openly they expected the imposter governor to be executed by a firing squad. Mutiny in the face of the enemy. It was too preposterous to be taken seriously.

But what did the President want? The letters from Jessie and the Senator had been vague—long, enthusiastic, loving, but still vague. It would be months before Carson's trip could bear fruit. Things were moving too swiftly. If the President chose to vest authority in Kearny, of course Frémont would submit. But where would that leave California? The province again seemed on the edge of revolt. Did Pico exaggerate? Maybe—but the seeds certainly were there. And what about the debts—what did Kearny really mean? Would good-faith debtors lose? Would he himself be declared liable, reduced in an instant from triumph to disgrace, ruined beyond repair?

He was ready enough to obey legitimate, clear orders. After all, his authority flowed from the President via Stockton. If Stockton's authority to appoint was flawed, if the President had other plans, that would settle the matter; he had said so repeatedly. But no further communications came, from Washington or from Monterey. He tried to contact Larkin, and was informed the consul was away on state business. He felt like a man shouting into an empty cave. There were fewer callers now, and they were fearful and angry. This was American governance?

There came a rumor of a proclamation, issued by Kearny and the new Commodore Shubrick. They were working together, then. The proclamation said that Kearny was governor, while the Navy was to control ports and commerce. Purely by chance, Frémont was able to lay hands on a copy. Most of it appeared to be an attack on his own administration. It referred to the oppression of Californians by the previous government and the ruffians of the Sacramento Valley. This apparently meant the Bear Flag men, Merritt and Big Fallon and the others. It seemed that Frémont and the settlers were the enemy from whom the new administration had rescued the populace! In the plaza people turned away when they saw him now.

He rode north to Monterey. Kearny was as forbidding as ever. The new regimental commander, Colonel Mason, was at Kearny's side; he stared at Frémont with savage contempt.

"Are there new orders?" Frémont asked Kearny.

"I don't discuss my orders with junior officers. Are you prepared to obey?"

Frémont hesitated. Kearny told him icily he had one hour to think it over.

On the street Frémont encountered Larkin. The merchant-consul studied him curiously. The new orders had come from the President at least a month earlier: did Frémont really intend to disobey them?

"*A month ago?*" he stammered. "A month—? None came to me—I had no word . . ."

The news was like a blow to the belly. *A month ago*—he had *offered* to obey whenever orders came; the simplest notification would have sufficed. But they had said nothing . . .

They had laid a deliberate trap, then. They intended to destroy him.

He walked back to the *presidio* in a cold rage. Kearny was waiting for him; it was as though the man hadn't once moved. He said: "Are you ready to obey my orders?"

"Yes, sir."

"Very well. You will return to Los Angeles and prepare all records of government and of the California Battalion for transmission to this office. Then report here for further instructions. That's all."

Two days after Frémont reached Los Angeles, Colonel Mason arrived with a sergeant and fifty men. Mason had a narrow mustache and a mirthless smile that was remarkably like a sneer. He was full of orders: produce the accounts, the executive-order book, the contracts book, the battalion roster, the disciplinary records. Casually he sat at Frémont's desk and opened its drawers. Pico and Godey listened in the anteroom; Godey's face looked cut from obsidian.

"Now hold on, Colonel," Frémont said. "My orders were to bring the records to Monterey. I'm obeying those orders."

"*I* give the orders, Frémont," Mason said. There were several exchanges before Mason jumped up and snarled, "None of your impertinence or I'll put you in irons!"

"Do not threaten me, sir," Frémont said. "I've come a long way over hard ground to be threatened by you or anyone else."

"Don't tell me about the ground you've covered," Mason said. "I know all about that. The famous explorer, rising through the ranks like magic—no service with troops, no military skills, no training, and yet it's *you* who's chosen, time after time. Don't you think the Army's noticed that?" There was something eager about him, some anticipation that shone in his face. "We understand your kind, Frémont. A man who knows just which ass to kiss." Deliberately, enjoying himself, he said: "The explorer who married his expeditions—every officer in the Army knows just what you are."

The venom in the man's voice was astonishing. Frémont took a step toward him, then said tightly: "You despicable bastard. I'll have satisfaction for that."

"I shall give it to you."

"Immediately."

"As soon as we effect the transfer of the records. You are challenging me?—I have the choice?"

"Yes."

"Very well. Double-barrel shotguns at twenty feet."

Even in his fury Frémont was staggered. Shotguns were murder weapons. Then Mason's reputation flashed into his mind: the man was expert with shotguns, famous for it. Was that talk of execution more than foolish chatter?

Godey loomed in the doorway. His face was very hard, his green eyes brilliant. He said to Mason: "Man calls for a shotgun, he don't want to fight, he wants to kill."

"Who the hell are you?"

"I want to tell you something, Mason. Cap'n Frémont, he has a lot of friends."

"That's enough, Alex," Frémont said.

"No, sir—I ain't in the Army. I don't have to eat none of his shit." He took a step into the room, his hand resting on his horn-handled knife. "If there's the slightest thing ain't right, and the Cap'n gets hurt—I promise you, you won't live out the day."

"You'll be punished for this," Mason said in a thin voice.

Godey moved as swiftly as a striking snake. Mason stepped back and bumped against a wall. Godey stopped a foot from him. "Don't you threaten me, you little chickenshit, or I'll spill your guts," he said. "Remember what I told you: fuck with the Cap'n and you won't see the sun go down."

The duel was postponed. Kearny ordered it delayed—indefinitely.

Frémont reported to Monterey. Kearny refused to see him. There was no work for him to do. No officer would speak to him.

He waited two weeks, three weeks, four. He addressed petitions to Kearny:

Permission to go overland to report to the regiment to which he had been nominally assigned with his promotion: denied.

Permission to assemble his exploring party and return to Missouri in a body: denied.

Permission to go to San Francisco to gather his instruments, journals and botanical specimens: denied.

He waited.

The Territory remained calm; Frémont had bequeathed stability even if the new administration would not acknowledge it. He mounted the big gray, Sacramento, and rode out every day; he would not hide. Now the Californians he met were savage. What about his orders, his promises, his debts? The new governor acted as if the old hadn't existed. Frémont promised them that Congress would confirm all that he had done. Congress would meet the debts. Sutter appeared at Frémont's quarters one day. He was disdainful of Kearny's regime and his threats, and full of plans for his domain. If he took any pleasure in Frémont's dilemma he gave no sign of it, and Frémont put his name at the head of the debtor list.

Kearny seemed to blame the California Battalion for Frémont's sins. Their pay for the whole period of their service was limited to ten dollars a month. The men denounced that as ridiculous—and so were discharged without pay and sent home to ranches that had sagged into disrepair during their service.

Ezekiel Merritt came to see Frémont. "Well," he said, "it's sort of a pissant ending for what began so big. But don't you forget, Cap'n—wasn't none of these arrogant bastards around when the going was hard. We done us a real piece of work—we brought the sweetest country God ever made under the United States flag. That's what we done—and General Kearny can kiss my Bear Flag ass."

And finally, finally came orders from Kearny: muster his men to march at the rear of the General's column under guard to Fort Leavenworth in Kansas Territory. *Under guard.* Kearny was going home; Colonel Mason was the new governor. Mason! That malevolent lickspittle had succeeded to command, usurped *his* place . . .

Well, he wasn't finished with California. He would be back. He asked Larkin if he would complete the purchase of the ranch that stood on those hills above Santa Cruz overlooking the Pacific, gave him power of attorney and a draft for three thousand dollars on a Washington bank. The money represented every penny he had saved over the last ten years. He told Larkin that Pico, who had returned to San Luis Obispo, could show him the place. The money probably would be enough for purchase; if not, Larkin was authorized to issue his note for the balance.

What remained of Frémont's Third Expedition now mustered as ordered. Half of the men were staying in California. Sagundai and the Delaware scouts were gone. Godey was there, Raphael Proue, big Dick Owens—nineteen all told. They stayed close to Frémont and he knew they saw themselves as bodyguards. They took their assigned places at the extreme rear of Kearny's column: they would ride all the way to Kansas choking in Army dust. He, of all men, eating dust. The dragoon wranglers handling the Army's herd turned curious, cold faces to the disgraced Colonel and his party; but no officer made the slightest move against him.

They crossed hard desert, struck the Oregon Trail, came through South Pass and down onto the high plains. A bitter moment. It was August 1847; Frémont was twenty-seven months gone from home, the summer sun burned the ground. But the wind was blowing, sweat dried in an instant, the sky was as high as infinity; you could see a million miles. He was coming home. They saw buffler, feeding in groups of fifty or so, grunting as they moved, and his eyes filled with treason tears. If only Louie were riding with them, it wouldn't be so bad; if only he had remembered to post a guard. . . .

At Fort Leavenworth the band was playing and families were out to greet their men come marching home; but not the Pathmaker and his scouts. At Fort Leavenworth there were orders too: report to General Kearny.

The general was in his Fort Leavenworth office. As at Jefferson Barracks, the window was set so that the light struck Frémont's eyes.

"Colonel, you will consider yourself under arrest," Kearny said. "You will go directly to Washington and prepare yourself for a court-martial on charges of mutiny."

"Yes, sir," Frémont said without expression. He wasn't beaten, and he knew Kearny knew it. He saluted then—held the salute five seconds, ten, while the old clock on the wall ticked ponderously and Kearny watched him.

"You are *dismissed,* Colonel. Didn't I make myself clear?"

"—You *will* acknowledge my salute!" he whispered in sudden cold savagery, and the adjutant's eyes rolled up at him, white with alarm, from the far wall. "Do you hear me? You *will!*"

With infinite deliberation Kearny raised his arm and returned the salute. *"Colonel,"* he said icily, the word itself a final threat.

Frémont whipped his arm downward, made a precise about-face and left the room.

Then he was on a steamboat slipping down the Missouri toward Westport, away from Kearny and the Army; free to breathe at last. At Westport the boat whistled and huffed toward shore. A woman stood high on the levee, her skirts blowing sweetly. Suddenly she waved. He stared: *it was Jessie.* His eyes filled with tears until the levee was a blur and then he was running, down the near ladder, along the deck, and he was across the bow and jumping for the levee before the boat touched, running, running up the levee, and he saw her coming toward him with her arms outstretched.

COURT-MARTIAL

THERE WAS NO HONEYMOON this time when Charles came home. She'd had it all planned: they would go for country rides, take a steamboat down to Memphis, drink wine and laugh and dance, explore each other's hearts and bodies again; but none of that happened. He was raging, on fire, and they set out for Washington determined to confound their enemies. The steamboat turning slowly up the beautiful Ohio might have served, but the general had preempted their sweet reunion.

The moment she saw him at Westport she knew he was changed. There were new lines in his face, gray streaks in his dark hair, a new hardness of manner. She saw it even more clearly at the open house Colonel Brant gave for them in St. Louis, Charles was older, tougher, a much harder man than the handsome, exuberant explorer who had left her. He spoke with more force and authority; after a while she realized that youthful, deferential note had utterly vanished. He was thirty-four and while to her he didn't seem older than his years, still she noticed that men much older than he did not look on him as their junior. Those twenty-seven months had burned him down to an adamantine core.

He was eager for the court-martial after all those weeks of humiliation. Let Stockton come forth and tell them he had given the order that Frémont had obeyed, as together they grasped that golden province for the United States. Let the Army—and the public—listen to the whole story, and judge whether Frémont had erred! Jessie liked that; Mr. T was so excited he couldn't sit. They were in his study on the third floor of the house on C Street, the sperm-oil lamp gleaming, and the floor creaked as he paced.

"To think that man would accept my friendship and patronage for thirty years—and then drive a knife into the very bosom of my family! It is abominable and it is intolerable, and Kearny will pay for it. We demand this trial—we *demand* it, I say!"

"Papa—"

"I haven't spent the past twenty-five years in the service of this country to be vilified by some ungrateful little tin-soldier despot who wouldn't recognize *real* initiative if it was spelled out in letters of fire across the great wall of the Rocky Mountains!"

"Papa," Jessie remonstrated softly, "it's *Charles* who's being court-martialed—"

"Oh, no!" He whirled around, his great face red with anger. "We are *all* of us on trial here—make no mistake about that! Look at this Fortress Monroe nonsense they've cooked up—a Godforsaken point thrust into the Atlantic, the press barred, no visitors. Secret proceedings indeed! On what grounds? Well, we'll see about that—there will be no star chamber in *this* Republic, not while I'm alive and kicking, anyway!"

"Papa," Jessie said in distress, "please calm yourself."

"I *am* calm, I am perfectly calm—"

"You'll give yourself a stroke if you go on this way."

"But you'll be vindicated." Her father abruptly thrust one quivering finger at Charles, nodding grimly. "They will *weep* for your pardon before this is over, you mark my words! Remember what old Palmerston said to Van Buren when he was rejected by the Senate: 'It is an advantage to a public man to be the subject of an outrage.' They know who sent you out there, and for what purposes—let the newspapers hold some of Polk's subterranean schemes up to the light of day, and *then* we'll see . . ."

Jessie had stopped listening to him. Mr. T was off on one of his finer frenzies; they might as well let him vent his rage and run down. But there was something deeply disquieting about it—it *was* as though he himself were on trial, as though it were some curious duel between him and the general, and Charles was merely an associate—almost a bystander . . . Idly she watched Charles, who was bent forward now, one hand gripped in the other, his mouth working beneath his mustache, and then Eliza's husband, who was sitting very relaxed, one leg hooked over the other, his pale face grave and noncommittal. William Jones was as quiet as Eliza, and as impersonal—no one ever dreamed of calling him Bill—but he'd made himself a solid reputation in the courts and now had offered his services in his famous brother-in-law's defense. It had shamed Jessie a bit, for she had often rather resented her cooler older sister; but God knew they needed cool heads and dispassionate minds as they never had before.

Her father had paused, was fiddling with a block of rose quartz on his desk. Jessie said: "What do you think, William?"

He glanced at her, his green eyes level and cool, then shook his head. "I think it's very doubtful that they'll let you introduce the whole story," he said in his rather light, clear voice. "Assuming it *could* be introduced, of course." He turned to Charles then. "We must assume they will try to limit you to a narrow view of the charges." The court-martial's essential specifications—mutiny, disobedience of lawful command, and conduct prejudicial to good order and military discipline—all stemmed from Charles' initial refusal to obey Kearny. "The Army will probably seek to hold you to that line."

"Well," Charles gave a terse laugh, "if the only issue is to be *whether* I disobeyed orders and not *why*—then I guess I'm guilty, all right. But that's certainly a mighty narrow view of the law."

"The law is subject to human interpretations," William answered quietly; he watched the explorer, his face impassive. "It always has been. That's what often makes it such a tortuous trail to follow."

"Well, this one is clear enough—you'll see. I'll call every Bear and Californio on the Pacific Coast as witness if I have to! *They'll* back me, all of them . . ."

Charles wanted to talk about everything at once. He wanted to tell them about his Homeric efforts to remain neutral during the early days of the Bear Flag Rebellion; he urged Mr. T to introduce legislation authorizing payment of the financial claims made by Californians; he told them about his plans for a railroad route to the Pacific—and for Jessie to join him in San Francisco and ride down to their ranch overlooking the sea.

"You'll love California, darling—it's as though God Himself decided to create a brand-new Garden of Eden, after the old one had come a cropper. I can't wait to show it to you!"

She caught the golden flash in his eyes, the lithe, impatient movement of his body. He was utterly certain of vindication—she could see it in his face, hear it in the vibrant ring of his voice: he would clear his name in the court-martial, and then go out and girdle the continent with hoops of steel. Sitting there she felt a wave of indescribable tenderness—and then a thrill of pure dread, paced by the measured, implacable tap of William's pencil on the desktop. She glanced at her father's heavy, aging face, the weary, lidded eyes that had been party to so many power struggles and compromises, seen so much avarice and duplicity . . . She thought of the day they had come into this very room to tell him they were married: defying him, fighting for her very life, she had told him his dreams were only dreams—but that Charles could turn them into reality; and now here was Charles caught in the same deadly web of intrigue. . . .

Next day Charles took her away for a week on the eastern shore of Chesapeake Bay. Just the two of them: Lily watched them pack with aggrieved resignation, but they had to be alone together now. They ran down to Annapolis on the cars and crossed the bay on a small lugger that threaded its way through an inbound skipjack fleet. There was an inn at St. Michaels with white clapboard cabins scattered in a grove of ancient oaks aflame with fall colors. The first geese were flying south from Canada, coming in low with whistling wings and then, on signal, settling toward the marshes in a silver rush of water. Solitary egrets and herons stalked the shallows. Charles taught her the subtle marks that differentiated the clouds of ducks, the eye bar, the flash of color on the shoulder, the underwing markings, the way a pintail shuffled its feet to drive food up from the bottom.

On the second day they found a place they made their own. It was an old skipjack driven ashore long ago and now lying abandoned, its timbers scoured clean by years of sun and salty wind, cast at just such an angle that the side of its cabin made a cradling seat and its deck a back rest full in the autumn sun. Here they made love as if to make up for all the lost time, as if to hold off the danger that awaited them. Here they returned each brilliant day to renew their bond.

The calm before the storm. Was it? Jessie watched her husband's face against the flame of autumn foliage, the hard brightness of the sky. She was twenty-three, six years married, five years a mother; a long, long way from the girl who had grinned impudently across the Brant drawing room at the man she would marry. Four out of her six years of marriage had been spent apart from her husband; and when he was home the findings of his expeditions had dominated them. And now this trial—there was nothing easy about life with John Charles Frémont, and she knew it would never be easy. But, resting in the autumn sun, reclaiming from each other two years of separation, she saw a closeness only this kind of life could give. For as he grew into the man he would become, he would need her still more. He was more interested in her opinions, more inclined to test himself in her reactions, more concerned with *her* feelings and needs. There was a hunger in his questions about her and Lily and their life at home, as if he felt as deprived by separation as she did, as though they were only complete when they knew each other perfectly. If he *was* an adventurer, as his enemies said, at least he made her part of the adventure: that was the meaning of his insistence that she come to California. He was a path-marker first of all. He didn't think of the risks, grim for her and Lily on the difficult fever-ridden Isthmus crossing to come, critical for him in the winter snows; he thought only of the goal, of reaching it together. No matter how much William Jones might discuss his cases with Eliza, they were still separate from her. But she and Charles had literally lived his journeys together, even when apart; and she valued that, for all its bitter penalties, far more than living the separate, humdrum lives most people spent together.

Their talk always circled back to California. Charles had been treacherously used. Kearny had hidden the new, definitive orders so as to seduce him into further disobedience. There had been no hint that Kearny intended to arrest him until they were far from California, where Charles might have gathered evidence and depositions in his defense. Kearny and his people had issued scurrilous newspaper reports defaming Charles and Stockton. His only failure was the failure to guess in advance which commander the President would anoint.

"You don't think . . . ?" She hesitated, put her hand to his face; there was a scar at the edge of his jaw that hadn't been there before. She said gently: "I mean, it isn't possible that part of it was you took a dislike to Kearny? that you were reacting personally to his high-handed ways?"

He glanced at her quickly, glanced away again; after a moment he nodded. "Maybe so. Maybe that was part of it. I've thought about that. I had a lot of time to think about everything—out there . . ." He took his hand in hers then, his blue eyes very intense and wide. "But I remembered, Jessie—what I promised you."

"Promised me?"

"Yes, what you asked me: I *was* cautious. I was deferential—I took more from that tyrannical old fool than I've ever taken from anybody! Amateur . . . Why, his odious toady Mason actually tried to euchre me into—" He broke off, studying the geese feeding in the shallows.

"Into what?"

"Nothing. Nothing." That implacable hardness had stamped his features again. "Just more Army tomfoolery. Look, he would have set it all afire, Jessie! Kearny—he'd have started the war up all over again; I *know* he would . . ." He skipped a small stone disgustedly at the water, watched the feathered pattern of splashes. "But it doesn't matter. I'm the one caught in the middle. Stockton told Kearny to go to hell—now that's the fact. But there's no court-martial for him."

"Oh, Charles," she said, confessing at last what had been pressing her heart, "maybe it's all my fault." She told him about her visit to President Polk, and recounted his angry denial of any implication, stemming from his political fear that the appearance of having conspired to seize California would be taken as proof of a conspiracy to expand slave territory. All right, she admitted it: she had thrust the President into a corner that day. Had she tied his hands? Not unless he was a political coward; but of course, politics was full of cowards.

She was watching her husband's face and she saw it brighten. He gripped her by the shoulders and said: "By God, honey, you're all right! It takes guts to walk into that man's office and tell him off. God, how I love you!"

She felt dismay rather than elation. "But the results—"

"To hell with him! Kearny's vindictive and the Army's myopic. Maybe Mr. Polk expects me to fight 'em off all by myself, and that's exactly what I'm going to do. Anyway, I want the trial now—I'm going to make them stand up in public and admit to what they've done."

At dinner that night he opened a bottle of champagne and toasted her: "To my sweet, courageous wife—it's a lot harder to face power than bullets." They took the bottle back to the cabin and finished it there, and she felt the quick, familiar fire leap inside her, flow out to her fingertips, her lips; curving out, out—like those shooting stars he had charted so often.

"Oh, Charles," she cried out softly in the night. "Oh, take me now. . . ."

Much later she felt something stir deep in her body. Could you ever really tell? Probably not, and yet somehow she was sure. "We have made a new Frémont this time, darling," she whispered. "I know it." She could tell he was pleased and excited.

"Just in case you could be mistaken," he murmured, "we'll try again."

It was a perfect week; they came back rested and at ease. She felt ready for anything—except for what, in fact, awaited her. At Annapolis they found the latest newspapers, and as the cars trundled toward Washington they read that the war was over at last. Scott had driven inland from Vera Cruz, with an army that rarely numbered more than seven thousand, facing thirty thousand men who were defending their homeland, and from entrenched positions. They had fought at Contreras and at Churubusco, and on a final desperate day in September they had swarmed over the walls of the Castle of Chapultepec and then raced across the great causeways to batter down the gates of Belen and San Cosme. Mexico City was theirs; the war was done, the fighting finished.

Her father met them at the front door with tears in his eyes. Watching his face she felt all at once cold as winter.

"*—Is it Preston?*" she whispered, knowing, begging him to shake his head.

He opened his arms to her. "I'm so sorry, child. So very sorry . . . He was killed at Contreras. Shot through the heart leading a charge. He died in Tom Callendar's arms."

There was a high, ringing noise in the room and she stumbled away from her father and caught herself on the back of a chair. She was vaguely aware of Charles' arm holding her upright. Preston, beautiful Preston, showing off his new uniform, laughing like a boy. Poor Millie. What would happen to her? She knew that the last of her old childhood had ended. The glorious war was over, the empire won, hurrah!—and Charles faced trial—for mutiny!—and Preston was dead and her world would never be the same.

When the court finally called Commodore Robert F. Stockton, Jessie saw a nervous-looking man with hollow, saturnine features threading his way up the crowded aisle; he bore no resemblance whatever to the vigorous, ebullient man of action Charles had described to her. In astonishment she glanced at her husband, but he was staring at the naval officer without expression. The courtroom, filled to overflowing, was astir now—spectators turned to watch Stockton as they might an actor making a stage entrance through the audience. They knew this was the climactic moment; their faces were marked with wonder, anticipation, and that peculiar taut avidity of the thrill-seeker. Sitting at the defense table between Charles and her father, and opposite William Jones, Jessie saw Stockton wink at someone on the court; then, when he winked again, she realized it was a tic in his right eye. Involuntarily she shivered; this was the man on whose testimony they had staked everything . . .

He came before the court without a glance at the defense table. Charles, who according to the rule of court-martial had to conduct his own questioning, rose as Stockton approached, but the Commodore immediately turned away and said in a hoarse voice that cracked on the last word: "May it please the court—"

"*Sir,*" Charles interrupted; he turned in amazement to William, who murmured, "Don't know," and shrugged. "He was perfectly all right a few weeks ago . . ."

"If you'll be seated, Commodore, the defense will direct its questions," the president of the court was saying. He was an austere brigadier named Brooke with a grayed narrow head who sat at the center of the high judges' bench. The other members of the court were ranged on either side while the judge advocate, an athletic-looking major named Lee, sat at a separate table. The major had a disconcerting way of jumping up like a squirrel, though he had already proved himself a formidable opponent; he served as both prosecutor and legal adviser to the members of the court, who were all line officers unversed in the law.

"General," Stockton said, "before I testify, may I say that my position is a delicate one. I feel that my actions in California are also on trial. Because the situation there was extremely complex, I have taken the liberty of composing a complete account of all that I did. I beg leave to read it as the form my testimony shall take." He pulled a thick sheaf from an inside pocket.

"Objection," Major Lee said, bounding up. "What the commodore did is not at issue here. Nothing is at issue beyond whether or not Lieutenant Colonel Frémont obeyed an order from his commanding officer."

"The devil it is," her father muttered loudly, wagging his great shaggy head. "This is preposterous, a perfect travesty of—" Jessie put her hand on his and he subsided.

As William had foreseen, the court had taken the narrowest possible view of the charges. They had stricken as irrelevant more than half of Charles' witnesses, and much of what he had hoped to prove. So they fought with one hand tied, which made Stockton's testimony all the more important. The sudden sharp pain in Jessie's lower belly came again, and she shifted in the hard wooden chair. This time the pain continued. She concentrated on keeping her face expressionless.

"We wish to show you all courtesy," Brooke was saying, "but the court fails to see—"

"I have a constitutional right against self-incrimination."

"But you're not on *trial* here," the general said, puzzled.

Leaning on the table, Charles said to William in an urgent whisper, "He's afraid . . . but my God, if *he* feels vulnerable—"

William answered something inaudible. Then he leaned toward Jessie and said behind his hand, "There's a rumor going round that he's met with Kearny and effected a rapprochement. I'd discounted it until now."

She nodded tightly, digesting this alarming news. The court refused to let him read his document, and Stockton took the stand with unconcealed anger. Charles posed his questions gracefully, but the Commodore ignored them and launched on a long recital of how he had conquered California. Major Lee objected repeatedly and the bench sustained him, while Charles tried desperately to bring his witness to heel. The members of the court looked bored and irritated. A soured displeasure settled over the courtroom as Stockton began to ramble through the afternoon. . . .

The trial had gone badly from the start. Jessie had wakened early on the first day to severe morning sickness; Lily had given her no such trouble. It was like an omen. The case had received wide notice in the newspapers and the courtroom was crammed with spectators when they arrived. She had seen reporters scrambling for places at the press table. As Charles followed her in, someone applauded and suddenly everyone had taken it up—a thunderous welcome as encouraging as it was startling. But watching the members of the court turn in hostile surprise, she had realized instantly that Charles' cause had not been helped at all.

General Kearny had not once met her eyes during his testimony. He was older, grayer, more cruel-looking, she thought; she remembered his respectful attendance on her father in St. Louis when he was hungry for rank and still needed him. On direct examination he glossed over his command controversy with Stockton as one of those little confusions of war, while presenting Lieutenant Colonel Frémont's part as heinous out-and-out insubordination. Mutinous conduct. Charles had been determined not to let him get away with this. His cross-examination was masterfully orchestrated.

"General, didn't my secretary of state, William W. Russell, go directly to your headquarters in Los Angeles from the plain of Cahuenga, where I had just accepted the surrender of the Mexican Army?"

"He did."

"And did he not inform you that I had sent him for the explicit purpose of ascertaining just who *was* in chief command at Los Angeles?"

"Mr. Russell came to my headquarters on the 13th."

"I believe we've already covered that point, General. Did not Mr. Russell specifically ask you whether your arrival in the area had *superseded* Commodore Stockton's, who had already been recognized as chief commander?"

"He asked me that question."

"And did you not tell him that Commodore Stockton was still in command?"

"Yes."

"And this was precisely *four days* before you ordered me to cease obeying Commodore Stockton and henceforth carry out your orders?"

"It was."

"Now, did you receive any orders from Washington between the 14th and the 17th of January, *changing* your status?"

Kearny's gaze moved coldly to the far wall. "No dispatches reached me during that period."

There was a murmur of surprise in the audience, then a faint spattering of applause. Beside Jessie Mr. T was saying, "*Admits* it, actually admits he arrogated command to himself! Nerve of the blackguard . . ."

"General Kearny, four days later, when you ordered me to cease serving under Commodore Stockton and obey your directives, did I not inform you that Commodore Stockton had refused to cancel my appointment in the United States Navy, and that he would consider me mutinous if I failed to recognize *him* as commander in chief?"

"As commander in chief of the California territory I was not bound by Commodore Stockton's assertions."

"But you *did* inform Commodore Stockton that he was no longer commander in chief in California, and that you were?"

"I so informed the commodore."

"And didn't he refuse to relinquish that command?"

"He refused to acknowledge my chief command."

"And as I had been appointed Governor of California, and was the next highest ranking officer to you and the commodore, weren't you trying to use *me* to settle your dispute with Commodore Stockton?"

The judge advocate bobbed to his feet crying, "Objection! Defendant is indulging in rank conjecture . . ."

"Sustained," Brooke said crisply. "The court will strike the last question."

Charles stared at Brooke a moment, then turned back to where Kearny was sitting. "When I sent my first letter to you, respectfully declining to obey your orders until this question of authority was settled, did you not say that the man who delivered my letter was a stranger to you?"

Kearny's eyes flickered away. "I don't recall."

Charles picked up two papers from the long mahogany table. "Here is your testimony, General, in which you've clearly stated that the messenger *was* a stranger to you. And here is my letter—which was brought to you at your headquarters by none other than Christopher Carson. Didn't you encounter Mr. Carson on the trail near Fire Butte, order him to guide your force to Los Angeles, and threaten to put him in irons if he refused?"

"I have no recollection of any such incident."

"You don't! Did you not spend many weeks on the trail with Mr. Carson, employing him as guide?"

Kearny's face was like stone. "The man who brought your letter was a stranger to me."

So he's perfectly willing to perjure himself, Jessie thought hollowly; her heart had begun to pound. What else are they willing to do to uphold the infallible sanctity of the United States Army?

The courtroom hummed; Charles shook his head in helpless amusement, demanded: "One of the great frontiersmen, famous as a western scout, known from St. Louis to Taos to Monterey—and you *failed to recognize him*?" He threw up his hand as if raising a rifle. "Well, there he sits, in the first row"—pointing at Kit's handsome, wind-burned face, which was stamped with the same amused incredulity "—do you recognize him *now*?"

The room broke into a roar of laughter, and Brooke irritably gaveled for quiet. Charles laid down the papers and approached the witness again; his expression was perfectly impassive again, almost serene.

"General Kearny, did you receive the final War Department directives confirming your chief command on or about April 15th?"

I did."

"Did you at any time after that date forward a copy of these directives on to me or to my headquarters?"

"I did not."

There was another murmur in the room, low, premonitory. Charles said softly: "General, may I inquire as to *why* you did not do so?"

"Objection!" Lee sang out. "Court cannot inquire into the orders issued by General Kearny to his command."

"Sir," Charles turned at once to Brooke, "this was a War Department directive issued *to* General Kearny, not *by* him. I maintain that his failure to pass it on crucially affected me and my command."

Brooke, frowning, gave a curt nod. "Overruled. Witness will respond to the question."

Kearny stared again at the far wall, his face harsh with contempt. "I saw no reason to pass on high-level directives to a junior officer. The orders were common knowledge throughout my command."

"General, your headquarters were then in Monterey, isn't that true?"

"Yes."

"It is nearly 350 miles from the *presidio* in Monterey to the Governor's house in Los Angeles. How would I have become aware of them unless you had forwarded them on to me in the south?" Then with sudden harsh force: "Then you admit you deliberately concealed from me the existence of orders granting you full authority over the interior of the province of California!"

"That is correct."

The courtroom burst into a tumult of shock; the judge advocate was on his feet again, calling something, inaudible in the racket, and Brooke was crossly pounding for quiet.

"Insufferable!" Tom Benton was saying hoarsely. "Now by God, he *has* gone too far."

Stunned at Kearny's admission, the sheer blunt arrogance of it, Jessie glanced at Charles; the muscle in his cheek had flexed, his eyes were snapping hotly.

"General, isn't it true that you informed the officers of your staff, immediately after my refusal of January 17th, that you planned to put me in arrest?"

"I may have mentioned something to that effect."

"And when did you instruct *me* that I was to be placed under arrest? Was it not on the 16th of August—*six months later,* after we had reached Fort Leavenworth?"

Kearny's eyes glinted once. "You were put under arrest at Fort Leavenworth."

"So that, by waiting until we had arrived at Fort Leavenworth, you deprived me of any chance to assemble data in California for my defense. I was unable to inform any witnesses that I might need them in Washington for this court-martial—isn't that true?"

Kearny's voice was as cold as the Sierra snows. "You were informed of your arrest in due time, at Fort Leavenworth."

"In due time." Charles' fist was clenched at his trouser leg, the knuckles white. "When you ordered me to return to Washington, did you not refuse me the right to go to San Francisco and collect the journals, maps and drawings of my Third Expedition?"

Kearny flared for the first time. "That was government property—"

"I am thoroughly aware of that."

"—it could not be entrusted to an officer who had been insubordinate and derelict in his duty!"

The courtroom burst into an angry roar; there were whistles and catcalls. A tall lantern-jawed man in a green woolen shirt was shouting: "Don't let the bugger bad-mouth you none, Colonel—*you* know what's right!" To Jessie's consternation her father had started to heave himself to his feet; she clutched at his sleeve and pulled him back down again. Brooke was angrily threatening to clear the room, his gavel rapping through the uproar like spaced pistol shots.

"Derelict in what way, General?" Charles asked tightly.

"The charges and specifications speak for themselves—all twenty-two of them." Kearny was looking at him savagely now. "You broke your word to the Mexican authorities, you seized mounts and provisions from the Californios and paid for them with bogus promissory notes—above all you led an armed force onto foreign soil on the flimsy pretext of a scientific survey, instigated American settlers to rebel against Mexican authority, carried out a campaign of military conquest, and assumed control over all of northern California without any official authority whatever. If that does not constitute dereliction of duty, I don't know what does!"

The room had quieted, bound in tension. Charles started to make an angry reply, and suppressed it; he threw Jessie one piercing, anguished glance, and looked down at his notes.

"All right, tell them!" his father was whispering hotly. "Go on—*say* it, let them hear what that conniving, cold-blooded Polk instructed you to do!"

"He can't, Papa," she heard herself say with heavy urgency, "—can't you see that? He *can't* . . ."

Across from her William was tapping his pencil against the wood. His eyes caught hers, his eyebrows rose; then he looked down again. He hadn't once moved. She knew what that look meant. She wanted to signal Charles any way she could, get him to break off this cross-examination. It was all going wrong now; couldn't he see that? With every outburst of astonishment and anger in the courtroom, Brooke and the other officers of the court were only hardening in their opposition. A general's motives were being impugned; that was all they saw. It was like politics—the most honestly impassioned action often defeated its own purpose; the slyly contrived attack gained its ends. Effect was more important than principle. It shouldn't be true, but it was. And Charles, honorable and impassioned to a fault, could never see that. . . .

And the half dozen words that would vindicate him utterly, he could not say.

The room had quieted, though there was still a low, tense buzz of conversation. Her husband's face was marked with the same wild, barely contained outrage she remembered from the morning Mr. T had accused him of marrying her to advance his career. Furtively she tried to signal him, couldn't get his attention.

"General, isn't it true you refused my request to join my regiment in Mexico to serve under General Taylor—even though General Scott had specifically instructed you to extend this privilege?"

"I know of no such advice from General Scott."

"I see. When I requested permission to return over a new route in order to complete my mapping for the Topographical Corps, isn't it true you refused that request, and forced me to march under guard, in the dust at the rear of your forces like a common criminal?"

Kearny's eyes dilated, but he had himself under control again. "You marched behind the Mormon Battalion."

"One last question: didn't you try to prevent Lieutenant Gillespie's leaving California, even though he was overdue here in Washington?"

"I have no authority over naval officers."

"But you *did* request of Commodore Shubrick that he *not* be allowed to make the overland passage?"

Kearny smiled grimly. "I informed the commodore that I did not think Lieutenant Gillespie ought to be wandering around loose in the province of California."

"Wouldn't you say, General, that these several actions—deliberately withholding the orders in question, declaring your intention to put me in arrest *prior* to the arrival of those orders, refusing my requests to recover my records or to serve in Mexico, and seeking to block the return of witnesses crucial to my case—wouldn't you agree that this constitutes palpable evidence of a personal hostility toward me?"

"Objection!" The major had bounced to his feet again. "The question is clearly an attempt to lead the witness—"

"Sustained," Brooke answered sharply. "Colonel, I must remind you that you are to confine yourself to facts, not speculation or personal opinion."

"Very good, sir. I apologize to the court . . . though in all truth, I fail to see why the witness should object to answering the question: he himself is often given to the most extraordinary speculations—when it pleases *him*."

"—Not so!" Kearny burst out all at once. *"I'm* not the one making false claims, the one who's unlawfully seized government property!"

"What—" Charles had whirled around, his hands clenched; for one terrified instant Jessie feared he was going to physically attack Kearny. *"What are you saying?"* he whispered.

"I refer to a twelve-pound howitzer you abandoned in the Sierra in '44, and to two field pieces you failed to return to me after the surrender at Cahuenga! They were the property of my command, and—"

Charles cried: "You lost those guns to the enemy when you were defeated at San Pasqual!"

Kearny's head came up. "San Pasqual was *not* a defeat, Colonel, and I resent your use of the word! The enemy was forced to retire from the field."

"General, I would hardly call the loss of more than a third of your men a glorious victory."

There was scattered laughter throughout the room, and more catcalls. Lee, again on his feet, shouted: "Gentlemen, I challenge these unwarranted aspersions on the combat career of a distinguished general officer! And I further question the relevance of this line taken by the accused."

Jessie found she was holding her fists to her face; her heart had begun to pound heavily, and the pains in her stomach were worse. Ah dear God, she almost cried aloud, if I hear one more word about a cannon I will go stark, raving mad. . . .

"Sir," Charles was calmly addressing Brooke, though his voice was shaking, "I did not introduce this subject—the witness did. Since he *has* seen fit to bring it up, however, I hope I will be permitted to say for the record that it was the California Battalion who recovered the subject field pieces the witness lost in an *engagement* at San Pasqual—"

He broke off in amazement. General Kearny had risen to his feet, his eyes fastened with a baleful glare at the accused's counsel table. For a wild instant Jessie thought he was pointing at her, his hand shaking. "I wish to draw the attention of this court to the fact that while I have been sitting here the senior counsel for the accused, Thomas Hart Benton of Missouri, has sat there making mouths and grimaces, clearly intended to offend, insult and overawe me!"

There was a heavy gasp in the courtroom, a sharp collective intake of breath, and a quick stirring of bodies. General Brooke was leaning forward, his eyes narrowed, saying:

"Surely you are aware, Senator, of the 76th Article of the Rules and Articles of War, which specifically prohibits the use of menacing words or gestures in a—"

There was a sudden violent commotion next to Jessie. She tore her eyes away from Brooke to see her father heave himself heavily to his feet, his face flushed and choleric, and roar: "Oh no! It is General Kearny who has looked insultingly at Colonel Frémont, not once but many times! And I determined that if he should again attempt to face down the prisoner in this contemptible way, I would look at *him*—"

"Senator Benton, I must warn you—"

"I did today look at General Kearny when he sought in this contemptible way to intimidate Colonel Frémont . . . and I looked at *him* until his eyes fell, sir—till they fell upon the *floor*!"

Listening to her father being reprimanded by the court, watching her husband's tormented face, Jessie pressed her hands against her stomach and bowed her head.

Things went from bad to worse. The trial dragged on week after weary week, snarled in wrangles and exceptions and technicalities. The War Department still further restricted the areas of inquiry, and refused to permit more than half of Charles' arguments and witnesses. Spectators fought to gain admission to the sessions, and more guards were needed to control them during some of the most stormy exchanges. The press was having a perfect field day with what it was calling "the court-martial of the century," the most sensational Army affair since the treason trial of Aaron Burr. Tempers grew short, the parade of witnesses continued inexorably; and in the jury box facing the counsel tables—where of course there was no jury—the Army officers sat in massed ranks behind Brigadier General Stephen Watts Kearny, their faces smooth with malice . . .

And now, four agonizing weeks later, they had the reluctant commodore. Ultimately, Charles forced the story from him, but the shock was that he *had* to force it. Worse, under Major Lee's cross-examination on the following day, Stockton became acquiescent and obliging. The major seemed to be enjoying himself, and the angry note Jessie had heard in his earlier objections was gone.

"Tell me, Commodore," Lee said at last, as if he were addressing an old friend, "What orders did you have for the establishment of civil government in California?"

"Why . . . I don't think I had any."

Jessie watched William scribbling on a legal pad, but she knew it was too late. If Stockton was willing to say he had no authority—

"But you did establish such a government?" Lee said gently.

"Yes, sir—by the right of the law of nations."

Jessie saw the members of the court look at each other. The answer meant nothing to them. Did it mean anything to anyone? Even to suave, oily George Bancroft, far away in London town?

"Let me put it to you this way," Lee said with his most appealing smile. "Probably the question of your authority isn't even at issue here. With that in mind, how much of your authority would you say transferred to Lieutenant Colonel Frémont after you left Los Angeles?"

There was a long silence. Stockton fixed his eyes on the trim major. "Well," he said at last, "I suppose it might be a question as to whether I exercised *any* authority at all after Lieutenant Colonel Frémont became governor."

A small sigh ran through the audience. Jessie gripped her hands together. She knew instantly that they were finished; their single line of defense was destroyed. She could see it in the faces of the men at the long table.

Urgently she leaned over to tug at William's sleeve. Charles had a pale, dazed look.

"He's dodging the issue. Why can't we force him to—"

But William was shaking his head despondently. "No—he's our witness. We're not allowed to impeach him."

Then Charles leaned toward her and said in a harsh whisper: "The bastard—he's afraid he'll be censured, afraid the Army will demand that the Navy hold a court of inquiry over him! That's why he's running. Chicken-livered son of a bitch . . ."

She was actively sick with defeat, with dread. All at once she realized he had never once doubted he would be acquitted; the alternative had only just hit him.

He was still staring at Stockton, then turned back to her in a raging whisper. "You know what? Kit knew from the start—told me you couldn't trust a man who had the crazy schemes Stockton did! Think of that—Kit knew from the beginning. . . ."

The verdict came like hammer blows, clearly audible in every corner of the chamber. For the first time since the trial had begun, the courtroom was utterly silent. Brigadier General George M. Brooke rose, resplendent in gold braid, and began to read aloud tonelessly:

"Of the first specification of first charge: Guilty. Of the second specification of first charge: Guilty. Of the third specification of first charge: Guilty."

He ran through all twenty-two charges, and the answer to each and every one was the same. There was a hushed, almost sepulchral pause, as though the audience was too stunned even to react, and then Judge Advocate Lee bounced to his feet and declared in his light, ebullient voice:

"The court finds Lieutenant Colonel Frémont guilty of mutiny; of disobedience of the lawful command of his superior officer; of conduct to the prejudice of good order and military discipline." He cleared his throat. "The court does therefore sentence the said Lieutenant Colonel John C. Frémont, of the regiment of Mounted Riflemen, United States Army, to be dismissed from the service."

There was another instant of shocked silence—and then the room broke into angry shouts. A woman's voice was crying, "Shame! Shame!" and a man flung off up the aisle shaking his fist at the bench. Brooke rose again, looking startled now, almost fearful, and referred the verdict to the "lenient consideration of the President of the United States"; and the case was closed.

Jessie stared straight ahead at the members of the court, searching for something in their faces—some touch of regret, sorrow, even vexation; but there was nothing she could detect beyond a matter-of-fact acquiescence. Justice had been done, then.

But the eyes of the West Pointers ranged in the jury box behind Kearny gleamed with malicious satisfaction as they leaned forward offering their congratulations. It was over. She rose to her feet to leave the courtroom, her head high, her eyes front—knowing with fearsome shock that if someone had put a pistol in her hand she would have fired a bullet into Kearny's grim, forbidding face without one touch of remorse.

"It'll be all right," Charles was saying. They were back in the yellow sitting room at last, she had removed her constricting gown, and he was pouring her a cup of tea. "You'll see, the President will turn it around. I went out there and did what he wanted done, and he'll remember that. It goes to him for automatic review, and he'll turn it around.

"Look," he said, warming to the idea with that characteristic buoyancy of his, "the Army was bound to find as it did—it's half-crazed with fear of a disciplinary breakdown. Discipline is the only thing that keeps a soldier's hands from an incompetent officer's throat—and don't think they ever forget it! And so the point has been made. The thing is, I *succeeded*—I did just what they all wanted done. And the proof is that California is a stable, peaceful United States territory today. The only fact the court-martial *proved* is that I didn't do a blessed thing wrong except misjudge which officer finally would be declared in command."

She was nodding as he talked; she wanted to be comforted.

"You see?" he said. "He's let the Army have its day. Now he'll reverse it—nothing else makes sense."

Of course he was right. Give the President time to make an appearance of a careful review and he would reverse it. A week went by, and another. The President was busy. The treaty that would formally end the war with Mexico had been signed and the President sent it to the Senate with much fanfare. Another week passed. Secretary of State Buchanan said Charles' case had been discussed at two cabinet meetings. He wanted his former translator of Mexican dispatches to know, he told Mr. T, that he had argued for reversal. The comment left her shaken: there *was* an argument, then, for not reversing? Charles took long solitary walks in the winter sunshine.

In mid-February a captain from the Judge Advocate General's office brought a sealed envelope to the house on C Street. Charles carried it upstairs as if it might explode. He sat sideways in her desk chair, holding the envelope in both hands. She was afraid to say anything. Then in one quick gesture he ripped it open and unfolded a single sheet.

"From the President," he said in a high, tight voice. "He's—let's see—he rejects the mutiny charge. As to the other two, he has studied the evid—ah, God!—he's *affirmed* them! Both—disobedience and conduct prejudicial—he's affirmed them both. *He's found me guilty!*"

She couldn't speak. The silence was unbearable. At last he said, incredulous and raging: "So I'm to be the goat. This is just a dirty little Army-Navy cat fight—and they want *me* to pay the whole bill! No one asks the War Department or the Navy *why* they issued conflicting orders—no one challenges that miserable Stockton . . . Sure—what's another unscrupulous adventurer—?"

"No," she answered softly, "there's more to it than that. It's the slavery issue. The President is *afraid* to favor you for fear the abolitionists will turn it against him. He's a political coward! He owes you, and he's afraid to pay—"

"He does *not* owe me!" His anger shifted suddenly to her. "Nobody owes me anything! I did this on my own." He glared at her. "Give me that, at least that, damn it all."

He was pacing up and down the little room like a caged animal, gripping the knuckles of one hand. She watched him a moment, said: "I only meant—they sent you out there without proper authorization to do their dirty work for them. They ought to acknowledge that, at least."

"I'm sorry, Jessie," he muttered, turning toward her. "I had no right to lash out at you like that." There were tears in his eyes; he was struggling with all his might to calm himself. "I don't need to be rewarded for anything! I know what I've done. I just—can't stand to see people acting dishonorably. I can't *stand* it, Jessie!"

"I know." A moment longer she watched him, caught in a turmoil of conflicting feelings. Finally she said, "You know—you wanted to go, Charles. To California." He was watching her intently now. "You'd never have gone if you hadn't wanted to. Just because Bancroft dropped those 'diplomatic' hints of his. You had to go. . . . Isn't that true, darling?"

Staring at her he nodded, and then gave her a flash of the old boyish grin. "It's true. You're right, sweetheart. You're always right. California's still there. And it's a rich, magic land, Jessie. You'll see. Maybe it's all for the best." He was calming down now. "I'll be on my own, this way. It's probably better. I couldn't have taken a Rocky Mountain expedition to California on my own—but once they turned me loose, then I was acting on my own."

They had changed positions suddenly, like debaters. She frowned. "That's all very well, but to allow you to be dismissed after such success . . ."

"No," he said, "he's not doing that. He affirmed the verdict but reversed the sentence. Because of my past service, he says. I'm to take up my sword and report for duty."

She was confused again—relieved but not sure if she should be. "Do you mean—it's all right, then?"

"Of course it's not all right! I won't accept his damned clemency—I'm *not guilty!*"

"But you just said he doesn't owe you."

"It's entirely separate. Don't you see? The *point* is that I don't mind acting on my own. And afterwards I'm willing to stand for what I've done. I won't whine for special consideration. What's infuriating about this is that I haven't done what they want to punish me for."

"What do you mean, you won't accept—"

"I mean I'll resign. *I'm not guilty.*"

"But Charles—"

"God almighty, Jessie, if I accept his clemency, then I accept his judgment of guilt. Then they really *have* whipped me. Don't you understand that? I tell you, the day Kearny first made his move I knew there was no justice in it—and there still isn't. It's the *Army* that's betrayed me, not the country—and it's the Army I'm leaving!"

"But what about the new expedition? Congress will never support it if you're out of the Army. Even Papa couldn't get *that* through. . . ."

"Yes," he said slowly, "I see what you mean." Then his face hardened. "But Goddamnit, I can't just take this. I *won't* take it! To hell with the expedition."

"But it's your life," she cried, "—it's what you can do better than anyone in the whole world . . ."

"Well, hold on now, wait a minute . . . we'll finance it privately, that's what. Raise the money in St. Louis. That's it—like the old fur-trade treks. Hell, Jed Smith never had a dime of government money, or Tom Fitzpatrick either. Well, this is business, too—those St. Louis merchants will make millions from a western railroad. Let 'em bear a little of the initial cost. They don't have to sweat out the trail. . . ."

PART FOUR

LOSSES

"I'M WORRIED, CHARLES," she said one raw, rainy afternoon. "It's all moving too fast. We ought to slip the whole expedition over a year."

"We can't, and that's final!" The strain in his face had intensified since the court-martial: nothing had let up for them.

"It's dangerous, you know it is. You won't even *be* there before the snow."

"Not if we know what we're doing and we're careful. And I promise you we will be."

Well, it wasn't just that, she thought, distressed; it was everything—her pregnancy, the lectures Charles must continue to give now his Army pay had stopped, the need to gather support in St. Louis—all aggravated by her fear of a Rocky Mountain winter. She felt as if she had never given the baby a chance to get comfortable in that warm sack in her belly. Never given him a placid moment. She should have felt better at least to have the court-martial over, but she didn't.

Mr. T had been stunned when they told him Charles had resigned within an hour of receiving the President's message. Probably it would have been more gracious to have talked it over with her father, but Charles had been in no mood to wait or hear advice. It was done, that was Charles' way, and if her father in his political caution thought it a mistake, she didn't want to hear about it.

Yes, he had said slowly, probably Pierre Chouteau could rally underwriters for the expedition. Jessie had wondered if his hesitation meant more than hurt feelings, but he had written a long letter to Pierre the next day. An enthusiatic if somewhat guarded answer was back in a month: Pierre urged them to start planning while he gathered backers in St. Louis. He thought that news of the court-martial had reflected well on Charles and badly on Kearny, even though St. Louis was Kearny's home. As for Polk, Chouteau said that he was finished and that anyone the Democrats nominated this year would have trouble running against Zachary Taylor . . .

To her surprise, Jessie found that most people shared Chouteau's view of the court-martial's findings. Interest had faded before the trial ended, and the treaties that closed the war with Mexico had seized public attention just as the verdict came in. The Frémonts were more in demand than ever at Washington parties.

The Senate passed legislation authorizing payment of up to seven hundred thousand dollars for the California claims, and a half-dozen senators made speeches lavishing recognition on Charles. John Dix of New York said flatly that Charles had kept the British out of California; Jessie thought it about time that someone in a responsible forum made that point.

His reputation as an explorer continued to grow, undamaged by the trial. The Royal Geographical Society in London gave him its Founder's Medal for services to geography. A gold-chased sword engraved as a memorial to his scientific work in Oregon and California came from the citizens of Charleston, who now considered him a native son. The Prussian government even struck a gold medal for him at the urging of venerable old von Humboldt himself. Charles was so moved at the formal embassy presentation that he could barely respond. He revered Baron von Humboldt, whose own explorations ranged over the entire world and for whom he had named a major American river.

And from the good old *Democratic Review*, whose editor had been so perspicacious in recognizing the nation's manifest destiny to drive westward, came a different kind of accolade. It complained that Frémont had received no rewards for his work, though Lewis and Clark had been granted "double pay, 1,600 acres of land each, promotion to general, and copyright in their Journals." Compared to Lewis and Clark—and high time!

They went to New York, where Charles gave a series of lectures before select audiences; every night there was a reception and dinner in one of the great town houses that lined Fifth Avenue. Watching the leaders of New York society and business listening respectfully as Charles talked of California's future was a balm that assuaged some of the court-martial's pain. Indeed, it would have been undiluted pleasure if she hadn't been so tired and ill, but there was never time to rest.

On one such evening she saw a man studying Charles. He was dresed in a plain black suit with rumpled linen, though he seemed entirely at home. He had cold, speculative gray eyes. After a while she caught him watching her, like a butcher estimating a calf's weight. He was interested in her. It wasn't sexual—she knew that look well from Washington—but he *was* interested.

She saw him several times, always watching, and then one night, across the room, he was talking to Charles alone and she knew immediately that was what he had waited for. Curiosity drove her to join them.

"John Bigelow," Charles said, introducing him. "He's editor of the *Evening Tribune.*"

Her eyes widened: that was William Cullen Bryant's paper.

"So that's my point, Colonel," Bigelow went on. "The court-martial made your reputation."

"Other way around, I'd say; it only failed to destroy it."

"No. You're a famous explorer, a great leader of men—but you don't know how the public mind works. Look, we ran reams on your defense. All about you taking California—you and Carson and that fellow Merrill—"

"Merritt."

"Merritt. Doesn't matter. Point is, you made yourself a hero—and we brought you out glistening like gold. Every paper in the country carried it. And then the treaties came in and crowded out the verdict. I gave the verdict three grafs on page nineteen. Nobody cared about it."

"But it's in the record."

"Sure—but who looks up the record? People make up their minds on what they hear—on how that makes 'em feel. They feel good about you. Do you think the public gives a pig's ear whether some tin-pot general is miffed? The man out there likes nothing better than someone who spits in a general's eye. Human nature."

"I didn't spit—"

"But the public thinks you did, and they're saying hurrah! You've got a lot of potential, Colonel. Pull off this new expedition and you're *in.*"

"In *what?*" Jessie asked. The man unsettled her.

"In whatever he wants," Bigelow said, turning that cold, measuring eye on her. "And don't think it hurts to have an attractive, intelligent wife—not one bit."

"You're an interesting man, Mr. Bigelow," Charles said.

"No, sir. Just good at spotting potential. Let's stay in touch, shall we?"

She saw their host approaching with new guests, and when next she glanced around, Bigelow was gone.

When they returned to Washington, Charles continued to lecture—he was becoming a graceful speaker, able to blend humor and adventure with evangelical descriptions of California—because the honorariums were their only income. Life without regular military pay already had altered their view of the ranch in California. It had shifted from a speculation to their chief resource.

"Suppose you did a real book—a big book," she said. "You could trace the new route to California and then go into detail after you get there. Do it all—the geography, the people, climate, agriculture, the 'feel' of the place. Tell the whole story of the conquest—the Bear Flag, everything. Call it *California!* Don't you like the sound of that?"

He was watching her with a pleased, indulgent grin, and she laughed out loud. "They loved your other Reports," she said.

"Your reports."

"No—thank you, sir—*your* Reports. But they did, Charles. Look how they sold. If we'd only had a royalty on those. Why should the publishers make all that money from your discoveries? You're out of the Army now—what you write will be your own. Anyway, this could be much bigger. The whole country is fascinated with California; and who would they rather read on the subject than the man who made it all possible?"

"The same as before? The way we worked?"

"Same way. You talk it out and let me get it down. We could structure it around the diary form again—get the new route anchored first, then the story of what happened there, and then open up for a report on the whole territory. It would be a wonderful book, Charles!"

The work was harder this time. The subject was much more complex than she'd expected. The diary approach didn't work and she had to invent a new structure. Their talk wasn't as easy as it had been for the Reports, either—it tended to slide off into heated, obsessive rehashes of the court-martial issues. Or maybe it was just that she was so tired. But despite everything, the book began to move. She made copious notes from their talks in the mornings and wrote in the afternoons while he made preparations for the Fourth Expedition.

Chouteau's letters were more and more encouraging, and word was coming in from the men. Alex Godey was going, and Charles was sure that Kit and perhaps Dick Owens would join him. He had written to old Tom Fitzpatrick. Fitz and Kit knew the mountains north of Taos better than anyone else in the West. Raffie Proue sent word that he would be waiting at Westport, and of course that led their thoughts back to Louie; and Charles looked saddened and grim. One day he brought home little Karl Preuss, the cartographer of the First and Second Expeditions. Preuss was in his forties now, and years of easy living in Washington had softened him, but he'd persuaded his wife to let him go out again. That was good news—once they found the best pass, a good map would be the crucial next step in establishing practicable grades for the bed of the railway.

Then one morning a letter from Larkin arrived in a packet of California mail. Charles opened it eagerly—then she saw his face change.

"What in hell is going on?" he said. "Larkin says he found me a great bargain. But that's not what—" He stopped and looked up at her. *"Jessie, he didn't buy the ranch."*

"He didn't? But why?"

"He bought something else with our money." Quickly he ran down the page and turned it. "A big tract back in the Sierras someplace. Eleven leagues, nearly seventy thousand acres—that's cheap, all right, but what the hell good is it? Indians still hunt there—you'd have to have an armed garrison to open it to cattle."

He consulted the letter again. "Says it's called Las Mariposas because of its butterflies—says the hills turn solid gold with them in the spring. Isn't that poetic! But I'm raising cattle, Goddamnit, not . . . Wait a minute. There was a letter from Jesús Pico, too. Let's see what he—" He tore open the envelope. "Ah," he cried savagely, "that's it! Pico says Larkin bought our ranch for himself! The son of a bitch took our land and wants to fob us off with a worthless wilderness. There's a Boston Yankee for you—I should have *known* I couldn't trust him."

He had a look she had never seen. She thought of sullen Purvis, Proue raging in anguish over Louie's body, Bladon and his great knife, and was filled with fear.

"Charles—" she pleaded.

"He's going to answer for this," he said between his teeth. "He's not going to *take my ranch*! Every son of a bitch around has had a go at me lately, and Larkin thinks he can join the crowd. Well, I'll have him in court the moment I get there—and by God, he'd better hope the courts are prompt! He'll like that a lot better than dealing with me personally . . ."

Then the very next day came a letter from Carson, written by a scribe in Taos. Kit said it surely hurt him to turn the Colonel down, but he had new ventures in Taos and Santa Fe that would go under if he left them now, and he couldn't do that to his growing family. Tom Fitzpatrick was the new Indian agent on the Arkansas and probably wouldn't be available. Did the Colonel really have to go this winter? He thought it chancy as all hell and suggested holding their horses until the following summer when he'd be free for the trail. Then they could scout several good passes in advance and return in the winter to see which one worked best.

Listening, all her fears came back. No Kit—steady, resourceful Kit. . . . Unlucky, an unlucky start. "Even Kit thinks it's dangerous, and if he says so you *know* it is. Please, darling, put it off, do as he suggests."

"I can't."

"Please . . . it would give us more time for the book. It would make for a better expedition." He shook his head. "Well, what about me? I'll be crossing that Isthmus jungle with a six-month-old baby."

"Maybe you're right about that," he said, softening. "Maybe you'd better delay your trip—join me later."

"I don't *want* to join you later! God, is a year so important?"

"Yes, it *is* important," he said, restraining his irritation. "Look, we've got enthusiasm in St. Louis now—will we still have it next year? The time to do things is *now*. I never got anywhere by waiting. And anyway, it costs too much to keep men in the field for nearly a year. It would change all the economics—we'd have to start all over again." There was more of Kearny's legacy, she thought bitterly; they'd never had to worry before about the costs of an expedition.

"I think you should wait until it's safe for the baby, but I've got to get on to California. I've got to get those debts I ran up settled—and I've got to take care of Larkin. I'm going to get that ranch if I have to take that bastard by the throat and shake it out of him!"

"Charles, you know you said—"

"I know, I know— 'the cautious seldom err.' But they never get anything *done*, either! I'll be prudent, within reason . . . But I'm through being baited and badgered, Jessie—I don't have to take that anymore. And I won't!"

He paused and his voice changed. "There's another thing. Zachary Taylor'll be elected this year. I hear he thought the whole court-martial was a mistake—including the verdict. Now, I've been thinking—there's a lot of exploration to be done in the West. And if I come through with a solid success about the time he takes office, he just might want to give me a real expedition . . . But a year later, he'd have other plans, the whole situation would be different. You know how Washington works."

She saw that he would not be persuaded. They were such ferocious mountains. But after all, he had crossed the Sierras in winter; and she had unshakable faith in his abilities. She decided she just couldn't afford worry—it was an indulgence for which she lacked the strength. It was May 1848, the sultry Washington summer was coming on, the baby would be born in a couple of months; she was so tired that she often felt faint. The book had become a terrible burden. She started work earlier each morning and continued later each evening, sitting curled in a chair in the yellow sitting room, her distended belly turned to one side, covering page after page in her neat, firm hand.

Late one afternoon he came into the sitting room. The light changed, and without looking up she snapped, "Don't move the lamp; I can't see." She dropped her pencil, leaned down to get it, saw her board and the pages falling—and then she seemed to be toppling after them into darkness and she realized dimly he had caught her. She felt him pick her up, the darkness crowding close around his face. . . .

Later she awakened in her bedroom. Sally was there looking frightened and said she had been asleep three days. Jessie got right up, or started to, and found she couldn't; and when she awakened again it was sometime later and Charles was there with a doctor who was convinced bleeding would help. There were hushed, angry voices, and then it seemed Charles had thrown the doctor out and she remembered her father believed it was the doctor's bleeding cups that had destroyed her mother's health. Oddly comforted, she went back to sleep.

She began to improve, though worrying about the book gave her a blinding headache. Charles told her not to think of it. He said he would draft a short geographical memoir to satisfy his obligation to the Senate, and they could deal with the book later. She thought about that for a long time, and a day or two later she whispered, "Get that phrase 'the Golden Gate' into the memoir. It's too good to last—someone else will use it."

From Charles' expression she might just have won a prize. "Oh, sweetheart," he cried, "you're going to be all right."

Every day she grew stronger. She ran her full term and when labor pains began they came very quickly. The baby was born in not much more than an hour. He wanted to come, he was ready, she thought; perhaps everything really would be all right. She wanted to name him after his father, but Charles surprised and pleased her by insisting they name him Benton.

He was a superb boy, perfect in every way, beautiful beyond expression. With his birth her own weakness receded and soon she was up. Lily, who was nearly six, spent hours with the baby. He looked like his father, Jessie thought, and shared his nature, too—intense, demanding, active. He fed lustily, pulling furiously at her breast until he was forced to stop, panting.

She laughed the first time. "Are you so hungry that you can't stop to breathe?" she asked, and gave him her nipple again. But the effort seemed to have exhausted him and he went off to sleep. He wasn't gaining weight as Lily had. Lily rocked him for hours and Sally fixed a sugar tit to stimulate his appetite. Sally assured her that he would adjust in a week or two. He would be fine; all he needed was rest and nourishment. But she couldn't rid herself of a stealthy anxiety. It had been such an ominously unlucky year. . . .

It was so damned good to be back in St. Louis putting the new expedition together. Even the fact that Chouteau had called a meeting of Frémont's backers without consulting him couldn't dim his mood. After struggling for months in the toils of military justice gone mad, Kearny glowering out his litany of arrogant protocol, the court-martial officers examining each technical nit as if to see how many could dance on the head of a pin—enough! it was time to get on to things that mattered. It was time to turn to his own ground: an expedition that went where protocol and privilege had no meaning because the only things that lay between any man and the wilderness were his personal skill and courage.

September now, and late—dangerously late—which was why this meeting of his investors came as an irritating interruption. He would have liked to come out to St. Louis in June, but Jessie's illness had precluded that. After his awful fear at the sight of her tumbling from her chair that day, he hadn't considered moving her. And then little Benton couldn't travel for a month after his birth. The child was delicate; Frémont knew Jessie was worried, though he supposed all babies were delicate. The frontier air should build the boy's strength.

When Frémont and the Senator walked into the cottage in the American Fur Company compound that served as Chouteau's office, the acrid smell of raw fur swept him back across the years. It was ingrained in the very wood, an olfactory monument to past glory. Here was where it all had started; he a novice to Papa Joe, Louie strutting in his go-to-town buckskins, old Provost remote in the dour, unassailable superiority of a senior mountain man. . . . Now, after less than a decade in years but a lifetime in experience, Frémont himself had grown to Provost's stature. . . .

Benton knew the men assembled. Frémont warmly greeted Bob Campbell, the ruddy, red-haired trader-merchant who had helped provision his previous expeditions. Chouteau introduced the others: O. D. Filley, who manufactured ironware, a lead-mine operator named Lemuel Frincke from down toward St. Genevieve, Cap'n Ed Milby, whose fleet of river boats had reached fifteen, Rossman from the Planter's House, and the pink-faced Mr. Slagle, who looked more like an overfed baby every year—and who controlled two banks with an iron fist.

They sat on straight chairs with rawhide bottoms and listened with steady attention as Frémont, speaking in the easy manner he'd developed for his lectures, blocked out the expedition. Thirty-five men, half of them already signed up, the remainder waiting to join the party at Bent's Fort. Livestock and basic supplies were already in hand. From there they would head into the mountains, check several passes, choose the most suitable one, and be out in the spring with a sound route to California. Six months—and St. Louis would be the jumping-off place for a railroad that would tie the nation directly to the fabulous West, and the Golden Gate to the Orient.

On that flourish he ended and was about to invite their questions when Mr. Slagle spoke up. The old banker had a remote, frosty voice.

"I hear you didn't get your California claims bill through Congress after all," he said.

Surprised by this digression, Frémont hesitated, and Tom Benton interceded. "It passed the Senate easily. The House delayed on it."

"I heard they'd turned it down," Slagle pursued.

"They voted against acting on it in this session. Just a formality. We'll get it through next year."

"Think so? Seven hundred thousand is a lot of money."

"It's a shitpot full of money," the lead miner, Frincke, said suddenly. He looked a lot like a ferret. "I hope you ain't planning to spend anything like that this time."

The idea was so ludicrous that Frémont laughed and shook his head. "That was for two years. We went to California, raised an army, fought a war. We ran a government on that. And it was cheap at the price, actually. But no—nothing like that this time."

"I don't know that it's so funny," Frincke said. "We wouldn't want you to forget you're spending *real* money now."

Frémont's smile disappeared. "Mr. Frincke," he said levelly, "when you've operated on military budgets, you have to know the value of money."

"Horseshit, Colonel, no offense. The Army doesn't know a thing about real money. Or about the real world, either."

Frémont looked at the man closely for the first time. He was a pissant, but there was a mean force in him. His mines would not be happy places to work.

"I think I can say the Army is real enough," Frémont said mildly.

"Nah. You know what the difference is? In the real world, if you haven't got the money to pay, you don't eat. That's the biggest difference there is."

"You think that's all there is to it, do you?"

Benton coughed and shifted his feet, but Frincke ran on. "All that counts. Now, you take old Kearny—you've had some experience with him, ain't you?" He gave Frémont a smug, malicious look. "What do you think he'd do if he had to meet a payroll? He wouldn't know whether to shit or go blind. And why? Because for all his airs, he ain't never lived in the real world."

Frémont looked down at his hands. There was a silence, and Campbell said, "Kearny's in town, Colonel. Did you know that?"

Frémont kept his face expressionless. "No—I just got in."

Chouteau said: "He's been with Scott in Mexico. Got sick there—yellow fever or something. They say he's going to die of it."

But Frincke didn't intend to be diverted. "You know why government money ain't real?" he demanded. "Because the government don't have to work for it. We work for ours."

All at once Frémont had had enough of the man. "Don't tell me about work, Mr. Frincke," he said shortly. "Not when you're home sleeping in a warm bed every night."

"Well, now, I don't know about that, Colonel," Frincke said softly. "Long as you're spending our money, you're likely to hear a good deal about work."

Frémont knew then that Frincke had been waiting for this. "You're likely to hear about the cost of supplies, too. We don't want to hear about any pretty little brass cannon left along the way this time. Or stock and wagons shoved over a cliff, either. Not as long as you're spending our money."

No one spoke. Rossman, the hotel man, was examining his fingernails, and suddenly Frémont realized that Frincke had spoken for them all. He was angry: now was the time to stop this.

"I don't like that kind of talk," he said coldly.

"Well, you better learn to like it," Frincke said, his voice now so small that it was hard to hear. "Or maybe there won't *be* no expedition. You thought of that?"

"Now, boys," Benton spoke up quickly. "Are we here to put a great project in motion, or are we just going to wrangle?"

Chouteau said: "All right, Lemuel. You don't want to push Colonel Frémont—he's not a man who pushes easily." He gave Frémont a pleasant smile. "And Colonel, you want to try to see this our way, too. The Pacific railroad is fine, but it's all off in the future—won't come for years. Hell, we haven't even got a railroad to the East, as yet."

"But when we do get it," Frémont said, "you'll profit handsomely—"

"Of course, and the future is promising, too. We know that, that's why we're sitting here. But you see, you're used to thinking in national objectives. Now, that's a luxury for a businessman. Maybe that's what government ought to be doing. But what a businessman's got to do is mind the till or he'll be out of business. And all those long-term grand objectives won't matter a jot. So businessmen, when they don't see an immediate profit—why, you've got to hold their feet to the fire to get 'em to go along. And that's what we've done."

"Amen," said Milby. "And it wasn't easy."

"All Lemuel is saying," Chouteau said gently, "is that we want you to understand it the way we do. If you don't . . . well, hell, just say so and we can all back out and no hard feelings."

There was a long silence. Frémont saw that Benton was gazing at the floor. Benton was still a national power—though that, too, was slipping through his big hands now—but at home he had no voice when money talked. It had surprised Frémont to learn that the Senator was a poor man. He remembered the flush on Jessie's face when she had explained: in nearly thirty years in the United States Senate, old Toller Tom had never accepted a dime of outside income. Most politicians became rich, and not necessarily through thievery; it was easy to arrange things so profit flowed your way; indeed, given the nature of power, it was hard for a man in Mr. T's position not to take advantage of it. He had worked at *not* profiting. Look at the great Daniel Webster with his magnificent oratory, his grand vision of America—and his stipends from the bankers and industrialists whose causes he supported. She was proud of her father but—and her eyes had filled suddenly—the result was that he could never clear the mortgage of their St. Louis home, and finally he'd lost it. That was why they always stayed with his cousin, Joshua Brant—they were staying there now.

A slow flush had crept over Benton's face. He was humiliated and the pain that gave Frémont was greater than the worst that Frincke could do. It made him realize in the hardest terms that he loved the old man.

He swallowed. "Well, Pierre," he said slowly, "with my background and the Senator's, I'm a little surprised that you gentlemen need reassurance." He swallowed again, and found a smile. He was glad that Jessie wasn't there today. "I will say that in the last few minutes my appreciation of money has become more acute than ever. So, specifically, be assured that I will husband our resources. I guarantee costs won't get out of hand."

Sally burst into the room, and at the look on her face Jessie started up.

"Miz Jessie, you better come! The *baby*—."

Jessie ran up the polished walnut stairs of the Brant house toward the nursery. Lily was crouched by the crib, rubbing the baby's little hands and arms.

"He's cold, Mama. Benton's cold." Tears were streaming down her face.

Jessie saw it in an instant. His eyes were open and sightless, his lips drawn back. She brushed past Lily and picked him up. His head lolled. She jerked up his gown and pressed her ear to his chest. She could feel his tiny rib cage against her cheek. So cold. So very—

"Oh, Mama," Lily whispered, "Mama, is he—"

"Be quiet, Lily—I can't hear."

But there was nothing to hear. The silence stretched and grew monstrous, a silence that folded over her, over her daughter, the house, her life.

Slowly she pulled down his blue flannel gown. She closed his eyes and wrapped his blanket around him. She sat down, holding the tiny bundle to her breast, and put out a hand to Lily. The small girl fell on her knees, put her head in her mother's lap, and sobbed.

Sally rushed into the room. "We've sent for the doctor. His poor lil heart just stopped beating, Miz Jessie."

"No," Jessie said, looking up. She was dry-eyed. It was like a stark, measureless dream. "No, his heart was broken before he ever had a chance to be born."

The doctor came. Reluctantly she let him open the blanket and touch the little body with his stethoscope. He shook his head. She wrapped him and held him to her breast again.

"Mrs. Frémont," the young doctor said gently. "I'm sorry. Your baby is dead." Jessie nodded. Her eyes were still dry.

"Let me take him, Miz Jessie," Sally said. She had a frightened look.

"It's all right, Sally," Jessie said. "I know he's gone. Just let me hold him until his father comes. I've had him for such a little while."

Half an hour later Charles found them there. And still she had not wept.

The dragoon captain was wearing his dress blues. She thought of the three officers in this same room, the afternoon she'd first caught sight of Charles arguing with her father, his face young and eager and impassioned.

The captain—she missed his name, hadn't wanted to hear it—was very uncomfortable; he sat on the edge of a chair in the Brants' drawing room. He couldn't know that she had come to hate that uniform. She was immensely glad Charles was down at the riverfront drawing supplies.

"General Kearny sent me, ma'am," he said. "He's very ill. He would—ah, he would appreciate a visit."

"I think not," she said.

"Please, Mrs. Frémont. It troubles him that there are hard feelings. He remembers you fondly."

She watched him a long moment; then shook her head.

The officer was agitated. He kept turning his hat in his hands. "Let me be direct," he said. "The general is gravely ill. What he wants . . . he's asking you to—come and forgive him. Won't you do that?"

Dying. Yes. Well. And had *he* thought of forgiveness when he'd hidden the President's orders from Charles all those weeks? when he baited him, mocked him, put him in arrest and charged him with mutiny, tried to destroy him? when she'd felt that knife thrust of pure pain deep in her belly . . . No!

"No," she said, and shook her head again. Her face was hard as flint.

He stared at her, his mouth working. "For God's sake, madam, don't you understand? The man is *dying*. Can you refuse forgiveness to a dying man?"

She stood up then, the officer rose immediately.

"Tell the general," she said, "that it is quite impossible." She could hear the iron in her voice. "Tell him—that a small grave lies between us."

PARTING

THE LAST MORNING CAME QUICKLY, as in a dream. It seemed impossible, but here the men were lining up in the final departure camp on Boone Creek to tell her good-bye. She had come up to Westport with them; she and Charles had stayed with Major Cummins and his wife at the Delaware Indian Agency. Charles had reclaimed Sacramento from a year's pasturage in Westport and was busy assembling the last of the livestock and supplies. Each morning she had accompanied him over to Boone Creek. The men had treated her like some rare ornament.

They were thirty-five strong, mostly Charles' old men, Godey and massive Raffie Proue, and young Henry King, who'd married a girl in Georgetown just before they left Washington and worked every conversation with Jessie around to his bride. Most of them had been on the Third Expedition, a few on the Second—and Raffie had been on them all.

"I wish Louie were with us," she had told Proue softly, and he'd looked pleased, as if due had been given, and said, "Yes'm, I know . . ." but they hadn't spoken of it again.

Ned Kern, now a veteran, had brought his brother, a Philadelphia physician. On her first day in camp he'd sketched her portrait and handed it to her with a flourish, and she'd seen that he had made her very beautiful.

It had been a happy time there on Boone Creek. Two of the party were French *voyageurs,* survivors of a dying breed. Antoine Morin and Vincent Tabeau, called Sorrel for hair that once had been red, had given her reassurance. Years of experience and hard times lay behind them; nothing could go wrong with such men. She chatted with them in French, which had moved even old Sorrel to a smile and a quick, oblique compliment.

And there was Captain Andrew Cathcart, one of those whipcord Enlishmen with a fine education and a taste for action, who had just given up a commission in Prince Albert's Own Hussars and come to America for a bit of adventure. He was a Scotsman, actually, one of the Cathcarts of Carleton, and he'd charmed her with his tales of growing up in Killochan Castle. He had come over in the spring with that dashing British adventurer George Frederick Ruxton, who'd written so nobly of the West. What Jessie hadn't known was that only two months before, Ruxton had died of dysentery in a Planter's House room at the age of twenty-seven while Cathcart bathed his face. Cathcart had buried Ruxton in St. Louis, and signed on with the expedition, anxious for his own taste of the West.

Alex Godey built a lean-to and dug a fire pit where he roasted the quail the young hunter, John Scott, brought down with his scattergun. She knew that she would never think of quail without remembering Boone Creek and the lean-to and Godey's silky hair. It was the first thing she'd noticed about him, falling to his shoulders, black and shiny, and impulsively she'd said: "Why, Alex, you have the most beautiful hair . . ." She had stopped, fearful of offending, and he had only laughed easily, his face tilted back to the light.

"So they all tell me, ma'am," he'd answered, and she'd seen in an instant she had won his heart.

And now they were leaving. The dreamy, pastoral quality remained. She was like a statue, a princess caught in a spell, as the clock ticked down to zero. They came past her in line, taking her hand, and all the while she watched herself from a distance, smiling, blurred and uncertain as a figure seen through glass.

Godey held her hand, shaking it gently from side to side in an oddly intimate gesture, and said, "You look out for yourself down there in Panama. And remember, we're gonna throw you the dog-*goned*-est *baile* you ever seen when you get to California. Yes, ma'am!"

She rode along for a few miles, the men strung out ahead, her little mare keeping pace with Sacramento. She watched her husband. He was looking ahead, his mind already on the trail and the problems of the mountains. Part of him had already left her. The reins curled between his strong fingers, his whipcord breeches taut over thigh muscles. His hat was cast onto his back so that its rawhide tie pressed his throat. The leather cord emphasized the strength of his neck. She wanted to touch him, clasp his neck in both hands, press her lips to his throat. The thought made her lonely; the year lay ahead like a mysterious canyon, its bottom menacing and dark.

Major Cummins was beside them on his rusty buckskin. If Marjorie Cummins had been there she would have told her husband to drop back, but she wasn't there and he went on, pacing them step for step. A bank of October clouds lay heavy and dirty on the north horizon. The horses stirred fallen leaves, a dry, shuffling sound. Why this mounting sense of loss, of fathomless pure dread? She shivered; the sun was climbing in a bright sky, but it had not broken the morning chill.

"You'll have good weather for now, at least," she said with an effort. They were on the brink of parting and she talked of weather. She cast about for the right thing to say but her mind was empty.

"Usually have bright autumns in this country," Major Cummins said amiably. "Usually do. 'Course, you can't tell. I've seen blizzards in September. I 'member the fall of Thirty-nine—two foot of snow and the leaves still green on the cottonwoods."

So they talked like spendthrift idiots until at a high place Charles stopped and dismounted. The ground ahead sloped into a grassy swale a mile across, open but for the line of woods that marked a stream along its middle. The grass was already golden. She saw it ripple, and a breeze came chill against her cheek.

"We'll leave you here, sweetheart," Charles said. When Cummins dismounted too, Charles thrust out his hand.

"You've been mighty kind, Major," he said. "You know I appreciate it. I'll tell you good-bye now."

"Oh, of course," Cummins said, looking at her in sudden dismay. "Well, sir, good luck to you on the trail. We'll see to Miz Frémont, never you fear." He took the mare's reins from Jessie. "I'll just walk the horses off a bit."

The line of men was smaller, moving across the expanse of grass. She saw Godey turn once in his saddle and look back. It was time.

"Oh, Charles," she said, "there was everything I wanted to say—and here I'm saying nothing."

He was holding both her hands. Sacramento cropped grass around the bit, obedient to the dropped rein.

"We don't need to say it," he said, smiling slowly. "We know it, don't we? We know what we are together." He hesitated, looking carefully at her face, always reluctant to admit doubts. Then he said, "Look, Jessie, nothing will happen to me. I'm lucky, you know. Basically a lucky man." He grinned. "Even when my luck turns sour for a spell. I won't let anything happen. And remember what I tell you: the sun always shines in California. Always—even when it rains. You understand?"

"I understand, darling," she said. "I do. I'll be waiting for you in California."

He glanced at the line of men swallowed up in the great distance.

"I love you, Charles," she said.

"I love you," he answered, "and I always will. That's what matters."

When he kissed her his lips were rough, already chapped. It was a kiss of departure. Then he caught Sacramento's reins and was up in the saddle.

"Charles—" she said suddenly, lifting her arms to him. He leaned down to her. Her arms went around his neck and her voice was barely a whisper.

"Good-bye, my darling," he said softly and released her. He looked at her for just another moment and then he lifted the reins and Sacramento sprang off. She watched him go, the horse's long rocking gait stirring the grass. The first of the line had gone into the woods at the stream, and by the time the last man reappeared, Charles rode at the column's head. She watched them move toward the distant rise, and it seemed that they reached it immediately. The big gray, tiny now with tiny rider, turned off the trail and stood on the crest. She knew that Charles was looking back at her. The line passed him and the men sank steadily out of sight until only horse and rider stood outlined against the sky. She saw him stand in his stirrups and wave his hat in a slow arc over his head, and even as she threw up her hand in answer the stallion wheeled and broke into a lope and almost immediately disappeared. The ridge was empty, the sky burning white with sun haze that danced as she stared.

Cummins cleared his throat uneasily. She had forgotten him. She knew she was pale, and when she tried to smile she felt her lips tremble. She shook her head sharply but just the same she didn't trust herself to speak; and they rode back to the agency in an awkward silence. She could not shake this feeling of dread.

The agency was a strange, rambling structure of logs with butts squared and notched. Parts of it had been added at different times so that it had a haphazard quality, its walls turning whimsically here and there. Cummins had given the Frémonts a room at the far end. She heard Sally singing inside. The trunk and the three wicker hampers stood open. Sally stood on a chair, unpinning one of the sheets that Jessie had hung against a bare log wall to collect the light.

"Oh, Sally," Jessie said, "not yet. Leave them up and we'll take them down tomorrow just before we go. It's gloomy enough without looking at that dark wall."

A shaft of sun drifting with dust motes lay across the tiny room. It was different now. The heavy logs pressed close, dark and rough. For the first time she noticed that the mirror over the washbasin had a cloudy look. The basin was cracked. Those sheets ("like the palest French wallpaper, don't you think?" she had said, and Charles had laughed) were the room's only civilized touch. Charles' ivory-handled razor and the small tortoise brushes she'd given him were gone. The peg by the door where his greatcoat had hung was empty. The room looked unendurably bare. She took down the red velvet dress she'd worn the night before and spread it on the bed to fold it. It didn't fold well and she shook it out and tried again. The cloth slipped and unfolded in her hands. She saw Sally watching her.

"Well," she said, smiling self-consciously, "we won't leave until tomorrow. Major Cummins says that'll give us plenty of time to catch the steamer."

"And will I be glad to see that boat start down that rolling river. . . . *Away, I'm going a-way—across the wide Missouri . . .*" she sang in a deep, creamy voice. "I don't know about this frontier life, Miz Jessie—I like the big house in St. Louis. Back on C Street, too."

"Well," Jessie said, more sharply than she'd intended, "you'd better get used to the frontier. What do you think California is?"

"I'm afraid a bad old grizzly bear will eat me in California, Miz Jessie."

It was an old joke that reflected Sally's indecision about going West, but this time Jessie did not smile. She stood looking at Sally somberly, saying nothing, and Sally said, "He'll be all right, honey. I never knowed a man better able to take care of himself than Colonel Frémont."

"I know—but I never felt so lonely, the other times."

"You still grievin' over lil Benton," Sally said gently. "That casts a sadness over everything. Can't be helped."

"I know."

"But that's natural, it's the way life is. It don't mean nothin' but natural grief, Miz Jessie. Ain't no bad omen. It's just seein' things dark for a time."

Am I so obvious? she thought, and sighed.

"Miz Jessie, don't you fool with this packin'. I haven't another livin' thing to do. You go see Miz Cummins. She's makin' you a nice dinner—said to send you right around. You go on, now."

It was a robust midday meal, well served on Limoges hauled clear from Philadelphia, and Jessie tried to eat it. Watching her move the food around on her plate, Marjorie Cummins looked meaningfully at her husband and said: "Why don't you take Mrs. Frémont for a ride after dinner? I think the air would do her good."

Cummins, ladling gravy over a rough-cut slab of bread, looked up in surprise. "She was out this morning."

"Well, Richard," his wife said more slowly, "perhaps she'd like to go again. Perhaps she'd rather not spend the afternoon in that little room."

"That would be nice," Jessie put in diplomatically. "If the Major has the time."

"Well, indeed," Cummins said, his glance shifting between the women. "I'll take the time. Indeed I will. I'll have Jackson get the horses."

Mrs. Cummins smiled. "Exercise settles the mind."

Jackson had the mare saddled when Jessie stepped into the corral. The foreman was a stocky Delaware with heavy black braids dropping from under his hat. He let the mare drink and then held the stirrup for Jessie. Cummins led a big bay from the barn. Three little black-haired boys burst out of the barn just behind him, perched on a corral rail and watched Jessie, solemn as owls. Cummins and Jackson talked for a moment. There were two new cases of diphtheria among the Delawares; a needed consignment of supplies from St. Louis was late.

"And that last shipment was wormy and half-rotted," Cummins said to Jessie. "These folks live awful thin." He shook his head, looking discouraged. "But what can *I* do? I'm just—"

He broke off when he saw an old blue-tick hound hobble gingerly from the barn. "Well, look who's here," he said with a note of pleasure Jessie hadn't heard before. He knelt and the old bitch crept close, her tail low and sweeping. "Want to go hunting, do you?" He pushed the other dogs away and rubbed her grizzled head. "Gonna get you some birds? Well, I'll tell you what: how about this time you stay home and give these pups some lessons? Turn 'em into hunters. Will you do that for the old man?" The hound's tail brushed faster; she looked pleased.

They mounted and headed back to Boone Creek, and that proved to be a mistake. The campground was dead as a deserted house. Soon the lean-to would fall and disappear into the earth. The cottonwoods were almost bare; she remembered them full of green and gold. A gust of wind flung leaves into the fire pit in a dusting of dead ash. Clouds from the north had advanced over half the sky.

"Come along, Miz Frémont," Cummins said unexpectedly. "I'll show you something interesting. It'll take your mind off of—of things."

The creek bed opened onto a plain approaching the river. He reined his horse toward a prominent line of bluffs, and she followed. She heard a killdeer cry.

"We been losing a smart of lambs to a wily old she-wolf," Cummins said.

"She was killing so regular that I figured she had her a den of pups. Probably got a little wild dog in her—a fall litter is unusual for a wolf. I seen her a few times, but she's smart and won't let a dog approach her. Well, I knew that den had to be somewhere hereabouts, and sure enough, Jackson tracked it down with the hounds this morning.

"Here we are," he said, reining up. He helped her down. "See that trail?" He pointed up the face of the bluff. "It's real faint, but that's her lookout trail. A wolf always wants to be able to see a distance."

He gestured toward a low, innocuous boulder partly covered by a bush. "In the bluff right behind that rock, clever put as it can be—you'd never find it without dogs—is her den. You can just make it out. And look what I took out of that den this very morning, after we came back."

She followed him around the rock. There, laid in a row on another low rock, were the bodies of three pups. Their soft, fluffy fur was chocolate brown, their chests white. Their blue eyes were open and sightless. She saw damp marks on their fur.

"Ain't that something to see?" Cummins said.

Jessie could not answer.

Cummins peered more closely. "I declare," he said. "I believe she's been here trying to lick 'em back to life. That won't do her no good. I knocked their heads for sure."

Jessie saw movement in the distance, a pale gray flash turning against the bluff. The wolf was there, watching them; they had interrupted her. She heard Cummins grunt.

"Just out of rifle range," he said. "Knows her way around all right. But here's three little devils that won't grow up to be sheep killers."

Jessie stared at the wolf. It was moving among the boulders below the bluff, appearing and disappearing. It sat down for a moment in the open, deliberately showing itself, and then vanished again. She was waiting for them to leave.

"Pups too little to skin. Too soft, too young. Pelt's no good, you see."

Suddenly Jessie began to shake. "Oh, for God's sake, leave them to her!" she cried.

Cummins' eyes opened wide. He looked confused. "Well, I didn't mean—"

"At least let her mourn them!"

He had her meaning now. His face reddened abruptly. "Now, hold on, Miz Frémont, I'm at no fault for having killed these pups. I'd kill that she-wolf too, if I could get the range on her. She's been taking lambs my Indians depend on for food. Yes, and for what little things of comfort they can buy. Don't you understand?"

"Yes, yes," she said.

But he wouldn't stop. Something in her face had stung him. Her pain was a reproach. "God knows, it's hard enough getting Indians to a settled life after we've taken their lands and forced them to come a thousand miles to start over new. And it's even harder to keep whites hereabouts from coveting their land and euchring 'em out of their poor herds. It's just too damned much, begging your pardon, to have wolves feeding off 'em too. I'll kill every wolf I can find and all her pups as well. Lord! You're a Missouri girl, you must know that!"

Jessie watched him, unblinking. "I know all that," she said. "It's just that some die so much sooner than others." She turned away toward the horses. "Just leave her their bodies, Major. Leave her that consolation. . . ."

The trunk was packed, a nightgown and her robe left out, her brush and comb by the cracked basin under the yellowing mirror. A wicker hamper stood open by the wall, space left in it for the sheets that would come down in the morning. The wind had turned full to the north and it blew damp and chill around the loose window. The twilight was almost gone when she heard the first raindrops spatter on the glass.

They built the fire to a bright blaze and then Jessie sent Sally to her own room. She put on her robe and her rabbit-fur slippers and pulled a chair close to the fire. She tried to think about the morrow's departure and the fearsome journey ahead, the passage to the Isthmus. She should be planning everything, but her mind would not obey. Instead it drifted back to Charles mounted on the gray stallion, the image of the hat string pressed against his strong neck cord. She sighed. Another gust of rain, harder this time, beat on the glass. She was cold. She shook out the big Hudson's Bay point blanket Charles liked and wrapped herself in it. It had his smell; she held its rough fabric against her cheek.

The parting had gone all wrong. She should have sent him off with smiling confidence. Instead she had pressured him into reassuring her. He'd always hated doubts but now it was more than that: he couldn't afford them. He was stretched too thin. He had seen her need and he had spent willingly from his own meager stores. . . .

But she didn't doubt *him.* What, then? Herself, that's what—her own bereft heart, the crushed, empty feeling of the last year. Her old self was gone; she was as different from the girl on C Street as any woman could be. She was swept with losses: Kearny and Bancroft, Stockton and the President, ingratitude and betrayal—*and wasn't some of it her fault? hadn't she compounded it that day in the White House?*—and her baby, innocent as new snow, had paid. . . . They'd all paid—Charles plunging into winter snow, the pain in Mr. T's face after the meeting with Chouteau and the underwriters, her own anguished spirit—but little Benton had paid everything.

She didn't doubt Charles; never had, never would. Why in God's name had she lost control just as he was going? She began to compose a letter, the lines running fluid in her mind. Then she remembered that he already was beyond any post; he would be at Bent's Fort and on into the snow before a letter could reach him. All the way through the mountains he would bear her weakness and she would bear, at sea and across the Panamanian jungle, the knowledge that when he had needed her most she had failed him. The rain beat more steadily, directly from the north. It was beating on him, too, now, somewhere in the open prairie, soaking through his clothes, cold against his skin. She was hardly aware of the tears. They worked slowly down her face and she surrendered to them. They were a last indulgence; in the morning they would have to be gone. But tonight she let them flow and she huddled against the wall, wrapped in the trade blanket, watching the fire die down to coals.

Then she heard the wolf. It was close and she recognized its lament instantly. The sound seemed half-howl, half-moan, full of grief and defiance. The animal was moving, circling, crying against the night. There was a long pause and then the voice came again, much closer, and now she heard a sound of rage woven through grief like steel threads. The younger hounds in the kennel beside the barn began to yap and mew, and suddenly Jessie was frightened. It was as if the animal knew, as if she understood too well. As if she and the wolf were one.

The next call was more distant, but she listened to the bleak grief thrown on the night, distant again and then close, a tireless lament until at last she drifted into sleep.

The dogs awakened her, sounding a purposeful alarm that was dominated by the voice of Cummins' big shepherd. Then she heard horse's hooves and then her husband's voice, loud and high-spirited.

"It's Colonel Frémont, Jackson! I've come a-calling this splendid evening . . ."

For an instant she thought she was dreaming, but she came cleanly awake and heard the horseman sweep around the other end of the building, around Cummins' quarters to the corral, and she knew Jackson had lowered his shotgun. She was up then and calling for Sally and jerked the window open to hear Cummins call, "Is there trouble, Colonel?"

"No, no," Charles answered in the same exuberant voice. "We camped only ten miles out—and it struck me that a ride back would be just the thing. The moonlight was so lovely and bright."

Another gust of rain lashed her face. She heard Cummins laugh, and his reply surprised her.

"You're a born romantic, Colonel—I reckon that's why my wife thinks you're such a marvel."

And in a moment she saw him coming quickly through the corral's back gate, his greatcoat swollen with rain, water streaming off his hat brim. She threw open the door and then he was inside, big as a furry bear, holding her, wetting her robe with his drenched coat. "Oh, darling," she whispered against him, "how nice to have you home."

"Glad to see me?"

"Oh, darling, yes, yes, yes," she said, and felt tears start in her eyes. He hung his coat on its peg by the door and she saw that he was soaked to the skin.

"Out of those clothes," she said. She stripped him naked and tossed him the blanket from the bed. He wrapped himself quickly and lay stretched, male and beautiful, on the bear rug close to the fire. She added two logs and stirred them into flame and heard him sigh, pleased with himself, pleased with everything.

"A wonder horse," he was saying, "a perfect horse. We came ten miles through the blackest night this side of Dante, and he didn't falter once."

"And after he went all day, too," she said.

"Oh, no. I didn't ride him. As soon as I was out of sight, I switched to Weed." Jimson Weed was a rawboned brute, somewhat crazy but inexhaustible.

"Charles Frémont, you devil," she said, "did you know all along you were coming back?"

He grinned. "Well, the thought may have crossed my mind. But I couldn't know until I saw how the day went." They'd found a good place, an oak grove in a draw, ample grass, wood and water. Scott had brought in an elk and they were already talking about buffler. Godey built a lean-to and they'd stretched canvas sheets: everyone was dry tonight. The day had been good too—smooth, steady. Later they would do thirty and forty miles a day, but ten was right at the start. What mattered was that the men had shown an easy, competent air some parties needed a month on the trail to achieve.

"That's why I felt safe in leaving them, tell you the truth. Some men, you wouldn't want to leave 'em on the first night. So it's a good beginning, a good sign. I can go all the way through with these men. I know it. We're not going to have any problems we can't handle."

It was as close as he would come to reassuring her, and it was enough. It was just what she wanted to hear.

"You are a sweet, good man, Charles Frémont."

"You couldn't tell it," he protested. "Hard as I'm treated. I wouldn't have believed I'd be treated so, after riding all night to see you."

"How's that, Charles?"

"Leaving me alone in this blanket. You wouldn't believe how lonely it is in here."

"What shall I do about it?"

"You could come inside it with me."

She pretended to ponder. "Why, I suppose I could—I hadn't thought of it."

He opened his arms and the blanket and she fell slowly against him, moving as he drew the blanket around her.

"Ah, that's ever so much better," he said. He was on an elbow, cradling her. "You know, sweetheart," he said in a different voice, "life is good. It's also hard. It's terribly unfair, too. In spots. You just go on. You look for the good, you bear the bad . . . You know that, don't you?"

"Yes, darling," she said. She felt her heart unlocking. Her head was on his shoulder. Gently she caught his neck cord in her teeth just where the hat string had been; gently she bit down. His hand found her calf under her gown and moved up her flank, the robe and gown slowly lifting with it, until she was naked against him. She could hear his breathing.

"Oh God, Jessie," he murmured close against her throat, and she turned her face and found his mouth and they toppled back on the bear rug and began to laugh, merry as bells. Then she slowly rose to her feet and stood. The fire lighted her body and he stood quickly.

"You're so beautiful," he said, and she heard his voice tremble and they stood pressed together. Then he picked her up in that easy way that always made her feel as if she were flying and swung toward the bed. He eased her gently on the feather pallet and lowered himself beside her; and her arms were around him.

"Ah, Charles Frémont," she whispered, "I needed you so badly. I want you so badly. You can't imagine—"

"Yes I can."

The fire roared, filling the room with heat and light. The rough log walls were golden and she felt as coveted as a princess and swept with love. Rain beat on the window and she knew that the wolf was gone. She was full and afire, she who had been empty and cold, and she cried aloud in rapture that was as sharp as pain and as sweet as honey, and he was telling her what she so needed to hear, his voice a whisper captured in her hair so that it would echo in her heart for all the year to come.

DISASTER

JUST OUTSIDE PUEBLO, Frémont told Vincenthaler to set up camp and then rode on in with Godey and King and Cathcart and Ned Kern. The little trapper settlement clinging to the underside of the mountains was no more than a handful of adobes scattered about as their makers had pleased; a large building with a barn served bravely as general store, hostelry and saloon.

It was cold in the pale sunlight. The very feel of the air against Frémont's face was like a hand raised in warning. Dead ahead of him the Southern Rocky Mountains crowded the near horizon in towering white masses; they had a menacing look—mountains piled upon mountains, whole independent ranges receding into misty infinity . . . They weren't at all like the Sierra, with their single great spine to be breached in one hard rush—and then down to a valley of warm sunshine and lush green things. At Bent's Fort, Tom Fitzpatrick had told him the Indians were expecting a winter worse than any in memory: bears had gone to ground weeks early, squirrel coats were strangely thick, the buffalo herds had pushed far to the south. It was no time to head into the high mountains; Fitz had urged him to wait till spring. But that was out of the question. Frémont needed a guide, and he needed him yesterday.

Broken Hand had insisted that Old Bill Williams was his man: only Antoine Robidoux knew these mountains better, and Robidoux had gone East. Old Bill was wintering in Pueblo, Fitz had said; he'd drunk up his money and more than likely he'd be hungry for work. Frémont grunted—the old coot had led the Third Expedition through this area three years before, and in that ten days Frémont had had more than enough of him. It didn't pay to start a venture as crucial as this one with a man you disliked, but there wasn't anyone else.

Williams opened his door with a surly jerk. "Well, how-de-damn-do, Colonel," he crowed. He was tall, skinny, rope-hard, with a long nose that seemed to point at his chin. "I hear they fucked you around pretty good back East."

"Something like that," Frémont said shortly.

"Tinhorn blue-leg bastards. You should have kicked 'em *all* out, and set up your own private bailiwick, with plenty of beaver and rivers of booze and all the fancy gals coming a-running!" He gave a shrill giggle—*hee-hee*—that Frémont remembered instantly with intense dislike.

Then Williams spotted the jug in Frémont's hand. "You boys come right on in." He spoke in Arapaho to a woman who was cooking, and she produced earthenware mugs. She gave Frémont a shy smile and he saw that she had been very pretty once. Williams filled the mugs, took a huge slug and snorted.

"Waugh!" He gestured them toward benches made of pegged puncheons. "That'll start a fire in the cellar!" He drank again. "What the hell're you boys doing in Puebler?" He had small eyes, shrewd, suspicious, somewhat feral; he was wearing a worn, greasy serape cinched in at the waist with a hackamore of plaited horsehair; his head was covered by a dirty yellow woolen sock whose toe and heel dangled playfully beside his cheek. He smelled powerfully of sweat, whiskey, meat gone ripe.

When Frémont told him, Williams grunted. "Not this winter you ain't." He spoke to the woman, gesturing at Frémont, and she shook her head with a forbidding smile. "This winter is going to be a piss-cutter."

He refilled his cup, his spirits rapidly improving, and began to talk about cold: cold that made him dance a jig to keep alive, cold that made beaver pelts thick as buffler's robes, cold whiskey couldn't cut, cold that had made him so careless he like to have throwed his life away—so cold all he could think of was sleeping it off, and three Blackfoot coming out of the sleet with their arrers cocked . . . Frémont had heard a thousand stories like it: a moment of terrible cold or unbearable heat, hunger or exhaustion, the trapper careless, the Indians waiting . . . Williams' voice had changed.

"What the hell are you up to, young feller?"

Ned Kern had his sketchbook out. In one long stride, Williams pounced on Kern and snatched the book away.

"I don't care for *no* man taking my likeness," he said in a deadly voice. Kern's face was pale. "Indians'll tell you—you can take a man's soul that way and make it your slave, and I don't know but what they're right." He tore off the sheet, tossed it in the fire and handed the book back to Kern. "You put that Goddamn pencil away now, hear?"

Glowering at them, he drank and belched. Gradually his good humor returned. "Them Indians is right smart about these things. You know I started out a Baptist preacher? Couldn't tell it now, eh? But when I went to convert the Osage, they damn well converted me instead. You boys heard about the panstrigrating of souls?" He hacked and spat into the fireplace. "Tell you how I'm coming back—had me a dream wunst of a grand elk, a mighty beast with a white diamond blaze on his forehead. Now when I'm gone under, do you come on such an elk in the high country, I want you to hold your fire, for that'll be me, a-cropping away on the sweet grass with never a whiskey care in the world." He sighed and drank. "Still, you know, when you ponder it all out, Indian faith and Baptist—it don't mix too bad. God looks down on us all, now ain't that right?"

Cathcart was gazing at Williams, fascinated. He'd come all the way from London to hear just such talk, Frémont thought; it was the kind of thing his friend Ruxton's books had caught so well. Alex Godey glanced at Frémont and winked. But Ned was still smarting over the sketch, and Henry King was downright troubled.

"My pappy preached Baptist some," he said, "and he sure never preached anything like that."

"Well," Williams said, "back East with the slickers—likely he hadn't heard of it."

"No," King said sharply. "The Lord's teaching comes out of the Good Book, and there's nothing there about coming back as any beast. That's—hell, that's pure blasphemy."

King had an eager, guileless manner, but when their quartermaster had gone on a toot in California, King had taken over so effectively Frémont had left him in the post. He'd persuaded him to come out again, even though it meant leaving that pretty young bride.

Now, watching warily, Frémont saw Williams give King a look from the edge of his eyes, half-hostile, half-puzzled. Then he said with surprising mildness: "Well, son, when you've talked to God as often as I have, maybe you'll see the light," and before King could answer he'd downed another mouthful of whiskey and was back in his story.

It was a good one—even a connoisseur of wilderness tales would agree; how cold had dulled his senses and left him desperate for a fire; how the three Blackfoot had jumped him and he'd fled; how he'd circled back and tracked them on foot, with no weapon but his knife; how they had filled themselves with meat on the fourth day and fallen asleep . . .

His hand flicked behind him and reappeared with the long, razor-bright steel, point out and flat, the knife fighter's stance, and there wasn't a sound in the room but the bubbling of a pot on the stove.

"I come in soft as a cattymount," he said into the silence, "jammed my sticker into the first one's throat and clamped my hand over his mouth to keep him quiet." All at once he sprang across the room in a long, fluid motion and landed crouched over Cathcart; the knife flashed in a short, bright arc half in inch from Cathcart's handsome face. The Englishman didn't once flinch; his cool gray eyes had narrowed a little, but he was still watching Williams with a bemused half-smile. It was an impressive performance and Old Bill, satisfied with his little test, grinned down at him approvingly, nodding, then completed the pantomime; and they could all see the dying Indian's struggle.

Williams was sixty-one years old and he moved like a boy. Fitz had said he was tough as old strap leather. A loner, he always trapped the most dangerous country, and never a word on where he'd found his beaver, no matter how drunk he got. So, he was saying, he'd killed two Indians and kicked the third one awake to show him their bloody scalps.

Captain Cathcart, still smiling coolly, said: "That's the way Her Majesty's forces did it in India: always leave one of the buggers alive to tell the tale."

"You got it, John Bull. You're all right."

Frémont said suddenly: "We've got work for you, Bill. I want you to guide us over the mountains."

Williams' eyes swiveled toward him over the rim of his cup like gun barrels. "You think I'm getting drunk, young feller. Well, you're right as rain! . . . Only I ain't getting *that* drunk. Not by a long sight!"

Frémont felt a surge of impatience. Deliberately, he said: "You wouldn't be running out of sap, would you?"

Williams glared at him. Then he sighed. "Colonel," he said, "you'd better let me give you a lee-tle guided tour." He took a stick from the fire and began sketching on the table with the burned end.

The Rockies in this neck of the woods consisted of three separate ranges: the Wets, just to the west, were substantial but not difficult to cross. Beyond *them* lay the Sangre de Cristos, which trappers called the Sierra Blanca; they were something else, but they could be breached best through Robidoux's Pass.

And then beyond *them* you ran up against the Rio Grande del Norte. Yes sirree. Williams drew a wavering black line to the west. Now you were spank in the *real* Rockies, with the Continental Divide on ahead and a thousand creeks and canyons running every which way. They were high, dangerous, almost unknown; there you were in *big* trouble. The San Juans were tough old granddaddy mountains. "Maybe they'll open up for you in winter, and maybe they won't."

Williams had another long drink, and drew small X's along a winding line representing the Divide. They stood for three passes. The first was the Pass of the Del Norte; Williams had discovered it himself: it was shortest and most direct, but also the highest and steepest. "You ain't going to put no railroad through *my* pass." *Hee-hee.* Next was Carnero Pass, farther but easier, and then Cochetopa, descending on the far side to Cochetopa Creek, which ran to the Colorado. The Cochetopa was the easiest.

"That's the one we'll take, then," Frémont said.

Williams studied him a moment, drank again and wiped his mustaches. "What you just don't quite grasp, Colonel, is how mean this winter is fixing to be. Folks has got through the Cochetopa in easy years—a few of 'em—but this year even the snowshoe hare'll be in a sling." He nodded confidently. "So I tell you what you do, bucko. Either you hole up till spring; or you run down past Taos, skirt the southern edge of the mountains, and run for California from there."

"No, Goddamn it! I just *told* you—the southern route is no good to me. And we're not waiting, either—the whole idea is to find a winter pass . . ." He glared at the guide, tapping his boot; the old man's obstinacy irritated him. Waiting would double the costs—Christ almighty, Williams ought to sit down with those people in St. Louis if he wanted to learn something about real cold! He *had* to move—he had to get to California, he had to find a route and catch Zachary Taylor's attention *now;* there were a thousand and one things he had to do . . . To his intense surprise, the anger ignited in a flash of real rage and had nothing to do with Old Bill Williams. They had abused him, God damn them to hell, gotten out of him what they wanted and then dropped him, and his child had died and his wife had suffered and it was time to turn things around!

"I am traveling along the Thirty-eighth Parallel," he said grimly, "and we're leaving in one week. Now are you coming with us—or are you fresh out of balls?"

Williams set down his cup with a bang. "Say, who in hell do you think you are, telling what all you'll do in these mountains? These mountains are like Godalmighty Himself, and don't you forget it! You don't tell God nothing, mister—you pray, and you hope He'll see fit to grant! Mountains do all the deciding. Who gets through and who don't!"

Shaken, Frémont said shortly: "There's no mountain that can't be beaten."

"You need a little Goddamned country humility, that's what *you* need!"

Frémont got control of himself again. "Look: you know the ground, you've wintered up there. I've got good men, good stock, good equipment, plenty of supplies."

"Lot of good they'll do you!"

"And I've got good money for guide hire."

Williams' mad little eyes opened wide. "What you paying?"

"Five dollars a day."

"Five dollars! Shit, Colonel, now why didn't you *say* so?" Frémont had never paid Carson more than three. Williams' face turned canny. "You'll have to buy my riding mule, though. Likely enough we'll end up eating him—and the others, too."

"Set a fair price."

Williams emptied his cup again and picked up the jug. "You done bought yourself a guide, Colonel." He uttered his high, whinnying laugh. "Let's drink hearty. No sense wasting it—won't a Goddamned one of us ever get back to finish it off."

In late November the expedition started up Hardscrabble Creek into the Wet Mountains, scouts and hunters ahead and behind, in a long pack line that folded itself against the massive contours of the land. Frémont had calculated carefully with Fitz, and again with Williams: it was about two hundred miles from Hardscrabble over the Continental Divide and down to a valley low enough to promise game and grass. A good party could make it in a week in summer, two in winter; Frémont had allowed four weeks—a full hundred percent margin of safety. He'd swapped their horses for mules, which were stronger and surer of foot, though slower; and sent the big gray, Sacramento, down to Taos with Fitz. The hundred mules would carry, in addition to the baggage and extra food for the men, 130 bushels of shelled corn for their own feed on the heights. It also meant the men would walk from Hardscrabble. . . .

Eighteen days later, more than half their time used up, the corn supply dwindling, they had not yet found an approach to the Continental Divide. Frémont felt a pressure growing behind his eyes. He already had been forced to abandon his plan to use Cochetopa Pass. Now he was far up the narrow canyon of the Rio Grande, climbing steadily into Old Bill Williams' granddaddy mountains, the San Juans, still uncertain of his route.

Everything had gone badly. The snow had been waist-deep when they crossed the Wets at nine thousand feet. Robidoux's Pass had taken three times as long to traverse as expected. And then they had met the murderous wind that scoured the barren sagebrush flats of the valley lying between the Sangre de Cristos and the San Juans. They had camped dry that first night on the flats. Godey had killed two deer, but a sagebrush fire in a wind won't cook and they'd eaten the meat raw. The wind screamed all night and the temperature had fallen to minus twenty. It was killing weather. Frémont had cut blanket strips for the men to wrap about their faces for wind masks. But neither these nor their heavy sheepskin coats, hooded, the fleece turned in, had prepared them for the next day. He started them up the valley but by noon they were near collapse, the mules braying in pain, the men blinded, the flesh on their faces abrading, their hands and feet beginning to freeze. Killing weather. At last he turned them south, away from the Cochetopa, toward the trees visible in the distance along the Rio Grande. The river meant browse, firewood, water, sheltering bluffs—and it meant that now they must aim for Carnero Pass. Williams thought it over and decided that maybe Carnero was superior to Cochetopa, anyway.

But that was small comfort. Frémont had begun to suspect that his guide was half lost. It was a devastating thought—and he thrust it away. None of the men seemed concerned, not even Godey with his sensitive nose for terrain, and Frémont hoped he was just suffering commander's nerves. But Williams didn't act like a man who was confident about the country. The farther west they pushed up the increasingly tight canyon of the Rio Grande, the more morose and silent he became. He'd scout each creek that entered from the north and return in an hour or two with his face a little longer to say still again: "We'll go on upriver a ways."

The difficult Pass of the Del Norte, which Williams had discovered, was up ahead. The abandoned Cochetopa was now far to the north. Carnero lay somewhere between the two. The problem was to find the passage that would lead to the Pass, and not into some deadly maze—and to find it while there was still time to use it.

Of course, the equation that calculated the days of life left the mules was not entirely precise. There had been occasional grass in the windswept places, and each mule they lost became a kind of negative advantage—its absence left more corn for the others and its carcass provided meat for the men. Frémont already had reduced the corn ration, but that reduced the animals' strength and made them more vulnerable to the cold. The harsh fact was that he had about ten days left to get over those mountains and find grass. Sometime after that—soon after that—his mules would begin to die.

They were camped in an alder grove where a creek entered from the north. It was near dark when Williams came out of the narrow canyon.

"This is it," he said. "We turn up here."

This way? Frémont tried to feel elated. The canyon looked narrow and steep, as bad as they'd seen.

"It'll get better," Williams said. "It straightens out after a while. It's Robidoux's old road." Trappers called whatever route they used a road; it didn't mean that it was improved or blazed.

The river muttered at Frémont's feet. The mules had found a little browse and were stamping through snow to clear it. Somewhere at a distance a tree split in the cold with a sound like a gunshot. Frémont studied Williams' face; it showed none of the relief and pleasure you would expect in a man who had found the way. His shrewd little eyes were narrowed to cracks. He had taken to wearing for headgear a piece of orange blanket with the corners sewed into points like a wolf's ears; he had the aspect of some mad tribal shaman—half animal, half human.

"What do you think?" Frémont said to Godey.

The guide scowled, but Alex said easily, "Bill can read this country. We'll be all right."

"I sure as hell ain't going to go looking for another route when I already know the right one," Williams said. He felt challenged, and that made him dogmatic; but Frémont knew that he was still unsure. "If you don't trust me, why don't you get yourself another guide?"

They were a hundred twenty-five miles from Hardscrabble. Godey said quickly: "Don't you go threatening us, Bill."

"I didn't mean it that way a'tall," Williams said. "But if I'm guiding, then *I* say how we go. You want some other road, you find it on your own. That just stands to reason."

"All right," Frémont said. "We'll take your road."

" 'Tain't mine—it's Robidoux's. But it's the right one."

The first sun came rocketing up the canyon in the morning. It made the dark cleft that was the creek opening look ominous as a bear cave. Williams finished a bowl of mule-meat stew, wiped his hands on his wool pants and started up without a word, Godey behind him.

Ned Kern was cinching his last mule. Watching Williams over his shoulder, he said, "If that's Robidoux's Road, I'd hate to see the ones he rejected."

"It looks so—so closed," added Doc Kern, glancing uneasily at Ned. Frémont had welcomed having a physician along, but there had been no illnesses, and despite his brother's coaching, Doc seemed unable or unwilling to learn.

"It'll be like a staircase, Doc," said Carver, who'd been bouncy when they started. "Just imagine you're creeping up the attic stairs to the parlormaid's room—that oughta warm you up. Right, Colonel?"

Frémont grinned: they were still intact.

Vincenthaler cinched the last mule tight and tossed the lead line to Carver. "Shake it up!" he said. "I want to get over that damned mountain and line up some elk meat."

The canyon turned left, right, left again; it might have been chopped from the earth by a cosmic axman. The column moved single file, and Frémont ranged its length, checking, encouraging, lending a hand in the tight places. He saw no birds or game tracks in the snow, heard no sound but that of water running under ice and the mules grunting and stamping. Blood smeared the rock edges where men or animals had fallen. Once he found Proue on his knees nursing a cut cheekbone. It made him think of a tavern brawl in Westport that Raffie and Freniere had started, and he said, "How'd the other fellow look?"

"I wish there *was* another fellow," Raffie said without smiling. "I'd kick the living shit out of him." He had changed vastly since they'd lost Louie; he'd stuck close to Frémont through California, but there had been something resentful in him, like a man who felt tricked and didn't know what to do about it. The happy-go-lucky spirit of the Oregon Trail had never returned.

The way seemed steeper. The *voyageurs,* Tabeau and Morin, posted themselves at a bad place and helped the mules past, shouting and popping short ropes. They were solid veterans in their late forties, still strong and very experienced, and Frémont knew that he could rely on them. He stopped to talk with them in French, which always pleased them.

They made only three miles and camped in a small aspen flat. Vincenthaler doled out corn from the shrinking supply. It wasn't nearly enough. The mules gnawed at tree bark, which was worthless, and Frémont saw them biting each other's manes and tails. Another had failed on the trail, but that was a mixed blessing, for mule meat was a lean diet and now diarrhea was endemic. He had the sense that all the lines were converging—time, weather, distance, corn, strength of flesh and spirit—and he was trying to slip through before they met.

Karl Preuss was bracing the barometers against a lodgepole pine. His terrain sketchbook was jammed in the pocket of his coat. He hadn't changed a bit, Frémont thought—he was full of querulous complaint when things were good, high spirited when they were bad. Just under nine thousand feet, he announced with a smile, temperature just above zero.

Williams came in after dark from up ahead and didn't have much to say. The canyon had opened slightly, the fir and blue spruce standing with branches snowy and interlocked wherever soil had collected among the rock. But the rock edges were just as cruel, and now the men knew it wouldn't get any better. No one spoke to Williams.

"This isn't Robidoux's Road," Frémont said quietly to Godey. "One whole day to make three miles? No one would come this way willingly."

Godey agreed, but he thought the old mountain man's instinct for direction and terrain would prove out: Williams had stayed alive a long time. "He maybe got confused on the canyon, but I expect he's headed right."

Frémont went to sleep listening to the mules moan and chatter with hunger and Andrews cough in his sleep. Andrews was a slender young midshipman just out of the Navy; he was a navigator and at first had been fascinated by the charting process. Since leaving Hardscabble, though, he had grown increasingly quiet as his cough became more violent. Looking at his flushed face one day, Frémont had realized that the man was tubercular, westbound in hopes of a cure. Doc Kern had recognized the signs, too; but there was nothing in Doc's medicine kit that would help Andrews.

The snow in the canyon's channel grew steadily deeper: four feet, six, drifts to twenty. Too much snow, Williams said, more than he could remember, the winter's promise proving out. And too deep for mules: Godey led them up the slopes, searching for ground that was too steep to hold much snow and yet negotiable. As the canyon turned, the open side often steepened into cliff while the other side shallowed out. Then they had to maul a path down to the frozen creek and work their way back up the other side. The men hated these crossings; someone was sure to get wet, and then frozen feet were an immediate and deadly danger.

Frémont heard shouting and hurried to the head of the column, to find that Ned Kern had led four mules too far onto an icy slope that turned a corner and abruptly became a cliff.

"Goddamnit, Ned," Godey bawled from the far side, "I *told* you to come down and cross over!"

"Thought I could get through, Colonel," Kern called, ignoring Godey. He was trying to calm his mules as he backed them, but the two in the rear were alarmed and fractious. One bit the other's rump and then both lost their footing and slid down the slope. The first went safely into deep snow but the other struck a boulder. Its leg broke with a loud snap and it trumpeted shrilly.

Vincenthaler had come up and was watching. "You stupid son of a bitch!" he shouted.

"You watch your Goddamn mouth," Kern cried. He and Vincenthaler had had trouble at Sutter's and it still lay between them.

"That's enough, now," Frémont said; the sound of his voice cut them short. Henry King lunged through snow to the floundering mule and worked it back to solid ground. Vincenthaler called up the mauls to beat a path down and across the creek.

"Come on, Beady," George Hubbard said to Ben Beadle, "Let's make meat before that son of a bitch freezes stiff." They cut the injured mule's throat and began to butcher it; Beadle cursed when his knife slipped and cut his hand, but he continued to work.

Proue started down the tamped path and his first mule broke through the ice. It stumbled and Proue put his shoulder under it; all at once his legs buckled and the mule fell on top of him. Frémont darted forward, but Proue squirmed free and stood trembling, drenched in icy water.

"What the hell, Raffie?" Frémont said.

Proue looked puzzled. "M'damn legs give out," he said slowly. "Never had that happen before."

Breckenridge had a fire ready and a supply of deadwood which he chopped to size with clean, steady ax strokes. They helped Proue out of his wet clothes and hung them on sticks to dry over the fire. As Proue wrapped himself in a blanket, Henry King stepped into the water to guide the mules across.

He was laughing, his teeth chattering, slapping his hands together. "Keep 'em coming," he sang, "keep 'em coming! My legs feel like they're gonna bust right off." But his hand on the mules meant that the rest of the men could cross on unbroken ice, remain dry and continue up the canyon.

When the last mule was through, King could scarcely walk. Frémont and Breckenridge helped him to the fire and stripped his pants and moccasins.

"Next time I'll build the fire, Tom," King gasped, "and *you* jump in the creek."

Up above, Frémont found Cathcart rigging lines from a big lodgepole pine to guy the mules past a steep place.

"A little trick we learned in the Himalayas," Cathcart said. He was a good man, Frémont thought, cool and unflappable. He had come along as a sportsman, supplying his own kit and taking no pay, but he was willing to work and he knew how to get things done.

At midafternoon on the third day off the Rio Grande the canyon belled out at the top. The last trees, limber pines gnarled by life on this frontier, ended abruptly. This was timberline, the top of the world, opening up at twelve thousand feet, and it gave Frémont a giddy sense of freedom and then, almost instantly, of vulnerability. A broad, flat-topped mountain rose before them, unmarked but for the wind whorls in its snow; in his mind's eye he could see himself and his men—tiny specks on the edge of this glittering white universe. An evil wind curled around the flank of the flat mountain. The mules huddled together with their heads down, whispering and complaining. Vincenthaler gave them a corn ration; about two quarts per animal remained. Some seventy mules had made it this far.

Frémont worked his way to the end of the flat-topped mountain with Godey and Williams, driving against that wind. It had a distant sound; the scuffing of their snowshoes was near and personal. A long, treeless swale of about three miles came into view, and ran up to a saddle in a ridge well above them.

"There it is," Williams said. His voice was hoarse; it had been a long time since Frémont had heard his raucous giggle.

"You mean the pass. Carnero?"

"Well—or right on beyond." He hesitated. "But that's the way, all right." He stood staring at the ridge, his eyes squinted.

"Well, is it or isn't it?" Frémont snapped.

Williams turned on him. "God damn you," he cried, "you think there's any man knows every foot of these mountains? Shit, no—we know *directions,* that's what. Over yonder, on a bit, that'll be Carnero. You'll see." Angrily he started back toward camp.

"He doesn't know where the hell we are," Frémont said.

"I wish I'd kept my mouth shut, down below," Godey said somberly, "Don't know what we do now."

"Do? What else? We keep doing."

In the morning they started mauling toward the ridge. The old pain began in Frémont's hips and moved up his body. Well, they'd gotten over the Sierras. All right: this was worse, much worse—higher, colder, farther, and dear God, so uncertain—but they'd made it before: don't forget that. He forced himself to maul on. Fitz had faith in Williams. So did Kit. And Godey was right—that the crazy old bastard was still alive was a testament to something. Maybe he had a feel for ground, as Louie'd had for buffalo.

Frémont refused to think about the pain—maybe Williams' sense of terrain was accurate after all, and over the ridge they would find—

He went to his knees, swept with vertigo, his arms numb, the wind driven out of him; someone else took the maul. Dark was falling when they stopped five hundred feet short of the ridge, to camp in the head of a timbered draw. The trees were limber pine but for a single massive white fir, oddly out of place; *White Fir Camp,* Frémont dated his journal that night. Five more mules were down. Now the poor brutes gnawed at ropes and straps, and snatched at each other's manes and tails while trying to protect their own. Whimpering, they tried to eat the blankets on sleeping men.

In the morning it was snowing, the sky dark and low, the flurries driven on a whipping, changeable wind. Frémont looked back along the trail they had cut the day before and then up at the ridge. Spots kept floating before his eyes and he had to stop from time to time to breathe; he realized his nose had begun to bleed. Once over the crest they would know; perhaps Carnero would be just beyond, a gentle saddle leading up to it—perhaps they'd be over by afternoon! Over and probing down its far flank for grass and game and rest. . . .

Near the crest, the wind grew harder, the snow heavier. As he came over the ridge, Frémont realized they had seen only spillover from the real storm that boiled against the top of the mountain. Now the wind roared and buffeted and blasted down until the very air turned milky. Filled with wonder and horror, he stumbled forward. Carnero might be right there, but he was blind. The wind staggered him, threw him down. Distantly he heard cries—men down, mules loose and falling, one animal trying helplessly to crawl back over the ridge.

Williams loomed beside him and shouted, the words faint in the wind. "Gonna take a look-see." He slipped a mule's pack, forked himself into its back, set off to the right and immediately disappeared. Frémont wondered idly if they would see him again.

He saw Kern on his knees, holding his face in both hands. "Get up, Ned," Frémont shouted. Kern didn't move. "Get up, God damn you!" he shouted, and kicked him hard. Slowly Kern started getting up, a man in a painful dream. Breckenridge appeared beside them, caught Kern around the body and lifted him. Frémont heard shrill cries over the storm's roar and realized the mules were screaming in despair. Beadle was down, the blanket strips unpeeled from his face, Andrews was down. Proue—good old Proue, who had buried Louie that dawn near Klamath Lake, and then paid the blood debt among the blazing huts—was still crawling forward; Raffie would follow him into hell and out the other side.

Neither men nor mules could survive an hour here in the open. Nothing living could. Frémont collided with Godey, seized his arm. *"Go—back!"* he yelled. "Start them back." He stumbled around the ridge, waving men back toward the last camp, sanctuary in timber. Williams' mule came out of the gloom then, like an apparition, the old man clinging to its neck, unconscious and half-frozen.

Six mules died on the ridge, but Frémont got the party off and back to

White Fir Camp. By a fire at last, he felt blinding waves of pain in his hands and face: frostbite. He saw Doc Kern whimpering to himself. Men went from fire to fire, too agonized to remain still, wringing and beating their hands, tears streaking down their faces. Frémont told Vincenthaler to give the mules their final ration of corn. Not many days were left.

The next morning was like spring—sunny, wind fallen, temperature at twenty degrees. Now, at last, he would know. Frémont tried on his snowshoes. His hands were shaking, his fingers clumsy on the rawhide. With Godey and Williams he swept up the slope, moving swiftly in the soft air.

As they broke the crest, an incredible panorama opened before them. The ground fell off and a mile ahead Frémont saw a draw in which timber grew. Beyond that lay a vast stretch of open ground, great sparkling snowfields far above timberline that would have to be mauled, gaping chasms that would have to be descended and reclimbed, ridges on ridges of glowing ice. It ran on and on—and then in the distance it reared into a chain of mountains awesomely, fearfully higher, two thousand feet higher, than where they now stood. In an instant Frémont realized that was the main spine, the Continental Divide, the great challenge, the place of the crucial passes—Merciful God and *it was twenty miles away. . . .*

He saw Godey cross himself, heard him whisper, "Hail Mary, full of grace—"

Williams' voice was a croak. "Little farther than I figured, but it's right over yonder. Ten miles, I reckon."

"Twenty," Frémont bit off. He couldn't manage another word.

"Less'n that. And it's downhill, lots of it, see. Timber, probably some grass. Game maybe. We'll rest up and then try the pass."

Old fool! Frémont had a wild, ungovernable impulse to kill him—pull his pistol and shoot him down, right here—in the snow. He clenched his hands in a spasm.

The Kern brothers came onto the ridge on the lead maul. They stopped and stared.

"Oh, my God," Doc cried. "We're done for! We'll never get over that." He didn't even seem aware of Frémont's presence. "Ned, Ned, what are we gonna *do*?"

Ned flashed a murderous glance at Frémont, looked away. The others came onto the crest then. King, Stepp, Hubbard, Beadle, all staring in silence, faces blank with shock, Proue looking as if he were somewhere else, Cathcart without a trace of his charming hussar's smile; Tabeau was murmuring something to Morin in French, Preuss had his old look of sardonic amusement. All at once they began to babble, curses and prayers and lamentations intermingled.

Frémont shouted harshly: "All right! We camp in that timbered draw, there. . . . Move on, now!"

Tabeau and Morin took the lead. Frémont walked along the column, trying to talk them calm. "It looks rougher than it is," he kept saying. "Downhill for a bit, then up and over. Hell, boys, we're halfway to California . . ." No one answered him. Cathcart nodded at him mutely; he saw Carver's quick, bright eyes fastened on his with a stark, importunate intensity—a look he remembered from the Sierra crossing, and Hawk's Peak. Fear was clutching at their throats; he fought off its clammy touch. Would they turn on him, and flee? Intuitively he knew they wouldn't if he kept his own courage. Faith in him was all that they had left. "I tell you, we're halfway to California," he repeated.

Williams went scouting down the draw on one of his look-sees. He was back in three hours. "Gets a little tight, but we kin make it. Then we'll swing over to the next creek, and the next—we'll get there all right."

"Any grass?"

"Didn't see none. On up ahead, I expect." He moved off without meeting Frémont's eyes.

The temperature was down in the morning. They broke camp, started down the draw and had made a half-mile when heavy clouds coming out of the west on a hard wind blotted out the sun. It was like a suddenly drawn curtain. The air turned immediately colder. The draw shelved suddenly—and he saw a cloud slipping toward them, an advancing wall that blotted out the ground behind it.

It enveloped them with a roar. Frémont had a sudden sense that the mountain had lifted them into the heavens where men didn't belong, where all the dimensions of wind, cold, snow, violence were scaled to the gods. In the gloom and whirling snow he could see barely a dozen feet. Things crashed at him from every direction; he was knocked sprawling. He thought a man had hit him and rolled over to meet an attack, but there was no one near him. He saw two mules crumple at the forelegs as though scythed. He got up, staggering, and pulled the nearest man erect, saw it was Godey.

"Go—back!" he screamed. The wind seemed to shred his words. "Back to—last camp! Get 'em turned around . . ."

He found Cathcart trying to raise a fallen mule. Both of them kicked the animal's ribs and thrust their shoulders under its shaggy sides, and it managed to stand, swaying, its legs shaking terribly.

"Head back!" he yelled in Cathcart's ear, pointing. His words emerged as mumbles. He realized his face covering had unwrapped. His face was freezing. He rewound the blanket strips, staggered to another man who was down and kicked him hard in the rump. It was Beadle, completely ignorant of where he was.

"Get up!" Frémont bellowed. "God damn you, get up and go back!"

Vincenthaler loomed up beside him. "Boys're turning around, Colonel."

"Mules can't live in this!" Frémont shouted. "Nobody can. . . ."

Vincenthaler disappeared in the gloom. Frémont ranged in a circle. He found three mules down, motionless, probably already dead. He started back, bringing up the rear, and almost fell over Andrews. The midshipman was on his hands and knees, coughing hard; Frémont saw a crimson spray on the snow. He tried to lift Andrews, and the wind drove them both down. He got his arms around his thin body, lifted him again, held him like a child against his chest until the spasm ended, and led him stumbling back.

The fires were up when he got in. Godey ran a head count and reported everyone present.

"We got between forty and fifty left," Vincenthaler said. He had been with the mules. The storm blatted crazily about their heads. Vincenthaler's voice sounded oddly far away. He'd taken the packsaddles off, stored the baggage under tied tarps. "I don't know how long they'll last."

At last Frémont could fall shudderingly by a fire, his hands and face pulsing with pain. The fires were sinking into the sheltering fire holes, casting nightmare shadows against the snow. Williams and King were in one with Preuss and Creutzfeldt; Cathcart shared one with the Kerns, Andrews and a few others; Vincenthaler had a group by his fire—the stronger men seemed to gather around him. Frémont checked them: none were crippled, though all were frostbitten and in pain.

They were seven days off the Rio Grande.

The storm raged unbroken all that day and the next, and the mules began to die in the drifting snow amidst the limber pines. There was no helping them. They stood with their heads down, moaning, too weak to gnaw bark. Frémont was watching when one raised its head; it brayed, a weak, quavering noise, and tottered away from the others. Its barrel contracted suddenly, arching in a spasm, and then it toppled sideways on stiff legs, its heart already stopped. That night more than half the remaining mules died.

On the morning of the tenth day off the Rio Grande, the last mules were dead. The men huddled by the fires, motionless, waiting for nothing. They didn't talk, didn't even look at Frémont any longer; their faith had flown away on the cold and the wind, sunk deep in the snow with the dead mules. They were past panic now, beyond mere fear; they crouched close to the all-succoring fires, locked in suffering and despair.

The storm stopped. The clouds dissipated and the sun was brilliant; the very cold seemed to glitter and crackle. It was well below zero; it might be so for days. Frémont sat staring into his fire, facing the incontrovertible fact. The mountain had won. It had killed the mules. It had destroyed their dreams. It had broken their will. Now it was ready to kill them.

"All right, boys," he said. His voice sounded like some other, different man's. "We've had enough. We're going back. —Back over the ridge, down to the river."

Slowly, like men too near death to think, they began to creep out of their holes and breast the fresh snow, while he watched them hollowly.

Action had failed him. All his life he had believed that if you drove ahead, you won. If you were forceful and resolute and utterly refused failure, you conquered. And here he was beaten, broken, his dreams in ashes; a tiny two-legged organism trapped in a pitiless wilderness of ice. The men in St. Louis flashed into his mind, impassive, coldly accusing. And then a thought he'd never once entertained: had his luck turned fatally with Kearny and that damned court-martial? Was his lifelong conviction about his destiny no more than a capricious roll of the dice?—was it all simply a gambler's streak, a run of the cards that now, malignantly, had decided to turn against him?

And what would he say to Jessie now?

SANGRE DE CRISTO

GET OFF. That was the only issue. Get off this part of the mountain where the gods ruled. An overwhelming urgency goaded him—if the weather crashed down again, locked them to their fires again, they might never get away. So move—get back over the intervening ridge and down to White Fir Camp—just that far would return them to the comfort of territory that was scaled to men. And then they would hurry on, down that dreary canyon, down to the certainty of the Rio Grande. . . .

He forced himself to organize things. Half the men would haul baggage, half would butcher the mule carcasses for which Vincenthaler and Godey were probing in the snow. Get them started: they would have to carry what the mules had carried. And there wasn't one minute to spare.

They made pack straps out of harnesses. Ned Kern lifted fifty pounds, took a few staggering steps, got his balance, and started toward the ridge and the camp below it. Henry Wise took one step under load and fell with an agonizing cry. Frémont inspected his feet and found that the misnamed fool had let them freeze; his toes were black; the soles were separating from the pulpy undersides. He'd lose those toes, but in the meantime he'd walk; and if he couldn't walk, crawl. Frémont watched Raffie and the *voyageurs* raise their loads on trembling legs; even his stalwarts were running down on this diet of lean mule meat and terror. But they were moving; Frémont had faith in a moving man.

Vincenthaler had shoveled down to a carcass, a set, determined expression on his face, his breath frosting in a wet cloud. The temperature was still below zero but there was no wind. When the carcass was cleared, Vincenthaler called Hubbard and Beadle to help him butcher. Frémont decided to work with them and dropped into the hole, which now was four feet deep. King and Rohrer followed him. A flour miller who lived near King in Georgtown, Rohrer had a sustaining belief that an expert mechanic would make a fortune in California.

Vincenthaler shouted toward the fires: "You, Wise, get over here and cut meat. If you can't haul, you can cut, Goddamnit." He chopped the frozen carcass apart with a sound like an ax against oak. His exertions in the thin, cold air made him gasp. King and Rohrer rolled the carcass over and disembowled it. The men worked on their knees with knives, grunting and growling with pain. Frémont's left leg began to ache, and he chafed it absently. A small cloud slid over the sun. Hubbard looked up in instant alarm.

"Jesus!" he cried. "More snow?"

The cloud passed over swiftly but it had tipped Hubbard's mood; he threw down his knife.

"Shit!" he said. "We got plenty of meat."

"That's right," Beadle agreed. "We been cutting up mules fast as they died for three days."

"We ain't got no meat problem."

They looked alike and now they sounded alike; Frémont heard the whine of real panic in their voices. Their faces were sunken, their eyes hollow and shifting. The mountain was wearing everyone down.

"You give me a pain in the ass," Vincenthaler said, too fiercely, as if they had touched something in him that he didn't like. "Talking like old women."

"Oh, yeah?" Hubbard cried.

"Easy, boys," Frémont said. "We need all the meat we can find. Then we'll haul our gear off the heights and get going. We'll be all right."

"Not if that damned cloud means more snow," Beadle said.

"Damned right." Hubbard glanced sideways at Vincenthaler. "We ought to get the hell out of here."

"Run for it," Beadle said eagerly. "Get off this fucking mountain . . ."

Rohrer stopped working. "I think they're right," he said in a low voice. He was the first man to look at Frémont. "Maybe we ought to run while we still can."

"But we can't—run," Wise said in alarm. "I can't move too fast. You wouldn't leave me, would you, Colonel?"

"Come on," King said. "Nobody's running anywhere. You won't get left."

"You men pull yourselves together, now," Frémont told them sharply. "We'll get down to the river all right. But we still have to eat when we get there."

"But what'll we do *then,* Colonel?" Rohrer whispered.

Frémont stared at him. He hadn't thought of what came next. It was a hundred sixty miles to Taos. Thirty miles this side of Taos was a settlement of sorts—there might be help there. But they couldn't make that distance. They couldn't carry enough food on their backs—and tools, weapons, blankets—to see them through. Without livestock, they were in almost as much peril on the river as they were here. *He hadn't thought . . .*

They'd read his face. "We're trapped, ain't we?" Beadle cried shrilly. "Don't matter how much meat we cut—we can't get out anyways!"

"Ah, Jesus," Hubbard moaned.

Frémont saw Vincenthaler and King watching him, waiting.

"Shut up!" he said coldly. "What's the matter with you? We need all the meat we can salvage—because as soon as we're over the ridge and set up in White Fir Camp, I'm sending out a relief party."

The logical answer had just popped out of him—but why hadn't he planned it, announced it? Why had he needed their panic to jolt his mind into the obvious? The lapse alarmed him deeply—was he losing control?—of the expedition, of himself? Suddenly he saw himself as no different from Hubbard and Beadle—whining and desperate to get off this terrible mountain, with never a thought of what came next. He willed his voice steady and set out a logical plan: a small party traveling light could go fast enough to get through—and in two weeks they'd be back with twenty mule loads of beans and bacon.

"We ought to—*all* of us get out," Hubbard said stubbornly.

"No," King said. "Colonel's right. A few strong men moving fast will make it. Big party's too slow. Too much to carry." He glanced at Wise. "Some couldn't keep up. What would you do then?"

"Leave 'em," Hubbard said.

"And suppose you was the one to get left?" King retorted.

"Now, that's enough of that, Hubbard," Frémont told him. "A relief party'll be back in no time. With plenty of food. So let's get to work—now is what counts; later will take care of itself."

On that note he went off to check on the others. He was painfully conscious of having lost control of things, his mind paralyzed by this uncaring immensity the gods alone ruled. It left him with a feeling he knew he'd remember. But the quarrel had freed him; immediately a new idea burst forth: the relief party could change everything. Maybe they could go ahead after all—*maybe he wasn't beaten!*

The details fell swiftly into place. First, get the men into a good camp on the Rio Grande. The relief party would return with ample food, even a few luxuries—sugar, coffee, plenty of flour, tinned fish if it could be found. Then, while they fed up and rested for two or three weeks, he and Godey would ride down to Taos on the relief mules. There he would load a hundred fresh mules with ample new supplies—and if those tight-fisted buzzards back in St. Louis complained, to hell with them. He would talk over his route problems with Kit in Taos and then he'd come upriver with the new pack train, and this time he and Alex would locate the right pass, wait for the right weather and push through to California with a serviceable railroad route in hand. And Bill Williams could go to hell in a handcart. He turned the idea over, liking it better and better. By God, he hadn't failed yet!

The new plan buoyed the men, even as the labor of ferrying the equipment back over that ridge at twelve thousand feet reduced them; Frémont could see them deteriorate from day to day, growing more gaunt, moving more slowly, falling more often. He decided that when he went down to Taos on the relief mules he would take the worst of them with him—Wise, Andrews, perhaps one or two others.

He put Henry King in command of the relief party. Despite the hardships of the past month, King hadn't lost that youthful strength and spirit. He would never give up; he would drive the group if necessary, but he would get them through. King was a natural quartermaster. He began making lists—new mocassins, a small keg of whiskey, soap, a firkin of marmalade if he could locate one. He would hire a half-dozen fresh hands to speed the return.

They agreed that a strong party should make a hundred thirty miles on flat terrain in less than a week—and the return trip on mules in four days, maybe five. Call it two weeks to be on the safe side, and add two more days for margin.

"So," Frémont said, "if you're not back at nightfall on the sixteenth day, I'll take it that something's gone wrong."

"We'll be back, Colonel." King hesitated. "Keep an eye on Willy Rohrer, will you?—he don't look so good. He's got a family, you know, five or six kids. I could've been doing something else when I talked him into coming along."

Frémont worked out the rest of the party with King. Four men, he decided; small enough to move rapidly, big enough to support each other in trouble. He decided on Tom Breckenridge, always strong and willing. Then he chose the botanist, Frederick Creutzfeldt, who had stood up well physically. Scientific training had given a steady, practical cast to his mind that might be very useful. The fourth man . . . the fourth man would have to be Old Bill Williams.

The guide had been out searching for a better route down. The new canyon was a little longer, he said, but considerably easier. There was no more talk of Robidoux's Road.

"You understand," Frémont said, "everything depends on your not getting turned off the most direct route." He could hear his voice get an edge in it every time he spoke to Williams.

"Well, hell," Williams answered brightly, "can't *miss* when you're following the river, now can you?"

God, Frémont thought, how he hated the crazy old bastard with his loony antics and his phony poses. How he hated him! Williams seemed to read the thought, for he smiled ingratiatingly and said, "Look, Colonel, this didn't maybe turn out as good as expected, but now I got the lay of it. The *winter* is what turned us back, and I give you fair warning of that, didn't I? Any other year, we could've made it in a breeze. Now I'll admit it ain't the easiest route, but it would have worked." Frémont did not trust himself to speak. He read the change in Williams' manner: the coony old son of a bitch didn't want it spread all over Taos that he'd lost his way in the snow. "But anyway, now I got it all straight. Now I seen it from up here—why, hell, whenever you say the word I can take you right to the pass. Can't miss. . . . Don't you fret about a single thing."

Frémont turned away with his fists clenched, wishing with all his heart it wasn't so infernally easy to kill somebody in this godforsaken wilderness, and thanking God Himself that the opinionated old imbecile would be out of his sight for a while.

Next day he started down to the Rio Grande to set up the haven camp, where the men would recuperate for a new assault. This canyon was straighter and more open—a great improvement over the tortuous route of their ascent—but it emptied onto a dangerously unprotected flat. From the mouth of the canyon the stream meandered to the river through what proved to be six miles of frozen marsh and meadow with only occasional stands of trees. The combination of an easy canyon and the open flat made good traveling now, even with heavy loads; but in a storm the wind would be deadly here. All the more reason to hurry.

He located the camp in a tight bend, with a sheltering bluff on one side; on the other he built a windbreak of fir branches, which would become a snow fence after the first storm. The camp would be as protected as an uncovered camp could be, and it had ample water and wood; with fresh supplies the men should be fairly comfortable here.

Back in the canyon he found them staggering under their loads all along its length; they looked measurably more worn and answered him in monosyllables. That day the temperature began to fall, and soon clouds as hard as gunmetal were blowing over in great trains out of the west. There was still baggage at White Fir Camp, and Frémont drove the men hard, packing along with them. They strained under the heavy loads, groaning in pain, crying out when they fell, their faces set in sullen lines. The air took on a heavy, gray, menacing quality. But still the weather held—five days, six days, seven since the relief party had gone out, and the weather didn't break.

When it was nearly dark on the seventh day, Frémont and Godey set down their loads in Vincenthaler's relay camp, midway down the canyon. There were three fires, now deep in their melt holes. In the nearest, Carver was crouched over a pot of boiling mule meat. His buoyant, chirpy manner was gone; the skin was tightly drawn over his wide face, which gave him a mean, apprehensive look in the firelight; his lips were cracked and bloody. The other men in the hole moved to make room; no one spoke. Frémont saw that Cathcart was chewing at the inside of his mouth, as if to bite back some violent rejoinder; the Kern brothers wore a surly, embattled look, two against the world. Raffie Proue had a blanket drawn over his shoulders to his eyes and Andrews was half-lying on the fir boughs that covered the ice on the hole's floor.

His mind fixed on his hunger, the compelling odor of cooking meat, Frémont said: "How you boys doing?"

"Getting mighty hard, Colonel," Ned Kern answered in slurred tones.

"Keep falling down," Carver said.

"Goddamn ice. Fall and it messes up your hands."

"Right—hands're no good no more."

Silence. Bloodshot eyes met, locked, wavered away again. The wind hissed in the firs overhead.

"Shit," Kern said, "how come the damn meat ain't ready, Carver?"

"Because it takes time to cook, Goddamnit!"

"Should've started it earlier, then."

"Would've," Carver said angrily, "if I hadn't had to dig Raffie out of the snow. I come on him halfway down—floundering on his face like a beetle flipped on its back. He'd be there yet if I hadn't got him out."

Frémont looked at Proue. "Couldn't you get your pack off, Raffie?"

"Funny," Proue said dully, "I didn't even think of that. M' hands're bad, but it wasn't that. Truth is I didn't much give a shit, one way or the other."

"That ain't right, Raffie," Godey told him quietly. "Ain't right to think that way."

Proue made no answer. He still looked as if he'd been stunned by a blow to his head. Frémont thought of the time at Sutter's when Raffie had supported eight one-hundred-pound bags of wheat on his back while Louie, who had set it all up and lured the suckers in, collected more than fifty dollars. Doubtless great strength required more fuel; he wondered distantly if that made a big man more vulnerable.

"Well, Carver," said Taplin, who had just joined them, "you ain't got much to say. *You* fell in that snowbank so deep I had to dig for you like we dug for them mule carcasses."

A dark look crossed Carver's face. "Scared me shitless," he said. He turned to Frémont. "I was on this rock, see, had the snowshoes off, and I stepped onto a snowbank, and Jesus!—I went straight down. Over my head! I must've stepped off a cliff or something—I thought I was gonna go all the way down. Snow over my head!"

"I heard him yelling," Taplin said. "Took a shovel to get him out."

"Warning," Carver said with the same dark look. "Like it's a warning. You know? Solid rock one minute, buried in snow and ready to die the next—maybe it's a message."

"Oh, for Christ's sake," Kern said.

Without warning, Andrews began to cough. He sat bolt upright, his blanket fell away and he bent forward, both hands pressed to his chest, the spasm shaking him like a scarecrow. The men stared at him. He looked up as if to reassure them, and the paroxysm seized him again. There was bright fresh blood on his lips, the blanket.

"God damn you," Carver cried in sudden rage, "you got the consumption, don't you? What the hell you *doing* up here?"

Andrews looked around the circle with a frightened, eager expression; death shone in his face. All of them wanted him out of their sight.

"Leave him alone," Doc Kern said with an effort. "Often a man doesn't know he has a problem till it acts up."

"Why the hell don't he go to some other fire?" Carver demanded.

"Shut up!" Ned Kern told him savagely. "The kid's sick, he can't help it. You don't like it, why don't you haul your ass off your ownself?"

" 'Cause this is *my* fire!"

"The hell it is." To Andrews, who had regained control, Kern said: "Get up close to the fire, kid. Ignore that asshole."

"Now, look—" Carver squealed.

"All right, all right," Cathcart broke in for the first time. "You boys better save your energy for packing all this equipment." The Englishman's usual good humor was gone; he turned a hostile look on Frémont. "If you ask me, you're wearing your men out, to no good purpose."

Godey said, "I didn't hear nobody ask you."

"By God, I don't need anybody to ask me!"

"Then say it—don't go pretending somebody else started it."

"I will," Cathcart said. His nose was thinned down to a white line and his eyes were murky and hot. "I think we should get out while the weather's holding. If we get caught in another blow, some of these men will be in real trouble. And what the hell good is all this hauling?"

Frémont held his voice steady and low. "The camp on the river is ready and the relief party'll be here in a week. But that still leaves us in the wilderness, so we'll still need supplies, won't we?"

"I can't believe all this materiel is essential."

"Well, you'd take the food?"

"Don't mock me, sir—I'm not a fool! Of course I'd take the food. What I'm talking about is all—*that* . . ." He swept his arm back to include the great mound of strapped packs and bundles. "You find all that absolutely necesary, do you? Worth risking body and soul for?"

"Now, listen—" Godey began, but Frémont cut him off with a gesture. He saw the men's faces brighten and realized that they'd been talking about this, that Cathcart was speaking for them all.

"I don't think you understand quite what it means to be a hundred thirty miles from the nearest settlement in midwinter, Captain."

"Don't I? I've been in wild places, Colonel, some very wild places indeed. And you simply do not—"

"You wouldn't leave the weapons, would you? Or the blankets? Or our axes and picks, ropes and strap leather—you wouldn't leave them?"

"Of course not!" The Englishman's face was stiff with anger. "I'm talking about the trade goods, the baubles and—"

"Would you want to meet a Ute war party downriver and have nothing to trade with?"

"Yes, we *might* run into an army of Hottentots—I suppose even some *Indians* are fool enough to be abroad in this weather. But *you're* risking lives just on the chance . . . And what about your precious instruments? Do you intend to barter those with the heathen?"

Frémont's head came up. "Are you actually suggesting we throw away the *instruments*? Why, they give us our location—"

Cathcart laughed harshly. "Why man, we haven't the foggiest idea where we are in God's universe—you haven't even been able to *use* them in days. What earthly good do you think they'll do you if you're as stiff as those mules?"

"And just what do you suggest, Cathcart?"

"Why jettison the gear, man! Cache it, and come back for it when there isn't ten feet of snow and winds that tear the skin from your very back . . . Is that so preposterous a thought?"

"They'd be ruined in a season—the weather would do them in." Frémont could feel his jaw set. "It's out of the question."

Cathcart nodded tightly. "I thought as much."

"That's what you did in Her Majesty's Army, did you? Just throw your gear to the four winds and run like rabbits?"

The captain of hussars became very still; then he smiled a cold, thin-lipped smile. "I think you know better than that, Colonel . . . This is all beside the point, isn't it?" He went on in a lower voice. "That isn't the real reason you want everything packed out. It's because you intend to regroup and go on. Isn't it, Frémont? Isn't that the real reason?"

Frémont could feel the tension in the air around the fire; he clenched his fist under his coat. All right, then. Head on. "Captain, we are safeguarding the supplies necessary to keep us alive in the wilderness. It is that simple. As for going on, we will reach that decision after the relief party arrives. Anyone who likes will be free to turn back—and that most emphatically includes you, sir."

Cathcart's eyebrows rose, his lips still curved in the bemused smile. "You're saying that I am no longer welcome because I speak my mind?"

"Not at all. You're a valuable member of the expedition, and you're more than welcome." He looked calmly around the ring of faces. "The fact is, I've been ordered to chart a *winter* route through the central chain of the Rocky Mountains—and I still intend to do just that. You all knew that when you signed on." He made himself smile then—an immense effort at that moment—and murmured to Cathcart: "But they'll never forgive you back in bonnie Scotland when you have to tell 'em you didn't make it to California with Frémont."

Cathcart laughed. "A trenchant point—maybe I'd better stick with you a bit further, at that."

"Carver," Ned Kern said, "dish up that Goddamn mule meat. I ain't gonna wait any longer."

The storm broke late the next afternoon. The temperature fell, and wind and more snow burst against them. Frémont counted his men as they brought in the last loads from the heights: all present but Proue, Carver and a couple of others who had been relaying down to Kern's camp at the canyon's bottom. At first its very violence let him hope the storm would blow itself out, but by next morning he knew they would be locked by their fires for days. He forced himself to be calm, to save his strength, to wait. *Waiting*—it seemed a test devised for the intemperate, a punishment for the impulsive. He lay on boughs around the fire with his men, watching them deteriorate, watching the meat supply shrink, taking his turn at digging out and cutting wood to force the flames against the snow. There was almost no talk; the snow came gusting down without end and they gave themselves up to dreams.

. . . Jessie would be on her way to California by now. It was early January, and he had left her in late October—ten weeks. It seemed like a thousand. She'd have returned to Washington, she'd have seen Henry King's bride—trust Jessie to do as she promised—and, yes, now she'd be on the high seas, bound for Panama with Lily and Sally, carrying an open wound deep in her heart for little Benton. He had been such a beautiful baby. There was pain in his own heart, too—but it was mingled with shame. Obsessed with the trial, Kearny's shocking malice and Stockton's equally shocking betrayal, his own hunger for recognition and the deliberate denigration of his achievements, he had scarcely been aware of his firstborn son until he felt the still body as deadweight in his arms. Then, forever too late, everything had been clear: Jessie had known; he had seen it in her face as he took the child. She had forgiven him—she would always forgive him his worst crimes—but he could never forget the shame of having opened his heart only after the child was gone. And here he was, pinned to this accursed mountain with his men failing all around him and his wife bound for the singular perils of Panama, alone when she most needed him because his soaring ambition had driven him to stake his life on the faulty memory and rusted skills of a half-crazed old fool. . . .

But next day, watching the snow drift ever deeper into the notch of the canyon, he decided that the important thing now was to take *hold*—get on to California, get the ranch settled and a home started, get their future charted. This time he would find the right pass, and go on to California. But if he couldn't, so be it: whatever happened, he *must* be there when she arrived, ready to care for her at last. And if having to reach California by the southern route certainly would be failure, it would be bearable failure. He was bringing his men out in good order, every man intact except for Wise's feet; that alone was a kind of triumph, considering the odds.

So he reassured himself as the storm thundered on around them. Ten days since the relief party had left, eleven, twelve—the same storm would have caught King coming up the river with his mules and his fresh hands. Henry would need that extra two days, but he would come, and then the world would begin to turn again.

The snow stopped late on the thirteenth day. The clouds were thinning but a murderous wind still lashed the mountain. In the morning Frémont decided to go down to Vincenthaler's camp at the canyon bottom, though it was much too early to start the men again. He thought the temperature might be ten degrees below zero—Preuss had the thermometers in the river camp—and he tied a blanket strip close to his face.

Vincenthaler stood up with a surprised look when he saw Frémont. New lines in his face had aged him frightfully.

"Too cold to travel, Colonel." His tone was half-accusatory, half-defensive.

"Just checking," Frémont said.

"Too damned cold. That's what I told that fool Proue, but he went on anyway."

"This morning?"

"An hour ago."

"The wind'll be bad on the flat."

"That's right—but he was gonna go. Said the relief party would be at River Camp. It's been two weeks today—he'd notched a stick. Said they was eating good down there." Vincenthaler glared at nothing. "Hell, King ain't there yet. He couldn't move in this weather no more'n we could."

"You shouldn't have let Raffie go."

"*Let* him? Shit, Colonel, there wasn't no stopping him 'less I knocked him down. I ain't his daddy."

The two *voyageurs* were listening. In French, Tabeau said, "The wise man waits. Everything is possible for the man who waits." Morin wagged his head sagely. "*Peut-être,*" he said. "One can also wait *too* long . . ."

Frémont said: "I've got to find him." No one made a move to join him. Had they offered, he'd have told them to stay by the fire and wait; but they didn't offer.

He followed Proue's snowshoe track onto the open flat and immediately found that it was worse there than he had imagined—much worse. The cold seemed to suck the warmth from his lungs. The wind had a shocking force, square on his back, boring through his heavy sheepskin coat, thrusting him along. The left leg began to throb painfully, and his eyes burned like fire. Before he had gone a mile he realized he was beyond the point where he could turn back and hope to survive against the wind. His hands and feet felt leaden and he hurried on in the snowshoe-shuffling, bent-kneed gait, flailing his arms against his body, keeping his blood pumping hard, nagged by rising worry.

The stream folded away to the right, and then returned. He saw a pile of deadwood deposited by a spring freshet; a man could stop there, build a fire and stay alive. Proue's tracks were wandering, swinging left, then right; there were marks in the snow where he had fallen, got up confused, started in the wrong direction and then tried to correct himself. There—he'd fallen again, and a little farther, again. Frémont was in a clumsy shuffling run now, panting, beating down his fear.

A hundred yards ahead he saw a dark lump lying across the tracks he followed. Not a quarter-mile beyond, the stream came looping in from the right; there was a stand of trees there and another pile of deadwood, dry and ready to fire. Why hadn't Raffie gone on?—a man can always make another quarter-mile, if he has to crawl on hand and knees. But Proue was down, square body curled in the snow, his back to the wind; his arms were folded, eyes closed. Frémont seized at his shoulder in panic. No: he wasn't stiff, wasn't dead yet.

"Get *up,* Raffie."

Proue opened his eyes. "We there yet, Colonel?" The wind moaned across the flats. It battered Frémont as he crouched over Raffie, shaking him.

"Get up, you Goddamn fool—you'll freeze to death!"

". . . King's there, ain't he? Coming after—"

The words were blown away. Frémont slapped his face hard. "Of course," he panted, "waiting at the river. Get up!—We'll go on down—"

Proue raised his head and looked around as if recalling where he was. "Wind took me down," he mumbled. "Pretty bad, before. Getting better now—"

"*Not* getting better, damnit—you're freezing!"

"Don't know . . . I'm feeling better, somehow—needed—rest . . ."

"Raffie, for God's sake—look, there's wood—just a little way. We'll make a fire—"

"Not right now, Colonel. Got to rest now. . . ."

"Just up there!" He thought desperately. Proue was far too big to lift or carry, or even drag. The cold poured over Frémont's back with evil force. His legs and arms were numbing—he was beginning to freeze. A still man—a down man—could not live in this; he himself had no more than ten minutes. Maybe not even that.

Proue shook his head, muttered something he couldn't hear. Frémont bent close, heard him say, "Ask Louie—he'll know what to do. Louie always knows . . . take care of things."

"Stop it!" The words burst out of him. "Louie's dead—out in California."

Proue stared at him. "That's right, ain't it?" he said quite clearly. "Louie's dead." He shook his head again. "It don't pay to ride with you, do it?"

Frémont couldn't answer.

"Louie loved you," Proue said in that same clear voice. Frémont could hear every word over the wind. "Figured the sun rose and set on you. That's why I come this time—'cause Louie would've. . . . I figured I owed *him.*"

The voice seemed as hard as the wind, as implacable. "He loved you, but you didn't do him no good. And I reckon you ain't going to do me no good, neither." There was a dreadful pause. Frémont had never in all his life felt such pure anguish. Raffie's eyes closed and then opened again. With an effort he said: "You know what, Charlie? Louie was wrong. It costs too much to ride with you. . . ."

"Oh, Raffie—"

Proue shut his eyes. His head moved as if he was settling himself into sleep. Frémont shook him frantically, called him again and again, but there was no response. Five minutes left. Firewood a quarter-mile off, but it could be ten miles, a hundred. His legs were stiff, his feet completely numb. Time running, racing. He laid his head on Raffie's shoulder, threw an arm around his big chest, tried with all his might to hold him for a moment and stood up. The bad leg hurt so he cried out. He stamped his feet, swung his arms in a paroxysm of despair. The wind drove against his back. Raffie lay motionless. Frémont, weeping, stepped around him and left him there in the snow. Shuffling along in the wind, snowshoes throwing clouds of powder ahead of him, he began to run, willing his movements, willing warm blood to pump hard to his legs and arms and head, running from the wind. He did not look back at the man lying curled in the snow.

King didn't arrive the next day, or the next. That was the deadline: sixteen days since he had left with Williams, Breckenridge, and Creutzfeldt. Trouble, then. Toward dark Frémont stood on the bluff, sweeping downriver with his glasses, blinking away the pain in his eyes, the constant blurring. The wind had slackened. The river was flat and white, winding among stands of black trees, and as far as he could see there was no movement, no wisp of smoke. The men had been straggling down the flat all day, and now they watched him with slack, hollow faces, their courage seeping away with their hope.

Frémont capped his glasses and came down from the bluff. "I expect ol' King's hung up in the snow," he said easily. He saw a flash of real terror in Carver's eyes. "I'll start down in the morning with Godey and Preuss to hurry 'em along." King couldn't be more than a few days off, and he was sure to find him within two days and be back within another two. "If I'm not back by then," he told Vincenthaler, "all of you start down to meet us. Meanwhile, see if you can get the rest of the baggage in."

He divided the rations. There was only a little meat left. Every day over the deadline would come out of the men's flesh and life force; their reserves were already gone. His, too: an awful lethargy that was beyond the fierce, constant griping of hunger now dogged him.

Hurry, then: they were away by starlight, far down the river by dawn, strung out in single file, walking fifty minutes and stopping ten, mile after grim mile. The weather was bitter but the wind had gone; the smoke from their fire that night rose straight as string. They had seen no living thing all day. He set the same hard pace in the morning, his scuffing snowshoes the only sound, scanning ahead for the dark specks of loaded mules, a trail of smoke in the sky. A peculiar ache radiated through his body, a palsied trembling. It was disconcerting—he was thirty-six years old and he had never felt his age before. Ruthlessly he thrust the thought away. Never admit tiredness—if you refuse to admit it, you are not tired. It is a question of will, *willing* the flesh to obey, put one foot before the other, all it is. *Will.* You will. Raffie could have made it for just a quarter-mile, made a fire. The food was coming and they'd have gone on to California, together. Only man who'd been on all four expeditions with him: that matchless strength, always reliable, always willing . . . What in Christ's sweet name had happened? *It costs too much to ride with you.* No, that's not so! Find King, get the rations, rest and rebuild—rebuild the party and drive on, to California—

There were tracks in the snow. *Tracks.* He stopped, blinking and squinting in the glare. No, it was no trick. Godey was a hundred feet behind him, Preuss behind Godey. Horse tracks, man tracks. The relief party; but where were they? Had he passed them, not noticed them in the screen of trees? Impossible. Bewildered, he whirled around and saw the tracks behind him curving off, away from the river. Had they wandered off, then? Something was wrong; as Alex came up, he realized the tracks were running in the same direction they were headed, downriver. Someone had come in from the side and turned downriver, someone up ahead. Crouching, he peered at the tracks. Unshod ponies, three or four, a man leading them. An Indian, then; not his party at all. An Indian headed south.

Horses! The meaning penetrated in a flare of relief, of hope. Horses meant life now. Hurry, catch them up. He set a furious pace; in an hour they came to where the Indian had camped earlier. So the man was farther ahead. The pace had drained them badly—for a frightening moment Frémont wasn't sure he could get up—and he decided to camp there. The slivers of meat they allowed themselves weren't enough to restore strength, let alone to slake hunger. They had been two days on the trail without any sight of King's party.

In the morning they started along the Indian's track, but now their stops were more frequent. Twice Frémont found himself on his knees in the snow, not sure how long he had been there. Once he realized that Godey was shouting at him, shaking his shoulder; another time he and Alex were lifting little Preuss, holding him upright until he could get his body working again. Will. There was only will now. The leg burned like hell fire.

Late that day they saw a smoke column ahead. A fire flickered among the trees. They unslung their weapons and came on slowly. An Indian was bent over the fire. He saw them and reached for his bow. Godey snapped up his rifle and shouted, "No!"

The Indian was just a boy, slender, hardly sixteen. Alex talked to him in a mix of Plains Indian tongues and sign language, and the boy's fear ebbed.

"Says he's been hunting," Godey said. "No luck. He's got a little grub left, but damned little."

Then, to his surprise, Frémont heard his own name, the Indian pronouncing it in the flat, Anglo way of the prairies: *Free-mont.*

Alex grinned slowly. "Well, I'll be damned. Remember them Utes we met north of here, coming back from California the first time? One of 'em was this boy's pap. His pap says Frémont could have killed him and didn't—gave him his life and some tobacco to boot. Says he'll be honored to help us. Don't know as he has much choice, but I think he means it."

Bread upon the waters. How wonderfully strange. "Tell him he'll be rewarded," Frémont said.

"Oh, he's counting on that."

The horses were too poor to ride, but they could carry the packs and that left them feeling light as birds. They went on and on, stopping when one of them fell, camping when they realized it was dark, movement and halts running into an indistinguishable pain-ridden blur . . . and finally, as they followed a long loop of the river, Frémont saw a string of smoke rising from timber ahead. King's party? The Indian boy said something. Godey listened a moment: the boy thought that it would be other hunters from his tribe. But it *must* be King! It had to be. . . .

They hurried forward, fresh caps on their pieces, studying the trees. The pillar of smoke continued to rise on the still, cold air, but it was from a single fire. There was no sign of mules.

Three men lay by the fire, wrapped in blankets. Rifles stood against a tree. Then one of the men stood, dropped his blanket, and started toward them across the snow, stumbling, tottering. A white man. When he was nearer they saw he was emaciated, his face skull-like under his beard, his eyes hollowed and staring. The man said something Frémont couldn't understand, his voice a rusty croak. He fell on his knees, his arms still stretched toward them.

"*—Herr lieber Gott!*" Preuss cried. "Frederick!"

Creutzfeldt? Frémont stared in horror as Preuss ran to him and caught his hands. Then the others must be . . . Frémont hurried forward. Yes, there were Breckenridge and Williams, sitting by the fire, watching him.

"Where's the relief party?" he cried; he heard his voice shake. "Did you come on ahead?"

"Never got no farther than this," Williams said dully.

For one long, fearful moment, Frémont simply could not comprehend any of this. *No farther* . . . then they hadn't gone out—got only halfway out and then gave up and stayed here, by this fire. . . ?

Then there was no relief party on the way.

Staring into their gaunt, wolfish faces, he thought with a dart of agony of the rest of the party holed up back in the canyon, out of food now, waiting; Andrews coughing his lungs out on the snow, Carver with his bad back,

Wise's frozen feet; all of them hanging on there because they believed in him, in what he'd promised; waiting for food and clothing and mules that would never come . . . The expedition was dead. They weren't going to rest and reoutfit and push on, thread that pass to California. They'd be lucky to get out alive, any of them.

"What the hell do you mean?" he cried at last, incredulous and raging. "Why *didn't* you go on?"

"Fell on starving time." Williams wagged his head. "Run out of meat, had to slow down. Slow down. We couldn't carry enough to start with, you know that. Took a shortcut across the big bend in the river. Wind come up and caught us in the open, and we went under blankets four days. Hurt us bad. Yes, sir."

Breckenridge looked up in sudden defiance. "We cooked our parfleches, ate our Goddamn belts and moccasins! . . . You had plenty up there with the mules, but we run down. Can't you see that?"

Suddenly Frémont realized there were only three of them. "Where's King?" he said, hope flaring once more. "He left you and went on?"

"King gave out," Williams said. His eyes would not meet Frémont's. "Folded up a while back. We took a shortcut, come in from thataway." He gestured vaguely off to the right, away from the river. "King give out—we had to leave him in the snow."

"He was pushing too hard," Breckenridge added. He sounded angry. "Always pushing us, wanting to go faster."

"Don't pay to hurry in this kind of weather," Old Bill nodded somberly.

"He talked hard to us—he was plumb crazy over making time." Breckenridge stared at Frémont, his eyes bright and out of focus. "Wore hisself out. Said he was going to rest a little, told us to go on and make camp and he'd be down."

"You left him there—?"

"After we got a fire set, I went back for him," Williams said, "but 'twasn't no use—he was dead."

"How far?" Frémont demanded. "Where is he now?"

"A mile back," Breckenridge said.

"Two miles," Williams corrected him. "Three maybe." Now he was glancing sidelong at Frémont. "You'll find him in bad shape. Ravens been at him. I seen 'em circling as we left. When I got back they'd been at him. Cut him up some."

"Didn't matter to him," Breckenridge said with sudden vehemence. "He was dead. Didn't make him no difference."

Frémont gazed at them in silence—a moment of great confusion through which a horror-filled awareness slowly burned . . . Henry King: that smiling, willing lad with his bright eager face, his bride awaiting him in Georgetown, younger than any of them, stronger—*he* had collapsed, and not the others? He'd been driving them, he understood the desperate nature of the situation, of course he'd pushed them; and finally they'd turned on him, and struck him down . . . and then taken their knives and—My God, they had—had—

Williams smiled, his lips red and obscene in his beard, a terrible glitter in his eye. "He didn't know shit!" the old man was saying savagely. "He didn't know how to manage in this country. He didn't deserve to live."

Frémont took three quick steps, seized Williams by his coat and jerked him up. "You vicious old bastard!" he screamed. "God damn you to hell—I trusted you, and you got us lost."

"Now, listen—"

"You filthy fraud—you ruined everything, and now you can't even get out for relief with good men waiting for you, their *lives* in your filthy hands! You crap out around a fire—you kill Henry, and then you . . . You rotten fucking *beast*!"

With surprising strength, Williams threw up both arms and knocked Frémont's hands away.

"You chickenshit son of a bitch," he said in a hoarse, deadly voice, "don't you talk to me none." His long, bony finger came out and pointed at Frémont; he towered over him. "Don't you lay it on me! I *told* you about this winter. I told you about them mountains. I told you they was like God! It was *you* didn't give a shit about them—no, nor about God, neither. . . ."

He was like an Old Testament figure of wrath, his gray hair flying, his eyes blazing and demented; Frémont stared at him, speechless.

"It was *you* said you could go where you pleased, you didn't have to ask nobody. Yes, said you was bigger than God." His voice sank to a hard, vibrating whisper. "It was you."

"I just can't get it out of my mind," Frémont said. "What happened up there. To Henry." He took another sip of Josefa Carson's hot chocolate, held it in his mouth. Hot and rich and sweet. Three weeks off the trail, most of his body tissue restored, and he still had an overpowering craving for sugar.

"Let it go, Colonel," Carson said. "Let it go, now." They were sitting in the living room of his adobe house in Taos. Piñon logs crackled brightly in a fireplace outlined in red tile. The massive furniture had comfortable buckskin cushions and Frémont sat with the frostbitten leg propped on a chair and stretched toward the fire. He raised the cup to his lips again. It was impossible; impossible that he could be sitting here in the house of a good friend, warm and well-fed, healing while out there on a celestial arrow-flight under the same cold moon, lay that snow-whipped mountain of the indifferent gods where he had beat his hands against his thighs, groaning in pain . . . where he had left good men to—I never used to have thoughts like this, he wondered morosely, I used to take even disaster in stride. . . .

He said aloud, stubbornly: "I know Henry King didn't wear out back there. I *know* what happened."

"But you said Raffie wore out. Raffie was strong, too."

Frémont shook his head. "Raffie was the exception. He wanted it . . . Not King. And it would've been easy—a quick blow from behind, leave him to freeze, come back when he was dead. It wouldn't have been hard—for *those* bastards."

"Well," Kit said slowly, "I'll tell you this: I'd never walk in front of Old Bill Williams in starving time."

Frémont let the enormity of that remark sink in slowly. At last he said: "I could bring charges, but in the end I couldn't prove anything. No jury would convict on suspicion."

"You can't do nothing, Colonel. It's best to let it lay."

Frémont sighed. He wished he had gone back with Alex for the men. He had led a sullen, fractious Williams and the others safely into Socorro, the tiny settlement north of Taos, though he couldn't remember the last couple of days very well. He had been falling often by then, and he was nearly blind. When Godey was ready to go back with horses and fresh hands, he'd insisted that the Colonel's physical condition would slow him; but the truth was that he had been easily persuaded. Anyway, Alex would be here soon—he should have been in yesterday.

"But to kill a friend," he murmured somberly. "Cut him down and leave him to die, *in order* to eat him . . . Jesus."

"Well, it's happened before," Kit said shortly. "And it will happen again."

Frémont could see the subject made the scout master uneasy but, shaken to his roots, he pursued it obsessively.

"Well," he said, "could *you* do it?"

"I couldn't say. I've never been quite that hungry."

"No—and you never would be. By God, *I* wouldn't do it! No matter what."

"Maybe so." Carson's voice was hard, a touch sardonic. "Maybe, if a man happened to get hungrier than he could stand, felt himself going under, lying trapped in deep snow, say—and right beside him is a man who's dead or dying . . . We're not a hell of a long ways out of the jungle, Colonel."

"The devil we're not! We've developed standards, principles, all the rest of it—or we're supposed to've, anyway."

"Fellow off a whaler I run into in San Diego told me they still eat each other, out in those coral islands. Serve each other up every chance they get."

"That awful Donner party," Frémont muttered. "Two years gone, and people are still whispering about it, everywhere you turn. I'm damned if I want them talking that way about *my* expeditions."

Carson said sharply: "Nobody's going to talk that way about you. First off, you don't *know* King got et. All right, there may be talk, but no one's ever going to know for sure. You can bet your bottom dollar Old Bill ain't going to shoot his mouth off! Or Breckenridge, either. The Donner people kept talking about it. Eighty-nine went into the Sierra, forty-five come out. Hell, they'd be famous if they *hadn't* touched human flesh . . . You lost two men. Nothing out of the way about that. Maybe if you'd—"

As though his words had been some sort of signal, there was a muffled commotion outside. Kit was on his feet in a bound and moving toward the door. Godey came in quickly, knocking snow from his hat, stamping it from his boots.

"Great Jesus, what a winter," he said.

"Alex!" Carson grabbed him with both hands. "Josefa said you'd be in tonight. You eaten?"

Godey shook his head and shrugged out of the fleece-lined jacket wearily.

"I came straight here. Left the whole party at Jameson's in Socorro, borrowed Tom Baxter's filly Pretty Baby and rode over." He glanced across the room at Frémont. "I knew you'd want to hear right away."

"Josie," Kit called, "get Alex something to eat, muy pronto!—Want a drink?"

"I could use a shot all right." He came up to Frémont and took his hand. "How you making it, Colonel?"

"All the comforts of home," Frémont answered, smiling. "God, I'm glad to see you. Found 'em all, did you?"

"Yes, sir." He sat down then, and gripped his big hands; his face was streaked white with cold and fatigue. "But the boys, uh, had some trouble after we left."

"What kind of trouble?"

"Several kinds, I'm afraid."

The party had started downriver on the fourth day, as Frémont had instructed them; but an immediate altercation had arisen between the strong ones, who wanted to get out fast, and the weak, who couldn't. The food had been about gone by then. Vincenthaler had set a hard pace, and when Ned Kern protested, Vincenthaler told him to go to hell. Ned figured their best chance overall lay in a slow, steady pace, the strong helping out the weak. Cathcart, who never could abide Vincenthaler anyway, had stayed with Ned, and so had good old Stepp and Charlie Taplin, who said straight out it wasn't right to abandon the weak ones.

"Ned figured Vincenthaler was trying to shake 'em off, he set such a pace. And then there was the deer. Seems Vincenthaler called a halt for hunting, and by God, one of 'em got a deer. But Ned says they didn't bring it in—they ran downriver, cooked it and ate it. By the time Ned and Cathcart figured out what was happening and got down there, 'twas all gone but a shoulder blade. Next thing they knew, Vincenthaler's bunch ran on downriver and left the others for good."

"For Christ sake," Carson said disgustedly. "What got into them?"

Godey raised the tumbler and drank, put it down softly. "I asked Vincenthaler about the deer; he says Ned's crazy. Says when Ned *didn't* come, he couldn't keep starving men from eating. Damned if I know—but Ned's in a fury about Vincenthaler."

He had the uneasy sense that Alex was avoiding something. "These squabbles aside, though, you brought them out, didn't you?"

"Yeah." Godey stopped and looked at Frémont squarely for the first time. "If you can call it that."

Frémont felt his heart racing. "Maybe you'd better give it to me from the beginning," he said quietly.

In the kitchen Josefa began singing in her soft contralto about a man named Jaime who had left his lady with *dolor de corazón, dolor grande y mal . . .*

"Well, I traveled pretty fast, and I come on Vincenthaler's bunch early on the fourth day. He had a half-dozen men with him. Funny thing is that though he run off, he didn't get all that much farther than Kern's bunch—

the strong ones wore theirselves out running, seems like, and they slowed down, too. Vincenthaler told me that Hubbard had give out a ways back. They'd made him a good fire and left him, and then did the same for Johnny Scott, who said he couldn't do no more. So I went on up to find 'em, and Vincenthaler come with me. After a while we see Johnny, and his fire was still going and he was alive."

"Left them?" Frémont whispered, feeling hollow. "Left them there?" Suppose someone can't keep up? King had said. Leave 'em, Hubbard had said. And King: *What if you're the one to get left?* "And Hubbard?" he said aloud.

"Dead. Fire was out and he was stiff. Froze to death—or starved. Or both."

"Both, probably," Kit said.

Hubbard dead. He gazed at Godey.

"So I pushed on upriver. Cut across a big bend and come on Ferguson sitting by a fire. He looked pretty bad. He had Beadle with him, but Beadle was dead. He said Beadle'd gone two, three days before."

Hubbard and Beadle. Looked alike, talked alike, died alike—but not together.

"Mi corazón, mi corazón," Josefa sang softly.

"Ferguson insisted that the Kerns was downstream from him. I figured they must be in that loop I'd cut across, so I went back down and found 'em. They was in pitiful shape. They hadn't moved for six days—they looked like walking dead. You could see their skulls under their skin. I've never seen nobody quite like that.

"Andrews was dead. He collapsed on the trail, went down unconscious, and they carried him in. He never come to again. Died the next day. Poor bastard—he did good to last that long, I reckon."

"Tinhorn fool—he never should've signed on in the first place," Kit said.

"Rohrer, too." King's friend; watch out for Rohrer, Henry had said. Sweet God. "Seems Rohrer tried to run off with Vincenthaler and played out and lagged back to Kern's. But directly he went off his head. He was raving all night and they seen he was going to die."

Godey stopped. Josefa set a plate of elk steak and biscuits in front of him; he looked at it and then began to pick at the rough wood of the table with the point of his knife. "Ned and Cathcart both said the boys talked about eating Rohrer," he said in a low, uneven voice. "They decided it wasn't the Christian thing to do. I brought his body back and checked it out good—it didn't have no marks." He paused for a moment and then added very carefully, "I found King's body too, and brung it in. It was cut up pretty bad. Of course it could be a number of things."

No one said anything for a time; Alex pushed the plate of food away from him silently with the point of the knife.

"There were others?" Frémont asked heavily, knowing the answer now, knowing everything.

"Well, Wise. He fell out the first day. Couldn't walk good, but he was game—he kept going. Ned said he all of a sudden threw down his piece and his blanket, took a few wobbly steps, and fell over, like them mules did up on the mountain. When they got to him, he was dead.

"And Carver—you know how he was always excitable?—he went kind of crazy. Raved all day and then in the night when no one was looking he wandered off. Ned said they was gonna follow him, but then Vincenthaler lit out and they figured they had to stick with the strong group if they could. Anyway, he was dead—he couldn't have gotten through a night without fire." He paused. "I didn't find his body, though."

Frémont felt deeply, physically sick; his face was numb. "God . . . that's how many?"

"Well, and then Tabeau and Morin."

The *voyageurs,* the old reliables. Frémont stared at him blankly.

"Ned said as soon as we didn't get back on the fourth day, they lit out alone, running ahead of everyone. Just took off. Panicked, I reckon—that surprised me."

What had Tabeau said, sounding so wise? Frémont could hear the husky voice, the rolling French: Everything is possible for the man who waits. And then Morin had said—

"Well, running broke 'em and they dropped back and joined Ned. And directly Tabeau said he couldn't go no more and he sat down in the snow. Then Morin seen Ned and asked where was Tabeau. Ned told him and Morin went back without a word and built a fire and never left. I found 'em that way—Tabeau stretched out in his blankets, Morin still sitting up against a log like he was on guard. At least they went together."

"Sweet Jesus," Frémont whispered. Tears stung his eyes. "How many, then, all together?"

"Ten, Colonel. Eight after we left—and King and Raffie." He hesitated, looking uneasily at Frémont. "I went back up the canyon. Got the instruments and journals. But I couldn't find Raffie's body. There'd been more snow, and I reckon he got buried. I looked hard—I want you to know that."

In the spring, Raffie's body would reappear and the scavengers would come. Raffie had laid the Hawken with the buffalo carving in Louie's arms so he would arrive prepared wherever he was going; had wrapped him and covered him with packed earth and stones and obliterated the grave so that no scavengers would disturb him. . . .

"A third," Frémont whispered. "A *third* of the party gone."

"They were an awfully mixed bag, Colonel," Carson was saying in a low, gentle voice.

"But they were *my* men!" he cried softly. "Mine! . . . If only you'd been up there, Kit," he went on, knowing it was foolish, a perfectly foolish thing to say, but having to say it anyway. "None of this would have happened . . ."

"Sure it would. They're a different breed, most of them. Iffing's for greenhorns. It's no fault of yours. You did all you could."

There was another heavy silence.

"Colonel," Alex said, "I'd give everything I own if I didn't have to tell you this. Colonel—"

He realized he'd begun to weep, silently, uncontrollably; he couldn't help it. The intolerable shock of finding Old Bill Williams sitting by that fire in the bend of the river, defiant and cunning and mad; the desperate march out through the cold, hobbling half-blind, savagely beating down his terror of losing the bad foot; the slow, painful convalescence, and the relentless worry—all of it overpowered him. For the first time in his life he felt *old;* old and defeated, broken past mending. Ten men. Ten good men who'd trusted him, believed in him, followed where he'd led—

"You know what, Charlie? It costs too much to ride with you. . . ."

He put his hands over his eyes, heard distantly the two men softly leaving the room. In all his life there had never been a time as bad as this. Not even riding in the choking red dust as Kearny's prisoner or listening to old Brooke's dry voice droning out the verdict of the court . . . Rock bottom. He'd fallen to rock bottom. In his boundless brash innocence he'd dreamed of blazing a comet's trail across the great, free face of America—and he had brought about a disaster. . . .

Jessie, he murmured like a prayer, holding her sweet face in his mind's eye, blotting out other faces, other scenes; the need for her presence was a boundless ache in this still, alien room. God, how he needed to hear her voice, feel her hand on his cheek, feel her arms around him hard, sustaining him, comforting him. And she a thousand jungle miles away. Ah Jessie, he thought in bottomless anguish, forgive me. . . .

REUNION

THERE WAS A STEEL BAND CLAMPED around her head, just over her eyes, and it was tightening. She lay there panting, her mouth open, her fists clenched, and after a while the pain receded. She opened her eyes again. Lily was standing by the bed in the pale light that filtered through the wooden shutters closed against the tropic glare. Lily was six now, getting that thin, gangling look, her little face plain and very worried. Jessie saw she was crying.

"Teresita said you're going to die," Lily said.

"Oh, Lily, darling, don't be silly—I'm not going to die."

"Madame Arcé slapped her for saying it, but she said it again after Madame left."

"Teresita is an old fool," Jessie said. The headache beat in her temples, and her head began to swim. "I've just got a little fever." Not yellow fever, thank heaven—she had waited anxiously for the dread black bile yellow fever victims vomited—so it must be a malarial ague contracted as they crossed the Isthmus.

"What'll become of me, Mama, if you die?" Lily cried suddenly in a squeaky voice, "I'll be all alone . . ."

She shook the child as fiercely as she could. *"I'm not going to die,"* she repeated, hearing the tremor in her voice. "We are going to California." That was, if a ship ever came, they were; they had been trapped here in Panama for seven weeks.

"Benton died, Mama. Anyone can—"

"Oh baby, that was different! Benton's little heart was broken." She heard the mounting fear in the child's voice and knew she should deal with it, but not now: she was too sick now. And too worried. Not a single ship had come in from California. Why was that? Charles would be there by now—what would he think when she didn't appear? "Come on, sweetheart," she said, "help Mama up, now."

The tile floor was cool against her bare feet. The sweating, palsied shaking had retreated again, but she was still faintly dizzy, and weak as water.

She saw Lily gazing at her anxiously, and she smiled reassuringly. She wished fervently that Sally had come; at the last minute she'd backed out—her man wouldn't go and she couldn't leave him.

Jessie had landed blithely on the Atlantic side of the Isthmus without the least idea of what the crossing would mean. Up a jungle river by small boat for four days, sleeping in tents on the riverbank, then across the mountains on mules—it had sounded a lark about which she would write dashing letters home.

And so it had seemed at first, with monkeys swinging on flowered creepers, green parrots sounding harsh alarms, iguanas with flickering tongues, and Lily laughing and pointing at each wondrous new sight. But as the river wound into the interior the jungle grew dense, dark, ominous. The boat was tiny and very slow; the nearly naked crewmen poled against the hard current with rhythmical grunts. Away from the sea the heat was crushing, the air still and fetid. Mosquitoes poised in brazen clouds on her netting, their long probes straining toward her flesh; vivid welts arose where they reached her. Lily seemed to thrive on it all, but Jessie could feel the jungle miasma sinking into her lungs, her very blood, breeding fever . . .

Then the mules: three more days of lurching over a narrow jungle trail Spaniards had built centuries before to haul the gold of Peru across the Isthmus—but that was another story, sighing off into fever's mists. Still, looking down from the heights onto the sweep of the Pacific, she wasn't too ill to notice that not a single ship stood in the harbor. Then they came down the last sheer slopes, each step of the mule jabbing a separate needle in her head, and passed through an immense wall of mossy stone; dimly she realized she was quite sick, more sick than she had ever been. But she was carrying letters of introduction; Madame Arcé Costa welcomed her like a lost daughter and put her straight to bed. There were spells of quaking chills followed by fever, Madame Arcé's worn, handsome face hovering over her through each crisis; awakening, she would find herself in the cool, dim room with its jalousies, and drift off into a grim, recurring dream of Charles, shapeless in shaggy furs and wearing a headdress with buffalo horns, disappearing into a whirlwind of flying snow no matter how desperately she called for him. The line of figures kept walking away from her, stumbling, vanishing one by one; she could never see their faces . . .

Lily tugged at her hand now and she stood, swaying, her eyes full of sharp edges, all her joints swollen and mutinous. Still, she felt better after she had brushed out her hair and let Lily help her dress. The headache was receding. She could hear Mr. Gray's voice downstairs. He was a banker from New York, going to California for his firm; a stout, fussy man who had been caught here with everyone else.

He jumped to his feet when she entered the drawing room. "The mystery of the ships is solved, Mrs. Frémont! The crews have deserted them in San Francisco Bay, and run off to the gold fields." He waved a handful of fresh newspapers. "The bay is a forest of masts, ships at anchor going to the worms, not a soul on board. Even the officers have deserted . . . Gone to the greatest gold strike in history!"

Madame Arcé, sitting in a splendid fan chair that rose behind her like a halo, gave Jessie an ironic glance; she considered Mr. Gray a bore, quite lacking in masculine vigor. Tiny, in her seventies, with a very straight back and dark hair drawn into a severe bun that belied her affectionate manner, she was embroidering little blue flowers on white cambric clutched in a hoop.

The papers were from New Orleans, and had the full story, Mr. Gray was saying, spreading them before him, half reading and half telling. Apparently it had all begun when Captain Sutter hired a man named Marshall to build a sawmill. One morning Marshall saw glitter at the bottom of the tailrace—and there was the gold. How wonderfully fitting, Jessie thought, that Sutter, always broke and always the entrepreneur, the dreamer with pretensions, should have his own gold mine! Would he send a barrel of gold to the family he'd abandoned back in Switzerland? Sutter had tried to keep it all quiet, but you can't keep gold a secret anywhere for long. Still, people had hesitated at first, as if afraid to believe it, until a big Mormon named Sam Brennan had come into San Francisco with a glass bottle full of gold dust.

Jessie could see it clearly: the big man in a battered hat waving the bottle and shouting, "Gold! Gold from the American River—laying there for the taking!" and men crowding around gaping, their faces igniting. Then, utter conviction had seized hold of all California and propelled everyone into the Sierra foothills around Sutter's grant. It seemed so strange no one had ever noticed it. Charles had camped along those streams. A faint memory tugged at her; while they were writing the Second Report, Chales had told her about Bushnell showing him these golden flakes from a stream. He had explained why iron pyrites are called fool's gold, and laughing they had tossed them back into the water. . . .

Gold fever had spread like a disease, Mr. Gray was reading. Sailors abandoned ship, soldiers deserted, shopkeepers bolted their doors, farmers left fields half-plowed. Shovels sold for five dollars, ten, twenty. A cannon could be fired down any main street in California without risk to a human soul—everyone had gone to "the diggings."

"Imagine that—just putting a shovel in the dirt and turning up . . . real gold, right in the dirt."

"Then it's bigger than just Sutter's find?" she asked, grasping it at last.

"Oh, yes—this writer mentions three or four rivers . . ."

"It sounds insane," she said slowly. "Doesn't it?"

"They're talking about nuggets as big as your fist," he said. "About streams with golden bottoms. Solid golden bottoms!" Startled by a sudden tremor in his voice, she looked at him sharply and saw an expression of naked avidity that made him look years younger. Had a woman ever stirred him so? she wondered.

Mr. Gray had recovered himself; it struck Jessie that his own reaction had frightened him.

"It's very ugly, Mrs. Frémont." His voice was flat now, forbidding; he was a banker again. "Very dangerous. Sudden wealth—there for the taking—

that changes men. It can turn them into animals. Think of it—some of them rich beyond imagination in a day, a week. A king's power with none of a king's responsibility. It will give them wrong ideas . . . And the others—they don't all strike, you know. Those who don't will be insane with disappointment."

He stopped and swallowed again. He folded the paper as if its contents had contaminated him, and said primly: "All I can say is, I'm glad Colonel Frémont will be there to protect you. It doesn't seem at all the place for a young gentlewoman."

Three days later there was mail. Madame Arcé brought the letters upstairs herself.

"Two were from Colonel Frémont," she said.

"Oh, thank God," Jessie cried. "There's been a ship from California, then?"

"No, my dear. The letters are from Taos."

Alone and with trembling hands, she spread the letters flat and read the one with the earliest date. He was alive, safe, down from the mountains, in Kit's house; they were nursing him. He had a badly frostbitten leg, and was suffering from snow blindness; but it would pass. Alex had gone back to bring out the rest of the party while Kit had put him to bed for a spell. It had been a hard winter. Very hard.

Raffie and Henry King were dead. The paper quivered as she read the words. She looked again at the date of the letterhead, shaken by the bitter temporal anomalies that had turned young Mrs. King into a widow even while she still believed herself to be a happy bride.

The second letter dealt the heaviest blows of all. Ten men—their faces rose in her mind from the Boone Creek camp; friends, men who had smiled at the very sight of her—all struck down by starvation and cold . . .

Fighting for control, she reread the letters. He had tried to be matter-of-fact, but it was obvious that the expedition was finished. Destroyed. All their dreams had crashed to earth. They had wanted to raise a railroad triumph over the ashes of his career, reclaim what Kearny and the court-martial and a temporizing President had stripped from them—and he had come reeling out of snows with a third of his men dead and not a thing to show for it. There would be no special attention from Zachary Taylor, no commisison to explore the rest of California, no momentum for starting a transcontinental railroad. There would be no more credit from those flinty men in St. Louis for new projects in California. She thought of the Donners and the way everyone talked about them, voices in low respectful register, eyes alight with prurient fascination . . .

But what about Charles? He had expressed himself cautiously in letters that anyone might well read before they reached her, but his anguish was clear—and so was his need for her. With the hollow dismay of someone discovering the irreparable loss of some cherished family heirloom, she realized she had never believed it possible that he could fail to find his pass and cross the mountians, that he could be hurt—even that he might die . . . On that gift night at Boone Creek when he had come back to her through the rain, she had felt nothing could hurt them—and now he was in Taos, injured in body, wounded in spirit. Needing her as never before.

Fear pressed her close, borne on the fever, slipping off into chill; she drew the bed jacket around her shoulders. She felt so *vulnerable.* She had been gliding through a mirrored hall of illusions—and now the real lesson had followed; she *wasn't* special, wasn't protected. Like Charles hobbling lost and despairing through a wilderness of ice, she was vulnerable to every lash laid across the back of humankind. Wasn't that precisely Lily's fear?

But it was Charles who mattered; what if he couldn't go on? He said he would leave shortly for California by the southern route—she snatched the letters up again to be sure—but how badly was he hurt? Was he lying to her, making light of his condition to allay her fears? If ten men had died . . . Could a frozen foot hold the stirrup across a thousand miles of desert?

What if he couldn't be there when she arrived?

A single gun cracked through the city like a trumpet cry just before dawn. Jessie came awake with a start. Signal gun. A ship in, from California. She impatiently dressed and waited till the sky was light. She was still very weak, but she had neither fever nor headache when she stepped out of Madame Arcé's door. Here the streets were almost deserted. She turned through the plaza, past the bandstand and the *paseo,* where pigeons fluttered out of her way. The town had a cool, washed look; a pearly green sky glowed against the pearly concavities of oyster shells set in the cathedral tower.

Far below, framed between two-story buildings, she saw a small steamer at anchor, and her heart sank; it wouldn't take one in ten of the men who wanted passage. Mr. Gray said there were more than two thousand, roaming the streets, trading rumors and growing daily more desperate, fearing they wouldn't get a ship before their money ran out, or they caught fever and joined the procession to the graveyard behind the alcázar . . .

At the foot of the street Americans were crowded around a waterfront building of ancient stone on which a fresh-painted sign hung crookedly: PACIFIC MAIL STEAMSHIP COMPANY. Policemen with truncheons and shotguns cleared a way for her. A rough voice said, "Well, now lookit Missus God-damn Fancy Drawers," but she didn't let her expression change. The crowd of men pressed forward. They were almost silent, but she sensed the desperation in them, the barely checked ferocity; they were like wolfhounds in that instant before a keeper slipped their leashes. She was acutely aware of being the only woman among such men, but she held her breathing steady and tried to work her way through the press to a harassed clerk behind a makeshift counter.

After twenty minutes of being jostled to and fro, her strength began to ebb; there was that light-headed swimming sensation as the fever returned, and her legs were weak. She was about to turn away when she saw a face she recognized—a man by the steamship company's door talking to someone. For a moment she wondered if it was the fever, if she so wanted the comfort of a familiar face that she had invented one.

"Ned?" she asked uncertainly, gazing up at him. "Is that you?"

He turned on his name. "Jessie!" he said. "Why, I've been looking for you . . ."

Yes, it was Ned Beale, dear Ned Beale, as handsome as ever, his dark ruff of beard neatly trimmed; and she felt a surge of pure relief. A naval lieutenant, he'd been at San Pasqual with Kit; the two had made the night march through the Californians' lines for the force that saved Kearny—and he'd said as much, too, when he testified for Charles. But what in the world was he doing in Panama?

"I thought you'd be here," he said, "but I didn't know how I was going to find you." He peered at her and his voice changed. "You've been sick."

"Touch of fever, that's all. Did you come on this ship?"

"Just landed. I'm going on to Washington with dispatches from the commodore in San Francisco. I've got a dozen men, well equipped—and I'm going to escort you—home."

She felt confused. The crowd seemed louder, more hostile; there was a scuffle near the center, and several policemen moved to stop it. Ned seemed oblivious. Had she heard him correctly?

"But I'm going to *California,*" she said.

"I know, but it's dangerous there now. Things are—very volatile. Really, Jessie, it's no place for a woman and child alone."

"But Charles—"

He shook his head. "That's the point. Charles isn't in California."

"Not there?" Her knuckles pressed against her lips.

"Not when I left, three weeks ago. The reports from Santa Fe say that his feet were seriously frozen—he may not be able to travel for a year." He hesitated, as if realizing only now that this might alarm her, and added hastily: "Of course, I'm sure he'll be all right." He took her hand. "Look, Jessie, I wish I could tell you he's pacing the dock in San Francisco. But the way things are, I think he'd want me to head you off here."

His hand was comforting. "What's it *really* like there, Ned? We've been hearing such ridiculous tales . . ."

"There's a very rough element, no doubt about that. There must be fifty men for every woman. It's—"

"Are there hotels?"

"Yes, but they're vile places, and they charge a king's ransom." He stopped. "Oh, San Francisco's operating, such as it is. It's all made of canvas, you know—raw and very rough, but functioning. They're not exactly ravening through the streets, but there've been some very ugly incidents. A man feels a lot more comfortable going about armed."

"We've got to see about the ranch," she said. "It's all we have left now, you see."

He looked worriedly at her. "Jessie, you don't understand. The men there, they're like—that . . ." He pointed to where another scuffle had broken out, shouts and curses: a man in a torn cutaway coat was holding a hand to the side of his head; his assailant in a buckskin shirt ws being led away by two police. "Only worse—because these poor devils are held in line by fear. In San Francisco they're drunk with gold, and dreams of gold—they've gone crazy."

"But Charles will come on, I know he will! And I must be there when he arrives."

"But it's not the California we knew before—the way it was when Charles left. Believe me, Jessie, it's no place for a woman alone! If he'd known what's happened, he'd have insisted you wait till he got there. He'd agree it's my duty to protect you from that."

The sun had come up; it was blazing in her eyes, dazzling her, fusing with the fever. Her early morning strength had vanished utterly; she wanted to go away somewhere and sit down.

"I must think about it," she said.

"I'm sorry—time is the only thing I *can't* give you. I'm under urgent orders. I can wait while you collect your trunks, but I'm afraid I must have your answer now. Please, Jessie, let me get you out of this—let me see you home. Out of this lawless, lethal sinkhole."

Bells were ringing for morning mass; they seemed to echo bells in her head. Home. The house on C Street, Mr. T at his desk at dawn—she ached to be there.

"Dear Ned," she said at last, "what a joy it is to see you. But I promised Charles I'd meet him in California. And there it is."

He started to protest once more, then stopped himself. "You are a very gallant lady," he said. He touched his forehead in an odd little salute. "God go with you."

Down in the street below, a voice was calling: "Lassiter, Colonel, Slim Lassiter—you remember, from Zeke Merritt's company. Good to see you again, sir. Yes, your wife's in the hotel . . ."

Lily ran to the window and jerked it open with a crash.

"It's Daddy," she cried. "He's getting off his horse. He's—he's limping, Mama." She leaned far out and pealed, "Daddy! Daddy!"

Jessie, at the window now, seized her by the waist. Over the girl's shoulder she saw Charles looking up, standing foreshortened, smiling vividly and waving, and then he disappeared from view.

Lily squirmed back into the room. "Let's go meet him," she said, and raced from the room.

Jessie started to follow—and then stopped, seized by a restraint that surprised her. She had been waiting here for days, longing for this moment for months and months . . . and now she wasn't ready at all. She snatched up the ivory mirror and began tucking away stray strands of hair. Her face stared back at her, thin, haggard, her eyes huge and burning—she looked as ratty and ill-put-together as this dreary room in this miserble hotel in this hysterical, tatterdemalion city of tents and shacks. Their room had canvas walls; it was no place to receive her husband after eight famished months. Canvas walls. One could hear everything in the next room, where apparently a half-dozen men slept, until Lily had said loudly, "Mama, those men are saying bad words," which had produced a squawk from next door and after that muted whispers.

She coughed and the mirror shook in her hand. This incredible damp cold rolling off the Pacific—after Panama's heat it seemed to have compounded her fever with a rattling pleurisy. It was June, but like no other summer she'd ever known. When their ship had steamed into San Francisco Bay the wind was hurling dust about like a desert sandstorm. Boats had put them ashore; sailors standing knee-deep in water had carried them the last few feet, and they had arrived in California. Everyone seemed to know her and welcome her: Yes ma'am, the Colonel's in California, he's back on his feet; yes ma'am, fella named of Jensen said he saw him in the mountains riding that big gray hard, you know how the Colonel can ride . . .

She heard Lily's voice, suddenly shy, and then Charles—and then Lily again, clearly, accusingly: "Mama almost died. We needed you so, and you didn't come."

That child! Like this excuse for a hotel—everything wrong . . . And then Charles was in the doorway, Lily in his arms. She had a quick impression of his face—lean, harder than before, new lines in his cheeks, something inexpressibly sad in his blue eyes. Then she flew to him, tears choking off her words; his arms were around her, and he was kissing her, and Lily was crying and laughing too, and the whole hotel was listening through those canvas walls—and she simply didn't care . . .

They talked and laughed and reassured each other all at once; no she didn't almost die—she had fever, that was all; no, his feet weren't frozen, he had a bad case of frostbite and his eyes had gone bad in the snow; yes, the leg still ached when it was cold or the wind was off the sea; Lily had grown whole inches and inches, she was a big girl now; and that cough of Jessie's, he didn't like that cough. Well, they were here now, the three of them, together at last; they would love California, it was warm and sunny and full of good, solid people along with the inevitable riffraff. Everyone had welcomed him; if they remembered the circumstances under which he'd left, no one had said a word. That was all behind them. . . .

So many hilarious, sad, frightening things to talk about; so very many. He drew a chair close to the bed where she sat. Lily lay with her head in Jessie's lap, listening, and as their voices settled into an even rhythm, she dropped off to sleep.

"I'm sorry I'm so—unpresentable," she said.

"You're the most beautiful girl I've ever seen. You look tired, that's all." He reached and touched Jessie's cheek then, tenderly. "What Lily said—were you that sick down in Panama?"

She smiled faintly. "I was pretty sick, Charles. And such a long way from home. Lily was frightened, and I was too. I realized I could die—I'd never really known that before. It was . . . kind of a shock, feeling that."

"Yes," he said. "I know."

"It was very bad in the mountains, wasn't it?"

"About as bad as it could get." Talking softly, he told her about it—what

Raffie had said to him in the snow, and the way Old Bill Williams had looked when he talked about Henry King, and how Alex Godey's voice had trembled back in Taos. But there was more to it, something more lying in the shadows of his eyes.

"You were frightened," she whispered. "Weren't you, Charles?"

He nodded. "I'd never felt that way before. That mountain—even when we gave up and turned back—it didn't let up. It *wanted* to kill us all. To the very last man. Yes, I was scared." He was looking at his hands, his fingers laced and taut. "But that wasn't it. The thing is . . . I'd always been so *sure*! And we were whipped down off that mountain the way you'd swat flies with a dishcloth."

She leaned forward to touch Charles' hands—they were rigid, straining against each other.

"Darling," she said. "Oh, my sweet darling . . ."

"But Jessie, don't you see?—this is my *field*! Look—when Bancroft wanted me to come out here, that day in your father's office, and I forced him to say he spoke for the President . . . it meant nothing—not a thing. When they kicked the trapdoor and left me hanging, I didn't even know I'd been led onto the scaffold," He paused, watching her face, and she knew he was coming to the root of it. "But this was different. This was *failure*. I know the mountains—that's my trade. If you go ahead—if you don't let anything stop you—you get through. I've never missed. And this time, when it meant more than ever—I was going to turn it all around, Jessie, don't you see? I was going to throw it in all those bastards' faces. And I gave it everything I had—everything!—and it didn't work."

"But *nobody* could have gotten through that snow. Even Kit said so."

"Who knows?" He gave a hard, bitter smile. "What matters is that I didn't get through."

"It's not failure if it was impossible . . ."

"It is never impossible. If we'd found the damned pass, if I'd picked my people a little more carefully, if I'd husbanded supplies just right—no, Jessie, you're *never* innocent in your own failures."

"But what difference does it make now? You did your best—that's the point."

"It's just not so easy to bring a failure like this home to your wife."

"You mean, I might—think less of you?"

"You've been raised on success, Jessie."

She felt her eyes fill. Dear God, but she loved him. "Oh, Charles, my sweet husband—everything I learned in Panama belies that. Success, my foot! I found out how utterly, horribly vulnerable I am." She whispered: "Don't you know that all I care about is that we're together? Don't you know yet that nothing else matters, or ever will?"

She opened her arms then and he came to her, his face on her breast, his arms around her and the child; she held them both.

"How I love you," he said.

Lily sat up suddenly. "I can't breathe with all this hugging," she said, and looked irritated and yet pleased as her parents broke into soft laughter.

After a time Jessie asked him about the ranch: had he been able to take any steps toward recovering it?

He shook his head. "It seems the title's not clear—Larkin says that's why he bought the other property for me."

"And took the ranch for himself. Trust a Boston Yankee."

"Well, he *says* he merely took an option on it, to hold it for me. In fact he offered to trade it for the other property anytime I wanted."

She was puzzled, there was a curious, bemused glint in his eyes that she couldn't read.

"You mean we have it, then? It's ours?"

"No . . . I decided to hang on to what we've got." Then to her amazement he laughed, a swift catch of breath, and seized her hands. "Oh Jessie—you won't believe what's happened."

They'd been following the Gila River, he said, heading west at last, making good time, when they'd encountered a tremendous cloud of dust and held a hurried conference. It certainly wasn't buffalo; no Apaches would ever move this way . . . Cautiously he'd ridden ahead with Alex.

"It was a party of Sonorans, Jessie—more than a thousand of them. Men, women and children, cattle and wagons—it was like some wild, biblical exodus there in the desert. I said: 'What has happened? Where in God's name are you going?' 'For the *gold*!' they cried. 'The *gold* . . .' It was the first I'd heard of it. They began telling me of the strike at Sutter's, and above Auburn—and all at once I remembered Bushnell that day at the river, and the grant Larkin secured for me, and put two and two together. Right there on the spot I hired twenty-eight men to work the streambeds: half for them, half for me." He laughed again. "I've just been up there. Every creek is running yellow with the stuff! It's—it's uncanny . . ."

"Gold?" she whispered. "You found gold on *our* land?"

"Look at this." He drew a buckskin bag from his coat pocket and hefted it in the palm of his hand. Slowly he opened the pouch and poured a glittering heap of yellow flakes and dust and little nuggets onto a paper from his notebook. She had never seen anything like it.

"Gold from the Mariposa," he said. "We're rich, it seems."

"Rich?"

"Just like that. Very rich."

She glanced at the canvas walls, suddenly uneasy. "They'll hear us, Charles."

"Doesn't matter—everyone in California's running around with some of it in his pockets."

Lily was standing with her face at the level of the table, staring at it. "Can I touch it, Daddy?" she said.

"Of course you can, sweetheart."

Slowly Lily pressed her hand into the pile, moving it about. There was an expression on her serious little face that made Jessie think of Mr. Gray. Lily's fingers were damp, and when she lifted them they were coated with gold dust. She turned her hand to catch the light, looking at her golden fingers.

"This is what those men in Panama were fighting over?" she said in wonder.

"Why in the world didn't you tell me about this the moment you walked in?" Jessie said.

He looked surprised. "Why should I?"

"It changes everything."

"No it doesn't," he said, and his face hardened again. "This is just luck. We've had some bad luck and now we've had some good." His eyes fastened on her, blue and intense and unbelievably sad.

"But the other was important."

MARIPOSA

It was midafternoon; the sun spread a golden haze across the rolling foothills of the Sierra Nevada. She watched the mountains rising in the distance, already vast but still miles away. The sun warmed her, driving away her cough, restoring her youth. It burned the hills, streaking the grass with buff, bringing out blazes of wildflowers. A dense live-oak grove looked almost black, the trees so like the apple trees back in Virginia that she looked for red fruit on the ground. The road turned between walls of thorny chaparral, impenetrable and mysterious, opened again into a field of poppies which flooded her eyes with color. A wooded stream ran below them and the carriage started down, its wheels spinning dust into the sweet sun haze.

She heard the mules snort as they approached water. The carriage rocked gently on its leather throughbraces, a little like a boat on an easy sea. It was a gorgeous thing, this carriage, its wheels a brilliant red, its body lacquered in brown with golden scrolls, its cushions and rolled curtains in matching red leather; it produced a sensation wherever they went. It had come around the Horn and Charles had brought it to the hotel the morning after he arrived. He had been so pleased with her stunned surprise that he'd insisted on demonstrating immediately—for her and the friendly crowd that gathered—how the cushions folded ingeniously down to become a bed. The boot in the rear was big enough to make a bed for Lily when the luggage was removed. This, Charles had said, would be their home on the way up to Mariposa, and they'd set out in a little cavalcade; Charles rode Sacramento, Godey was on a ragged buckskin, and Juan and Gregorio, two Indians from the California Battalion, came along as wranglers. Juan drove the carriage, Lily perched beside him, and in the afternoons Charles put Sacramento on a lead rope and sat inside with her, talking away the months of separation. They were in no hurry: they were together again and newly, astoundingly rich; they turned to the sun to draw away their hurts.

They passed into a grassy glade for the night and again she saw the smooth effectiveness of men accustomed to the field. Juan led the animals to water and grass, Gregorio fetched firewood, Alex set the coffeepot to boil,

Charles unloaded bedding and placed a leather cushion on the grass for her seat. She studied Alex as he worked; he was older, she saw, harder and more quiet than she remembered; she thought of him riding back into the mountains alone, finding the men strung out along the frozen river, wrapping the bodies of the dead and bringing them in. But his smile was as ready as ever; he looked up at her, laughing silently as his eyes streamed over the onions he was slicing. He speared beef and tomatoes on spits, thrust potatoes into the coals. Charles took a trout from the stream, Lily exclaiming as its rich iridescence faded, and dropped it into the pan with the onions. In startingly quick time the six of them were dining on stoneware plates and Charles was drinking a cup of hot chocolate. He couldn't seem to get enough of it.

The snow had aged him terribly. Sometimes he muttered in his sleep, but he would never tell her his dreams. The gray in his beard was more pronounced. With a start, she realized he was nearer forty than thirty. She lay flat in the sweet grass, feeling luxurious, listening to the men talking about gold. It was a presence in her mind—smooth, shiny, malleable to her needs. Of course it didn't line the stream bottoms, as they had said in Panama. It sought the low places, under rocks, in crevices, in the river sand itself. Miners dug into banks and bars in the rivers, into streambeds that dried in the summer; they went down and down, washing the gold-permeated sand as they moved toward bedrock where pockets of gold might be taken with a spoon. Spooning gold like oatmeal—the image delighted her.

"It isn't so obvious as all that," Charles told her. "That fellow Marshall wouldn't have found it at Sutter's if he hadn't been building a mill. He stirred the bottom making his tailrace, and the next morning he found the gold dropped all along the race."

"Isn't it incredible that Sutter's right in the middle of it? He must live a charmed life."

"He wouldn't say so—it's about ruined him."

She could hardly believe what he told her. After a lifetime of self-promotion built on air, solid gold in Sutter's hands had paralyzed him. He had done nothing to capitalize on it, and when the rush started men swarmed over his land, took the gold, trampled his crops, slaughtered his beeves. In a year he had lost control of most of his property and was facing ruin.

"People can just *come* on your land?—on our land, too?"

"You can't keep people away from gold lying on the ground. That would take an army—and then the army would take the gold." The men laughed. "Anyway, they regard these mountains as free land, public domain, like a frontier that's always open to settlers."

"But we have a grant—we have title, don't we?"

They did, but the Spanish title appeared even more ambiguous than the French titles had been in old St. Louis. First, their Mariposa grant wasn't precisely bounded; it authorized them to "choose" a huge area—about a hundred square miles—within a much larger area, and Charles hadn't done that yet. And then, the grant had no real standing until it was ratified by United States land commissioners, who hadn't even been appointed.

She felt a deep, pervasive alarm. "We could lose it, then?"

"I don't think the courts would abrogate a valid grant, though we might have to fight for it."

"But if anyone can take our gold, how are we—"

"I've grubstaked a hundred men on the land, that's how. These Sonorans are professionals—there's plenty of gold in Mexico—and they know just what to do. I stayed long enough to make a pouchful and get 'em set up. And then I came looking for you."

Over the next few days the road to Mariposa steepened and grew steadily rougher. Cottonwoods and chaparral gave way to white fir. Sometimes the road was such a narrow cut that from the carriage she could see only the drop. It was better not to look down at fir trees aimed at her like arrows, and she leaned back instead to watch the great range filling the eastern sky. She knew the Appalachians, and knowing them made these mountains all the more stunning. This was what Charles had led his party across in hard winter with no assurance that he could get down; she had written the whole story, but she saw now she hadn't felt it at all.

Then the carriage tilted down into Bear Valley, and far below, on a flat where the streams slowed into long, lazy loops, she saw a village of some twenty tents and houses made of canvas nailed to frame. There was one solid-looking log cabin. The buildings stood haphazardly against a steep bluff, flanking a two-story public house made almost entirely of canvas. It was a hotel; the upper half of its first story stood open in lieu of windows, and red calico curtains fluttered half in and half out. Prospectors in flannel shirts and low-crowned hats, their boots caked with mud, were milling around in front. The settlement depressed her hugely—all scraps of unfinished lumber nailed higgledy-piggledy, the ground littered with tin cans, broken miner's tools, discarded clothing, everywhere abandoned mine pits filled with water.

A loud voice cried, "Well, God damn, it's Colonel Frémont! You come in the nick of time, Colonel." Immediately the men crowded around Sacramento, shouting greetings, pumping his hand; how well known he was in California continued to surprise her. A big miner with a red beard called something and the others yelled in approval. An intelligent-looking man in a frock coat was talking earnestly to Charles; in a moment he came over to the carriage.

"They're holding a man they think killed his partner," he said. "They're going to try him, and they want me to preside. The doctor's wife is the only woman in the area—she'd like you and Lily to visit her while I tend to this."

"You're going to try him for *murder*?" Over his shoulder she could see a young fellow standing awkwardly; his hands were bound. Even at this distance she could sense his terror. "What if you find him guilty?"

"Maybe we won't."

"Charles, surely that's a matter for the authorities—the sheriff or—"

He grunted. "There *are* no authorities. There's not even any government in California. Miners' courts are all they have—but it'll work out. Come and meet the Steffansons."

The doctor led her toward the log cabin she'd seen from above. The men opened a way for her, pulling off their hats and staring at her with a respectful fascination that made her acutely aware of her sex. June Steffanson was a small woman hardly older than Jessie, though strain lines drew down the corners of her mouth.

"It's so good to see you!" she cried. "You can't imagine how dreary it is, being the only woman in town." She fussed happily over Lily as she led them inside. "My three are all boys," she said. "It does get lonely. I don't mean the men aren't nice to me—they treat me like a pet." She picked up a fruit jar. "Look—Ab Simmons found this swimming in his water glass at the river, and nothing would do but I must have it." Jessie saw a two-inch trout circling in the jar. "But even being a pet gets tiresome."

The cabin was twenty feet square with a dirt floor. It had no windows, though a course of logs had been replaced by chinked fruit jars to admit light. Mrs. Steffanson had lined one side of the cabin in calico spotted with roses and stacked her traveling trunk on two boxes for a dressing table. Jessie saw a silver mirror there, with cut-glass bottles.

Stirring the fire under her teakettle, June Steffanson said, "I'm so glad Colonel Frémont came. That Johnny Hoffman is wild."

"What's it all about?" Jessie asked.

"Oh, Billy Claxton's partner disappeared. Joe Robson. They've been working a claim over here no one thinks much of. Billy says Joe's gone off to San Francisco. Billy's one you'd find it hard to believe if he told you the sun was up at noon—always studying his boots. So they searched him and found four hundred dollars in dust. They think that can't be a half-share from such a sorry claim, so they figure he must've killed Joe and buried him."

"They would hang a man on no more evidence than that?"

"Well, Colonel Frémont'll know what to do. Those wonderful reports he wrote! Claude and I came out two years ago in Mr. Ebsen's wagon train, and all the way across, those reports were our bible. Clear as day they were; as if he was right there at our shoulder, explaining it all." She poured the tea into finely translucent china traced with pale anemones. Jessie commented on the cup's beauty, and Mrs. Steffanson looked pleased.

"They were my grandmother's. We brought them all the way from Indiana in that wagon, and we didn't crack one." She laughed and added, "I thought all my bones would shatter, but I never regretted coming for a moment. Truth is, after reading Colonel Frémont's reports, we decided California was the place for us. 'Claude,' I said, 'we've just got to go,' and he said, 'All right, Juney.' He was going to practice in Sonoma, but when everyone came to the gold fields, so did we."

"Is the doctor mining?"

"Oh, goodness, no. The miners are always sick. And they pay him lots more than he could make panning."

Jessie was surprised. "People aren't getting rich, then?"

"Mining? Oh, my dear, no. You hear some wonderful stories, the pocket of dust that yields five thousand dollars in an hour—that's the crazy appeal of mining. You never know but what the next shovelful with give you a nugget big as an apple—I've seen one myself big as a fat plum. But most men are lucky to get an ounce a day, and it takes that much just to live. Why, a man and his wife worked up north of here and she made twice as much taking in washing as he did taking out gold."

She sighed, watching the men outside through the open canvas door, which hung on leather strap hinges. "Doing brute labor," she said. "I don't know why they don't all go off. I wouldn't doubt that Joe Robson did just what Billy said—got tired and decided to go home."

"They couldn't convict a man just because he had four hundred dollars, could they?'"

"I don't know. They convicted one of theft last week and flogged him. Oh! I've never heard such sounds and I never want to again . . ." She stopped, glancing uneasily at Lily. "But you see, Mrs. Frémont, that's why Congress just *has* to give us a government. Those idiots in Washington!" She stopped, coloring. "Oh, dear, I'm sorry. I forgot that your father—"

"That's all right," Jessie said. "Senator Benton has fought to get California admitted. It's the southern men who block it."

There it was again. What a marvelous irony—the western empire for which Mr. T had fought so hard had only inflamed all over again the awful issue between slavery and free soil. An increasingly powerful movement in the North insisted that slavery be banned in any territory acquired in the war with Mexico, and the South was resisting this fiercely. The same old, grim, implacable issue. Before she was born her beloved Missouri had entered as a slave state, balancing the free state of Maine. And until some solution was worked out, the new territories would have no real—

"Lord ha' mercy," June Steffanson cried, "there he is!" She darted outdoors, shouting, "Claude! Claude! Johnny Hoffman! Look who's here, you idiots!"

Following her out, Jessie saw the doctor's wife pointing at a man who was staring at the crowd with dull-eyed surprise.

The red-bearded miner pushed angrily toward him. "Where the hell have you been, Joe?" he demanded. "We're fixing to hang Billy Claxton for killing you."

"Why, I aint' killed, Johnny. You can see that."

Charles was just behind Hoffman. "Hold on, now," he said in a voice that Jessie rarely heard; it produced immediate silence. "Are you Joe Robson?"

"Always have been."

"All right!" Charles said. Jessie recognized the flash in his eyes—very pleased, burdens lifted—then he'd jumped onto a packing case and called: "Here's the court's ruling: since the murder victim is alive and kicking, the murder case is dismissed; but since these two have made a plain nuisance of themselves, I'll open a nuisance case against them. Now, having heard the evidence, I find them both guilty of being pains in the backside."

There was a roar of approval.

"And here's the sentence: jointly and severally, the defendants should stand the crowd a round of drinks!"

"You're our kind of judge, Colonel," Hoffman shouted.

June Steffanson gave Jessie a triumphant little hug. "Didn't I tell you Colonel Frémont would know just how to handle it?"

They started out again in the morning. The way grew so steep that Jessie and Lily left the carriage to ride little mules who placed their tiny hooves as daintily as dancers. The dominating ridge of the Sierra stood high above them; white fir marched up the slopes like armies; she watched a bald eagle carrying something in its talons settle into a roost a hundred feet above ground. As they started down toward the Mariposa River she had the oddly comfortable feeling that she was coming home to country she had never seen.

At the river two Mexicans were shoveling dirt into a wooden box and flooding it with water. They raised straw hats courteously and one called upriver in a high, carrying singsong.

"That'll fetch Miguel," Charles said, "but first I'll show you where we'll live." He led the way up a broad slope that shelved onto an almost level bench a mile long. Here a grove of stout black oaks clustered around a spring that bubbled from the mountain's base. The water wandered across the flat, forming a pond about halfway to the edge. Grass grew to her stirrups. Charles handed her a cup of water from the spring; it was stingingly cold and had no mineral taste. They would build the house here, surrounded by oaks, its back to the spring, its veranda overlooking the pool where, just then, she saw a fish rise.

"Look," Charles said. They faced directly toward a huge rough-shouldered mountain three or four miles away. Its shape was very distinctive; she knew that it would burn itself into memory and become a talisman of home.

"I thought we'd name it Mount Bullion," he said, and she laughed, nodding. She knew how her father would prize that—Old Bullion, the battler for hard money, was his favorite nickname—and she decided immediately to sketch the mountain for him, showing how it stood apart from the main chain of the Sierra Nevada, rugged and alone.

Then they went down to the river. Miguel Reyes of the long black mustachios caught Charles in a bear-hugging *abrazo,* bowed gracefully over her hand and told them that the Mariposa was proving much richer than expected. His men had worked fast, taking creek after creek and skimming off the accessible deposits before the inevitable rush of strangers arrived. He thought they had preempted the best claims; already they'd taken at least four thousand pounds, and there was plenty more.

"Pounds? Of gold?" She stared at him.

Miguel was packing it in buckskin bags, each about fifty pounds; he hadn't bothered to count them.

"I *told* you we were rich." Charles laughed. "That'll teach you to believe me. Come on, I'll show you how it's done." He led her over to a box several feet long, open at the top and the low end. It was mounted on rockers and had a hopper box with a mesh bottom. One miner shoveled dirt into the hopper and then poured in buckets of water while another rocked the box. The dirty water sloshed about the cleated bottom and poured from the open end.

"Remember, it's not ore—the gold has already separated from the rock, but it's mixed with dirt. When we get the dirt moving in the water, the mesh in the hopper stops the big stones, the cleats catch the gold, and the dirt washes on out. Look . . ."

Sure enough, grains of gold lay behind the cleats. She passed the top of her fingers over them, feeling faintly dizzy, very strange, bound in a golden dream. "Does this get it all?"

"Some washes out. Later we'll set up long toms—they've got a bigger hopper with a series of riffled sluice boxes under it—so the gold'll have to wash over forty or fifty cleats to get away."

"So you don't use a pan at all."

"Well, sure, it starts with the pan. That's how you learn if the dirt's worth working." He took a flat pan of about eighteen inches diameter with rounded sides, half-filled it with dirt and scooped it full of river water. Then, holding one edge lower than the other, he rotated the water so that it slopped over the edges, spilling the lighter dirt. When the water was gone he picked out the remaining stones and showed her the shiny flakes on the bottom.

Just then the edge of the bank gave way under him. He threw out a leg to catch himself and slipped into the icy water to his knee. Instantly his face turned white and strained.

"Oh, my God," he gasped. He held out a hand to her. She braced herself and pulled him up. He wrenched off his boot, his breath coming in shudders, and thrust his foot into dry sand the sun had warmed. The exposed skin was laced with the ugly blue welts of swollen veins.

"Oh, my dearest," she murmured, crouching beside him, holding a soaked handkerchief to his forehead.

"Ah, sweet Jesus," he muttered. "That's better." Gradually the color returned to his face; he gave her a small smile. "Too soon, after frostbite," he said.

When he could stand again he insisted on seeing the gold, though he limped as Miguel led them to a small log structure. Inside she saw buckskin bags, each the size of a small pumpkin, stacked waist-high. Miguel opened one, rolling down the sides to show the heavy yellow dust. She couldn't pull her eyes away.

". . . How much is four thousand pounds' worth?" she asked at last. Her voice seemed stuck in her throat.

"Well, sixteen ounces to the pound, ten dollars the ounce, half our share . . . nearly a third of a million."

Third of a million. Dollars. Sitting there in those buckskin sacks.

"Mr. Larkin did us a favor," she heard herself say humbly.

"He put us in beans for the rest of our lives."

She laughed wildly then; she could not understand how he could sound so casual about it. That was what had been warming her, she realized; the sun had helped, but it was the gold that had bathed her in such peaceful assurance. It did not matter that Washington was an enemy camp, that they had been spurned and humiliated; gold was proof against every calumny, gold would insulate them from the pain of betrayal. For months she had carried deep within her a kernel of worry; how were they to live with Charles out of the Army and denied his true vocation so cruelly? Maybe it *was* all pure luck, as he claimed; but maybe it was something more—maybe the gods, having veiled their faces so ruthlessly for so long, had at last relented, and proffered a kind of consolation.

They were secure forever.

It was Jessie who focused their attention on the quartz outcropping. Later, Frémont was amused. He had noticed it a half-dozen times in passing—like reddish glass, with streaks and whorls of white, purple, green, orange, black—but it was Jessie who pressed them for a piece of it to decorate the table in their tent.

"It's gorgeous," she said, "and that whole slab looks ready to break off. Alex, see if you can't work it loose."

They were on the open flat a quarter-mile beyond where Jessie wanted to raise a house someday; a small stream cut a gully toward the river. Frémont had been a little unsure as to how Senator Benton's daughter would like life in the open, but after a couple of months in a tent, she seemed as content as he. Her color had returned and her weight was restored—he could see it in the rounded perfection of her upper arms.

Godey slid his knife blade in behind the quartz slab and began to prize it loose from the main body of stone. In a moment there was a crack and a piece a foot square and a couple of inches thick fell into his hands.

"Well, I'll be damned," he said. He looked up at Frémont. "It's full of gold."

The rock had split along a thread of gold that balled into a good-sized nugget in one place. In the unusually translucent quartz Frémont saw other threads gleaming straight through the slab. That meant that runners of gold were coming out of the mountain—and then he was on his knees, picking at the exposed face of quartz with his knife. Yes: the gold ran deep back into the rock.

"I'd better go get some tools," Godey said in an oddly tense voice.

"What does it mean?" Jessie asked as they waited.

"Maybe we've found where the gold comes from," Frémont answered. "It's a vein." He was trying to adjust to the idea. A vein meant gold concentrated in one place—it would be *their* gold, not free to whoever came along, because it was their ground and they controlled its source.

"It couldn't *all* come from here," Jessie was saying in wonder.

He saw Godey with the tools. He wanted to open this up; he had to know. "There'll be others. I've seen several quartz outcroppings . . ."

The glassy rock broke readily under their picks and fell on the canvas Godey had brought. Frémont stopped often to examine the face. It was unchanged—gold threads stranded through the rock, emerging from the mountain, with here and there isolated flakes and occasional nuggets.

Back at camp Jessie put the original piece in their tent. Frémont spread a clean canvas and set out an anvil and a small sledge from the tool shop he had had sent around the Horn. He weighed out twenty-five pounds of broken rock.

"Let's see what we've got," he said to Godey, and began beating the rock to powder against the anvil. It reduced to perhaps a third of a bushel, which they washed with a pan. When they were done, Frémont weighed the gold. It held the scale at precisely two-tenths of an ounce.

That was rich, awesomely rich—.05 percent, when gold mines back in Georgia were counted good producers at .005 percent. There was eighty cents worth of gold in every pound of raw rock. If that held up as the rock ran back into the mountain, he was sitting on a fortune that would make the placer mining in the streams a penny-ante affair—all the gold they'd taken so far might be only prelude. Frémont had assumed that when the winter rains began the Sonorans would have cleaned out the Mariposa's streams and the gold would be finished. He'd expected to use his continually mounting share to stock a fine mountain ranch. But now . . .

"Alex," he said quickly, "there's a mineralogy professor from Harvard College studying the fields up north of here—Adelbury, I think his name is. Around Hangtown, maybe—wherever he is, find him. Tell him what we've got, and tell him we'll meet any fee if he'll come give us an opinion."

Frémont discovered four more quartz veins, all gold-bearing, while Godey was away. An underlay of excitement stirred him at odd times; he sidled up to the idea, nudging it like a forbidden pleasure that might disappear if grasped squarely. The Mariposa had some hands by now and was beginning to take shape as a working ranch. The men had come drifting up looking for wages. They were men who lacked a nose for color or whose grub money ran out before they struck or who didn't care for the risk of ending a week with no dust in the pan and no food on the table.

Frémont hired them at ten dollars a day, a king's wage in the East but about what a decent claim would produce out here. He started a barn, raised a corral, sent crews to mountain meadows to make hay. He put up a cookshed with a roasting pit and one day there appeared a cook who had jumped a Boston ship in San Francisco Bay and found that shoveling wasn't his art. A cook should cook, said Long John Bartholomew, just like a cow should give milk and a woman give trouble. Godey taught him the Spanish art of the barbecue. The Sonorans continued to work the river and the most promising streams, and though the golden flow was slowly diminishing, Miguel added still another fat bag to the others every few days. Frémont padlocked it behind the stout doors of the new barn.

June Steffanson came to visit with her boys. Lily was delighted and Frémont found the children's voices as sweet as music. Watching them pile onto her pony Daphne, he thought how Benton would have been a year old by now; in his mind's eye he could see a little boy following the older children. June Steffanson was good for Jessie; it struck him that both women were lonely, and he began to wonder if Mariposa really could be their permanent home.

Then Godey rode in with Dr. Festus Adelbury of Harvard College. The professor had a bulbous nose and a drooping taffy-colored mustache; he wore a high collar and string tie. He squinted at the outcropping a long time, then at the surrounding rock. At last he opened a rucksack and took out an oddly shaped hammer and chisel. He knelt on a leather apron and gouged out chunks of glassy rock, which he then broke with deft hammer taps that shattered it cleanly on its crystal lines.

"Um," he said at last. "Perfect. Classic quartz, classic pattern. But the richest I've ever seen."

"More than just a pocket, you think?"

"Quartz in a pocket? Don't be ridiculous. It doesn't occur so. This is a vein, sir, a damned fine vein. You understand a vein, do you? Molten quartz, carrying gold, has been laid among other rock. It may be a couple of feet deep, it may be ten, in width it might be narrow or it might spread out to a hundred feet. May run a mile or it may pinch right off. Gold may run through all of it or just a little of it. Quartz is ubiquitous, you know—if there was gold in *all* quartz, we wouldn't care much for gold, I can tell you." He gave a shrill laugh, and his eyes glinted behind his steel spectacles.

"Then we have something, you think?"

"Who knows?" He stood there patting his mustache. "Now I must be alone, if you please." He told Godey to fetch his horse. "I will look around, measure, estimate. We will see what we will see." He cocked his head, sniffing the odor that drifted from Long John's pit. "Fat beef, eh? Capital! Nothing stirs one's hunger like good quartz."

The next morning Dr. Adelbury started the men on test shafts cut toward the veins. The first vein was about four feet at the outcropping; twenty feet in it had widened to nine feet and its gold content remained high. Quite singular, the professor said, filling several notebook pages with calculations as he led the men to the next vein. A few days later he was ready to talk.

"Greater sulfide problem, naturally, as you leave the surface, but well within tolerable limits," he said, polishing his glasses. They were sitting at a slab table near the cookshed; a mockingbird's fluid notes came pealing down from the live oak. Jessie brought three cups of coffee on a tray; she sat down on Frémont's side and leaned against him. He felt preternaturally alert, as though facing danger, and her closeness irritated him.

"Then what do we have?" he asked.

"We tested three veins. All of them get considerably wider and hold their gold content. That's what counts—no sign of the gold petering out. I can't say how far in it runs, but my professional opinion is that those veins will hold up deeper than you possibly can follow."

"Can you put that in concrete terms?"

"Dollar figure? In the ground?" Adelbury gave him a sly, wicked smile. "Doubtless there are veins not yet discovered—they come in groups. Tens of million of dollars, certainly. Fifty million. Maybe a hundred million. Enough, though. Wouldn't you say?"

Frémont couldn't seem to draw enough air into his lungs. Adelbury's eyes were searching his; there was something mischievous, almost malicious in the man's expression—or maybe it was just envy.

"But the real question," Adelbury went on, "is: how much can you get out? You'll have to cut shafts a mile long, oaken shoring all the way, drill and blast, lay tracks to haul out ore. You'll have to set up stamp mills to crush the ore, washers, copper plates with mercury bed—" His eyebrows shot up. "It should be interesting to set up an industrial empire where everything must be hauled up in parts by muleback. . . . But when you get it in place, when you begin to produce, you will be rich." His head was nodding rapidly, his eyes glinted wickedly at them. "Yes, Colonel and Mrs. Frémont. Very, very *very* rich."

"I don't know how to calculate the cost of developing," Frémont said evenly, willing himself to show no emotion in front of the man, whom he'd begun to dislike intensely, he didn't know why.

"Why, roughly speaking, you should make a good start on capital of a half-million dollars or so."

The figure was stunning—it was every penny they had taken out so far, and more. Adelbury began ticking off figures. "Hundred men minimum, that's a thousand a day, say two hundred days the first year of operation. A hundred thousand for stamp mills, rail equipment to move ore, donkey engines, steam pumps, blowers. Another hundred thousand or so to get it set up; and the rest for the unforeseen—ah, contingencies . . ."

Frémont, in a turmoil of emotions, didn't respond. Adelbury said with a high, thin laugh, "And then millions upon millions. In your hands." He paused again as the mockingbird's song spilled down in the sunshine and added brightly: "Provided the veins don't peter out, of course."

Jessie shivered suddenly and rose from the bench. "I've got to see to the children," she said. Frémont watched her walk quickly away, her skirts snapping.

Late that night he said to her, "What a fantastic turn of fortune! This morning we were well off—this evening we're rich beyond imagining. There's no way even to grasp the figures."

The evening chill had fallen down the mountain and she was in bed, a blanket drawn under her chin. But her voice had an edge in it. "Funny," she said. "I was thinking just the opposite. This morning everything was secure and nothing could touch us. This evening everything's a risk. Everything."

He was in the saddle at dawn, restlessly prowling the Mariposa. He didn't have to decide immediately, he told himself, there was no hurry. In fact, his decision had followed instantly on Adelbury's words. It was the chance of a lifetime—of a score of lifetimes. He already had sited the stamp mills in his mind, and was planning rails for the ore cars. He felt a bite of fall in the morning air. Winter would be along before much could be built, but he might start cutting out some ore.

A few days later he and Jessie took June Steffanson back to Bear Valley. As they topped the ridge at midmorning, he knew the ugly little hamlet would be bigger next year, it would feed on a growing Mariposa, and it struck him that he ought to buy land here. The makeshift street was empty now—everyone was working against the coming fall—but he saw a stout-looking wagon drawn up before the canvas hotel. When he handed the women down at the Steffansons' cabin, Jessie asked him to be back in an hour for dinner. Frémont strolled toward the hotel, seeing brick buildings in his mind's eye, a mercantile establishment, a livery stable, a hotel with real windows.

The wagon was muddy, but Frémont made out the legend MINERS' SUPPLIES on the side. The team was standing out of harness and two men were sitting on the veranda of the hotel. They were strangers, but they recognized Frémont and came down to greet him. Peddling must be a chancy affair in such rough country, he thought, and said as much. The younger man, a big fellow with a black beard and an oversized head, wanted it known immediately that he was a good deal more than a peddler. His name was Collis Huntington, and he had the biggest miner-supply store in Sacramento. He left his partner to tend counter—he liked to get out among his customers. "Find out what they're wanting, worrying about. That's how you figure what's needed before your competition does. I've done a plenty of peddling, though. Used to run a wagon from Oneonta, New York clean out to Indiana and back. There's a life that'll teach you a little about business."

"Are you in hardware, too?" Frémont asked the other fellow. But he already knew the answer. He was a little older than Frémont, with a saturnine face, and he wore a suit, his coat open in deference to the sun. His name was Trenor Park, he said with just the right graceful touch of modesty. There was something comfortable about him, a matter of class: Trenor Park was entirely different from the rawboned hardware peddler.

"Brother Huntington sells the real implements of mining," Park said. "Good oak and sharp steel. My business is more ephemeral—dreams, you might say. I'm a trader, and a bit of a banker. I match folks' needs—over here at A they've got too much of something and at B too little of it, and I bring 'em together, and usually there's a little left over for me. It's like a grand game, and at the same time it lets you do a little something for your fellowman, which isn't the worst thing."

"But you're a banker, too?"

"In a sense. My twin brother back in New York City—he and I were in investment banking when I decided I just had to see California . . . Well, I collect dust out here and give the miner a draft on my brother that his folks at home can cash. And every so often I send a gold shipment home under guard. It's a service to the miners—gives 'em some protection for what they've worked so hard to gain. And there's a little margin in it for me, you know."

He bobbed his head, deprecating himself with his quick little smile. "You wouldn't remember," he added, "but actually we've met. At Colonel Barnabas' home in New York."

Frémont remembered Barnabas, an imposing figure in shipping with vast muttonchop whiskers who had given him a dinner party when he was lecturing in New York. But he had to admit he didn't recall the meeting.

"I was the smallest fish in the room, Colonel. But it meant a lot to me. I got hold of your Reports next day, and stimulated by meeting you and reading your adventures—well, that's what decided me to come to California. My brother just couldn't understand it—but now I bet he wishes he'd come too."

Huntington interrupted rather impatiently then to ask if the Colonel needed any supplies up to his place. The question decided Frémont. If he was going to start taking ore, he would need more shovels and pickaxes, rock drills, blasting powder, a small steam compressor. Huntington scribbled in a little notebook, wetting his pencil on his tongue.

"That'll be, let's see," he said, totting rapidly, "it may vary, but say $1,325, less twenty percent for volume order plus say, $325 for haulage. Call it $1,385. If I can find the compressor for less, you'll get the difference; if it's more, I'll give you an accounting. Delivery in two weeks. Fair enough?—or do you want to compare prices?"

"Sounds good," Frémont answered. "Let's shake on it."

There was a moment's awkward silence and then Huntington said, "I didn't hear nothing about how I'm gonna get paid." He was smiling, but there was a raw, aggressive look on his face that irked Frémont.

"I thought that would go without saying."

"The question of payment don't *never* go without saying."

"Why, we're taking out more gold than that every hour."

"In gold then?"

"In gold," Frémont said, now thoroughly irritated. This wasn't the way gentlemen did business. He saw Park watching as if embarrassed for his friend. "In gold, ten dollars the ounce, on my scales—and you can bring your own to compare. Now, I suppose you'll want *that* in writing?"

Huntington shook his head. "Nope. I don't doubt you'll pay me. It's just good business to get the hows and wherefores straight." Neither distressed nor embarrassed, he said: "Let me ask you something different, Colonel. We heard you was planning to push through a railroad pass and got turned back. Does that mean you think it can't be done?"

"No," Frémont said, his temper fading; the man just didn't know any better. "I still believe Cochetopa is the right pass. We had a guide who lost his way, and an uncommon winter, and we lost some men. But I'm planning another expedition to establish the route once and for all."

Huntington said the railroad was essential to California's future, advancing arguments Frémont himself had often made with considerably more skill. Then, to his real surprise, Huntington added that he would like to build that road himself.

Hardware peddler cum railroad magnate! "That would take some capital, wouldn't it?" Frémont mildly inquired.

"A whole hell of a lot more'n I've got," Huntington said simply. "Still, it ain't never going to be till some folks with get-up-and-go start it. I reckon I can make a place in such a group." He put a foot on the hitching rail and scratched his ankle down into his high-topped shoe. But first, California had to get busy and make itself a state. The present situation was intolerable. What government they had was a half-baked mix of military rule, old Spanish laws—

"And *ad hoc* rule," Park said, interrupting without seeming to. "But you don't need to tell Colonel Frémont about that. He was our first governor—I expect he understands California politics better than either of us."

"Well," Huntington said, "the real problem ain't political. It's business. You can't do business without solid rules of law, and courts to enforce 'em. You write a contract, you want to know under what body of law it's to be interpreted, right?"

They talked about the convention that would open soon in Monterey. California already was big enough—Huntington was sure it had a hundred thousand people—to be admitted directly as a state, if those dunderheads in Congress would quit shuffling over slavery. . . .

"Will you play a role in the convention, Colonel?" Park asked.

Frémont frowned, and gripped his belt in both hands. "Not me, sir. My days of mixing in politics are over."

"That's too bad. Everyone's talking about you, over there. I'd guess they need someone with your experience."

"Oh, they'll get it done, all right," Huntington said. "The new legislature'll pass a body of law we can rely on. . . . Hell, you talk about railroad capital—there won't be any of that till we get some government."

Park said thoughtfully: "There are countless problems with a railroad—engineering, route, land grants and politicians, even Indians—but capital is never a problem. Capital's easy."

"Easy!" Frémont thought of the ring of tight, distrustful faces back in St. Louis. "Easy, you say?"

"Colonel, it's not hard to find money. What's hard to find is sound projects. New York and London—why, they're waiting with money that wants to invest in California. These old financiers hear all this gold talk and they want a piece of it. It's exciting, romantic—makes 'em feel young again. But at the same time they want assurances, names they know and trust. Give 'em that—and they come begging you to take their money."

"I may have some capital needs myself," Frémont heard himself say. "The Mariposa has considerable potential beyond the immediate placer mining." Both men were watching him intently now. Well, why not? He would have to face it sooner or later. Why not right now? "I can demonstrate that."

"Colonel, a man of your name and reputation wouldn't have to prove anything. The way you brought your party over the Sierras—*that's* the proof that counts. As for resources, if someone like Dr. Adelbury were to look it over—"

"Adelbury has examined the—the terrain," Frémont said cautiously. "He's drafting a report."

"Then capital will flock to you, no problem at all. Seems to me the real question is whether you'd want to take it."

Frémont saw Huntington glance at Park; it struck him that the two men didn't know each other well. "I don't know that I follow you, sir," Frémont said.

"Well, sir, money's trouble. It's an old adage, but it's true." Park hesitated and then with an apologetic little grimace said, "I feel a little presumptuous, talking this way, but money *is* my business, after all."

"I'd like to hear what you think."

"Well, sir, they'll give you their money—but then they'll dog you. They'll charge too much interest and they'll want to put deadlines on you. If it takes you a little longer to get set up than you planned, if you have a bad turn of luck, if a flood knocks out your mills, if labor is scarcer than you expect, they won't be understanding. They'll try to squeeze you. Now, I don't mean you'll squeeze easily, but what you want to remember is that what a money man desires most of all—after his investment, you know, he always wants a fair return on that—what he *really* aims for is *control.* He wants what's rightfully yours." Park cocked his head; his pale blue eyes were very clear. "Ownership. I'd say—stop me if I'm speaking out of turn."

"Go ahead."

"Well, I'd say: stay out of it. You've got a magnificent property from what I hear." Frémont wondered if Adelbury had been telling tales. "Why not develop it slowly, pay for improvements with what you take out of the ground? Sure, the capital's available, all you have to do is nod—and you could make your place an empire, you could be as big as big can get in American business—but you'd always be fighting off the wolves."

"I've dealt with wolves before," Frémont said wryly.

"Not *these* wolves, Colonel. These are the granddaddy timber variety." Park shrugged. "The point is, for a man with national position and all—would it be worth it?" He gave the self-deprecating little laugh. "Listen to me, telling a man like you these things. But it's what I believe, Colonel: never get involved with money men if you can help it."

So money was available as all that. He thought again of Slagle, and Chouteau, and old Frincke's pinched, ferret face. Well, that was probably the difference that gold made. It had been an interesting morning.

"Come on, Daddy," Lily said, running up to tug at his coattail.

He looked down at her. Nothing in this world had ever seemed so eager and innocent and trusting as his daughter's face.

"All right, honey," he said.

PART FIVE

THE GIANTS

"WHAT DO YOU THINK?" Jessie whispered as the great oak door closed. In spite of herself her heart had begun to pound uncontrollably and her throat was dry. From where she was standing she could see Merritt and Snyder moving away up Alvarado Street, their hats pulled low, collars turned up against the driving rain. "Is it actually *possible*—!" She faced her husband. "What do you think, Charles?"

"It's certainly something to think about, isn't it? The fact is, I'd put the whole thing out of my mind."

But his eyes flashed at her darkly, and she could see the old, high excitement dancing in them. He stirred the logs in the big fireplace and when he looked at her again his face was smooth with concern.

"What's the matter, Jessie?"

"I'm—scared, Charles," she said softly. "And I don't really know why . . ."

It had begun quietly enough—like all momentous occasions. The constitutional convention was due to convene in the morning; delegates had been streaming into Monterey for the past three days. With the onset of winter Charles had shut down mining operations and they'd moved into Señora Castro's handsome, spacious adobe. The long drawing room had an odd, bulging fireplace of plaster and floors of red tile. Its walls were white but she had filled it with bright colors and warm leather; it was a room for comfort and pleasure. She had been looking forward to the social life, and planned to give several dinners, even perhaps a ball. The Mariposa had restored her health over one glorious summer—but it was an undeniable joy to be back where houses had stone walls, and friends gathered to talk and laugh.

But there was nothing social in the meeting Ezekiel Merritt had wanted. He had arrived in midafternoon with Jacob Snyder, Elisha Crosby and other old California Battalion men. They had filed in quickly, their boots leaving water marks on the polished tile, and after a few lively reminiscences over the Bear Flag days Merritt had come straight to the point.

"Colonel, I remember when we didn't know how to handle that horses business—well, now we've come up against another situation. We're fixing on making California a state, whether the Congress likes it or not. And we need your help."

"You see," said Snyder, "we're like the old trapper who wakes up in the morning to find a couple of bull grizzlies fighting in his camp." He had fierce eyes, though his voice was moderate, and Jessie saw that he was the real leader of the delegation. "Now, the trapper don't care much which bear wins—he just don't want to get et up himself. 'Pears to us the Congress is a natural bear pit—the northerners ain't going to let in any new territory that *allows* slavery and the southerners won't take any that *bars* it. We got to figure out how to slip in betwixt 'em without getting ourselves chewed up in the process. Know what I mean?"

"Let me ask you something, Colonel," Crosby said. "There's talk the real reason for the war with Mexico was to acquire more territory for slavery. Texas is slave country and now it's trying to take over New Mexico. Polk was a southerner. . . . Think there's anything to that?"

That was radical abolitionist talk. Jessie thought of Bancroft with his tart Massachusetts accent—Bancroft as a tool of southern slave manipulators was ludicrous. She glanced at her husband as he said easily:

"I don't believe that for a moment. But what the war *did* do in bringing in so much new territory was kick over the balance between slave and free soil—and *that's* a mischief I certainly never contemplated."

"You were reared in the South, Colonel. What's your own feeling about slavery?"

"I hate it. I grew up with it and I know it for what it is—I'd never have anything to do with it."

"Under any circumstances?"

"Under any circumstances whatever."

Snyder said: "There's a story going round you've got slaves working for you at the diggings."

Charles' head came up. "That's a plain and simple lie, and I'd like to meet the fellow who concocted it. Matt Saunders was an ex-slave I met right here in Monterey. He told me his case, and I took him up to the Mariposa. He worked there until he'd earned the $1,700 he needed to purchase his family's freedom. Which he promptly did. He was a good worker, too. The best."

"And what do *you* think, ma'am? Missouri is slave territory."

"But lots of Missourians oppose it," Jessie answered. "Senator Benton has always opposed slavery—but he doesn't want to see the Union shattered on the issue."

"Amen to that," Charles said. "It's dangerous."

Elisha Crosby said softly, "But you could make slavery pay big on the Mariposa. I hear you're going to need lots of manpower for what you've got planned."

"Slave miners?" Charles said. "I doubt it would even work. But in any case it doesn't matter, I'd never do it. I'll tell you, gentlemen, it would be a terrible mistake for California to accept slavery. The South likes to talk as if it's just a matter of choice, but it's not. There's no way you could have slaves on one property and hired labor on the next. Slavery will drive out free labor. And it will debase everyone it touches."

She saw Merritt and Snyder look at each other: that was what they had come to hear, then.

"All right, Colonel," Snyder said briskly, "here's the situation. We can pass a free-soil constitution—the problem'll be to get Congress to swallow it. We're going to get us a legislature, and it will elect United States senators. Their first duty will be to take our constitution to Washington and get us sworn into the Union, so to speak.

"Now, you know William Gwin?" Charles shook his head. "Well, he's a Mississippi man, he's heading up the proslavery group. He will probably nail down the second seat—he's experienced in Washington and well respected here even by those who disagree with him. But the truth is he don't know California, and he don't speak for the majority. So we want to make sure our first senator is a free-soil man who knows California, but at the same time has some connections in Washington. We figure you—and your missus—fit the bill perfectly. Fact is, Colonel—you *are* California, and every Bear and homesteader and Californio knows it." He paused and gave Charles a long look. "If you're willing," he said at last, "we can promise you the seat. . . ."

The cold rain kept rolling in from the sea, thundering on the tile roof. The sky was gray as stone; it would be dark soon. Charles came behind her, caught her shoulders, and held her against his chest. His hands were firm, reassuring.

"You're *not* scared," he said. "There's no need to be. You want this as much as I do. And by God, I want it—I do!" He turned her around, his hands at her waist. "I *want* to go back there, and with position. Those bastards on the court-martial tried to destroy me, just to save Kearny's face. I don't give a damn that he's dead—he was wrong, he tried to slander me! Found guilty as charged, without so much as a thank-you . . . and little Benton—"

He broke off, went pacing across the room. "Look, Jessie, getting driven back in the snow, losing those poor devils—that's my fault and I won't walk away from it. Ever. But *why* did I have to move out on such short notice, press on against those weather warnings? I just couldn't wait—not after all the things that had happened and those money men on my back. Sure, I'll always believe it was my fault, but Goddamnit, now the shoe's on the other foot. We've a fortune in gold behind us, and now *California* is ready. We're going to overturn everything that was done to us back in Washington. Turn it all around! By God, I want that!"

She understood him perfectly. Vindication. He wanted it with his heart's blood—more than that, he needed to restore himself. It struck her that they had been hurt even more than she had realized. But would vindication do that?

Before he could answer, she said: "But that's the trouble—that's only to show others, and that's pretty hollow in the long run, isn't it?"

"I'm not sure how hollow it is," he said with a tight, grim smile. "I wouldn't mind swinging some weight in Washington—calling a hearing, letting Colonel Abert and a few others testify. I wouldn't mind putting Bancroft under oath and letting a few things out in the open, for all to see."

He was still smiling but his eyes were hard, and it increased her alarm. Yet she understood him utterly. She had watched too many political battles not to know the intense pleasure in wielding power.

"Would you do that?" she murmured.

He shrugged. "Probably not. But I wouldn't mind coming to town and let them sweat a little, wondering if I *would.*"

"Then it is hollow, if you wouldn't do it."

He didn't answer. The fire was burning low and he put on a log and stirred the coals; the flames made leaping patterns on his face. He sat in a chair with his feet on the hearth and his hands behind his head, watching her.

"What's really bothering you, Jessie?"

"The Mariposa," she said immediately. "Shouldn't we stay here and deal with it?"

"Why?"

"Why? Because there's so much to do—open those veins, get the stamp mills in place, lay all that track you were telling me about. Who's to see to it all?"

"Well, we won't be in Washington forever. Maybe there'll be delays, but Trenor can move some of it along."

"What does Trenor Park know about stamp mills? There's so much that can go wrong. I don't trust him, anyway." She stopped, surprised, realizing the thought was true, though it had just come to her. "He's too smooth—he wants something."

"I don't know what. He doesn't think we should raise *any* capital. When I insisted, he persuaded me to limit it to two hundred thousand. Adelbury urged a half million, but Trenor showed me we can make a good start with a lot less investment and less risk."

"I don't remember meeting him. Do you, really?"

"No, but I hardly imagine he'd make it up. And we *were* at Colonel Barnabas' home."

"The papers reported everywhere we went."

"Oh, Jessie, that's pretty farfetched! Why are you so cynical about it?"

"Because they took everything away from us once," she said slowly. "Washington has changed, Missouri has changed, Mr. T is getting old—he is, that's the truth. And then we came out here and the gold was like a gift. It scares me to risk it."

He kicked indolently at one of the andirons. "Jessie, it's only money, you know. A pile of money."

"But it's what's given you this new power—"

He came to his feet in a bound. "No!" he cried softly, and his eyes flashed in the old way. "No! It's the Sierra crossing, and Hawk's Peak, and the California Battalion—*that's* what put the power in my hands, *that's* why they want *me,* and no one else. Didn't all those mornings with the Senator teach you that? It's not what you have, it's what you've done that matters." He struck his open palm with his fist. "I have to *do* things," he said vehemently, "I'm nothing unless I'm doing them, that's all that counts. Money isn't the answer to anything, Jessie—not at bottom. Money doesn't set anything right, it doesn't make a man a man. Huntington—that's his obsession: money. All he's good for. . . .

"That's the greatest thing about your father," he went on, his voice passionate and low. "That time in St. Louis, with Slagle and Frincke and the others, I felt so badly—I felt I'd shamed a great man. But later I saw I had it all backwards. Everyone in that room had more money than the Senator, but *he* was the great man—and they were pissants, nonentities. They were rich and they were nothing; but *he* will live on down the years."

He began pacing up and down, the way he had when he dictated the Reports. "Take Bancroft. Granted I was naive when he turned to us—but just the same, he *did* turn to us. And we made something of it, too—we were a part of great events." He was hot with energy, his moccasins scuffing against the red tile floor. "Listen, Jessie, just look at what's happened in the last five years. The Oregon issue settled, Texas in, California and all the territory between—this country has near doubled in size. That's something! Your father always said it was an empire, and he's right. With the new territory, we're going to become one of the great powers in the world—we'll be too strong to live in Europe's shadow. And you and I have been right at the heart of it. The expeditions, the reports you wrote, California—we've been central to the whole thing. Maybe we won't get the credit, but by God, *we know,* and that's a lot."

She felt tears sting her eyes. He was right. It *was* a lot. If Mr. T had simply wanted money, he'd be a wealthy lawyer in St. Louis right now.

"Now, the slavery issue," he said. "It's got to be settled by compromise—or it'll be settled in blood. You know that. So does the Senator. I'll tell you, love, we've had a real say in this country's history over the last five years, and I don't want to quit now. Being rich is fine—but it doesn't hold a candle to trying to keep this country out of civil war . . ."

She frowned. "If the people of Missouri turn on Mr. T, maybe he'll wish he'd been a fat lawyer in St. Louis all along."

"Do you really believe that, Jessie?"

"No," she said reluctantly. "No, I guess not. But still, when we've been handed a gift as rich as the Mariposa, it seems like tempting fate to fly off and abandon it." She sighed. "One part of me wants to stay here and watch over it, make sure nothing goes wrong. And the other part wants to be at the thundering center of things again."

"And that's the real part, darling. That's the bold, adventurous side I love." He reached down and caught her hand, raised her and danced her around in a circle. He was humming, and all at once she recognized the tune—it was what the hurdy-gurdy had played on Pennsylvania Avenue when they were courting, when she'd had one eye cocked over her shoulder for the fearsome Senator B. Nothing had stopped them then . . .

"Godey's up there, he'll watch the property," he was saying. "Going to Washington may mean some delays, but that's all. It'll take time to get the equipment, anyway."

He released her and stood by the window, looking out. It was dark now and she saw his reflection staring back at him; he was more like a hawk than ever, his face thin and intense. He had gained a little weight on the Mariposa, but it hadn't changed the hard lines of force—and the hunger.

Then he shrugged, smiling. "Anyway, it's all academic—you can't argue with destiny."

She laughed once, gazing at him.

"Sure," he said. "We *are* the West—what Snyder said. We both are, we can't back away. Why did it all come together around us—who had a bigger hand in it than we? Kearny tried to take it all away—and the people of California intend to give it back again! That's the nature of destiny, don't you see? That's how it works." He took her in his arms, his eyes fiery and darkest blue. He had never looked so vital, so handsome. "We'll *go* to Washington—and it'll be a hell of a lot different from the last time I left California, choking in Kearny's dust . . ."

"Yes," she said. "Oh, yes, Charles." All right—they would march into the big arena again, move together down the long reaches of power. They would try to right a few wrongs, and serve this cumbersome, wonderful, maddening republic as best they could—and if they couldn't find their own Cochetopa Pass, still they would have tried. Being who and what they were, it would be cowardly of them *not* to try. . . . His hands were firm at the small of her back. She began to sway faintly; the magic trembling that swept her breath away.

"Oh, darling," she murmured. "I want you very much . . ."

He smiled softly. "Yours to command, ma'am," he said, and together they were moving toward the stairs under the insistent drumming of the rain.

Frémont and Jessie walked into the great ballroom and paused. The room was crowded, women in velvets as bright as jewels, men in evening dress or uniforms on which medals sparkled. Soft light spilled from chandeliers and there was a warm sound of talk and laughter that gradually stilled as heads turned with the avid, critical glances he remembered. Then Daniel Webster detached himself from a group and hurried toward them, his massive head cocked to one side, his hand out. He walked with small steps for so solid a man—he seemed to skitter across the floor; he had aged markedly since the day in '44 they had dined together.

"*Senator* Frémont," Webster said in that rich, resonant voice that carried effortlessly to every corner. "Welcome home!" He leaned close and kissed Jessie's cheek. "You're as captivating as ever, my dear. That California sunshine has made you bloom." He linked his arms through theirs. "Permit me, as one colleague to another, to present you if I may."

Frémont had awaited this moment, but it had not occurred to him that it would come on the arm of the great Whig. He glanced at Jessie's radiant face; the Mariposa seemed more than a continent away.

He met senators, congressmen, committee chairmen, leaders from both sides of the aisle; everyone seemed to be there. The room's lively buzz resumed; musicians tuned their instruments in another room, and across the way a woman laughed too insistently. Waiters circulated with wineglasses on round trays. Following Webster, they were presented to their old friends the Crittendens (John was now Attorney General) and Secretary of State John Clayton (it was rumored President Fillmore was going to replace him with Webster himself) and Supreme Court Justice Wayne of Georgia, who greeted them with surprising warmth—and found themselves before a mountain of a man in a brilliant uniform.

"General Scott," Webster said, "have you met Senator-elect and Mrs. Frémont?"

Winfield Scott cleared his throat gruffly. "I already know Colonel Frémont."

"From other days," Frémont said easily, smiling. "And vastly different circumstances."

"Ah, of course." Webster put palm to forehead. "I'd entirely forgotten." He held the conqueror of Vera Cruz with a droll glance, his massive eyebrows lifted. "General, you should never have let Mr. Frémont get away—but perhaps the Army's loss is the Senate's gain. I expect he'll ask for a seat on Military Affairs—that would be quite fitting with his background, wouldn't you say?"

And he led them away quickly, chuckling. "You must forgive me—I simply couldn't resist that. He's a great general—that campaign into the Valley of Mexico was a masterpiece—but Old Fuss and Feathers doesn't know the least thing about politics. And he wants to be President, alas."

When they had circled the room, Webster's tone became businesslike. "Now, I'm sure Tom'll move to give you the privilege of the floor. Tell him I'll be pleased to second the motion—it'll give it a nice bipartisan flavor. You won't have a voice, of course, until California is admitted and you're actually seated, but you should be there—California is at the core of the Great Debate." The leonine head came up and Frémont saw the force in his deep-set eyes. "Well, it's no longer a debate, I'm afraid."

"It's very serious, then."

Webster's smile disappeared; he looked haggard and grim. "Absolutely deadly. The United States is in more peril at this moment than it has been in all its sixty years of life. This time the South means it. You understand, you're a southerner—they're good Americans, they love the Union, it would break their hearts to secede. But they believe slavery is fundamental to their lives."

"They've talked secession before," Frémont said.

"You know they've called a convention in Nashville for June third? That, sir, is a secession convention. If we don't defuse this situation by then, it may be too late to avoid civil war. That's what Clay's compromise proposals are all about." A lovely woman nodded to them then, and in a flash his mood changed. "But you'll hear more than enough about that. Now's the time for dancing and"—he winked—"perhaps a glass or two."

But there was a whiff of national danger in the air that Frémont found as charged as those summer nights on the high prairie when the lightning walked on stilts. He talked to a score of men about politics and slavery and

California, but oddly, what interested them most was his gold. They knew no one else who owned a great gold mine! And gradually he realized that the fascination he read in their voices was . . . envy. The Mariposa was not a continent away, then—it was right here in this glittering citadel of power and privilege.

When the music began he danced with Jessie. She seemed to glow, her radiance undiminished, and he found something flirtatious and exciting in her manner. Her hand gripped his tightly, her breath was hot against his ear:

"Charles, it's a triumph! Can't you *feel* it? They're not just being gracious—it's more than that. They've been seeking me out all evening . . ."

It was just that—a triumph. They had sailed from San Francisco on the *Oregon* with William Gwin and other emissaries of this raw, new empire—and three million dollars in closely guarded gold dust. A British man-of-war off Mazatlán had fired a salute in their honor, they had been feted and cosseted at Panama City, and not even a recurrence of Jessie's malaria or a bout of rheumatic fever in his frostbitten leg had been able to dampen their sense of sheer jubilation.

"I know it's sinful, Charles," she was saying. "But I love it! I just love it! After all those terrible months . . ."

He swung her lightly through the waltz, conscious of the covert, envious glances all around them; the leg still hurt, but he would have cheerfully died rather than show it now.

"Let's revel in it, darling," he said. "It's really rather harmless sinfulness. . . ."

The following Monday Frémont was granted the privilege of the Senate floor. California's admission was trapped in the larger debate that now engrossed the Senate, but it gave Frémont an opportunity to listen and learn. Sometimes he joined Benton at his desk; more often he posted himself on a leather couch at the Democratic end of the chamber.

"Understand, Charles, the founding fathers—great men though they were—left one big structural crack in the timbers . . . and passed it on to us." Benton had wandered over to join Frémont on the couch; he sat with one ear cocked to the debate. But then, he went on, there wouldn't have *been* any nation if the northern states, which had outlawed slavery years before the Revolution, had insisted that the Declaration of Independence meant precisely what it said. The South would have walked out.

"But the situation's held for sixty years," Frémont said.

"Aye—because in the beginning it was a regional matter." Frémont thought that Benton was most likable when he was lecturing: dispassionate, analytical, but not overbearing. Most northerners found slavery distasteful but not their responsibility, so long as southerners kept it at home. And as the nation grew—Carolina to Tennessee to Missouri—the balance had held; formalized in the Missouri Compromise, Missouri slave and Maine free, the line of 36°30′ the demarcation between slave and free into the future. "And I sat here on this bench waiting for admission so I could take my seat, just the way you are now."

"So the West—and all our dreams for it—are what blew the balance apart," Frémont said.

"Well, life means change, Charles. The Mexican war forced the change as much as anything—it shifted people's focus from their state to their nation, and of course it brought in vast new—"

He broke off, called suddenly: "Point of order, Mr. President," and was on his feet, hurrying to the center of the floor. "The gentleman errs, and it grieves me to say it, because the senator from Alabama is an honored colleague and friend . . ."

The debate spun off into arcane depths and Frémont's mind drifted back to the South. His work, his dreams had made him a westerner, but his home region's new terrors and pride were giving him the same shocks of recognition the smell of sweet grass at dawn gave him when he went there. But atavistic feelings aren't necessarily true. He had never accepted southern premises. The British had imprisoned his father and set him at hard labor on a West Indian plantation for no reason but that he was French; and blacks were never faceless beings to him nor, perforce, to his son. Still, Frémont understood the tragedy that had enveloped both races. Enlightened southerners once had hoped that slavery would wither away, though all chance of that had died with Eli Whitney's cotton gin, which made cotton a practical crop. King Cotton, they called it now—it had spread across the lower South; the European textile markets depended on it and now southerners considered slavery to be economically crucial. It was hard to remember that there had ever been talk of ending it.

Nothing drew Frémont south now. His mother was dead, his old friendships withered. He could still remember his naive surprise the first time he'd left the South. The North was sharply different—alive, active, booming—and very appealing. The South was slow—surely the effort of keeping half its population under the dominance of the other held it back? Now the North's population was nearly double that of the South, and it had full control of the House of Representatives; only the Senate remained roughly equal, for the South had maintained a balance between free and slave states. No wonder the men at Mr. Poinsett's breakfasts had held the Senate in such reverence . . .

Frémont had long held a theory that since slavery was pernicious and anti-Christian on its face, it had been necessary for his fellow southerners to invent a mass rationale to justify it. The stability of King Cotton had supposedly helped the South to build a classic society in the Greek mode, which they claimed was of equal benefit to slaves because in time it would lift them from savagery to civilized Christianity. Frémont remembered Jessie's surprise on their first visit to Charleston. It had never occurred to her that the slaves on the McDowell family plantation were there for their own good, she said coldly. Now, though, the attitude had crept north through Virginia; to her horror, Jessie's cousins insisted that slavery was divinely inspired.

And yet, for all that, the South was fearful. Everyone seemed to talk of slave rebellions. White southerners were convinced that only the control slavery imposed kept blacks from slaughtering whites—"a holocaust of blood" in the orators' phrase. Those Frémont knew had talked themselves into a dangerous corner: paralyzed by fear on the one hand and a sense of superiority on the other, they now believed that life itself depended on maintaining slavery—which was why they saw northern abolition talk not as a moral position but as a knife at their throats. The irony of this was that most southerners were much too poor actually to own slaves. But once when Frémont had pointed out that the whole quarrel was over the interests of rich men and large landowners, a Charleston friend with whom he once had gone to Sunday school replied: "You know what your trouble is, John Charles? You done become a Goddamned Yankee. Maybe you'd better go on back up where you kin suck around 'em all the time."

His native South seemed determined to rub the foul institution into northern noses. That was Daniel Webster's view. Frémont encountered him in the halls one afternoon. Webster was going down to his hideaway office, catercorner from Benton's rooms, for a small nip.

"You know what this fugitive-slave question is doing?" Mr. Webster said. "It's radicalizing the North. I tell you, sir, it's one thing to disapprove of slavery and quite another actually to see some poor cowering wretch who's made his escape led back in chains. And then to learn that your own police must assist—indeed, that you yourself can be *compelled* to cooperate in his capture—now that, sir, will make an abolitionist in the afternoon of a man who was a states'-righter only that morning! Pursuing fugitive slaves is the worst thing they can do—and yet they believe they have no choice."

"No choice?"

"None at all. From their point of view, to let slaves run off without trying to recover them would undermine the very concept that they are property. It would be as good as admitting that slaves are what in fact we all know they are—prisoners held by force!"

He sighed. "Now we're heading for showdown," he said. "The extremists on both sides are in the minority, but they're hardening, growing rapidly. All southerners feel under attack, but a fanatical core already believes that secession is the only answer."

A page passed outside with a hand bell signaling a roll-call vote. Both men hurried up to the floor. Almost as an afterthought, Webster muttered, "I remember when abolitionism was a voice crying in the wilderness; today it speaks in thunder. Collision course, sir." He sighed impatiently. "We're trying to reconcile the irreconcilable. But what else can we do?"

It was damned ugly irony, Frémont thought, that the Western dream should become a battleground for North and South. California would be free, of course, if the Senate ever got around to admitting it; it had voted a free constitution. Oregon had been admitted as a free-soil territory. But would slavery be permitted or barred on the vast ranges of New Mexico and Utah, which ultimately would become several states?

A Pennsylvania congressman named David Wilmot had crystallized the radical northern viewpoint almost accidentally by introducing a resolution to bar slavery in any territory that might be acquired as a result of the Mexican war; Frémont had been out getting the Bear Flag waving, but even in California he'd heard reverberations of the fight that followed. In the end the resolution had been defeated but the Wilmot Proviso became antislavery's rallying point. When Frémont met this man who had become a hero in the North, a devil in the South, he was astonished to find him a plump young fellow of no particular force or intelligence. Old Benton was amused at his reaction. "History is crammed with men whom circumstance taps once—and never revisits," he said. But each move echoing Wilmot struck the southerners to whom Frémont talked as another unacceptable nail pounded into the coffin of the Union. Southern radicals looked forward to the convention at Nashville with sharp anticipation, moderates with dread, but none seemed to doubt that the end of the Union was near. And every northerner knew that southern secession meant civil war.

Into this caldron stepped Henry Clay. Benton hated the old Kentucky Whig—they had fought for years—but Frémont readily saw why Clay was admired and even loved. Harry of the West, men called him, the Great Pacificator who had shaped the Missouri Compromise, a towering figure who had hungered for the presidency for thirty years without finding the combination of circumstances that would reward him. Frémont recognized that Clay and Benton, Webster and Calhoun were the giants. Benton accepted that. He liked Webster, disdained John C. Calhoun, the great southern strategist, and hated Clay, but he was honest and he knew a great man when he saw one—himself included.

Clay was seventy-three, tired, ill, passed by ambition; now he intended to save the nation. He introduced a series of moves that, taken together, amounted to a canny blend of giving each side what it wanted most. Frémont listened carefully, ticking off the key provisions. California would be admitted as a free state, of course, and the rest of the territory would be admitted without reference to slavery—which was less than the extremists on both sides demanded but was attractive to moderates. And the North would agree to a fundamental southern demand—a more effective Fugitive Slave Act that would recognize slaves as property and provide for their return when they fled North. There was an ugly rumble when Clay reached this point, and the gavel rang through the chamber.

Clay spoke for compromise, the civilized way to settle differences, neither side asking the impossible, each recognizing that the other was composed of decent men who honestly disagreed. Frémont thought it brilliantly stated, but Benton listened with a series of sour grunts and said he would vote against it.

"At a time of such crisis?" Frémont asked, shocked.

"Well, what about it? The question is whether we really deal with it now or paper over again what won't stay repapered. Yield too much, and compromise becomes surrender." But Frémont thought that his dislike of Clay had blinded him. And Benton was in real trouble in Missouri, where proslavery men were stronger than ever.

At last Daniel Webster took the floor. "He'll be for it," Benton murmured. "Clay wouldn't have moved without his support." The great voice soared to gild the image of compromise with splendor and righteousness: he even sought to make the Fugitive Slave Act sound as noble as possible. His first cause was preservation of the Union, now and forever. "There's no finer speaker in the world," Benton said "How it must have hurt to find himself speaking for that damnable act. Courage, too—raw, gut courage. He's ruined himself with a large part of his abolitionist constituency. You'll see—it'll cost him the Presidency. They'll pillory him in Boston."

Calhoun was too near death to stand. He sat expressionless while a colleague read the speech he had written. The great South Carolinian had been the voice of the South and states' rights for as long as Frémont could remember. Senator, Vice-President, he, like Clay and Webster, had always expected to be President. His cold intellectual force overwhelmed his opponents; he and Mr. Poinsett often had opposed each other, but Frémont had never heard his old mentor speak disrespectfully of John C. Calhoun.

Listening to the definitive southern position in the hushed chamber, Frémont realized that Calhoun wasn't even bothering to address Clay's proposals. Instead he was gloomily acknowledging that the tide of events was running against his region. No matter how the new territory was organized for the moment, they all knew that slavery was not practical there, and so would not take hold. Ultimately, then, this great area would mature into free states and the South's balance of power would erode until it would be powerless to keep its enemies from abolishing slavery by constitutional amendment. In horror Frémont understood that Calhoun was not talking to the Senate at all. From the edge of his grave he was trying for the last time to rally his people—and the message was: Secede! Secede while there's yet time!

Calhoun died a few days later. Frémont wondered if the eulogies shouldn't really be for compromise itself. The voice of the South had spurned compromise. Webster's own constituents had burned him in effigy on the Boston Common for advocating compromise. Did anyone really want it? Yet the alternative was war . . .

At last Clay's measure came to the vote and in a series of devastating moves it was undermined, broken and finally defeated. The day of the giants was over. The organizers of the Nashville Convention cheered and the running tide for secession seized the South like a foul undertow.

Frémont was in despair. "But what about California?"

"Oh," Benton said flatly, "it'll work out. It's only a side issue right now."

Clay was exhausted, but now, unexpectedly, a moderate Democrat stepped forward and took command. Frémont had met Stephen A. Douglas of Illinois and wanted to know him better. Douglas was a small man with a big head which some said he needed to house his massive brain. "The Little Giant," they were calling him. Frémont enjoyed his quickness, for he was friendly and he had that quality—uncommon in brilliant men—of making others feel more rather than less intelligent. He had quietly withheld commitment through all of Clay's maneuvers; now he staked his reputation on his capacity to succeed where Clay had failed.

"Can it possibly work?" Frémont asked him one day in the cloakroom. "I don't believe they want compromise."

"You are right, sir," Douglas said with an easy smile. "But yes, it will work. You're perceptive—more so than Mr. Clay, I might say. His bill failed because, as you say, they don't want compromise. Mr. Clay thought they did—he thought they would give to get. He was wrong. But in another sense, he was right. There is a small group for whom compromise is the *only* issue. And that small group will prevail."

"I hope so," Frémont said doubtfully.

"Wait and see."

Frémont found Douglas' technique formidable to watch. The Illinoisan split Clay's compromise measure into individual bills, each of which drew support from a small bloc of men, from both North *and* South, who believed compromise so vital that they were willing to vote for measures they otherwise abhorred. Piece by piece, Douglas crafted a majority for each of Clay's points; one by one they passed and became law.

On the crucial issue of the Fugitive Slave Act, Benton abstained. "I'm damned if I'll vote *for* it," he told Frémont, "and if you know anything about Missouri, you know why I can't vote *against* it." That the grand old man would duck a vote struck Frémont in the pit of his stomach; he couldn't keep the sheer disappointment out of his face. After a taut silence, Benton growled: "God, boy, but you've got a lot to learn!" and Frémont realized fully how desperate things had become in Missouri.

The whole nation celebrated, and the Nashville Convention piffled off into oblivion—no one but the hottest of the red-hots really wanted secession. California was admitted and Frémont was seated, Benton formally presenting him, Jessie watching from the family gallery. At last, at long last—taking his own seat in the Senate of the United States, rising to make his maiden speech, glancing up at Jessie's radiant face, this was more than he'd ever dreamed might happen to him. He felt tireless and inventive, flooded with energy; it was like outfitting a different kind of expedition. There were only 21 working days left to the session, and he introduced 18 measures—including aid to western homesteaders and to impoverished Indian tribes and the federal regulation of mining claims. Some of his senior colleagues began to look at him with interest when he rose to speak.

Yet deep in his heart he knew he was no politician—he could not sustain the necessary cool responses on the Senate floor. When hotheaded Henry Foote of Mississippi insinuated that his mining-legislation bill was self-motivated, he was filled with rage: to impugn the motives of a senator and colleague! He formally demanded a full retraction or the inescapable alternative. This made Jessie frantic and even alarmed old Benton.

"You can't react that way, my boy. Don't you see what he's doing? He's simply testing you . . ."

"Then he's chosen a very dangerous way to do it. I will not have my motives called into question among my peers."

Jessie cried: "But Charles, he's not like that sly Jefferson Davis. He's a Unionist, like you—he's an ally!"

"There *are* no allies when slander is the issue."

"He's fought half a dozen duels already," Benton said in a wary voice. "They say he seldom misses."

Frémont smiled grimly. "Well, when it comes to pistols I *never* miss—Mr. Foote apparently needs to discover it's hazardous to try to blacken a man's good name."

In the end the affair blew over; Foote replied with a handsome disclaimer (if not an apology), maintaining his remarks had been misconstrued. But Frémont never felt quite the same after that. If this kind of personal attack was seen as tactical maneuver . . .

The other bone of contention was the "short seat." Either he or Gwin would have to relinquish his seat at the end of the session and stand for election at a later date, to satisfy electoral procedures. Gwin suggested drawing straws for it; Frémont agreed . . . and drew the short straw. When Jessie heard about it she was wild.

"But *you're* the first senator—you received more votes than Gwin at the convention—why on earth did you agree to it?"

"It's commonly accepted practice."

"But that's ridiculous—to leave a matter that important to mere chance! Oh, there are times I simply don't understand you, Charles . . ."

Chance. He started to reply, held his tongue, remembering . . . He owed so much to chance, good and bad, in spite of good intentions, in spite of audacity and fortitude. In the end perhaps everything was chance.

In any case he'd stand for reelection when he got back, and he'd win—he was the best-known, the most respected figure in California. It was a minor matter. There were so many other things to do, too. There was the new plan to send five separate expeditions to seek negotiable passes through the Rockies for a transcontinental railroad; he intended to lead one of these right through Cochetopa Pass. There was no incompatibility between great deeds and a Senate seat; couldn't each enhance the other?

On the last day of the session he came into the reception room with its black marble and scarlet draperies and saw a man in a rumpled suit talking to the senior member from New York. Instantly Frémont recognized him—that newspaper editor he'd met in New York, the one who'd sought him out, talking about his potential. Bigelow, his name was. Make that expedition a success, he'd said, and you're *in*—whatever that meant. Well, mad Old Bill Williams and the demons of the San Juans had settled that. But now the editor was approaching him, his hand out.

"John Bigelow."

"I remember you well, sir."

There was a contained force in the fellow's manner, as if he had honed himself so that no motion was wasted. "Nice to see you here," he said. "I *knew* you had possibilities." Their previous talk might have been last week. "Now a lot of men know it. You've made a considerable impact on this city."

"I doubt that," Frémont said. "I wasn't even seated till the main action was over."

"So much the better. Webster's destroyed himself. He'll never be President."

"But his courage alone should—"

"It won't. I have something to say in the Whig party. Webster's finished as a national figure. Whereas you, Senator Frémont, *you* have a large future. And I mean nationally."

The naked directness of it disconcerted Frémont. "Mr. Bigelow, I have some pressing projects. I've gold mines to develop, a railroad to push through to the Pacific."

"Excellent. Couldn't be better."

"I'm not a Whig, either. I'm a Democrat."

"Does that matter?"

"Not to me, if it doesn't to you. Anyway, I drew the short term, as you probably know."

"I'll tell you something, Senator," Bigelow said in the flat, cold voice. "Being out of public life a spell wouldn't hurt you one bit. This slavery-secession issue eats up public men. Look at Clay, look at Calhoun—look at your father-in-law."

Frémont frowned. "Let's hope the compromise has put all that behind us."

"Do you believe that? I don't. Now, of course, if that's so, then the country will seek out a President as dull as Zachary Taylor. But if the issue is as alive as I think it is, it'll continue to tar every man in politics—there's no way a public man can avoid identifying himself with one side or the other. Then the time will come when a bright fellow riding out of the West on a fine white horse—a horse named Sacramento, say—with his shield unmarked by the mud of the battle, would be damned attractive." He smiled—a sardonic, rather unpleasant expression—and his eyes glinted.

It made Frémont uncomfortable. Irritated, he shook his head. "Perhaps so. In any event I've gold and railroads and a Senate seat to reclaim."

"Exactly," Bigelow said. "But great days are coming—momentous days. I'll be keeping one eye on you, you can bet on it." He nodded and an instant later vanished through the door.

GRAND TOUR

"EVERYTHING'S CHANGED," Jacob Snyder said. The fierce light had gone out of his eyes and he looked tired, bored, a little disgusted. "I'm getting out of politics. Merritt got out last fall. Most of the old Bear Flag crowd have gone home—they're leaving the field to these jokers." He gestured disdainfully about the big room.

He and Frémont were in the bar of the Miner's House in Sacramento. It had been rebuilt since the flood, the boards still pitchy, and the floor shook when men tramped by their table. There was a piano playing, a raucous poker game nearby.

"Would you listen to 'em?" Snyder said sourly. He banged his whiskey glass on the table until he caught a waiter's eye. "Population has doubled since you went east. They don't know a damned thing about the old days, and they don't care. Look around—how many of these men do you know? More important, how many know *you*?"

Frémont had just ridden over. Jessie had stayed in Monterey; she was pregnant again, and ill.

"Let's face facts, Colonel." Snyder was shaking his head dourly. "All these newcomers—drifters and tinhorns. And the slavery boys getting stronger every day. And that big place of yours around your neck. Add 'em up. Especially that spread—and you getting set to go to court and tell the world about it. These boys are Missouri squatters; they think a hundred-sixty acres is about right, a quarter-mile . . . and what've you got, seventy-odd *square miles*? They figure a man with a spread like that must be a prince or a thief, one—and they ain't going to vote for neither."

"Well, I'm sure as hell not giving it up," Frémont said. He felt dangerously angry, as if he'd been challenged at his roots. "I've opened it up, I bought it, I paid for it—my taxes are supporting Mariposa *County*, for God's sake. Anyone who doesn't like it can—" He stopped, glaring at Snyder, who grinned and raised his whiskey glass in mock salute.

"Just laying it out for you, Colonel. Times change, and folk's feelings change—and California's the changingest place of all . . ."

He found he didn't have three supporters in the new legislature; the men were polite but cool. Go stump the state, they suggested, let the folks see you, build up your support. But Frémont was no stump speaker. He could lead, he could act, but he couldn't blow his own horn; it ran against his grain. He refused to withdraw his candidacy, but he knew he was finished. It was bitter, though; the Bear Flag days were only five years back. *Five years* . . . The great compromise of last year was already showing signs of collapse, the country was more desperate than ever for statesmen, and he was out. His mood sour and sullen, he headed for the mountains: if the Mariposa had cost him his seat, then by God, he'd make it pay.

Godey was awaiting him, as honest and unequivocal as ever. Alex had married a pretty Indian woman and built a log cabin on the place. He didn't know much about mining, but he knew how to kill a man, and there was that mercury point in his eyes that said he'd do it if you pushed him. That was important around gold; gold brought strange visitors. The Mariposa looked glorious to Frémont, the river running with spring melt, balsam scent in the air, the men happy to see him. Godey and his skeleton crew had finished a wagon road to Bear Valley and a bunkhouse, the barn was full of hay. They recanvased his house for when Jessie came. He saw a trout rising in her pond. On beyond stood Mount Bullion. The old man had been wonderfully touched by that.

The Sonorans were long gone. Broken rockers lay along the river where they had worked. Placer mining was playing out now, and there were plenty of men interested in day wages. Frémont summoned his old engineering skills and went to work. He decided to open five veins, choosing those from which the ore cars could run by gravity down to the stamp mill. Mules would haul them up and men would ride them down, braking as they came. He put a crew on each vein and soon timbered shafts were driving into the mountain. The stamp mill operated on steam, but he sited it on the river to wash the gold from the crushed rock by water. He built a flume of rough-cut planks that intercepted the river at a higher point and brought water gushing down in a straight shot through the mill and into long sluice boxes with multiple riffles. The mill machinery arrived in pieces on wagons and took two months to assemble. It was a marvel of efficiency. Five round stamps, each weighing a ton, were attached to poles held loosely in greasy sleeves. Cables fixed to the poles wound around drums in the rafters. The power ascended a marvelous complex of belts, turned the drums, lifted the stamps and let them fall a full six feet against the quartz ore, reducing it to powder. It battered the eardrums, but that was the sound of wealth.

Trenor Park sent up a man named Jack Hopper who he thought might do for a manager. Hopper was Australian, a rough, hearty fellow about Frémont's own age who had run mines in Peru and Mexico. He had a tendency to enforce discipline with his fists, but Godey approved him after watching Hopper clean out the Placer Saloon down in Bear Valley singlehanded—Alex insisted he'd done no more than stand by with a pistol to keep things honest. Hopper kept the ore cars running and the stamps falling; and the gold began to flow.

Jessie's time was coming, and Frémont rode hard down to Monterey. A week later he was holding in his arms a sunny little boy. This time Jessie prevailed: they named him John Charles, Junior. When she was well enough, they moved back to the Mariposa. He found the shafts already deep, the stamps thundering, the sluice boxes glittering with gold. He felt like Midas . . . but each day the stamps sounded the same, the shafts advanced another foot or two, the gold kegs were a little fuller, and like Midas he began to wonder if there was a catch to it after all. Or perhaps he simply had too much time to think.

He remembered the look of the great high plains when the West stretched to infinity waiting to be conquered. What if that red-haired Californio officer with his great mustaches had rallied his men and mounted an all-out charge on Hawk's Peak? Suppose Kearny hadn't stepped in and prevented that shotgun duel with Mason? What if *he,* not poor Henry King, had been walking in front of Old Bill Williams through the snow? So many narrow squeaks, so many reprieves. . . . Chance. *Was* there a divine Providence that decided in its infinite wisdom to spare you, hold you for some momentous occasion further on?

Knitting swiftly under the soft gold light of the whale-oil lamp, Jessie watched her husband, traced the course of reminiscence and conjecture in the play of his features: the roving, restless glance, the intent frown, that flexing of a cheek muscle she knew so well. His neatly trimmed beard and hair were flecked with silver, his face was scored harshly, his lips thinner and more compressed. He was not physically powerful like Alex, or intellectually formidable like Papa, or even dashingly picturesque like that Lieutenant Joe Hooker she'd run into in Panama City. But he had this other thing—this intangible mixture—an intrepid resilience, this burning *excellence* they all turned to in the desperate moments. Even now there was something in him which seemed to be on watch, holding him in readiness for some great event to call him to action.

His eyes flickered at her; he'd become aware of her glances. He turned and faced her directly, somberly, and she knew he was marking the passage of years in her own face. She was still young, but her vivacity had seemed dulled lately—perhaps even her beauty was beginning to fade. Was it? A long, naked exchange. Then she said lightly:

"A penny for your thoughts, Colonel."

He caught himself up, and grinned. "Gold nugget, you mean! We think big, out here in the Mother Lode country."

"Not too big, I hope."

He frowned, peering at his strong, supple fingers. "Jessie, I've been mulling over something. A new project. A big one."

She composed herself. "Really, darling?"

"Yep. It has to with the Golden Gate. You remember my Golden Gate."

"You named it," she answered brightly. "And *I* reminded you to use it in the Report."

"Well, I've been thinking. I think we ought to hire a strong, workable cutter, lay in a good supply of tackle, hoisting gear mostly . . ." He paused, weighing the alternatives; she waited stoically, her head lowered a little. "Now mind you, it would mean a lot of hard work, a lot of planning, we'd have to rough it a bit—"

"For heaven's sake, Charles!" she burst out. "Come to the point!"

"Right." He scowled darkly at his hands. "Well, to cut it short, I think we ought to sail out through that Golden Gate—and head for Europe."

She stared at him in amazement as he burst into laughter, wagging his head at her.

"Oh, you tease!" she cried. "You infernal miserable tease! . . . Oh, could we, darling? Could we, really?"

"Not only could. We will. The Grand Tour—isn't that what they call it?—with all the trimmings." With a flick of his hand he knocked over a pewter cup of bore samples, and the gold dust and quartz fragments spilled across the table. "What's the good of all this yellow stuff if you don't use it for something? Then it really *is* fool's gold . . ."

He stared at her again—a curious, almost defiant glare. Laughing together, they peered at the powdered rock glittering on the smooth wood.

Another expedition, then. But one for pleasure and replenishment; and this time she was with him. They sailed on the Cunarder *Africa,* in staterooms bright with gilt fretwork and rosewood paneling. They were rich, they were famous; Europe opened its arms to them. Jessie was presented to Queen Victoria; they met the Duke of Wellington, and the grand old conqueror of Napoleon nodded with severe approbation and said: "Ah yes—the brilliant explorer. I envy you, sir." Lord Murchison of the august Royal Geographical Society gave a dinner in Charles' honor, and made him a member.

Paris provided even greater triumphs. They leased Lady Dundonald's mansion on the Champs Elysées, took a brougham and pair with an Irish coachman, engaged governesses for the children, hired a platoon of gardeners and maids, cooks and butlers, and despite a new pregnancy, Jessie gave a round of stunning dinner parties. The Comte de la Garde, an engaging old courtier from the last days of the Bourbons and a Bonaparte by marriage, became Jessie's most fervent admirer and appointed himself their sponsor. They danced in the mirrored halls at Versailles, they were part of the American delegation when Louis Napoleon took the emperor's scepter, they even came as guests to his marriage to Eugénie de Montijo. Dressed sumptuously in green velvet, watching the Emperor lead his Spanish beauty to the altar, Jessie marveled at the capricious turns of fate that could lift an impractical insurrectionary from political prisoner to Emperor of the French in six short years. She glanced at Charles, knowing that he, too, was thinking of power and chance, and destiny; but his eyes were slightly narrowed, and she knew he was also measuring his man, assaying his qualities. In certain ways he and Charles were alike—former army subalterns who had known deep disgrace and high triumph. But there the similarity ended. There was something subtly insubstantial about Napoleon III; something vain and mercurial and unsound. He lacked . . .

Charles' abiding sense of honor. The Frenchman's fortunes were at the flood now; how would he do when the tide turned, and the hammer blows began to fall?

It was the grandest of Grand Tours. Charles was in his element, speaking his father's tongue again. He kept himself fit fencing or riding in the Bois de Boulogne, talked with princes and foreign ministers and financiers; they took a box at the Opéra, danced away the nights—and the Mariposa veins paid for it all. A glorious, voluptuous, undreamed-of holiday.

There were some shadows, of course. One evening at the Duc de Morny's she found herself dancing with a tall, narrow man named Napier who had a slued eye and a thin, cruel mouth.

"Do you ever wonder, madame?" he was saying in an overly soft voice. "At certain—intimate—times—do you ever reflect on your husband's culinary tastes? In human flesh, that is to say?"

She looked up in amazement; at first she thought she must have misunderstood his French. But his expression of pleasant malice was unmistakable.

"I pay no attention to vicious gossip, monsieur," she said slowly in her father's voice. "No matter which side of the Atlantic it comes from. And now, if you will excuse me . . ."

Perhaps she should have made a special effort to warn Charles, but it was a very formal affair and there was no easy occasion. But later she saw Napier move up to a group of men talking with Charles. There was an exchange; Charles gave a smile she knew was no smile at all; there was a swift, subtle stiffening in the group, a tensed silence, and then Napier moved away.

"What happened?" she asked in their bedroom later. "With that odious Napier?"

Charles looked at her, his eyes flat and very hard. "The gentleman asked me if I found it diverting to dine on human flesh."

"Oh, my God. What did you say?"

"I asked him if *he* found it diverting the last time he'd made love to his mother."

She gasped. "Charles, you didn't!"

"One vicious insult deserves another." He smiled grimly. "Besides, it all sounded much more *comme il faut* in French, don't you know."

"But—but then he must have—"

"Not quite. He said I was not now in barbarous America, that in France such a remark *might* require satisfaction."

"Oh, no . . ."

"I told him that was true in barbarous America, too. And that I was entirely at his disposal if he *might* be so inclined."

The gentleman apparently was not so inclined—in any event Charles never heard from him again; and the episode was forgotten. Jessie loved the soirees, the thrust and parry of wit; it was like the state dinners of her childhood, but refined tenfold. And across the room she would catch sight of Charles, surrounded by uniformed dignitaries and décolleté comtesses—and as if on signal his eyes would meet hers, he would smile the old, charming smile, and she would flutter her eyes at him; and the faces of cynical, licentious, weary Europe would turn blank with surprise. Flirting with one's own husband! *Comme c'est amusant, ça . . .*

In May the new baby came, a beautiful girl with gold ringlets, who smiled at all she saw. The old Comte de la Garde was enchanted. "*La petite Parisienne!*" he would cry, kissing the point of her snub nose. "If only the Marquis de Lafayette could see her—he would declare all those frigid winters at Valley Forge were worth it!" Life slipped back into its leisured, elegant round—balls and races, weekends at estates on the Loire . . . and then there came a letter from home that brought Charles to his feet, his eyes burning.

"It's come through," he said tersely, and she saw then how bored he'd been through it all, how deeply out of his element. He had done it all for *her.* "They've authorized the five separate expeditions at last! To find and chart routes for a Pacific railroad. I've got to get back! We have to catch the next ship home . . ."

"Of course, Charles," she said.

He could not believe it, simply could *not* comprehend it. But there it was. Franklin Pierce was President now; he was a New Hampshire man, but the southerners held him captive—and Jefferson Davis of all men was his Secretary of War. Davis, who had decided that if there was to be a railroad it would follow a southern route only; Davis, a West Pointer who had served with the Regular Army until 1835—who had no interest whatever in a maverick engineering officer who'd been court-martialed for insubordination and believed passionately in a route along the Thirty-Eighth Parallel that would serve equally North *and* South . . . Frémont had been passed over for all five expeditions. The heaviest blow of all fell when he reached Washington. His father-in-law, sick and failing, defeated for reelection in '50 and now serving as a congressman, informed him gloomily that the new chief of Topographical Engineers was none other than Colonel William Emory. Who had served on Kearny's staff in California, who would remain Frémont's implacable enemy till hell itself froze over . . .

"That's it, then," he said grimly. "I'm shut out."

Doggedly the old man shook his head. "We must do it ourselves. War is coming, Charles. I'm told Davis has already begun secretly shifting federal arsenals to the South. We *must* have a proven, central route from St. Louis: it's been the gateway—it always will be."

"But the financing . . ."

"You have money yourself now. I can sound out people, secure backing—but it'll have to be under the table. I—don't carry the weight I used to." The weary, skeptical eyes flashed once with the old combative fire. "But there isn't much time."

They set out from Pueblo in crackling cold, twenty-two men as well-equipped as Mariposa gold could manage, and started up the San Luis Valley toward Saguache Creek. It was good to be back where issues were starkly defined: terrain, astronomical sightings, horses, leather—not the elusive abstractions that had begun to plague him, such as promissory notes and bills of lading and collateral securities. He was forty now but he felt fit, confident, at the peak of his powers. *This* was what he was meant to do. It was a normal winter and the cold, though intense, was bearable. Storms forced them to hole up twice, a dozen pack animals died, but they found their way to Cochetopa Pass in good order, crossed over and started down, Frémont setting his teeth against old memories.

The snowfall diminished at the Green River and they made good time. He missed the old crowd. Little Karl Preuss couldn't come—his wife had adamantly refused to let him go—but there was a talented photographer named Carvalho, and he'd signed on a first-rate topographer in Egloffstein. This new breed were a curious lot—more educated, less sandy. They were superb at surveys and starsightings, but they saw disaster behind every ridge. When a band of Utes surrounded the camp one afternoon, brandishing rifles and whooping up a storm, they began to come all apart.

"What the devil's the matter with you?" he harangued them crossly, hands on his hips; he was standing in full view of the Indians. "They aren't going to do a damned thing—they haven't got any ammunition."

"*No ammunition?*" Carvalho asked him, openmouthed. "How do you know that, Colonel?"

"Because they'd have hit us, instead of parading around like a county carnival. It's all show—I guarantee it! Now pull yourselves together . . ."

They shook down with time, hardened and steadied on the trail. The snow was mercifully light. Beyond the Green River the country turned bleak and dry, with little game; they ate mule meat again, fought the debilitating spasms of dysentery; and finally even the mules ran out.

"Parowan," he told them calmly, pointing to a notch in the distant mountains. "Right through there."

"But . . . how far away is it, Colonel?" Egloffstein said in a panicky voice.

"We will reach Parowan in three days," he said. "I guarantee it. What's three days? Anybody can walk three days without food, especially if you know there's plenty of it at the other end." He paused; he didn't like the way their eyes kept flickering back and forth at one another; it stirred his worst memories.

"All right," he went on flatly. "I know what you're thinking. Let's make a pact, right here and now: no one will resort to—to cannibalism, no matter what. *No matter what,*" he repeated, holding them all with his eyes. "We are *men,* God's highest creatures—we are not wolverines. Let's behave like men." He thrust out his clenched right hand. "Put your hands on mine!" he ordered. "And make the pact with me . . ." They crowded up around him almost eagerly, gripped his hand and wrist.

"All right, now," he murmured after a pause. "Now let's walk over to Parowan."

He made a perfect landfall, as he knew he would, and they straggled into Parowan in exactly three days to the hour. The Mormon homesteaders gaped at them in amazement. By then they were swaying, fighting down hallucinations, their tongues so swollen they could hardly talk. But they had made it. The rest of the expedition was comparatively easy, following the long slope to the Pacific.

Frémont was jubilant: the winter route was a reality. He wrote a detailed and enthusiastic report to Secretary of War Davis, but there was no response. As the silence grew from weeks to months, it was as if this great effort in the snow, the winter desert, had never been; he might have been pouring spring water into the great salt sea . . .

He turned again to the Mariposa. Godey had a couple of youngsters now. Hopper's wife and children had come up from Mexico and there was a little settlement of log cabins on the river above the mill. The Mariposa threw him a great fiesta: the *patrón* was home again.

But the place had a shabby look. The ore cars were dented, the equipment patched. The flume was leaking seriously; sections of it needed to be replaced. The stamp mill's steam engine had a voracious appetite. They were consuming timber that could be better used to shore up the hundreds of feet of shafts now boring into the mountain. Logging had denuded nearby slopes, leaving them rutted and ugly, and the labor costs had doubled.

There was a more subtle problem, too. Production was falling and expenses were rising. the shift was insidious but clear when he studied the books: year by year the margin between income and outgo had narrowed. Surprised, he saw that his annual capital and interest, plus what he'd taken out for his own use, hadn't all come from current production—it had cut into his reserves. He remembered Miguel once, smiling sadly, repeating an old Spanish adage: *It takes a mine to run a mine . . .*

The year turned. Jessie arrived from back East with the children. Baby Anne, the beloved petite Parisienne, had died suddenly in April of heart constriction. A second boy, Frank, came the following spring. Lily was nearly twelve, as tall as her mother, with skinny legs and a huge appetite. She'd always been a serious child; now she was moody and often sullen, though she watched over her brothers with a maternal care almost equal to Jessie's. Jessie had found a fine French wallpaper with a print rather like that in Lady Dundonald's dining room, and she covered the house's canvas walls.

"As good as the Champs Elysées," she said, laughing, "except it's more original—the walls quiver when the wind blows!" Frémont watched her, in tender amusement—she made a home wherever she was with whatever she found.

August came. The mountain breezes failed and the Mariposa lay gasping under a beating sun. One blazing morning Frémont found a bee in his office. It had got in and couldn't get out. Thinking of that bee high on Frémont Peak, long ago, he looked again at the bill for nearly $3,000 that the mechanics from Sacramento had handed him. The mill had lain idle for twenty-two days while those worthies overhauled it. The lost time had left him no margin: he would barely make the annual payment next month.

He ran through the figures again, sweat blotting the paper. Yes: it was limited, cautious—a pissant operation. He threw down his pencil in disgust.

No wonder the nation ignored him—he was doing nothing to merit notice. He went to the door, staring out. Not a sound. Jack Hopper must have stopped the mill to grease the arms again. The Sierra Nevada filled the eastern sky. The morning he'd set his men against that mountain, all stone and ice in the winter light—by God, he hadn't worried then about overreaching, about consequences! *Let's go,* he'd said, and they'd gone.

Why not, Goddamnit, why not? He spread out his map of the Mariposa's elevations, and began to calculate. His shirt was wet; he folded a piece of blotting paper under the heel of his hand. He could reach all twenty-nine veins by installing . . . yes, three miles of rails on which a steam locomotive could run. He would need a much bigger mill—say fifty stamps—and he'd run it on water power and stop wasting timber and scarring the slopes. He'd need a dam to channel the water through the mill and a whole new system of washing sluices. He was sure he was losing gold now—the rock inadequately crushed, inadequately washed—so he'd expand production tenfold and improve efficiency at the same time.

But the cost? On a fresh sheet, he began adding: a dam, a new mill, a locomotive, three miles of track heavy enough to bear its weight. Before long he was past a million dollars.

A million dollars.

He stared at the figure, feeling chilled in the fierce heat. He threw down the pencil again—and heard a rattling crash followed almost immediately by the shriek of metal on metal, and then a man's scream. Up the mountain somewhere. The scream continued, hoarse and lonely, and then he heard shouts of other men.

Outside the sun blinded him for a moment; the shadows looked black. Far up the slope two ore cars were on their sides. Tiny figures were making long, bounding strides toward them, and the cries stopped suddenly. He caught up a mare and galloped bareback up the mountain.

The injured man lay on the ground between the cars, partly buried in spilled rubble. Quartz dust from the crash glittered in the still air. The first car had gone off the track and the second, following too close, had struck it. The brake platform was on the rear, so the first man had been caught between. Frémont pushed someone aside and saw Rufus Fairchild on his back, his boy's face white and frightened. Blood was soaking his trouser leg just above the left knee, pulsing right through the cloth. Tourniquet—he whipped his belt off, but something seemed wrong as he tightened it around Fairchild's thigh. Then he realized that the boy's leg had lifted too easily, the lower part had scarcely moved. He looked at it and grunted—the foot was *backward.* Bartsinger cut away the cloth and Frémont winced. The leg was severed above the knee, the bone shattered, twisted muscle strands and a little flesh all that remained attached.

"What happened?" Fairchild moaned. A Mississippi boy, he'd come out a year ago looking for adventure. He plucked at Frémont's sleeve. "What happened to me?" Then his eyes cleared, his grip on the sleeve tightened. "It's all right, ain't it, Colonel?" he whispered.

"Easy, son. Rest easy, now." Frémont gripped the boy's shoulders. "Doc will be here." He felt nauseated. The quartz gouged his knees. Awful, awful. Where was Jack? They had to get some morphine into the kid and send for Doc Steffanson to square off that jagged bone and give him a stump he could live with. Tightening the tourniquet again, he decided then and there to fix a settlement on the boy, give him a place for life. . . . Another expense, another drain. The thought shamed him, but it was there.

Frémont organized a stretcher party and then went with Hopper to inspect the track. Spikes were loose and the rails had moved enough to spill the cars on the turn. They'd have to reset the rails, he told Hopper grimly.

"We won't haul much ore for a while."

"Won't matter—the mill's broke down again."

"But we just fixed it!" Frémont cried. They'd miss the payment. Rage washed over him, borne on the mounting worries. "Don't you do any God-damned maintenance at all? Look at that track!"

Hopper looked stunned; then his temper flared. "Maintenance!" he shouted, his face reddening. "Bloody fucking right we do maintenance. Don't do nothing else!"

"Doesn't look it."

"You put the Goddamned rails in too light for the load, that's the bloody problem!"

"This is a hell of a time to tell me that. If it needs to be rebuilt, why didn't you say so a long time ago?"

"Because you ain't been here. That's why! You been off skylarking in Europe and dreaming about railroads, while *we* been trying to keep this junk heap running!" Frémont saw anger in his face—and a kind of fear as well. He knew Jack was right. Jack felt vulnerable—it was the only job he had. They were all vulnerable, God knows, he felt suddenly with harsh reality.

Shaking his head, he mounted the mare and started downhill. Immediately his mood improved, as if the burst of anger had washed out the horror of the ugly accident. Fairchild was lucky in a way—he'd have bled to death in another couple of minutes. As for the mounting bills, let the damned bankers wait. He rolled his shoulders, working the tautness from his neck. He decided to get Godey and ride down to town.

Bear Valley had become a quiet little hamlet, reflecting the violent change that had transformed California. Frémont wished again he had bought property here. The old canvas hotel was gone, replaced by the Valley Palace, solid brick and two stories. There were numerous homes of brick or logs. He ought to order a load of bricks and build a proper home for Jessie. The streets were empty when they rode in. Though stores still kept dust scales, most prospectors now worked others' diggings for wages. They would come straggling back toward dusk, swinging lunch pails like any eastern laborer.

A single building served as stage and freight station.

"Some supplies come in for you, Colonel," the expressman said. He had a purple smear on his lip from licking the indelible pencil. The shipment included a box of shovels, and Frémont took one out.

"How much we paying for shovels?" Alex asked him.

"Dollar-fifty, I think." Frémont hefted it, liking the solid oak handle, the balance, the sharp blued blade.

"Glorietta Mine's getting 'em for a dollar-fifteen, Bill Hendricks told me."

"Maybe ours are better."

"No—same shovel. American Ironworks Standard."

"Yeah? Who supplies the Glorietta?"

"Huntington."

Huntington. Frémont had seen the big hardware merchant not long ago in San Francisco at the new Union Club, which antislavery men had started, and Huntington had said—

"Colonel Frémont?" A stranger in a travel-stained suit stood in the doorway, blinking in the sunlight as he peered in. "I'm Curtis Rollins, New York *Post*. John Bigelow asked me to look you up."

Rollins was touring California to write a newspaper series on gold. Frémont led him to the Valley Palace and called for a whiskey punch, light on the whiskey.

"Shed your coat, Mr. Rollins," he said, "or you'll take a stroke in this heat." It was a relief to talk to someone new. He felt the last of the morning's tension ebbing as young Rollins asked intelligent questions about gold mining. After a while the talk turned to the prospect for the western railroad.

"Bad as ever," Rollins said. "The whole country wants it—everyone's crying for it—but it'll never be built till the route's decided. And Jeff Davis has dug in his heels—he won't hear of anything but a southern route."

"We're going to have to start the railroad here and run it eastward," Frémont said. "They'd *have* to deal with us then. Remember, that's how we got California into the Union—we organized it and then presented 'em with the accomplished fact."

Rollins listened, nodding, but made no notes; he'd heard the idea before, then. That was Huntington's plan, too. Frémont had been startled and impressed when they'd met in San Francisco to find that the merchant had anticipated his own vision. More powerful than ever, with hardware operations in several California cities and other enterprises as well, Huntington was a long way from starting a railroad, but he'd put together a group of men who wanted to begin the surveys; he recognized the value of the Cochetopa. No longer amused at Huntington's pretensions, he had wondered if he could fit him into his own plans—and then the fellow had spoiled it all.

"How much you paying for supplies up to your place these days?" he'd asked. Frémont had smiled and dropped any idea of including Huntington. He was small-time after all. When Frémont quoted what prices he remembered offhand, Huntington had said: "I can beat that twenty percent across the board."

"I'll bear that in mind next time I'm ordering, Collis," Frémont had said coolly.

"You know about Kansas?" Rollins asked Frémont now. "It's terrible—bleeding Kansas, they're calling it. I've just come from there. Jesus God, those slavery boys from Missouri'll slit your throat if they catch you alone, and the Yankees aren't much better. No one moves unless his friends are along. I tell you, Colonel, when Douglas put Kansas-Nebraska through he tore the scab right off, and I don't know if it'll ever heal."

What Douglas had done struck Frémont as criminal. Apparently for no more reason than his desire to run a railroad west from Chicago, he had pushed through bills establishing Kansas and Nebraska as territories in which slavery was neither allowed nor excluded. It sounded like another compromise, but it wasn't because Nebraska was *north* of the old Missouri line of 30°30′. What Douglas *really* had done was repeal the Missouri Compromise itself, after it had stood as a rock-solid bulwark against the northward extension of slavery for thirty-odd years. The already battered Compromise of 1850 had shattered like glass. Slavery men in Missouri and free-soil men in Massachusetts had organized, and each group sent settlers flooding into Kansas—Rollins said they were heavily armed.

"War going to start right there in Kansas, sir, if the settlers don't kill each other off piecemeal first. It's a killer issue." Rollins wiped his face with a kerchief. "Clay and Webster both dead, Douglas has cut his own throat on this, and that Pierce is a damned fool. The North'll never take him again. The country's going to hell in a bucket, Colonel. The Democrats are reeling, the Whigs are a spent force. Mr. Bigelow's written the Whigs off altogether."

"Has he? But who's to take their place."

"Mr. Bigelow says something new is coming."

"Like what?"

"Don't know—no one knows. New parties? New ideas? Secession? War? One thing's sure—the old pattern's broken. Something new has to take its place." He glanced directly at Frémont, his eyes bright and intent. "New faces—new men who aren't tarred with the proslavery or abolitionist brushes. Mr. Bigelow's got some interesting ideas about that . . ."

At the Mariposa, setting new ties in the roadbed, helping Hopper hammer the curve back into the rail, Frémont kept thinking about what Rollins had said. Bigelow knew what he was talking about. Opportunity—the times were ripe for it, full of bright possibilities when strong men could move swiftly to the fore in national affairs, when the prizes would go to the men who acted. And he couldn't even keep a stamp mill operating. The worm gear regulating the belts had shattered, the chief mechanic said; he'd have to take everything down to reach it.

"I can't tell when a piece of metal'll go." His tiny close-set eyes gave nothing away. "That's God's department"

Worm gear—Christ! What was he *doing* here, being told off by mechanics while the whole world went off like a rocket in the distance? What was he doing?

"We've got to expand," Charles said. "Build up the place, make something of it."

She looked at him in surprise. "What do you mean? It's something now."

The children were in bed, it was dark outside but no cooler, and the tree frogs were shrill. Someone was still working at the forge, steady hammer taps that plinked against her nerves.

"Well . . . put it on a sound footing," he said.

"It's sound enough, Charles."

"We're going to miss our annual payment, with the mill down."

"Then we'll incur a penalty—that's not so fatal."

He got to his feet and began pacing up and down in front of the fireplace, and she saw the fierce restlessness working in him. "You can't stand still, Jessie. You reach a certain level and you've got to expand—or shrink away to nothing. That's how business works."

"Well, we can liquidate something else, and make payment. I don't see why we—"

He made a sharp, dismissive gesture with his hand. "Look, the Mariposa has vast resources we haven't even touched. Good God, Jessie, we've got twenty-nine gold veins here! Suppose we opened them all up—suppose we dammed the river for water power, installed a locomotive, and laid some real track—"

"We'd be up to our eyebrows in debt," she broke in. "It'd be risking the whole thing!"

"No, we wouldn't—the gold's there, we know it's there."

"But the *expense!* Have you costed it out?"

He looked away, across the valley. "It would run . . . it might run to a million or so."

"Dear heaven! You can talk of risking a million dollars, just like that?"

"For God's sake, Jessie, calm down!" But she could see he was even more agitated than she was herself. "I'm only talking, projecting. . . . What in thunder are you so afraid of?"

She looked up at him then. He flushed, but his eyes still glittered with that impulsive fever she feared; he was very serious about this.

"That's not fair, Charles," she said quietly. "We have a very good thing here. Enough and to spare. And all of it our own control. A million dollars—that would put us in other people's hands. I'm not sure I like that."

"Jessie, you have to give something to get something—that's the way the system is. . . ."

"Look at Papa," she said flatly. "He served Missouri voters for thirty years, and they turned him out without so much as a thank-you."

"That's different," he said tersely. "That's politics."

"It's the world, Charles. That's what it is. If he'd spent more time looking out for himself and less for the people of Missouri, he'd be a great deal better off now."

"Yes, and if he'd racked up a pile, like Chouteau or that old weasel Frincke, he could have told those voters where to go and how to get there!"

"Oh no!" she cried, and her eyes filled. "You said . . . back in Monterey, when Merritt came to you about the Senate seat, you said the money men were pissants and nonentities, but Papa was the great man—and now you say this!"

The muscle in his jaw flexed; his head came down. "I was wrong," he said heavily. "I didn't see it until I was there, in the Senate. *They're* running the country—the big financiers. Old Vanderbilt, the Astors, Russell Sage, Peter Goelet, the Schermerhorns. They've always held the real power. They call the tune, and everyone jumps. Everyone."

"That's not true! My father never kowtowed to the money men in all his life, and you know it! He was his own man, and so was General Jackson. Remember that!"

"Why," he came back hotly, "must you always and forever hold your father up to me?"

"I have *not* held him up to you! You're the one charging him with subservience, with—with bowing to money power. It's not true—and it's a rotten thing to say . . . For God's sake, Charles! Isn't having your own private gold mine enough? Do you have to be Lord of the Mother Lode?"

"Well, I'll tell you this—there's one hell of a lot more to life than accepting whatever's handed out to you, penny-pinching in some backwater."

She stared at him a moment, wide-eyed and speechless; then her jaw set. "Ah," she said. "That's it. You want to go back. To Washington. Have your revenge. Is that it? And the money would—"

"With a fortune, a sizable fortune, I could *force* my way," he said between his teeth. "Yes! *My* transcontinental route is the right one—I know it better than anyone else. I could ram it through, then, in spite of that West Point son of a bitch Jefferson Davis and everyone else." His face was contorted with anguish. "I mapped half the continent! They'll have to recognize John C. Frémont!"

"It won't work, Charles. Don't you see what you're doing? They've turned on us back there—we're the *enemy.* No amount of gold will change that. We're out of favor, and that's all there is to it. Let it go."

"I can't," he said.

"I see. . . . You know, it wasn't so long ago we were frantic because Larkin had taken the ranch and left you with this worthless patch of mountain. And then, you had plans for stocking the spread in cattle—before you found the veins. Whatever happened to that dream?"

He said nothing, he was staring off into the Sierra night. She said softly: "Let it go, darling."

He shook his head. "I can't let it go," he muttered. "Not a chance like this. Look, honey, everything's changed—this country's coming apart at the seams. War is coming, very fast now: this Kansas-Nebraska business has ripped off the lid, there's no going back. It's a time of transition. Bigelow says—"

"Bigelow?" She stared at him in consternation. "You've been in touch with John Bigelow?"

"No, not directly. But he thinks it's a time for fresh ideas, new men. He feels—"

"I know what Bigelow thinks—I've known all my life! He wants to use you, and you've fallen for it."

"I haven't *fallen* for anything! But by God, I haven't simply given up, resigned myself to holing up in the Sierra for the rest of my life . . ."

"All right!" she cried, beside herself, fighting back tears. "Go on, then—sink a hundred shafts, buy a locomotive! Borrow a million, two million, put your life in the hands of the eastern bankers—I don't care!"

"Oh, for God's sake, Jessie!"

"Only remember—they'll own you then: body and soul!"

He flung out of the room. She heard his boots thump hard on the porch beyond, and thought: All right, then! If he won't face facts, let him stew over it. I'm *not* going to agree meekly . . .

But much later, lying beside him naked in the still, dry heat, she felt despondent and contrite; she reached over and placed her fingers on his chest.

"I'm sorry, darling."

His hand closed over hers. "So am I, honey."

"We mustn't quarrel like this."

"No. We mustn't."

"If you want to try it . . . if you've thought it through, and you're sure it's what you really want . . . I'm just afraid of it, that's all."

"We've never been afraid before, Jessie. Not at the worst times—we've never backed away from a challenge. Why should we now?" He passed his free hand tenderly through her hair. "It's just that I can't end it like this," he murmured, "grubbing gold out of a hillside. Great events are coming—terrible times, demanding times. I was meant for more than this, honey. Don't you see? I've got more to do—a whole lot more. I *know* it . . ."

Stirred to her very core, loving him utterly, she gripped his hard, spare body. "I know," she said. "I love you, Charles."

Yet even at the sweet moment she was more afraid than she had ever been.

The mechanics spent two weeks on the mill. Frémont worked with them, though he had no feel for machinery. He liked horseflesh, terrain, tactics, live things; metal against metal on a skin of grease seemed dead. But men work better with the captain on hand, and the annual payment was upon him. The sun glittered outside, brilliant yet cooler. He was at the mill one morning when he saw Trenor Park approaching on a fine bay mare. How did the man keep his boots so clean? Frémont had been half-expecting him; the payment would worry him. He leaned against a sluice box with his arms folded. The box was dry, its seams gaping.

Park gave him that wry, deprecating smile and raised a hand, half salute and half wave. He dismounted and slipped his saddle girth.

"Trenor," Frémont began, "I think Turkel's overcharging us on supplies. Collis Huntington offered prices twenty percent lower. The Glorietta's paying substantially less than we are."

"Why, that scoundrel." Park never looked more at ease than when being questioned. "I'll speak to Turkel. Get him straightened out."

"Maybe we should switch to Huntington."

"Well, maybe. I don't know how long his prices would hold, once he had you."

"You don't think Huntington's honest?"

"None of 'em are, really, unless you keep 'em that way. Turkel'll tighten up, we put it to him. It makes a fuss when you change—it'll scare the boys in New York."

"How's it their business? Anyway, they ought to see it as an improvement."

"It'll scare 'em that things *need* improving, get 'em asking questions. Better to let sleeping dogs lie, you know? O.K.?"

The old slogan amused Frémont. When he was courting Jessie and General Harrison was running for President as Old Tippecanoe, the desperate Democrats had nicknamed Van Buren "Old Kinderhook" for his hometown in upstate New York. *"O.K. Means All Right!"* they'd sung, until Harrison had bowled him over. "With a slogan like that," Benton had snapped, "who'd want him?" Jessie had used the term occasionally to irritate her father.

"Anyway," Park was saying, "with the mill down, I take it we'll be explaining a late payment?" Frémont nodded. "How late?"

"Couple of months."

Park shrugged. "Not bad. Let me handle it—I'll put it in the right light." He hesitated. "Production's down a little, eh?"

"The place is sucking in money faster than it's turning out gold right now, that's the trouble," Frémont said. He told Park about the accident with the ore cars. Fairchild was recovering nicely, but Frémont didn't want to talk about the look on the boy's face when he'd understood his leg was gone.

"Give him a tin cup and turn him loose," Park said. He gave Frémont a sidelong glance, then chuckled. "Just a joke, Colonel—of course you'll have to look to him. Find him a sit-down job." He picked up a stone, round and smooth as an egg, turned it in his fingers and then threw it. It fell neatly into the dry sluice box with a hollow rattle. Eyes glinting in satisfaction, he said: "Kind of a blow to miss a payment over a pulled rail, isn't it? For lack of a nail, there went the war, that sort of thing, eh?"

"We're too small," Frémont said suddenly. "We can pick away at these few veins and never get ahead. Not with our mill down half the time."

"The boys at the Glorietta are hauling out gold aplenty, they tell me. Of course, they went all-out from the very start."

"That's what we should do." Frémont sketched the plans he'd been evolving. Park listened quietly, his eyes alert. He looks like a cat at a mouse hole, Frémont thought.

"Why not?" Park said. "We've been at it awhile, got some baselines now. It'd probably help with the railroad plan, too—folks'll want to know you've got your own property booming 'fore they'll get behind you on something big as that. 'Course, that'd change the position some: debt's around three-fifty now, with what you've repaid. You kick that up to a million-three or four, that's something else. They'll want assurances—guaranteed production schedules by dates certain. But with all the veins open, a big mill, dam, power railway—hell, you won't have any trouble meeting 'em. I can handle that, if you like."

"I was thinking of raising fresh capital in Europe," Frémont said.

He saw something indecipherable in Park's eyes, but the entrepreneur said easily: "You got special money in mind?"

"Baron Jarnac of the House of Rothschild was interested when I was in Paris."

Park nodded. "I guess I can keep them happy back here." Frémont gave him an inquiring look. "Well, you know, Rothschild money scares folks: it generally winds up taking over. I wouldn't recommend it myself, but you know 'em, and if you feel good about it—well, hell, it's your gold mine. But your other creditors'll be jumpy. The boys in New York—they won't be eager to share with those Rothschild sharks. They'd figure to get eaten alive—and so would I!" He laughed pleasantly.

"What other creditors? I've kept up-to-date, but for this current payment."

"Some Californians have been carrying you too, you know. Old Turkel—now, we don't want him overcharging, but he's been mighty good about carrying your account—"

"Wait a minute—he's been paid regularly."

"Well, Colonel, my obligation is to you, not to him. I don't get him paid any faster than I have to—every day he waits is a day *you* get the use of the money. That's standard."

"No," Frémont said. "I like to pay on time, keep accounting up-to-date."

Park looked at him curiously. "You've been away a lot, Colonel. That New York money doesn't come in all at once, you know. The Mariposa needs something, it needs it now. I've carried you a good deal myself, for that matter. Twenty, thirty thousand at a time. I'm glad to do it—the Mariposa's good business for me too, you understand, and the association doesn't hurt me round the state. But with Rothschild money . . . well, we'll see. Maybe it'll work out."

"Suppose we went back to the well in New York?"

"They already wonder why we haven't gone for more." Park had never talked this way before. As if the thought had been transmitted, he added, "I've always told 'em you were going slow and steady. That's sensible; no one can quarrel with that. But sure—with a whole *mountainside* of gold, you can meet a few guarantees. Maybe I'm too cautious. Banker's nature, you know. My brother always claimed I was too busy looking back to see ahead."

Frémont pushed himself off the sluice box and stretched. There was something keen in the air and in the shadows that lay as sharp as straightedges. This was the California he loved, the sky depthless and vast, the ground sun-drenched. It made him want to saddle a good horse and strike across open country—it made him want to *go.* He glanced at Park's smooth, handsome face, set in its diffident smile. Things constantly shifted with the banker, bending this way and that, just the opposite of the iron edge of shadows at his feet, but he made you feel easy and assured.

"Let's do it," Frémont said. "Let's make this place hum. I'll write Baron Jarnac. You put it up to the New York people. If they get uppity, we'll let the Rothschild threat knock some sense into 'em."

"Now you're talking, Colonel," Park said. "Catch 'em in the crossfire. Use Rothschild to whipsaw those New York bastards. Just the way to play it."

Then he said, so slowly and distinctly that it was uncomfortably like a warning: "You understand, Colonel—for that kind of money they'll want you to give the place your full attention."

TEMPTATIONS

NATHANIEL BANKS CAME THROUGH the main lobby with a quick, lithe step, head cocked to one side, a tentative smile on his alert face. Banks would be good on the trail. He had that willingness to venture. He saw Frémont, waved, started toward him, and then was stopped by a man who caught his arm. Cast Nat Banks ashore on a desert island and he'd find someone he knew; meet him in the Astor Hotel in Manhattan and certainly you'd share him.

It was a fine fall morning. Frémont had breakfasted early and been out in the park for a canter; now he sat in the Astor's elegant lounge where the walls were of red brocade and the stately windows looked across Broadway to City Hall Park. . . . There, Nat had broken away. Speaking to other men but not quite stopping, smooth and politic, Banks came across the room. He was a rising star in the United States Congress from a Boston district. They had been close since Frémont's Senate days.

He started to get to his feet, but Nat was caught again. It was—yes, of course, Seward. *No one* passed Seward, when New York's senior senator wanted to talk. He saw Banks nod in his own direction, and Seward turned with a smile and tossed him a small salute. Seward's expression was intent as he plunged into conversation with Banks, his macaw's beak of a nose almost touching his cigar.

There was tension in the air these days—everyone seemed affected. Washington had been prickly with it, a disturbing mix of fear and opportunism that always accompanies change, and a vindictive savagery that had astonished him. Their southern acquaintances had been particularly hostile—so much so that he and Jessie had decided to change residence in the East to to New York City. Bill Preston, Jessie's cousin, had been palpably nervous when he'd asked Frémont to meet with Governor Floyd and some other Democrats. Floyd, the former governor of Virginia, had married Sally Preston. Momentous things were afoot; they clearly wanted his support. Jessie had gone off to Nantucket with the children, but he had held in New York; he would see the governor in an hour.

Banks was listening to Seward, his face interested but watchful. It made Frémont think of his own days in the Senate, the strategy sessions with his father-in-law. The old man had lost even his congressional seat now; his vehement opposition to the Kansas-Nebraska Bill—some said it was the most memorable speech of his career—had cost him dearly. He was writing his memoirs all over again. The handsome old house on C Street had burned to the ground—Jessie's sister Eliza had risked her life in a vain effort to rescue Volume II of *Thirty Years' View.*

Earlier in the year the Senator had sent them an alarmed message that Mrs. Benton was failing, and they'd hurried back from California. The day after they reached Washington, Elizabeth Benton, leaning on her daughter's arm, had gone to the Senator's study. There, her ravaged face full of emotion, she had laid her thin hand on the desk, on the silver candlestick the old man had swung at Frémont, on the back of the chair where he'd sat so many years preparing for political combat she had never understood. That mute expression of love, so surprising and wondrous, and her father's utter desolation when his wife died, had stunned Jessie; it was always humbling to find unexpected depth in others. . . . Banks had broken away at last, Seward clapping his shoulder.

Frémont stood. "Señor *Popularidad,*" he said.

"They love me," Banks said dryly. "They can't help it."

"Still solving everyone's problems, I see."

"All but my own." A waiter brought him coffee. "So," he said, "and how's California? Gold still pouring out of the magic mountain?"

"Some magic!" Frémont laughed. "It hides up in the rock and we claw at it—no necromancy there."

He and Park had secured further underwriting from the New York bankers, in return for certain production guarantees and other concessions. Some of the new equipment had arrived at the Mariposa. An engineer had started on the dam, and another so-called mechanical genius had been erecting the new mill when Benton's letter had come. It was a bad time to be away, his backers wouldn't like it, but Frémont knew his limitations—maybe it was better to leave it to the experts after all. Still, he felt uneasy.

"I envy you that gold mine," Banks was saying. "I often think of you in sunny California surrounded by heaps of gold, dribbling it on your head, throwing saturnalian orgies whenever Jessie's not looking—"

"Hold on, now—I'm a very sedate fellow."

"You can't fool me—a man who's got all the gold in California can hardly be denied."

"Come on—three thousand miles from the center of the world? It's you power brokers who have it all your own way, you demons on the Hill manipulating the rest of us and telling us it's for greater Democratic glories. I know your kind, Mr. Congressman."

"Trapped in my own web of intrigue," Nat said lightly, but his face had changed. "I'm not a Democrat anymore."

"No! You've gone to the Whigs?"

"God forbid! I'll do anything to get elected, granted, but not that. Anyway, the Whigs are dead. Absolutely moribund. But so are the Democrats—in the North, at least. No one in my district will even talk about a *modus vivendi* with the South. Mention compromise and they laugh in your face. Or curse you roundly. And the reports from Kansas drive a new nail into the Democratic coffin every day. They're fighting a regular civil war out there—and don't forget that most of the northern men were set up out there by Massachusetts emigrant societies."

"So what did you do?"

"Switched to the Native American party and got reelected."

Frémont laughed. "You—a Know-Nothing?" The Native American party had started as a secret anti-Catholic organization for men alarmed by waves of Irish immigration. Its members had been instructed to answer queries by saying, "I know nothing about it." Suddenly this narrow-minded, ignorant group had ballooned into a party of frightening national significance.

Banks gave him a mock glower. "That's a very outmoded term, sir."

"Nat, do you actually believe there's a Vatican plot to control and use the Irish to influence Congress?"

"No, no—the party's dropped that tack, anyway. I admit it's pretty anti-Catholic—"

"Bigoted, you mean."

"Well, sure, that's the ugly side. But this flood of Irish immigration since the famine—they're rough and rowdy, full of fight . . ." He was plainly embarrassed. "I don't know, they scare the less-educated old Protestant stock."

"Well," Frémont said, easing up, "some of the Irish are rough, all right. I watched a few of 'em rescue a black man from a Charleston slave hunter this very morning."

It had been over on the west side, near the docks; he had turned a corner and seen the black, his hands bound, being prodded along by the slaver, with three federal marshals in sour attendance. The Charleston man was wearing an incongruous white plantation hat and the black's face was contorted with utter misery. Just then the Irishmen had appeared, dock wallopers on their way to work. One stiff-armed the slaver. Another seized the black, slashed off his bindings, and shouted, "Begone!" The slave hunter started to draw, and a tall fellow with a red face kicked the piece out of his hand and slammed him against a building. "Kill the bastard," someone called. The marshals waited until the slave disappeared and then drew their truncheons. "All right, boys," one of them said, and the Irishmen, now in high humor, backed off. "But what about my prisoner?" the Charleston man cried. The marshals shrugged and the red-faced man said: "Take yourself home, you murdering sod. We'll bust your back if we see you again." Frémont had been ready to jump in on their side.

"Well, of course." That was the emotional storm that had driven Banks to a safe harbor.

"The Know-Nothings. Any port'll do, eh?"

"Kindly don't look down your nose at me," Banks said firmly, not smiling. "These are dangerous times and they're going to get one hell of a lot worse. You've been sitting out there on your golden mountain—we've been back here wading knee-deep in threats and slander." He sighed "Oh, hell, I'm sorry, Charles. Politics isn't very much fun these days. But who knows? The night is darkest just before the dawn, hey? Seward's talking about starting something entirely new."

"A new coalition, you mean?"

"Don't know, exactly. He's damned mysterious, but *something's* going on."

Frémont set out on foot for the meeting with Governor Floyd, pondering what the Bostonian had said. Nathaniel Banks a Know-Nothing! Genial, liberal, intelligent, and here he was tied up with a bunch of nativist bigots. Still, he knew a lot more than he was telling. Frémont liked him immensely. What strange, cruel times, the future like wild, uncharted seas. It was good to be back East, where things were humming. Maybe he *had* sat atop his gold mountain too long. . . .

The St. Nicholas was one of those small, elegant hotels that made the Astor seem rather gaudy. Bill Preston was just inside the door. The McDowell family resemblance struck Frémont; Jessie would be on the Nantucket beach with the children by this time of morning. As Preston led him into a second-floor suite, Frémont saw John Floyd rise from a chair by a tall window. Two other men stood up. Frémont liked the former governor; they had hunted together with old Colonel McDowell at Cherry Grove. Floyd had the easy assurance of Virginia gentry—his father had been governor before him—but an essential warmth of nature gentled any arrogance.

"How good of you to come," Floyd said. "May I present General Mitchell Murdock of Kentucky."

A big man with a wide, hard face, skin drawn tight over cheekbones, put out his hand.

"And Judge Elkins of Maryland," Floyd said.

"I know you by reputation, sir," Frémont said, surprised. "I'm honored." Elkins gave him a dry, frail hand. He was seventy or more, with a slight quiver in hands and voice. Frémont knew him as one of the most powerful men in Maryland, with tobacco plantations on the Eastern Shore and in Delaware. He didn't know Murdock, who had a rough, aggressive look.

Frémont took a chair by the second window, putting the light at his back. Murdock sprawled onto a sofa and Elkins sat carefully on a straight chair as if his back hurt.

They had just been in New England, Floyd said, and they were more alarmed than ever. The nation seemed bent on a separation course. Abolitionists were calling secession a bluff, while secessionists declared openly that the North lacked both the means and the will to resist them. The old ties that once held the nation together were fraying. Churches were splitting into northern and southern branches that didn't speak; books and journals no longer circulated; men traded invective instead of ideas.

"Now our national political parties are tottering too, reeling under the divisions," Floyd went on. "The Whigs are finished. The Know-Nothings are a joke. Of course, our good old Democratic party could restore these bonds, but I guess you know we've been hurt in the North."

Frémont listened quietly, letting the ex-governor state his premise, but the curious tension in the room irritated him; it seemed inappropriate among gentlemen. Elkins sat so still he hardly seemed to breathe. A pulse beat in Murdock's right temple; his foot, thrown over the sofa arm, flexed up and down.

"But this separation isn't necessary," Floyd continued. "Moderates still control in the South, and we place great hope in two concessions the North has made. The Fugitive Slave Act grants us our rights of property, which is only simple justice. And the Kansas-Nebraska Act recognizes our rights in territories that are the property of the whole nation."

"Well, Governor," Frémont said, "I'm sure you're aware that the Democratic party's problems go straight to Kansas-Nebraska."

"Yes, but it's not the *act* that's at fault—it's the northern *perception* of it. It's the radical reaction in the North—the constant drumbeating against the South—that erodes the position of southern moderates and feeds our own extremists. Look, Colonel, you know slavery will never flourish on the high plains. We're not trying to implant it there—we're merely seeking to hold the line, to protect it at home."

"That's not how most people see it here."

"But that's simply because Kansas has been allowed to become a battleground. Kansas isn't a North-South problem at all, sir. It's a national problem; it's not a question of slaves against free-soil, it's a question of political courage in Washington! Desperate, frightened men from both sides are slaughtering each other in Kansas, but the real question is, what are *we* going to do to stop it? Let me put it flatly. The national administration lacks the courage to take a firm hand. What's wrong in Kansas lies at the feet of a craven President—and that's precisely why the Democrats will never renominate Mr. Franklin Pierce. He's avid for it, you know—actually claims he deserves it—but I assure you we'll never give it to him."

Floyd paused portentously. He leaned forward, hands on his knees. "And that is why we asked you to meet with us, sir. Everything now depends on a strong man coming to the fore who can take charge, bring order to Kansas, and begin to heal this country, knit it back together again. We believe you are that man, Colonel Frémont."

"You want *me*?" The overture, the very possibility, had taken Frémont utterly by surprise.

"Yes. And we are prepared to assure you the Democratic party's nomination for President of the United States."

Murdock put both feet on the floor with a thump and said: "And this time, nomination is the equivalent of election. The South is solidly Democratic—there's no opposition left there. In the North there's opposition, sure, but it's fragmented. There's simply no way the Democratic nominee can lose."

Frémont's consternation, the first thunderous excitement, was washed away in a surge of anger. Did these politicians actually think they could toy with him like this?

"You must take me for a fool, Governor, waving the Presidency at me like some sort of gift. I'd have thought better of you, sir."

Floyd flushed; Frémont saw his eyes go flat and hard. Elkins was smiling faintly.

"Perhaps I present things a bit awkwardly," Floyd said stiffly. "I've never offered a man the Presidency before. But I assure you we're serious. Do you doubt that we can deliver?"

The whole thing was preposterous. Frémont had supposed they wanted an endorsement of some sort. Buying time to consider, to think, he said: "It's rather a large order."

"Well, so it is. But I still have a little influence in Virginia. Judge Elkins can speak for Maryland, as can General Murdock for Kentucky. There are others, of course. And I might add that we don't look on you as some sort of savior—rather, you happen to make irrefutable political sense." Softly, still angry, he added: "If I took you for a fool, Colonel, I wouldn't want you for President."

He expected an apology, but Frémont didn't offer it. And still . . . they were serious. They actually meant it! He felt a rush of sheer exhilaration, as intoxicating as the rarefied air on the Sierra peaks; for a moment it was actually difficult to breathe. He knew that it showed on his face. He saw Elkins glance at Murdock with the flicker of a gambler who has drawn aces over kings. The look steadied Frémont and he was able to say: "Why me, gentlemen?"

Murdock stood up, slapping his hands together, rolling his heavy shoulders. "Because we want a western man for a western problem," he said, his voice rasping. "Someone active, vigorous, strong—someone with guts. Someone who doesn't mind stepping in shit, to put it square. That's how people see you. They know you cut those trails by making a quick, sure decision—and then acting on it. No ifs, ands, or buts."

"But there's no shortage of decisive men," Frémont said with irritation. Murdock was puffing him and he didn't like it.

"Well, there's more to it than that," Floyd admitted. "Remember, we're going to win; what we *want* is a win that will bring the North along. Maybe your greatest value is that you're not already locked into the controversy. You haven't been in public life that much—haven't had to commit yourself. So you're flexible, you can strike out in new directions. You're famous, but you're not a politician—politicians are not in very good odor just now. Why, your image—frontier hero renowned for decisive action—is stamped in gold in the public mind! There's no mystery in why we want *you.*"

When Frémont didn't answer, Floyd shrugged. "Look, I'm not telling you anything new. Who are the likely candidates? Pierce has destroyed himself trying to please everybody all the time. Douglas will never do, with Kansas-Nebraska around his neck. That leaves Buchanan, if only because he's got the fewest enemies. But hell, Colonel, you know Buchanan."

Oh, yes, Buchanan. Frémont had an indelible memory of Polk's Secretary of State refusing to take a stand when the court-martial verdict was before the cabinet. There would be a certain cold pleasure in taking the White House over Buchanan.

"He's a decent enough man," the governor said, "but he won't be able to bring North and South together. Let me say it again: we need someone who isn't tarnished by all the failures of the past."

It made sense. He could rally the North as Buchanan or the others never could. He understood southerners by instinct, even when he didn't share their views. And once in, by God, he could ride into Kansas with disciplined troops behind him and knock some foolish heads together there. He knew men and how to handle them. He would get the factions into one room, lay down sensible rules, and see that they were obeyed. Hell, yes—as President he would know how to stop the fighting in one quick thrust. He could lead as no other. The country would love him for it and so would Kansas—nine out of ten men didn't want to go night-riding; they wanted to work their land. There'd be precedent for it, too. Zach Taylor had been ready to lead troops, and so had Old Hickory in '32 when South Carolina was talking secession. The people wanted a strong, fair President. Why not Frémont?

But these men hadn't asked him for his own views on the issue, and it struck him suddenly that they didn't want to know. So there was more to it: now he saw their faces, tentative, waiting, on edge.

"And what do you want of me?" he asked quietly.

Then Elkins spoke for the first time, surprising authority in his dry voice; the old man's quaver had vanished.

"There's just one more element. I expect you can carry the North, just as the governor says. But first of all, of course, we have to keep the South solid." He paused a heartbeat—two, three, for emphasis. "Now, you're a sensible man, sir, a southerner by birth and rearing. You understand the situation. To hold the South secure, the Democratic nominee must support wholeheartedly the Kansas-Nebraska Act and the Fugitive Slave Act. They're right and proper, and the South will accept no less."

Again that little smile, cold and superior, a look of power that had nothing to do with the old, frail body; the look of a man who has just drawn his third ace.

"Agree to support those two acts, Colonel, and we'll assure you the nomination—and I promise you that a year from now you will become the fifteenth President of the United States."

"But what are *their* conditions?"

She had that penetrating Benton look, and he knew the question had been in her mind all the time he'd been talking. But there was more, too. She was cool, but he had seen the light flash in her eyes.

They had reached the point where the Nantucket lighthouse stood rooted in granite that rose from the sea. Waves broke gently on the stone, rising with lethargic power and sighing away. The tide was falling and the sea grass was still wet. Later the nor'easters would send spume thundering up the rock to challenge the light itself, but now the sea lay docile, muttering at their feet.

Frémont had come out from New York by train, taken the ferry and then a hack out to Siasconset and the cottage on the beach they'd rented for the season. He'd felt as if a fever were rising in him, as if all his senses were keyed to every click of wheel on rail; every voice in the car seemed clear, precisely detailed. The leaves were changing as they ran east, red and gold and umber flashing in the late-afternoon sunshine. He saw a man in a black suit reining back his carriage horses at a crossing, a doctor, perhaps, and in a station a woman with a child obviously worried about her trunk. All these people, those outside, those across the aisle, were his people. If he were President he would be responsible for them, *to* them; they would look to him to bring them through the dark days ahead.

All his life he had lived by action—and this was the ultimate action. He bore Destiny's mark—he remembered that dream image of himself on Barney setting out across the vast sunshot plains, a tiny figure riding westward toward great things. Sequences grand and petty swept through his mind. He was riding into Kansas at the head of his troops, bringing peace, accepting the cheers, a woman in a sunbonnet was crying out her gratitude as tears streamed down her wind-roughened cheeks—and the next instant her face became the face of Colonel William H. Emory, USA Topographical Engineers commandant, at the instant he learned who would be his next Commander in Chief. The uncommon jubilation, the flooding sense of opportunity, the hot ambition rising in him until he trembled—and then, again, those conditions like cold sleet against his face when camp was still miles away. . . .

"Walk with me down to the light," he had said to Jessie after tea. And on the hard-packed sand still wet from the tide he'd caught her hand and told her: the White House, so it seemed, could be theirs. The White House!

Her eyes had gone wide, her hand tightening convulsively on his, that eager light in her face. For just a minute, clear as a crystal mirror, he knew she had seen herself as First Lady of the United States, had sat at the great desk in the President's office and spun on the swivel chair while her husband stood laughing. Tom Benton's girl. Frémont could see it all in her eyes; he knew her so well, he loved her so much. And on New Year's Day she would stand with the President in the great foyer and greet the citizenry—and all of Washington, which had become an enemy camp for her, where the practiced ease of her girlhood had fled, would approach with bow and curtsy. She and the President would talk over the great problems and set them straight with one wise, swift action after another. All this flickered across her face like flames in a prairie campfire . . . and then that piercing, practical look came, and she had asked her question.

"Of course," she said, surprised despite herself at his answer. "That makes sense, they need to hold the line there. . . ."

She listened then, asking occasional questions as he detailed the meeting. He could see she was enjoying the political symmetry, the sense of tactic and maneuver, but there was a wary tension in her face, too. Her capacity for political analysis often amazed him. He fancied he knew something of this interweaving of issues, personalities and ambitions, but she always saw more than he did. Could they really assure the nomination? She thought so—because they had come to him together. Separately any one of them might tell him anything; together they were committing themselves and their prestige, not just to him but to one another. Anyway, selecting Frémont made overwhelming political sense—it could stitch together a party that was badly cripped in the North; and who was there to defeat such a unifying candidate?

They strolled along the hard-packed beach under the lighthouse talking politics as if only theory were involved, but her face was strained; at last she said: "Then what did you tell them?"

"Nothing as yet."

"Neither yes or no?"

"Of course not. Would I make such a decision without talking to you? We've always worked together."

She squeezed his hand. "But what do you want?"

"I'm sorely tempted. Think of all you could *do,* Jessie! Your father would tell me to take it."

"Yes—he'd be out campaigning for us. Think of that! Above all else he's been praying for someone who can hold the Union together."

"He's a wise old man," Frémont said. "You think he's right?"

"Right?" she said, staring at him, that hard Benton force in her eyes again. "Who's to say what's right in such a situation? What do *you* think?"

"I think his view is right for him, and wrong for me," he said immediately, surprised at the clarity of the thought. He realized he'd been avoiding the decision, shying from it like a colt. "Ah God, Jessie, I don't want to turn it down. I've never wanted anything the way I want this." Far out a sail caught the setting sun, a coastwise vessel out of Long Island running for Boston.

"The Fugitive Slave Act is plain wrong, morally and practically. Kansas-Nebraska is a disaster. We've been placating and appeasing the South for years—and all it gets us is closer to war. I'd try something different if I had a chance, but—no, I can't support either one. I just can't."

She had stopped and turned to him, head back; there was something peculiarly intense in her features, the late sun glowing on her face, and for once he couldn't read her thoughts.

"You'd really give up the Presidency?"

The question firmed him; he'd lived by swift decisions, hard commitments. "It gives *me* up, doesn't it? It wouldn't work. If it was just holding my nose and signing a pledge, maybe I could swallow it. But I'd have to speak for it, argue it, answer questions on it, explain again and again why it should be supported—and all the time I'd be lying. People sense dishonesty quicker than anything else—I've seen it. They'll forgive everything before they'll forgive that. It wouldn't work, Jessie."

She struck her fist against her thigh. "I knew you were going to say that!"

"But don't you see—in the end I'd never be nominated *or* elected, because everyone would know I was lying."

"Oh, God damn!" she cried, her fists doubled. "God damn them down to hell!"

He was stunned; he'd never heard her swear like that. Her eyes had filled with tears.

"Do you want me to take it?" he said, troubled. "Anyway?"

"Oh, for God's sake, Charles! No—I knew it wouldn't work the moment you told me." She set off down the beach, walking fast. He hurried after her, saw her staring harshly into the sinking sunlight, tears streaming down her face.

"Jessie . . ."

"Those bastards—with their rotten damned conditions! I'm so *sick* of the South and their demands, their arrogance, their stupid sensitivity, their damned self-serving blather about their noble, *honorable* way of life—when all they *really* want is to live like lords on the backs of other human beings! Look at them—dancing on the edge of Armageddon, armored in their pride. Everything—*everything* has to turn on that! The West, statehood, the railroad—this one vicious issue has dominated our lives . . ."

She stopped and turned on him, her cheeks tear-streaked but her eyes flat and angry.

"What a miserable irony," she said. "We've never even thought of this, and then they dangle it like forbidden fruit—as if God was laughing at us. This is our own party that's doing this to us—the dear old Democrats who can do no wrong. Asses!"

Her face was so hard he was startled; she was Tom Benton's daughter, all right. "That's the joke," she said. "They're *exactly* right—you could save their hides, you're the new broom that could sweep it all away, start over again—and they throw it away. Maria Crittenden was right, all those years ago—they're just plain stupid. They throw everything away. Stupid! *Stupid!*"

She fell against him, weeping again, her face against his chest as he held her. The sun dipped into the sea, the lighthouse took on a blued, somber hue. He saw movement behind the glass; they'd be firing the big lantern now. She was quiet then, and he held her, stroking her back and kissing her hair.

"I'm sorry, honey," he murmured. "God knows I am."

"It's all right." she straightened, managed a shaky laugh, and said, "Well, I'd have liked to live in the White House. It's a good address, you know—nice house, pretty grounds, interesting work." And then, fiercely: "And we'd have shown 'em, too—we'd have shown *everybody*!"

CANDIDATE

OLD FRANCIS BLAIR WAS WAITING for her, looking gaunt and grand and wonderfully familiar when she stepped down from a carriage at the Music Fund Hall. A huge Philadelphia policeman saluted her with his baton and waved the coachman along. A man wearing a sandwich board hung with campaign emblems sidled toward her. It was June and already hot.

"Just in time," Mr. Blair said, hurrying her into the building, up several flights of stairs and along a dim passage. "The convention's ready to vote. It'll go for Charles, but we need you."

"Need me?" she asked uncertainly.

"Of course. The delegates are crazy about you, Jessie." He looked at her quizzically, a big turnip watch in his hand. "Don't you realize what a public figure you've become?"

He had insisted that she come to the convention, though protocol barred Charles. She followed Mr. Blair, a little breathless, and midway down another corridor he opened a door. As they entered a roar washed against her like a tide and she hesitated. She was on the podium. A thousand delegates milled about on the floor below, talking, laughing, shouting to one another. The chairman sat in the box just above her and a speaker was clamoring for attention. Clouds of tobacco smoke billowed toward windows open for ventilation high above; there was a catwalk up there, and boys' small faces peering down.

The texture of the noise changed. She saw heads turning and men pointing. An excited enthusiasm rippled through the crowd, and with a jolt that took her breath she realized that it was for her. They had seen her now. It was a mass of movement, signs, bunting, color—but the faces focused on her. A huge portrait of Charles in buckskin hung from the balcony over the Massachusetts delegation, and then, startled, she saw a matching portrait of herself at the other end of the hall.

"Hey, Jessie!" a bass voice boomed, and a chant began.

"JESSIE! JESS-EEE! JESSSSS-EEEEE! We're—for—you . . ."

Cheers, whistles, banners waving—and that same booming voice: "We love you, Jessie!"

Nat Banks appeared beside her, face alight, and cried, "What do you think of the Republican party now?"

She shook her head. Of all the events that might have followed that anguished afternoon on the beach at Siasconset, this was the one she could never have imagined. It was as if they had slammed the door on Destiny—and Destiny had kicked it open again and reached in and seized them by the collar.

"You have thrown away the greatest opportunity of your life," Governor Floyd had said to Charles back in New York. "I had thought better of you, sir. I had imagined you were interested in serving your country." He had cut off Charles' explanations curtly. "You understand what will happen now—Buchanan will be nominated and elected. But he won't be able to deal with the situation."

Nat Banks had snorted at this. He had waited with Jessie at the Astor House while Charles took his answer to the Democrats.

"Floyd's an anachronism and an ignoramus. He has absolutely no idea what's really going on." He had urged them not to return to California. He'd met with Seward again; a new national antislavery party was starting, with big men behind it, movers and shakers—Seward, John Bigelow, Edward Everett Hale, Francis Blair . . .

"Why," she'd said in amazement, "Mr. Blair is the staunchest Democrat ever. He and Papa—"

"Well, so was I," Banks had retorted, pained. "So are you. But didn't you just turn them down? Don't you see—everything's changing, nothing's as it was."

They had taken a handsome brownstone on East 9th Street just off Fifth Avenue. And soon John Bigelow called. He had turned the same cool, appraising look on her she remembered, as if again calculating what she could do for him.

"I always knew you had potential, Colonel," he'd said to Charles, pleased with himself. "Now I'm going to prove it. Everyone who hates slavery is turning to the new party, and *you'll* be our man."

He refused food or drink and she'd had trouble getting him to sit down. "Be ready, Colonel. Seward likes you. Banks is working actively in your behalf. Blair is amenable—let your friends speak for you. We're going to make you President." And with hardly a good-bye, he was gone.

She hadn't taken Bigelow very seriously, but Francis Blair's participation in the fledgling party had reassured her. Her earliest memories included Mr. Blair; at times he'd seemed like a second father; there had been talk that she might marry his favorite younger son, Frank, until a handsome lieutenant had blown in from the West. Mr. Blair had been almost as angry about that as Mr. T; it had been two years before he'd spoken to her again. And then one day it had dawned on her that his own heart had been involved. It wasn't Frank who'd been angry, after all, but his father. . . . The notion had disconcerted her strangely, but her intuition told her she was right and that a residue of that feeling remained in Mr. Blair to this day.

In any case, it served to increase the affection she felt for the canny old publisher. Frank, as dear a friend as ever, was now a whiz-bang attorney in

St. Louis, for whom his father had developed awesome ambitions: Mr. Blair wouldn't mind seeing Charles in the White House for the nonce, but he intended to put Frank there ultimately. And he *was* a power, no doubt about that. He and his Washington *Globe* had prospered after General Jackson had brought him to Washington to start an administration newspaper, and Mr. T had welcomed him to the Jacksonian wars. In fact, the *Globe* had done so well that Mr. Blair had purchased an estate at Silver Spring near Washington, where she'd spent many a happy summer visit.

It was there, as 1856 began, that the new party was founded in an excited first meeting and adopted the name Republican. It still made Jessie uncomfortable to call herself anything but a Democrat, but it helped that the Republicans had begun in Mr. Blair's parlor.

As spring came in, the new party caught on. Northern Whigs and Democrats joined en masse, and the South began to denounce it. Newspapers wrote glowing articles about Charles and referred to her approvingly. "Our little Jessie," some called her, which irritated and charmed her at once. It was all great fun, but she gave the Republican party little chance and wasted no time imagining life in the White House. She had had enough of that in one turbulent hour under Nantucket lighthouse.

But as the nomination convention approached, events began to take control. "You've heard about Sumner?" Bigelow snapped on a May afternoon. Of course they'd heard; what she couldn't understand was why Bigelow was so pleased. A southern congressman named Preston Brooke had walked right onto the Senate floor and caned Charles Sumner of Massachusetts after one of his more vituperative abolitionist speeches. Apparently he'd crushed Sumner's skull—they said there was blood everywhere—and it wasn't clear that Sumner would live. Right on the Senate floor—*what are we coming to*? And like a dark answer came the news from Kansas: a mad old Abolitionist named John Brown had murdered five proslavery southern men on Pottawatomie Creek, claiming he was the instrument of God's will. Word of the Pottawatomie Massacre swept the South into an orgy of rage and fear.

"This Sumner business shows the South's true nature," Bigelow said. He was gloating and it angered her.

"That's absurd. What about Pottawatomie?"

It was the first time she had seen Bigelow smile. "What about it?" he said. "Both score points for the Republicans. Combine poor Sumner with the South's ravings over that idiot in Kansas, and it says there's no getting along with 'em."

So the impossible had come to pass: when the Republican nominating convention opened in Philadelphia, the party had become a force to be reckoned with . . .

Now, standing on the platform, the cheers crashing through the great hall, the chairman's gavel a thin, furious tapping against the uproar, she saw at last the overwhelming force of Destiny—when it wanted you, it beat down all barriers and came and took you by the hand.

A band she could hardly hear was playing below the podium, its director sweating, the instruments flashing. Gradually the tumult slackened and the gavel regained supremacy. As she took her seat the speaker finished up with the party's new battle cry and the crowd picked up the chant—

"FREE MEN, FREE SOIL, FREE SPEECH, FREE-MONT—and VICTORY!"

The cheers faded and the seething ant hive on the floor resumed. She saw a man edging along with four coffee cups in his hands. Another man backed into him. Hot coffee sloshed over his wrists and he dropped the cups, cursing. Anyone who'd carry four filled cups onto a convention floor must be a political novice, she thought. For all this hoopla, what chance did they really have? The floor was a forest of signs, but in fact this was a sectional convention for a sectional party that had no strength south of Pennsylvania. She was, after all, her father's daughter. No one was here from Missouri. Mr. T was in St. Louis, holding hard to the Democratic standard; her pleasure would be complete if only he were here, approving by his presence the course she and Charles had taken.

It was time for the vote. She could see that Mr. Blair was nervous. John Bigelow was whispering urgently to the chairman, who turned the gavel over and over in his slender fingers and nodded as if taking instructions. The trouble was that several states were interested in John McLean, an elderly Supreme Court justice Jessie remembered well from a boring evening when she had drawn him as a dinner partner.

The break came when a very tall man with a shock of dark hair and a bony, cavernous face took the floor. "Mr. Chairman, with deep regret that a great American, John McLean of Ohio, must be asked to stand aside if he is best to continue serving his country"—the voice was raw, squeaky, rurally accented, but she found the phrasing appealing—"Illinois casts its vote for John C. Frémont of California, the American Pathfinder, in the fervent belief that as he discovered those paths that opened the American West, so he can now best lead this troubled nation into new paths—"

The rest was drowned in the delegates' roar as they grasped the significance of the Illinois commitment.

"Who is that man?" Jessie asked Blair.

"I'll find out for you."

It was Bigelow who had, typically, invented "The Pathfinder" title and had almost lost Charles on the spot.

"I'm *not* a pathfinder," Charles had said to him sharply. "Path*marker,* if you will—the trails were already there. Tom Fitzpatrick, Jedediah Smith, Bridger, old Provost, those were the men who showed me the way. What I did was open them to everyone, chart them."

"Same difference."

"Not at all. It makes me look the fool, claiming too much—when I've given legitimate service that I'm damned proud of! Everyone in the West will know—"

"But the votes are in the East," Bigelow had said coldly. "People need the heroic, Colonel—they want their leaders bigger than life. Look at George Washington—he had to relieve himself like any other man. But that's not what people want."

"People are not stupid. It'll blow up in our faces," Jessie had warned him.

"Nah—by the time anyone raises a fuss, you'll be elected."

"The hell with that," Charles had snapped in his trail voice. "It's *my* reputation, and I want it stopped. Understand?"

Bigelow had backed away, instantly apologetic. It was catching on, he'd said, but he'd do his best to kill it. That rural Illinois voice using the term showed her how hard he'd tried! She glanced around now and saw Bigelow watching her; slowly, brazenly, he winked. She jerked her eyes away; it was like looking inadvertently into some stranger's bedroom. She imagined what dear old Kit would say about a man like Bigelow. She'd like to be back in California, she thought suddenly, riding up toward Mariposa, Alex Godey coming down to meet them through the high sunburnt grass. . . .

A man was whispering to Mr. Blair, who turned to her and said: "The speaker's name is Lincoln. Downstate lawyer—Billy Herndon's partner, apparently—I understand Billy waited till he was out of town and then signed his name to a Republican call, so Lincoln said what the devil and joined up. They tell me he's got a future."

Now state after state fell in line—Massachusetts, Michigan, New York, New Hampshire, Ohio.

"We've got it," Mr. Blair said sharply. He stood up, waving his tally. "By God, we've got it!"

The crowd knew it too; she heard a new force in its voice. She saw the chairman point his gavel and nod. Someone was moving to make the vote unanimous, and then the hall erupted. The band burst into victory music as if to get a head start, and on the overhead catwalk those small boys ran along unfurling a huge banner: JOHN C. FRÉMONT FOR PRESIDENT. Paper streamers unrolled from above in long, curving streaks of color. The Massachusetts delegation surged out of its seats in a snake dance that collected more celebrants as it passed each delegation.

Someone pulled Jessie up and led her to the lip of the platform, toward that awesome noise and motion.

The chant began. "FREE MEN, FREE SOIL, FREE-MONT—"

"And Jessie!" the huge bass voice cried. The crowd roared.

"FRÉMONT AND JESSIE!"

"FRÉMONT AND JESSIE!"

"FRÉMONT AND JESSIE!"

Suddenly she felt entirely alone on the platform with the whole terrible force of those screaming faces focused on her; the very sound was crushing. For an instant she was terrified—she took a step backward in a wild urge to flee. Desperately she fastened onto a single face, round as a dish, bulbous nose, a man standing just below the platform, and she realized that it was suffused with hope and admiration—and yes, love! At once she was reassured, and she felt surging up in herself a profound counterforce of love for every person there. Oh, if only Charles could be here, to see these faces, hear these voices! How it would restore him . . .

"Oh, Mr. Blair," she cried, "isn't it wonderful?"

His look cooled her—it had none of this hot joy. For a moment she saw herself mirrored in his eyes—flushed, excited, looking like the girl she no longer was. It gave a discordant feeling, as if she were masquerading.

"Aye, wonderful," he answered flatly, barely audible over the noise. "I hope it'll be worth the price."

She shook her head, not sure she'd heard him. The hall was alive and she was at its center, noise and love and excitement rushing over her, enveloping her in a creaming flood.

FRÉMONT AND JESSIE!
FRÉMONT AND JESSIE!
FRÉMONT AND JESSIE!

The campaign began with a rush. Good news rolled in from all across the North; FRÉMONT AND JESSIE banners were draped across storefronts from Maine to Iowa. *Free soil, free men, free speech, Frémont—and victory!* To a folk tune, people sang, "We go for our country and Union, and for brave little Jessie forever." It was all nonsense, of course, but it delighted her.

She was lamentably unprepared for what was to come.

Bigelow opened a headquarters in the crumbling ballroom of the old Sebastian Hotel—a block from the Astor House in distance, miles from it in style—but Jessie liked it immediately. Its long tables were heaped with unsorted mail, handbills, posters, lithographic portraits of the candidate. Schedules were tacked to faded wallpaper, and bits of plaster from the disintegarating ceiling ground underfoot when she walked. The nearby window opened onto an alley that smelled of stale beer and urine, and she gave the porter a dollar every morning to wash it down. New York politicians wandered in and out; newspapermen came to see Bigelow and stayed to talk to Jessie. Parade marshals, ward heelers, men who worked the taverns crowded in laughing and telling stories, while the headquarters staff ignored them. One of the volunteers was a young girl with vulnerable brown eyes named Nora Pemberly, who wore little round collars that gave her a virginal look. Summoning the courage to volunteer nearly undid her—she immediately attached herself to Jessie; yet she showed a surprising sense of authority, and soon Jessie relied on her.

The only flaw was that Mr. T was opposing them actively. He'd warned them—he said the new party endangered the nation because it would drive the South to secession—but she'd never believed he would hold out against her. Or maybe she just hadn't been willing to face the irony of their undertaking such an uphill struggle without the support of the man who should have appreciated it most.

Poor Nora was stunned. "But—how could he?" she faltered. "Your own father . . ."

"You don't know Senator Benton," Jessie told her. "He would calmly cut off his right arm if he thought it posed a threat to the Republic." But she was furious, all the same.

Bigelow was writing a campaign biography of Charles and asked her to gather information for the early chapters. She planned no more than a few notes, but soon found herself writing again. The old skill returned, and the delight; it swept her back to the Reports. Bigelow seemed a different man; he wrote with easy skill at a breakneck pace. Even his manner changed when he talked about the book. In the professional editor she saw the more attractive man concealed behind the cynical politician. He made suggestions that improved her copy, but proposed using it largely as she had written it.

"You're good," he said. "You've got a fine, natural style. We can smooth it a little, sure, but the main thing is that it's *alive*—there's no faking that, you know."

Things were going well. Whig and Democratic organizations in the North began switching to the new party. Huge crowds attended the first Republican rallies, drawn by parades, fireworks, bountiful food and drink. There would be no shortage of speakers. Mr. Blair planned to reserve the important ones—Banks, Seward, Horace Greeley, Salmon Chase, Chandler of Michigan, Trumbull of Illinois, Wade of Ohio—for the big rallies and send others touring the small towns to stump for the candidate. Every voter would hear a speech and have his chance to ask questions. Jessie headed the committee which answered the mail that poured in and planned letters—along with paid advertisements—for friendly newspapers.

Presidential candidates rarely spoke for themselves, but Charles was so attractive that Jessie dreamed of setting up a campaign train. She liked to imagine them rolling across the country, greeting hometown crowds from the rear platform; but the men hooted down the idea. The Democrats had nominated Buchanan as predicted, and he was staying close to his Pennsylvania home. Charles met almost daily with delegations from various states, who came to hear his views and take them back to their constituencies.

Charles said this was a hell of a way for a grown man to spend his time: "Truth is, as the feller says, if'n it weren't fer the honor of it all, I'd as lief be on a horse bound for South Pass,"—but they both knew their chances were very real. The strategy sessions bore that out. They wrote off the southern states, of course, for the Republican party was uncompromising in its stand against slavery. But in the North they could begin with a solid block of 114 electoral votes—New England, New York, Ohio, Michigan, Wisconsin, Iowa—against the 149 needed to elect. The decision would lie in the doubtful states, Pennsylvania the key with 27 votes. If they could carry Pennsylvania with Illinois or Indiana, they had the White House. It hurt that Buchanan was a Pennsylvanian, but there was strong antislavery sentiment there too. Pennsylvania's early election added to its importance: it would elect state officers two weeks before the presidential vote. If the new Republican state ticket won, it would be a clear signal that Frémont could win two weeks later and would give the campaign a rocketing momentum. In a sense, everything rode on Pennsylvania.

Then, abruptly, the Democratic campaigning began to turn vicious. It was as if the Democrats had awakened from overconfidence, enraged to find the Republican threat real. Democratic speeches, newspapers, handbills, even the letters that flowed over Jessie's desk were filled with a new rage.

She had been in Missouri campaigns all of her life, but this was different: she had seen partisanship, excessive zeal, even outright personal attack, but never such savage vituperation.

A Democratic theme began to develop: The South would never live under Black Republican rule. Elect Frémont and you will shatter the Union, for the South will surely secede. "If you love the Union, don't vote for the man who will destroy it." Northerners were listening; most of them opposed slavery, but they weren't ready to see the Union broken over it. The whole thing was poppycock, of course. Jessie knew that the Democrats were merely playing on southern fears—it was cold-blooded politics. Her father believed secession to be an imminent danger, but he'd thought that for years. He was too influenced by those Missouri hotheads on the Kansas border. Southerners didn't want to secede—nor would they need to, with Charles in the White House. He would bring the regions together. He could do it because he was unmarked by the issue, not bound by any promise: free to bring sense into an insane situation that could tear the nation apart.

"Mrs. Frémont," Nora said with a troubled look, "have you heard about your father?" Jessie looked up in alarm. "He's addressing a Democratic rally at City Hall Park at noon tomorrow."

So Mr. T would speak against them, barely a block from their very headquarters. Well: it had to happen. That was what politics meant; he'd taught her well enough. At midafternoon next day she saw a carriage turn off Fifth Avenue. It stopped at their house and Mr. T stepped down heavily. She opened the door and hesitated—then ran into his arms.

She put him in her chair in the bay where the three open windows gave a little breeze. He looked very tired—and oddly frail; he who had always seemed so ageless, indestructible. She sweetened cool tea and dropped in ice chips from the sawdust chest. A spasm crossed his face when he drank.

"A little stomach upset—one of the minor perils of old age . . ." His eyes rolled up at her. "God, I wish we were on the same side—I'd campaign for you till I dropped."

"I know that, Papa."

"I tell my audiences that it tears my heart to speak against you." She knew he did; ironically it made him even more effective because it proved his conviction and laid bare a family drama that made them listen more attentively.

"You don't hold it against me, then, that I put conviction ahead of family?"

"Papa, of course not." She knew that was what he had come to ask her. "It just hurts that we're on opposite sides, that's all. . . . I was mad at first."

He looked pleased at that; it struck her that he was very lonely. "Remember the way you'd bring in the tray and we'd plot out those old battles? Those were wonderful days—before the world went crazy. I think about them all the time; especially since I lost your mother." He stopped and blinked, staring at the glass in his hands. "She didn't understand politics, she couldn't be—well, a partner, the way you were—but that dear woman's love sustained me my whole life. She was such a—a comfort to me . . ."

Suddenly he was in tears. He stopped, dabbing at his eyes with a handkerchief. Jessie sat still, bound in affectionate surprise. Her parents had been much older when they'd married; their courtship had been a long one, there hadn't been the all-consuming fire of her passion for Charles—but weren't there many different kinds of love in this capricious, uncertain world?

He was gazing at her fondly. "You've grown into a fine woman. Remember when you cut your braids? That was the first time I saw you as a person, not a child—willing to sacrifice for what you believed, willing to fight. Conviction. That's what's brought us here today."

He sipped the tea; she saw pain flicker in his eyes. "I'll turn into a weepy old man if I'm not careful. What would they say in Washington?" He hesitated. "Well, I want to say that you've been a perfect daughter. I love you, Jessie. And Charles—he's like my own son . . . You were right, you know; I was wrong."

"I knew him," she said.

"Yes, and I didn't. I'm proud of him—I'm proud of you both. What he's done in the West has lasting value. And being nominated for President is no small thing—even if it is by the wrong party."

"You should be in it too, Papa," she couldn't help saying. "The people you're supporting are the very ones who stole your Senate seat."

He shrugged and sighed through his nose. "Well, that's Missouri politics. It hurt for a while, granted, but I don't think much about it anymore. Anyway, my day is over. Everything has changed. I've made many an opponent sorry he tangled with me, but it wasn't vicious, it wasn't destructive." He paused. "There's a new savagery afoot. It's not just that I'm getting old, either. You know, Jessie, the system only works when you grant the goodwill of your opponent. What I see now—on both sides—is an assumption of basic evil. And then the subsequent distortion. Seeing your opponent as evil is the first, irrevocable step toward being willing to destroy him rather than live beside him."

He leaned forward, the great gnarled hands gripping each other. "I'm afraid for you both. I am. Hatred is murderous—you know, Jessie, there are wounds to the heart and soul that are far worse than wounds to the flesh," he said. "It's going to get worse, you know. Much, much worse. Brace yourselves."

There was a clatter outside and the two boys burst through the door, Lily right behind them.

"Grampa!" they cried, climbing onto his lap, hugging him, and she saw a look of benign peacefulness settle on his face. Lily leaned forward and kissed him decorously on the cheek; she was a young woman with budding breasts, yet part of her was still a child; Jessie saw she wanted to be on his lap too.

He was catching a train to Boston—to campaign against them there in Nat Banks' hometown—and she rode with him to the station. "I dread the days ahead," he muttered. "The South will secede if Charles wins—not because of him, but because they're in terror of the Republicans. What terrible decisions you both would face then." At the station he held her close. "Take care of yourself, child," he whispered hoarsely. "Take care of your husband. Try not to let him be too hurt by what is sure to come."

The campaign grew hotter, more clamorous. At Alton, Illinois 35,000 people turned out to hear that young lawyer Lincoln speak for Frémont. There were more than 30,000 at Kalamazoo, 50,000 at Indianapolis. Jessie could hardly believe the accounts of the rally at Indianapolis—cannon firing all day, a parade that took hours to pass a single point, 4,500 men marching in a single delegation, five speakers' stands going from morning to night. From Maine to Iowa there were Frémont clubs, banners, bonfires, bands, cider busts, Frémont picnics, marching companies of Wide-Awakes, Frémont glee clubs. A song to the tune of "Camptown Races" swept the North:

There's an old gray horse whose name is Buck,
du da, du da!
His dam was Folly and his sire Bad Luck,
du da, du da day!
We're bound to work all night,
We're bound to work all day!
I'll bet my money on the mustang colt,
Will anybody bet on the gray?
The mustang goes a killing pace,
du da, du da!
He's bound to win the four-mile race,
du da, du da day! . . .

Yet Jessie clung to the good-humored naiveté in the song, for the ugly aspects of the campaign grew more and more intense. Hecklers began to appear at Republican rallies; fights broke out and spilled into the streets. When Democratic and Republican crowds collided in Pittsburgh, it tripped off a riot. In Maryland and southern Indiana Democratic toughs chased the speakers from the platforms. Furious, Bigelow talked of organizing bands of Republican toughs in reprisal, and he and Mr. Blair had a fearful row over it.

And then came the handbills. They appeared in orchestrated waves, printed by the hundreds of thousands in different cities, passed out on corners and nailed to posts, trees, walls, so that a coordinated attack appeared everywhere on the same day with the same simplistic message: FRÉMONT MEANS DISUNION. FRÉMONT MEANS WAR. Never mind any idealistic theories on slavery—think what will happen to you if your country is destroyed . . . The air was shrill with hysteria.

Late one hot, sodden afternoon, facing another batch of telegrams—accusations, appeals—she decided she'd had enough. She wiped her face with a damp cloth, turned the most pressing messages over to the indefatigable Nora and set out for home.

Muggy heat struck her as she left the hotel; her clothes clung to her. She stopped on a policeman's signal, found herself swaying and realized she was exhausted. She thought of her father, rattling about in trains in this heat; she remembered that spasm of pain in his face. Broadway was a tangle of hurrying people and carriages wheel to wheel, but not a single hack was free. Foul odors clung low to the streets. She had an overpowering desire to be home on the Mariposa, sitting on that makeshift porch with Charles, watching the sun sink into the soft, magenta hills . . . .

And then, coming directly toward her, not ten feet away, she saw a familiar face. It was . . . why, it was Millie Townsend!

"Millie!" she cried, and saw the startled look on the girl's thin face. Millie, who'd been engaged to Preston—she had never married after he had been killed in Mexico; she still lived down the road from the McDowell plantation.

"What are you doing in New York?" Impulsively she seized Millie's hands. "Oh, what a sight for sore eyes you are! Come home with me—Charles would love to see you."

"No!" Millie jerked her hands away sharply. "No, I can't."

"Then let's go in the tearoom and sit down. I want to hear everything, how you've been—"

"I have nothing to say to you, Jessie Frémont!"

Jessie knew she had gone pale. "What do you mean?"

"What you're doing is *evil*!" People flowed around them but Jessie saw nothing; she felt numb with shock. "How could you, Jessie? I can understand your husband—men will do anything to advance themselves, and he's nothing but a common adventurer, anyway. But you're a southern girl. You're a McDowell! Or you *were* . . ."

"Millie, you don't mean that!"

"I do mean it! What do you want? For the niggers to rape and kill us all? Don't you *know* what'll happen if you win?"

"Millie, for heaven's sake . . ."

"I don't want to talk to you—I don't want to be *seen* with you! But I'll tell you one thing: don't ever come back to Virginia. Don't ever come back to Cherry Grove. There isn't a McDowell who'll admit you're related. As far as we're concerned, you're dead!"

For another instant Millie glared at her; then she turned and ran, colliding blindly with someone and running on. Jessie stood still, watching her; only when she saw a woman eyeing her curiously did she realize that she was standing on Broadway weeping.

She wrote to the McDowells. There was no answer. She wrote again. By return mail came a note instructing her to send no more letters: the family found it distasteful even to hear her name.

Two nights later Charles handed her a letter from Edward McCrady, an old Charleston friend for whom he had named a western river. It was very short. *After your course in reference to the Presidential election, any correspondence with you is painful to me, and nothing but the necessity of vindicating myself and family from a suspicion of a gross indelicacy could have induced me again to address you . . .*

She remembered the day that dear little Preuss had proudly inked in McCrady's name on the map. Karl was dead now; unbelievably, he'd hanged himself in the woods near Washington, in grief, she thought, because his days of freedom on the open trails were finished. So much was dead and gone now—old memories, ties, loyalties. These were their own people who had renounced them, their own Democrats. Doubtless Buchanan didn't approve; but being Buchanan, neither did he do anything to stop it. He was at his Pennsylvania country home with Harriet Lane, placidly awaiting the election. Harriet would be her uncle's hostess in the White House if he won; Jessie remembered her ease that night at President Polk's dinner party. After the court-martial Harriet had made it a point to come to tea, and they had talked away the afternoon. That memory warmed Jessie, but she was glad there would be no occasion to test the friendship further. Charles still resented Buchanan, but Jessie had never expected him to speak up when he was in Polk's cabinet—he had never been capable of taking a stand. She remembered when he had asked her to translate the Spanish dispatches because he feared he had a spy in the State Department—but also feared to say so.

The old gray horse when he goes to trot,
du da, du da!
Goes round and round in the same old spot,
du da, du da day!

Charles wasn't afraid of decisions, and he'd managed to swallow his hot pride in this matter of personal attacks. He was full of plans for easing the tension. After he'd settled the trouble in Kansas, he intended to replace the Fugitive Slave Act with a bill to recompense the owners of escaped slaves at fifty percent of value. Jessie thought that a brilliant solution. Then he would move toward purchasing the freedom of slaves in the border states. Once southerners saw that freed slaves didn't mean racial war, passions would subside and the program could move farther south. It would mean accepting for a time the repugnant concept of human beings as property, but it also would release millions of black Americans from bondage. Overcoming southern fear and the radical Republican hunger for overnight abolition would be difficult—but the alternative was civil war!

Walking downtown one sweltering evening later that week, numb with exhaustion, she felt a broadside flung into her hand; an urchin in torn knickerbockers and a cloth cap had already turned away, seeking other clients. She peered at the flier, which was printed on noxious orange paper. The headline leaped out at her: FRÉMONT, THE FRENCHMAN'S BASTARD.

Are we to be ruled by a Frenchman's bastard who despoils our city with his conception on a couch of illicit love, who dishonors the Sovereign State of South Carolina with his illegitimate birth? Does the Republican nominee suppose that southern free men will submit to tyranny from so flagrant a degenerate? Does he imagine that we are too witless not to have uncovered the truth about his roving Don Juan of a father and his slut of a mother? Bastard . . .

There was more, but she had shut her eyes, crushed the sheet in her hands. She felt sick—actively, intensely sick. She hurried home in a turmoil of rage and incredulity. Charles was in his study, writing. She thrust the broadside before him and cried:

"*Look* at this! Is there nothing they won't stoop to—*nothing* they won't invent, in their madness?" She watched the muscle in his cheek flex once, again; his hand holding the sheet began to quiver.

". . . So they dug it up," he muttered. "The swine. I might have known."

She stared at him, incredulous. "What do you mean?" she said. "What are you saying?"

"I should have laid it to rest. Tried to, anyway." His eyes rose to hers, dark with misery. "It's true—in a way. There's—just enough truth—"

"What are you saying—!"

"My mother was once married to a Major Pryor—a Revolutionary veteran, a sour, peevish old man. It wasn't a happy marriage—her family had fallen on hard times, they'd pushed her into it, and Pryor took advantage of it . . . And then my father came along, and they fell in love. She told Pryor about it honestly, she begged him to release her, but he wouldn't hear of it. He flew into a rage, even threatened her physically. So—they ran off together." He tried to grin, but it was a bitter effort. "The way we did. Except that the circumstances were rather different. After a time Pryor even petitioned the Virginia legislature for a divorce, but they wouldn't grant one. Mother's family had disowned her by then. And so . . ." He cupped his fist in his hand. "I was born—out of wedlock. As the saying goes."

"But—why didn't you *tell* me?" she cried at last. *"Why,* in all these years . . . ?"

"She was of very good family, you know—my mother. My father was an émigré artist, a teacher, a dashing, imaginative person—they were romantics, that's all. Do you see? And they *did* marry as soon as they could . . . But who would have accepted that?"

She whispered. "How could you have believed you couldn't share this with me?"

"I thought you'd never have to know—I never wanted you touched by it." He stared down at his hands. "You were a McDowell—and Senator Benton's daughter . . . I kept waiting for your father to bring it up—you know, that time in his study." He smiled again, the saddest smile she'd ever seen. "Perhaps it was—a kindness on his part. Perhaps that's what it was."

"But it wouldn't have mattered to me . . ."

"It mattered to *me,"* he said, and now the naked anguish in his face was devastating. "You don't know how people treated us in Charleston, what my mother suffered, what I endured. Those sidelong glances, the silences, the amused contempt—you haven't the remotest idea!"

"But—it was just a matter of timing, Charles—an accident . . ."

"Accidents decide our lives," he answered, his voice all at once hard. "Accidents determine whether we are legitimate or baseborn. Whether we sit in a comfortable room drinking hot chocolate or lie under ten feet of snow and ice. Whether we rule as governor or are found guilty of mutiny. *Chance,* you see . . ."

His eyes remained locked on hers, as though if their gaze were broken he would be consigned to some eternal limbo. "And then, later, I—just never brought it up. Maybe I had to bury it, I don't know. But it began to seem unimportant, in terms of what we shared together. I know I should have. . . ." He shoved the orange flier away from him with the heel of his hand. "I'm sorry you had to hear it this way. Deeply, deeply sorry."

She came up to him then and pressed his head against her, hard. "It doesn't matter, darling. It never could have—you *must* know that. You must. They—they would have invented it, or something like it."

"Yes, but that was the thin edge of the wedge, you see. As Kit would put it. This is true—more or less. And it will hurt us."

"Charles," she cried softly, "you can't *think* that way! They're simply out to slander you, discredit you in the public eye . . ."

"Yes," he said tonelessly. "Aren't they. And I'm afraid they've only just begun. I never thought I'd see the day when I'd be glad that my poor gentle mother is dead," he said.

After a time Jessie went downstairs to talk to Lily. She must explain this to the children now, before they heard elsewhere. But how explain the vulnerable complexities of love, the cold cruelties of politics? Lily listened dutifully, nodding, but her face had a stricken, forlorn look; there was no more to say. They, who were so proud, must now live with this public humiliation. Frank and young Charles must endure mocking taunts. Jessie took two bowls of soup upstairs. She and Charles ate in the dark. Outside the gaslights made a harsh lacework of the trees.

Now the mood of the campaign darkened. Bigelow maintained they were still ahead, but day by day, as she sat at her long table in the shabby ballroom, she saw signs that the tide was running against them. In addition to the viciousness of the personal attack on Charles, the Democratic campaign was making the fear of southern secession real to a great many voters. Republican rallies seemed more somber, friendly newspapers more cautious. And their money was drying up—a critical sign; big contributors always had long antennae, Jessie knew too well.

An angry Republican circuit speaker came in from southern Pennsylvania to say that a crowd there had threatened to tar and feather him, while the Republican supporters—if there were any there—had kept their mouths shut. And as for his going back, Mr. Bigelow could try whistling up a rainspout. It was hard to ask men to carry the campaign from town to town when they faced hostile crowds, cool newspapers and a shortage of expense money. Jessie read and reread the mail; she judged they were still strong in New England and New York, but their people were losing heart in the crucial border states.

Bigelow spent most of his time trying to reassure their backers. "Don't worry," he told Jessie. "Southern Pennsylvania is edgy, granted, it's butt-up against Maryland and practically slave country, but we're gaining in Philadelphia and Pittsburgh. We'll take that early election, and you'll see, the coffers'll pop open again and we'll go full-tilt into the last two weeks. That's when elections are won anyway, you know that."

Or lost, she thought.

New attacks struck from the West. She had imagined that savaging Charles' mother, turning a national hero into a mere bastard, was the ultimate personal attack. There weren't many votes in the West, Bigelow had been right about that, but she and Charles were vulnerable there in ways he couldn't imagine, for their hearts were in the West.

In Missouri, her father wrote them in an agitated letter, and all over the West, people had now seized on that absurd business of Bigelow's calling Charles The Pathfinder, and were denouncing the candidate himself for it. Even Chouteau had made a deprecatory speech. It hurt terribly that Pierre would attack him. Charles' brilliant western career had begun in Pierre's compound, and some of her fondest girlhood memories were of its bustle as steamboats crowded its levee and fur bales were wheeled into the limestone warehouses.

I only warn you of this, Mr. T wrote, *because while it probably won't matter much in the East, it's hurting Charles badly out here. You know how many big talkers we have already; consequently people resent a man who claims too much credit. A suspicion has attached itself to Charles; whether it will evaporate when this is over, I cannot say. It's perverse, too—there's no Republican strength out here, so this attack reflects a personal hatred that's been carefully spread, not a general political purpose.*

His handwriting had trailed down to an exhausted slant; he added only: *You know I've always believed in the political process, but I fear it has been fatally corrupted. It's as if that process itself is rotting and dying—but daughter, it is all we have!*

Kit had written in a similar vein: Frémont was being bad-mouthed all over New Mexico for a braggart and a four-flusher.

"Maybe winning is the only revenge," Charles said. He was sitting very still; she saw a nerve trembling at the edge of one eye. "If I could settle the Kansas business, nothing else would matter." He sighed. "Wouldn't it be grand to forget the whole thing? Go out and spend a week or two with old Major Cummins at the Agency, ride out on the prairie every day?"

As though they had already scented victory, the Democratic attacks on Charles redoubled; they fell like hammer blows, all the more painful for their very absurdity: *This abolitionist renegade has not himself been above owning slaves—as witness some of the poor devils shackled deep in the gold mines of his vast Mariposa empire . . . His cruelty toward the defeated Californios during his "rule" as self-appointed sultan is well known: hidalgos imprisoned without cause, ladies of gentle blood imprisoned and assaulted by his bravos . . . What this unprincipled adventurer has managed to conceal most craftily is his religious faith. For Frémont is nothing less than a Roman Catholic! He and his strong-willed wife were wed by a Catholic priest, and he has been seen on many a Sunday genuflecting in the aisles of Catholic churches in the city of Washington . . .*

Charles had been right: it had been only the beginning. There was no end to the odious parade of slander. He was a confirmed drunkard, he had been married illegally, he had enriched himself at the expense of the conquered Californians, he had sold government beef to the Indians and pocketed the profits. To crown it all, a fellow named Clark Melling came east from California with a letter from Collis Huntington, who was running the Republican campaign there, to report even more flagrant rewritings of history.

The Bear Flag Revolt had been recast—suddenly the California settlers, Merritt and Fallon and the others, were self-serving ruffians, and Charles a filibuster acting on his own initiative, in hopes of emerging as California's despotic ruler. His refusal to submit to Kearny was cited now as evidence of other intentions, and the outrageous court-martial verdict was taken as confirmation.

"I don't like to bring bad news," Melling said. "But they're saying that Larkin had the Californians all ready to swing over to the United States peacefully, when the revolt touched off the war. And they're blaming the war for all the hard feelings that followed."

Jessie could see the perverted logic in it. So many newcomers had flocked to California in the gold rush that the native Californians had been reduced to a small minority and badly abused by these interlopers—and now people would rather blame this on Charles and the war than on their own greed and cruelty.

"People actually believe that?" Charles demanded, incredulous.

"Too many of them do."

"And Larkin, does he—"

"No. He's issued a good letter supporting you."

Jessie thought of Bancroft's cool, remote expression at the White House dinner. But she knew Charles wouldn't claim now an authority that Polk himself had repudiated when he let the court-martial go forward.

"You know, Mr. Melling," Charles was saying, "at one point I thought I'd enjoy running for President. That shows you just how much I knew about politics, doesn't it?" He shrugged. "Well, sir, what can we do about this?"

"Collis Huntington would like a full, explanatory statement from you. We've got Larkin's letter and one from Jesús Pico. We'd also like letters from Stockton and Gillespie."

"We'll get those," Charles said. "Try Sutter, too—I don't think he has any hard feelings. Kit Carson will send a statement. What about Ned Kern?—he ran the fort at the time."

Melling gave him an odd look, his blue eyes flashing wide. "Don't you know about Kern? He's supplying this idiot, Pickett."

At their puzzled look, he said: "You haven't seen this?" He opened his case and tossed out two copies of a pamphlet. "It must have reached the East by now; it was out a week before I left."

The title jumped off the booklet's cover—FRÉMONT: BLACK REPUBLICAN HUMBUG.

"Oh, God," Jessie murmured. It was an attack on the Fourth Expedition, written by one Charles Pickett, who stated that he relied on information supplied by a participant in the disaster, Edward Kern.

"Who is he, this Pickett?" she asked.

"Friend of Kern's," Charles said. "I remember him vaguely at Sutter's—I didn't much care for him."

The brutal message of the pamphlet was simple: *Frémont was vain, arrogant, selfish, cared nothing for his men; he set out in deadly winter in mad hopes of a* FEAT *to overshadow the* DISGRACE *of the court-martial.*

"But why would Ned do this?" she whispered.

"He's hated me ever since Doc got killed." Charles looked at Melling. "His brother, a physician, went out with Old Bill Williams a month after the expedition, and the Utes killed them both. The Army had hit a Ute village the day before. I was already in California by then, but Ned blamed me." He shook his head. "Doc was an awful greenhorn. Ned should have blamed himself for bringing him out, but he couldn't face that."

Arrogant, uncaring, mad with AMBITION, *Frémont had refused his guide's advice and driven his men into the mountains, higher and higher, the food running out, his honest guide protesting but staying with the men, whom he refused to leave to their terrible fate . . .*

"Honest guide!—That old murderer—got us lost from day one!"

Then, beaten at last, FEAR *overcoming his own greedy ambition, the commander had tucked his tail and run. He had taken the food for* HIMSELF *and run for safety—abandoned his men to die while he saved himself.*

"Ah, Jesus," he said. "It wasn't like that. Not like that at all . . . The relief party quit on us, lay down, ready to die. Williams, too." He was looking at Melling but she knew he was talking to her, to himself, maybe to Proue lying there in the snow. "We'd all have died if Godey and Preuss and I hadn't gone for help. This man is crazy. He's—"

But how had the commander remained so STRONG *that he could stroll out of the snow when all around him better men, stronger men, were dying? Reckon the whispers that long have attended this fateful expedition: that men ate men, the ultimate degradation. How else did the commander remain so strong but that he* FEASTED *on the bodies of his men as they died? One by one they died, the commander putting them to his horrible use as he fled toward safety.* THIS *is the man who now asks us to put our future in his hands . . .*

Charles turned away and gazed out of the long ballroom windows; his hands, clenched together at the small of his back, were trembling, the knuckles white. Bigelow came in with a sheaf of telegrams in one hand and read the pamphlet. "Jesus, Colonel, we've got to hit 'em back, hard. We've been too damned nice, that's our trouble." Jessie could hear a note of hysteria in his voice. "God damn 'em, they want to play dirty—what about Buchanan and his bachelorhood, so called? What's his relationship with that little bitch Harriet Lane? By God, we'll—"

"Be silent!" Charles stood very straight and slender, his face white as cuttlebone, unbelievably cold and threatening. Bigelow did not move. "*We will do nothing.* Is that clear?" His hand closed on hers so hard it hurt. "Come on," he said. Bigelow, his mouth open then, stepped aside quickly and they went unseeing across the ballroom, through the hotel lobby, and onto the street, walking very fast; he held her hand as he might have a life preserver. He made for City Hall Park and its trees, the sight of the river, the open sky.

"I never wanted to be President," he said tightly. They were in the park, her heels loud on the bluestone walks, pigeons fluttering out of their way;

an old man was sunning himself, a nanny watched three children play. "I never even thought of it. Hell, I turned down the Democrats. I wanted to open the West, that's all I *ever* wanted, and by God, I did it—we all did it together! Me, you, the Senator, the men. That's what matters—we paved the way. . . ."

She found his face frightening; she wanted to put her arms around him, to protect him, but his anguished rage was too great even for that.

"But those bastards don't understand. It's just something for them to use—making me out a windbag, a charlatan—a cannibal . . . Christ! Ten good men dead—and all it means to them is another chance to say something filthy." He struck his hands together fiercely; his eyes had filled. "Well, I don't give a good Goddamn for the presidency. The West is what I am—what I'll always be . . ."

Then he stopped so suddenly that she was ahead of him. She turned and saw his face close and tighten. Deliberately he reached down and brushed a pigeon fleck from a wooden bench, motioned her down. He was very still and she didn't dare speak. At last, as if some tremendous inner tension had broken, he sighed.

"It's not fair," he said with a touch of the old verve. "Your father never told me politics was such fun. Did he?"

She wept then, her head on his chest.

"Yes, it hurts. Hurts us both." He hugged her, took her hand. "Well, to hell with 'em."

He was himself again. "We've made some mistakes. One or two. But we've always done an honest day's work. I'm proud of that. And I have no intention of slinging mud back at them, whatever anyone says. Dignity. Yes, and honor—they're what we believe in, Jessie. . . . When I think of all you've suffered, all you've achieved—and now for you to have to take *this*. We haven't asked any favors. And we won't. And when this is over we'll go back to the Sierra, where one man can't slander another without running the risk of paying for it. What a relief *that*'ll be."

"Oh Charles," she murmured, "you're such a good man. Noble . . ."

He laughed then, and squeezed her. "Don't you try flattery, now. Nothing noble about me. Hell . . ." He turned serious again. "Look, Jessie, every bad place I've ever been, it's always been the same: you have to figure out what seems best and do it. Maybe it'll be a mistake. Maybe it just won't work. But even if you fail, it won't really matter. It's the dream itself—do you see? If you hold to *that* you'll be all right, no matter what comes. No matter what."

"Well," Jessie said as brightly as she could manage, "this is one family argument that Senator Benton won!"

Lily began to cry. Frank and young Charles gaped at her in dismay; then their faces crumpled and they cried too. They were all seated at the breakfast table on the morning after election day. Charles and Mr. Blair looked at each other helplessly.

"Lily!" Jessie said. "You stop that this minute."

"But Mother, I *wanted* to live in the White House . . ."

So did I, child, so did I. "We don't cry over our losses, sweetheart. Wipe your face now and go for a walk in the park. Take your brothers and think about how many people *did* want your daddy to be President."

As Lily went for her coat, Jessie said to Mr. Blair: "Well, you warned us. Everyone pays the price."

He smiled an old man's smile. "The dark side of politics. I'm sorry you had to go through that fire."

"It was worth it," she said, glancing at Charles. "Even with all the venom, it was worth it."

She had thought their chances real until that early gubernatorial election in Pennsylvania had gone against them. The loss had been very narrow, which made it hurt even more. The pain of it surprised her and made her angry. She realized she had let the insidious dream creep in after all—like Lily, she'd been seeing herself in the White House.

There had been a bitter meeting later that night: Mr. Blair, John Bigelow chewing chalky heartburn tablets, Senator Seward and his cigar, Thurlow Weed who'd caught a train down from Albany, and the national chairman, Ed Morgan. Then Nat Banks had come in, straight from Philadelphia, Ed Davis with him. Davis was one of her favorites, a handsome man with jet-black hair. They had counted on him to hold Pennsylvania. He had waved to Charles and taken her hand as she extended her other hand to Nat.

"Sorry, Jessie." Ed looked haggard. "We tried."

"How's Nancy?" she asked, trying to smile. "Not undone, I hope."

"Oh, you know Nancy. She went shopping."

Jessie laughed at that. She was fond of Nancy Davis. "That's not fair. I'll bet she's hurt."

"We're all hurt, sweetheart. Ask Nat."

Nat rolled his eyes. "Kick in the belly."

Charles said: "But can we turn it? Margin of 3,000 votes—that's 1,500 to turn around and two weeks to go. What do you think?"

Ed shook his head. "Sorry, Charles—the tide's running against us. The electorate seems to have bought that damned Frémont-and-war message. They're running on fear. Two weeks ago we might've won—two weeks from now I think we'll lose by ten, maybe twenty thousand."

He'd been right, of course. Toward the end the tide against them had been like the sea rushing into the cove at Nantucket. Even then it was close. When it was over, they found that they had carried every state they'd considered certain—but not one of the others. Yet for a new candidate running with a new party against the most agonizing question in American history, Charles had managed what Jessie knew was a triumph: 1.3 million Americans had voted for him, against 1.8 million for Buchanan. And sour, embittered old Millard Fillmore and his die-hard Know-Nothings had siphoned off 870,000—the votes that would have made the difference. Defeat, yes—but it was defeat with honor.

Charles stood up. "C'mon, kids," he said, "before you go, I want to tell you a story about mountains—and why you don't always get to the top of them."

From the table, she watched him sit on the settee by the front door, Lily beside him, the boys spread-legged and grave before him.

"You're one brave girl, Jessie," Mr. Blair said softly. "Women shouldn't be subjected to this kind of thing. All those vicious stories . . ."

"That's the democratic way, isn't it?" She smiled wryly. "Anyhow, fire hardens one, I'm told."

She knew she was right. She felt a strength within her that was new. She was exhausted, her nerves were raw and tears were very near the surface, yet she felt stronger than ever.

There was another thing, too, that lay deep in her mind; a curious consolation taken. She wouldn't mention it to Mr. Blair, and probably not to Charles; but now they wouldn't have to face the terrifying possibility that the South would carry out its threat. Not a day had passed that she hadn't thought of what her father had said as they approached the station: *What if you win?* Probably he'd been wrong—she'd thought so then and did still—but now it wouldn't be put to the test.

"One thing, though. I've learned a lot more about slavery. It really *is* evil—I always knew that, but now I know just *how* abhorrent it is. It corrupts everything. Look at the hatred it unleashed on us. In a way it thrust us into the same category as the Negro: something almost but not quite human, to be branded and reviled at will . . . Not that they aren't a million times worse off, of course; but the point's the same. Slavery denies humanity—the humanity in all of us."

The old publisher looked troubled. "Oh, I'd hardly go that far, Jessie. The Negro is a—"

"No. That's it, exactly. It isn't simply 'slavery.' " She had just caught sight of something she'd never seen before. "It's the *premise* that's so evil: you start by denying humanity in the black man, and the next step is to deny it in Catholics, in the Irish, the Italians, and then Germans—and finally . . . and finally everybody who doesn't think precisely the way you do. We're really going to have to put an end to slavery, and soon. I never saw that so clearly until now."

Francis Blair looked rather alarmed at this. "End it? All at once? That's a bit frightening. Limit it, I think. Stop it from spreading—and in time it'll die of its own accord."

"I doubt that. I don't think it can wait. Mr. T has always said nothing is more important than preserving the Union; but I'm beginning to wonder if it's worth saving, at the price of tolerating slavery, and the cruelties it brings in its wake."

Plenty of Republicans, maybe a majority of them, believed it too. The new party would have to be reckoned with in the future. The idea brought her some comfort on that bitter November morning, though Bigelow had infuriated her when he'd said roughly the same thing that night at party headquarters. Ed Morgan, the party chairman, had been full of asinine ideas. He was a heavy man, assertive, with that quick, unreflective confidence that grows from success in business; he proposed that the candidate issue some dramatic, inflammatory statement. Charles naturally refused and there had been one of those rows that arise from acute tension and exhaustion.

"The trouble with you, Frémont," Morgan had said, his face livid, "is that you're an amateur politician—you haven't the belly for the hard stuff."

Jessie had looked up at her husband in alarm, but Charles had only said quietly: "Better an amateur if you call yourself a professional, Mr. Morgan. Fear of me is what the Democrats are selling: you're asking me to prove their point."

"Doesn't matter," Bigelow had interrupted in his cold way. "The Republican party is here to stay, and that's what counts. If we don't win this time, we will next time. And"—his bright little eyes rolled around to Charles with hard disfavor—"with a different candidate, I might add."

"You're damned right, with a different candidate," Charles had snapped.

Now, though she didn't like Bigelow one bit better, she knew he was right. The Republican party would survive because it had started with a credible idea and a credible candidate. That was what Charles had given it.

Charles had returned to his seat. "They're all right," he said. "They'll steady down. I think it was that miserable orange handbill that got to Lily. She thought living in the White House would answer all the attacks."

"Would have, too," Mr. Blair said. "According to Seneca, success makes all crimes honorable."

She saw Charles' eyes flash at the publisher in the old proud way. "Montaigne says there are some defeats more triumphant than victories, Francis."

She laughed then, surprised at herself. "Well, when you're attacked on this scale and nearly half the country says: 'It doesn't matter, we don't believe it, we're with you'—that draws a lot of the poison."

She felt so *free*. It was over, done with, settled. A great national party had chosen them and an immense outpouring of votes had ratified that choice. That never could be taken from them. It set them free. She was sure of it.

"You know," she said, "I never really got over the court-martial. That trial was so unfair, we were so helpless. The Army used us to cater to Kearny's cheap pride, President Polk used us." She saw Charles' warning glance, but she had no intention of spilling the agonized heart of that story. "After all," she added smoothly, "the plain fact was that Mr. Polk wanted California. And you got it for him."

Charles poured more coffee in their cups. His face was neutral, calm; he was waiting.

"It's as if the fires of the campaign burned it all away," she said. "As if that marvelous outpouring of votes—it doesn't matter at all that it wasn't enough, not at all . . . I don't think the court-martial matters anymore." She was still talking to Mr. Blair, but she was watching Charles; and in a moment he nodded and got to his feet.

"Tom Benton says losing the Presidency is something no man ever recovers from," Francis Blair said suddenly. "You think that's true, Charles?"

He turned, smiling, and shook his head. "Even Old Bullion can't be right every time. . . . All right, honey," he said, his eyes burning, and she could see he felt as free, as vindicated as she did herself. "Let's go down to headquarters and wrap this up—we have to head for California!"

GOLDEN GATE

"COLONEL! *Colonel . . .*"

He came awake with a violent start, the voice—tensed, insistent—mingling with the tag end of a discordant dream. He was on his feet without thought, swaying slightly, the rough pine boards cool against his toes. Jack Hopper's bare head was at the window, silhouetted against the dark.

Frémont said: "What is it?"

"They've jumped the Black Drift. In force."

"Right." He dressed hurriedly, yanking at his boots. Behind him Jessie stirred, rose on one elbow.

"What's the matter?"

"Just some mine troubles, honey. Go on back to sleep."

His eyes had grown accustomed to the dark now. He quietly slipped his gun belt off the top peg by the door and buckled it on, lifted the Winchester off the elk antlers, and plucked his hat from another peg.

"Charles . . ."

He turned. Jessie was standing now, in her nightgown, her hair down, looking ghostly and appealing. "Be careful."

"I'm always careful," he answered lightly.

"No. I mean it. Remember about 'The cautious.' "

He grinned in spite of himself. "I will. I promise."

The air outside was soft as a woman's breath; the summer heat clung close on the western slope of the Sierra, baked by the long afternoon sun. Jack Hopper was standing in the yard with half a dozen hands; they all had weapons.

"What happened?" Frémont asked the foreman.

"They came up from Bear Valley in a body, surrounded the shaft."

"How many of them?"

"Hundred, hundred and fifty maybe."

"Who's on duty there?"

"Taffy Caton and Jack Evans, couple others. They tried the same shit they pulled off over at Lone Pine—told them they'd make it worth their while if they came on out quick and easy. Taffy told 'em they could go to hell in a wine barrel." He cursed and spat. "Lousy fucking claim-jumpers . . . Piccadilly heard it all."

"Piccadilly" was Douglas, a slender sixteen-year-old boy their friends the Foxes had sent out from England in the hope that the outdoor life would rebuild his frail constitution. Frémont turned to the boy; in the soft blur of first light his face looked fragile. He'd been leading a burro loaded with tools down to the maintenance shed when he'd heard men coming, he related in his high, clear English accent.

"When I realized how many there were, I knew it was the Hornitas League."

"What did you do then?"

"Abandoned the burro and hid in some rocks, sir."

"Good boy." Frémont thought rapidly. He could muster 40 men, perhaps 45. But if there were 150 of them . . . and it would mean stripping his other shafts, leave him vulnerable everywhere else. He thought of Alex Godey, running a horse ranch now, down in the sleepy Santa Inez Valley. He'd been happy enough to back Godey in the venture—but God, how he missed him.

"We've got to go get us some help," he said aloud.

The Aussie foreman shook his head. "I sent Bracken. They opened up on him, killed his horse and caught him. They've got every frigging trail out of here blocked."

"I see."

"They mean to break you, Colonel. Right here and now. If they can take over the Black Drift, they figure they can take 'em all."

"All right. Saddle up," he ordered. "We're going over there." He turned to young Fox. "Douglas . . ."

"Yes, sir?"

"I want you to ride to Coultersville. You'll have to go the long way round—up cross-country through the notch between Catamount and Old Bullion, and then down Fletcher's Creek. The way we rode that Sunday. Remember?"

"Yes, sir."

"Take Lily's Ayah, and string Mrs. Frémont's Mariposa Belle. Follow the creek beds, use manzanita and madrone for cover wherever you can. And cross your ridges with care." He put his hand on the boy's shoulder. "A lot depends on it. Think you can get through?"

"Yes sir, Colonel. I do." The boy looked steady enough, and eager. Well, he could spare him better than any of the men if it came to a fight—he owed that to the boy's parents; and like so many Englishmen he was a superb rider, and intelligent.

"Good lad," he said. "Tell Mr. Lawson I formally request the governor to send the militia. He'll know what to do. Good luck."

Riding hard through the dawn light Frémont grappled with the problem. He had come home to an avalanche of troubles. Much less work had got done than he'd expected. The new dam was nearly finished, but most of the machinery for the new mill was lying around in crates, strangely shaped cogs and pistons and rocker arms. His ownership of the Mariposa had still been clouded; after months of frustrating depositions, his old friend John Crittenden had bested Attorney General Cushing in a masterful plea before the Supreme Court, and only the other day the title came clear at last. Then there were continual headaches with the new stamping machines. The railroad bed crept down the mountain with maddening slowness. The rock encasing the primary vein proved much harder than they'd expected, which slowed things and required even heavier equipment. To maintain production he opened new veins, but that raised labor costs. Harder rock slowed the stamps and they had to be reset. A drought reduced the water level and settlers downstream begged him to open his dam, leaving the mills operating at half-capacity.

And the gold: it either gushed forth in torrents or dried up to a trickle—but the bills never slowed, and interest charges of two to three percent a month meant that debts tended to pyramid. What an irony—here he was, one of the richest men in California, and again and again he had to ask some creditor to wait until the gold flowed again. More than once the Mariposa County sheriff had ridden out, pulled off his hat politely and served Frémont with a writ attaching his property. Then he would have to wire Trenor Park to find funds to keep his head above water.

And now, on top of everything else, this damned Hornitas League . . .

The law—or rather *non*-law—lay at the heart of the trouble. In their infinite wisdom the California courts had ruled that anyone could take full possession of any unoccupied mine—no matter who owned it and had been working it an hour before—nor how much he'd already invested in its operation. Then there were the squatters: they had drifted into the Sierra by the thousands, a very different breed from the early settlers. Rowdy, rootless, spawned in the San Francisco taverns, they would work listlessly for a few weeks and move on again. They provided a huge, if undependable, source of men for exploitation by any unscrupulous malcontent with grand ideas—and lo, this Hornitas League was born, its sponsors claiming that mines were like all unmarked land, ripe for homesteading. They claimed only rapacious land barons like Frémont kept the common man from owning his own gold mine in this great land of opportunity.

The only problem, of course, was to render a shaft *unoccupied;* and there the League had been quite resourceful. Two months ago they had bribed that old simpleton Tom Parry to leave Mariposa's Lone Pine shaft, and Frémont had found himself helpless. He'd put $40,000 of his hard-earned money into that mine, it was *his* equipment those claim-jumpers were using, and there wasn't one single thing he—

The crash of the gunshot was shockingly loud, echoing and reechoing down the valley. He ducked involuntarily and reined up. Ahead on a great knob of rock a man waved his rifle and dropped out of sight. Hopper cursed under his breath, and an engineer named Pearson was looking at him worriedly.

"They mean business, Colonel."

"Yes. Well, so do we." For a moment Frémont studied the terrain, fastened on a harsh granite peak considerably to the west of the mine, out of easy rifle range. Dismounting, he drew the Winchester from its boot and hung his field glasses around his neck.

"Let's get up there," he said, pointing.

"Up there? But why, Señor Coronel?" Juan Ramirez asked.

"Get up above 'em," Hopper told him with his hard grin. "Look down their throats, the sons-of-bitching dingoes."

Climbing hard through the heat, the chaparral and manzanita tearing at his shirt, Frémont felt the old excitement catch at him, lodge high under his wishbone. All right! He was damned if he was going to give up his beloved Mariposa to a bunch of drunks and ne'er-do-wells! Not after all he'd put into it. If only he had Alex here beside him—Alex was the best man in a fight he'd ever seen, except Kit. Why couldn't they all have stayed together, gone on doing what they were good at? Goddamned world, the way it turned everything all around, in spite of everything you did . . .

He'd reached the top. The sun was up now, burning into the back of his neck. Thinking of Louie he dropped to his knees and crept forward, raised the glasses. The mine shaft was a solid black oval against the granite. In among the boulders and ridges of rock he could see two frayed pup tents and several ponchos spread on sticks; here and there he made out a hat or a rifle barrel. There was no movement at the mouth of the mine.

"All right," he called through the morning stillness, "who's in charge of you?"

There was a scurrying ripple of movement, a fevered clicking of rifle bolts and hammers. Then a voice, hoarse and deep:

"*I* am in command, and my name is Dennis O'Brien. Withdraw your men from this shaft at once, in the name of the Hornitas League!"

"*Whore*-nitas league, you mean, O'Brien!" Hopper shouted.

"That's enough, Jack." Frémont got to his feet, hands on his hips. "Now you listen to me, all of you!" he called. "This is *my* land, and *my* mine, by deed and title. You are committing armed robbery—"

"*You're* the fucking robber, Frémont!" O'Brien roared.

There was a shot, another; a ricochet sang away from the rock below him.

"Get down, Colonel!" Jack was saying in an angry, fearful voice. "For Christ sake, lower your bum."

"Want them to see me," he answered evenly; he was still bound in the tense exhilaration. "They can't hit anything anyway—there isn't a decent marksman among them. . . . I will tell you this!" he called. "I am not going to give you this mine without a fight. There's a battalion of state militia on the way—and they will string you up for common highwaymen when they get here."

There was a chorus of shouts and curses, and a ragged fusillade for answer.

"Stop it!" O'Brien was bawling at them. "Don't you see that's just what he wants? Save your lead . . ."

"For the love of God, man, get down!" Hopper was hissing at Frémont, who only cupped his hands and shouted at the shaft:

"Hold on tight now, Taffy! Don't let 'em faze you. Help is on the way!" He stepped down then. Pearson was shaking his head unhappily.

"Won't work, Colonel," Jack said. "They plan to camp here for as long as it takes. Starve 'em out."

"We'll see." Frémont squinted into the rising sun; the sweat was already soaking his collar. "Wait'll they've sat out in this heat for eight hours. We'll see how enthusiastic they are."

They settled in for a siege. Hopper and Ramirez took a party back to the barracks for food and water and some light tentage. Gregorio reported that young Fox had made it over the pass without being detected. Good; it was just a matter of time, then. The white California sun climbed high above them and held there, in all its midsummer force. Any movement was an effort; the rock became too hot to touch. There was some stirring among the Leaguers; a heated argument broke out under one of the pup tents, and two men walked away down the trail from the mine shaft to jeers.

"There's two have had enough," Frémont remarked. "And tomorrow won't be any easier."

"Or for Taffy and them, either," Hopper muttered. "How long can *they* hold out? Hell, all they got in there is water."

After a torrid eternity it was dusk. The sun sank into distant ridges; great blued shadows swept up the slopes, and the air turned faintly cool. They ate dried meat and corn cakes and lay on their ponchos smoking. Watching the stars come out, identifying them one by one, faithful old friends, Frémont thought of the high plains north of Fort Snelling, and Papa Joe, and found himself smiling. . . .

Three more men deserted the Leaguers next morning right after sunrise. The heat was worse on the peak; their eyes were puffed, their tongues swollen in their mouths; the rock shimmered and swam, lizards scuttled in the shadows. Around noon Jack cried suddenly:

"For the love of Mike—it's a brace of Sheilahs."

Frémont rolled over and peered down. Two women were coming up the trail toward the mine mouth, their bonnets drawn low, shading their faces; they were carrying wicker buck baskets and a tin billycan, walking quickly, the dust kicking away in tiny puffs from their heels.

"It's Taffy Caton's trouble-and-strife," Hopper was saying. "I don't know the other one." He gave his harsh laugh. "Bringing 'em up some nip-and-tupper."

"They'll never let them through," Pearson muttered. "They're crazy . . ."

A figure had stepped out of the shadows, another, three more—and a big red-bearded man pointed back down the trail contemptuously. The foremost of the two women, the slimmer one, advanced on Redbeard. She was wearing blue calico, she had a—

Frémont snatched up the glasses—and now there was no mistaking his wife's white, oval face, the huge, flashing eyes.

"—*Jessie,*" he gasped. He started to shout something, gagged on it. *Jessie*—

Redbeard had thrust her back roughly. Jessie's free hand dipped into the buck basket and came up again; the long-barreled revolver glinted in the hard flat light.

"God stone the crows!" Jack whispered.

My old Sharps. Frémont felt hollow-sick with fear. His vision blurred, cleared again strangely; he was incapable of any movement at all—could only stare and stare as Jessie said something more, something infinitely cold and scathing, her head back like Old Benton's . . . and then Redbeard had given way, the others moving back too, and the women had passed through them like a dream and entered the shaft.

"Will you glom to that!" Jack Hopper was pounding little Juan on the shoulders. "What a larruping, Fitzroy!" Then his eye caught Frémont's. "What's wrong, Colonel?"

The women had come out of the tunnel, empty-handed now, were walking swiftly past the Leaguers and away down the trail, their skirts snapping against their legs. Frémont put his hand to his mouth.

". . . Jessie," he heard himself say feebly, while they all stared at him.

"That was—Miss *Jessie*?" The Aussie glared at him in utter disbelief—then burst into a roaring fit of laughter. "Why, we ought to let *her* settle it, Colonel—what a bonzer stunt!"

Frémont nodded dumbly while laughter spattered all around him.

Later that afternoon a messenger rode in hard; there was another conference under the pup tent, and then O'Brien emerged and called to Taffy Caton and the others to come out or suffer the consequences.

"What do we do now?" Jack said. "They're going to rush 'em."

"No, they're not," Frémont told him. "It's a bluff. They've had some bad news, and he's trying to force the issue."

And sure enough, in half an hour a knot of riders approached the base of the peak. It was Arthur Bentham, one of his old California Battalion NCO's, with the Coulterville Home Guard, 87 strong, and news that 500 troopers led by the state marshal were only a day's march away.

"That's more like it!" Jack Hopper exulted. "Now let's go take 'em, Colonel—let's mince those dingoes!"

The cautious seldom make mistakes.

He shook his head. "No need for that. They've had the message. Leave the road to Coloma open for them," he said to Bentham. "I'm going home and get some sleep."

When he saw Jessie standing in the doorway of the crazy little whitewashed cabin (her White House, she'd called it once, laughing: "You see—I got one anyway!") he felt himself turn trembling again, as weak in the knees as the rawest tenderfoot after a firefight.

"That was a very, very foolish thing you did," he said in as grim a tone as he could manage. But she wasn't fooled in the least.

"Worked, though. Isn't that what you used to say?"

He held her against his chest so hard she groaned; he didn't ever want to let her go again. "Honey, you gave me one awful scare," he murmured.

She threw him the quick, mischievous glance. "Did I?"

"I was *watching* the whole thing!"

"You see, you're not the only one who can scare people, John Charles Frémont. It's my Mariposa too, you know. . . . Charles, I couldn't let Annie Caton go up there alone. I tried to dissuade her. She was very determined."

"You looked pretty determined yourself. What in God's name did you *say* to him?"

Her chin came up in that proud way he loved so. "I said: 'We have nothing to do with this stupid quarrel over mines and gold. Our business is to see that our men are properly cared for. You can blow each other to bits, for all I care—but right now I am going into that shaft and see those men have a decent meal. It may be the last one they'll ever have. And if you are brave enough to shoot a woman down in cold blood, now is the time to prove it!' And I looked him right in the eye—and in a moment he stepped back. And that was all there was to it!"

She laughed once—her high, jubilant laugh—and then she gripped her hands together and stared at him gravely. "But it was such a *long* moment, Charles. . . ."

"I know," he said. He pressed his mouth against her hair. "You're something, honey. You're the bravest of the brave."

Trenor Park came up to the Mariposa two weeks later, attracted by all the hullabaloo, Frémont supposed. It was all over by then. The state militia had arrived and camped around the White House in their conical mustard-colored tents; there was a little aimless shooting and a lot of patroling, and the Hornitas League had evaporated into thin air. Frémont was elated—he planned to go to San Francisco next month and appeal this outrageous claim-jumping law—but Park had other matters on his mind.

"Haroldson, Mulholland, and a couple others have got together," he said nervously. His face had a suety look; Frémont wondered if he was drinking too much. "They're talking about calling their notes."

"Jesus. Can they do that?"

"Well, sure—we're pretty badly behind."

"How much is involved?"

Park stirred. "Four hundred thousand or so. Thereabouts."

Frémont had an intolerable sense of being nibbled to death by these damned rodents of finance. First claim jumpers, now note jumpers—everyone wanted a piece of him. "I ought to go over to Paris and set up a European syndicate," he said. "Pay off everything with long-term money and get things in order. I was going to, before I got caught in that damned campaign."

"That's an indulgence, Colonel. You've got problems *today,* tomorrow. They're not going to wait for you to arrange things to suit yourself."

"Where's the indulgence? The Mariposa's worth ten million if it's worth a penny—probably a hell of a lot more."

"But it's all in the ground."

"Listen, Trenor, I'm not going to let these penny-ante bastards niggle me into bankruptcy."

"I'm not saying you can't fight 'em off," Park said irritably. "But they're in a position to give you fits. That'll shake up your New York backers and *they're* your real money. Those frog financiers—how'll they react to paper troubles here? They'll maybe drive a harder bargain than you want, eh?"

"What the hell's the matter with you, Trenor?" Frémont demanded. "Don't come up here talking tough to *me*."

"But see, I'm out on a limb too. Caught in the middle, so to say. You're not the only one gets stretched thin, you know." Park cleared his throat. "Look, Colonel, I've been shuffling this paper around, keeping it all afloat. I've made commitments, too. This is more serious than you seem to think. But there's different ways to skin a cat, you know."

Frémont sighed and rubbed his eyes. "All right. What do you have in mind?"

Park leaned back and laced his hands behind his head, his face suddenly as smooth and guileless as he had looked ten years ago.

"There's a thousand ways to develop a property, but they really boil down to two. You stay small and safe—what I always recommended, you remember—or you go *all* the way: raise real capital . . . and make it hum."

"Which is what we've done."

"Not really. Look at the Glorietta. The Mariposa's never hummed like that. No, Colonel, your real trouble is you're betwixt and between—too big to be small and safe but not big enough to go full blast." He clapped his white hands on his knees. "I'd say restructure the debt, raise another million and a half, two million, and go to town. It's too late to go small, so you might as well go big."

"Hell, the debt load's already—"

"I'm not talking debt, I'm talking capital. It's debt, sure, but it's not all yours—bring in some associates who can help you raise money and guarantee it. That way you'll make your pie four or five times as big—and when it's ready to eat, you'll all have more to slice."

"Give up ownership, you mean?" Frémont said, frowning.

"Colonel, if you don't mind my saying so, retaining *full* ownership is restricting, self-limiting. Maybe you've gone as far as you can on your own. If you took partners, their role'd be to raïse money and stand good for it. That gold in the ground will pay it off eventually—but meantime you're not being pecked to death for it. Interest isn't killing you. See what I mean? Right now it's to these fellows' advantage to call their notes. But give 'em a share in the final bonanza and you've put 'em on your side. Then it's to their *advantage* to see you succeed."

"How much ownership?" Frémont demanded.

"Say, three-eighths."

"Good, God, Trenor—that's nearly *half*."

"No, miles from it. Half loses control, five-eighths assures control. That's the crucial difference." He gave his deprecatory smile. "You've got to be in command—that's what everyone counts on. But if at the same time you can get a new surge of money, get men behind you to hold things steady till you're fully developed, that changes the whole picture. All that really happens is that you're giving up a minority share of the ultimate profit in return for getting the place on its feet, making your immediate profits four or five times as big. You can't lose."

Command was what counted: Park was right about that. He'd never thought of success on the Mariposa simply in terms of dollar profits, anyway—he thought of it running smoothly, realizing its potential. He wouldn't mind sharing profits—there'd be more than enough for everyone if volume was increased. But command was everything.

Still, three-eighths of his beloved Mariposa in the hands of money men, strangers . . . How would Jessie take it?

"I'll have to sleep on it," he said.

"Well, fine." Park stood up. "Only reason I came hotfooting it up here this afternoon, I have to see Mulholland day after tomorrow. If you're willing to explore this, I can give him a signal that'll hold off the wolves, you know what I mean?"

Frémont nodded. The grim fact was that he was in a bind. They'd lost Lone Pine to the League, Lily Belle One was shut down because of a faulty stamper, the vein in Bowie Knife was running thin. You expanded or you shrank away to nothing. If they shut him down now with their blasted foreclosures and attachments, he was through. He would have to do it.

It takes a gold mine to operate a gold mine, Señor Coronel.

"All right," he said. "Let's move on it." He caught the banker by the shoulder, almost spun him around. "Only make damned sure you check with me every step of the way—I don't want any surprises."

"You can trust me, Colonel," Park said, and smiled his thin, diffident smile.

Frémont came onto the terrace, coffee cup in hand, and caught sight of Jessie far down on the point. She was gathering roses; her shears flashed in the sun as the last of the fog burned off. The air had a washed feeling and the hills across the bay were sharp. A grape arbor outlined the L-shaped terrace; its pale leaves contrasted with the black of the banks of mountain laurel that ran down to the point. Off to the left stood the headlands of the Golden Gate, the Pacific swell surging between them.

She turned to clip another blossom, saw him, and waved. Black Point was their first real home, and she took extravagant pleasure in it. Frémont had bought it on impulse. He'd been lunching at the Century Club with Mark Brumagin, marveling at the city San Francisco had become in the turbulent decade since the gold rush: it was the undisputed queen of everything west of St. Louis, just as old Tom Benton had foreseen. Frémont could remember it as a handful of adobes when the Bear Flag was flying. Over their abalone steak and chablis, Brumagin had mentioned his twelve-acre plot that jutted into the bay only a stone's throw away; it had a comfortable stone house and he was thinking of selling. They walked over to see it after lunch. Frémont took one look down the point where the mountain laurel was blazing white and pink and lilac against its nearly black leaves—and bought it before he went inside the house. The cost had been $42,000, shockingly high for a single piece of property. But it had been worth every penny for the look on Jessie's face when without warning he had turned their carriage off a busy thoroughfare, handed her down, and shown her that blooming point thrusting into the bay . . .

She turned now, her skirt swinging in a lithely feminine gesture that stirred him profoundly. He smiled, watching her. It pleased him—wanting his wife at five hundred paces: his greatest fortune had been the lucky chance of his marriage. He remembered how she'd looked that first time in St. Louis—fresh and innocent as a fawn, yet alive with that sensuous force that had taken his breath away. He'd come off the trail that very day; almost any girl would have attracted him, but no other could have reached him as she had. What right had they to be so happy nearly twenty years later, when they had first hurtled together like two blazing comets? Anyone might have predicted that when the early heat passed they'd be only cold iron going to rust; instead their love had deepened, tempered, impervious to strain, infinitely richer than in those days when they had literally burned in each other's presence. They were so lucky—no matter what happened to them, they were incomparably lucky in their love. . . .

She started up, her basket full of flowers; he saw her looking out toward the Golden Gate. After all the rigors and privations of Bear Valley she deserved a home like this. The Washington she'd known was gone, the political wars of her girlhood had become history, the party she loved had turned on her. Her family had never forgiven them—her letters to Cherry Grove went unanswered. When the house on C Street had burned, most of their papers had gone with it. The old man had been dying even then of stomach cancer; the signs they hadn't read seemed obvious enough when it was over. Jessie had been standing by a rail fence on the Mariposa with new grass and spring flowers at her feet when Frémont had to tell her that her father was dead. He'd thought the presence of such abundant new life must cushion the impact of death; but watching that sweet, oval face turn haggard with memory, he realized it had made death seem even more obscene.

Her face was flushed now from the walk; her cheeks like the roses in her basket. "Oh, darling," she said, "you wouldn't know I was a Missouri girl—I've put down my own roots with my rosebushes. I'm a Californian now." Then, "I'm home. Really home—for the first time. Oh, Charles, promise me we'll never leave."

"I promise," he said, touching her cheek.

"You know, I wanted to be involved in everything—to do, do, do. I remember telling Marie Crittenden that. Now I want to let the world go by, and tend my roses. Do you think I'm getting old?"

He drew her to him, said in Kit Carson's lazy drawl: "I'm plumb downcast to hear that, ma'am—it ain't fittin' fer a spry young dude to be sparkin' a creaky old gammer like yourself."

"You look out, now—I'll take you inside and show you who's an old gammer!" She nestled her head against his shoulder, looking seaward; he could feel her heart beating under his hand. "I never see the Golden Gate," she said dreamily, "without thinking of you and Kit rowing across to spike those guns. The day you named it. We really *are* California, aren't we? What Jake Snyder said that night in Monterey . . ." She looked up at him eagerly. "Wouldn't it be good to see Kit! Write him, Charles—tell him to come and see us."

Ed Davis emerged from the house. "Cuddling in sunlight means the marriage is sound," he said. He had come out from Philadelphia with a shipload of merchandise and was thinking of opening a branch in San Francisco.

"California's full of love," Jessie said, disengaging herself. "Where's Nancy?"

"Making herself beautiful. What else?"

Frémont said: "She's beautiful already. You married far above your looks, Ed. How'd you manage that?"

"Swiftly, Colonel," Davis answered him, deadpan. "You're not the only one with a talent for decisive action."

Lily came out on the terrace with Nancy Davis and said: "Mother, will Bret be coming?"

Jessie gave her a quick, searching glance. "Mr. Harte will be here, yes."

"Good." Lily nodded simply and looked at Frémont, who winked back. She was wearing her best linen frock, and her hair was done up in a new way Frémont liked. His view of his daughter was almost belligerently protective. He thought her much prettier—in spirit, in heart—than her plain features admitted. She was a somber girl, given to sudden rebellious outbursts. Sometimes he wondered if the strain of the early years had been too much for her; and of course she was overshadowed by Jessie's native vivacity.

The party was to celebrate the unveiling of a painting they had commissioned from Albert Bierstadt. The artist was spending a year in California; his reputation was booming in the East, where the new technique of drenching landscapes in stunning light was sweeping the art world.

"He's been working on it for weeks," Jessie was saying to Nancy, "but he's so secretive! No one can see his work until it's ready—and then he expects a dramatic unveiling with half of San Francisco in attendance. A new Bierstadt is an event."

"What if you don't like it?" Nancy asked.

"It won't bother him a bit. He'll just write me off as utterly lacking in taste. In his mind, you know, it's still his painting. I guess that's the way artists are."

"Well," Frémont said, "you're a writer—don't you feel the same way?"

"Flatterer!" She smiled at him from under her brows. "But I'm not one, really."

Nancy stepped out from the grape arbor into the sun and threw up her arms; the light blazed on her pretty face, her rich blond hair. "Look at that view!" she cried. "Feel the sun! Ed, it's *winter* back in Philadelphia. Let's stay here—let's never go back!"

"What!" Davis said. "Who'd mastermind the party? With Charles and me both here, the Republicans would sink right out of sight."

"Is that such a grievous loss? Then perhaps you'd have time for your suffering family." Nancy turned to Jessie. "Truthfully, aren't you tired of political widowhood?"

"I'm tired of *everything* about politics," Jessie said softly, and Frémont knew she meant it from the depth of her heart.

The first guest to arrive, not to Frémont's surprise, was Bret Harte, the impoverished young reporter on the *Golden Era* whose writing Jessie admired. Harte claimed to be twenty-three and looked seventeen—probably because his only square meals appeared to be the ones he enjoyed at Jessie's parties. Mark Brumagin arrived and greeted Ed Davis like an old friend, despite the fact that they'd parted coolly after a contentious financial session the day before. Amused, Frémont watched Davis slowly unbend. Everything ran to extremes in the unbuttoned West: a businessman would gouge you unmercifully in the morning and then cosset you at dinner—and see nothing untoward in it at all.

The room was beginning to fill; Callahan, the Irish butler Jessie used for her parties, was serving champagne. Frémont saw Monsieur D'Aubisson hesitating at the door and went to greet him. Anatole D'Aubisson was a concert pianist on world tour; he would be sailing to the Orient after a series of Bay Area concerts sponsored by the ubiquitous Tennyson Palmer, who had also arranged Bierstadt's dazzling debut. Even as Frémont chatted in French with D'Aubisson, he saw Palmer's carriage glide into view. Ten Palmer was a very successful lawyer, which he liked to dramatize in the ornateness of his brougham, though in person he was unfailingly modest. Frémont watched him help down his carrot-haired wife Betsy, who called in her high, girlish voice, surprising in so big a woman:

"Oh, Colonel, *when* are we going to see the picture? I'll bet Albert's charging you a leg and an arm!"

"He is, he is." Frémont laughed. Betsy Palmer considered it a virtue never to think before speaking, but she was so palpably goodhearted she rarely offended anyone.

The long parlor was almost full now; Jessie had again achieved the creative balance for which her soirees were celebrated. Albert Bierstadt, with his liquid, emotional eyes, was surrounded by a woman whose poetry was published locally and whose name Frémont always forgot, and several minor artists properly humble in the presence of the Lion. Edward Baker, who had defeated young Lincoln for Congress back in '44 and was expected to win a Senate seat from Oregon next year, was in earnest discussion with Horace Greeley, the controversial voice of the New York *Tribune* and an enthusiastic supporter of Lincoln for the presidency. Ed Davis was talking to Collis Huntington; the big man still had that rawboned look, but now he wore a well-cut suit and his grammar had noticeably improved; the two merchants had clearly found common ground for exploration. John Sutter stood far across the room, glass in hand, his round face flushed and congenial, listening to the captain of the steamship *Royal Neptune;* catching Frémont's eye he nodded warmly, and Frémont smiled and nodded in return. He'd been working with Senator Gwin to induce the Congress to recompense Sutter for his lost land; he had never forgotten the way the Swiss entrepreneur had supported him during those bitter days of humiliation as Kearny's prisoner . . .

It was late afternoon now and the western sun bathed the room in a deep, golden shimmer. It seemed to match the conviviality and exuberance Frémont could hear in their voices, the easy laughter, the soft clatter from the dining room where the buffet was being spread. Charley and little Frank were peeping out from the kitchen, and Frémont waved to his sons. The butler passed, bearing stem glasses festive with white wine and champagne, and cut-glass cups that glinted darkly with a whiskey punch. Frémont took a glass to have something in his hand—he rarely drank—and stood a little apart, watching Jessie move from group to group, flattering Bierstadt, teasing Palmer, drawing out D'Aubisson, tying everything together, enjoying herself hugely.

Artists loved Jessie—her quick enthusiasm and guileless empathy drew them—and the gatherings at Black Point had become very popular. The city seemed all at once crowded with artists and patrons; its rough vitality sought the healthy vanity of art's reflecting mirror, and Jessie's little salon was at the center of things. Frémont smiled, watching her, remembering her astonishing poise and easy wit at the elegant, power-heavy dinners of her girlhood. Well, at least he'd been able to give her a faint echo of that, a chance to shine after privations aplenty—let her spread her wings a bit. The gold had been good for this, at least—even if it did bring more headaches and pressures than a winter crossing.

Park had set up the Mariposa deal with his eastern contacts. They'd sent out an oily-tongued fellow named Hoffman, and the lawyers were now off working out the stock allocations. It had been the only thing to do—another three months and his creditors would have shut him down for good. As it was, only Mark Brumagin's stepping in to indemnify O'Campo's liens (in return for a whopping one-eighth share) had saved the situation.

But it was hard to share control of your own operation, unbelievably hard. . . .

At the other end of the room he could see young Harte standing alone by a window, looking forlorn. He started over, saw Lily move up to the journalist diffidently; he gave her an awkward little bow. Lord, I hope she doesn't get interested in him, Frémont thought; he hasn't got a penny to his name—and God knows if he'll ever be able to earn anything from those mining-camp stories Jessie's so excited about.

Bierstadt had managed to shift his bulk casually from the big rock-faced fireplace to his painting; resting on a large easel, mysterious behind its elaborate draping, it drew anticipatory glances. The artist in society: full of sensibilities others could hardly share—yet mindful that half the people in this room could commission works if they chose. Frémont wondered if the painting really could be worth the $4,000 he was paying for it. Maybe Betsy Palmer was right—it was nearly ten percent of the value of Black Point itself. Still, the new school did do magnificent things with light; they caught not so much how the country looked as how it made you *feel* when you rode a good horse into uncharted territory. And Jessie had wanted her own Bierstadt with a passion that had surprised him; the idea of the painting served to anchor Black Point's permanence for her somehow.

There was a small commotion at the door and Thomas Starr King arrived with his radiant smile. "Forgive my tardiness, dear Jessie," Frémont heard him say. "We had a funeral St. Peter himself will have to take cognizance of. Not Catholic-grand, of course—but what we lose in pomp we atone for in determined sincerity." A Unitarian minister who had come out from Harvard, King attracted people of all faiths with a combination of poetry and crisp contemporaneous ideas that made his sermons memorable. Jessie was inordinately fond of him. Frémont liked him, too—though he suspected that, like many ministers, King was more at ease with women.

"Bret," she said, "did you send that story to the *Atlantic*? I wrote Mr. Field—I told him you were the best writer in California."

Harte flushed with pleasure, looking suddenly rather handsome, if fragile. Before he could answer, Jessie said: "Have you thought of a new title? I thought 'Hangtown' was awfully blunt."

"Do you like 'The Legend of Monte del Diablo'?"

Diablo. Carson's little mountain. In an instant Frémont was swept back to that agonized moment on the pass when Kit had looked down into the Sacramento Valley, seen familiar ground, and restored them all to life with a single word.

"Perfect!" Jessie exclaimed. " 'Legend' says 'enchantment' to me, something fascinating, out of the past—immediately I want to read it."

June Steffanson approached them with her frank, easy smile. "Hello, there, storyteller." She gave a mock curtsy to Frémont. He knew Harte had drawn much of his material from her vivid recollections of life in the gold fields. "Bret," she said, "did I ever tell you how I met Colonel Frémont—the day they were going to hang Billy Claxton?"

"Don't you dare," Frémont protested. "That story further tarnishes my tarnished reputation."

June laughed. "You weren't cut out to be a judge, that's for sure."

The Steffansons had moved back to Sacramento, where Claude had made a reputation in gunshot trauma and was often called to San Francisco.

There was a lull in the conversation, one of those breathing spells that occurs at every gathering; like a bubble through oil, Brumagin's query rang through the room: "But how serious *is* the situation back there, Davis? Aren't things looking up a little?"

Heads turned, then; other conversation faltered and died. It wasn't the subject for a gathering like this—but it was the question all of them wanted to ask. And more than a question, Frémont knew; it was a plea, evident even in the way Mark had couched it: public posturing aside, can't you, a sensible fellow, tell us things are better than they sound? That the compromises *are* working, that the awful danger can be averted?

Frémont saw Nancy Davis shake her head at her husband, but Ed had no choice. Smiling politely, his tone casual, he said, "They're looking down, I'm sorry to say. Looking perfectly awful, in fact." He hesitated. "And I'm afraid people in the North are getting fed up, too."

"The North?" said Tennyson Palmer, his voice equally pleasant and neutral. "I thought it was the *South* that was objecting." He was from Maryland; Frémont remembered that Betsy's people owned large tobacco plantations.

"Well, as you know, the North gave way to the South in '56—which is why our charming host isn't President today, more's the pity."

"Then none of us would be here, awaiting the glorious unveiling!" Jessie broke in lightly, though Frémont could see her eyes tighten.

But Palmer wouldn't let go. "It was hardly a case of *giving way,*" he returned. "The South had to hold to its principles."

"Of course. It's only that the South seems—well, a bit like a bad winner, if you see what I mean. It's been pushing us pretty hard ever since."

"Ed," Nancy said, "this is hardly the place for—"

"Just a moment, Mrs. Davis," Palmer said with his gracious smile. "I'm interested in what he means by pushing . . ."

Davis glanced at his wife and shrugged. "All I meant is that a feeling is growing in the North that the South had Buchanan and the Democrats in its pocket. Look at Buchanan pressing to get Kansas admitted as a slave state. Look at Dred Scott."

"He's right," Huntington said in his low, harsh voice. "If slavery was illegal in the territory, then Scott's going there made him free. If he was free, then it was illegal to ship him back to slavery in Missouri. They can't have it both ways."

"Oh, that Dred Scott," Betsy Palmer broke in irritably, "what does it matter whether some nigger can run off to Wisconsin or not?"

"It isn't a party subject," Nancy said coldly, though she clearly didn't agree with Betsy's sentiments.

Frémont saw Jessie start forward to seize the situation, when Starr King said in his best pulpit voice: "But it does matter. Our highest court has cast it as a moral issue—and that places it squarely on everyone's conscience." Jessie had stopped: Frémont knew she would not challenge King. "The Court decreed that Scott has no right to sue because a slave can't be a citizen; and neither can the descendants of slaves. Now, in a nation which holds that all men are created equal, this can only mean that blacks are not considered human beings. But we know they are children of God; and to deny that is to deny God's dominion. It is a moral, not a legal matter."

He spoke with such quiet authority that he carved out a moment's silence. The man had more force than Frémont had realized.

"Well, Dr. King," Davis replied mildly, "I do not question your moral case, but Dred Scott has plenty of legal consequences all the same. For nearly fifteen years the key question's been whether slavery can move to the territories. Now—just like that—the court says it can."

Frémont sighed. He saw Jessie biting her lower lip, but a man who has run for President has obligations; he knew he would have to take a hand. And maybe he could avert a serious argument.

"Senator Benton was a great constitutional scholar," he said quietly, "and he grasped instantly what the Court had done. It was one of the last things we talked about. The whole *idea* of America was that its people would be free—the Constitution chartered that freedom. The most that Americans would concede to slavery was its right to exist locally, in particular states."

King's expression was absorbed, Palmer's skeptical. Greeley was nodding emphatically. D'Aubisson was bored—this benighted country's tensions were none of his concern. Betsy Palmer looked cross; she still thought the issue was whether "niggers" could run off to Wisconsin.

"But the South—and now the court—have reversed all that," he went on quietly. "By insisting that southerners with slaves can't be barred from federal territories, they're saying that slavery is a national condition, freedom a local one—that slavery can go everywhere it hasn't been specifically voted down. Now, believe me, Americans at large are simply not going to accept or tolerate slavery as a basic tenet of their society."

"That's very neatly put, Colonel," King said in surprise. Like many orators who enjoyed captive audiences, he never expected coherent thought from anyone else.

"An interesting analysis," Ten Palmer said judicially, though there was an unmistakable undercurrent of emotion in his voice. "But you also must recognize its opposite side: your *implication* is that a way of life southerners believe in deeply is to be denied."

"Limited, I'd say, not denied," Frémont answered.

"But Mr. Davis, here, makes it sound as if it's a southern plot." Palmer jerked his head toward the Philadelphian, but his eyes held Frémont; the anger was clear in his voice now. "You know the pressure the South has been under. You know how fanatical the abolitionists have become. The South's not initiating, it's reacting!"

"That's an old argument," Davis said tersely. "The fact is, our southern friends are feeling their oats. They want to start the African slave trade again—after we abolished the importation of slaves half a century ago! Plenty of northerners feel the South will try to legalize slavery in the North."

"They'll never get away with it," Brumagim growled. Frémont saw Huntington listening carefully, but this time he made no move to speak.

"Maybe," Davis said, "but if the Court can deny a territory's right to bar slavery, the way it did with Wisconsin, what's to stop it from denying a *state's* right?" He spread his hands amelioratively. "All I'm saying is that the North is getting alarmed. It gave in to the South in '56, and I don't think it will again. The Republican party is stronger now, and it wants to be led to victory."

There was a brief silence. June Steffanson asked innocently: "Will that be you, Colonel?"

Frémont saw Davis and Baker exchange embarrassed glances. Quickly he smiled and said: "No, no, June—I don't want it again. I haven't done anything to stay in line for it. And anyway, there aren't many second chances."

"I'd vote for you—if I could," June said, and Nancy added gallantly: "So would I, my dear."

"Ladies." He bowed, trying to lighten the moment. "I'm overwhelmed."

"Who *will* get it, Colonel?" Brumagim asked him.

"I'd say Seward. He practically founded the party, and he speaks clearly for its best instincts." Frémont saw Huntington smile in agreement; an upstate New Yorker himself, the hardware baron was a passionate admirer of Seward.

"Exactly," King said. "Seward calls a spade a spade on the slavery question."

"Perhaps too much so, Dr. King," Davis replied. "He's a radical at heart."

"The times call for a radical," the minister declared, and Frémont realized that he agreed. They had worried about southern sensibilities for too long—but everyone knew of the South's vicious personal rejection of him three years before, and he didn't speak. He saw vexation on Palmer's face. The lawyer felt shunted aside, what he saw as the real issue buried in talk that assumed his defeat. Frémont waited for a later chance to intercede.

"But things are so tense," Davis said, "one radical might well drive the South to secession—when only a handful of hotheads really wants to—"

"Whom do you like, Ed?" Frémont broke in. Better to keep it on party politics.

"Lincoln's awfully attractive. He grows on you. In those debates with Douglas last year, he made it clear he believes slavery is a moral issue—"

"Bless him for that!" King said.

"—but he's clearly a moderate. Douglas tried to lure him into extreme positions and failed. He wouldn't surrender, the way Buchanan has, but he'd be a lot less alarming to the South than—"

"He'd be alarming enough, I can tell you that!" Tennyson Palmer came in hotly, his anger boiling into the room. "The South will never let itself be ruled by the North—never! We will not play the vassal to an industrial overlord."

His outburst startled the company; Palmer had never lost his urbane manner like this before.

"That's overstating things a bit, isn't it, Ten?" Frémont said gently.

"I don't know that it is. Mr. Davis talks about a few hotheads. Try putting in some radical party that's fundamentally opposed to the southern way of life—and by God, every man, woman, and child in the South will be ready to secede!"

"We've been hearing that talk forever," King snapped at him.

"Go on, then—elect a Republican President," Palmer cried, "and you'll hear something else—you'll split the Union apart like the rotten tree it is!"

There was a curious flutter in the room, a low murmur of consternation. Someone called, "Hold on, now . . ."

"Starr!" Jessie was saying. "Ten! Please!"

Frémont was staring at Palmer's face, which had gone white as paper. The man was standing right in his living room preaching disunion! He had tried to grapple sensibly with the subject, had thought himself dispassionate—but Goddamnit, he had been *in* this battle, had taken the fire, and this arrogant, epicene fool . . . His fists knotted, he took a step forward. Palmer backed up and bumped against a small table.

"I cannot condone such sentiments, sir," he heard himself say flatly. "No one will talk treason in this house. No one!"

"Treason!" Palmer cried. "What do you mean, treason—I was merely expressing a political opinion."

Jessie had moved forward and seized his arm. "Charles, for heaven's sake! Let's drop this . . ."

Frémont locked his hands together. The entire company seemed frozen in time—faces stared back at him, frozen in fear and approval and vindictiveness . . . It was a party of friends. Guests—Tennyson Palmer was a guest in his home. For a happy occasion—

"Betsy," Palmer was saying fiercely, "we don't need to take this, stay where my opinions are maligned—"

"No, Ten," Jessie cried. "Please don't go . . ."

Frémont cleared his throat. In another instant the party would be beyond repair. "Well, Ten," he began; his voice was unsteady. "We both feel very strongly on these matters. I'll give you that, if you'll return the favor." He forced himself to go on. "Let's not allow the issue to destroy our friendship." He essayed a smile but he wasn't sure how much of it showed in his face. "Shall we leave it at that?"

"Of course we can!" Jessie broke in. She gripped Palmer's hand as if to hold him physically. "You'll stay—won't you, Ten?" She turned to the room. "Now, see here!" she cried, making a valiant effort to sound lighthearted. "No more politics! This is an artist's party—and art, thank God, is apolitical. Look—the sun is setting . . ." Hazy golden light was pouring into the room. "Let's go out and watch it. Ten? Come on, now. Ed?" She drew them both with her toward the terrace. Frémont saw her catch Nancy's eye and nod vigorously toward Betsy Palmer. Awkwardly the company followed her.

Outside, Frémont stood a little by himself. The sun lay on the western horizon, the light booming almost flat across the sea and pouring into the bay, so that those gateposts seemed made of solid gold. His Golden Gate. The grape arbor laid heavy stripes against the house. Callahan brought a tray of fresh glasses and Frémont took one, conscious that his mouth was dry. He had dealt with savage political attack in the past and kept his head—why had Palmer's foolish outburst undone him so? It had very little to do with Ten and his witless wife; the gods themselves were hostile, the battle lines were hardening . . .

Jessie's action had broken the tension; guests had clustered in new groupings. He saw Davis listening to young Harte; Nancy had drawn Betsy Palmer into an animated exchange. Palmer was talking to Anatole D'Aubisson, and looked calm enough.

Collis Huntington came up to Frémont then. "If the North is really going to stop letting itself be whipsawed by the South, d'you think that means it might pull itself together and support a Pacific railroad?"

"Might," Frémont said. "How far along are you?"

"This engineer, Ted Judah, has a route laid out, and we've raised some money. Can't really move without land grants from Congress to support long-term bonds, but we're getting there." He looked down, scuffing his boot against a flagstone. "You'd be a mighty big asset to us, Colonel. Your eye for terrain, your political background, reputation . . ."

Frémont said: "I'm going to put in a railroad myself, as soon as I get the Mariposa in good running order. Perhaps you could join in my plans to our mutual profit."

"Colonel," Huntington answered, careful but blunt, "you'd be very important to any railroad operation. But in our case you would not be in control."

Frémont was startled; the residue of anger from the secession quarrel stirred again. He'd been in command of every enterprise since he'd crossed the Missouri as a green lieutenant under Papa Joe Nicollet. In the mountains, on the Mariposa, as Senator from California, as candidate for President, he had given the orders—and here was this Sacramento hardware peddler offering *him* a job.

"No offense, Colonel," Huntington said uncomfortably. "But railroading requires a very hard business head. Very hard. Now, you take me: I've never known anything but business. It's all I care about, all I think about. And every day I learn something new about it—find new angles, some brand-new way of doing things. You see, Colonel, you're good at a whole lot of things. But business is very narrow, very specialized. That's how it works."

"I expect to command my own enterprises," Frémont said; his voice sounded harder than he had intended.

"Command." Huntington shook his head. "We're just talking a different language. I don't think you quite grasp the situation here. There's four of us, you know. Leland Stanford'll be governor before long . . . Mark Hopkins, Charley Crocker . . . we're all equals in the deal, you see, handling different aspects. It's too big for any one man—you've got to see that."

"It's all right, Collis," Frémont said. He softened his tone; there'd been enough friction already today. "I'm going to run a railroad across, and I'll be in charge. That's the only way I'd be interested."

"Well, sure, Colonel, of course," Huntington answered. "No offense, eh? I wouldn't for the world—"

"You two stop butting heads," Jessie said, coming up to them. She liked Huntington; she always said he was honest. "Enough business talk! We're going to see that painting now."

She was clapping her hands. "Come on, everyone—we're going in and let Albert show us what marvels he's done! Come along—Ed, Betsy . . . Bret, come on now, art awaits!"

The sun was gone, the sky crimson and the blue and green of bird's eggs, pearly as oyster shell. Bierstadt, looking as if he'd thought the moment would never come, made a graceful little speech to which Frémont didn't listen, about the artist's eye and the integrity of nature. The conversation with Huntington had forced his thoughts back to Mariposa—heavily he wondered again if giving up three-eighths of your holdings wasn't the first step on the road to perdition. He'd kept command—so far—but what would come next?

He watched Jessie listening intently to Bierstadt, and felt a rush of affection for her; he'd given her such a wild, tumultuous life and she'd taken it all in stride, never faltering, never once complaining. He could see her father in her face—the long nose, the imperious forehead—and he had a sudden intimation of the woman she would become as she grew older. She looked—strained; had he done that to her? His ambitions, his certain, fanatical sense of destiny, the crushing failures that kept pace with his achievements, that couldn't be averted—even this last heated exchange that had fallen across her party—it struck him now that she deserved so much better.

Bierstadt had finished. He held out the draw cord to Jessie with a little bow. "Madame," he said. Slowly she pulled the cord. The draperies swept open: a gasp and then a soft, collective sigh ran through the room. It was the scene they had just been praising—Bierstadt had painted the Golden Gate from Black Point. It was magnificent, as blinding and strange and wonderful as that faraway afternoon he'd rowed across the strait with fire points blazing off the chop and the water as black as ebony. The artist had given him back that very day, out of his triumphant youth, arrested forever . . .

Bierstadt was surrounded by guests now, eagerly accepting their congratulations. Jessie however had turned toward her husband. Oblivious of everyone she came to him, her arms open.

"Oh, Charles," she whispered, "I love you. I do, you know."

"I'm sorry," he murmured. "About the quarrel with Palmer."

"It couldn't be helped. It's the times." Her hand tightened on his arm. "This afternoon, the painting—it's all very *special,* somehow. Special and fragile." And her gallant face turned infinitely sad. "It's about to close in on all of us. The storm's coming, Charles."

He drew her nearer to him. "Yes, honey," he said. "I know."

PART SIX

COUNCIL OF WAR

IN THE UNIFORM OF A MAJOR GENERAL, United States Army, Frémont strolled along Pennsylvania Avenue on a July morning in 1861, bound for the White House. He was early and he walked slowly; he didn't want to present himself to President Lincoln with sweat wilting his collar.

A column of soldiers came toward him down 14th Street, marching to a snapping drum. Maine volunteers, carrying old smooth-bore muskets and looking cock-a-hoop devil-may-care. A towheaded boy saw Frémont and grinned.

"Lookit the goddamn ginral," he said loudly, and called, "Howdy-damn-do, Ginral?"

"Shut up, Morrison," his sergeant said, saluting smartly at Frémont. "And align your piece."

The boy winked as he passed. Frémont crossed behind the column. There weren't many smiles in wartime Washington. The city was torn between the grossly overconfident and the faint of heart. Underneath, the capital had a nervous, stricken air; he had been here a week, and every day the confusion seemed a little worse. There were soldiers everywhere, few of them any better trained than this lighthearted kid from Maine. They were bivouacked in tents on the Mall, in camps that lined the hills above the city. They crowded into taverns and brothels, wandered drunk in the streets, slept in alleys. Staff officers galloped about, spattering pedestrians with mud. Cannon practice rumbled in the distance and the crackle of musketry had the sound of popping corn. What did it all mean? The soldiers were boys, half-larking and half-frightened. There were Confederate troops not far into Virginia; rumors spread that the Union troops would go out and challenge them—one of these days.

Amidst all the apprehension and easy optimism, mouths were tight and faces closed. Who was unionist, who was secessionist? Whom could you trust? The impossible had taken place: the South had seceded, Fort Sumter had fallen, civil war had commenced, but so far there had been only light skirmishes, as if neither side was entirely serious about it all.

Frémont could remember promenading on this very block with Jessie and her sisters, one eye cocked for the formidable Senator; it was all sunshine and music in his memory, a concert of organ grinders. He had bought her a collection of sonnets in Pishy Thompson's bookstall. Now the stalls were full of Halleck's *Tactics* and Clausewitz and Jomini's *Art of War,* and if Pishy were still alive, doubtless he'd be a secessionist at heart, like most of Washington's merchants.

Frémont passed the New Treasury extension that broke the classic plan for Pennsylvania Avenue. Ten minutes early. He went beyond the White House and circled the little brick building that housed the War Department, where so many of his problems rested in the hands of paperbound fools who couldn't comprehend a crisis even when it was about to blow them away. He needed men, and arms, heavy guns and professional artillerymen, horses, wagons, medicines—he had an army to build! With an irritated sigh, he turned up the circular drive toward the mansion's north portico. A trooper in an impeccable uniform brought his rifle to salute, bayonet flashing. He gave his name and the soldier turned with professional polish and announced him. By his accent, the man was German; Europeans understood soldiering in a way that Americans never could, Frémont thought wryly—and maybe that wasn't such a bad thing, either.

One of the President's secretaries, a young law clerk from Springfield named Nicolay, led him up a curving staircase into the cross corridor on the second floor. Portraits of Jefferson, Jackson and Monroe surveyed benches of velvet and a scuffed carpet; half-round windows blazed with light at each end—a place for great deeds. The irony pierced Frémont. *He* should be in residence here, not Lincoln; he should be receiving generals, planning campaigns, punishing the rebels, restoring the Union. He felt like the butt of a grisly joke: the country might as well have elected him, since the South had gone out after all. Nothing had been gained by the delay—the Secessionists in fact had used the time to build up their stores of arms—and now the nation must face the crisis under a man who had never run anything bigger than a Springfield law office.

He suppressed the thought: that was no frame of mind in which to meet his Commander in Chief. His role was important enough, for that matter. He was one of four major generals—only old Winfield Scott outranked him—and on his way to St. Louis to take command of the Western Department. He knew that his, though removed, was actually the important command of the war, the theater from which the rebellion could be broken most effectively.

The secretary opened a door and said: "Major General Frémont, Mr. President." They were in the Cabinet Room. Chairs with pale blue seats were drawn back carelessly from the long table, which was littered with maps and muster rolls. Dark green wallpaper with evenly spaced gold stars gave the room an oddly muted look despite two tall windows through which Frémont could see the Potomac. Lincoln came across the worn green carpet, his hand out. The President had a gangling farmboy's way of walking, all arms and legs, though there was something forceful in his movements, too.

Frémont wondered if Lincoln deplored that "Railsplitter" sobriquet as deeply as he himself had resented the "Pathfinder" nonsense; but the man did look as if he'd split a few rails in his day—and still could if he had to. Frémont had seen him in December—they'd met for a half-hour at the Astor House when the President-elect first came to New York. Lincoln had seemed as out of place in that elegant hostelry as he did here.

"Good morning, Frémont," the President said. "We've just been talking about General Lyon. He's set Missouri on its ear—I don't rightly know if that's a blessing or a curse."

Frémont saw his old friend Montgomery Blair standing at the far end of the cabinet table. Blair was Postmaster General, but he also spoke for Missouri in the cabinet. He nodded, his flat, smooth face impassive, his thin lips curving in a faint smile. Beyond him General Winfield Scott was slumped in an armchair, looking as if it would take a crane to get him out of it. Frémont had called on Scott twice in the past week. Old Fuss and Feathers hadn't made much sense. His gout had been bothering him, he said.

Montgomery Blair said deferentially: "Frank says Lyon saved Missouri almost single-handed, Mr. President."

Lincoln grunted. "Well, it's not saved yet, but to the extent it *is,* I'd say it's more Frank's doing than Lyon's." He sat in a black horsehair chair by an open window, his long fingers clamped on the arms. Frémont knew Lincoln was close to Frank Blair; he was the younger of the brothers, the apple of old Francis Blair's eye. Springfield was near St. Louis, and Frank had been a prime mover in Lincoln's candidacy.

"Lyon did save the arsenal from the Secessionists, sir," Blair offered easily. "And he routed the rebels at Booneville . . ."

"Oh, he's *active* enough—I'll give him that. Sit down, General." Lincoln turned to Frémont, who pushed a straight chair back from the table. Blair sat astraddle another, his hands on its back, his slim face alert. General Scott's eyes were fixed in the distance. "Lyon's a West Pointer, with a fine record in Mexico—I jumped him from captain to brigadier," the President went on. "But he's a roaring abolitionist. He's inflexible and insensitive—he drives people away just when we want to draw them in. I don't mind telling you that Frank wanted him to command the Western Department. When I balked on that, he and Montgomery both turned to you." He smiled. "It was an appointment I was happy to make, Frémont."

Lincoln was telling him he'd been the second choice. Well, that was all right, too. He'd been in Europe, and Lyon had been on scene; though he did sound pretty headstrong.

"I'm pleased, of course, Mr. President," Frémont answered. "I look forward to serving the Republic again, in any way I can." Scott's heavy-lidded eyes swung up to his, cold with aversion, fell away again. The President didn't answer and Frémont added: "I've known Montgomery and Frank for years. Their father was a tremendous source of support in '56—my wife has always looked on him as another father."

He saw the President frown slightly at this, and wondered if he had offended. Did Lincoln want more appreciation for the Blairs' part in his appointment? Or was he jealous of old Blair's power in Washington? Frémont shrugged to himself. Commanding in Missouri was hardly a plum—it was a hardship post, taken at considerable disadvantage to himself. Seward had suggested to Lincoln that he appoint Frémont Secretary of War; and at their December meeting, Lincoln had talked vaguely of making him Minister to France.

Frémont hadn't been in London on Mariposa business a week when the first thunderclap of news arrived: South Carolina, his native South Carolina, had seceded. The hotheads there hadn't listened to Lincoln's assurances, hadn't even waited for him to take office. That a Black Republican had been elected was enough for all those posturing fools. Every week brought new dispatches: the cotton states were following South Carolina out in lockstep—Alabama, Georgia, Florida, Mississippi, Louisiana, Texas. On February 8, 1861, they met at Montgomery, Alabama, and formed the Confederate States of America. Frémont, reading the New York papers at the Athenaeum Club, felt sick with dread. They had threatened and threatened, they'd said they'd go out in '56 if Frémont won, they'd held it to the head of the North like a cocked gun—but still it didn't seem possible. He waited, but no more states joined the militant seven; Virginia and Missouri and the others stood on the sidelines, trumpeting fellowship and warning the federal government against taking action . . . And nothing happened. Nothing at all. That timid, pussyfooting Buchanan dithered around, as he had for four years, and after Lincoln's inauguration in March, all remained quiet. In Paris, where Frémont was trying to raise additional capital for the Mariposa, Baron Rothschild buttonholed him: Was there a war or wasn't there? Frémont could only shake his head.

The crisis came over Sumter, the federal fort in Charleston harbor. South Carolina troops had ringed the place with heavy guns. It was time to force the matter, but Lincoln still wanted to give the Secessionists room to back away; he announced that he was sending an unarmed ship to resupply Sumter. At the Athenaeum, Lord Dunraven had been mightily impressed with that move.

"Ruddy good, eh?" he'd said to Frémont, clutching a copy of the New York *Times*. "If they allow it to be supplied, they can't be serious about taking it, and that means they won't fight. Ergo no rebellion. If they *are* serious, they must sink an unarmed merchant ship loaded with food and medicine—and if they're going to do that, they might as well go ahead and reduce the fort itself. Then the Union'll know they mean it, and set out to punish 'em. This fellow Lincoln must be a damned clever chap. I'd say it portends badly for the rebels." He had paused, frowning. "D'you suppose those idiots at Whitehall will hold firm? The Confederate emissaries are pressing hard for recognition, you know. And our mill owners are worried about the cotton."

And a new ship had brought word that after a bombardment of a day, Sumter had fallen. Lincoln had called for 75,000 troops to punish the Secessionists—and immediately Virginia, North Carolina, Tennessee, and Arkansas seceded. The Confederate capital had moved to Richmond. The last four slave states—Missouri and Kentucky, Maryland and Delaware—had bucked and swayed, but they hadn't gone out. Not yet. By that time Frémont had forgotten his Mariposa troubles and started frantically buying weapons he knew the Union would need, underwriting his purchases with personal IOU's: $75,000 worth of British cannon, 10,000 stand of French rifles. Charles Francis Adams, Minister to London and a clearheaded Yankee, just the man you needed in a pinch, cooperated with him swiftly, drawing on government funds to cover additional requisitions. It was no time for the niceties of protocol. Then word came that Lincoln had sent Frémont's name to the Senate for confirmation as major general. He must return immediately, Jessie must close Black Point and come east at once—and he had caught the first ship for home, reading Napoleon's memoirs and studying maps of the Mississippi as he crossed the Atlantic. . . .

Frémont knew his face had tightened. Blair was saying something in a low voice to Scott, who looked disgruntled and peevish. Gratitude for the chance to do his duty wasn't quite what Frémont had in mind; they had a war to fight; they might get on with it. Lincoln, catching himself up, asked if he'd had time to formulate any plans.

"Yes, sir. I plan to assemble a force at Cairo, two brigades and naval auxiliaries, and drive down the Mississippi for—"

"First, though," the President interrupted, "you must make sure of Missouri."

"Granted, but I don't expect much trouble."

"Don't you?" Lincoln inquired politely. "It's touch and go there, you know."

"We won't *let* them go, sir."

Lincoln grunted. "They decide to go, they'll go. And then you better look out. I know 'em better than you do." Frémont made no reply. The President threw a long, bony leg over the chair's arm and said in a more relaxed voice: " 'Minds me of a farmboy I knew near Hannibal." He grinned, suddenly genial. "Now this boy, he was on an old plow horse name of Buck when that cayuse took fright at his own shadow, lit out running and didn't stop till he got to Salisbury. Well, 'twas about dark when the lad reached home and his Pa says, 'Boy, where in thunder you been?' And the boy says, 'Over to Salisbury.' 'What in thunder was you doin' over there?' 'Well,' says the boy, 'ol' Buck was heading there anyway, so I thought I'd go along for the ride.' "

The President gave a loud, braying laugh, slapping at his knee. Montgomery Blair's face wore its cool, pleasant smile, Scott was frowning into space. Lincoln's laughter trailed off into a sigh. "Now, you see, what we've got to do is head those folks off, before they get the idea of going to Salisbury." He leaned forward, scowling, in bad humor again. "Hell's bells—slavery or no slavery, they aren't southerners, they've got the sense to see *any* war is going to be hardest on people along the border. What they really want is to be left alone."

"But that's not possible, is it?" Frémont said.

"That's exactly right! And the *rebels* aren't letting 'em alone either, believe you me. Claiborne Jackson, that scoundrel—calls himself a governor!

You should hear his answer to my troop call." Lincoln stood up, unfolding the storklike frame, and began riffling through papers on the stand-up desk. "Yes . . . now, here . . . listen to this: says my call is 'illegal, unconstitutional and revolutionary in its objectives, inhuman and diabolical—not one man will the state of Missouri furnish to carry on such an unholy crusade!' That's the governor of the state! Now, that's nothing but plain and simple *treason*!"

Watching, Frémont was impressed by the man's rude, spare power. He listened quietly as Montgomery Blair filled him in on what he already knew—how Lyon had marched on the state capital, the governor had turned the state militia into a Confederate army, and the two forces squared off against each other. But it hadn't worked—the governor and his militia hadn't been enough to swing everyone away from the Union, and Missouri was still—shakily—in the loyal column. But now guerrilla warfare had begun to flicker. Unionist farms burning, bushwhackers at work . . .

"Mr. President," Frémont said firmly, "I'm not saying it'll be easy, but I do expect to hold Missouri." He paused. "I would hope we could discuss offensive operations."

"All right. Let's hear it." Lincoln sat down on the horsehair chair and folded his hands across his stomach. General Scott hadn't moved or spoken in several minutes; Frémont saw he was sound asleep. Lincoln looked once at the old man but said nothing. Montgomery Blair's gray eyes cut to Frémont, then to the ceiling. Scott had been great in his time; that campaign into the Valley of Mexico had been magnificent, but now the Hero of Lundy's Lane was seventy-five years old and Washington was whispering that his trouble wasn't just gout.

Succinctly Frémont outlined his plan. Organize an army, train it, equip it with the best weapons. Bolt cannon to steamboats, run down the Mississippi, take Memphis, then Vicksburg; drive on to New Orleans and cut the Confederacy in half. Louisiana, Arkansas, and Texas would be peeled away and held in place by garrisons stationed along the river and the naval blockade of the coast. Then he would wheel east and roll up the gulf states, while an eastern army struck south through Virginia and the Carolinas. A grand envelopment, hammer against anvil.

"Well," Lincoln said mildly, "that sounds fine."

Frémont hesitated. It wasn't the enthusiastic response he'd expected. He wondered if the President had grasped the soundness of the plan. "To carry it out," he said, "I'll need troops. A hundred thousand stands of rifles. Cannon and a regiment of regular artillery to man them. Appropriations to construct gunboats. And so far, I'm afraid I'm not getting much cooperation. The Quartermaster General doesn't seem to—"

"Out of the question."

Everyone turned. General Scott hadn't moved; but now, wide awake, he spoke in angry little bursts. "Quartermaster General Meigs is acting on my express instructions. Arms are in very short supply. We must train and equip our eastern armies *first*. I can spare no weapons for the West. Perhaps in ninety days the situation will change. Perhaps not." He gave Frémont a belligerent stare and looked out of the window.

"Well," Frémont said, "since General Lyon was quick enough to hold the St. Louis arsenal, that gives us 60,000 stands of rifles."

"They've all been shipped east."

"East?" Frémont stared at Scott, incredulous. "Then, sir, they must be shipped back!"

"Impossible!" The old man seemed to retreat to some impenetrable place. "You don't know what you're asking for, Frémont."

"We have a desperate shortage of arms of all types, General Frémont," Lincoln said heavily. "I thought you understood that."

"Yes, sir, I do. I arranged for shipments from Europe—"

"They'll go to the Army of the Potomac. A drop in the bucket, I'm afraid."

Lincoln stood and Frémont started to rise, thinking he was being dismissed. But the President crossed to the detailed map on the opposite wall.

"The enemy's here in force at Manassas"—he tapped the map—"twenty-five miles from Washington. Under Beauregard. Nearly twenty thousand troops spread along this waterway they call Bull Run. Just a bare twenty-five miles from the capital." His finger roved along the elevation lines. "There's another Confederate force over here in the Shenandoah Valley under Joe Johnston. Now, in the next few days, General McDowell—"

"He has no need whatever to be privy to this," Scott broke in sourly. "Man has never commanded a large body of troops in combat."

Frémont looked at him directly, his eyes snapping. "That's true, sir. But I've been in some exceedingly rough places, if I say so myself. And I like to think I have a good appreciation of the value of terrain."

Scott grunted without amusement.

The President turned. "Now General, we have McDowell commanding in the East and Frémont in the West—don't you think each ought to have some idea of what the other one's doing?"

"If you say so, sir," Scott replied grudgingly.

"I say so. Now, the Army of the Potomac will march out in short order. We hope it'll be quick enough to cut the Orange and Alexandria Railroad, here, so the Shenandoah force can't use it to support Beauregard. Then, if things go as planned, McDowell will knock Beauregard back and eliminate the threat to the capital. You see the situation: until we render the capital secure, we can't undertake anything else."

Frémont glanced at Montgomery Blair, who didn't meet his eyes. *Of course* they should secure the capital—they should have done it twelve weeks ago. The question was whether they really intended to prosecute this war. He was sure he'd kept his face impassive, but he saw now that the President had read his thoughts.

Deliberately Lincoln leaned against the cabinet table, his arms folded. Blair busied himself with some documents, and Scott's face, now fully alert, still wore that disapproving stare. Frémont had a sudden feeling of being back in the old arsenal, hearing the court-martial charges. Some wars were never over. . . .

"First things first, General," Lincoln said calmly. "And the first thing is: I don't want a full-scale war if I can avoid it. The southerners have made a big mistake—maybe they'll come to their senses. We want to give 'em that chance. We want to forgive and forget if they'll come home. Kill the fatted calf, so to say."

Frémont stifled the impulse to shake his head. You've got a full-scale war on your hands right now, Honest Abe, he thought somberly; you just aren't willing to admit it. He knew the South—he'd felt its venom. The only way to deal with it now was with force: attack, seize control, hang the leaders and warn the people. *Then* bring them together. Lincoln hadn't been on the firing line four years ago, or he'd understand how arrogantly assured, how spoiling for a fight the South was.

"Thing is, we're between a rock and a hard place," Lincoln was saying. "Maryland is slave country—I had to throw a regiment into Baltimore to break up the Secessionist mobs attacking our troop trains. As long as they can threaten our very capital, they don't have much reason to feel discouraged. And the British, the French: they're watching it all—trying to decide which way the cat will jump."

Frémont listened quietly, leaning against the map of Virginia. If this is the way we're going into this brawl, he told himself morosely, then God help us. Old Provost would have crossed the Arkansas by now, and Kit—Christ almighty, Kit would have gone roaring down the Tennessee Valley and be halfway to Marietta . . . Beyond the President's shoulder he saw that the Kellogg portrait of General Jackson had been hung in the place of honor over the fireplace. It had been Benton's favorite portrait of the great old man, who couldn't be pushed into *anything* he didn't want to be—but who moved like chain lightning once he'd made up his mind. Lincoln said he'd warned the European nations to stay out of internal American affairs, and so far they were heeding him. But if they thought the South would prevail, they might recognize it to protect their cotton source. Then their ships would try to run the blockade and the nation could find itself fighting a foreign as well as a civil war. "And the southerners *won't* be coming back, so long as they think London and Paris will get behind them."

"I understand, Mr. President," Frémont said. "And I won't forget that Missouri is my first priority."

As if pleased with this reassurance, Lincoln sighed and stretched. One hand rapped the globe of a gas lamp that hung from the ceiling. His trouble, Frémont thought, is that he can't see the forest for the trees. Of course the war is complex, but the best way to deal with complexity is to cut to its very heart. Give his Army of the West a hundred thousand men and a fleet of gunboats, let him slice through to New Orleans and halve the Confederacy like an apple under a knife—and a hell of a lot of this *complexity* would vanish like morning fog. But Lincoln was at the helm, not he.

He took Monty Blair's cool, dry hand and said to Scott: "My respects, sir." The Conqueror of Vera Cruz dismissed him with a brief, contemptuous gesture.

"I'll see you out, General." The President was moving him toward the door. They walked together along the cross corridor and down the curved stairs. Lincoln moved with a loose, shambling gait, arms dangling disjointedly. Men in his own administration called him "the ape"—a jape to appeal to Washington's southern sympathies. Frémont was swept with a profound sense of the peril the country was in. We could lose this war; it was possible. . . .

Sparrows were splashing in a puddle beyond the portico. The sentry snapped to attention and Lincoln waved a hand at him, looking faintly embarrassed. Frémont asked if the President had any further instructions.

"No," Lincoln said, "I'm giving you *carte blanche;* a free hand—and not much to grip. You must use your own judgment and do the best you can." A look of profound melancholy darkened the mobile, expressive face. "Maybe a bloody nose'll bring 'em to their senses, but I don't know. God help us, maybe they'll never come back till we drag 'em back by the scruff of the neck . . ."

From the deck of the ferry bringing them across the Mississippi, the first thing they saw was the Confederate flag flying over downtown St. Louis.

"Strange," Jessie murmured. "Gives you a—a chill."

"Judge Berthold's house," Lieutenant Gaines said. "He let 'em make a sort of headquarters there. They're recruiting."

"Recruiting?" Frémont demanded. "In the open?"

"Afraid so, sir." Gaines was a neat young man, very assured, West Point '57. He'd been waiting when Frémont and Jessie stepped down from the train on the Illinois side of the river.

The boat moved with a thrumming noise, stern wheel thrashing, bow crabbing upstream against the swirling brown current. A white egret flew alongside, lazy in the cool morning. It was late July and the cloudless sky said that it would be hot by noon. Frémont stared at the rebel flag. There was no more respected name in St. Louis than Judge Berthold's. He remembered a Fourth of July party at that great pile of a mansion on Pine Street; it had been the first time he'd ever tasted mint juleps. . . .

"I don't see *our* flag," he said.

"No, sir."

"They recruit publicly—and we don't show our flag?"

Gaines looked uncomfortable. "There's a lot of hard feeling just now, General."

Out-and-out Secessionists in this divided city were a minority but, it seemed, militant. No one wanted to cross those prominent business and financial leaders who were oriented toward the South. Perhaps they weren't exactly rebels themselves, but they supported the rowdy secessionist toughs who roamed the streets.

"There are ardent Unionists too, but most people play it safe. They're smack in the middle," Gaines said. "Call themselves 'conditional unionists.' "

"What in hell is that?"

"They don't want to secede, but they don't want to see any action taken against the South, either."

"Fence straddlers."

"Yes, sir."

"That won't work, you know."

"Yes, sir. General Lyon's trying to make that clear. But he's been in the field with most of his force for six weeks, and lessons wear off fast around here."

"Is Frank Blair in town?"

"No, he's in Washington, sir. He's expected this week."

Jessie said suddenly: "Have you noticed this is the only boat on the whole Mississippi River?"

She was right. A long row of steamboats were snubbed hard to the levee; not one was making steam. The levee itself looked deserted.

"It's all shut down, ma'am," Gaines said. "No goods coming in. Manufacturing's come to a standstill. Lots of men are out of work, and some of 'em are a little desperate—we've had several ugly riots over food. Problem is, no one dares plan ahead or make commitments."

"Why don't they?" Frémont said. He didn't like the sound of this.

"They're waiting to see what happens, sir. If the state goes South—"

"Good God! It's not *going* South!"

"No, sir. But . . . ah, they don't know that for sure. Especially not after Bull Run."

The news had come over the telegraph wires just as Frémont and Jessie were leaving New York. New horrors had awaited them at every stop on the way west. Frémont remembered Lincoln saying McDowell's forces were to move quickly, but in fact it had taken them days to cover the twenty-odd miles to where Beauregard's Confederates waited on the banks of Bull Run. And that Confederate army under Johnston over in the Shenandoah Valley had evaded Patterson, commandeered locomotives and raced over with safety valves tied down and fireboxes glowing to join Beauregard before McDowell arrived. Everyone knew the battle was set. The Washington gentry put picnic hampers in carriages and went out with their ladies to view it all from nearby hilltops.

"War as spectator sport," Frémont had said in cold disgust to Jessie at Wheeling as he scanned a paper. "Sip a vintage Moselle, nibble pâté de foie gras and watch young men kill each other." No one in the East even understood what war meant. Sometime in the afternoon Kirby Smith's brigade came up and the battle had turned against the Union forces; the picnickers, seeing knots of bloody, powder-blackened soldiers drifting past, bethought themselves of home. Fancy carriages and cannon and beaten soldiers locked into a mammoth snarl and retreat had turned into rout that didn't stop until they reached Washington's defenses. In Cincinnati and Louisville and Cairo, Frémont anxiously searched the papers, asked for news. Had the capital actually fallen in this shameful defeat? No—the Confederates hadn't been able to follow it up, though the door was wide open; they, too, had learned something about war at Bull Run.

The difference was that they had learned while winning . . .

"There was quite a celebration here," Gaines said. "Bonfires and speeches and all. A secesh mob roared around, shot up the town. Figured the war was over."

"And our people?"

"Stayed home, sir."

"But the *army* must've—"

"No, sir." Gaines's face was expressionless. "It laid low."

Headquarters proved to be a former dry-goods store three blocks from the ferry landing. It was temporary, of course, but Jefferson Barracks was too remote to serve St. Louis in the midst of crisis. Jessie went on to Colonel Brant's house—they would stay with her cousin as they always did in St. Louis—while Frémont and Gaines walked to the storefront-cum-command-post. Shelves, counters and glass cases were still in place. Soldiers playing cards at the counters straightened uncertainly. Several officers lounged in a small room at one side. Frémont could hear a piano plinking away in the tavern across the alley. A dog appeared in a doorway to the alley, yawned, raised a leg, and wet the doorframe.

An old colonel with white muttonchop whiskers and a mottled red face hurried forward and said: "General Frémont, welcome to—"

"Are you in charge?"

"Yes, sir."

"Your name?"

"Jeter, sir."

"Colonel Jeter, why don't you have a flag outside?"

"General, this is a temporary headquarters. The flag—ah, you see, it stirs up the—well, the subversive element."

Subversive element. "Captain," Frémont said to a slender officer who was listening with a small smile.

"Sir!"

"Take a half-dozen men to the nearest boatyard and get a spar. Nail it to the front of this place. I want the biggest, brightest damned flag in St. Louis flying from it in half an hour."

"Yes, sir!"

"Gaines," Frémont said. "Do we have a headquarters company?"

"Yes, General."

"Turn out twenty men, please. Full loads, fixed bayonets. Ten minutes." Turning to Jeter he said in a kindly tone: "Now, Colonel, tell me about the command."

Jeter had led a company in the Black Hawk War of '32, and had farmed in Indiana since. The Indiana troops had elected him, and here he was—befuddled, apprehensive, not quite sure how command had devolved on him. That Lyon had left Jeter in charge told Frémont a great deal about Lyon. Jeter said he had some 3,500 men, with one weapon for every fourth man, while untrained recruits dribbled in daily.

"Walking up here from the ferry," Frémont said, "I saw a fight in front of the old Green Tree Tavern. Some men were in uniform, or partial uniform. Who would they be?"

"Probably some of my boys, General."

"At this time of morning?"

"Well, it's hard to keep track of 'em."

So that was how things stood. Frémont stared at him. "Where's your cantonment?"

"Haven't really got one, sir. The arsenal won't hold many, you see. Boys are scattered around—houses, barns—it's hard to keep track."

"My God, man, you need *grounds* for an army! Tents, mess halls, firing range, drill fields . . ."

"I know that, General," Jeter said indignantly. His face quivered; for a moment Frémont thought he might weep. "Don't you think I know that? There's plenty of ground around the arsenal and we drill there, too. But we've got no tents, you see. I don't like to have the boys sleep in the open, in garrison. It's not like we was in the field—"

"No tents! Isn't there a sailmaker in St. Louis?"

"Yes, sir—name of Sam Rogers. He's got a place on—"

"Get him over here."

Jeter blinked at him. "You mean . . . that is, you want me to—"

"Send an officer for him. *Now.*"

"Very good, General."

Gaines reported troops from the Headquarters Company formed outside. Frémont started out. He paused at the door. "Gaines, I need a good steamboat man. A captain, a pilot—preferably a man who owns his own vessels. Someone who knows river people and something about building boats, too. Anyone come to mind?"

"Captain Maxwell might do. He's been steamboating . . . oh I guess thirty years. His boats run on time and his men like him. Solid Union man."

"Go find him."

Twenty troopers stood neatly at ease in the street. A plump captain called them to attention; his voice cracked slightly. Frémont studied the men. Each had a bayonet in place and their pieces looked clean.

"Can you use that bayonet, son?" he said to a tall boy with sandy hair in the front rank. He was spare but his heavy wrists suggested strength.

"Sure thing, General—stuck many a frog back in Arkansas."

"Arkansas?"

The boy's eyes narrowed. "Missouri frogs stick just like Arkansas frogs, General."

"Good. What's your name?"

"Briggins, sir."

The captain's name was Dolberry. Until seven weeks ago he'd been running a general store in a crossroads town in Illinois. He was older than he looked; he might be thirty.

"Let's go," Frémont said. He jerked his head toward Pine Street.

Marching, the men had a ragged look. Their sergeant, Riordan, a big man with a broken nose and a full black mustache, watched them with a disgusted expression.

"Dress your ranks, Sergeant," Frémont said sharply. "Can't you count cadence?"

"Yes, sir!" A smile crossed Riordan's face. "Dress up, boys. Guide right! You there, Yancey—straighten that piece! You look like an old woman. Huh! Hoo! Hee! Hor! *Step* it out, now!"

There were people in the streets, but Frémont saw none of the giant dray wagons and other signs of commercial activity that once had hummed about the waterfront; the yards before the stone warehouses stood empty and silent. The door to one yawned open, showing small stacks of boxes dwarfed by empty spaces.

They entered an area of houses and small stores, still below the bluff. The men's boots scuffed the cobblestones; they were eyeing the houses warily now.

"Sergeant Riordan," Frémont commanded, "have them all call cadence. And pick up the pace."

Faster, bootheels loud now, held on a rolling cadence, the detachment looked stronger, more purposeful. That was better. Windows opened, men appeared in doorways. A boy ran out of the yard to follow and his mother ran after him, carried him back squealing. "You stay away from those Bluebacks, Johnny Adams!" she cried. Three men were glaring from the opposite sidewalk. On the corner ahead a half-dozen more had gathered. A bull-shouldered man with a checked cap pulled close to his eyes, a red kerchief around his neck, took a step into the street, hands hanging like hooks, and bellowed: "You Yankee fuckers just wait! We gonna give you a Bull Run—Missouri style!" He glanced back at his friends, grinning. "That means we skin 'em *before* we run 'em!"

There was loud laughter and someone yelled, "You tell 'em, Spurge . . ."

Riordan said quietly: "You wanna take him, General?" Frémont shook his head. "Boys are getting tired of these bigmouths," Riordan murmured.

The cadence had gone ragged and he brought it together again. A livery-stable door stood open ahead and Frémont saw a man hastily throwing a saddle on a horse. The group of men had begun to follow them. Frémont studied Riordan's face, the high-ridged broken nose, the flat amber eyes. He'd seen him somewhere before—he never forgot a face, a trail or a river.

"Do I know you, Sergeant?"

Riordan's eyes flickered at him. "Sir, I was riding horse guard behind General Kearny's battalion when he come back from California."

"So *you*'re the one who made all that dust!" Frémont smiled. "What a time. . . ."

"Well, you won't be eating anybody's dust from now on, General." The sergeant's glance held all that needed to be said. Here he was, running Kearny's old command, starting at a rank one grade higher than Kearny's highest—and he wouldn't need any glaring window at his back, either . . .

"This army's growing fast," he said aloud. "How come you're still a sergeant?"

"Beats me, sir."

"Could you handle a company?"

"Yes, sir."

"A battalion?"

Riordan's eyes cut to his again, excited but troubled. "That'd take some getting used to . . . but maybe—yes, sir."

"We'll see," Frémont said.

They turned onto Pine Street. Twenty-odd men were following them now; Frémont saw others ahead. If there was a friendly face in St. Louis, he hadn't met it yet.

"I want to hear that cadence, Sergeant!" he said sharply. "I want 'em to *know we're here.*"

"Yes, sir! Pick it up, boys!" Riordan began to sing the cadence. He sounded loud and aggressive, and the detachment picked it up. Their boots crashed against the cobblestones.

Dolberry looked at him, his face damp with worry. "Up ahead, sir, that's the Berthold house. That's where—"

"Where did you think we were going?"

"Sir, these seceshes, they mob up in an awful hurry."

"That's what the bayonets are for, Captain."

"I could send a couple of men back for the rest of the company."

"Captain, this rabble seems to think it runs St. Louis. If it takes a whole army to deal with 'em, maybe they're right."

The man's eyes went whitely from side to side. "General, I think we're making a mistake. You just got here—you don't understand—"

"One more word, Captain, and I'll relieve you."

The Confederate flag was whipping in the morning wind off the river. Frémont recognized the house immediately. Two men in civilian clothes were seated at a table on the veranda, talking to several youths. Recruiters, sure enough.

The troopers followed Frémont through the gate. Riordan expertly fanned them into a half-circle, rifles at port, bayonets pale blue slivers in the sunlight. Frémont went up the steps, Dolberry behind him. A man with bright yellow hair and a soft, full face, his silk cravat elegantly tied, lounged at the table. He did not bother to stand.

"I don't believe you've been invited here, General," he drawled carelessly, his very smile contemptuous. "Now, I suggest you take your people—"

Frémont reached down, clutched shirt and cravat in his hand, and jerked the recruiter erect. "Come to your feet when you speak to a superior officer! What are you—captain? sergeant? Or some common bushwhacker—"

"Captain!" the man cried. "You take your—"

"—of an outlaw army?"

"Of the Confederate States of America, God damn you to hell!" The secessionist swung at Frémont, who snapped him off-balance and threw him down the steps.

"You're a prisoner of war now, Captain," he said. "You're also out of uniform." To the other onlookers he added: "You're all under arrest. Don't move." The rebel officer had struggled to his knees, cursing.

"Briggins," Frémont said. "Watch him."

"Yes, sir!" Briggins' rifle swung down, the bayonet tip stopped an inch from the small of the man's throat. "Whyn't you just keep your peace now, cousin?" Briggins said.

A crowd had gathered along the fence. Frémont heard a hoarse yell; the man in the checked cap stood in the middle of the street, windmilling his arm to others in the distance. Frémont slashed the lanyard with a clasp knife and hauled down the flag.

"You bastards better look out!" someone yelled, but no one entered the yard. Dolberry held the flag taut while Frémont cut it in long strips.

"Fuckers are cuttin' our flag!" the man in the cap roared. "Look at 'em . . ."

"Twist these up and use them to bind the prisoners," Frémont ordered.

A black man peered hesitantly from the front door; there was no other sign of life in the house.

"You, up there," Frémont called.

"Yes, sir." The man stepped onto the porch apprehensively.

"You tell Judge Berthold, compliments of Major General John Charles Frémont. This is a loyal city in a Union state. If he lets this happen again, I'll seize his house and quarter troops in it. You got that?"

The black man gave him a sudden immense grin. "I'll tell him, yes *sir!*"

On the street Riordan formed the men in a hollow square with the bound prisoners inside. Sixty or seventy idlers had gathered, a tough-looking crowd. They held back a little way from the soldiers, lowering but uncertain. Two men wore revolvers; several had bowie knives; no rifles were visible.

The man in the cap bawled to the others: "You going to let these bluebelly bastards get away with this?"

"That's right!" shouted a tall fellow with long arms who wore overalls over a union suit. "Let's gut 'em."

Riordan glanced at Frémont. Frémont nodded.

"Briggins," Riordan said. "Yancey. Look sharp, now." He took a few quick steps and seized Checkered Cap by his shirtfront. There was a short, violent scuffle, Riordan hit him twice, and he went down. "All right, chickenshit," the sergeant said. "You're coming along."

The man in overalls started forward. "Now you wait one damn minute!"

Briggins was in lunge position, the bayonet point quivering at the overall snaps. "Jump on that, you ugly son of a bitch," he said with a tight smile.

Then they were swinging down Pine Street again, rifles at the ready and prisoners in the box, roaring cadence, boots ringing on stone.

"Worked out all right," Frémont said. "You see?"

"Yes, sir," Dolberry answered morosely.

"You like leading troops?"

"No, sir. I liked my store better."

"What would you do if someone tried to take your store away from you?"

A look of outrage flashed across his round face; at once he seemed older, harder. "I'd fight him—I wouldn't let him!"

"We've got as many problems with supplies as with men," Frémont said. "Maybe you should be a quartermaster."

Dolberry blinked in relief. "Yes, sir . . . I'd like that."

At headquarters a squat, powerful man in a leather apron jumped up as Frémont came in. "I'm Sam Rogers," he snapped. "What do you want with me?"

"Mr. Rogers, I want tents and lots of 'em—and fast. You'll be paid, don't worry about that. But for now get your crews together and start stitching a—"

Rogers was shaking his head, gray eyes stubborn. "Can't do it, General," he said.

"What do you mean, can't?" Frémont said ominously. "I *said* you'd be paid. Or do you mean you won't?"

"Hell, no! If your boys'll fight these secesh bastards, I'll put tents over 'em all right. I mean I've got no tenting!"

"No canvas in all of St. Louis?"

"One place. There's a shipment in Snively's warehouse. But he's a dyed-in-the-wool secessionist—he'll never release it."

"Dolberry," Frémont said, "here's a quartermaster problem. Think you can get us that canvas?"

Dolberry nodded firmly. "I do, General."

"Very good. Let Briggins show him that frog-sticker of his. Then be sure to give him a receipt."

"Yes, sir!"

Thomas Maxwell turned out to be just what Gaines had promised—an experienced steamboat captain with the calm confidence that comes with years of command. He listened quietly to Frémont's plan for building a fleet of gunboats and enlisting a corps of river men to run them and agreed that it sounded feasible enough. Frémont told him to come back in two days with specific proposals.

"If I give you the command," he added, "it'll carry the rank of colonel."

"If I take it," Maxwell answered evenly, "I'll keep the rank of captain. Ain't nothing higher on the river, General."

Frémont sat down with Colonel Jeter and the rest of the staff to devise training schedules for the recruits and plans for fortifying St. Louis and procuring more arms. Three hours later Gaines interrupted with a message from General Lyon.

"He's calling for reinforcements, sir."

"Where is he?"

"Down in southwest Missouri," a quiet major named Holtzmann said. "About a hundred miles beyond the last railhead at Rolla."

"Rolla . . ." Frémont couldn't believe Lyon would extend his lines that far. "What's his situation?"

"He's got six thousand men," Jeter said. "He's been chasing the Missouri rebels, but now they've joined up with McCulloch's army from Arkansas—they outnumber him two to one."

"We have much the same situation at Cairo," Holtzmann interposed. "General Prentiss reports a powerful Confederate force coming upriver."

Cairo. That was serious. The town lay at the juncture of the Ohio and the

Mississippi—it was the key to his strategy and the linchpin securing Missouri. Whoever held Cairo controlled the Mississippi Valley.

"Maybe Lyon had better fall back," Frémont said.

"He's not the kind of man who likes to retreat, General."

Frémont looked at Jeter, then Holtzmann. "He will retreat if he's ordered to," he said quietly. "But we'll see."

DARK HOUR

THE WOMAN LOOKED VAGUELY familiar as she came down the long hall of the Planter's House with tiny steps, leaning hard on an ebony cane. She wore a veil and a fine gown, old lady's purple, with a strand of matched pearls whose roseate luster would have shone in any city in the world. She and Jessie were momentarily alone in the great hall.

"My dear, would you help me?" Her voice was at once plaintive and used to command. She assumed obedience, stopping and bracing on her cane near a tall plant in a burnished copper pot. Then Jessie recognized her. What *was* her name—she'd had a son, a tall boy, rather handsome . . .

"Mrs. Boileau!" she said with a rush of nostalgic pleasure.

Surprised, the old woman raised her veil. Jessie saw her eyes widen. Then she dropped the veil as if her privacy had been invaded and took a quick step backward.

"What are you doing here?" she said sharply.

"Why, Mrs. Boileau—"

"Don't you speak to me! Your Daddy would turn in his very grave if he knew what you're doing! He would never have gone against his own people—he'd have stood with us!"

"We're standing for our country, madam," Jessie said evenly. "I think he'd have done the same."

"I remember you as a little girl." Mrs. Boileau put both hands on her cane and shook her head forbiddingly. "I remember you in a pretty gingham dress . . . it was that vagabond you married. Running off with a man twice your age! We all knew then what you were—"

"Madam—"

"Pathfinder, indeed! Let me tell you one thing." The scratchy voice rose tremulously. "You'd better enjoy that husband while you've got him—he'll never leave St. Louis alive!" Then a look of horror swept her face. She put her hand against her mouth and took another step back so that the plant's green spears pressed around her head like a witch's crown.

Jessie turned from her and walked home quickly, cold in the knowledge that many old acquaintances would now be enemies.

They had turned the Brants' house into military headquarters for St. Louis—rented it entire so as to have everything, including their own quarters, under one roof. A sentry stood at the gate and two at the door. The big formal parlor had been converted to offices, with situation maps and bulletin boards; a telegraph station was located in the basement. Captain Gaines—jumped a grade as Charles' aide-de-camp—had a desk there, though he was usually with the General; and so was John Howard, who had worked for Charles in the '56 campaign and on the Mariposa. Jessie ran up the broad steps to the second-floor family parlor that was now Charles' office. Gaines was with him, his lips tight, as if he'd just been reprimanded.

"Jessie, where have you been?" Charles snapped at her. "I need you here, not gallivanting around St. Louis . . ."

"Charles," she began, "I've found a building we could use as a base hospital, if the—"

"I don't care what you found! There are requisitions, correspondence, directives—I can't do everything, Jessie!"

She bit her lip, drove Mrs. Boileau's shrill, vindictive voice out of her mind. Charles had looked down at his work again; his hand holding a War Department directive was trembling slightly. Captain Gaines was studying the floor in embarrassment.

"Of course, Charles," she said calmly. "What do you have for me?"

There was everything to do, and no time at all to do it. Charles had the men billeted in Chouteau's old fur warehouses or bivouacked in the new tents, but training facilities were still inadequate and the shortage of rifles was acute. A central depot had to be built, unifying all of the haphazardly placed railroad lines to facilitate troop movements; the commandeered river boats needed to be iron-plated, the city itself fortified. The 90-day volunteers threatened to go home en masse if they weren't paid; Henderson categorically refused to release any funds for the purpose, and Charles had gone to the supply depot with an armed detail and seized $150,000 from the enraged quartermaster to pay them. Confederate sympathizers began to terrorize the city, especially at night, and Charles was forced to declare martial law. A cavalry arm had to be activated. Everything had to be done from scratch; and over and above it all came the incessant demands from Washington for men and more men. To his own urgent pleas to be allowed to retain his own scantily trained troops, and for weapons and supplies, the only reply was Montgomery Blair's terse wire: "I find it impossible now to get any attention to Missouri or western matters from the authorities here. You will have to do the best you can."

It was after midnight when he came slowly up the stairs to their living quarters. He was white with exhaustion: he was not fifty, but tonight the new gray in his neatly clipped beard and the lines in his cheeks seemed deeper. She herself was too exhausted from the sea of official correspondence to raise his spirits. He sat down to a late supper but couldn't eat; he drank his tea and buttered a slice of bread, pushing the rest aside.

"Another message from Scott today," he said wearily. "He must think Washington's in danger again—he wants 5,000 more troops."

"But—you can't spare such a number," she said, shocked. Ever since

Bull Run the government had been in a panic—all it could see was the Confederate Army in Virginia. It was draining the West of men and weapons—tragic shortsightedness since the campaign Charles had planned obviously would relieve pressure on the East. Old Fuss and Feathers, who had exploited so brilliantly the Valley of Mexico, was blind to the crucial importance of the Valley of the Mississippi. But even without any cooperation from Washington, Charles was accomplishing wonders. Captain Maxwell already had gunboats on the ways. The training camp for the new recruits was operating; Benton Barracks, Charles called it, though the men were living under the new tents. He'd put Riordan, now with a major's leaves, in charge of training.

"What will you do?" she asked.

"I will have to comply. It's a direct order, Jessie. It means Lyon will have to fall back." He rubbed his eyes. "I can't reinforce him *and* Prentiss at the same time. I'm taking Starrett's Brigade downriver in three days."

"But the boats aren't ready . . ."

"It can't be helped. I must do it anyway, with what I've got. I can't risk losing Cairo—no matter what."

Charles poured himself more tea. He wasn't eating, he was hardly sleeping. This wretched job is wearing him down day by day, she thought with raging resentment; he can't possibly cope with all the problems—no one could. A horse clattered by in the street below at a hard gallop: some courier bearing news of another crisis, more demands . . .

"Isn't it odd," she said lightly, "to find ourselves here again in this old house. Remember that day on the veranda when Louie showed us that dreadful buffalo on his rifle stock? And Papa surprised him so when he picked it up and aimed it?"

He gave her a slow smile. "I remember." She thought of Lily holding up her fat little arms to Louie that day. Lily was nearly twenty now. The same grave, plain-featured little girl, given to those unpredictable outbursts of temper. She had become hysterical at their departure from Black Point, crying if they left they'd never see it again; Jessie had been utterly unable to console her. Thank God she and the boys were in Boston. St. Louis was much too dangerous a place to bring youngsters; but it was lonely without them.

"Do you know," she went on, "I worked out the exact place I was standing, that day I first saw you—I was in the dining room talking to those three boys from Jefferson Barracks—"

"You could find it? The exact place?"

"Yes—Bob Gaines' desk is right over it. I told him he had the luckiest spot in all St. Louis. And then of course I had to tell him the whole story."

"What did he think?"

"He seemed a little scandalized. The General?—engaging in such romantics? Only young people are passionate, you know—and he knows we never were his age."

"Of course. He is very young. With all of life out there ahead of him . . ."

"And so are we," she returned. "We'll put this all behind us one day—

you'll see. And go back home and look across the bay to your glorious Golden Gate . . ."

He glanced at her sharply then, and a shadow crossed his face. Something else is wrong, she thought with sudden dread.

"What is it, darling?" she whispered.

"They've taken Black Point."

She stared at him, not comprehending. "Taken? Who's taken—?"

"The Army. I didn't want to tell you. At least until things settled down a bit. They're mounting guns there, to command the bay. To stop Confederate raiders."

She shook her head, wordless, gripped in a sense of loss she'd never felt before; not quite like this. *They had taken Black Point.*

"Can they do that?" she said.

"They've done it. A message today."

"But—can't we stop them?"

He shook his head. "It's legal—right of eminent domain, war powers—"

"Oh Charles. They'll ruin everything—the garden, the trellis . . ." She gazed at him. "We'll have to make them post a special guard . . ."

He looked at her, looked away again. "Jessie, they've torn down the house. To make room for the guns."

"Torn down? Our house—they've destroyed our *home*—?"

"Look, darling," he said quickly, "it's all right. We'll rebuild when this is over. It'll be all right, I promise you."

But he was wrong. She knew it. "We'll never get it back. They'll never give it up—it's too beautiful."

"Of course they will. After the war—"

"No. They'll find some reason to keep it. Men in power never give things up."

"Jessie—"

"They won't!" She was on her feet with no sense of having stood, her sight darkened with rage. "What are you going to do about it?" she cried. "Are you just going to sit there and let them take away our home?'"

"Jessie, sweetheart—"

"No, Goddamnit! My home! Wire the President—tell him we won't *let* them take it!"

He was standing too, a hand stretched toward her.

"What the hell good is it being a general if they can steal your home?" she cried. "Tell them to come out and run this stupid war themselves if they haven't anything better to do than steal—"

"Honey, the government feels—"

"You're the government! We're the government—what right have they got to take away the only thing we . . ."

She was unfair, she knew she was unfair and she didn't care. She stood there clasping her arms, turning from side to side. He started toward her and stopped, irresolute.

"Damn them," she said. "Damn all of them to hell!" The campaign of '56 still lay upon her like a fresh burn. She'd never gotten over it and she never would. Black Point had been her balm, and since they had come to St. Louis the memory of it had been her one comfort. And now it was gone and she and Charles had been set down among enemies.

And then, for all her determination to be resolute, she was weeping, gripping her arms with all her might. "Damn them!" she cried again. In that instant Kearny's malignant glare, Polk's face cold with duplicity, and now Mrs. Boileau's terrible, spiteful attack all melted into one. "Why is it everything we love, everything we touch," she sobbed thickly, "why does it all have to be torn out of our hands?"

His arms were around her then; the buttons on his tunic chafed her forehead. She wept because in her exhaustion and despair she couldn't seem to do anything else, and his strong, spare arms held her here in the late night; the only comfort. "God, I'm sorry," he murmured. "I wouldn't have had it happen for the whole world . . ."

Far off, out west of the city toward Webster Grove, she heard a gunshot, another. Charles' head went up, she felt him stiffen.

". . . They hate us here," she said.

"What? That's not true."

"Yes, it is. We're among enemies. I see them! Every day. The Blairs, too."

"Honey, they're doing all they can . . ."

"They've changed. Frank's changed, Charles—he used to be so lively and devil-may-care. Now he's so willful, so—*hard.*"

Charles was smiling wryly. "He's caught the fever."

"What fever?"

"White House fever. His father's told him he's going to be President for so long he's finally begun to believe it. He's just been used to having everything his own way out here. He'll learn."

"I hope so. . . . They'll tear out my rose beds, won't they, Charles?"

"I don't know, honey."

"Yes." She nodded to herself. "They'll tear them out by the roots. Roses and guns cannot live together. Not possibly." This war would go on and on, she knew it in her very bones. There was too much hatred, too much savagery and pride. It would rage on for years, and thousands on thousands of young men would be slaughtered and maimed, and even if the Union were preserved it would never be the same again. Never. She shivered uncontrollably, and gripped the rough cloth of his tunic.

"Hold me, darling," she said in a tone that was like a prayer. "Please hold me, now. . . ."

"What the devil is he up to?" Frémont rattled Lyon's dispatch as if to shake a better explanation out of it. "He says the enemy is near him 'in overwhelming numbers.' Then he says: 'I shall hold my ground as long as possible.' Goddamnit, I *told* him five days ago to fall back if he felt threatened."

"It galls him to pull back," Gaines said, standing not quite at attention before Frémont's desk with a clutch of papers. It was midmorning; Frémont had been at the desk since before dawn. "He's a very rash man—he's too proud."

Frémont didn't bother to reprimand his aide. Nathaniel Lyon did have a way of infuriating people; he was a fiery little man given to feisty pronouncements. Frémont believed in strong action—the situation was clearly beyond that amelioration for which the President still yearned—but in the early months, trying to hold Missouri, Lyon and Frank Blair had touched off deadly opposition. Frank maintained it was there anyway—best to force it into the open where it could be fought directly. Long before Frémont had arrived, when Lyon was still hoping for the western command himself, he had led his troops out to arrest a state militia unit camped in St. Louis. The militiamen were secessionists, all right, but the arrest hadn't done any good, since Lyon had paroled them next day and they'd rushed off in a body to join the Army of the Confederacy. And by then the riots had started. Twenty-eight people died—among them a babe shot accidentally in its mother's arms. And the damage was done. Countless men who'd been wavering or indifferent had made up their minds: If them bluebellies gonna shoot down helpless women and babies, I reckon we'll have t'fight, boys. Many who chose to stay at home were fighting too; guerrillas and nightriders, all the dark-hearted men with grudges had slipped their leashes and run free ever since. Every day new outrages and alarms occurred in the city itself.

Now Lyon was down in southwestern Missouri, in pursuit of those militiamen turned Confederate soldiers. Old Governor Price, who'd been a general in the Mexican War and knew a thing or two about soldiering, had rallied to the southern side and shaped his boys into an army as they moved. He had also linked up with McCulloch's division from Arkansas—which put a formidable force at Lyon's front. Lyon simply had pursued too far—the railhead at Rolla was the last point of strategic value.

Irritably, Frémont tugged at the bell pull. When Jessie came in, he gave her fresh orders for Lyon: "He is to pull back to Rolla, where I can reinforce him by rail. Tell him if he fights, it will be on his own responsibility. Try not to ruffle his feathers, but make it firm and unconditional."

He watched her face as she wrote, brushing back her hair with a tired gesture. She hadn't slept well since he'd told her about Black Point. She hadn't mentioned it again, but next morning he found the Bierstadt painting hung in his office. He was surprised: he hadn't realized she'd brought it from California. It was hardly the right note for a wartime general's office, but seeing the set look on her face, he hadn't said anything. There it hung now, ablaze with light, reminding him of the Sierra and Monterey, beckoning him with the old fierce longing—

"Three court-martial verdicts for your review, sir," Gaines was saying. Frémont set the paper aside. "And a third of the men at Benton Barracks on sick call this morning—some gastric flare-up, the doctor said."

Frémont grunted. The training camp had gone up almost overnight. The privies had been dug too close to the well—instinct told him he was right. Any mountain man would know to put the crap hole away from the spring.

"Tell Dolberry to have new privies dug—well away from the water source and the cook tents this time."

"Sir, that'll play hob with the training schedules—"

"Which is more important—two days of close-order drill or half your command down with the quickstep? Use your head, son. Tell him to hire some of these unemployed laborers, too—it'll get 'em off the streets."

The windows were open against the early August heat. Frémont could hear the telegrapher's key pounding away downstairs. It ran late every night, a cascade of messages in and out. The whole first floor was crowded with young officers wrestling with the endless details of building an army. There was so much to do! Take horses, alone—you had to find a nearly endless supply when farmers didn't want to give them up; then rustle up saddles and harnesses, liniments and blankets, precast horseshoes and blacksmiths with forges mounted in wagons who could set up shop wherever the army stopped. You needed a saddler wagon with strap-leather supplies . . . He stopped to scribble a note to make sure that each wagon carried a spare tongue and two spare axles slung underneath.

"When the *Louisville Lady* arrived yesterday, that four tons of gunpowder wasn't aboard," Gaines informed him.

"Damn!" Frémont said. "We had a firm promise on that. Wire Cincinnati—I want to know just what in hell went wrong." The aide was making notes. "Ask about that surgeon, too." They *must* have a trained military surgeon who could organize a medical corps. Local doctors had seen plenty of gunshot wounds, but they had no idea whatever of the kind of damage sixteen-pounders or canister could do.

"Then today's troop drafts," Gaines went on, "125 from Illinois, 10 stragglers from the Second Iowa, 97 from Michigan."

"None from Missouri?"

"Missouri enlistments have nearly stopped, General. The boys say the guerrillas are so bad no one dares leave his farm."

Frémont tapped a pencil on the desk. Those damned guerrillas balked him at every turn. He had imposed martial law on St. Louis and it had worked wonders. Maybe he could extend it. . . .

The door popped open with a loud bang and Frank Blair walked in, unannounced and uninvited. "Morning," he said, not smiling. He looked at Gaines and jerked his head peremptorily. "I want to talk to the General." After a second Frémont nodded and Gaines left, his impassive face brick red with anger. Blair threw himself in a leather chair and hooked a bootheel on the corner of Frémont's desk. He was rangy, with a fleshy face and restless eyes; a sandy mustache drooped around the corners of his mouth. There was something brash and testy about him, even in repose. There was certainly no trace of the debonair, carefree boy Jessie remembered.

"I heard from Lyon again," he said now. "Sounds like he needs help. You'd better get some support down to him pronto." He nodded, confirming the value of his judgment. "Muy pronto."

It struck Frémont that it would be a tremendous pleasure to throw the Honorable Frank Blair out on his ass. His brother Montgomery had continued to serve faithfully—if ineffectively—as Frémont's conduit to President Lincoln, but Frank had proved an utter disappointment. Frémont wondered again why Jessie and the Senator had so admired him—certainly they had never practiced his brand of politics.

"I've had to reinforce Prentiss at Cairo, Frank. Four thousand of the—"

"Cairo! What the hell's the sense in that?"

Frémont wondered if he had been drinking. He knew the signs: the over-hearty laugh, a certain heightened intensity in manner. Monty and his brother both believed that a brilliant career awaited Frank—the old man had predicted Frank would be President within a decade. The idea afforded Frémont wry amusement. Maybe Francis Blair was slipping into his dotage, scheming to recapture through this immensely improbable son those glory days when he had sat in Andrew Jackson's kitchen cabinet.

Patiently Frémont again explained the strategic realities: Pillow still threatened Cairo with 12,000 men; Price and Hardee were moving against Lyon with more than 35,000. To oppose all this he had less than 23,000—with 8,000 of them three-month volunteers whose terms were expiring—and nearly all inadequately armed and equipped. Washington's urgent demands for some 7,000 were still unfulfilled; the new recruits were absolutely worthless until they'd had some training; the detachments stationed along the Missouri were barely enough to restrain the guerrillas—

"I know, I know all that," Blair broke in impatiently. "Well, Nat Lyon's facing the *real* threat, I'll tell you that."

Frémont shook his head. "Lyon's ground has no strategic value. He can pull back to Rolla, and his position actually improves. But if we lose Cairo we lose the rivers—and then we've lost it all." He paused to write another note to himself to check on the battery of 24-pounders and 1,000 men dispatched to support Marsh. Had they got there? If Girardeau fell, it would be almost as bad as losing Cairo. . . .

Blair said suddenly: "Loudermilk tells me you rejected his bid. Why's that?" His eyes were hot with resentment; Frémont saw he had come to his real purpose. This matter of Army contracts had been a continual bone of contention. Blair argued that rewards cemented politics and that it was politics that would hold Missouri for the Union; Frémont felt such favoritism was not only wasteful but a corrupt way to conduct a war that was being waged for the nation's very soul.

"He wants to sell us uniforms and equipment for 40,000 men," Frémont answered carefully. "That's much too big."

"You'll need it eventually."

"Then we'll buy it eventually."

"But it's economical, buying in volume . . ."

"Not from Loudermilk it isn't. I have another bid to equip 10,000—which is far more realistic—and it's nine percent lower."

"Tell me, General," Blair said with heavy sarcasm, "this other bidder—is he from California, too?" Blair took it as a personal affront that Frémont had awarded several contracts to California men.

"No—as a matter of fact he's from Illinois."

Blair slammed the chair arm. "Goddamnit, you still don't see the point. What good is it to reward a man who can't give you any help back? We got problems enough holding this state without running off the men on our side. Now listen—Loudermilk is a good friend of mine and I *want him on that contract.* You signed on the other?"

"Not yet." Frémont was determined to keep a firm hold on his temper.

"Well, don't. Loudermilk will come back with a different proposal. Now, if he's still out of line, all right—but I want him considered if he's anywhere near the other figure. He can do us a lot of good right here in Missouri, where we need it."

Before Frémont could answer, he heard an oddly familiar voice protest loudly in the anteroom: "Listen, Captain, I've come all the way from California to see him and I'm gonna see him!"

Blair heaved himself up and gave Frémont an ugly smile. "Your California friends do manage to reach you, don't they?"

He walked out, pushing brusquely past an orderly, and Frémont saw Trenor Park in the doorway, gesticulating; Lieutenant Howard was trying to restrain him.

"I'll see him, John," he said stiffly, filled with foreboding. "Thank you."

Park came into the room, still ruffled and glancing back angrily. The very sight of him vexed Frémont. There wasn't even time to breathe as he struggled to build an army out of nothing—but the Mariposa's problems never failed to track him down. Was Collis Huntington always dogged by worry? . . . But Huntington had the sense to stay out of the gold business. All Frémont knew were ledgers and red ink and idle machinery coated with rust . . . and that wretched dam. It had looked so grand when it was finished; it filled, the machinery turned, the gold poured out, and the Mariposa had begun drawing ahead, settling those maddening short-term, high-interest debts . . . Then a freak spring heat wave had unlocked the Sierra Nevada snowpack all at once, and the water had come thundering down. The news had arrived by wire and Frémont had saddled a fast horse and ridden all night, driving two spares before him, California fashion. At dawn Jack Hopper had shown him the open floodgates, the sandbags, the shattered stone cavern and silt-clogged rubble that was all that was left. All that summer he had struggled to begin operations again, and in the fall he had set out that last time for Europe to raise money—only to find doors slamming shut in the European credit markets. He'd bought arms for the Union instead. Now the dam remained half rebuilt, production at a third of its potential, he was trying with all his might to run a war—and Trenor Park had the gall to come barging in on him like Napoleon III.

"What's on your mind, Trenor?" he said crisply.

"We're in a big bind, Colonel—General." Park sat on the edge of the leather couch beyond the map table. He was pale and his hair was too long, but his suit was expensive; his belly bulged against his coat and he slipped the button and wiped his face with a silk handkerchief. "A regular crisis, you could say."

"Indeed." Frémont listened stonily to Park's litany. The interest was destroying them: the war had driven short-term rates still higher, gold production was down; every month they fell further behind. The notes were coming due, and with the wartime credit squeeze it would be hard to renew them. The new machinery was ready, but the manufacturer was demanding immediate payment—in cash. The company was retooling to make cannon; there'd be no new mining machinery till this war was over. Park thought the new machinery would go to someone else if the company didn't get a substantial payment soon.

"I'd sue their socks off," Frémont said.

"What? In the middle of a war? How long'll that take? And what happens to the Mariposa in the meantime?"

Gaines walked in with a requisition form. "Sorry to interrupt, sir, but Captain Maxwell needs an immediate signature on that order for 80 tons of armor plate for the gunboats. It should go out on the *Louisville Lady*, and she's under way in 30 minutes."

Frémont leaned over his desk to scratch his signature. Gaines said: "Sir, that 500 stand of rifles we located up in Minnesota—General Scott has ordered them all east."

"Oh, for God's sake!" Frémont exclaimed. You'd think the Huns were sweeping down on Washington the way that senile old fool was screaming for every soldier, every weapon. "Send a wire to the governor up there begging him to hold those pieces till I can get a clarifying order from the President."

"Yes, sir."

"Let Mrs. Frémont draft it. Then tell her to write Postmaster General Montgomery Blair, explaining everything—we absolutely *must have those rifles.*" Park was watching him like a squirrel on a fence post. "So?" he snapped.

"General," Park said in that soft, ingratiating voice, "whyn't you give up this military foolishness and come back and tend to business?"

Frémont stared at him. "Are you out of your mind? It might interest you to know we are engaged in a life-and-death struggle for this nation's existence. I've been put in command of the Western Department—"

"Well, Jesus sake, can't somebody else command it? What about all these professional Army men? They been waitin' a lifetime—why do *you* have to do it?"

"Because the President appointed me, for one reason."

"Maybe you should have told him your fancy gold mine was about to sink under you. You ever stopped to calculate how little time you really give that place? You're always off chasing after some other rabbit." He gestured toward the painting. "You oughtta look at that view more often."

Coldly Frémont said: "Since I cannot and will not abandon my post in time of war, what do you propose?"

Park gave him a curious little smile. "I knew you wouldn't. You'll never do what's good for you. Yeah, I've worked out something."

The solution had to be long-term bonds. In spite of the war's uncertainties, there were buyers for fifteen- and twenty-year bonds well secured by gold in the ground. They weren't easy to find, but Park had already lined up the best man in New York—George Opdyke, the former mayor and a prominent speculator and financier. Frémont nodded: he knew Opdyke, a corpulent man whose hand was damp when you shook it.

"Now, he and Morrie Ketchum are willing to put together a combine to sell Mariposa bonds—they guarantee 'em. See what that gives you?—the buyers know the deal's sound if George and Morrie are behind it. With the war and all, buyers want someone they know personally, see?"

"And what does Opdyke want in return?"

"Well, a fee, of course—just to cover expenses. And then, naturally, he can't promise buyers it'll succeed if he hasn't any say in its operation."

"Ownership, you mean?"

"Just a quarter interest."

"I see," Frémont said tightly. "You and Mark Brumagin and the others are holding three-eighths—another quarter would put me in a minority position in my own property."

"Only technically, General," Park answered quickly. "Only technically. You wouldn't actually lose operating control. See, the California boys understand gold mining—they naturally would vote with you. And George and Morrie aren't going to try to run the place from the East Coast. I'll tell you frankly, they have a lot of irons in the fire—they wouldn't touch this but for the strength of your reputation. Truth is, they're trusting *you*—it's not the other way around!"

The sheer effrontery of this startled Frémont; he gazed at Park's bland face, his anger rising.

"Sir!" Gaines was in the doorway, holding a message scrawled on a yellow telegrapher's pad. His face was strained. "Sir, General Lyon has engaged. Near Wilson's Creek."

Frémont felt a stab of dismay. "Price attacked him?"

"He's attacked Price, sir."

The message was from Lyon, written the night before and sent by courier to the telegraph office at Springfield. He would attack at dawn, he said, a third of his force under Colonel Sigel circling around to strike from the south, the main body straight at Price. Alarm pulsed through Frémont. Lyon had divided his force when he was already outnumbered two to one. If anything went wrong on the flank, he'd be facing *three* to one. The yellow sheet quivered in his hand. Why had Lyon attacked? He'd clearly already received Frémont's order to retire. It didn't make sense. Doubtless he'd perceived a weakness in Price's dispositions, but what good was a piecemeal victory on meaningless ground? It would be good for morale, it might draw a few fence-straddlers into the Union camp; but the risk was too great to justify it. The whole plan was to *conserve* troops for the downriver invasion that lay ahead. . . .

The telegraph was hammering again, its distant thud echoing through the big house, and Gaines hurried off. His stomach churning, Frémont tried to grapple with the consequences of a prolonged battle, a possible defeat. Now everything was at hazard. If Lyon were driven from the field, the railhead at Rolla would be exposed, and then . . . Park was watching him from the leather couch with that glint of speculative cupidity, and it drove him to fury.

"Goddamnit," he said, "I already turned over three-eighths to you people to cover these problems! You can damned well work out this bond deal yourself."

Park was on his feet at that, his face mottled. "That was before the dam went out! You were in trouble and we bailed you out of it—we *got* the place back on its feet, and then that blasted dam went, floodgates and all, and there wasn't a thing . . ."

The floodgates. All at once Frémont thought of Alexis Godey's letter. It had arrived several weeks ago, forwarded from New York. It was written in the polished hand and ornate phrases of a professional scribe, but its gist was clear enough. Alex had heard from two of the Black Drift crew that Jack Hopper hadn't opened the floodgates until *after* the dam had started to go. If that was true, Hopper had deliberately wrecked the dam. For some time Godey had thought Hopper was stealing from the Mariposa—that was the primary reason he'd left. Maybe he should have spoken up earlier, but he had no proof. "As to the dam, I can't understand how its loss profits him, but I trust the men who told me." He'd closed by asking if Frémont knew that old Kit was a colonel now himself, with his own Union regiment in New Mexico. Pressed by the mountainous crush of work, Frémont had set the letter aside and thrust it out of his mind. Its implications were deeply disquieting, but on the other hand, it was hearsay. Now, watching Park carefully, his tone impersonal, he began to relate Godey's charges.

Park had sat down again; his face took on an alert, judicial expression, a confident circumspection that made him seem much younger.

"Well, now . . . Godey . . ." he said when Frémont had finished. "I like him and I know you do. So it grieves me to say what I've got to tell you. And I never would have, but now . . ." He shrugged sadly, laced his hands behind his head. "You see, General, the real reason Godey left the Mariposa was Jack Hopper caught him stealing gold."

Frémont watched him, the smooth face, the diffident, deprecatory smile. "He was taking it out of the run at night, and caching it on those deer-hunting trips of his. Jack didn't want to tell you, so he came to me. We both talked to Godey and he decided to go into the horse business. Didn't you ever wonder how he paid down on that ranch?" Park hesitated, added gently: "I'm sorry to break this to you."

Old Alex. Frémont had ridden a lot of miles with Godey. He thought of the day Alex had slammed that conniving brute Colonel Mason against the wall in the governor's residence at Los Angeles. They had ridden together right into death's doorway, he and Alex, and they had ridden out again. Godey had insisted on going back alone; Frémont remembered his face that terrible night in Taos, the look in his eyes. "Colonel, I'd give everything I own if I didn't have to tell you this. *I'd give everything I own . . .*" It came to Frémont simply, irrefutably—as clear as creek water when the first snow melts.

"You filthy little swine," he said quietly. Park's mouth fell open, he pushed himself backward against the couch. "You *wanted* that dam to go. Didn't you? You *wanted* me in the box."

"That's ridiculous. It hurt my three-eights just like it hurt—"

"No! It let you set your hooks deeper." Frémont took a step toward him.

"Godey's a liar!"

"No. Not Godey. Not in a million, million years. He'd put his hand in a flame before he'd take a copper penny that wasn't his." The thing was opening up like campfires flashing on the high plains. "Hopper's *your* man—you sent him to me, and you've been paying him ever since. Those funny real-estate investments of his—"

"That's crazy talk, Colonel! You don't know what you're saying."

Frémont gazed at him as if he'd never seen him before. "No," he said. "You always wanted in, you whipsawed the place. All that machinery breaking down, all the things that kept going wrong. Hopper *ran* it down—stole from it, milked it so I'd *have* to come to you. Didn't he? And you were always there, always waiting. . . . You told me yourself, the day we met—said the money men would always try—"

"Yes, I told you!" Park cried; his lips were drawn back from his teeth like a prairie dog's. "But you were too smart to listen. You were too full of yourself, with your fancy European airs, your presidential dreams—"

Frémont reached for him; Park half-turned, trying to scramble around the couch. Frémont seized him by the lapels and jerked him upright.

Park squealed, "Let go of me!" His soft white hands were clawing at Frémont's face.

"Sir!" Gaines cried from the doorway, and the note of alarm in his voice stopped Frémont cold. "General Lyon has been defeated! They're falling back, in full retreat . . ."

Frémont thrust Park away from him. "Is Lyon reporting himself?"

"No, sir. The telegrapher at Springfield is sending on his own."

"Rumors—it's just rumors, then?"

"No, sir. The main body's falling back through Springfield. Sigel's flank attack was broken immediately. The Second Kansas and First Missouri fought for five hours, but they couldn't hold. Took terrible casualties, they're saying . . ."

Frémont shoved the other maps onto the floor and spread southwestern Missouri on the table. "Gaines," he said as calmly as he could, "send Lyon a message. Tell him to order his force and try to go on the defensive at Rocky Run, just east of Springfield. Send that this instant."

"Sir . . . to tell General Lyon how to conduct his retreat—"

"He didn't know not to attack and get whipped! He didn't know not to split his force. *Send that message!*"

"Yes sir."

Frémont stared out the window, trying to marshal his thoughts. Lyon's men were the heart of the whole Army of the West—how many had he lost? Was he retreating in good order, did he still have his guns? Could he hold? Had Sigel's brigade been overrun, was it finished as an effective force?

"Don't push it off on me, mister," Park was saying in a low, spiteful tone. "You never gave that place a gnat's ass worth of attention. Most folks, they watch over their gold. But not you, oh, hell no—off climbing mountains, chasing railroads. Running for President, for Christ sake—President! And now this damned war. Couldn't *anybody* but you run this war—of course not."

He'd better put Marsh and Prentiss on alert—this might embolden Pillow to attack up the Mississippi again. He'd better issue powder, lead, rations to the St. Louis garrison, have a train standing by to deploy Riordan's people if he had to. He could divert maybe a thousand men from Girardeau . . . He would *not* strip Prentiss at Cairo—he was damned if he would, no matter what! He'd have to submit a full report to Washington as soon as he heard directly from Lyon. The fool, the damned impetuous fool! What could he have been thinking of?

"Don't put it on me—blame it on your ownself," Park was still saying. He leaned forward, knuckles on the map table, glaring at Frémont. "I told you the dangers. Know why you couldn't see 'em? 'Cause you don't know shit from applesauce about business. I saw that the first day, way you talked to Huntington." His lips were curved in the sly, hard half-smile. Watching him coldly, Frémont realized Park had wanted to say these things for a long time. The thought was troubling: I never read him at all. . . .

"So don't you come on indignant with me," Park said. "You don't *deserve* to be rich—you're lucky you got anything! Truth is, I kept you in business all these years—"

"Get out," Frémont said.

Park blinked vacantly. "What—?"

"Get out of here. Out of St. Louis."

"But—wait—what're we gonna do? I'm an owner, too—we've got trouble, we've got to do something . . ."

Jessie swept through the door, a telegrapher's yellow in her hand. Gaines was behind her. "Charles," she said urgently, "Lyon is dead. Killed instantly. They say here he was leading a—" She saw Park then; her eyes went very wide, then hardened. "What's *he* doing here?"

Frémont said to her: "How do you know this?"

She caught herself up. "They've just brought his body into Springfield."

Lyon killed. That feisty, fierce little man. Impossible—! He tore the flimsy from her hand. It was from the same telegrapher, still reporting on his own. Men had been streaming back through Springfield—weapons gone, cannon abandoned. Some units were still together, but preparing to evacuate Springfield immediately. Rumors put Confederate troops twenty minutes away. This would be the last message: the telegrapher was shutting down, preparing to flee himself.

Frémont stared at the sheet. In less than an hour . . . *Why had Lyon attacked?* Things kept crashing about him. There was nothing now between Price's Confederate forces and Rolla—and the railroad ran from Rolla straight into St. Louis. . . .

"Gaines," he said in a low, steady voice, "put all troops on immediate alert. All of them, trained or not. Instruct McKinstry to issue all available weapons, three days' cooked rations for each man. Ready a train—we'll move straight on Rolla." He hesitated. Could raw recruits hold them at Rolla? He just didn't know. "Better get the sappers moving," he added, thinking hard. "I want every trestle between here and Rolla rigged for demolition on one hour's notice. They are not coming into St. Louis on *our* railroad."

Jessie said again, pointing at Park: "What is he *doing* here?"

Frémont said then, "And Gaines."

"Yes sir."

"Have this man thrown out. If he resists, put him in irons at once."

"Now wait a minute," Park cried. "We've got to do something about this, we can't leave it hanging—"

"Briggins!" Gaines shouted through the doorway. "Come in here and get this man."

The Arkansas boy, now wearing corporal's stripes, entered with easy haste and took Park's arm. "Come on, cousin," he said.

"You'll regret this!" Park cried shrilly, twisting in Briggins' grip as they went through the doorway. "You'll pay for this, Frémont. I promise you!"

"I want to see Colonel Buechner, Majors Zagonyi and Riordan," Frémont told Gaines. "All regimental and battalion commanders. In one hour."

Messages kept pouring in all afternoon. The retreating army—what was left of it—was well north of Springfield. Along the route people were packing wagons and joining the soldiers, clogging the roads. From all over the state came frantic rumors—places 300 miles from the battlefield sent urgent demands for a regiment to protect them. Union supporters everywhere were leaving their homes and heading for St. Louis or Illinois; and secessionist guerrillas, newly bold and celebrating, were running loose. Reports, reports: farms burning, street mobs roughing up Union sympathizers, men flogged, three deaths already and more certain to follow. Send troops. . . .

Gaines was back: the train was assembled and making steam, troops had mustered at Benton Barracks, they could roll before nightfall. Frémont drafted a preliminary report to the President. A newsboy was hawking an extra on the streets outside. From the window Frémont could see crowds gathering. "Gaines," he said, "better detach 200 regulars—I think they'll be needed. And put out an order right now to close the saloons."

Frank Blair burst into the office, his face flushed, clutching a new broadside in his fist. "*Now* see what you've done!" he roared thickly, his mouth slack under the sandy mustache. "I told you to reinforce him, I *told* you . . . and now this! Call yourself a general—"

"Look, Frank—"

"He's dead!" Blair slammed the paper to the floor—and then started to weep, wringing his hands. "Nat's dead—the finest man that ever wore this country's uniform—and you killed him!"

"Frank!" Jessie gasped.

Frémont said: "Frank, get hold of yourself."

"You had plenty of men, lolling around—you could have supported him anytime you wanted, but no!—you didn't *want* him to win a brilliant victory, did you? No, of course not, because then he might take over your command, and you couldn't stand—"

"Get hold of yourself! You're going to have to deal with the city while I hold Rolla."

Blair straightened with a lurch, wiped his mouth aimlessly; his eyes had turned baleful and wild. "You're going to pay for this, Frémont," he shouted, "—this is *my* state, *I* command here—and by God, you're going to find that out! I'm going to see that you pay for this for the rest of your life . . ."

"Frank!" Jessie was pleading with him. "You can't mean these things."

"Oh, can't I! We'll see what I mean!"

"Frank," Frémont said with still, icy calm. "Go get your people together—see what you can do, here in the city."

"You bet I will, Frémont! I'll *show* you what I can do!"

He was gone in a clatter of bootheels. There were more men in the streets now, milling around and shouting threats. The boy had sold out his extra, was running off toward the print shop. Frémont could hear laughter; yes, there was actual jubilation in the air. Where in God's name were the Union men?

A bass drum boomed funereally in the distance. He went over to the window again. The drumbeat grew louder, a new crowd came into view. A half-dozen men were carrying a black box draped with Confederate colors. A straw figure in blue dangled above it on a hangman's noose snubbed to a long pole. Nathaniel Lyon—St. Louis was full of people who hated him. The man holding the pole kept making the figure dance obscenely.

Jessie was beside him at the window. "We are among enemies," she said dully.

"Howard," Frémont called, "send the boys out to break that up. No one is going to make a mockery of General Lyon's death while I can help it."

"Yes, sir."

"And get that damned flag! I will not have the enemy flag shown in St. Louis." Howard started out and Frémont called him back again. "I want troops in the streets now. Curfew at dark. No assembly of more than—say, five persons. Any more than five who gather will be arrested. We're not going to have mob rule in St. Louis."

Frémont stood there, trying to assess the implications. It would shake the whole country—it would even reverberate through Europe. And in Missouri now, a Confederate army was free to roam at will: Secessionists would draw strength, Unionists would wonder if they were on the wrong side, enlistments would shrink, the guerrillas would become front riders and scouts for Confederate troops—and what was he going to do about it? What could he do?

Jessie had put her arm around his waist.

"Our own Bull Run," he whispered. "Total disaster." He gripped his hands. "Maybe it's a kind of retribution."

She turned sharply. "What do you mean?"

"What irony—that *another* man's rash action should come down on my head. Maybe the gods are finally angry—for the Platte, the Sierra . . . even Sonoma and Parowan. Maybe—"

"No," she said fiercely, "they're not! It's Lyon's fault. You *ordered* him to pull back—he attacked on his own initiative . . ."

"It doesn't matter." He shook his head. "He's a brave officer, and a popular one. And a West Pointer. And I am in charge here—it will all come back on me."

"And on Lincoln," Jessie murmured.

"Of course. On Lincoln, too."

HIGH POLICY

JESSIE WALKED QUICKLY down the long hall of the Brant mansion and tapped on Ed Davis' door. There was a pearly sense of dawn in the windows; a moment ago they had been black. She knocked again, harder. Sleep clogged Ed's voice when he answered. Frank Blair had given him dinner at the Planter's House and she knew it had been a late night.

"Wake up, Ed." She set his door ajar. "There's coffee in the parlor. Charles will want us in half an hour."

His shirt was open at the throat when he joined her; she saw he'd cut himself shaving in the lamplight. Poor Ed: he wasn't used to wartime hours. Charles had been up well before four; during the night she'd heard him pacing, seen his figure passing and repassing in front of the windows.

"Want to talk?" she'd murmured.

"No. Through talking." His voice taut in the darkness, edged with that restless excitement that always gripped him when he'd seized on some arresting new idea, some compelling plan. "Now it's time to act."

Ed drank his coffee in silence. A lock of smooth black hair fell over his forehead; he brushed it back and sighed. "I don't know how he stands this pace. You, either. Up before dawn, working till the small hours . . ."

"You do what you have to."

"I wouldn't last three weeks. Even Nancy would have thrown in the towel by now."

He smiled at her. He had been in St. Louis three days; he was making a survey of western recruiting for the War Department. She wished he'd brought his wife with him—she was genuinely fond of Nancy, and she found this fractious, violent city intolerably lonely. Outside, the brightening sky made a grim black lacework of the trees. She tied back the curtains.

Ed cleared his throat. "Jessie, this fellow Ulysses Grant—the one Charles has put in command at Cairo. That's a pretty crucial post, isn't it?"

"It certainly is—it controls the rivers, the whole valley . . ."

"I've heard some disturbing things about him."

"Have you?"

"It seems—he has a past."

"Oh, we all have one of those, wouldn't you say?" He laughed with her, but his eyes were wary. "Anyway," she went on, "he impressed Charles with his grasp of strategy, of what needs to be done. You know Charles has always believed the Mississippi is the key—that's why he gave Grant the command."

"And put a lot of noses out of joint, I'm told."

She watched him a moment. "There are always noses to go out of joint, Ed. Whenever anybody moves up. You've been around enough to know that."

"Yes, but—it seems there's a problem with the bottle. They say Grant left the Army under some sort of cloud several years ago, and has been nothing but a failure since."

"Ah, *failure!* That depends a good deal on who's keeping score. In the eyes of narrow-minded, carping—" she broke off.

Her hand shook a little when she raised her cup. Exhaustion was building in her, she knew, her control shakier than it ought to be; what little sleep she got no longer seemed to help much. Sometimes, late at night, she could see a tic in Charles' right cheek, pulling at his mouth. Everything had been worse since Lyon's death. Forcing a smile, she said: "Perhaps it's General Grant's destiny to play an important role in this war. Who knows? And maybe destiny let him suffer a bit first."

"Do you believe in that sort of thing?" he asked curiously.

Soberly she nodded. "I think some people are—oh, I don't know—meant to *do* things, special things."

"Like you and Charles, eh?" He was mocking her now, but gently, affectionately.

She shook her head. It wasn't something to talk about—not casually, not at dawn, not with any friend, even an old friend. Destiny. Success, failure . . . Vindictive old Kearny had put an end to the California governorship; Jefferson Davis—now, incredibly, President of the Confederacy—had thwarted any further government exploration; the Senate seat hadn't lasted; the run for the White House had only paved the way for Lincoln; the transcontinental railroad wasn't quite practical—not yet, anyway. So they had taken refuge on a jeweled point of land thrust into the western sea. Very well: she could have stayed at Black Point all her life—and she'd have tried to make sure that Charles was happy, too. But suddenly great events beckoned—wasn't that destiny? They had been called back to center stage to play an important role in the national crisis . . . and wasn't that really what they had believed in their hearts they might do, from the beginning?

Ed was watching her with a faintly quizzical look. Impulsively she started to convey this sense of what St. Louis meant to them just now. But she didn't like the garrulous, tensed edge in her voice and stopped herself; she *was* tired, ill with weariness, trying to express thoughts that were most clear when they were not expressed.

To change the mood, she added lightly: "If we'd known how hard things would be, maybe we'd have had second thoughts."

"Go on . . . you two are firehorses."

Firehorses straining to the bell. She smiled: yes, that about covered it. But second thoughts did, too. Very little had gone right in the three weeks since Lyon's defeat. The only redeeming part was that Price's Confederates had been so disorganized by their victory that they had been unable to advance on Rolla and St. Louis; instead they'd started moving up the western side of the state, toward the plantation country along the Missouri River. But their victory had been enough to touch off a perfect firestorm of guerrilla warfare in Missouri. It was Bloody Kansas all over again, only magnified a hundredfold.

At the same time a howl of national outrage arose, under which could be heard a clear note of fear. The defeat had followed hard on Bull Run—two Union failures in a row, Union armies east and west broken by audacious, tatterdemalion Johnny Rebs who fought with shotguns and hunting rifles and wore butternut to war. Wouldn't northern armies fight, couldn't northern generals lead? The war already had lasted longer and cost more than expected. Would the people stand the test? And jubilation had raced through the Confederacy—how they must have danced at Cherry Grove, where her name had been stricken from the family rolls!—while Union hopes that southerners would return to the fold began to fade. . . .

Death had absolved the rash Lyon; the blame fell inexorably on Charles. A storm of abuse that left her heartsick and angry was still raging from Boston to St. Louis itself. Newspapers denounced them, preachers berated them, politicians attacked them—and their friends, if any they still had, remained silent. Members of Congress paused in condemning Lincoln to hound after this new quarry. They cared nothing for strategic realities. And why, sir, had Frémont abandoned the brave Lyon and his gallant little army? Because, sir, this Frémont was an incompetent charlatan, no military man at all but a mere explorer—and one, pray remember, sir, who followed other men's trails. In the same way he had left real soldiers to die in the field while he postured at headquarters. . . . How Mr. T's mighty voice would have drowned these mice of men—but Mr. T was gone. . . .

It would take weeks to rebuild Lyon's units and make soldiers out of the green recruits streaming into St. Louis. Charles spent most of his time in the field now, returning saddle-stained and muddy long after dark. Colonel Riordan was in charge of all training. The men were learning to take orders, to form in skirmish line, to fire by volley, to serve cannon at three rounds a minute, timed. They came knowing how to shoot—Charles said that was in their blood—and now they were learning to swing a saber from horseback, to use a bayonet. They were learning to trust their officers, one another, themselves. They were becoming soldiers. One day he came in laughing, exultant, his face alight.

"They cheered me, Jessie! Can you believe it?" It had been impulse, contagious, rippling from unit to unit, a gathering roar of fealty and esprit. "They'll be as good as any army in the world," he told her. "I mean it!" But they needed another month—a month at least. . . .

She wished with all her heart that he could bring Washington along as well. The government remained in myopic panic, overstocking the eastern armies at the expense of the West. But Lincoln was a *western* man—he should understand. He simply wasn't being told of western threats, western needs. Powerful personages—yes, and that went for Montgomery Blair as well—had his ear; they were blocking Charles' messages.

She tried to explain to Ed; he listened noncommittally, spreading marmalade on a piece of cornbread. What he should understand was the dilemma they faced. While Charles was getting the army ready, the impression had overtaken the Missouri countryside that the Confederates were going to win—and this, of course, had galvanized the guerrillas into new action. Farmers by day, marauders by night, they wreaked outrage upon outrage; and each depredation served to convince more Union men that safety lay with the other side. She had monitored the reports that streamed into headquarters. A man tarred and feathered at Grand Pass. In Liberty, a former mayor named Caldwell horsewhipped in the square when he said he sympathized with the South but thought secession a mistake. In Carroll County nightriders barred the doors and fired a barn; the trapped horses screamed for hours. Men settled old grudges and vented old hatreds; they flogged men and raped women, plundered and stole. Union supporters were pulling out, secessionists were already established on their places.

Charles had small troop contingents who rode themselves ragged in pursuit of the guerrillas, but even when they caught men with weapons in hand, instead of following their inclination to string their prisoners to the nearest tree, the soldiers must take them to a magistrate, knowing that they'd likely be free within the hour. The magistrates had been amply warned—death threats nailed to their doors, shots fired through their windows—and the soldiers couldn't stay to protect them. There was the dilemma. Soon the main army would be ready to move, but what was to happen in the meanwhile? And all of it flowed directly from Lyon's impulsive, disastrous attack.

"Jessie," Ed said suddenly, "in all truth, couldn't Charles have reinforced Lyon?"

Her head came up at that. "Frank Blair has really been at you, hasn't he?"

"It's not just Frank. They say—"

"I know what *they say,*" she broke in crossly, "—they say a lot of things, different things on different days. They weren't sitting up there at Charles' desk with the decisions to make."

Ed bit his lip. "They say Lyon was begging for reinforcements and Charles never even answered him."

"What?" She gave a short gasp of amazement. "That's simply not true. Charles ordered him in no uncertain terms to fall back on Rolla. I wrote out the order myself, I can show it to you."

"But then—why didn't he publish his orders?"

She looked down. "He said Lyon died bravely, a hero's death. And nothing must detract from it."

Ed set down his cup with a smart click and sighed. "Ah Charles. The last cavalier. It'll be the death of him yet—do you know that?"

"It's been the *life* of him—I know that . . ."

"Touché." He smiled, again turned solemn. "But still . . . there weren't other troops? here and there?"

She bit off a sharp reply, composed herself. "Ed," she said, "you know, you really can't trust what Frank Blair says."

He looked surprised. "Why, I've known him for years—we worked together to swing the nomination to Lincoln."

"Frank and I played together as children. But he's our enemy now."

"Oh Jessie, you don't mean that."

"I'm afraid I do."

Ed fiddled with a spoon, looking unhappy. "He said there's been some—friction . . ."

"Indeed there has."

A week ago Frank had brushed by Gaines and flung his riding crop on Charles' desk and demanded to know why Cale Sterrett was in jail. Jessie had recognized the name at once: Sterrett was one of Frank's ward captains.

"Because he was picked up three hours after curfew, trying to leave the city without a pass," Charles had said calmly.

"What difference does that make? He's a good Union man."

"Is he? In fact, he's a big slave owner."

"Well, Jesus Christ, owning slaves doesn't make him a rebel!" Frank's face was flushed; the big vein in his right temple had begun to throb. How tired she'd grown of Frank Blair's opinions, Frank Blair's drinking, Frank Blair's rages! He'd hated martial law from the moment Charles had necessarily imposed it on the city, because any of his friends who ran afoul of it expected him to rescue them; and Charles wouldn't bend the rules for anyone. Missouri was full of loyal men who were friendly to slavery, he was saying; the trick was to hold their loyalty to the Union. Curfews and soldiers questioning anyone they pleased were making them feel as if they maybe belonged on the other side.

"Hell's bells, the city isn't in any danger anyway."

"Sam Rogers should be here to answer that," Charles snapped. The tentmaker's factory had burned after Lyon's defeat. In the morning his body had been found inside, his throat cut.

Blair dismissed this with a wave of his hand: "Rogers asked for it—running around bragging about how much he was doing for the Union."

Charles looked at him—that hard, level gaze. He said: "It doesn't prove your point very well, does it?"

"I'm not saying there's no secessionist sympathy here, Frémont. But the danger cuts both ways. You're driving good men out of the Union."

She shook her head angrily. That was exactly the line Governor Gamble had taken when he refused to impose martial law throughout the state: You'll alienate people. Timid, temporizing old fool. Chaos had followed.

"Now, Cale Sterrett," Frank was saying. "I don't deny he's got some tender feelings for the South. But in the end he's loyal, and that's what counts. Now you've put that loyalty to some strain."

"It's been strained all along," Charles said dryly. "He's behind some of the guerrilla raids that are cutting down good Union men out in the country."

"Sterrett a *guerrilla*? You're crazy!"

"Supporting them. Look, Frank, these night-riding scum who go out and do the dirty work can't operate on their own. They've got to have horses, guns, money. They've got to have protection. Why do you think nobody ever sees them, knows who they are? It's not just fear of the men themselves. Powerful people support them—powerful people *want* them out riding. Without the Cale Sterretts behind them, we'd be catching guerrillas right and left."

Frank's mouth had drawn down to a hard, straight slit, his eyes narrowed. "Can you prove that on Sterrett?"

"I've no courtroom proof, if that's what you mean."

"Then Goddamnit, don't say it!"

Charles' hands were flat on his desk, but the knuckles were white. "Frank, I don't *have* to prove it. Under martial law I can try him for curfew violation—and believe me, I will."

"And set another man against us! You're so Goddamned pure, you two—everyone who's not a thousand percent for Frémont, anyone who isn't rigid and holy enough is the enemy. Measure up to The Pathfinder's purity or get out! Well, let me tell you, a hell of a lot of 'em'll get out before they'll knuckle under to you."

"That's where you're wrong. The Sterretts will go, anyway—they're already disloyal. I'm not interested in begging men to be loyal—I want to show them that disloyalty's expensive."

"Now you listen to me, mister—"

"No—you listen!" Charles was on his feet. "Don't come in here and lecture me. You want to be helpful for a change, use your family influence in Washington to get me the means to rebuild the army your fine friend Lyon destroyed . . ."

"Don't talk of Lyon to me," Blair shouted. "You're not fit to speak his name!" He snatched the crop from the desk, and for an instant Jessie thought he was going to hit Charles with it. His forehead was slick with sweat, his eyes held that fevered, baleful glare; Jessie could smell the whiskey now. "Nat Lyon's a hero—something you'll never be, no matter how much you puff yourself up! And the men who died with him, they were St. Louis men—they'll never forgive you here. Every time your martial law roughs them up, they hate you all the more."

"Yes, and you're encouraging them," Jessie burst out. "You're whipping up opposition to us!"

He turned to her, his mouth slack with contempt. "No, you don't, Mrs. General Jessie. You've got it backwards. The worst thing that can happen to a man in St. Louis is to be known as a friend of mine—the Frémonts'll fix him for sure! Look at Loudermilk."

"Loudermilk is a thief," Charles said.

"Thief? Jesus, the contracts *you've* let are a disgrace—you're going to answer for them in court yet."

Jessie was wild at this. Of course some of their contracts were faulty—who could build an army under such pressure and make certain every transaction would satisfy the auditor general? But to openly countenance plain peculation . . .

"Frank," she cried, "you care nothing about the war, do you? It doesn't matter that Loudermilk's a thief and Sterrett a traitor—just so they can deliver! It's all politics to you—"

"Don't talk to me about politics, lady. I *am* the politics in this town. And more than that." He turned to Charles, malevolent and savage. "We'd better get this straight, once and for all. I've got a lot of support here in the Mississippi Valley. I'm going to ride it right into the White House when Lincoln's done—and I'm not going to let any tinpot armchair general challenge my authority in the meantime. Now I'm warning you—stay out of the road!"

For a terrible moment Jessie was afraid that Charles would hit him. In a very low, flat voice, he said: "Get out of this headquarters. That is a direct order."

Frank stood up. He leaned on Charles' desk. Jessie could see his mustache quivering. "Worst mistake I ever made was putting you in this job. But I'm going to remedy that right now."

"I will put you in irons if you interfere with me again," Charles said softly.

At the door Frank turned. "There's an old saying in my family, General," he said. " 'When the Blairs go in for a fight, they go in for a funeral.' You remember that . . ."

She looked up. William Dorsheimer, Charles' junior aide, was standing in the doorway now. He nodded to Ed Davis, said to her, "The General would like to see you both, ma'am."

Charles came around his desk holding several sheets of paper. His face was animate with that contained excitement she'd learned to recognize: he'd decided on something. Something momentous and bold. She knew it before he spoke.

"I've made up my mind," he told them. "It's out of hand—the guerrillas are destroying the state county by county, looting and killing, chewing up Union authority . . . I'm putting the whole state under martial law."

"Thank God," Jessie murmured.

"But Charles," Ed was saying, "can you do that?"

"Of course I can. I've got the troops to back it up."

"Well, I meant *legal* authority."

"If you mean do Missouri statutes permit a general to assume power normally held on the civil side—no, probably they don't. They don't permit the actions the secessionists are taking, either."

"But the governor—"

"Look, I've asked him repeatedly to take this action—it's well within the governor's emergency powers—but he's too spineless for the job. So now I'm doing it."

Ed cocked his head at him. "And what'll you do when you catch them?"

Charles raised the paper and read: *All persons who shall be taken with arms in their hands within these lines shall be tried by court-martial and, if found guilty, will be executed by firing squad.*

"*Shot?*" Ed exclaimed. "That's a bit drastic, isn't it?"

"They're shooting *our* people, right and left. You haven't been out here on the griddle, Ed. Let's see how they like the other side of the fire."

Jessie was still watching him intently. "There's more," she said. "Isn't there?"

"As a matter of fact, there is." He raised the sheet of paper again. *The property, real and personal, of all persons in the state of Missouri who shall take up arms against the United States, or who shall be directly proven to have taken an active part with their enemies in the field, is declared to be confiscated to the public use*—he paused, and looked full at Jessie, his eyes glinting—*and their slaves, if they have any, are hereby declared free men.*

He lowered the draft, and there was a little silence.

"Oh, Charles," she said, and felt her eyes fill. She believed she loved him more at that moment than she had in their whole tempestuous life together. "That's it—that goes right to the heart of it all."

"Gosh, I don't know, Charles . . ." Ed Davis was rubbing the side of his jaw in alarm. "When you talk about *emancipation*—that's a very touchy issue back in Washington, you know."

"No more touchy than it is right here."

". . . But have you the power?"

"Ed, I am Commander of the Department of the West."

"Yes, but have you the *right*?"

Charles' head came up. "The moral right, you mean?" He shrugged. "That's something every man will have to decide for himself."

"But then why raise the issue? The administration has a—"

"Because," Charles broke in, and for the first time she felt the heat in his voice, "these people know they can go out burning and murdering all night long and then sleep all day—because their *slaves* remain at home to do the farmwork, that's why! That's what's at the core of the trouble. And it's always been the moral right they want to forget, back in Washington City. Ed, I'm fighting a *war* out here! Or trying to, anyway . . ."

"But emancipation isn't a war aim." Ed was leaning forward, troubled and intent. "We're fighting this war to keep the South from destroying the Union."

"True," Jessie answered. "But what's *behind* the South's intention? What has torn the nation apart for forty years, set state against state, friend against friend, brother against brother?"

"Seward won't like it," Ed mused. "And neither will Cameron."

"They don't have to deal with my problems," Charles came back. "If they did I expect they'd whistle a different tune."

"Charles, you want to remember that Governor Gamble is close to the Attorney General. They're brothers-in-law."

Jessie glanced at her husband. Edward Bates was a St. Louis man—Lincoln had named him Attorney General. And of course there was Montgomery Blair . . .

"Bates doesn't understand the situation here very well," Charles said. "Or he doesn't want to. . . . The trouble is, Lincoln listens to the wrong people most of the time, if you want my opinion. He doesn't think enough for himself."

"He's not the down-home bumpkin a lot of people take him for," Ed said carefully. "This business with Seward—you know about that?"

Charles shook his head.

"Well, it seems Seward as much as tried to take over the government. Yes! Considered Lincoln incompetent, you see, and envisioned a sort of super managing director—himself, of course. I've got this on very good authority. Seward drew up a plan on paper and presented it to Lincoln; actually expecting him to be grateful, you know. Old Abe put the kibosh on *that* in a hurry! But the marvel is that he was big enough to put Seward in his place—and at the same time recognize his value, keep him in the administration. Seward has no illusions about who's in charge now, and he's been making himself mighty useful ever since."

"Too bad the President's not so forceful when it comes to settling on military commanders or strategy, much less the problems out here," Charles said dryly.

"You must remember, he has problems everywhere."

"Obviously. But here's where it counts. *Here's* where the war's going to be won. Not in the Shenandoah or Virginia—here, the Mississippi Valley, the deep South. Ask Grant, ask Cump Sherman; they'll tell you the same thing. They've agreed with me from the start." He smiled somberly. "Don't worry, Ed. The President gave me *carte blanche.* He told me it was up to me to save Missouri, and he wouldn't try to tell me how to do it. I'd say that's authority enough, wouldn't you?"

"I suppose so," Ed said slowly. "But all the same . . . don't you think you'd better clear something as important as this with Frank?"

"No!" There was such hard force in his voice that the room shook. Ed, staring at him, had gone pale. Jessie had seen this expression on Charles' face only once before—during the court-martial confrontation with Kearny—and it made her pulse race. "Frank Blair has done nothing but defy me, undermine my authority. From now on he will stay out of my way or I'll run over him! He has no say here in anything at all! I have the authority—and by God, I will assume the responsibility . . ."

There was a short silence. Ed Davis folded his hands. "It's your Department," he said.

"You bet." Charles turned to her then, his face calm. "Let's get this set in type. I want it on the streets in one hour."

The second day, she saw, was going to be much worse than the first. She had left St. Louis before dawn the previous morning and now her train was in Ohio, slowing as it bit into the first grade of the Appalachians. Cinders streamed past the open windows. The sun came up; it was going to be another scorcher. Her hair was already damp and the black linen traveling dress bound her like a corset, twisted and intolerably wrinkled. The rhythm of the wheels half-mesmerized her, jolting in and out of her thoughts: *trickery-TACK, liberty-BLACK, bivou-atTACK, jittery-bickery-bigotry. . . .* There was another burst of drunken laughter from the other end of the car, and across from her the bald fat man slept, his snores like a death rattle. The baby in her arms stirred fretfully and she hummed a lullaby, rocking to the train's rhythm, thinking of the White House, trying not to think of James Polk's cold, forbidding face long ago, telling herself resolutely, urgently: You must not lose your objectivity this time, your poise and balance; everything hinges on the *manner* in which you present our case, your timing and grace; you are your father's daughter, you know how these things work, you must not let yourself forget that—above all, you must not lose your poise . . .

There was a private car forward occupied by several Chicago merchants, war profiteers in checkered vests and mouse-colored derby hats; they kept sending the porters out for whiskey and beer at station stops. The cars in the rear were troop cars, crammed with soldiers rolling east—instead of west, where they were needed. There were soldiers in her car, too. The conductor had led her to her seat at Union Station and then one wounded man after another had crept painfully aboard. Soldiers going home from war. As they rolled across southern Illinois bound for Washington, she had watched a boy feeling the stump of his leg as if he couldn't believe his loss. He'd caught her eye and given her a hot angry look that had shamed her. When she'd glanced covertly at him again he was gazing out at a solitary mule in a cornfield, tears silvery on his cheeks. One of that fool Lyon's men, perhaps—she thrust the thought away. It had all been Lyon's doing . . . She had remained alone, her provision basket beside her, but in the night when the train had shaken to a stop in some dark, lost station, she had felt a hand on hers.

"Ma'am, kin I sit alongside you?"

An innocent face, overlarge eyes, straw-colored hair neatly braided. The girl wasn't a day over seventeen; a baby was cradled in her left arm and she was carrying a carpetbag.

"Of course, dear."

Her name was Ella Reeve; the baby was Benjy Junior: five months, fourteen days. Benjy Senior had gone off to the war and died. With Lyon? Jessie wondered. No, he'd died of cholera in some recruiting camp only ten days after he'd joined.

"I am sorry, dear," Jessie said.

The girl nodded. "They don't want me at home." The words fell out flatly; she was going back anyway, to Pennsylvania. "Paw says he has too many mouths to feed already; now I'm bringing him a new one."

Jessie slept then, and awakened a little after dawn. Ella was rocking the baby, who had begun to cry, and she gave him her breast, but he continued to cry. The fat man woke up and glared at them. Jessie glared back and he looked away.

"Let me hold him," Jessie said. She took the baby and rocked him, humming gently, and after a while he quieted, watching her with wide eyes. His little body was like a furnace in her arms; a damp spot spread on her dress where he rested. Ella had fallen asleep. The engine huffed and growled up ahead, the rhythm slower but more insistent as the train climbed into the Appalachians, straining, *rickety-liberty-trickery* . . . Out there, beyond those dense green hills, mighty armies were massing, moving toward terrible battles; it seemed impossible, a nightmare vision. . . . She had held Lily in her arms like this, as Charles proudly spread on her bed the flag that had flown from the highest mountain in the Rockies; and the impossible stillness of little Benton's body—*no,* she willed that thought away, fiercely, losing herself in the iron clamor of the wheels. Think about that magic moment in the Brants' living room; think about the inlet at St. Michaels, the geese soaring into the marsh in a scissored storm of wings, think about Charles riding in that night at Boone Creek in the rain, singing a snatch of song—think about anything but that single sheet of parchment bearing the presidential seal. . . .

It had all begun so promisingly. St. Louis had reacted to the proclamation with a rush of relief and approval—everyone sick of guerrilla outrages agreed that striking at slavery as the cornerstone of rebellion was crucial. Next day congratulatory letters and telegrams began to pour into the headquarters telegraph office in the basement—an approval that swelled into a roar of national acclamation. No single event had been received with such spontaneous enthusiasm since it had all begun at Sumter. There were torchlight processions in New England, huge rallies in New York and Philadelphia; recruiting everywhere doubled and redoubled; the mighty newspapers of the Northeast printed the proclamation on their front pages, and supported it with laudatory editorials: General Frémont had given point and focus to the war effort, he had united all citizens of the loyal states; he had rooted the national purpose in principle . . .

Only Frank Blair attacked the proclamation, raging that it had been issued without his permission, calling it a sensational political maneuver shrewdly calculated to draw attention away from Frémont's gross incompetence as a field commander and regain his fading prestige in the Republican camp—and the blatant viciousness of that stung; but his jeremiad was drowned in the mounting waves of praise. Charles Sumner of Massachusetts, who had finally resumed his seat after that savage caning by Congressman Preston Brooks on the Senate floor, telegraphed his warm approbation; and Simon Cameron, who had campaigned so vigorously for Charles in '56 and was now serving as Secretary of War, sent a highly congratulatory wire—clearly official administrative approval.

She had entered Charles' office to find him joking with Robert Gaines and John Howard. She had not heard him laugh like that for months. He waved another flimsy at her. "Listen to this, honey. *Am publishing in today's editions tribute to man who has made our war aims clear at last. Proclamation master stroke, setting precisely right tone, attitude, tactics. New York is cheering—Frémont is name on all men's lips. Your policy shames laggards in administration who draw back from sounding clarion call that summons men to nobler purposes.* Who do you think that's from?" She shook her head in happy wonder. "Horace Greeley, that's who!" He caught her up and swung her around merrily, while his aides looked on with shocked amusement. "*Now* what do you think of your grizzled old explorer?"

Then, six days later, the letter came from the White House; it was in Lincoln's hand—she recognized it immediately. She saw a shadow of perplexity cross Charles' face as he read.

"He doesn't understand at all." He bit his lower lip, staring at the paper. "Thinks if we shoot guerrillas taken red-handed, the rebels'll retaliate by killing Union prisoners of war. . . . But that's ridiculous—that would be barbaric. We're not taking action against legitimate *soldiers*—we're after the irregular, the criminal! How can a few months in Washington so isolate him from reality?"

She found she'd been holding her breath. "What about—the emancipation clause?" she whispered.

"He doesn't like that, either. Not one bit. Says *it will alarm our Southern Union friends and turn them against us; perhaps ruin our rather fair prospects in Kentucky."* He lowered the letter, his face grim, while she watched him.

"He wants me to withdraw it."

"*Withdraw* it—!"

"Yes. Wants me to do it on my own responsibility." He slapped the stiff paper sheet hard on the desk. "Damn! He's a decent man, but he doesn't understand anything. To withdraw it now will destroy all Union authority in Missouri—the atrocities'll double."

"Yes, of course, Charles, and the best minds in the country are with us—Greeley, Sumner, all the rest of them. What'll Greeley say if we back off now? What about Simon Cameron?"

"Exactly! It's folly—I'll be damned if I'll do it. He has the power to order it done, and that is just what he'll have to do. I won't compound his folly. If he wants this proclamation rescinded, he's going to have to *order* me to do it—I'm not going to do it on my own."

"Frank's behind this," she muttered.

"Isn't he though." Charles glanced at her. "Montgomery's coming out."

"Montgomery Blair? Coming here? Why?"

"A general inspection trip. With Meigs." His lip curled. "To check on the overland mails. That's what the wire said, anyway."

"He's coming to snoop," she said grimly. "You know the kind of report he'll write."

"Of course. He'll support Frank. What else?"

Montgomery Blair with his cool gray eyes and distant smile; and his brother-in-law, Quartermaster General M. C. Meigs. That meant—that almost certainly meant the administration had decided to withdraw its support from Major General John C. Frémont. "I think now that's why they sent Ed Davis out."

He struck his thigh in frustration. "They've got Lincoln boxed in—I'm convinced of it. They're simply not letting him see the truth of things out here. It's hopeless! If only your father were there . ."

"I could go," she said suddenly. He stared at her, biting his lip. "Why not? I could explain it to the President—the need to rebuild the Western army, the campaign against Price, your strategy to encircle Memphis with Grant. . . . You must write him a letter first, explaining it all, then let me put it right in his hands—no one else's. And I'll be there on the spot to answer any questions."

"Perhaps," Charles said gravely. "First, he'll order my proclamation canceled. He's going to do that anyway—his mind's set on that. Then, once he's had his way, maybe he'll listen to me on the military operations." He hesitated, peering at her. "You'll have to handle him carefully, though. Ed's right—he's no prairie clown. When I talked to him at the White House he was—well, not quite the same man I'd talked to before."

"Presidents never are," she answered. "I'll be careful. But he needs to hear the other side of the story for a change."

It took her a couple of days to get ready. The President's order canceling the proclamation arrived and was released, to a whirlwind of resentment and rage. The northern liberals were wild, the press scathing over the government's craven repudiation. Up in Boston James Russell Lowell, the venerable editor of the *Atlantic Monthly,* cried: "How many times are we to save Kansas and lose our self-respect?" Blair and Meigs were on their way—maybe they even carried a recall order with them. There was no time to lose. Charles drafted a careful review of his plans and strategy, which she folded into her case. And now she sat listening to the rhythms of the wheels as the crowded train labored into the Appalachians, a strange baby sighing at her breast . . .

Ella and Benjy left the train somewhere in Pennsylvania. Impulsively Jessie embraced the girl and gave her a gold piece. "Don't be frightened by your father, dear," she said. "When he sees the baby he'll change." By late afternoon the train was running downhill through western Maryland with a following sun lighting the rolling hills. She rose, feeling stiff and clumsy, washed her face and brushed out her hair, sponged the black dress. She was running on nerve now, she knew. But that was how it would have to be.

It was nearly nine that night when the train squealed to a stop in Union Station. Edward Coles, an old friend from New York, and his daughter Peggy were waiting for her on the platform. He was a judge now and looked very distinguished. Then she was hugging Peggy, conscious of her age, her weariness, her own disheveled state. Late-summer heat clung to the Capital. At the splendid new Willard Hotel she paused in the lobby to send a short note to the White House explaining her mission and asking when she might see the President. The Willard—wonder of wonders—actually had a bath connected to every room. There was a warm message of welcome from the manager, there were fresh cut flowers in her suite. With an almost tearful sense of anticipation she asked a maid to fill the tub. She was at the door of the suite thanking the Coles for meeting her when the messenger she'd sent to the White House came bounding up the broad staircase and handed her an envelope marked The White House. With a feeling of uneasiness she drew out a card on which was written in a strong hand: *Now. At once. A. Lincoln.* There was nothing more.

"But," she said, faltering, "I can't go like *this* . . ." She could hear the water splashing into the tub.

Judge Coles took the card from her hand. "You can't keep the President waiting, Jessie. He's under tremendous pressure."

He was right, of course. But why this urgent summons? Her uneasiness deepened. There was no need for such haste. "Would you come with me, Judge?"

"Of course, Jessie."

It was three blocks to the White House. The streets seemed bright as day under the brassy new gas lamps; stately landaus rolled by, sleek phaetons drawn by matched bays, couriers in spanking new uniforms galloped by carrying important messages; diners in fine clothes emerged from fancy restaurants. Washington looked sprucer, more bustling, richer than she remembered. Did war do this? As she hurried along with her hand on the judge's arm, the oppressive sense of dread left her; she was filled with ebullient confidence: Let's waste no time, let's get matters settled; she could rest later—and if that was the cost of participation in great events, she would pay it gladly enough. As they turned between Treasury and the White House, she decided the President's urgency was a good omen; he must be eager for information that came straight from the source. Charles was Commander of the West, the man on whom the war depended, and she stood at his right hand. Lincoln was Commander in Chief—but he depended on them as much as they on him; that was a point that probably should be made during their meeting . . .

John Nicolay was waiting for them at the north entrance, his manner rather remote and disdainful. They went along the great Cross Hall to the familiar Red Room, in which the walls and furniture were covered with the same rich crimson damask. The vivid color had always pleased her, but tonight it made her think disconcertingly of blood. The secretary disappeared and she and Judge Coles stood mutely; they were like capped candles, she thought. She saw Dolley Madison's portrait with her rouged cheeks, the one she herself had saved when the British were coming. How the old lady had loved to tell that story—

The half-doors to the state dining room opened slowly and the President entered. He left the doors ajar. Jessie saw one of them open farther; someone was standing there, then, posted to listen. She thought it a curiously hostile gesture and glanced quickly at the President. He seemed even taller than she'd remembered; there were deep new lines in his homely, unsmiling face. His black suit was shabby and ill-fitting, but there was an aura of authority about him, a supreme quiet confidence; she had forgotten what force the office conferred. As Judge Coles withdrew to the oval Blue Room next door, she started to ask after Mrs. Lincoln, but the President gave her no opportunity.

"Well?" he said without preamble.

"Mr. President, General Frémont asked me to deliver this letter to you personally." She started to explain its purpose, but his large, bony hand was out and she gave it to him, and broke off, shaken at his rudeness. There wasn't a trace of the famous country geniality. Without a word he moved off under one of the chandeliers and began reading. His mind had already been turned against Charles, then. Had it? She glanced away uneasily—and caught her own reflection in a convex mirror set in a gilt frame. Her father's face looked out at her; in a flash she saw how she would look when she was old. Deliberately she studied herself. Her body was thickening a bit as her father's had, her face had filled—the slender, vivacious girl of C Street was gone forever. Her dress was rumpled and dusty, she should have redone her hair—would have if there'd only been time. But surely he wouldn't take offense—he'd known she had come directly to him . . .

Lincoln went on reading. Standing there silently, waiting, her ebullient excitement deserted her; she knew that she simply must sit down. After another tense ten minutes, even though he had still not asked her to, she stepped back and seated herself on the crimson sofa. The President seemed oblivious.

At last he dropped the letter on a small table. "This is all very well, but it's nothing new. He discussed all this when he was here." He stroked his coat lapels. "*Missouri* is the problem, Mrs. Frémont. I fail to see why the General has so much trouble grasping that simple fact."

"We—he *is* dealing with Missouri," she protested. "He's *saving* Missouri for the Union. That's why I'm here—to give you an accurate report on what he's doing there under appalling conditions—"

She broke off. He was pacing restlessly, frowning into space; he wasn't listening to her.

"I'd hoped General Frémont would have taken the field by now," he said after a moment. "It's been almost eight weeks since I sent him out there. We need to turn things around." He stared ahead gloomily. "General Lyon was a great loss to us. A great loss . . ."

"Sir, my husband's had to rebuild the army—it was virtually shattered after the—the engagement at Wilson's Creek. A great deal of its equipment was lost." He was watching her now, with what appeared to be a puzzled half-smile, and it irritated her deeply. "There were the fortifications for St. Louis, Cairo had to be held at all cost, the guerrillas have been a continual danger . . ." She added carefully: "That's why General Frémont wanted me to come in person. We fear you're not being given a true—that is, a comprehensive—picture of western affairs."

His heavy brows rose. "How could it be more comprehensive? I hear from General Frémont almost daily—always to the effect that he wants more support. He seems unaware that there are any theaters other than his own."

She felt oddly disoriented, faintly dizzy, and gripped the arm of the sofa. If he was getting their letters, if he understood the situation . . .

"I support him to the extent I can, madam. With that he must make do. The Armies of the Potomac and the Cumberland must have priority; the Capital must be secure. Anyway, his problems are not just men and arms. There are those dubious contracts, the excesses of martial law, his quarrels with good Unionists, influential men . . ."

Stung by the implications she said: "If I may say so, Mr. President, that's a highly biased view."

"I have complete confidence in Mr. Blair, madam."

"—Frank Blair is an arrogant, vindictive man," she cried all at once, "—a braggart and a fool! He will say or do anything to destroy Charles, he said as much!"

Lincoln had stopped short; the deep-set dark eyes bored into hers with an expression she couldn't read. "As a matter of fact, I was referring to the Postmaster General," he said.

Montgomery. Of course! How could she have made such a stupid blunder? "I'm sorry, sir," she stammered, "I misunderstood you."

"So I see."

"But that still doesn't alter the fact that Frank Blair is a headstrong, self-serving opportunist who has opposed my husband from the very beginning!"

The President shot her a warning glance. "Frank Blair," he said very slowly, "is chairman of the Military Affairs Committee in the House—same position your own Daddy held on the Senate side. I depend on Frank to hold the Congress in line behind this war."

"But that doesn't give him the right to spread slanderous—"

"Just a moment." One arm reached abruptly toward her, dropped back to his side. "I gather Frank and General Frémont are at hammer-and-tongs with each other. I'm tired of the whole subject—I haven't time to monitor personal wrangles. Both of them should put their energies to constructive uses. There is no place for that kind of squabbling in this crisis."

"If that's your feeling, sir," she said, knowing she was only compounding the error, but unable to stop herself now, "why do you let Montgomery Blair come out to spy on us?"

His face took on an immense hardness that shook her. At last he said: "That is a contemptible statement, madam, which I shall ignore—except to say that my right to send my cabinet members where I choose and for such purposes as I may decide is absolute, and I will accept no questioning."

He'd misunderstood; she was in a panic. "Mr. President," she stammered, "please forgive me—I didn't mean to question your authority. I only meant that others are abusing their ties to your office. . . . It is not to your advantage that General Frémont's relationship with you has been undermined—"

"No, madam," he cried all at once, "he has undermined himself! The General should never have dragged the Negro into the war. This isn't a war against slavery—it's a war to preserve the Union of the United States!"

There it was. Instantly she saw the danger. He had been rude, irritable, even disdainful, but now he was furious—and the difference was frightening. It was the proclamation, then, that had enraged him. And the proclamation was theirs—it couldn't be attributed to Washington's indifference or the malice of the Blairs. It meant that a loaded cannon was aimed at them. He stood there glaring down at her, hopelessly out of his depth in coping with the eastern generals and the scheming politicians, apparently unable to understand—but he was still the President and it was well within his power to take St. Louis from them. She thought of Charles swinging down from the saddle, boots spattered with mud, his eyes shining. *As good as any army in the world* . . . and this gaunt, implacable, terrifying man could destroy it all with one word. At once everything changed: she had come to inform him; instead she must fight him.

"Mr. President," she said very quietly, "the war *must* be against slavery. It's the root issue. It's the single rock on which everything has split apart."

He had regained his calm. He stopped pacing and leaned back, hooking his elbows on the handsome marble mantelpiece President Monroe had brought over from France. His wrists shot out of his sleeves, as heavy as oak.

"It is the cause," he said, "not the objective. The South's quarrel with us was over slavery, but ours with the South is whether we'll let it break the Union. Let me put it plainly, madam. If I could save the Union without freeing *any* slave, I would do it; and if I could save it by freeing *all* the slaves, I would do it; and if I could do it by freeing some and leaving others alone, I would also do that. I would welcome the South back this evening, slaves and all, if it would come."

"I see. But you don't expect the South to return without coercion—and I can't believe you would let a coerced South *keep* its slaves so that the quarrel would start all over again."

"The issues are separate, madam," he said sharply. "If the South continues to resist, it may well become both right and politic to declare all slaves free. But not now! Now the issues are separate, and I intend to keep them so. This war is going badly for us right now—who knows it better than you and General Frémont? I do not intend to run the risk of losing Missouri and Kentucky."

"With all due respect, that is a mistake, Mr. President." His expression turned grim and forbidding again, and she hurried on, fearful but determined. "We can hold Missouri—and Kentucky cannot go without Missouri."

"In fact, Kentucky reacted violently to Frémont's proclamation."

"The slaveholders did, of course—they caused the uproar. But you'd be amazed at how favorably the very people you're afraid of losing in Missouri reacted to the proclamation. People everywhere are recognizing at last that the real issue is slavery—and that it's wrong, *morally* wrong . . ."

Politicians! Why had she ever admired them so? There was principle and there was expediency in every turn of life—but it was *principles* that men died for, not the temporizing reciprocities of lawyers and merchants . . . "Don't you see?" she cried. "It's the moral force in the issue that gives the true edge to the sword. Moral issues are what galvanize people—make them willing to fight. Why does the cause of the North lack fire? Why is the performance of our troops lackluster? Why do people hold back? Because their hearts haven't been engaged! Because so far it's been a political war, a governmental war. But if you put before us the great issue of simple good, simple right, against evil, you'll stir us to the heights. *Slavery is evil*—raise that banner, Mr. President, and you will rally the North . . ."

"My, my," he said. His elbows were still on the mantel; deliberately he hooked a heel on a polished andiron, watching her with slow, sardonic amusement. "My, my. You are quite the female politician, aren't you?"

She stared at him, shocked and raging. She had believed with all her heart that marriage should be a working partnership, that women could serve the nation as ably as men; she had risked everything for principle, offered up her marriage and her children and her very health on the altar of moral probity, personal honor—and this was her reward: to be called a female politician by none other than the President of the United States . . . The dizziness was worse; insects kept dancing in the air in front of her, black against the blood-red walls—they were in her eyes. *No:* she would not faint, she would not give way, no matter what. Her boots pinched her travel-swollen feet unmercifully, her collar was choking her; if only she could get some air!

He had thrust himself violently away from the mantel and was saying with a singular harshness: "There's not a single new thought in all you've said, madam. It's standard radical Republican cant, the constant theme of the abolitionists, of all those men of big voices and no responsibility. But it's not moral sanctity that drives them—do not delude yourself! They want an easy way out: Strike a great blow and the people will arise at once and end it as if by magic!"

He shook his head slowly, a look of heavy contempt staining the gaunt, expressive face. "But *you* know all about radical Republican cant. You know what they want—what'll please 'em."

Her hand went to her mouth; she shook her head. "I don't know what you mean."

"I think you do," he said knowingly. "I think you understand the radical sentiment and how to exploit it. That explains General Frémont and his proclamation quite adequately."

"No," she breathed. "That it was nothing more than a trick, a political gambit? No—"

"You're unaware, are you, of the dissatisfaction among radicals with my policies? The growing clamor for change—none of that has penetrated Missouri, eh?"

"Well—"

"But you did notice the hosannas of praise for the proclamation—you didn't miss that?"

"Well, of course—but that only proves my point. There's a hunger—"

"No. It only shows a difference of opinion. *You* are listening to the zealots. But there's no evidence the average man wants any more war than necessary—and certainly none that he wants to punish the South for its sins. No, that's the self-righteous Senator Sumner and his Abolitionist crowd. And you've made yourselves quite their darlings. I'd say that's what this really is all about."

"No, sir, it is not."

Very softly he said: "Then why wouldn't General Frémont withdraw the proclamation on his own responsibility when I asked him to?"

"Because . . . because it would have destroyed the Department's authority. And it was wrong. It was a mistake."

"No. Mistake or not, that decision had already been made. General Frémont knew that I would rescind his order if he didn't. So why did he refuse my civil request? Surely because his eyes were cocked on the crowd."

"Sir, that's not true."

"Will you sit there and tell me, madam," he said slowly, "that the rapturous praise of Horace Greeley and the other radicals had *nothing* to do with his refusal?"

She couldn't answer. It was as if her mind had stopped. No, they didn't want to shatter that warm approval, not after the cruel defeats they'd suffered over the past ten years, not after the desperate effort to hold St. Louis, not when they knew they were right! But the President's wish commanded, she knew that from the faraway days in Mr. T's study. . . . She saw him watching her now. He nodded slowly, the sardonic smile at the edge of his grim face again. Was it cynical knowledge of the human heart or sadness? Oh, he was so *wrong* here! He would discover it all too late. . . . She caught her breath, enraged beyond bearing by the sense that she had betrayed herself—and Charles.

He was wrong, she told him then in a loud, ringing voice. Wrong to suspect them, wrong in listening to their enemies, wrong in not recognizing the West's importance, wrong, wrong, wrong!—on the slavery issue. "Can't you see?" she cried. "You're making the Union vulnerable. We could lose this war, because there's no transcendent *idea,* no force behind us, no cutting edge." It amazed her that he could be so obtuse. "Can't you understand?—you're making *yourself* vulnerable . . ."

He stopped pacing and turned toward her. His voice was cold and utterly calm. "Now we come to it, I expect. General Frémont came close to this office once. Might he just be the man to take advantage of that vulnerability you scent so strongly?"

She was nonplussed. "But—we're on the same side," she protested. "We only want—"

"To achieve, if I must be explicit, what he couldn't achieve when he ran himself for this office."

Fresh anger drove her to her feet, her exhaustion forgotten. "That is the most undeserved, contemptible thing you could have said!" she cried. The harsh injustice of the insinuation blazed into new rage, higher, hotter, until the room seemed flooded with white glare crashing off the red walls; she could hardly see his face through the dancing black figures. The enormity!

"But he could," she cried. "He never would, but he could! He is a man—he acts, he commits, he sees the real enemy, and he has the courage to strike. He would never, ever do it, his honor would forbid it . . . but believe me, he could! Because the people are tired of dithering, they're sick of hesitation. They want leadership—moral leadership. They want action!"

The President had not moved. Now he said: "Thank you, madam." He took up the letter and put it in his pocket. "I have General Frémont's view, which I will answer in due course. And you, madam"—she saw a flash in his eyes, hostile and yet sardonic, almost amused—"you've said all you came to say, I take it? And so I bid you good evening."

He bowed and walked rapidly toward the half-doors to the dining room.

She stood there a moment in that blood-red room, and then Judge Coles appeared beside her and John Nicolay, looking even more disdainful, was ushering them out. At the Willard she kicked off her boots and lay down in the soiled black dress and dreamed of dragons creeping through the streets of St. Louis, breathing fire. . . .

Next morning she bathed and dressed and poured a second cup of coffee; she was staring at it dully when old Francis Blair arrived. She wanted to throw her arms around his neck, but one look at his face checked her. He stood in front of the fireplace and turned on her like a hanging judge.

"Whoever would have thought," he said, "that you would come here and make Mr. Lincoln your husband's enemy?"

"But I didn't!" She was ill; she didn't want any more talk.

"The President says General Frémont appears ready to—to 'try conclusions,' was the phrase he used."

But no—what had she said? She struggled to remember and couldn't. The whole interview kept whirling away in a gust of angry, vituperative phrases. "I never said any such thing. I said the very opposite—I told him Charles' sense of honor wouldn't permit him to do it, even if he . . . I said—"

"For God's sake, why are you saying anything? Forcing your way in on him late in the evening, haranguing him. Why are you even *here*?"

"Because he doesn't understand!"

"Oh, he understands, all right. It's you who doesn't understand. Way you act, I'd never guess you grew up around politics."

"You've been listening to Frank," she said.

"No, not in this. Frank has greatness in him, but he's too hot-tempered and he wastes himself in quarrels. He has no business fighting with General Frémont—I've told him that."

He sighed, shaking his fine silver head. "Look, Jessie, I came down here when your father was young. I sat in Andrew Jackson's kitchen cabinet, hammering out policy around the coffeepot. . . . We're not talking here about whether to make slavery the issue of the war—that's already been decided. Now, if the South doesn't come to its senses in another year, then slavery'll become the enemy because there'll be no reason for restraint. Personally, I'll be surprised if the war ends with slavery intact, but that's for the future. What's at issue now is whether General Frémont will support his Commander in Chief."

"There's no one more loyal—"

"No—disloyal. He showed that when he refused to rescind the proclamation. Jessie, Jessie, grow up, won't you? Charles incurred vast political costs with that stupid proclamation. The least he could have done was pay them himself."

"But—"

"Don't 'but' me. You know the rule of political capital: every leader possesses just so much, and he'd better spend it sparingly. That's what underlings are for—to absorb attacks, not inspire them. But Charles deliberately focused all the radical rage on the President, instead of shouldering it himself. Good God, they hanged Lincoln in effigy on Boston Common three nights ago! Did you know that?"

She shook her head.

"That was Charles' fault. He stirred it up. It'll make it much harder for the President to govern. And that's simply unforgivable."

He stood looking down at her with an old man's black disapproval. "Charles is a fool," he said. "I suspected as much in Fifty-six. Now I know it. And so are you. I can't believe you're Tom Benton's daughter."

"Francis, that's unfair, and it's cruel. Charles has held Missouri when no one could. He knows how to win in the West. You have no idea what—"

He bowed to her. "Good day, madam."

"Good day, sir," she said. The door closed behind him. After a while she picked up the cup of cold coffee and drank it; and her eyes finally filled with the bitterest of tears.

RECALL

AT A CREST overlooking the Osage Valley, Frémont called a halt. The river turning in great sweeps below had an angry, swollen look; here and there he could see floating debris. Commands went rattling down the long line. A horse whinnied and Franz Sigel's piping Germanic accents rose above the clamor. The army always collided on itself when it stopped, like boxcars rattling together. Watching the blue ranks rippling, dispersing, the organized confusion, Frémont smiled. It was good to be in the field again.

Horsemen were galloping up the hill, Colonel Tucker on his big roan in the lead. Tucker tossed off a loose salute when he was near, the gesture of a civilian not much impressed by military courtesy. He was wearing a worn buckskin jacket that had probably seen service on the Oregon Trail.

"No way over, General," he said. He looked weary and his beard was gray with dust. "Last scouts came in an hour ago. Every bridge burned. Cable ferries cut, flats sunk. They did a right good job."

"I was afraid of that. No boats, I expect."

"Bottoms chopped out of every skiff for fifty miles. We swam our mounts over. Same on the other side. Too bad." Tucker chewed at his mustache. "Had a brush with a rear guard near Deepwater, caught us a couple of Johnnies. You're right, General. Price is fixing to make a stand at Osceola. If we could only get across that *river* . . ."

Frémont absently patted his horse's shoulder, staring down. Thirty thousand men and a five-mile string of supply wagons and artillery to get over a river rising toward flood. It was the end of October, corn cribbed and wheat in, the fall rains finally tapering off . . . and time was running out on him.

"We'll get across, Rufus," he said. "I've got Mosely working on it. You take any casualties?"

"Two wounded. Scratches is all. They're still riding." Tucker had an old tear in his left cheek, partly hidden in the beard. Frémont took it for a flinthead arrow wound—Tucker'd been out twice with Kit and ridden with Etienne Provost as a boy—but it wasn't the kind of question you'd ask.

Gaines had his glass trained downstream. "Colonel Mosely's coming, sir," he said. Feigning patience, Frémont watched his chief engineer approach. The man was an execrable rider; he had a way of flopping on a horse's back that punished him and horse alike.

"All set, General," Mosely called when he was still forty feet away. "Got a bridge designed." He wore round glasses in gold-wire frames that made Frémont think of Preuss. He forgot to salute: his head was always full of angles, stresses, weight-bearing members, cosines and what-all. He was forty years old and already a famous civil engineer; apparently he'd erected half the public buildings in Chicago.

"Where'll you put it?" Frémont asked.

Mosely twisted awkwardly in the saddle, pointing downstream. "At the bend."

"For God's sake—it's a half-mile wide down there . . ." He felt a flash of concern; was this another expert whose good sense fled the moment you put him in the field? "You can cut that width in two, right here in front of us."

"We'll be using pontoons, General," Mosely said patiently. "There's twice the width all right, but half the current. That's crucial with pontoons." He stopped to make a quick entry in a leather notebook with brass corners; the page was a scrawled tangle of figures. "I'll use those two little islands," he said, pointing, "sling chains from one to the next, secure pontoons to the chains. In effect, three bridges, eight hundred feet overall—with the current slackening, it'll hold. I compute a stress factor of—"

"All right," Frémont said, relieved. "How long will you need?"

Mosely hesitated, made another entry. "Give me a thousand men and I'll do it in . . . well, say under a week."

Price was running hard, fifteen miles a day, maybe twenty. A week without pressure and he'd be deployed below Osceola, fortifying positions. He had to catch Price and hit him quickly, full force—he *had* to. Frémont said: "Suppose I give you five thousand men and you do it in a day?"

Mosely wasn't at all taken aback. Sheer pleasure flashed in the engineer's eyes; he felt challenged, excited. In St. Louis he'd proved himself startlingly attractive to women—and all at once Frémont saw why.

"Say thirty-six hours," Mosely said, snapping shut the book, "and we'll do it."

"Good."

The brigade commanders—Sigel, Asboth, Schofield, Riordan—reported and Frémont began shifting his army from fighting to working force: a thousand men to fell timber, five hundred to rig horses and mules to snake out the logs, another thousand with sledges to split the rails for rough planking, two thousand more to join Mosely at the riverbank. He heard a rumble behind: the engineer wagons had broken from the line and were coming forward at a fast trot, the mules' harnesses jingling. They passed him in rolling dust and went down the long slope to line up along the water's edge.

Frémont sat his big steel-gray stallion a little longer, watching with genuine pleasure the frenzied activity he'd set loose; he eased the reins to let the horse crop grass around the bit. . . . Kit's face on the day they'd inflated the rubber boat to cross the flooding Kansas flashed into his mind. Buffler guts ripening in the sun, Kit had said derisively—he hadn't forgiven the Cap'n for weeks. Those had been the bright, triumphant days of his life, when he'd faced west over free and open country. Hell, he'd always been a field man, ill at ease with desks and stacks of paperwork and devious, calculating men. Those last weeks in St. Louis he'd felt as if that office was draining away his life's blood. Even the Bierstadt in its handsome gilt frame had prodded him: he'd been as free in those happy days when he'd named that glittering gate as the gulls the painter had caught in high, wheeling arcs, black specks against sun glare . . .

Well: he *had* escaped St. Louis at last—escaped in more ways than one. From the moment he'd caught sight of Jessie's exhausted, despondent face and listened to her anguished account of the interview with Lincoln, he'd known he was finished if he didn't get into the field, and quickly. Montgomery Blair's inspection tour had only driven another nail in the coffin. He and Meigs had pored over the rations and clothing contracts in disapproving silence, frowned at the hastily erected fortifications around the city, studied forbiddingly the troop training programs; Frémont knew all too clearly the report they would submit. Frank Blair lashed away at him in his private paper, the *Evening News,* charging him with arrogance, incompetence, flagrantly corrupt administration. Frémont had pushed Riordan and McKinstry hard, balancing what time he might have left against the crying need for more training, a few more precious shipments of arms.

Then Mulligan had taken his Chicago Irish Brigade and rushed off to Lexington, where Price with a vastly superior force cut him off; he was screaming for reinforcements—and Frémont had nothing to send him. Nothing. There was another uproar in the press. The Blair clique was savage: here was the Emperor Frémont, with 40,000—nay, 60,000—crack troops at his beck and call, and he refused to spare a handful of them for a heroic, doomed detachment! Even Schuyler Colfax, his old friend and supporter from the presidential campaign days, taxed him with indifference. How could he turn his back on his own people? Without a word he passed Schuyler his muster rolls, which revealed the confidential and unhappy truth of the matter: instead of this rumored grand army of 60,000 men, he had less than *7,000* for the defense of the most important city in the West. While the Indiana congressman was digesting this fact, Frémont handed him two War Department wires—one of them from Scott himself—ordering him to detach 5,000 men without a moment's delay for the defense of Washington!

"But General," Colfax said, "Mulligan's situation is desperate—there are Indiana boys in that brigade . . . Can't you protest this order, inform them you simply cannot comply?"

Smiling sadly he shook his head. "That would be insubordination, Schuyler. I've always been charged with that, and found guilty. Remember? No, I have to obey this order, whatever the consequences. I have no choice." And to his deep chagrin he felt his eyes fill with tears . . .

And so Mulligan, surrounded and overwhelmed, had surrendered after a battle, and Frémont found himself the target of another torrent of abuse. It was worse than Lyon's death. The northern newspapers, which had so recently showered him with praise for his emancipation proclamation, turned hostile; the New York *Times* even called for his relief. That pinch-gut, purse-mouthed Congressman Washburne ranted away about the "horde of pirates" waxing fat off Frémont's favors. The last straw was a thinly disguised editorial by Frank Blair blaming him personally for Mulligan's surrender, calling for his immediate removal on grounds of timidity, accusing him of planning to create an independent western military nation, with himself as emperor!

"Now, by God, he *has* gone too far," Jessie cried. "That's nothing but vicious slander!"

"I'm guilty of an awful lot of sins, Jessie. But disloyalty to my country has never been one of them."

"Charles, you have to put a stop to this! He's undermining your authority with the Army, with Washington—he's obstructing everything you're killing yourself to do here." She was leaning over his desk, the newspaper clenched in one trembling hand. "You have to *shut—him—up!*"

"What do you suggest—I take him out and shoot him?"

"You could arrest him. And you should!"

He stared at her. Ever since her return from the Capital she'd been like this—tense, sleepless, filled with a raging anxiety. The pressures of this post—the mounting avalanche of requisitions, correspondence, the ceaseless parade of contractors, favor-seekers, above all that ominous silence from Washington except when it wanted men, and more men, and still more men—it was all bending her to the breaking point. She needed a rest so badly . . . but he needed her even more. He simply could not handle all of this military-civilian confusion without her; there was no help for it.

She was still running on, about Frank Blair's ruthless ambition, his arrogance and vindictiveness, his drinking, his threats. "Emperor—*he's* the one who wants to be Emperor of the West. He cares nothing about the war, or the evil of slavery, or preserving the Union—he'd destroy the country itself if it would satisfy his own selfish, conniving ends."

"All right," he said; he held up one hand to stop her. Well, why not? It couldn't go on like this—he could get nothing accomplished with this drunken madman snapping at his heels all day and all night. The man was a menace. A menace, and insubordinate into the bargain.

"All right," he repeated. "I'll do it. Let him cool his heels in the calabozo awhile."

Next day Montgomery had sent a polite wire asking him to release his brother, and urging him to save combat for the enemy. Frémont had complied—he'd already begun to regret the action—but Frank had refused to accept release; he'd insisted on a court-martial until Frémont ordered the jailer to charge him hotel rates for bed and board. Then he'd stormed out and filed criminal charges with the War Department. The newspapers had a field day. Lorenzo Thomas, the Adjutant General, was a petty, obsequious man, but Frank was chairman of the Military Affairs Committee, and so Thomas had rushed out to St. Louis, contacted every Blair supporter he could find, and returned to Washington with a blanket indictment of Frémont's conduct of the war: neglect of duty, disobedience of orders, conduct unbecoming an officer, extravagance and waste, tyrannical conduct—and capped it all with a citation of incompetence for command from, of all people, David Hunter, still another West Pointer, and Lincoln's favorite general in Chicago . . .

Mulligan's surrender and the Thomas report had decided Frémont. To save his strategy in the West, to rescue himself, he must gain a decision in the field—and swiftly. It was now or never.

It hadn't been easy. The roads, drenched in the autumn rains, were knee deep in mud. That gimlet-nosed, pontificating John Pope, still sulking over Frémont's appointment of Grant to the command he'd coveted, criticized and delayed in a spirit that bordered on insubordination. The troops were still inadequately armed, there were shortages of horses and mules, over a thousand wagons made of rotten wood had collapsed into kindling. Half the time the men were traveling on half rations.

But their morale was high: they marched now in good order, kept their pieces clean and dry, their boots greased. When he rode down the line they would wave and call out to him with that note of familiar warmth he remembered. One afternoon Sigel's brigade had actually cheered him. They would follow him, they would fight for him. He knew it. He was a symbol to them—a symbol and a hope. He had crossed the Sierra, taken California on a shoestring and a prayer, he'd saved St. Louis for the Union in two strenuous months—and they knew it. No other general in all the Union armies was searching out the enemy. George McClellan had managed to shove senile old Scott into retirement, but nothing whatever had changed; the Army of the Potomac was swollen with men and arms, but McClellan, fussy, dogmatic, unimaginative, the compleat engineer, still sat in his tent, insisting on vast new training programs and tactical studies before he would move. The President was said to be frantic in his desire for action. After Bull Run, Ball's Bluff and Wilson's Creek, the North desperately needed a success.

"I'm going to catch Price and break up his force," he'd told Jessie the night before he left. "I know it. I can feel it in my bones."

"So do I." She had clung to him fiercely; he could feel her body trembling with tension and fatigue. "I know you will. Don't let anything deflect you, Charles. Anything or anybody. Promise me."

"I promise." He wouldn't fail. He wouldn't fail the country, or her, or himself. They'd been swimming against the current ever since Kearny had blunted his spear—now was the time to turn that all around: now he had a well-trained, confident army at his back for the first time. A glorious opportunity awaited him. This was a promise he was going to keep. . . .

He gathered the reins and sent the big gray loping down the hill. Lines of men were drawing axes from the wagons. Dolberry, now a major, was anxiously checking off lists. Frémont grinned in spite of himself. A moving army was a supply officer's despair: he was happiest when all was neatly stored, nothing in use! Engineers were already in the woods, blazing the trees they wanted. He saw a group milling around aimlessly, and cantered over to a fat captain who looked baffled, unsure of himself. Frémont sorted out the tangle, got the men moving. Farther on an alert young sergeant had appointed himself traffic master and was expertly dispatching teams into the woods.

"What's your name, son?" he said.

"Martineau, sir."

He nodded. Same name as the fellow who kept tangling with Bladon on the Minnesota; a good omen. He might just bust the captain and put this lad in his place. Dolberry was moving his empty wagons; he'd distributed the tools in quick time.

Frémont loved the Army's bustle, its variety, its sheer confident force. The troops were cheerful and excited, working hard. The axes bit into the wood like corn popping on a griddle; there was a high, admonitory cry and then the surf-crash of a tree falling. Some of them waved and yelled as he approached and he waved back.

"Keep those chips flying, boys!" he called. "Time's a-wasting." There was a chorus of hoots and groans, and a boy with a sweaty face and dark, sparkling eyes cried, "General, ol' Price ain't going to last any longer'n this here shagbark hickory when we ketch up with him!"

Briggins appeared beside him. "There's a civilian just drove up with an escort, General." He had a disapproving look. "Claims he's the Secretary of War. I told the boys to keep an eye on him."

"Thank you, Sergeant." Pleased, Frémont rode off at a gallop. He'd been looking forward eagerly to Simon Cameron's visit. He'd known the affable Pennsylvanian for years—they'd served together in the Senate, and Cameron had worked hard for him in '56—and while Cameron had no talent for military matters, he was a superlative politician who knew how to associate himself with a success. In another ten days he'd be back in Washington talking about "my army in Missouri." As Frémont approached his headquarters tent—it was well set, he saw, center pole true, corner poles at identical angles, flaps neatly tied, benches lined outside—Cameron came toward him with that slightly swaying walk Frémont remembered. He was a tall, slender man with Scotland engraved on his long face.

"Welcome to the front, Mr. Secretary," he said, swinging down. "How are things in Pennsylvania?"

"Benefiting from my absence, I don't doubt," Cameron answered with his small, tight smile. Frémont knew he continued to run Pennsylvania politics with an iron hand; was that why he'd been so lax about reorganizing the War Department?

"Let me get you a good mount," he said as they shook hands. "I want to show you everything we're doing here."

"I'm very anxious to see it."

"We've been making wonderful time, all things considered. Did you have any trouble catching up with us?"

"None at all. I came straight to you from St. Louis."

From St. Louis. Frémont glanced at him, but the Secretary's face showed nothing. His small gray eyes held a shrewd intentness that completely belied his folksy manner.

The riverbank was a frenzy of activity. They found Mosely directing the emplacement of a log anchor on the near bank; from it a great chain would run to a similar anchor on Island Number One, where troops were busily rigging block and tackle to trees to haul it over. Frémont introduced Cameron to Mosely, who showed them the long, coffin-shaped boxes covered with tarpaulin and heavily tarred.

"There are your pontoons, General," he declared. "Green wood won't carry much weight, but the air chambers will." He turned to the Secretary. "I've calculated this very closely, sir. The guns are the only problem—they'll be close to maximum limit. But everything else will breeze across. I guarantee it."

Some men were already holding pontoons in place, straining half-naked in the swirling, muddy water, cursing and calling to one another, while others were hurriedly laying balks across the pontoons and spiking them fast. A forage wagon had drawn up nearby and several soldiers were wolfing down half-loaves of bread or plucking apples out of a barrel. Blacksmiths had dropped the sides of another wagon and were firing its forge, the flames flaring and sinking redly under the bellows. Frémont felt the old prideful exaltation the trail always gave him when things were going forward vigorously and well.

"Look at them!" he exclaimed. "He's promised me a highway over the Osage in thirty-six hours. *Thirty—six—hours!* They'll do it, too. What do you think of that?"

The Secretary frowned. "The men look—unkempt. They lack the—the formality, the snap, you look for in soldiers."

Frémont laughed and slapped his crop against his thigh. "Spit and polish, you mean! Oh, they've turned woodsmen for the day—and engineers and riggers and carpenters and anything else that's needed. They'll go right back to soldiering as soon as we get across—don't you worry about that!"

"Look at that fellow, there. He's all rags. . . ." Cameron was pointing to Martineau. One of the sergeant's underwear sleeves had torn loose; he'd ripped it off and tied it around his forehead for a sweatband; his cap was gone, and his trousers were crudely patched at the knees. "*Half* of them are in rags."

"Well yes, we've had some trouble getting uniforms—you know about that. Contracts haven't been honored—"

"That boy over there in the water—he has no undershirt at all."

Frémont glanced sharply at Cameron—then stared at the boisterous, frenzied scene around them, trying to see it through the Secretary's eyes. Accustomed to honor guards at the White House and parades down Pennsylvania Avenue, he couldn't recognize this private's good sense in braving the chill water in order to keep his long-handled undershirt dry and whole; Cameron saw only a dirty young man out of uniform.

"They're soldiers, Mr. Secretary," he said quietly. "They're no Prussian *garde du corps,* I'l admit. They're short on equipment—and right now they look pretty raggedy-ass and nondescript to you. But their *weapons* are spotless. And their bayonets." Dismantling a stack he swung up a rifle at random, checked the trigger and hammer assembly, the bore, the ramrod, and handed it to Cameron. "You'll find them all like that. I won't tolerate dirty or neglected pieces."

"I'm told you had ration trouble at Jefferson City."

"Yes, Haverstraw promised me two million rations by the eighteenth—they weren't there. But our foraging parties have shown good initiative, they know how to—"

The scream was shocking in the still fall air—hoarse and shrill, filled with terror; then it stopped, as if a hand had been clamped over a mouth.

Cameron pulled up his horse in alarm. A moment later Colonel Cadwallader came out of the hospital tent, his hands running blood, and washed them in a tin basin.

"Well, what do you expect?" he demanded testily. "Tree can crush a man's leg as thoroughly as a ball . . . He came up out of the anesthesia too soon, that's all." Frémont thought he was shaken, though he would never admit it. He was the best military surgeon west of the Appalachians; Frémont felt himself lucky to have him. "We spill ether on gauze clamped to the nostrils," he was telling Cameron in a cross voice. "You can use too much—I've lost patients who couldn't tolerate it. But too little, and they come up in midstream. And there you are."

Cameron swallowed and looked away, and Cadwallader fixed a stern eye on him. "I was with Scott from Vera Cruz to Chapultepec. We sawed bone the whole way, I want to tell you."

"How's the—the sickness rate, Doctor?" Cameron managed to ask.

"Damned low, Mr. Secretary. General Frémont runs the healthiest army *I* ever saw." Frémont knew that Cadwallader liked him. "Virtually no malingerers at all. Best sign of morale there is. I know what I'm talking about. Of course, they haven't met the elephant yet, most of them. Why, at Cerro Gordo we had to lay them out like cord wood. . . ."

Frémont got Cameron away from Cadwallader, back to the headquarters tent, and explained his plan of campaign over a simple Army meal of beans, beef and coffee, with johnnycake dipped in sugar and fried until it gleamed like caramel.

"We'll have men over the Osage before nightfall tomorrow," he concluded. "We'll cross all night by torchlight. The lead units will move out next morning—the whole army will be marching by noon. I mean to hit Price before he can link up with McCulloch, and destroy him as an effective fighting force. The whole war will turn in our direction."

The Secretary lighted a cigar with slow care. "I hope so," he said.

"They'll do it, sir—they're as good as any army in the world. . . . Perhaps you'd like to turn in—tomorrow will be a hard day for everyone."

"Well," Cameron said, "there's this other matter."

Frémont's head came up. "What's that, sir?"

"General . . . in politics, things are always more complicated than they seem. Always." He squinted at a plume of blue smoke, his features marked with that expression of troubled reticence, of constraint Frémont had noticed at the riverbank. He started to say something, checked himself and sighed. "Oh hell," he murmured, drawing a single folded sheet of paper from inside his coat. "You'd better read this."

Frémont's fingers felt stiff. He opened the paper slowly, his eyes leaping along the lines. It was signed by the President. It was—it was an order relieving him. Brigadier General David Hunter would assume immediate command of the Army of the West—

It was impossible.

"But—but it makes no sense . . ." He felt actively sick with disappointment, with loss. Here, right now, just when he was about to pull it off, prove his plan for the West—to be *relieved* now. He thought of Jessie waiting at the mansion, hoping for him, praying for him, pacing in the night. "Christ, you haven't got a single army in the field—not McClellan's, not anyone's—isn't that right?"

Cameron nodded.

"And you're going to relieve your only active general. That's ridiculous—it's ridiculous and it's unjust . . ." Then the pitiless mechanics of the action ground in on him. "This is all Frank Blair's doing."

"Of course. What did you expect? Would you mind telling me just *what* was in your mind when you decided to throw him in jail? The President is sick to death of you both, I'll tell you that."

"But he still listens to *him,* it seems!"

"Naturally—for a hundred and one reasons, and you know most of them perfectly well." The Secretary rubbed his eyes. "But it's not just Frank. It's that damned proclamation of yours."

Yes, and your first reaction—before you learned Lincoln's view—was a wire of warmest approval, Frémont almost said aloud; he looked down at his muddy boots.

"And then there's Thomas' report."

"Lorenzo Thomas is a toady and a fool! Claiming I've 'lost Missouri'—at the very moment when the state is fully under Union control for the first time—and the only Confederate force is in headlong flight south . . ."

"Right on both counts," Cameron answered. "I'd give my gold watch to be rid of him. But his report's official—and now the press has got it, God help us all. It can't be ignored. God almighty, Charles, can't you see—you've managed in three short months to alienate or infuriate everybody in North America except Santa Claus!" He leaned forward, his eyes snapping brightly. *"The Blairs are the biggest political force west of the Appalachians.* Lincoln thinks the world of the old man—and his paper. What did you *think* he'd decide to do?"

Frémont gripped his hands together, hard. So there it was—all of it arrayed against him, all those charges and allegations accepted as gospel; and his solid achievements belittled or ignored. He felt a high, hollow coldness in his chest, and then the burning coal that never left him.

"Very well," he said flatly, "if that's the President's wish, there's no more to be said. But for the record, I ask you to remember that I came out here at Lincoln's request—without a moment's hesitation—and at considerable sacrifice, since of course the Mariposa needed me—it's in deep trouble. The President gave me *carte blanche*—he asked me to save Missouri. And I've done it. In three months flat I've held the state, I've built an army out of scratch, I'm on the razor edge of winning the first major victory of the war—and now I'm to be sacked, like any—"

"Hold on, Charles. Hold on." The Secretary held up a hand. "That's not all."

"What do you mean? I suppose he wants me to make a public—"

"It's not final." Frémont stared at him, blinking. "The President left it to my discretion." Cameron peered up at the tent roof through skeins of cigar smoke. "I'll be honest with you, Charles—which is more than you can say of anybody else coming out here from Washington. I came here prepared to execute this order. It's clearly what Lincoln wants. Your men are in need of proper clothing, discipline is lax, some of your contracts are a shambles, the camp looks like one of those trappers' rendezvous you used to tell me about. . . . But I like your plan for attacking Price. I like the way you get things done. That doctor—now he's a tough customer, and he sounds happy enough to serve under you." He shook his head, rolling the cigar between his long, expressive fingers. "I just don't know. They're all riding me back there, you understand. . . ."

The silence lengthened. Frémont hooked his hands in his belt. In the distance he heard a sentry's cry: "—and all's *welllll*. . . ." and he could see the whole sprawling camp in his mind's eye: all these farmboys and clerks and plainsmen in their thousands, ready to hike across that bridge tomorrow and fight for this unique, glorious republic. He loved them, they were his to lead—and they loved *him*, he knew that, too. They were embarked on the greatest adventure of their lives; and the victory that would cap it was so close. . . . It couldn't end this way. It couldn't!

"Please, Simon." He was beyond amazement, hearing himself. "Let me stay. Give me another month—two weeks. We'll break Price, I promise you! We'll open up the Mississippi, it'll be the beginning of the end. It'll fire up the nation."

Cameron made no reply, kept staring into the tent's roof. At the river's edge they were singing "Annie Laurie," the young voices carrying on the still night.

"Please, Simon. I know they're badly clothed, short on weapons—but their hearts, Simon. Their hearts! This army—it's *my* spirit I've given them. Don't you see? Why do you think they're throwing up that bridge in thirty-six hours? Do you think they'd work like that for anyone? Don't take them away from me now. Give me the chance, at least." Cameron still was silent. "Look—if I fail, I will resign instantly. I give you my word. Please, Simon . . ."

"—General Frémont, sir . . ."

He turned, exasperated. A gangling private stood in the doorway entrance, blinking in the lamplight. His tunic was hanging open, he was covered with mud and wood chips; he'd lost his service cap and was wearing a dirty felt hat with the brim turned up in front, the way Kit used to.

"Yes, soldier. What is it?"

"General, we've made it over to Island Number Two! Colonel Mosely wants you to test her out."

Frémont gripped his knees hard. "Thank you, private," he said. "Give Colonel Mosely my compliments and tell him I'll be down directly."

"Yes, sir."

"Wait a minute." Cameron had swung forward in the camp chair again and was pointing his cigar stub at the boy, who'd stopped. "Tell me something, lad. How do you think this war's going?"

The boy stared at Cameron in stark incredulity, as though he couldn't believe his ears. He glanced at Frémont, and his eyes flashed. "Why, mister, we're going to bust those rebs to smithereens! And then we're going to steam down the river and take New Orleans, wind up this danged war and be home in time for spring planting. That's what we're going to *do*! Why, General Frémont here has—"

"All right, soldier," Frémont told him. "You may go now."

"Right, General." The boy ducked out of the tent.

Cameron chuckled once; then his lean, handsome face sobered. "All right, Charles. You win. I'm not going to fly in the face of that kind of paprika." He folded the sheet of paper neatly, slipped it into his coat. "Keep on going. I'll go back and try to hold the President off. Maybe I can, maybe I can't. You've got two weeks, maybe three. *My* head's on the chopping block too." He stood up, and for the first time the strain of the office showed in his face. "But for God's sake, Charles, *give us a victory* . . ."

Colonel Tucker came in at noon. He had pinned epaulets with silver eagles to the buckskin jacket. A cold wind was blowing from the north, and Tucker had the jacket buttoned to his throat.

"They're there, General. Waiting like hens in a henhouse."

The army was below Springfield. Just as Confederate stragglers had admitted, Price had dug in at Wilson's Creek—the very spot where he'd defeated Lyon. What an irony! But this time the outcome would be different. Frémont had pushed his men hard after they'd crossed the Osage. The last of the column had come in after midnight, blundering and cursing in the dark, and the men had slept where they'd fallen. The army could rest today because it would fight tomorrow.

Tucker walked into the tent, pulled off his gauntlets and began to warm his hands over the iron stove. "By God," he said, "I could use a drink."

Frémont smiled, and Gaines produced a brandy bottle. Tucker ran the heel of his hand over the top and took a huge pull.

"Waugh! That puts life back in a man." He ran a blunt finger along the map. "They're camped right in here, all along the creek. They may be down to 8,000 or so, and they're poorly. The locals have been in and out of their lines."

"How close could you get?"

"They've got pickets in force a mile to the north, here"—he tapped the map. "We pushed 'em hard enough to draw fire."

So Price had finally turned, his numbers shrinking, his men hungry, their ammunition certainly low. They would fight—they hadn't come this far to give up—but they couldn't last against fresh troops and odds of three to one. He was going to deliver the victory he had promised Cameron. The Secretary had left for Washington the next morning and wished him luck cordially enough. But since then the silence from Washington had again been ominous: no directives, no queries, nothing. Just one more day of grace . . .

"Bob," he said suddenly to Gaines, "I want the camp sealed. No one in, no one out. That clear?"

"Yes, sir."

At two o'clock he called in the division commanders and senior staff. They would march in two columns, he heading one and Sigel the other. Reveille at midnight, march at one, in position before dawn, attack at first light. He would initiate; Sigel would engage only on the sound of firing.

"I want a close personal inspection this afternoon. Instruct your officers, examine each man's cartridge box individually. See every man has three days' cooked rations. Make sure they eat this evening and again before the march—men don't fight well on an empty stomach."

As Tucker took the pointer and explained the routes of march, Frémont watched his officers. Alexander Asboth, the impassive chief of staff; Franz Sigel, as peppery as his red-gold beard; Riordan, as confident a colonel as he'd been a sergeant; Charles Zagonyi, his cavalryman, dashing in his hussar's uniform, stirring restively; John Schofield, Lyon's old chief of staff and a good dispassionate operations officer; John Fiala, Mosely's chief, like Asboth a Hungarian, and a crack engineer. Too many foreigners on his staff, the West Pointers said scathingly; too many dreamers. Well, Asboth had served with distinction under the great Kossuth, and Sigel had led an army larger than this one in the Revolt of '48; it was Franz who'd organized the German regiments in St. Louis when the rest of them were standing around wringing their hands; they hadn't cooled *their* heels in two-battalion posts in Arkansas or Wisconsin—they weren't lagging behind like the West Point stickler Hunter, or that carping, incompetent Pope.

Toward sunset, Frémont rode slowly from regiment to regiment. There was a subdued air over the whole camp, which lay scattered along streams and in open meadows. Men were whetstoning knives and bayonets, greasing their boots; rifles were dismantled on blankets. The cold wind had died; he knew there would be starlight to move by and later a quarter-moon. He came to an Illinois regiment; its colonel called the men to attention. Frémont put them at ease and walked about, peering into cartridge boxes, testing the edges of bayonets. "You can shave with that sticker, General," a corporal told him proudly. It made him think of Briggins that first day in St. Louis. Beyond those woods Price's men were sharpening their bayonets tonight, too.

They expected him to say something and he climbed onto a wagon bed. They'd come a long way to square accounts with these rebels, he told them; now was their chance. Stay together, watch your officers, listen for commands, aim low. Aim for the knees, he told them, knowing that inexperienced troops always shot high. Remember that we outnumber them three to one, remember that our cause is right, remember that we've come here to win! They gave him a roar that went crashing through camp.

Frémont jumped down and found himself facing the round-faced, dark-eyed soldier who'd been making the chips fly the day they'd built the bridge.

"Are you ready for them?" he asked.

"Yes, sir," he said, but his expression was somber. He really was only a boy.

"Scared, son?"

"No, *sir*!" But his eyes dropped. "Yes, sir . . . a little."

"That's normal enough," Frémont said. "Everyone's a little scared." The boy looked up then, interested. "But your friends will stand with you, your officers in front of you. You won't be alone. Just do what the others do and you'll be all right."

"Yes, sir." Frémont was about to turn away when the boy said suddenly: "General, are you scared?"

Frémont hesitated an instant. Other men were listening carefully; he saw the strained inquiry in their faces. The good field general led his men into battle—and Lyon's death had shown them bullets made no distinction between the mighty and the lowly. He wanted to be truthful, but he didn't want to shake them unduly, or patronize them either. "Well," he said, "I bleed as quickly as anyone else. But I've got a lot of good men behind me and I know it has to be done. I know I'll be all right when the time comes—and so will you."

When he had visited every regiment, walked among the men, reassured them with the quiet reserve of his presence, he mounted the gray and started back to his headquarters tent. The men were all right: tense, running on that well-controlled edge of natural fear that would make them sharp and quick. He could feel it in himself—the testing sense, the memory of the hot, winy rush that came with danger. They were ready: nothing could stop them.

The guard's fire outside the tent was blazing. Frémont saw a civilian in a slouch hat and homespun warming his hands.

"Sir," Gaines said, "a perimeter guard brought this man in. I thought you'd want to see him. He's a Webster County farmer, says he has vital information on Price's intentions."

"What is it?"

"He won't give it to anyone but you, sir."

"All right. Bring him in."

The civilian was young, with a stubble of whiskers rather than a trimmed beard, and intelligent eyes. His coat was filthy; he looked like a pig farmer.

"Who are you?" Frémont asked.

The man came to rigid attention, something sly and triumphant in his face. "Thomas J. McKenny, sir—Captain, First Cavalry, detached, United States Regular Army. I have orders for the General."

Before Frémont could react he had opened his coat, ripped its lining and produced a long War Department envelope. As if in a trance, all his actions ordained, Frémont took the envelope and thumbed it open, unfolded the sheet and saw the signature: *A. Lincoln.* It was a field order: Major General John C. Frémont was relieved of duty; Major General David Hunter was on his way to assume command of the Army of the West.

He slammed the orders down on the table and said: "Sir, how did you gain admission into my lines? By some damned subterfuge, by lies! *Webster County farmer*—"

"Sir, I was West Point, class of Fifty-five, but before that—"

"Were you, now!"

"Begging the General's pardon, I grew up on a Webster County farm. I didn't—"

"Be silent!—or I'll have you bucked and gagged! You're Army enough to understand *that,* aren't you?"

In the silence the lamp hissed and guttered, the flame restless in its glass chimney. A small envelope accompanied the President's message. He opened it and read in Simon Cameron's hand: *Maryland and Missouri have overwhelmed Pennsylvania. Sorry. S.*

The Blairs. They had won after all. In for a fight, in for a funeral. Leadenly he picked up the orders again. Yes, he was stripped of the command that he had built so arduously. General Hunter, Lincoln's favorite and a West Pointer, would inherit what he hadn't remotely earned . . . He started, turned the orders to the light. . . . *subject to these conditions only, that if General Frémont shall then have, in personal command, fought and won a battle, or shall then be in the immediate presence of the enemy in expectation of a battle, it shall not apply*—

He expelled his breath in what was almost a laugh. That native political caution which had kept Lincoln from acting after the stormy interview with Jessie had saved him again. A weight fell from his back. He *was* in the immediate presence of the enemy, and about to give battle; by nightfall tomorrow, the North would have its victory and the President could forget these orders. He had faced the cannon at point-blank range—and been overshot. The fabulous Frémont luck was still holding.

"Gaines," he said crisply, "I want this man held under close guard. He is to speak to no one; no one is to speak to him."

"Sir," the officer cried, "I protest—"

"Put a rifle butt in his mouth if he doesn't obey. Now get him out of here!"

He folded the document with Simon's note; a keepsake for Jessie. He needed sleep for the morning. He went to his tent and rolled himself in a blanket, fully dressed. But his heart was still pounding in his throat, and after a moment he jumped up and went walking hard through the night. The stars seemed brighter than gemstones, the constellations as familiar as the maps on his table. He could see fires here and there about the camp, soft and orange compared to the hard brilliance overhead. The men would be asleep by now, most of them. He thought of the youngster in the Illinois regiment with the dark, earnest eyes. Some of these men, maybe many of them, would be dead by this time tomorrow. He gave a slow, deep sigh and rubbed his eyes. Well. He had prepared them, armed them, he'd gone to the very lip of his own personal precipice to give them more training; now they must trust to God and to luck. The taut, nervous flutter was fading from his chest. The thing was set; he had done everything he could do.

He was approaching the headquarters tent when he heard horsemen coming at a hard gallop. Tucker swept out of the darkness, the big bay lathered, a dozen men behind him, and was down before the horse could stop, flinging the reins to Sergeant Briggins. In a guarded but angry voice he said:

"They've skedaddled, General."

Frémont passed a hand through his hair. "You sure, Rufus? You're quite certain?"

"Yes, sir. Rode right through that picket position and into the camp. Not a soul. Fires all cold. They've headed for Pineville." He had turned up three Confederate stragglers and shaken Price's plans out of them. He threw his big gauntlets down on the table. "I've talked to some of the local folks. Roads aren't bad and we'll make good time. You'll still bag old Price in less'n a week."

"I'm afraid not, Rufus," he heard himself say quietly.

"Come again?"

"I've been relieved."

The cavalryman was staring at him, shaking his head. Gaines's mouth had dropped open.

"I've been relieved," he said more firmly. "General Hunter is coming to take command."

"But what in hell for? We've got them running—"

"The orders were not effective if we were in battle, immediate battle. Or about to be. A minute ago, we were; now we're not."

"Well, Goddamnit," Tucker protested, "they're just down the road, we're still going to fight 'em—that's close enough."

"Sorry, Rufus—it won't wash." He had thrust the temptation aside.

"General, I can put cavalry on their tails in twelve hours! Please . . . let's break out the best brigade, a half-dozen batteries, everything stripped down. We can corner 'em inside of twenty-four hours, thirty-six—that's 'immediate' in any man's language!"

"Rufus, Rufus . . ." Smiling sadly he shook his head. "Not good enough, and you know it. I've received the order, the enemy is not out there. I've got to obey."

"But what do they know, back in Washington—*we're* the ones here, on the ground! What damn difference do a couple of days make?"

"All the difference in the world."

Tucker cracked his hands together. "That isn't the way you ran things on the Sacramento—or Los Angeles, either . . ."

"That's just the trouble, Rufus," he answered somberly. "That's why I can't disobey now. Maybe you could. I can't. I've been convicted of mutiny once by this same Army. I can't make a habit of it. . . . Inform the brigade commanders and senior staff," he told Gaines. "We will not be attacking at first light, we will not be marching."

He leaned forward on the map table, staring at nothing. What a confused and murky world this was! The Army demanded immediate and unswerving obedience—it was, after all, what separated a military force from a murderous mob—and the good soldier lived by the book, following instructions to the letter, never deviating from the straight and narrow. Orders are orders. But the good soldier would never have taken India, like Clive, or captured an Austrian army, like Murat—or snatched California out of the caldron, for that matter—

He came alert, aware of a gathering murmur of many voices, punctuated by angry shouts, the drumming of running feet. He was buttoning his tunic when Franz Sigel burst into the tent.

"General!" he stammered thickly. In his agitation the little Austrian had actually, incredibly forgotten to salute, which amused Frémont and alarmed him. "You'd better come out! They won't listen to me—they're out of control . . ."

Frémont stepped past Sigel and left the tent. Men were running toward him from all over the camp. When they saw him they stopped in a jostling, unruly crowd.

"General," someone cried, "is it true they're sending you back?"

"Yes," he said. "It's true."

There was a low moan of sheer consternation, and then a torrent of violent cursing.

"Well, Goddamnit to hell!" A handsome giant of a boy with tow hair flung down the blanket he'd been wrapped in and stamped on it in a fury. "I signed to fight under General John C. Frémont—and *that's* who I'm going to fight under, and nobody frigging else!"

"Now, son," Frémont said.

"I mean it! They go and pull off a stunt like that, I'm going home!"

"Boys," Frémont pleaded, "boys . . ."

But they were crowding up around him now, inconsolable and raging, brandishing caps and blankets and tin cups: they'd followed General Frémont and nobody *but* General Frémont for many and many a mile, he knew by God how to get this war won, and they were winning it! He'd taught them how to march and shoot and live off the country, and he'd kept the chickenshit at a minimum—who in holy hell did these Washington lard-asses think they were, pulling him out? Let them waltz their fat asses out here where the fucking *war* was, where the bullets were flying; they God damn weren't about to shoulder a piece for any haystack fat-gutted armchair son of a bitch—by the great Jehovah, they were heading home! And the sons-of-bitching politicians, those loudmouth pork-barreling Blairs, could come out here and fight this war by theirselves!

Frémont dropped his hands. There was nothing to do but let them vent their shock and bitterness, pour themselves out in the chill gray dawn light. A swarthy sergeant was pounding both massive fists against his thighs, a sallow-faced boy was weeping openly, tears streaking the dirt on his cheeks. There was a nearby crash as someone kicked over a stack of rifles, and a lieutenant kept plucking at Frémont's sleeve and saying the same phrase over and over again, inaudible in the uproar. Frémont stepped back, jumped up on a bench, and held out his hands, and finally they quieted.

"Boys," he said. "Now you know . . . a soldier's first duty is to obey orders. Even the ones he doesn't like! You know that. Now, you joined the Army to fight for the Union—you've got pride in our cause, pride in yourselves as soldiers." Watching them, meeting their eyes, he felt perilously close to weeping. "Do you want to help me? . . . Then show the whole damn world that John C. Frémont's army can fight! Find Price and whip him! Driving the Confederates out of Missouri is the one thing that will help me now."

And finally, finally they subsided into mutterings and silence; but still they stood there, gazing at him, disconsolate and miserable.

"All right," the huge blond boy called. "We'll stay—but it's for *you* we're doing it, General. And that's God's truth . . ."

Major General David Hunter was a narrow-shouldered man with a broad, straight nose, sweeping handlebar mustaches—and the coldest eyes Frémont had ever seen. He rode up with a substantial entourage, sat at the head of Frémont's long table and wrote out his General Order No. 1, in which he formally assumed command of the Army of the West. Frémont was a guest at his own table, an intruder in his own headquarters. He reported on the army's numbers, units, commanders, level of training, supplies of food and forage, while Hunter listened carefully; one of his staff captains made notes with a scratchy pen.

Frémont rolled open the maps. He showed Hunter where Price had camped on Wilson's Creek, the roads he had taken toward Pineville, the route McCulloch was expected to use in his link-up with Price, the nature of the terrain the army would encounter. Hunter leaned back in his camp chair watching in a bored, desultory manner. The staff man's pen had stopped scratching. The West Pointer was simply waiting for him to finish. He wondered if Hunter saw his briefing as an attempt to cling to authority. Carefully he said: "I expect to leave for St. Louis immediately. But the army is ready to march."

The cold agate eyes rose to his. "I'll be frank with you, General. I don't plan to pursue Price at all."

Frémont felt as if the slenderest blade had slipped into his heart. He watched Hunter's hostile, vengeful face and knew he was destroyed. The chance was gone, all that effort for nothing, all hope forfeited, the war stupidly prolonged. Bound in a hard, hollow silence, his dreams cracking like glass, he knew that never had he wanted anything so much as the vindication now denied him.

He placed his hands firmly on the edge of the table. "May I ask why?" His voice was grave and steady, which pleased him greatly. "The enemy is near, he's vulnerable, there seems promise of a certain victory that surely would forward our cause."

Hunter shook his head stubbornly. "Price won't stand and fight. In any case, he no longer represents a threat to the Union."

"But Price *must* fight," Frémont said. "His militiamen will never cross the line into Arkansas. To do that would automatically turn them into regular Confederate infantry—they wouldn't be able to disband and go home to their farms. My chief scout, Colonel Tucker, has pried this out of Price's stragglers."

Hunter shrugged. "That's all highly problematical. In any event, I intend to replace Colonel Tucker at once."

Frémont stared at him. "I find it hard to believe the President would countenance terminating the only active campaign being carried on by the entire Union forces . . ."

"In point of fact, I am following the President's suggestion." Hunter's cold eyes rested on his with satisfaction. "His order leaves the decision to me, but he feels this *campaign*"—he laid emphasis on the word—"will only lure the Army too far from its base of supplies and reinforcements."

"But the foraging has been effective, the men can live off the land as they advance—"

"That is counter to accepted military procedure. Any excursion deep into Arkansas would only exhaust this force, and risk its very existence. The President clearly feels this is a wild-goose chase—a sentiment with which I wholeheartedly concur. In fact I've thought so for some time now."

"Along with General Pope."

Hunter smiled grimly under his mustache. "In essence, yes."

Frémont got to his feet then and picked up his slouch hat. "In that case, General, I'll take my leave. I'd wish you good luck—but of course you won't need any, for your *retreat* to St. Louis." He turned, said clearly: "I'll have your highly resourceful Captain McKenny released from arrest." Hunter blinked at him, startled. "He gained entrance to my camp through an ingenious falsification—doubtless something he learned at the Academy . . . He *is* an officer in your command, isn't he?"

Hunter's agate eyes glinted in cold malice. "That is correct."

Frémont smiled for the first time in many hours. "I rather concluded that." Standing before the table he drew himself erect and saluted smartly. "Good day to you, General."

The train lurched to a stop with a series of quick snorting sighs. He hurried down the iron steps through a steam burst—and there she was, in front of a milling, eager crowd, her arms raised full to him. He embraced her, clung to her for an instant like a castaway.

"My darling," she was murmuring. "Oh, my darling . . ."

A band broke into "The Girl I Left Behind Me"; there was a sharp, peremptory command and the familiar clash of rifles. He looked up in surprise.

People were crowding up to him, grasping his hand, their faces grave with sympathy, with respect.

"Bad cess to them, General," an old man in a leather apron was saying, "*we're* with you, all of us," and a woman wearing a Union blue bonnet gripped his hand and called: "God bless you, sir—my George told me about you, at the river . . ."

He was moving in a slow trance, past an honor guard at present arms, past the headquarters band, the crowd following them with a kind of gentle deference. He turned to Jessie, beyond amazement.

"But—why this reception? I *failed*. . . ."

"They don't think so. Look at them!"

Her face was so worn, so weary. Her hair was curiously dusty in the autumn sunlight—no, it was gray, streaked through with *gray*. But—when he'd left, it had been brown, that sweet coppery brown with flecks of amber. She was barely thirty-seven . . .

She was seeing him, too, with loving concern. "Your beard needs trimming, Charles."

"Does it?" He managed a smile. "I'd say it had been trimmed pretty smartly, all things considered."

Her face underwent a funny little quiver. "You're home, dear. You're home. Right now that's all that matters."

"Yes."

Emil Baumeister greeted him on behalf of the loyal German-American citizens of St. Louis; Robert Campbell, one of the Fourth Expedition's backers, offered his warm support; even crusty old Pierre Chouteau came forward and extended his condolences. He nodded, acknowledging them all. He'd come into this queenly gateway town a brash young greenhorn, facing west, dreaming vast, tumultuous dreams. Here was where he'd first seen Louie's quick infectious grin, old Provost's dour rocklike countenance, here was where he'd first caught sight of the dear oval face that was still so loving and resolute after all these strenuous, stormy years. . . . He'd been ordered to report back to Washington at his convenience, but there would be no further commands. He knew that. It didn't matter, really; St. Louis had been his greatest opportunity, and he had failed.

Had the proclamation really been such a mistake? They'd have to face the Negro question sooner or later, border states or none. They'd have to face the morality of it. Could he have handled Frank Blair more adroitly—could he have done so without knuckling under, without turning the state and the war over to him? Frank was a willful, arrogant bully—and the country would discover that, too, before long. Could he have taken the field a month earlier, and thrown half-trained farmboys at Price and beaten him? And in that case, would the President only have acted earlier than he had? He didn't know; he just didn't know. He'd acted, he'd done what he'd felt was best in the brief desperate time given him. When Hunter had stepped into his headquarters tent, it had been exactly one hundred days. . . .

He was all right until he saw the Zagonyi Guard. They rode into the square in perfect column, the survivors of the magnificent charge at

Springfield, their eyes rigidly front. Some were still wearing bandages; their once-immaculate uniforms were faded and frayed. They had been dismissed en masse from the service without pay, quarters, or rations on grounds of disloyalty, and charges that their commissions had been irregularly conferred. They wheeled into perfect line, and the babble of talk fell away to silence. Major Charles Zagonyi gave the command; the sabers flashed in the November air, drew down in a final salute. And standing at attention, returning it, Frémont could feel tears streaming down his cheeks.

SHENANDOAH

"YES, IT'S AN INVITATION, all right," Charles said; he'd drawn from its envelope the heavy vellum card embellished with lacy Spencerian script, and tilted it toward Jessie. "The White House ball."

"Oh, my!" She laughed once, without mirth; the card aroused a dozen harshly conflicting sensations. "Decided they couldn't quite pass us over, it seems. Of all the hypocritical dodges! Dear, duplicitous Washington—it never changes . . ."

They were standing in the guest bedroom of William and Eliza's house off Dupont Circle. They had come down from New York so that Charles could assemble his official records for the Committee on the Conduct of the War. The proposed hearing enraged her. Another court-martial—it *was* in effect one, they could mask it with all the congressional window dressing they liked—another trial in which Charles was forced to defend his actions, account for every order and expenditure during those desperate days when the fate of St. Louis and the West hung in the balance. As if it hadn't been enough for the powers-that-be to hound and humiliate him day and night, and finally strip him of—

"Well," Charles was saying, "they need all the support they can get."

"Don't they, though! Imagine—a White House ball, in the middle of this terrible war. Even pompous old Polk had better sense. And with their little boy so ill . . ."

"Yes. Poor Willie."

"Dorothea Dix told me it's very serious. . . . What can they be thinking?"

"It's probably Mrs. Lincoln's wish."

"Of course it is! Frivolous, willful creature. . . . Nobody's eager to go, I can tell you. Dorothea says Mary Lincoln's wringing her hands—they've already received more than eighty refusals. Senator Wade actually sent a letter asking if the Lincolns were aware there was a civil war going on! Eliza says they *have* at least decided to eliminate the dancing."

"Oh, they know there's a civil war, all right. . . . Hello: there's a note with it." He held it to the window. "It's signed by Lincoln—he wrote it himself."

He lowered the note and looked at her. "He especially desires my presence."

"*That* took nerve!"

"I wondered why it came over by special courier."

"He wants something, then."

"From *me*?"

"Well, it's something nefarious. . . ." She stared down into the black maw of the fireplace. Why this *personal* request? Had the Mariposa pressures dulled her awareness of the nuances of Washington maneuver—the circuitous ways alliances were forged, bargains sealed, accounts settled? It could even be a plan to heap on further humiliation: request the presence of the accused, then deliver the telling blow before the assembled company; she'd seen it done before. And they had so many enemies . . .

"Montgomery Blair's arranged it," she declared. "To discredit you publicly. That's what it is."

"Honey, *every* action in this town isn't taken because of venality or vengeance. . . . I wonder if Cameron will be there."

"He's already out, Charles. Eliza told me Lincoln's made him Minister to Russia—apparently the odor of graft got to be strong even for him. . . . Speaking of venality." All at once she turned. "You're not actually thinking of going—!"

He looked down at his hands. "He's my Commander in Chief, Jessie."

"But that's—that's ridiculous! After all he's done to you—withholding supplies, removing you that way . . . He tried to destroy you, Charles!"

"No, he didn't. The Blairs tried to destroy me. Lincoln acted on the reports he got."

"Yes, and they were the most biased, vindictive—"

"Hear me out now. When you look back on it, in terms of the donnybrook going on out there—Frank and I at each other's throats, Montgomery and the old man mixing in it, the charges of Thomas and Washburne and Hunter, not to mention your own lively White House evening"—he smiled at her faintly—"you could say old Abe acted with considerable forbearance. He felt it couldn't go on. He was wrong, but that's beside the point. From where he was sitting, he felt my relief was in the best interests of the department. . . . Yes: I think we should accept."

"Well, I don't."

"I gather that. It's a direct request from my chief—"

"But you don't have to honor it."

He turned serious then. "No, Jessie. I've never refused a request from a superior—never directly. Not with the cannon, not even with Kearny. They've branded me a maverick and a mutineer, but it's not true. I've played for time, I've stretched things a bit, here and there; but I've never spurned a request from my chief."

"You can't be serious," she cried. "Taking this as some kind of field order—it's a White House *party,* to enhance the prestige of the administration, nothing more! Charles, there are times when I simply don't understand you."

"Then try," he said in that immensely soft tone he always used when he was most serious, when most was at stake. "Try, Jessie. Lincoln's desperate. The war's going badly, the northern press is out to crucify him, his little boy's gravely ill. We know what it is to have a sick child. A mortally sick one. . . . Don't misunderstand me. I disagree utterly with his strategy for this war, perhaps I'll never like him personally—but right now he's pleading for loyal adherents to stand by him. It is our place to be there."

There was a silence between them. Jessie stared into the fireplace grate, thinking of Kearny's stony face, little Benton's blued, still body, Frank Blair, drunk and choleric, standing in the headquarters office, waving his arms . . . Where was the *truth* behind all the stealthy proceedings of high policy, the bottomless anguish of human loss?

". . . There's always been that thing between Lincoln and me," he was saying, more to himself than to her. "Maybe I'm a—a kind of conscience to him, don't you see? I raised the banner first, the antislavery standard—he came along four years later. He won because I took the arrows first, and lost; and he knows it. Every time he sees me he's bound to think: 'Frémont could be here, in this chair—maybe he *should* be. How would he handle this?' " He threw open his hands. "He's a border-stater, Jessie—he'll always be: trimming his sails, making deals to hold Kentucky, 'hold the border.' He'll never quite see the country whole, he'll never realize that *America means West*—that's where the war is, where the future is . . . Well, maybe we're all of us prisoners of our childhoods. Those early ghosts and shadows. In a way we're alike, you know. Humbly born, beset by many fears, huge ambitions . . . But he needs us now, he needs people around him who love the Union above everything else." He came up to her then and took her hands deep in his. "And that's why we're going, honey. Get out your best bib and tucker. We're going to attend."

She kissed the weathered cheek. He was so changed; he'd suffered so much—and yet he was freer of resentment, of malice than she. Adversity and injustice had tempered him, deepened him somehow. He was such an honorable man! And yet he still didn't understand the grinding mills of power. Perhaps that was the very reason. . . .

"All right, Charles," she said, and sighed. "We'll go. But I think we're going to regret it."

The carriage stopped with a soft jolt. Jessie gathered up the trail of her gown in a fierce little flourish. Charles helped her down and said to a smart young staff captain:

"Major General and Mrs. Frémont."

"Very good, sir," the officer said without expression, and moved away.

"*That* should set the sparks flying," Jessie remarked. She watched the slick black carriages rolling up to the White House entrance, soldiers briskly checking off arrivals. Wartime Washington. That telltale fluttering had begun high up under her wishbone, and it made her angry.

"Well," she said lightly, "once more into the lion's den!" They followed the company into the front hall and left the cloaks. At the foot of the great staircase the Marine Band, all brass and glitter, was playing the new "National Union March."

"That's to drown out the noise of the firing squad," she said.

He looked at her directly then, gave her arm a gentle squeeze. "Don't see shadows where there aren't any now," he murmured. "There are plenty of real ones to go around."

She caught sight of Lincoln at once. To her surprise he was standing at the very entrance of the East Room, towering over the slow procession, greeting arrivals. She took a deep, quivering breath; her heart was beating thunderously now, and it infuriated her. Why couldn't she be perfectly poised and at ease like Charles? Ah, but he hadn't been in the Red Room, exhausted and defiant, while the Railsplitter had given her that mocking smile and called her quite the female politician. . . .

Her eyes followed the arch of the vaulted ceiling, the classic fretwork, the festive chandeliers. This august edifice had stood at the heart and core of her life. She'd been able to see it from Mr. T's study, as a child she'd sat on grizzled old General Jackson's knee and made him laugh like a boy. Mr. T had hoped to move in here—not with the scheming avidity of Van Buren or Polk; but he'd hoped. Charles had come within an ace of it. She herself had bearded two Presidents in these stately rooms, and been taught the bitter lesson that her impressive tutelage had only given her a false sense of power. This saturnine young man John Hay, the lowliest clerk here, wielded more influence now than she would ever know. What had ever led her to think she could—

They had reached the President. He turned; the gaunt homely face cracked into a brief smile.

"General, Mrs. Frémont. Now, that's good of you to come. I appreciate it."

"Good evening, sir," Charles began. "Let me say we—"

"It's a hard time. A hard time for us." Lincoln raised one of his great hands to his forehead—a loose, distracted gesture. "Willie—our little boy Willie is . . . I'm fearful for the outcome. Mighty fearful . . ."

"Mr. President, we're both—"

Lincoln said suddenly: "You lost a boy."

"Yes, sir," Charles answered. "Our son Benton."

"Then you know. How it is. You know." And to Jessie's great surprise, with the pressure of guests gathering behind them, he gripped her hand in both of his. "It's an insupportable thought to me. I can't seem to—"

He broke off. For an instant she thought he was going to weep, but he only shook his head. His eyes were so sad! She had never in all her life seen such naked grief in a man's face. All the defiance went out of her; he was a frightened, agonized man, a fellow countryman, living through a terrible hour. Right now nothing else mattered.

"We both pray with all our hearts for Willie's swift recovery," she said.

"Thank you, ma'am. I thank you both . . ."

They passed into the ballroom; the blue uniforms made a somber foil to the bright splashes of the women's gowns. Jessie saw Montgomery Blair standing at the center of a small group—the narrow, high-domed head, the thin pursed lips—and her fierce defiance returned. Their eyes met; she nodded curtly, summoned her most icily patronizing smile, and looked away. That battle was not over yet.

Mary Lincoln was receiving at the far end of the room. Her bright, beady eyes leaped up to them, she called: "How *delightful* to see you! How very delightful!" her voice strained artificially high. She was wearing a white satin gown trimmed with black lace. She, too, looked as though she were on the edge of breaking down. Why in God's sweet name hadn't they canceled the affair?

They moved away, encountered with relief John and Maria Crittenden standing a little to one side.

"Dear Maria." The two women embraced, then drew apart in an awkward little silence, smiling. They hadn't seen each other in several years; Charles' candidacy and the Republican abolitionist platform had put distance between them. Yet there was still the memory of those afternoons in the gazebo, the confidences. Jessie said: "How are you, dear?"

"Trying not to be a hysterical female these dark days." Maria's lovely face was webbed with fine lines. "The men have taken over that department anyway, it seems."

"They didn't elect you," John was saying to Charles. "And it came anyway, God help us." His craggy face was terribly aged, his hair had turned pure white; he looked beaten and embittered. He had staked his whole career on a desperate, eleventh-hour bill to restore the Missouri Compromise line all the way to the Pacific, and its failure had broken him. He'd lost his Senate seat, returned as a congressman. Like Papa, Jessie thought. She knew John deeply disapproved of Charles' emancipation proclamation—he'd already introduced a series of resolutions defining the preservation of the Union as the war's sole purpose.

"My two boys are fighting against each other," he said suddenly, and his lip trembled.

"*No . . .*" Jessie glanced in horror at Maria, then at Charles; she could tell from the stern set to his face that he already knew. George and young Tom; to think they might actually find themselves on some battlefield, that they could actually . . . She shivered, said: "I'm so immensely sorry."

"It is the end of this nation," John said grimly. "No matter which side wins." His eyes bored into Charles'. "These fools—telling themselves it'll be over in a few months. Some skirmishes, a battle or two, then a quick-and-easy settlement. *You* know it won't, Charles—you know your people down there. And so do I. It'll go on and on, until the—"

He broke off sharply. Salmon P. Chase and his daughter Katherine had come up to them.

"Frémont, a distinct pleasure!" The Treasury Secretary seized Charles' hand. Tall, uncommonly handsome and distinguished—"a sculptor's beau ideal of a president," someone had called him—he'd lost out to Lincoln two years before, and he clearly had every intention of winning in '64. Jessie knew he maintained close relations with the anti-Lincoln wing of the Republican party. "That emancipation proclamation—a master stroke! It should never have been revoked."

The Crittendens eased away awkwardly; Jessie smiled sadly at Maria, thinking of a long-ago dinner and Charles' young face animate with expectation . . .

"Tell me, General. What do you really think of how they're running this war?" Chase was saying. "Be frank—you're among friends."

Jessie glanced at him in apprehension, but Charles only tilted his head and said gravely: "There are a great many things to do, and very little time in which to do them. We're not experienced at war, like the Europeans."

"Is that why you have so many foreigners on your staff, sir?" Katherine Sprague asked him. She was a stunningly beautiful woman, talented and shrewd—it was said she was her father's most effective campaign manager.

"I appointed them because they are competent, dedicated men—but let me assure you, Mrs. Sprague, they are also good and loyal Americans." And Charles gave her his most charming smile. "Except for the Indians, we were all of us foreigners at one time or another, wouldn't you say?"

Katherine Sprague laughed, and her father said, "Touché, Kate—he's got you there."

The Stantons came up to them then. Edwin M. Stanton had just replaced Cameron as Secretary of War—Jessie hadn't met him until now. She liked what she saw. Peppery and voluble, his eyes restless behind their steel-rimmed spectacles, he wanted to know Charles' opinion of Grant and Sigel as military tacticians. "After all, you first appointed Grant, didn't you?" He was particularly eager to learn how the construction of the central Union Station had facilitated troop movements through St. Louis. This led to a lively discussion between Chase and Stanton over the War Secretary's plan to place the railroad under military control, though it was clear they were in agreement; everyone knew they made common cause against Lincoln, both in the cabinet and the party.

Chatting idly with Ellen Stanton, Jessie studied the room. The party had broken up into small, subdued groups. The Marine Band was playing one of the gay new Strauss waltzes—but the President's dejection, the general discontent over the conduct of the war, and the knowledge that Willie was upstairs fighting for his life had cast a pall over the evening. Secretary of State William Seward greeted them with a geniality that belied his voracious appetite for power; he'd been passed over first for her husband and then for Lincoln, and was undoubtedly enduring the torments of Tantalus; but no trace of that showed in his cordial exchanges with Charles. Jessie detested him, but she had to respect the quality of his intellect and his passionate and sincere loathing of slavery. It was Seward who had earlier coined the term "the irrepressible conflict"—and now, sadly, he'd been vindicated.

More and more of the guests kept drifting toward Charles, seeking him out. There was Schuyler Colfax, always an ardent Frémont supporter, and now rumored to be first in line for Speaker of the House; there was the cool, urbane James Gordon Bennett of the New York *Herald,* and a uniform manufacturer from Chicago named Marshall Field. They all had something to say. Most were angry over the Army's lackluster prosecution of the war; others were even angrier at the administration's moral timidity over emancipation—and Charles, cashiered on both counts, had suddenly become the symbol of their disaffection.

"Far as I'm concerned, you ought to take over the Army here in the East, General," a weapons contractor named Tremayne was telling him earnestly; he had a face like raw beef. "Stop all this pussyfooting around, and go *after* 'em."

"That's hardly my prerogative, sir. Mr. Stanton is Secretary of War, and my superior."

"Well, then, that's just what *you* ought to do," Tremayne pressed Stanton, who regarded him with mounting irritation; Jessie guessed that the Secretary of War would not suffer fools gladly—or any other way, either. "I've just come from Missouri—you should hear 'em out there. Tell me he rides at the head of the troops. Tell me he had the war half-won, and then Washington had to recall—"

"All our generals take the field with their commands," Stanton replied tartly.

"Of course, there are ways and ways of taking the field," Schuyler Colfax said with his infectious grin.

"Gentlemen, gentlemen," Charles protested firmly. "The Army is filled with brave men, and able ones as well."

"Well, *somebody* had better take the helm pretty soon." Chase looked at Seward significantly. "Matters can't drift along like this."

"No more than the truth," Tremayne said. "And from everything I hear, General, you're just the man to step in and pull everybody's chestnuts out of the fire."

This was turning embarrassing—and dangerous as well. Jessie glanced around for the President or Mrs. Lincoln, but they were nowhere in sight. Deftly she eased her hand under Charles' elbow, but he had already begun to disengage himself, and they made their farewells. Slipping into her cloak she murmured between her teeth:

"This town is maddening—! Now you're out, they all want you back!"

"Chalk it up to human nature. If I were—"

"John! John . . ."

They turned. Charles Sumner was hurrying toward them, his heavily handsome face smiling.

"Charles." The two men shook hands; they had entered the Senate together in '51, and the Boston abolitionist had been a staunch Frémont man, and the most ardent supporter of his proclamation.

"Senator," Charles said. "I'm pleased to see you're fully recovered."

"Thank you, John. The President sent me—it's his wish that you return to the party, if you will."

"You're quite sure?" Charles said. "I don't know that it's the time . . ."

"Yes. He sent me for you. He specially wants you, John."

Charles' eyes flashed at her once—that fiery hawk's glance that stirred and frightened her.

"Of course," he said to Sumner.

As they reentered the East Room, Lincoln broke away from a small group and came at once toward them.

"You must forgive me," he said somberly. "I haven't been much of a host—I'm not myself this evening. General, I've just learned that you and General McClellan have never met. I'd like to remedy that."

George McClellan was short and stocky, with a broad nose and one of those scraggly walrus mustaches that completely obscure the lips. Jessie read him instantly: dogmatic, self-important, unimaginative. The consummate engineer, risen to great power. She'd heard the stories—how he'd kept Lincoln and Seward waiting for more than an hour, then on his return had actually gone upstairs to bed, leaving them *still* sitting there. West Point '46; a fine record in Mexico, railroad surveys—but apparently incapable, Charles said, of taking action, committing himself to—

The President was introducing her to Mrs. McClellan. She turned—and received a shock. The woman was wearing the secessionist colors: a broad band of scarlet velvet crossed her white gown from shoulder to waist; three scarlet-and-white feathers perched in her hair, bobbing. It was unpardonable, outrageous—it couldn't be an accident . . .

". . . The explorer," McClellan was saying to Charles in a high, colorless voice. "I surveyed the northern Pacific route myself through the Cascades—one of the river surveys for the Army in '53."

"I remember."

"I was surprised you weren't chosen for one of them."

The muscle in Charles' cheek flexed once. "Well, you see, General, I never had the special advantage of West Point."

"Of course. Tell me, what do you hear from David Hunter?"

Why, he's quite nasty, Jessie thought; a mean, petty man. . . . Charles' eyes glinted, but his face was impassive. "I have not been in personal contact with General Hunter. But my former chief of scouts tells me that the Confederates were only too happy to avail themselves of fine winter quarters when they reoccupied Springfield."

Jessie glanced uneasily at Lincoln—he himself had advised Hunter to withdraw to St. Louis; but the President's eyes were vacant.

"A negligible matter," McClellan said. "The war will be decided here—in the East."

"You're entitled to your opinion, General."

"It's not an opinion—it's a demonstrable fact." The engineer's voice rose, his mustache puffed eerily as he spoke. "Your pursuit of Price, I have no hesitation in telling you, violated all sound military procedure."

Charles' face had darkened perceptibly; even Lincoln looked distressed. Jessie braced herself; but then to her complete amazement her husband smiled his old expeditionary smile.

"Well, General," he said casually, "as the poet says, it's better to have loved and lost than never to have loved at all . . ."

For the first time during that long evening Lincoln laughed. "That's a good one." He nodded, pointing a long, bony finger at the perplexed McClellan. "He's got a point, George. A good point there. . . ."

Riding home through the raw night Jessie said: "He'll have to give you a new command now. Lincoln."

Charles stared at her. "Now, how in God's name do you figure that?"

"Politics. They want you back. Couldn't you feel it in there?" She smiled wryly. "Of course it could be a mixed blessing."

"There they are, General!" Captain John Howard called, pointing. "The whole kit and caboodle! Heading for Fisher's Hill."

"I see them," Frémont answered. Beyond the rise where their party had reined up sharply, the long valley swept away to the south, lush and green in the soft June sunlight, the Shenandoah meandering through it like a broad pewter scarf. On the far horizon the White Oak Ridge rose, the palest purple; and in the center of the valley Stonewall Jackson's supply wagons were moving, their canvas tops like tiny low sails, followed by darker masses of infantry. Frémont raised his field glasses—and now the horses were visible, the drivers, the rippling, snakescale glitter of armed men marching.

"Too late," Colonel Cluseret said, teeth clenched on his unlighted pipe. He was a stolid, imperturbable man, incapable of panic, but overly cautious; the two words, after these weeks of interminable, exhausting pursuit, irritated Frémont.

"No, it's not, Gus," he said tersely. "We can catch them—we *have* to catch them."

"Jackson won't turn now, sir. He's got what he wanted—he'll keep on running now till he's over the mountains."

"It's the bridge, at Port Republic. That's what he wants now." Frémont lowered the glasses. "He can't get across that bridge without giving battle—we won't give him time. We've got to push harder, pin him against the river . . . John"—he turned to Howard—"I want you to send two couriers around to General Shields."

"Yes, sir."

"Tell them to use Thornton's Gap. And send them separately, twenty minutes apart." He wrote rapidly in his notebook, tore out the page and handed it to Howard. "Tell them General Shields is to defend that bridge to the last extremity."

He rode hard back to the column, his staff strung out behind him; letting the horse's drumming rhythm, the clean rush of air clear his head, the way he'd done on the trail. To his boundless surprise he'd been given another field command. The congressional hearing in February on his conduct of the Western Department had ended in complete exoneration. Again he'd presented his own case—and this time there was no coldly malevolent Kearny; some of the faces on the committee were actually friendly. After a lengthy investigation they had absolved him from censure in his failure to reinforce Lyon or Mulligan, cleared him of all charges of extravagance, commended him warmly for his construction of gunboats and the appointment of Grant, and concluded that his administration had been "eminently characterized by earnestness, ability, and the most unquestionable loyalty." Senators Ben Wade and Zachariah Chandler with several others came up to him afterward and shook his hand. Frank Blair launched a vitriolic attack on the floor of the House, but Schuyler Colfax led a series of impassioned, masterful rebuttals. Powerful forces in Congress and most of the northern press had called for Frémont's reinstatement.

Jessie had been exultant. "Didn't I tell you? Lincoln can read the handwriting on the wall—you'll see."

And sure enough, in late March he'd been given the newly created Mountain Department, which embraced western Virginia, eastern Kentucky and part of Tennessee: mountain country for a mountain man. The new theater was a pet idea of Lincoln's—a roving force that could breach the Alleghenies, seize the railhead at Knoxville, and bail out the beleaguered Unionists there.

Jessie had also been right about a new command being a mixed blessing. It was cruel country: five hundred miles of mountain ranges running northeast to southwest—a wilderness one hundred miles wide, few roads, and most of those impassable. The foraging problems were fearsome—the country so poor there wasn't even enough fodder for the mules.

He'd been shocked at the condition of the troops. Their uniforms were worn to tatters; there was an acute shortage of blankets and tentage, and most critically of rations. His chief quartermaster, Moorhouse, a perpetually despondent man, told him almost tearfully that none of his requisitions had been filled; he'd protested and been icily instructed by Quartermaster General Meigs that he must make do with what he had: all available arms and equipment were to go to the Army of the Potomac. The soldiers consequently had outfitted themselves as they moved—a crazy assortment of frock coats, felt hats and farm quilts; they looked like railroad gangs at sunrise muster. Speaking to them, watching their sullen or indifferent faces, Frémont felt sore at heart. His Army of the West—he had breathed that army into life, built it out of whole cloth in one hundred strenuous days, imbued it with his own confidence and energy. These boys from New York and Pennsylvania and Ohio didn't know him, and they didn't want to; to most of them he was just another Goddamn general in good boots and a slouch hat . . .

Worst of all was the lack of a unified command. Nominally he was "head" of the Department, but in cold fact each area commander operated independently, subject to a stream of conflicting orders from Lincoln or Stanton. And they were alarmingly dispersed. His old friend Nat Banks from '56 campaign days had given up the Massachusetts governorship for a commission and was commanding at Strasburg in the Shenandoah Valley, with Shields' division farther south at Harrisonburg. McDowell, the victim of Bull Run, was encamped far to the east of the mountains at Fredericksburg on the Rappahannock. Milroy was tucked away behind Cheat Mountain at Elkwater. Frémont's own force had been placed at Romney on the upper Potomac, two mountain ranges away from Banks and Shields, guarding the

Baltimore and Ohio railroad line, which Jackson had raided the previous autumn, tearing up track and wrecking a dam.

The tactics of timidity—disperse and coil; Frémont didn't like it. In a day and a night he'd devised a plan: run south down the valley, catching up Milroy as he went, cut through the Cheat Mountain Pass to Staunton, link up with Cox at Gauley Bridge—and then, with a concentrated force, drive southwest to Knoxville. A workable scheme, if they could master the awful supply problem . . . but he'd never had the chance to put it in motion. That same evening Colonel Rufus Tucker, whom he'd brought east after Hunter had unceremoniously sacked him, entered his headquarters office and said: "Old Stonewall's loose again."

Uneasy, Frémont listened to his chief of scouts. The hero of Bull Run, who'd been last observed retreating east of the Blue Ridges at Stannardsville, was suddenly back in the Valley, moving rapidly through Staunton. Was it another raid? Or did Jackson intend to cross the mountains and attack Charleston—or even wheel north toward Morgantown and roll them all up? But he didn't begin to have enough men for that. . . .

"What's his strength?"

"Seventeen thousand, give or take."

"You sure of that, Rufus?"

"Yes, sir. They've given him Ewell's division for this one."

Not a raid, then. Well, he himself had nearly 33,000, not counting McDowell, who was too far away to be of any help anyway; he should be able to contain it. Jackson was facing two-to-one odds. Of course, that was on paper; the hitch was that he had a three-to-one advantage over each of their *separate* commands. This stupid splather! What had ever led Lincoln to believe he was a strategist?

He ordered Banks to send Shields farther down the valley on the double, and prepare to follow hard. He was wrestling with another supply crisis when Nat's wire came in that same afternoon: SHIELDS AT WARRENTON EN ROUTE FREDERICKSBURG TO REINFORCE MCDOWELL ON ORDERS WAR DEPARTMENT. Now what in God's name was *that* for? There was no impending attack on McDowell's lines. Frémont and Alex Asboth checked their maps in alarm. Warrenton was 25 miles on the *far* side of the Blue Ridges. That meant there was no one at Harrisonburg, or even at Luray—that meant there was a great, gaping hole where 10,000 men ought to be. . . .

He wired Washington urgently requesting Shields' recall, alerted Banks again, and prepared to march for Staunton at once. Jackson hit Milroy full force, as Frémont expected, and drove him back on Franklin. That was all right; Milroy was retreating in good order, his losses had been lighter than Jackson's, and his withdrawal would actually bring him nearer the link-up with Frémont.

Then, silence. Jackson clearly hadn't driven on west for Charleston; apparently he wasn't withdrawing to Staunton either. A spoiling attack, perhaps. Ashby's screens of Confederate cavalry cunningly shrouded all movement. Blenker's division, which Lincoln had promised him, still had not arrived; he decided not to wait any longer, but to push on southward.

The next thing he heard was a frantic message from Banks saying that Jackson had surprised Kenly at Front Royal and routed him; that he himself had pulled out of Strasburg and had been hit on the flank by Jackson at Winchester.

Winchester. He gazed at the situation map, beating down his consternation, tracing Jackson's route of march with one finger. That Confederate army had doubled back into the Valley, covered 170 miles in 17 days—much of it through mountainous terrain—and fought three battles into the bargain. Impossible. It was utterly impossible; but there it was. . . .

Filled with foreboding, he pushed his hungry, ill-equipped army on south. There was no communication from Nat for three days—and then a terse wire informing him that Jackson was preparing to assault Harpers Ferry, and that he was reorganizing his own forces below Sharpsburg.

"Sharpsburg—but that's in *Maryland* . . ." Frémont gazed at Asboth's ruddy, solemn face. "How far does Banks intend to retreat—Canada?" That meant he'd been broken, then—routed; there was no other explanation. And Jackson was shelling Harpers Ferry. The man moved like a phantom—a phantom in seven-league boots. Did he actually intend to cross the Potomac and envelop Washington itself, with that ragtag force of his?

Audace, tout droit! Louie's favorite slogan. Dare everything. Even in his acute trepidation, watching the troubled faces of his staff, he could feel himself smile at the curious kinship he felt for the man. Like me, he thought warmly. What I would have done, in '47. . . .

Now it was all up to him. He would have to cross two ranges, either north or south of Strasburg, and block Jackson's escape route. There was no one else to do it.

"Now he's gone too far," he said firmly. "Attacking Harpers Ferry—now he's bitten off *too* much, given us the chance to catch him. And that is exactly what we're going to do."

They watched him in uneasy silence. Even Charles Zagonyi, the fiery Hungarian cavalryman he'd brought east on his staff in the face of chill Army disapproval, looked dubious.

"But General," Asboth protested softly, "even if we *are* able to intercept him, and he gives battle, he will outnumber us—we have barely ten thousand effectives. If I may say so, sir, this army is in no condition to fight. . . ."

He leaned forward, gripping the table's edge, and looked at each of them in turn. "Then, gentlemen, we will have to accept the odds. We must do it anyway."

The little group was gathered at the edge of a cornfield near an abandoned farmhouse. Frémont recognized Tucker's gray plains hat and trotted toward them, conscious of sporadic rifle fire over on the Keezletown Road. Another rearguard action by Confederate pickets, buying time. For nine days he'd been chasing Jackson, straining every fiber. The Harrisonburg Road was littered with abandoned packs, blankets, even ammunition, and finally stragglers who'd been unable to keep up with Stonewall's furious pace. And men as hungry and weary and ill-clad, pressed after them, snatching up bits of equipment and clothing until, in the heat and choking dust, one army looked pitifully like the other . . .

"What's going on?" he called as he rode up.

"Straggler, sir," Tucker answered. "Found him holed up in a corn crib."

The group gave way, and Frémont saw a slim, fair-haired boy hunched over an improvised crutch made of an ash limb. His left boot was gone, the pants leg cut away; the exposed ankle had swollen to a great blue club streaked with ugly milky-yellow bands.

"Sit down, son," Frémont said. The boy eased himself to the ground, his teeth gritted. Half the buttons on his tunic were gone; the corporal's chevrons were so faded they were barely visible. "What's your name and regiment?"

"Orville T. Blankenship. Second Virginia." He paused. "And that's all I'm about to tell you."

"You watch your tongue, Corporal," Tucker told him sharply, "Or you'll regret it."

"How'd you hurt your foot?" Frémont asked.

"Took me a little fall north of Winchester."

Frémont stared at him. "You walked all the way from Winchester on that?"

The boy looked up at him—a droll, defiant glance. "No—matter of fact, I purchased me a magic carpet from that feller Sinbad . . ."

A sergeant from the Forty-fifth New York seized him by the collar and snarled: "You shut your frigging mouth, reb! You're talking to General Frémont . . ."

"That's all right, Sergeant," Frémont said. "Let him be."

The boy looked up at him again—a bemused, humorous squint that made Frémont think for a moment of Carson. "So you're Frémont. The mighty *ex*-plorer of the wild and woolly West. Why, hell's fire, we'd've been to Frisco and back before you'd hardly got yourself across the Missouri. . . . You're tangling assholes with Jackson's Foot Cavalry, Gen'ral. Now you see us, now you don't. You know?" His eyes passed over his captors with genial contempt. "Shoot, you Yanks're every bit as frazzle-assed as we are. Maybe a tad more so. Want to tell *you*, your best bet is to hightail it back over Massanutten Mountain before you get your tail feathers singed." For another few seconds he studied them, amused and scornful, while they stood over him in silence. Then he gave it up and doubled over the monstrously swollen foot, gripping it hard, his young face cramped with pain; his hair had fallen over his eyes.

Lord help us, Frémont thought. If they're all like this boy we're in for a hard time of it. A very hard time. . . .

The fields led down in gentle undulating grades to a stream called the Mill Creek, which fed into the south fork of the Shenandoah, then rose through woods to an open ridge east of the hamlet of Cross Keys. Columns of men moved down the Keezletown Road into line, plumes of smoke bloomed whitely against the massed green of woodlands; and over and under and through everything lay the thunder and crash of artillery, a pounding bass to the dusty rattle of musketry, the squeaky treble of human voices raised in entreaty, in rage, in terror . . .

Jackson had turned to give battle, as Frémont knew he would. Shields had finally, finally got back through the mountains and now sat astride the bridge at Port Republic. Jackson had had no choice; yet even then, harried as he was, hedged about, his troops exhausted and half-starved, he had still deployed them skillfully along the high ground commanding the road to Port Republic. At nine o'clock Frémont had sent Stahel's Brigade against the left flank at Beahm's Farm and then ordered Milroy and his West Virginians to advance on the right, where they cleared the Mill Creek and moved into the woods. Frémont, watching through his glasses, saw the woods erupt in continuous, coughing fire, and then men re-emerging in clumps of two and three. *No.* They had to get in there. They had to!

"Come on," he called to his staff, and rode hard down the slope and through the creek. The water was shockingly cold against the bad leg; how could it be so cold? It was June . . . Along the reverse slope men lay in grotesque attitudes, as though flung out of the clouds by some immense, malignant hand. Several men were running toward him, throwing fearful glances over their shoulders; two had no rifles.

"All right, now!" he sang out. "We're going back in there, boys!" They stopped stock-still, resentful, unbelieving. "*Here* we go now. . . . Come on!"

He entered the wood, was drowned instantly in gloom and chaos. Shells whined and crashed into the treetops overhead, leaves and bits of branches whirled upward in crazed fountains. An officer was sitting on the ground, both hands cupped hard over his belly; a colonel, glaring up at him. Donaldson; blood had smeared the side of his face. Men were milling around, crouching behind cover, a captain was leading a group off toward the left, cursing and roaring. Frémont thrust his way over to him, almost rode him down.

"No, no—that way! By the *right* flank! Fire right, march!" he roared. No one could hear him. He reached down, clutched the captain by the collar and pointed angrily *right, right.* To his amazement the officer gave him a quick, delighted smile and moved off to their right, still howling and cursing a steady stream. Frémont felt himself being bumped and shoved, glanced down in annoyance. Soldiers had surrounded him, were moving with him, staring straight ahead, their faces rigid with will. It's the horse, he thought, the bigness of the horse gives them comfort; God, how sad—and yet perfectly logical, too. . . .

They broke out of the woods: an orchard, edged at its upper boundary by a long, low stone wall, its round gray rocks like mammoth skulls. He turned, looked back again—and the whole wall bloomed into rolling puffs of smoke stitched with needle flares of flame. And an instant later a dun swarm of men was running toward them through the smoke, crouching and dancing, their bayonets glittering gaily in the sunlight; and now Frémont could hear snatches of cry—*"hooo! ya-hoooo!"* A flag, swirling red, went down, was caught up, again dipped down like a wild, wounded bird. He saw Charles Zagonyi, saber drawn and resting against his shoulder, talking casually to another officer, their eyes fixed on the oncoming infantry. Why not, he thought with a cold fatalism he'd never known before, why not? Now was as good a time as any. He drew his revolver, resting it on the pommel; seized in a measureless, depthless stillness, scarcely aware of the furious gunfire all around him, the frantic rituals of reloading, the shrieks and moans of wounded men. Let it come, he said, almost audibly, staring hard. He had never sought it, had always believed with frantic, prideful certainty he would evade its constant, deadly passes; but it had sought him often enough. So, now, let it find him. He was ready.

. . . They were stopping; they had wavered and paused, they were falling back through the stripped, spidery orchard branches, falling, turning, getting up again; they had reached the stone wall, were vaulting over it one-handed like lost schoolboys, the smoke drifting indolently over the brown lumps of bodies, the somnambulist groping of the wounded . . . And around him now men were shouting, thumping one another, chanting indecipherable sounds. He looked at them slowly. They had held them; they had held! Their physical presence closed around him like a woman's arms; he felt a rush of affection for them so great it made him tremble.

"Boys," he said. "Good boys . . ."

He had never known such anguished exaltation; he was very close to weeping. Hollering, cursing, crouched over hurt comrades, sucking on their canteens, they were magnificent in their tatterdemalion humanity; they lay at the very heart of all—

Someone was tugging at his shoulder, calling his name. A dispatch rider, the bill of his cap curiously crushed, his collar open.

"General! General Frémont, sir . . ."

It was like waking from a fantastic dream; sound came flooding back to him, cannon fire and human voices. He was soaked in sweat—it crawled through his scalp and eyebrows, stung his eyes; he realized his jaws had been clamped shut so hard they hurt. But his mind was perfectly clear.

"Yes, son," he said. "What is it?"

"Sir, General Stahel says to report he's under heavy attack on his left—he can't hold his position . . ."

"All right. Tell him to withdraw to Armentrous Hill—but no farther than that, you understand? I'll get someone over there to support him."

"Yes, sir!" The courier was gone. He dispatched Howard to tell Buell to move his battery to Armentrous Hill in support of Stahel, another rider to get Bayard to move his Pennsylvanians past the Union Church to the Ridge Road. But *here* was where it would be decided; he felt it deep in his belly. He was asking Zagonyi about Dickel's cavalry when he heard that high, premonitory *"Yip! Yip! Ya-hoooo!"* again and turned, thinking *NO*, they're not going to attack again—not after that first wild charge, the losses; not after hiking 245 miles in 35 days and fighting four battles, and now caught between the hammer and the anvil; they're not actually thinking—

They were coming again, down through the apple trees, the same battle flag swirling and dipping among the shattered branches; around him the firing rose to one stupefying roar. Frémont saw an officer in gray with a full black beard, waving his hat, his horse rearing, sidling—then the smoke had dipped down in skeins and streamers, shutting out all human life. . . .

"I hope you understand my position, General," Carl Schurz said in his clear, precise way; the German accent was much less noticeable than Frémont remembered it.

"Of course," he answered.

"It seems there is always an inquiry these days."

"Especially when things have gone wrong. Which they seem to be doing most of the time." Frémont gazed moodily out of the tent's entrance where a warm summer rain was falling, muting the camp sounds. "I'm getting used to them, Carl. Inquiries, investigations, court-martials. I ought to be, by now."

Schurz brushed fussily at his new, well-fitted tunic with one hand. "At least it's better than a firing squad, hey? That was what they had in mind for me."

Frémont smiled. He knew Schurz had barely got out of Rastatt when the Revolution of '48 had collapsed—and that he had again risked his life when he'd slipped back into Prussia and brilliantly contrived the escape of his old mentor Gottfried Kinkel from the formidable prison-fortress at Spandau. He liked Carl, for his fine impartiality as much as his passionate commitment to his ideals. The Wisconsin journalist had supported his candidacy vigorously in '56, and was credited with swinging the Northwest behind Lincoln in '60. From the very beginning of the war he had called for emancipation as the only choice which could give the North a high moral purpose. He'd just given up a post as Minister to Spain for a brigadier's stars.

Now he was here to pass judgment.

"Fortunes," Schurz mused; he had the Germanic fondness for metaphysical speculation. "So often they hang with the thinnest of threads: one hour, one cannon, one message sent—or not sent. . . . What a priceless blessing it is we never know what is in store for us, hey? We would be paralyzed with fear."

"It's all right, Carl." Frémont rose and walked over to the tent door. "Jackson got away. That's what matters. I understand."

At the end of that long, terrible day at Cross Keys they had not been able to dislodge the amazing Confederate army; they could not do it. Outnumbered, indescribably weary, low on rations and ammunition and lacking any hope of reinforcements they had held on, had met four furious assaults, the final one with the bayonet; they had held, and that was finally, utterly all they could do. That night Jackson had withdrawn and attacked Shields at Port Republic, Jackson himself rallying his Stonewall Brigade at the critical moment, and driven him from the bridge: the back door had been torn from the hinges. While Ewell held off Frémont's desperate counterattack next day, that irrepressible Foot Cavalry had made its escape across the Blue Ridge Mountains to Gordonsville.

"The man is a magician," Schurz was saying in wonder. "He will become one of the great tactical geniuses of the century, mark my words."

"If he lives."

"Of course—if he lives. The fire in his troops, their sheer unbounded love for him! That incredible forced march, the assaults . . ."

Frémont turned. "Yes," he said quietly. "They fight for him the way the Army of the West would have fought for me."

Schurz's huge dark eyes fastened on his—a long, piercing glance; his jaw moved restlessly under the broad black mustache. He looked more like a Caribbean freebooter than a German intellectual. "The President has personally asked me to make a report. There was the implication that it was to be confidential." He paused, and his lips twitched once. "But it was only implied. And because I have admired you for many years now, because you were the first to call for freeing the Negro—and paid a heavy price for it—I am going to tell you what I think." He set the heels of his long, expressive hands on the table, side by side. "So . . . my conclusions are: you did all you humanly could, given your situation. Lincoln's own troop dispositions here in the valley invited disaster. And his decision to send Shields over to McDowell was fatal—it presented you with a lost game, as we say in chess. Ordering you to make that forced march from Franklin to Harrisonburg was in my opinion impossible for *anyone* to carry out. Your people were starving and without proper equipment, as you well know. In no condition to fight—much less to engage a superior force."

He threw his arms behind his head. "Oh yes, a military genius—Frederick, a Bonaparte—would probably have reached Strasburg on the thirtieth. But we *have* no Bonapartes, we don't even seem to have a Murat. In all solemn fact"—he smiled wryly—"it's probably a very good thing you *weren't* able to place yourself across Jackson's line of retreat. There is the distinct possibility that if you had, your entire army would have been destroyed—and that is what I am going to tell the President."

"Thank you, Carl. I'm very grateful."

"It is no more than the truth." He smoothed his luxuriant black hair. "In any event, some good has come out of it all. Lincoln has at last decided to reorganize the forces here, consolidate them into one army."

"So he's finally got the message, has he? Well, who'll be in command—McDowell or me?"

"Neither of you." Very deliberately Schurz drew a sheaf of papers out of his dispatch case and handed it to Frémont.

> 1. *The forces under Major General Frémont, Banks and McDowell, including the troops now under Brigadier General Sturgis at Washington, shall be consolidated and form one army, to be called the Army of Virginia.*
>
> 2. *The command of the Army of Virginia is specially assigned to Major General John Pope as commanding general. The troops of*

the Mountain Department, heretofore under command of General Frémont, shall constitute—

John Pope. Pope, that insolent, carping prig, who had deliberately failed to carry out his orders at Wilson's Creek, who had lagged behind the line of march, intriguing with Hunter, undermining his authority and jeopardizing the campaign itself; Pope, whom that cunning traitor Jefferson Davis had given command of one of the five railroad survey expeditions, the most southerly one through El Paso and Yuma, who'd actually been made Chief of Topographical Engineers in '56—when he had been passed over—no! It was too much. It was more than any man should have to accept . . .

Schurz was watching him—a look of sorrowful intensity; he knew his own face was flooded with raging dismay, but he couldn't help it. "Perfect," he said grimly. "Afraid to sack me again—so he orders me to serve under an insubordinate son of a bitch who's hated my guts for years—"

"I know, it's hard, but the President—"

"—an arrogant, bigoted West Pointer, a Kearny man to the core, who will take every occasion to humiliate me in front of the men, until I'm finally forced to wipe that insolent smirk off his face, and court-martial proceedings can begin again—what a tidy solution! The one man certain to destroy me . . ."

"General, you must understand—"

"I understand everything! Believe me." He wrenched open the collar of his tunic; he felt as though he were choking to death. "The President will have my resignation in one hour."

Schurz came to his feet in alarm. "John, don't do this, I beg you! Don't act rashly—wait awhile, and see what—"

"No! I cannot swallow this—and I won't." Holding the damp, coarse canvas flap he peered out at the camp, watching a sentry, shapeless in his blue cape, his right shoulder distorted with the butt of the rifle slung barrel-down, and three privates running toward the cook tent, their mess gear jangling. To be forced to give this up, still again—after the creek bed at Strasburg, the orchard at Cross Keys; after all the worry and misery and sometimes glory . . . Lincoln had wired him: YOU FOUGHT JACKSON ALONE, AND WORSTED HIM. Which was not true, not remotely, but it had been a comfort in the bitter knowledge of Jackson's escape . . .

And now this.

"General." Schurz was standing close behind him. "I earnestly hope you'll reconsider—this war will be a long one, with many changes of fortune, many changes of command . . ."

". . . I can't." Smiling sadly he turned. "Some men could, I know. Perhaps *I* should—but I can't. There is no other honorable way." He gripped the Rhinelander by the arm. "Thank you for your support. . . . And now I'd like to be by myself."

"Of course, General."

For long after Schurz had left he hung by the tent doorway, gazing out into the camp, the rain.

COURSE OF HONOR

"LOOK AT THIS ONE." Charles handed a rose-and-ivory whelk from Jessie's shell collection to Nancy Davis.

"It's lovely. They all are."

"She's rich!" Ed exclaimed. "After all, the Indians used them for money."

"That's what we need." Zachariah Chandler laughed. "An easy, inexhaustible currency supply."

"We'll go beachcombing tomorrow," Jessie told them. "All of us."

They were gathered in the summer cottage the Frémonts had taken on the beach at Nahant, north of Boston. A September northeaster was driving gray surf against the pilings below the lawn; now and then it shivered the old house, flung puffs of smoke from the fireplace into the room.

Nancy said: "What a shame the weather's turned so foul!"

"What's a little gale?" Charles scoffed. "We'll wrap you in oilskins and give you Frank's knapsack. When the tide goes out, the beach is drawn clean as fresh slate." He turned to Chandler then, his eyes merry. "It's sort of like politics, Zach: when the east wind's blowing you never know *what* the tide'll bring in . . ."

Chandler grunted and sipped his sherry. A New Hampshireman, he'd made a fortune in banking and land speculation in Detroit before he'd turned to politics; one of the leading radical Republicans in the Senate, he ran the party in Michigan with an iron hand. "I wish it'd bring an end to this war, that's what I wish," he said in his low, harsh voice. "All the feuds and backbiting, the defeatism—we've got to put an end to it before it tears the whole North apart. What we need now, Charles, is *unity.*"

"I fear thee, ancient mariner, I fear thy skinny hand," Charles quoted with sly solemnity; and John Greenleaf Whittier, his long, slender figure supine in an old chaise by the fireplace—Jessie had thought he was asleep—chortled suddenly, and then subsided.

"Another country heard from," Nancy said.

"Don't you rag him, now," Jessie warned her. "He's composing an imperishable line. Aren't you, John?"

"No imperishable lines before dinner. My mind's on the steamed lobster."

Jessie laughed with the others. She was very fond of Whittier. He'd been an ardent supporter of Charles long before '56; the poem he'd written after Charles' removal as Commander in the West never failed to move her: *Thy error, Frémont, simply was to act / A brave man's part, without the statesman's tact, / And taking counsel but of common sense, / To strike at cause as well as consequence.* Yes—cause as well as consequence; that said it all . . . They'd become good friends with the poet since Charles had left the Army and they'd returned to New York City and begun summering at Nahant. Whittier had just brought out a new book, *In War Time;* Jessie thought it his best work, eloquent and heartfelt in its rude force.

Chandler was talking politics again; she only half-listened, watching him, watching the others. It was Zach who had telegraphed the day before: Ed and Nancy Davis were in New York for a week or so; could they and John Whittier come up to Nahant to confer with the General on a matter of some importance? She knew why they were here—or thought she knew. A curious trio: Chandler blunt and uncouth, the arch-politician; Ed as genial and urbane as ever; Whittier reflective and committed. Power, class and sensibility—Zach had chosen his emissaries with care . . .

Charles had caught her eye, winked at her gravely. The furrows in his face were deeper since Cross Keys, his neatly trimmed beard had turned completely gray. Fifty-two—her husband was fifty-two; it seemed impossible. He'd come back from the Shenandoah and slept for days—slept so long and so deeply she'd begun to fear for him. But he was only tired, he said; bone-tired, and he'd caught a chill during the drive down the Valley. She'd understood perfectly his reason for resigning—though part of her wished this time he'd buried his personal sense of injustice and stuck it out. In a few short months that arrogant fool Pope had spectacularly demonstrated his total incompetence at the second battle of Bull Run. Charles' old friend Franz Sigel, who'd commanded a corps there, wrote him about the contentious General Sam Sturgis riding up to Pope's headquarters tent after the debacle and roaring at him: "Damnit, didn't I tell you that all was necessary for you to hang yourself was to give you plenty of rope?"—and that at least was a satisfaction. But it was also the cruelest of ironies . . .

"It's all right, Jessie," he'd told her somberly. "They don't want me, they've made that clear—let's put it behind us. God knows we've problems enough right here at home."

Which was only too true. The Mariposa was in deep trouble. The debt load on the mines was shocking—well over two million; the interest charges alone ran to more than $13,000 a month. Harried by anxiety, chafing at his inability to get out there in the middle of the war and rid himself of what was clearly Trenor Park's calculated subversion, Charles put himself completely in the hands of the lawyers and the money men. The following year a company was formed, capitalized at 100,000 shares of stock with a par value of $100. Charles was to hold 37,500, but those paragons of financial sagacity, Opdyke and Ketchum, demanded 25,000 of Charles' shares—in addition to the 25,000 they already possessed—in order, Ketchum insisted, to empower them to maintain control for the New York group. It was only a temporary expedient, the lawyers assured him; when the bonds for defraying the debts had been repaid, they were to revert to the General. Merely a technicality.

The negotiations dragged on and on; the legal expenses were horrendous; David Dudley Fields charged the corporation $200,000 for his services. They'd got rid of that odious Trenor Park—but in the end Charles was left with only 8,500 shares in a 44,000-acre estate valued on a production basis of over ten million dollars. Jessie hadn't been able to control her dismay.

"I know, honey." He'd shaken his head grimly. "They had me over a barrel. It was the best I could do—I *had* to get that mountain of interest off my shoulders."

With time his spirits revived, the native impetuosity and enthusiasm she both loved and feared. Railroads were the answer—everyone down on Wall Street was talking about them.

"*Gold.* Jessie—what is it anyway but dead metal? That 'funny yellow stuff' of Lily's—remember? But railroads—they're the future, they're America . . ."

Railroads were speed, they were action—fluid motion, binding the land as precisely as those imaginary but absolute lines he'd once traced across the night sky with Papa Joe. A road to California was a certainty—Collis Huntington and his group had already started the Central Pacific eastward across the Sierras; somewhere in the Utah desert it would link up with the Union Pacific, driving westward. It was just a case of marking time until the war was over . . . How strange that Huntington, that prosaic hardware merchant, should be the person to bring the great dream to life! Charles engaged offices on Beaver Street in downtown Manhattan and busied himself with plans for the southern route he'd mapped in '54, grappling with financing for a small line through Kansas that would ultimately expand to connect the ports of Norfolk and San Diego. Coast to coast! Now and then she'd hear him humming that rude tune he loved: "*Singing through the mountains, buzzing o'er the vale, / Bless me, this is pleasure, a-riding on a rail!* . . ."

"McClellan's claiming victory already," Zach Chandler was saying gloomily now, chafing the toe of one of his high-laced boots against the fireplace fender. "Actually says he'll let the southerners keep their slaves—plans to *reimburse* them for any loss of their human 'property.' How do you like that for little green apples?"

"Arrogant pouter pigeon," Nancy said. "Who would ever have believed he'd actually be running for President?"

"Wants it all, but won't risk anything for it," Charles observed. "He's the same way in the field."

Jessie gazed out at the surf boiling dark against the bulkhead, the blown spume drifting downwind. So many changes. . . . The brilliant, formidable Stonewall Jackson had been killed in battle, as Charles had feared he would be. Her sister Eliza was dead; her dear friend Starr King had literally worked himself to death for the Union cause. Bret Harte, now employed by the United States branch mint in San Francisco, had written his plaintive, poignant poem "Relieving Guard" in the embattled minister's honor. Nat

Banks, who'd been beaten a second time by Jackson at Cedar Mountain (he'd become known in some Army circles as "Jackson's supply officer," from the equipment and supplies he'd lost to him—a brutally unfair aspersion, Charles angrily maintained), was now commanding a corps way out in the Red River country.

John Crittenden had died in '63; his two sons were still fighting against each other. Irony of ironies, the scheming General Hunter had resorted to his own emancipation proclamation to solve the terrible guerrilla problem in Missouri—and Lincoln had tartly revoked *his* order, too! He'd been given command of the Shenandoah, and been beaten roundly that July by the audacious Jubal Early, who'd crossed the Potomac on his spectacular raid and sent Washington into a panic—the Navy had actually dispatched a ship to spirit Lincoln off down the river. Frank Blair, who had managed—a patently illegal affair—to hold both a major-generalcy *and* his congressional seat at the same time, had run true to form that spring. He'd delivered a vicious, totally unsubstantiated diatribe on the House floor accusing none other than Salmon P. Chase of conspiring with his son-in-law over a southern cotton transaction by which, Blair claimed, the Treasury Secretary would make two million dollars. The liberal wing of the Republican party had flown into an uproar.

She glanced at her husband, who was following the conversation indifferently, his drawn, handsome face grave. What price vindication that came too late? Ulysses Grant, whose selflessness and tenacity of purpose Charles had spotted so swiftly in '61, was now commanding all the Union forces. The Mississippi strategy Charles had urged so vehemently all through that agonizing hundred days had nearly been realized—Vicksburg had fallen, the link-up effected at New Orleans with the Navy, splitting the Confederacy; and Union armies were rolling through the gulf states toward Atlanta. The war *was* being won in the West—it certainly wasn't being won in the East! And the President had finally issued his own Emancipation Proclamation—tardily enough, it must be said, and expediently timed to follow the victories at Gettysburg and Vicksburg—and at last the Abolitionists were satisfied. Well, up till now, anyway. . . .

"Ben Wade's still unhappy over the way Chase's candidacy fizzled,'" Chandler was saying. "I must confess I don't understand it myself."

"Women are attracted to him—which is why men don't trust him!" Nancy declared. "It's as simple as that." Her eyes sparkled mischievously. "Who do *you* think ought to run the country, Jessie?"

Jessie raised one arm dramatically. "Ladies and gentlemen, I give you an independent candidate, influenced by neither political or military ambition—John Greenleaf Whittier!"

Chandler scowled at the general hilarity. "Just what we need—a pipe-dreaming poet to show us the way."

"No, seriously, Jessie," Nancy pursued.

She shook her head quickly. "I'm done with politics."

"—But apparently politics isn't done with you," Ed Davis said with his affable smile.

She smiled back at him. Now they'll come to the point, she thought. Well, it was Lincoln's own fault—he'd always taken the conservative, the temporizing course; he'd never made any effort to conciliate the radical wing of the party, who still saw in Charles the forthright champion of emancipation, stern measures, a forceful prosecution of the war. Many German-Americans and most of the Abolitionists preferred him to all other candidates. In May a group led by Wendell Phillips and Schuyler Colfax broke away from the Republican party, held a rump convention in Cleveland and nominated John C. Frémont for the Presidency.

The act had meant nothing politically—the administration had been riding high that spring: Sherman was driving on Atlanta, Grant moving on the Chickahominy against Lee; it looked as though the war would be won by midsummer. The people were solidly behind the Railsplitter. But as a gesture it moved Charles, who'd accepted the nomination with pleasure. The wounds of St. Louis and the Shenandoah—yes, and the Kearny trial, too—hadn't entirely healed; they never would, she now knew. There would never be that grand righting of fortune she'd once believed would restore everything he'd been stripped of, give him his rightful place in the nation's heart—and this bitter knowledge had aged him subtly. And so it was nice to be honored again—even if it was only by an outraged phalanx of the party's uncompromising wing . . .

But it had turned into a summer of reverses after all. The mightiest Union force ever mustered had been beaten to a standstill among the Virginia jackthorns in a terrible place they called the Wilderness; the two armies had clashed at Cold Harbor, and still again before Petersburg, without a decision. And the casualties kept streaming back—men without arms or legs, bodies in new pine boxes. City papers printed the names in gray agate type, columns on frightening columns; every county courthouse had its bulletin board draped in black, with more names added day after day. The South had shown a bewildering resiliency, a Homeric will to resist. Recruiting had fallen off, the draft was wildly unpopular, paper money had skidded to forty cents on the dollar. People were war weary, grieving, angry at the slow parade of vacillation and temporizing. Discontent was rising everywhere—in the farms and factories, in Congress and in Lincoln's own cabinet, where Chase openly pushed his candidacy, and Stanton and Montgomery Blair lashed savagely at each other.

In the light of this general discord and despair, Charles' candidacy began to take on an unexpected importance. He could not win—there was no doubt about that—but he was suddenly a pivotal, perhaps a crucial force in the election. The Democrats, still trying to appease the Confederacy, had nominated General McClellan—whom Lincoln had fired for doing too little just after he'd fired Charles for doing too much—and who if elected was likely to welcome back the South with slavery intact; with Frémont in the ring McClellan's chances looked excellent. Alarmed, some prominent Bostonians issued a proposal that Frémont and Lincoln *both* withdraw in favor of a compromise candidate; Charles had indicated his willingness, but Lincoln had as yet made no reply . . .

"The President is in trouble," Chandler said all at once. Outside the wind had fallen, and his voice seemed heavier. "Big trouble. Fact is, his strength has been eroding badly in the past few months. Especially here in New England, the Northeast . . . That's why we're here, Charles. He needs your help."

"What help could I give *him*?" Charles asked levelly.

"Now you know full well you'll siphon off a lot of Republican votes."

"It's no more than a token, Zach. A complimentary gesture to an old explorer."

"It's a good deal more than that." Chandler threw out one of his big, square hands to include the others. "We're asking you to withdraw in favor of the President."

Charles got to his feet and settled a log deeper in the bed of embers. "I rather favored the Boston plan," he said after a moment. "I'm willing to step down if Lincoln does."

"Well, he won't," Chandler answered bluntly. "I've talked with him."

"We can't spare Grant for the Presidency," Ed came in quickly. "We need him too much in the field." Jessie wondered if he remembered his deep objections to Grant back in St. Louis. "Think about it, Charles. Who else has the—the sheer bulldog tenacity to bore in against Lee? Anyone else would be hopeless."

"You can't possibly beat Lincoln," Chandler said to Charles. "You know that, don't you?"

"Yes. I know that."

"But you could bring him down. And put Little Mac in. Do you want that?"

There was a pause. It's true then, Jessie thought; that's why they've come hotfooting it up to Boston: they're desperate, Lincoln's back *is* to the wall, as Horace Greeley says. Good! Let Lincoln find out power can ebb as fiercely as it flows, and leave you stranded like a piece of rotten dunnage . . . But her husband's face was only calmly inquiring—she could see no trace of the vengeful elation she herself felt in that moment.

"Maybe if the shift in popular sentiment continues the way it's been going, Charles *could* win," she couldn't resist saying.

Chandler's eyes closed in dissent. "Lincoln is still the President, the country's still at war. This Republic isn't going to embrace a third party—not now." He looked at her directly, unblinking. "You forgotten your lessons, Jessie? Birney and his Abolitionists stopped Clay in '44 and handed it to Polk, Van Buren's Free Soilers blocked Cass in '48—you forgotten how Fillmore's Know-Nothings tipped the scale against Charles eight years ago? No, all you can do is cause trouble—but you could do a hell-roaring lot of that . . ."

"Charles," Ed Davis came in again, "do you honestly want a copperhead down there running the show for four long years? with the South back in the saddle, dictating terms, dangling King Cotton in front of all Europe for bait? pressing for a slave-holding Southwest, forcing a division of your Golden State into a warring north and south? That's what McClellan will bring us if you split the Republican party."

"Yes," Charles came back sharply, stung by the allusion to California, "and maybe Mr. Lincoln should have thought of it when he yanked me out of Missouri, when he put Pope in over my head!"

"I know, you've been treated unfairly, more unfairly than anyone I know of, but that's over the dam. The issue is larger . . ."

To Nancy Jessie said with a laugh, "Have you ever noticed how the issues always swell in importance when *you're* being asked to give up everything!"

"He won't be giving up anything," Ed retorted, his face tight with irritation; he turned again to Charles. "You'll be gaining everything—you'll be helping save the nation! You of all people can't just let it drift now, sink back into states' rights and slavery, a perpetually divided country, an armed truce . . ."

Charles leaned forward, forearms on his knees. "Maybe you're right. The thing is, I don't have much left, Ed. I'd like to hold on to this—it's meaningless in a way, but it means a great lot to me, the unswerving support, you know, of a few who've never turned from the true course. . . . Let me think it over a day or so."

"I talked with the President two days ago," Chandler said in the silence; his voice lowered, shaded with complicity. "If you'll come along with us, we're prepared to make it well worth your while."

Jessie saw Charles' head come up fast, the old, fierce hawk's glance flare in his eyes. The fools. The fools! Didn't they realize that was the very *last* thing on earth to say to John C. Frémont? How could Zach be so blind!

"First off," Chandler was saying, "a high military command, active service in the field. That's firm." He still seemed unaware of Charles' reaction. "Second, the Blairs will be *finished* in the administration. Both of them."

Even now, raging inwardly at the Michigan senator's purblind venality, fearing the scene she knew must follow, she felt her heart leap. The fall of the house of Blair! They would never offer this unless they intended to carry it out. Frank would be stripped of either his generalcy or his House seat, and Montgomery would be brushed out of the cabinet. In for a fight, in for a funeral—and the service *this* time would be for vindictive Frank and arrogant Montgomery with their toadying to the slave-holding interests. Poetic justice! Freed of their malevolent scheming, Charles could have survived everything else—crooked contractors, Price, the guerrillas, even the West Point clique. Good, then: *in* for a funeral—so be it!

". . . The President is offering me the Blairs?" Charles was saying in that extremely soft voice that sent tremors down the small of her back. "Their heads—on a platter?"

Chandler grinned a politician's grin. "Well, they've been a hell of a thorn in your side for some time—that's common knowledge. I thought it might make the decision easier for you if you knew they'll never again be able to—"

He broke off in amazement. Charles had come to his feet, one hand extended toward Chandler.

"*Senator,*" he said and his voice rang in the room like struck iron. "Frank and Montgomery Blair have done me savage and irreparable harm, and I would dearly love to see them brought down—but I have never in all my life struck a bargain over a question of principle. I would not see even Frank Blair broken as some sort of 'reward'—I call it bribe—for my own compliance! You may tell Mr. Lincoln—if it is indeed his suggestion—that I do not *dicker* over matters like this. The offer is dishonorable, and it is insulting! As for the field command, the same argument holds; the President clearly does not consider me qualified to command a Union army—he has made that fact evident not once but twice. Why should I now become worthy because I leave the political field to *him*?"

"Now look here, Charles," Chandler said resentfully, "there's no need to put that construction on it. All the President is saying is that he's appreciative of—"

"*Be still,* Zachariah."

Everyone turned. John Whittier was looking at Chandler with his soft, good-humored smile. "I'm surprised at you. *Of course* he won't strike a ward-heeler's bargain—what on earth did you think? That's why he's John C. Frémont. That's why pipe-dreaming fools waste their time writing poems about him." He raised himself on the chaise then, his searching eyes very intent. "You've spent too long on the Senate floor—you think every man looks only for what he can get. That runs perilously close to the idea that every man has his price."

"Ah," Chandler said sardonically. "The poetic view."

"The poetic view is the humane view. Zachariah, in spite of what you think, poetry often does go to the heart of the matter. Often." He got to his feet and began to pace slowly back and forth in front of the seaward windows. *"To every thing there is a season, and a time to every purpose under the heaven: A time to be born, and a time to die; a time to kill, and a time to heal; a time to keep, and a time to cast away; a time of war, and a time of peace. . . ."*

His voice, musical and deep, reverberated through the rooms, dominating the surf, the storm wind. "I dreaded this civil war, and the bottomless miseries it would bring, as much as any man living. But the sword is drawn now. To welcome the South back *with* its slaves would be more ruinous than to lose it forever. It would be the blackest betrayal." He stopped and faced the explorer in the dying light. "It must not be in vain. It must not! Not all this terrible outpouring of blood and losses and anguish. You were *there,* Charles, in the Valley, where those awful sacrifices are being made. You have counted the bitter cost as none of us can. . . .

"You'd have been right for the country in '60, Charles. Swift measures, hard decisions, fire and fury—then was the time for it. Now you'd be wrong. Now it will need the healing touch." Chandler made a sudden movement of impatience and Whittier held up a hand. "I am as opposed to slavery and secession as any of you; but Sumner's vengeance is not what will be needed now. Now Mr. Lincoln's view will be the right one: the open hand, the bound wound, the soft answer. . . . And Lincoln will win if you step aside."

He paused again in front of her husband, who was watching him steadily, motionless in the dusk. "You see, Charles, you are one of those rare individuals from whom the fates demand more than from the rest of us. You have been chosen, God knows why, to walk the hardest road of all: it has somewhere been ordained that you must be humiliated in order to be vindicated, that you must accede in order to triumph. You were dragged back under guard from the coast, but you gave us California; you lost the Presidency, but you gave point and purpose to a political party; you were cashiered from a high command, but you sounded the first great clarion call for emancipation. . . . Now you will again fail for the Presidency—you cannot win it in any event—but you will ensure the triumph of another man's vision: victory without vengeance. And you will see the wisdom of yielding still again, because you have a larger spirit than the rest of us: you have been viciously used—and yet you bear less rancor than any man I know."

He dropped his hands to his sides. "And so I will lamely paraphrase that mighty preacher and poet and say: there is a time to do, and a time to stand aside. General, it is a time for you to stand aside."

There was a long silence, broken only by the moaning of the wind. Jessie watched her husband, the slow play of conflicting emotions stirring his features and fading again: vaulting dreams, radiant triumph, heavy injustice; and finally a decision that was almost serene. Her cavalier . . . perhaps one of the last. She loved him without reservation, she wanted to run to him and catch him in her arms, shield him from yet another defeat.

"Of course you're right, John," he said. "It is clearly the right thing to do." He turned to Chandler. "But not for any preferments—or retribution either. I absolutely reject that. Am I *clear*?"

"Understood." Chandler nodded coolly.

"Oh—one thing, Zach." To Jessie's surprise her husband's face had brightened with the impulsive, boyish smile. "When you see the President, I'd like you to give him a message. Would you do that?"

"Of course, General."

"I'd like you to tell him that it's been a certain pleasure, after all that's happened, to have him squarely in my sights . . . and that it's been an even greater pleasure to choose not to pull the trigger." Still smiling, he nodded to Chandler. "I think he'll understand."

PART SEVEN

IRON HORSE

WORKING IN THE ROSE GARDEN below the terrace Jessie could hear them coming—that rapid-fire drumming of hooves that never failed to thrill her. She lowered the pruning shears and turned. Below her Lily burst into view on Mariposa Belle. As usual she was bareheaded, the broad-brimmed plains hat Alex Godey had given her dancing on her shoulders from the rawhide thong across her throat. She was sitting elegantly erect, her knee hooked hard around the horn, swaying with the horse's driving rhythm. Such a fine horsewoman! Where the bridle path curved away toward the stables, she impulsively swung the filly toward the high, perfectly pruned privet hedge and sang out: "Hy-*yaaaah!*"—a wild frontier cry that made Jessie grin. Very intent now and confident, her full face flushed from exertion, Lily looked almost pretty. They swept toward the hedge; there was that curious, brief hesitation—a supreme gathering of forces—and then horse and rider flew over the barrier in a clean rush and cantered to an easy, sidling stop.

"*Good* girl!" Lily cried, and patted the filly's sweaty neck. Charley was next, on Tamerlane. Jessie watched her eldest son, crouched low in the saddle, his face caught in that fierce eagerness she remembered from his childhood. The horse cleared the hedge awkwardly; Charley fell forward against its neck and clung there an instant while Tamerlane shook his head at him crossly, blowing.

Lily permitted herself one word: "Disgraceful."

"Made it, didn't I?" Charley demanding, laughing. "And all in one piece."

"You rode better than that back home."

"No loss." He'd regained his seat now. "We don't ride horses in the Navy, Lil."

"More's the pity."

Last came Archer Wetherall on Charles' tractable gelding Barney. He saw the high hedge, the other two waiting for him on the far side. His face went blank with surprise; he reined up, swung the horse to the left and cantered through the break in the hedge where the driveway ran up from the Albany Post Road.

"Little barrier like that?" Lily cried coolly. "Why, it's nothing."

"Too much for *me,* I can tell you!" Wetherall laughed. He was tall, with a soft-featured face and a small mustache. "Wherever did you learn to jump like that?"

But Lily had already turned away and was galloping down toward the stables, sitting with that light, almost ethereal grace.

"Don't mind Lil," Charley told him. "Tell you confidentially—it's my belief she was sired by a centaur."

Their laughter faded as they moved off. Jessie, smiling, shook her head and mounted the stone steps to the terrace. Beyond it the great Hudson lay in sleepy midsummer stillness, gray in the haze; sloops and cutters speckled its surface whitely. Across the river Hook Mountain loomed like a slate sugarloaf, and farther south Piermont thrust its lean arm into the Tappan Zee. A lovely, lazy vista . . .

Her friend Hannah Lawrence had found the house for them. Weary from the years of work with hospitals, the slow parade of sick and wounded young men, resenting the fierce impingements of Manhattan, Jessie had found herself longing for green woods and distant hills; the Colonel Webb place had delighted them on sight. Built of gray stone, the huge, rambling house seemed to have been designed for their tastes, their lives in the East. There was a music room for Frank, a map room, a study, even a room devoted to Humboldt's mighty library, which Charles had purchased intact on the death of the venerable explorer. The large dining room could seat fifty, though they both preferred much smaller parties in the more intimate small dining room.

She called the house Pocaho—as Indians had once named these rolling hills north of Tarrytown—and filled it with pieces that stirred memory and affection. There were the silver services and Persian carpets they'd brought from Paris, a ferocious grizzly rug Kit Carson had sent from Taos, a Wedgwood vase given them by the Prince of Wales; there was the ceremonial sword presented Charles by the German citizens of St. Louis, and the flag he'd flown from the Wind River Peak, and that first quartz slab Alex Godey had pried loose from the Black Drift vein, mounted now in polished mahogany, beside a fist-sized nugget just as it had come from the creek bed, poised on delicate silver prongs. She'd positioned the table in the smaller dining room so that from her place she could always look through into the long drawing room and see Albert Bierstadt's painting centered there above the mantel. At times its incandescent western light seemed to set the very room afire.

Of course it was not Black Point; not remotely. Homes were like love—you loved only once in that way, if ever. But Black Point was closed to them for good: the Army, with its blind obstinate tenacity, had kept it, as she'd feared it would, though the war was five years past now. It seemed there was a plan to erect a *presidio* on the site, like the one on the hill behind Monterey. The government would never give it up. Theft by fiat. Even their efforts at reimbursement for the cost of the house and land had been unavailing. No: Pocaho would never give her that quick, deep catch under the heart, that warm sense of wanting to be nowhere else. But it suited them handsomely. There was the lively company of good neighbors—the Schuylers, the Phelpses, the Beechers; proximity to the occasional glitter of Manhattan's theater and opera; ample room to entertain old friends and new, such as the brilliant geologist Louis Agassiz or Collis Huntington; and the easy rhythm of long walks or rides, and winter evenings reading together before the fire. It would be as fine a place as any—well, almost any—to end their days . . .

In the music room the piano began: a few chords, tentative and thoughtful, and then the melody in brilliant, stately cadences. Frank, playing a Chopin polonaise. Dreamy, studious Frank—who would have thought that frail, troubled child had concealed this extraordinary talent? With what majestic caprice the gods bestowed their gifts! Her children's wildly differing predilections were still a source of wonder to her: Charley, obsessed with the sea and all things nautical since he'd been able to walk; Frank with his perfect pitch and astounding melodic memory; and Lily, the matchless equestrienne, scorning the easy social graces—

As if her thoughts had summoned them her son and daughter came on the terrace, Lily a step ahead of Charley, walking quickly, slapping the quirt against her leg; dismounted, she had reverted to her awkward, uncaring manner.

"Come on, Lil," Charley was saying. "It'll be fun—there'll be a regatta and then a dance."

"I despise dances—you know that perfectly well, Charley."

Slyly he said: "Spencer Pomeroy'll be there."

"Who cares." Frank's Scottish staghound trotted up to her, his tail wagging ponderously, and Lily bent down and ruffled his ears. "Hello, Thor. How's our noble protector?"

"Where's Mr. Wetherall?" Jessie asked her.

"Oh . . . he's gone." Lily went on petting the dog.

"What do you mean, *gone*? Didn't you invite him to stay for tea?"

"Sent him packing!" Charley rolled his eyes at his mother. "Another suitor that didn't suit."

"Don't be ridiculous," Lily said. "He's hopelessly insipid."

"Lil, you're impossible." His eyes flashed darkly at his sister, his slim, handsome face broke into the quick, roguish grin that instantly reminded Jessie of his father. "If the poor sod can't ride like John Gilpin he's out. And if he can, then there he sits, trapped in the saddle—with no occasion whatever for tender sentiments."

His older sister looked at him balefully. "Why don't you mind your own business, Mr. Jack Tar."

"You *are* my business, Sissie. We're all of us half-crazy racking our feeble brains to cure you of your equine obsessions, your—"

"That's enough, Charley," Jessie cut in. "True wit depends on simplicity and variety. You must try some."

"Touché, Maman!" He grinned at her, pleased with himself, the day, his life. He was in his second year as a midshipman at Annapolis and enjoying it hugely: he wanted to follow the sea, to command a vessel—he'd never doubted for a moment that he would. That irrepressible sense of certainty; so much like Charles . . .

"Well, I'm off to the Schuylers' *fête champêtre,*" he declared. "Wine, women, and song! Put a lamp in the window." He strolled off, whistling to the piano, out of tune.

Jessie said: "Aren't you going, Lily?"

"With those parlor types? Not likely. They're so boring." She threw herself into one of the rattan chairs, spanking the slate table with her quirt. Calmly Jessie studied her daughter: the heavy jaw, high-ridged nose, bold staring eyes. Like Mr. T, she thought; Lily got all his features, somehow—it wasn't fair; why couldn't she have inherited the McDowell delicacy of feature, or drawn Frank's fine Frémont nose?

"It's no fun without Papa around." Lily's foot was rocking swiftly under her long skirt. "He told us he'd be back yesterday."

"I know."

"Why can't he be *home* more?"

"It's his work, Lily. You know that. He has to devote all his energies to it now."

"Stupid, dull railroads. What earthly good are they?"

Jessie made no reply. Try as she might she could never grasp the murky complexities of business. The Mariposa troubles had grown into a notorious court case, brought about by Thurlow Weed's charges that George Opdyke and his associates had, among numerous other misdeeds, swindled Charles out of most of the Mariposa's gold. *Another* trial, with all the attendant exposure, fought by celebrated legal names avid for prominence. To see Charles in the witness stand, harried by lawyers, still gravely reluctant to accuse these predators in whom he'd placed so much confidence, was almost more than she could bear. The most shocking revelation of all surrounded those 25,000 shares Charles had transferred by proxies to Ketchum to ensure control of the mines' management for the New York faction. When Charles had tried to recover them, the lawyers now informed him he had in effect signed a deed of trust, making them over! He'd had to bring suit; and in the settlement these pillars of finance had offered to return 20,000 shares—provided he sold *them* the remaining 5,000 at half their market value—a loss of $125,000.

"The General was among friends," the brilliant William Maxwell Evarts sardonically informed the court, "and he may thank God that he did not fall among thieves!" The Manhattan courtroom roared with laughter, but there was nothing funny in the anguished flash of her husband's blue eyes . . .

The railroad ventures were, if anything, even more mystifying to her. Charles had sold out of the Kansas Pacific for the Missouri Pacific, then abandoned that line for the Memphis & El Paso.

"It's a magnificent opportunity," he'd exulted. "The Texas legislature has made an unbelievable grant—18,200,000 acres of Texas land, a veritable kingdom of land, ours when we complete the line. We already have substantial franchises—rights running all the way through Fort Yuma to San

Diego. The old trails, Jessie! It'll be the making off the Southwest."

His enthusiasm was unbounded, he'd regained all his former fire; but listening to him evenings she was troubled. The mere distances alone were terrifying—did they actually plan to lay one tie every three feet, over all those thousands of miles? And capital outlay was far worse than on the Mariposa. Financing became an obsession. Charles' brother-in-law introduced him to a French entrepreneur named Henri Probst; Charles liked him on sight, and talked the board into naming him agent for floating loans in France . . . and then it turned out that he and his French associates had proceeded to flagrantly misrepresent the whole enterprise, claiming that work had already been completed between Memphis and the Red River and that it was subsidized by the Federal Government as the Union Pacific had been. Charles had been wild with rage.

"They had no right to make these claims! That was the whole *point* of the line—I don't *believe* in federal subsidies. That's taking the public's money, drawn from their own taxes—we have no right to it for a private venture! And the line's funding is perfectly clear—that Texas land grant is printed right on the face of the bonds. They're trying to ruin my good name!"

He'd left for Paris at once and forcefully disowned and refuted the false claims, trying to set the facts straight. But the damage had been done: over five million in bonds had already been sold. Worse yet, that grim, vengeful Elihu Washburne, his old enemy from Missouri days, was now Minister to Paris. Still smoldering over the War Committee's complete dismissal of his charges that Charles had mismanaged affairs in the Western Department, Washburne had written Secretary of State Fish, urging a swift and thorough investigation. Old scores, new wounds. This had led to an acrimonious debate on the floor of the Senate that spring. Senator James Howard of Michigan thundered away, claiming "a more stupendous fraud never was committed upon a friendly people" and charging General Frémont with dishonest practices. Senator Sumner and Simon Cameron and a dozen other colleagues rose at once in Charles' ardent defense, but the press, as always hungry for sensation, rushed to call it the scandal of the decade.

Things kept going wrong. The French agents had pocketed a 40 percent commission—40 percent!—on all proceeds from the bond issues; a flood silted up the Red River channel fifty miles from the construction site; costs climbed and climbed beyond the original estimates. To cap it all now, the implacable Senator Howard was vigorously opposing the bill granting the Memphis & El Paso a right-of-way through the Territories, citing delays in construction. Charles, harassed and tense, was gone more than ever, closeted interminably with lawyers and contractors and financiers.

The truth of it was she resented the railroad—it excluded her, raised barriers between them that had never been there. She'd always been so close a part of his life—the expeditions, the Mariposa, politics of course, even the war—but railroads weren't challenges; railroads were money. Money, and how to raise more and more of it. Every day that endeavor seemed more pervasive in this booming, grasping postwar society, rampant with corruption, demeaning all the old dreams and sacrifices. She didn't care for the breed of men who pushed the railroads, either. They had no sense of the public trust she and Charles had grown up with; they carried about them a deep unsoundness—you had the disquieting sense that they would lead you astray and then betray you, not only out of greed, but for the sheer rapacious pleasure, the deadly game of it . . .

"I wish we could go home," Lily said suddenly; she was staring resentfully at the soft magenta haze over the Hudson.

"This is our home," Jessie answered quietly.

"Not to me. It never will be. Never. California's home."

"Lily, you have to put that behind you. . . ."

"I can't." She twisted the quirt brusquely into circles and bows, her face set in that barely contained impatience. It's sexual, Jessie told herself, surprised at herself, at the thought; all that energy, and no true outlet.

"He's right, you know," she said aloud.

"Who?"

"Your brother Charley. There *are* a few other things in this world beyond horseflesh."

"Of course."

"Life is full of wonders, dear—it is! But you have to reach out to them, *dare* a few things. With *people,* not just animals. Surely you can see that."

"You mean, now that I'm almost thirty?" Her voice was flat with disdain. "Now that I'm an old maid?"

"Now honey, I didn't say that."

"Of course you didn't. You never do. . . . It's all right," the girl went on in the same flat tone. "I know what I am. And what I want to do. That's more than most people can say."

". . . It's deliberate, isn't it?" Jessie asked softly. "You don't want it, do you? Marriage, a man?"

The girl turned then and fastened Tom Benton's cool gray eyes on her. "All right," she said. "You're always after me—it's true. Horses . . . animals. They don't betray you, ask anything back. You think marriage is wonderful—that's fine, Mother. For you. But I don't want it. I don't *want* to go through what you've gone through—all that waiting, the loneliness, the heartbreak. For Father, yes. It was worth it for him. But how many men are in his class? *I* don't see any."

"I see." She smiled sadly at her daughter. Yes—heartache, and to spare: the agonies of loneliness, the longing that bit at the very soul of you—but it receded, all of it, before the vibrant, triumphant *certainty* of their love; and if she had it all to live over again she would welcome it without a qualm . . . But then she had been fortunate. She had found the one man who could always strike the spark in her into a larger fire, make her whole. Perhaps Lily was right, in a way.

The piano broke off abruptly; Frank had left the music room, as dreamily as he'd entered it. . . . It was Panama, Jessie thought heavily; Lily had been terrified beyond fear—of my death, abandonment, the jungle, those half-crazed men. It was too much, it turned her away somehow from opening herself to love, and loss—to life. And what callow young man could hope to match the vitality of her father—explorer without peer, national symbol? He was especially close to his plain, forthright daughter. Or had it been *her* fault—had she clutched the frightened little girl too closely to her when she was still swept by her own youthful apprehensions? Or had her own confidence as a woman defeated the daughter she loved? Had she leaned on her too much, fought too single-mindedly for her husband's career when she should instead have protected her children? . . .

There was a sound in the living room, the sharp clink of glass on glass.

"That'll be Simmons," she said, getting to her feet. "Come along—I've got to talk to him about Friday evening." She hurried across the long flag terrace, thinking ahead. Nat Banks was coming down from Boston; the Phelpses and Beechers were coming for dinner Friday; Charles would rather avoid it, but they *must* return the Schuylers' hospitality before the month was out.

"Simmons," she said, entering the room, "would you send—"

She stopped short. Her husband was standing by the sideboard, a glass in his hand.

"*Charles,*" she exclaimed, watching him.

"Papa!" Lily said, behind her. "Why didn't you *tell* us you were home? We've been waiting for you for hours and hours . . ."

His head moved once—he gestured vaguely with one hand, set the glass down. It was empty. The look on his face filled Jessie with the deepest dread.

"What is it?" she asked softly.

"We are ruined." His face was white and very drawn; the muscle in his cheek flexed once. "They've taken our road."

"Taken it?" She gazed at him blankly. "What do you mean?"

"It's gone." He still hadn't moved from the sideboard; she saw with a piercing sense of alarm that his hand was braced against the worn wood. "The right-of-way bill didn't pass the Senate. Howard's killed it."

"Oh . . . I'm so sorry . . . But surely it could be brought up in—"

"There's nothing to appeal. We've gone broke. They've shut me out." He began to pace up and down before the French doors. "I figured they were trying to whipsaw me, pressure me out. The way they did with the Mariposa. I was damned if I was going to be taken again, so I called their bluff—told them to go ahead, put me in receivership and throw away that land grant. They'd only destroy themselves, they wouldn't get back a dime on the dollar." His voice was no longer steady. "Even when they went ahead with it, I was sure they were bluffing—I argued that the grant guaranteed my solvency. Clements ruled on it this morning—ruled against me. Eighteen million acres!" he cried softly. "An empire in land—that's half the size of all New England!—and he ruled me bankrupt. Two hours later the receivers were in my office."

"But why did they go through with it?" she asked. "All that land, all that work—it makes no sense."

"Lost their nerve." His lip curled down. "They were afraid to hang on, tough it out. Preferred to take a dime on the dollar and skip out. Cowardly scum."

She felt sick with anger, with fear, struggled to master it. She must hold herself in, help him with all her might. "All right," she said, "it's gone, then. If you ask me, you're well out of it. They're nothing but a pack of scoundrels, they'd sell their own—"

He made a low, inarticulate sound, deep in his throat. "You don't understand! This was it—*this* was our last chance. And it's gone!"

"Good God, Charles," she cried, thoroughly exasperated, "we've spent our *lives* snatching at chances—we live by chances, you and I!" She must turn this, somehow. Careful now, careful; this had hit him very hard—he didn't need recriminations now. "Look, darling, we've always taken grand chances by the hundreds. One more big chance doesn't matter anymore—of one kind or another." He started to speak and she overrode him. "We'll always find a new one—and meanwhile we'll just enjoy what we have."

He sighed, then—a tremulous sigh that was bleak with loss. "We haven't anything left to enjoy," he said finally. "I pledged it all. It's all gone."

She gazed at him dumbly. "But the—the Mariposa stock—"

"I threw it in. My working capital, all our assets." His eyes held hers, hollow with grief. "They tricked me—it was during the refinancing, after the trouble with the French bonds. They wanted a paper pledging my assets. It was just a formality, they said—I was glad to reassure them, give proof of the extent of my commitment. And now Gray—he's the receiver—says it's committed irrevocably. Legally binding. And Berryman and Shaw agree." His voice broke. "They whipped me, Jessie. We're ruined."

"—But we can keep Pocaho, can't we, Papa?" Lily cried out suddenly in the silence. "If we sell Nahant, and the house in the city, if we—"

He shook his head in a slow agony of loss while his daughter stared at him, her eyes huge with fear. Jessie watched them both numbly. They had been together, the three of them, in that ratty, jerry-built hotel in San Francisco when he'd spilled the glittering yellow dust on the table, and Lily had pushed her stubby fingers through it. Now here they were again, and the last vestiges of that dust were gone. Dust indeed. . . .

"You mean—we're really *poor*? We haven't *anything*?" Lily was saying in a thin, hoarse tone. "The house, the furniture—the—horses?" She was bent forward oddly, one hand quivering in the air. "You've lost it! Like everything else—we lost the Mariposa, you let them take Black Point—and now we'll lose this, too, for those cold dead iron railroads!" Her fists clenched, her voice rose in a shriek. "Oh, God, I can't bear it, I can't bear it!"

"Lily—"

"You never cared about us, not once! Only about your grand and glorious dreams! You left Mama to die in Panama, and now you've left us on the street, to beg until we—"

Jessie turned and slapped her once, hard. Lily stopped, glared at her a moment—then fell against her, sobbing.

"All right, honey." Absently she stroked her daughter's hair, staring at the gold-and-umber glint of the leather-bound rows of Humboldt's library, Charles' sword with its eagle-head hilt and blue tassel. "It's all right. Go up to your room and lie down. Rest awhile, child. We'll look in on you soon. . . ."

She led Lily out into the hall, returned to the drawing room. Charles still hadn't moved from the windows. Her panic, black as an abandoned shaft, had stopped; she felt only an empty despair heavier than anything she'd ever known. All the other disasters had been as nothing, then. Terrible as those times had been, they'd had youth, patrons, and the measureless, exultant dreams of westering . . . This, at their age, was fatal. They would be destitute. The enormity of their situation rushed on her like foul wings beating. How would they keep a roof over their heads? What in God's sweet name would they do?

"I had—I had such a dream," he was saying, his voice a monotone. "Linked to the old trails, don't you see? The trails I charted, and your father's dream west—the tracks curving out there along the riverbeds, through the passes, till they reached the Pacific, tying it all together: East and West, farmer and riverman and merchant. One undivided nation—all running on those gleaming iron rails . . .

"But they don't want that. I see it now. They don't care about westering, or America either—all they care about is money: piling it up until there's nothing left but stacks and mountains of green paper. They never wanted it to work, *my* way. That's why Howard fought me from the very start."

"But you never crossed him," she said. "You don't even *know* him—why should he want to destroy you?"

His face turned flint hard then, suffused darkly with blood. "Because I wanted to build a railroad without federal money," he answered with quiet savagery. "Because I believe a road should be like any other private enterprise—paid for by the men who expect to profit from it. But they don't. I've just seen that—more fool me. They want public money to build *their* road—and then they turn around and charge the people the cost of constructing it—*and* full fare. And so of course they're eager to pay off certain senators for the passage of bills giving them federal subsidies . . . and *that's* what Vanderbilt and Gould and the others can't forgive me for—or Howard, either. I was spoiling their little thimblerigging game for them."

She came up to him then, and took his hands. It was true—it was his dreams that were his glory and his anguish. He shouldn't have committed all their resources, of course; he shouldn't have taken the lawyers' oily assurances on faith—God help him, he probably never should have flung himself into the world of entrepreneurial schemes and corporate evasions at all . . . but he couldn't act any other way. His commitment was always total and honorable—nothing held back, no qualifications or exceptions; and what else but that unreckoning commitment could have held men together in the terrible mountain snows, fired them to grasp an empire? Half-measures never won anything, they never would. Perhaps dreams were too pure for railroad building. Charles had failed; Collis Huntington had completed the transcontinental railroad—they'd driven the golden spike at Promontory Point, Utah to the tune of speeches and marching bands . . . and all Collis had ever considered was the balance sheet, his every move predicated on profit. Collis knew no other gauge—and maybe there wasn't any other gauge in business. And even in that moment of triumph, the air had been clouded with rumors of fraud surrounding the Crédit Mobilier . . .

He was trembling, as though he'd caught a fatal chill; his eyes were hollow with pure agony. "It was all there, wasn't it?" he murmured. "The rubber raft. I've always run the rapids, without thinking—of you or Lily or the boys. She's right. Oh God, she's right. I've failed you terribly . . ."

"No," she said.

"Yes. Asked too much of you, risked you all. Again and again. That was wrong."

He looked more ill than ever, as if he was disintegrting before her eyes, and she felt a new shaft of alarm. "Charles?"

"I'm so afraid," he said.

"Afraid?" She stared at him. He had never been afraid—not of rivers or mountains or gold braid, parties or Presidents. He had driven ahead undismayed and undeflected, done what he thought was right and stoically accepted the consequences. "Afraid?" she repeated.

"Yes." His voice was barely audible. "That you might stop loving me. Because of this."

A slow, exultant sense of solace flooded her. His fear, his anguish was not over the lost fortune, or position, or their sudden, terrifying poverty. It was over the risk of losing her. He always cared—to a fault. Of course he'd acted as he had on the rapids nearly thirty years ago—why should she or anyone else expect differently? He had *acted*—it was the only way he knew.

"Oh, no," she said, holding him hard, willing the trembling away. "No. You'll never lose me. I'll never stop loving you, Charles Frémont. Utterly and completely. And I'll never stop believing in you. I know just how *right* you've been, darling."

Love was armor against all hurt, all disaster; it alone abided. The Kearnys and Blairs and Parks would never know it, and that was *their* loss, their pathetic poverty of spirit. Yes, *that* was poverty. Love was the only incorruptible armor, and nothing else in this venal, deceitful, pitiless world mattered. Nothing else at all. . . .

She stood there holding him while the summer breeze stirred in the beeches and the grandfather clock in the front hall struck off the minutes and the moments, stroking time.

"General—what a pleasant surprise!" Bette Kornruth exclaimed; she glanced at Jessie and laughed self-consciously. She was a tall woman whose long oval face was framed in rather silly yellow ringlets. She was the wife of Morton Kornruth, an investment banker who owned a country house in the neighborhood. "I didn't expect to find you here."

Frémont took her hand. "It's good to see you again. I had work to finish here at Pocaho."

"We'll sit in here," Jessie said, leading them into the little dining room, where only a few casual chairs and a tea table remained. "We'll find it more comfortable, I think."

The cottage at Nahant had gone first; then the house on 19th Street; and now the furnishings at Pocaho, preliminary to the sale of Pocaho itself: the Tabriz rugs and Sheraton tables, the Wedgwood and coin silver and Sèvres. When they came for Baron Humboldt's library it had felt as if one of his arms was being torn out of its socket; he'd had to leave the room. Jessie had been magnificent—steady and matter-of-fact, making lists, checking appraisals; he was amazed at her equanimity. Even Lily had taken it very well. She had broken down only once. When the horses were led away, Mariposa Belle had turned back and whinnied once, softly. The handler, annoyed, had jerked hard on the lead rope and the little honey-colored mare went docilely off down the road. Lily's face was shining with tears but she made no sound. Charley, defiantly buoyant, had gone back to Annapolis; young Frank had been visiting friends on the Jersey shore when they took the Bechstein, and that was a blessing . . .

The two women were chatting about a Players' Society production. Frémont held his tea in its Willow Ware cup and saucer, listening absently, swept by many despondent thoughts; then he realized Mrs. Kornruth was afraid to broach the subject.

There was a small pause, and Jessie said bluntly: "Well. You're interested in my Bierstadt, then?"

Both women looked through the hall to the painting mounted above the mantel in the great, bare drawing room. Frémont looked at his wife's face; it betrayed nothing.

"Why, yes," Bette Kornruth said, "I would . . . Oh, Jessie," she added in genuine distress, "I hate this."

"Why should you, dear? You mustn't feel that way. It had to go, and I'd much rather it went to a friend."

"Well . . . all right, then." Bette opened her handbag and produced an envelope. "But really, it seems far too little—so famous a painting . . ."

"No." Jessie shook her head firmly. "Four thousand dollars," she said with calm finality. "That is exactly what Charles paid Albert for it. We prefer it that way." At Jessie's gesture, Mrs. Kornruth handed the envelope to Frémont.

"Tell me, Bette," Jessie said suddenly. "Why do you like it?"

"Oh, for the colors! All those reds and golds . . ." She gazed awestruck at the great canvas, her guileless face perplexed. "Well, it's more than that, really. There's a feeling of—oh, I don't know; of life opening up in front of you—all those things it can be. . . ."

"Good." Jessie nodded. "You feel it, then. That's all that matters."

"But Jessie, it isn't as if you're losing it exactly."

"It's not?"

"I mean—" Bette stammered in embarrassment; she had caught the edge in Jessie's voice, sensed dimly that she'd said something wrong, "—that is, it'll always be there when you come to visit us."

Frémont saw a number of replies flow over his wife's face, all of them rejected instantly. She leaned forward and patted the woman's hand.

"Thank you, my dear. That's very kind of you—we'll look forward to it."

They would not be visiting the Kornruths. There would be an invitation, and another—even perhaps a third—and they would refuse them all, and that would be the end of it. There would be no more balls or theater parties or lively dinner parties here, with the setting sun washing the small dining room in rose and ocher hues, glinting on the brass candlesticks and pressed-glass goblets. The staff had been let go; only the cook remained, and soon she too would be gone.

"We'll have it sent over tomorrow, Bette," he said.

"Oh, my driver can take it—he's brought along the gardener to help. It'll go right in the carriage."

She meant to take it *now.* Frémont glanced at Jessie, caught the sudden rigidity around her mouth, the flicker of pain in her full dark eyes. With gentle authority he said: "It's too fragile for that, Bette. We'll get it to you tomorrow."

"Of course! I didn't mean—"

"I'll crate it properly. It's the best way."

"Of course, General." She rose awkwardly, collecting bag and gloves. "That will be splendid."

"Let me see you out," Frémont said.

Moving toward the smart maroon landau Bette Kornruth said: "I feel terribly about this—I do hope you won't take offense . . ." Like so many people, especially women, she seemed to view him with embarrassed and exaggerated veneration—as though he were a statue come startlingly to life; so strange—when here he stood, with nothing but the clothes on his back; just as he'd been when he'd walked the streets of Charleston half a century ago . . .

"Of course not," he said.

"I hope it hasn't upset Jessie unduly—I'm so awkward at things like this."

"It's quite all right, Bette." He took her hand, helped her into the carriage. "Mrs. Frémont is a very valiant lady."

He reentered the house and went up to the great painting, thinking of Carson in the boat that day, protecting the breech of his rifle from the spray with his sleeve, his hat brim flaring up in the wind, gazing transfixed into the gold that poured through that gate. *"We're in it now, ain't we, Cap'n?"* Kit was dead now. His horse had slid down some unforgiving slope deep in the San Juans and rolled on him. Kit had walked—or crawled—away from that but he'd never been the same, Alex said; the spill had cracked his heart, somehow. Well, we all took our falls—

The rap on the door sounded shockingly loud in the stripped rooms. A man stood on the threshold diffidently, hat held in both hands; soft face, pince-nez, waxed mustache. He stepped back in surprise.

"General Frémont!" he said. "I didn't mean to disturb *you*—I thought probably . . ."

"It's quite all right."

"My name is Chandler, Horace Chandler." A soft, pliant hand. "I understand the house is on the market. I was passing, and I wondered if I might have a look. That is, if it's no inconvenience."

"Of course," Jessie said; she had come up behind Frémont and now ushered in the visitor. They moved through the rooms, which suddenly looked alien to Frémont—a hostelry just entered, a home dreamed of; the stranger's presence had done it. Of course, it had never been home to him, not really; Pocaho had been blessed only because she had so enjoyed it. . . .

"It's so spacious!" Chandler exclaimed. "The rooms—so large and light. There's so much *light* in them!"

"Yes," Jessie said. "They are, aren't they? Well, you see, they held great happiness. There are very few shadows on these walls."

ECHOES

"MRS. FRÉMONT? The name's Donovan—Tim Donovan." He was young, with a short, upturned nose and shifting, wary eyes; a rust-colored derby was perched on the back of his head. "I'm with the *Trib.*"

"Oh, yes," Jessie said. "Horace Greeley's paper. We knew Mr. Greeley quite well."

"Uh-huh." The reporter glanced at her uncertainly. "Mr. Greeley's dead."

"I know." She pushed back an errant tendril of hair, pressed it in place. Mrs. Stanislaus and Mrs. O'Connell were sitting together on the porch next to hers, rocking and shelling peas, watching intently. Every house on this narrow, grimy street on Staten Island was exactly like every other one—pinched and frame-built, room behind room behind room: a shotgun house, Papa would have said.

"Won't you come in, Mr. Donovan." She led him into the little parlor and gestured toward one of the oak chairs they'd salvaged from the servants' quarters at Pocaho. "I didn't hear you at first—I was out in back, working in the garden."

"Garden?" He'd decided to remove the derby and was holding it in his lap with both hands. "You work in a *garden*?"

"Oh my, yes!" She laughed easily. "I put up beans and squash every fall—everyone here does. It's not Missouri River bottomland, but it bears, after a fashion."

"I guess so." He cleared his throat, and rubbed his nose with one knuckle. Horace would never have hired him. But Horace was dead now. To think of what peppery, embattled voice stilled—it seemed impossible. Horace, who'd supported Charles all those turbulent years, who'd felt he was better qualified to lead the country than Lincoln in '64, who'd battled Howard to the very end over the Senate committee's hostility to the Memphis & El Paso rights-of-way. Cranky, incorruptible Horace. He'd been one of the few who signed the bail bond to release Jefferson Davis from prison—a merciful action that had cost him half the *Tribune*'s subscriptions. He'd caught the Presidential fever, too, and been badly defeated by Grant. His bitter disappointment, and the concurrent death of his wife, had affected his mind; he'd died insane that fall. Another friend and champion gone. Well, he'd said: "Go West, young man, go West!"—and he'd be remembered for that, all right. Americans were still moving West in droves . . .

"How may I help you, Mr. Donovan?" she asked.

The reporter twisted his neck in the high collar. "I'd like to talk to you and Mr. Frémont."

"I see. I'm sorry, the *General*"—she emphasized the title—"isn't here. He's out west on business."

Donovan looked surprised. "Business?"

"Yes. Railroad business."

"I don't understand—I thought it had gone into—"

"Mr. Gray, the federal receiver, retained the General to assist in settling the affairs of the Memphis and El Paso. The Texas Pacific has assumed all debts and assets, which has naturally required a great deal of research and review. Perhaps if you'd care to return in a week or two . . ."

"No, no, that's all right. I'd like to talk to you, ma'am." He drew a brown notebook out of his breast pocket. "Would you tell me about yourself? your family?"

She examined her nails, which were grimy from her work in the garden. "Our eldest son, John Charles, is in the Navy; his younger brother Frank is a cadet at the Military Academy."

"I wondered about that—I understand General Frémont's always disliked West Point officers."

"He had disliked *some* of them. Others, such as Generals Sherman, Meade and Hooker he respected, as he did the Confederates Lee and Jackson. As I'm sure you know, he gave President Grant his first important command, in the West. He has always admired the Academy for the excellent training it provides in tactics and engineering. Frank is doing splendidly there."

"And your daughter? Is she still with you?"

"Lily has a position as a clerk in a law office in Manhattan—she's using one of those new typing machines." She paused. "I wasn't entirely sure that was a proper occupation for a young woman, but my daughter tells me that's a very old-fashioned attitude. In any event that's what she wants to do—and she is a very strong-minded person."

"More strong-minded than you, Mrs. Frémont?"

"Oh, yes!" She laughed easily. "Lily has always known just what she wants."

"And you haven't?"

"There are ambitions a woman cannot hope to realize, Mr. Donovan. The knowledge of those barriers is driven home in early childhood." She eyed the reporter mischievously. "But there were certain things I knew I wanted, yes. The General was one of them. We both fell in love at first sight—very romantic, very rare. We were immensely lucky, you see."

Half-amused, she watched him writing rapidly, in some kind of cipher. A story. Some editor had told him to take the ferry over here and dig out a story: the legendary explorer and Senator Tom Benton's daughter, living in a rented row house, living in straitened—

"I rode up to Tarrytown—to Pocaho," he said suddenly.

"Ah. Did you."

"It's very grand up there. All those mansions in the woods—it's hard to imagine it's so close to the city, isn't it?"

"Yes, it is."

"It must be a terrific change for you." His eyes flickered at her, flickered away. "I mean, after London and Paris—after all, you were billionaires!"

She smiled at the term; it was newly coined—there were apparently going to be a great many of them now. "Life is filled with change," she said lightly.

"All those grand occasions, coming within an ace of being First Lady, that empire out in California . . . and now this crummy little place, no servants—didn't all that high life spoil you for this?"

Ah. That was it. Of course.

"Young man," she said in her father's Senate voice, "I have bathed in a barber's basin under a woolen blanket, and stirred frijoles in an iron skillet over a hearth fire. I have shaken with fever in the jungles of Panama, and shivered with chilblains in the shadow of the High Sierra. Are you actually so naive as to believe living in a modest home on Staten Island holds any terrors for me?" She rose and clasped her hands. "And now, if you will excuse me, I have a great deal of work to do."

He got to his feet then, stuffing the notebook back in his pocket, catching up his hat. He looked contrite; he rubbed the base of his stubby nose again. "I'm sorry if I spoke out of turn—I didn't mean to give offense, ma'am."

"That's quite all right. None taken."

At the door he turned awkwardly. "Thank you for your time. I'm sorry I missed the General." For a moment he stared at her intently, his large mouth working. "—It's wrong!" he burst out suddenly, waving the rust-colored derby. "You two shouldn't *have* to live here—not after battling those blizzards in the Rockies, not after crossing the Sierras when Fitzpatrick and Carson didn't want to try it, when even that Indian guide was afraid . . ."

She stared at him. "You've read the reports?"

He nodded, his eyes shining. "What wouldn't I give to have been with him then! Jesus, Mary and Joseph, what a story. . . ." He raised a huge lump of a fist. "I'd give my right arm to have been walking along behind him then!"

She reached out and shook his hand. "I'll tell the General when he comes home," she said softly. "I know it'll please him. Very much."

It was a long, flat parcel, carefully wrapped and tied; she recognized Nancy Davis' handwriting at once. She started to open it, set it down and put on the teakettle and washed her hands.

She sat down at the kitchen table then and opened the package, which was lined with tissue paper. On the top was a note from Nancy and clipped to it a small blue envelope. The note said that Nancy's friend on the New York Committee, Eleanor Van Loudon, had taken a box at the opera in Philadelphia, and Nancy had returned the compliment. "I realize it's fearfully provincial and chauvinistic and all that nonsense, but I do like our opera better, and business keeps Ed pinned here in the city most of the time. Won't you and Charles and Lily keep this box at the Met from going to waste?"

There was a second sheet; the writing was looser and more hurried, as though Nancy had left the task and come back to it in a hurry. "And I found an incredible bargain in long gloves. I can't possibly use so many, so I'm dividing them with you. I know you won't be offended—we're far too good friends for that . . . but write me anyway to tell me you're not! And come down and visit us soon."

Very slowly she unfolded the tissue. The moment her fingers touched the satiny, pliant kid she burst into tears.

"The place had already been ransacked," Nat Banks said. He was heavier and his hair had turned gray, but there was still the old twinkle in his intense, deep-set eyes. "Chairs overturned, closet doors torn off, smashed crockery all over the floor. The pleasure men find in destruction! And Esterbrook said, 'Don't you worry, General, I'll rustle up something special.' He was the most undaunted forager I ever saw. 'Never mind, Jack,' I told him, 'I just want to find a place to sleep anyway.' 'No, no,' he said, 'there's food here, General—I tell you I can smell it!' He kept rummaging around, prying open things, and shaking his head; and finally he caught sight of a battered old wooden cradle pushed into a far corner. He got this crafty look on his face, pounced on it, flung back this rag of a coverlet—and there, packed in as snug as you please, were a ham and a side of bacon and a jug of molasses. 'What did I tell you?' Jack shouted. And all of a sudden right out of nowhere darted this old woman in a bindle bonnet. She fetched him a wallop with a laundry paddle that knocked him halfway across the room, drew herself up and screeched at me: 'Ah allus *heared* you good-for-nothin' Ya-ankees robbed the cradle, but Ah never did figure on livin' to see it with mah own eyes!' "

The three of them laughed easily, watching each other around the pine dropleaf table, reliving old memories. It was good to see Nat again. Charles had run into him on Fifth Avenue, peering into a shop window—and on impulse had rapped him smartly across the backside with his stick and said: "No loitering, son! Move along!" Nat had whirled around in a blaze, and then roared with laughter. Jessie was pleased Charles had brought him home for dinner—her husband looked more carefree and relaxed than she'd seen him in months. He was still traveling for the railroad, struggling to sort out its incredibly tangled finances. They paid him a salary—an extremely slender one—and there was the satisfaction of knowing he'd been fully exonerated in the congressional inquiry; the press attacks, too, had ceased since the far more shocking revelations of the Crédit Mobilier case involving the Union Pacific—a scandal in which their old friend Schuyler Colfax, then riding high as Vice-President, had been deeply implicated.

But it was melancholy work; the furrows in Charles' cheeks (his Sangre de Cristo lines, Jessie thought of them) were scored much deeper, the skin drawn more tautly over his fine nose. He was still as slim as when he'd left for South Pass, though his riding and fencing days had vanished along with Pocaho and Nahant. He'd located a bootmaker who was a minor artist at resoling, and he sponged and brushed his own clothes with care. Jessie trimmed his hair and beard whenever he was home. He looked as courtly and correct as ever; it only took a bit more effort now.

They were talking politics, inevitably. Nat had finished another term as congressman and just been made collector of customs for the Port of Boston—one of those remunerative federal jobs with which the faithful were rewarded. She served them an apple pie she'd baked, half-listening to them, thinking of her father, and Lincoln's shocking, untimely death, and Charles' face the afternoon she'd come home with that terrible orange broadside . . . All the Giants were dead and gone; where were their successors? All you saw on every hand were tinhorns and sharpers, as Kit Carson would have said. The Radical Republicans were in the saddle now; their ferocious Old Testament vengeance—Reconstruction, they were fond of calling it: *Reconstruction!*—had only piled up a mountain of bitterness and hatred. Worse, they were merely content to abandon the freed slaves, leave them to their own untutored devices . . .

"What a hog trough," Nat was saying tartly. "They've already stripped the South—now they've decided to raid the rest of the country. Either Grant has no idea about what's going on, or he doesn't give a hoot. . . . I'm told Belknap's behind it all—and that oily private secretary of Grant's, Babcock." He tossed his great beak of a nose in the air in distaste. "Politics has always had its seedy side—nobody knows that better than you two—but now it's running on *nothing* but under-the-counter deals and jobbery. There's no helm, no leadership—we're just drifting . . ."

"Generals in the ranks, and fools in command, Rufus Tucker used to say," Charles murmured.

"Isn't *that* the truth. Merit means nothing any more. The old maids and incompetents they've made Territorial governors—it's ridiculous. *You* should have been their first choice, Charlie—at the very top of the list. I talked to Sumner, but of course he's out now. And Delano just put me off. Told me 'the President has the matter under consideration.' And you gave him the command at Cairo! Shoot, if it hadn't been for you he'd have wound up cooling his heels as garrison commander at Port Hudson."

"Perhaps that's why," Jessie commented slyly. "Haven't you noticed? There are people who can never forgive someone for saving their careers at a critical point."

"Maybe it's Sherman," Charles said quietly. "He and Grant were always thick." His lips curved in the grave, mortified smile. "Sherman never approved of me—he always thought I entertained Napoleonic delusions."

"*And* made millions from fraudulent contracts," Jessie broke in, "*—and* siphoned off countless troops from Tennessee! There's another gentleman with a short memory. He never chooses to remember how I fed and cosseted him in Monterey when he was a frail, consumptive captain who didn't know where his next meal was coming from."

"Goes back farther than that, honey. When Kearny had me in arrest at Monterey, Sherman came out to my tent for a little chat. He seemed to feel I hadn't displayed a proper deference with that murderous toady Mason. My temper was running rather short those days. I reminded him that Mason was still alive only because I'd lashed down Godey and Carson and all the rest of my crowd, and that if he, Sherman, wanted to curry favor with his commanding officer that was his affair. Then I told him he had the simplest of choices: he could withdraw from my tent, or I could whip him to a frazzle and *throw* him out—it made absolutely no difference to me."

Nat gave his dry Yankee bark of a laugh. "I declare, Charlie—you've had more adventures than Marco Polo! Why don't you write them all up? Call it *Memoirs of an Unregenerate Sinner.*"

"I'd rather call it *The Bad Penny,*" Charles said with his old grin.

"Why, it'd be worth it just to send a few shivers through the high and the mighty! Did you know that fool Lew Wallace is writing novels? If he can, you can."

"Hell, I'm no writer, Nat. Never was."

"Why, look at the Reports—"

"I didn't write those. Jessie wrote them."

She stared at him, shocked; even Nat was watching him quizzically. "Charles," she cried, "what on earth are you babbling about?"

"No more than the truth," he said. He was very serious now. "Oh, I laid it out, all right—where we went, what we did: the feel and the smell and the glint of it. But I couldn't *write* it"—he was looking from Nat to Jessie as he spoke—"I couldn't make you see it the way I did. That's another kind of mastery. I didn't have that."

"—But you *did* it, darling," she said in a kind of exasperated distress, in rising fear. "That's what mattered . . ."

He shook his head, and put his worn, weathered hand on hers. "I did it, yes. But that's gone, that vanishes. What remains is the word." He smiled now. "Twenty years and settlers will clear those valleys and grow their wheat and drive their cattle, and never know I walked through there—or care either. And that's as it should be. I only showed the way. But *you* fired their hearts to the doing—made them see it, and dream it, and want to make it theirs. You struck it in bronze, Jessie, and that's the real triumph."

She leaped to her feet and fled from the room. If she hadn't left then she knew she would have broken down, in full view of her husband and his old friend Nathaniel Banks.

My Dear General and Mrs. Frémont:

I deeply regret to inform you that the earlier diagnosis has been confirmed. The lesion is not extensive; the condition is mild, but dangerous. Cadet Frémont has been placed on light duty, but I must warn you that the

Hudson Valley constitutes a grave danger to anyone with his affliction. I urgently recommend a minimum of six months' residence in a warm, dry climate such as Arizona, which I am reasonably confident would effect a complete cure. The Academy is prepared to grant your son indefinite leave without prejudice. I will wait to hear from you at your earliest—

She lowered the letter, conscious of a flat, rhythmic rapping outside; Mrs. Stanislaus beating her carpet again. Dear, dreamy, musical Frank. She sat very still, her head up, half-hearing the angry *thrap! thrap!* of the carpet-beater outside. A warm, dry climate such as Arizona—dear God, *Arizona,* the train fare alone—and he'd have to live when he got there—it would cost a thousand dollars at least. And what if it took longer than the post surgeon predicted?

A thousand dollars.

The government owed them $42,000—at least that—for Black Point and still adamantly refused to pay them for it; Nat had written the President in their behalf, Zach Chandler had pressed Secretary Belknap for restitution, to no avail. A thousand dollars. . . . She had ordered a gown of pale pink moiré from the finest dressmaker in London for her presentation at the Court of St. James; she'd given small fortunes to hospitals during the war, and anonymously paid the college tuition for half a hundred impoverished young people; a perfect river of gold had poured glittering through the baffles at the Black Drift . . . and they couldn't lay their hands on a thousand dollars to save the very life of their own son.

She bowed her head, gripping her hands tightly. Careful, now. Enough of that. There was no time now for resentment or remorse; those were luxuries too, their price was too high. What was it Papa used to say, those lines from Marcus Aurelius he loved so? *Be not disturbed about the future; for if you ever come to it, you will have the same reason for your guide which preserves you at present.*

Remember who you are.

A thousand dollars. There was nothing of value left to sell, they had no credit. She could cook for someone, perhaps, or clean house. Or sew: she was clever with a needle, always had been. But *a thousand dollars*—there was no time to earn that sum. Nancy Davis would give her a thousand dollars if she asked her; so would Hannah Lawrence. But they could never repay it. And you did not use your friends this way. You did not. If only Charles were home! It would be so much easier to bear. But Charles was two thousand miles away, inspecting repair sheds and twenty-seven miles of worthless track somewhere west of Fort Yuma. She would have to meet this alone.

The slap of the carpet-beater seemed to penetrate to the center of her brain, stopping all thought. Desperate for distraction she caught up an old copy of the New York *Ledger,* opened it at random and began reading the first thing she saw. It seemed to be a series of reminiscences about the Duchess of Bedford. Jessie remembered her—a gaunt woman with a horse's face and great yellowed teeth, a deep, braying laugh . . . but there wasn't even a hint of that woman here, in this simpering, toffy-nosed creature. How could they print such false trash? This writer had never even laid eyes on the Duchess of Bedford, let alone crossed swords with her over Harriet Martineau's waspish comments on America. Why didn't they assign these pieces to people who had been there, who knew what the grand eminences were really like?

She was on her feet then, staring at the Founder's Medal of the Royal Geographical Society in its glass case on the far wall, the delicate relief of Apollo striding across the zodiac; thinking of that unlicked reporter from the *Tribune*, Nat Banks, Charles' gentle smile. *"All those occasions!" "You've had more adventures than Marco Polo!"* "*But* you *fired their hearts to the doing. . . .*"

"All right," she said aloud, over the carpet-beater. "Nothing ventured, nothing gained."

An hour later she was on the ferry to Manhattan, wearing her last pair of good black gloves and the coat with the mink collar she rarely wore now because there would never be another.

Robert Bonner came out to her almost as soon as she'd sent in her card. He was Irish, enthusiastic, full of energy. He took her hand and asked after the General and Lily; they all used to ride together along the river north of Tarrytown. Horses were his pleasure, but his joy was the *Ledger*—she thought him the best editor in New York. They chatted a bit and then Jessie said:

"It's occurred to me that some of my experiences, both in Europe and the far West, should have a good deal of interest for your readers."

Nodding, he thrust out his lower lip, "I imagine they would at that, Mrs. Frémont. Just what sort of article did you have in mind?"

It was the kind of thing she knew how to do, and she did it well: the Duke of Wellington, eighty-four and still the grand old soldier of the century, wandering through the stately rooms at Sion House; the half-naked Indian woman bathing the infant Charley in an earthen bowl deep in the Panama jungles; the Hornitas League claim-jumpers walking toward her in the baked white dust, their rifles glinting; the impeccably aristocratic Comte de la Garde rocking tiny Anne in his arms and crooning a French lullaby; Andrew Jackson's gaunt, leathery face cracking into laughter at her own child's cry: "Hurrah for Old Hickory and the people's bank!"

She stopped then; she knew when to stop. His eyes were snapping at her, he was biting at the edge of his bright red beard. "It all sounds fascinating, Mrs. Frémont, absolutely fascinating. Of course, *writing* about it is another matter."

"Oh, I've done a great deal of writing."

"Have you?" His pale blue eyes studied her—speculative, a touch patronizing. "I didn't realize that."

"Why yes, you see I—" She broke off. She still could not bring herself to mention the Reports. Not to the world. Charles could say it to Nat; she could not. "Do you know my *Story of the Guard*? It was an account of the gallant war record of the Zagonyi Guards in the West. Ticknor and Fields published it in '63—it went into three editions."

"Yes, of course—I'd forgotten."

"I did much of the biographical material on the General during the presidential campaign in '56. John Bigelow praised my work—I know he'll be happy to corroborate that."

"John liked your work, did he?" Bonner made up his mind then, tapped the desktop. "Well, all right! Why not try a short piece, if you like?"

"Good." She took a slow, deep breath. "And now I'd like to talk about payment. What do you pay for such pieces?"

His brows rose, he looked blank with surprise. "Well, of course . . . *if* we liked it. I didn't realize it was a matter of—"

"If you don't like what I've written," she said, "we'll forget the matter. If you do, I will want the professional rate you pay."

"Of course, of course. Well, customarily we, uh, pay a hundred dollars for this kind of article."

"That will be satisfactory."

Still he hung fire, intrigued and amused. "But you'll have to be serious about it, you know."

She raised her head and fixed him with her eyes. "Mr. Bonner," she said, "you have no idea how serious I am." She paused. "I need the money, and I need it at once."

To her surprise he laughed out loud. "That's the best reason anyone ever had for writing anything." He rose and put out his hand. "I'll look forward to reading what you bring us."

At home again she built up the fire, filled the little Georgian inkwell she'd salvaged from the crash, opened her old calf portfolio, fitted a sheet to the blotter backing, and began. She wrote a page, and then another, waiting for that warm, familiar surge of satisfaction. It didn't come. She read over what she'd written and didn't like it very much. She was rusty, that was all; it was years since she'd done any serious writing. She drew a new sheet and started over again. It was better, but not much. Maybe writing was a young person's craft—she was past fifty. Nonsense: look at Cooper, look at Hawthorne . . . look at Dickens and Thackeray.

See the room, *see* Lady Bulwer's full, kindly face, hear her voice. Let it run naturally, easily, as though telling some old, trusted friend . . .

It grew dark; she lighted the lamp, rebuilt the fire and went back to her desk. Lily came in from work, her face red from the cold, and wanted to talk about the day in her office.

"Be quiet, dear," Jessie said, not unkindly. "I can't talk to you now. I'm writing."

"Writing? Writing what?"

"Never mind now. I have to keep my mind on it."

"But what about supper? Aren't you even going to stop to eat?"

"Later, dear. Perhaps later on."

Lily puttered around in the kitchen, finished up and went to bed. The raucous neighborhood noises faded, the late silence began to hum. She worked on, sharpening, remembering; holding the moment in her mind's eye, turning it before the mirror of her memory . . . and slowly, stealthily the moments, the sensations came flooding back, flaring like a phosphorescent night tide at Siasconset, teeming with life. Yes, their horizons had shrunk to a row house on Staten Island now; but they had lived the lives of a hundred, a thousand couples; they had laced the country and the hemisphere and half the world, had faced the captains and the kings, found greatness in the humble and pettiness in the great; they'd seen the very world shift on its axis—a continent convulsed with discovery, with migration, with the most terrible of wars . . .

Charles' life was action: he'd followed it, had done all he could, and more. Now it was up to her. Now the gentler virtues would have to serve. Their lives now were a memory solitaire, where the cards glistened with an occasional tear as she played, and shuffled, and played it again, alone in the humming dark. . . .

Bonner was clearly surprised to see her. "Run into trouble?" he asked sympathetically. "I told you it wouldn't be easy."

"It wasn't easy," she said. She opened the bulky package. "But here are ten pieces."

"Ten pieces? But it's only been a few weeks, it's only—"

"Sixteen days, to be exact."

He laughed, more in irritation than amusement. "When did you eat? or sleep?"

"In between drafts." She smiled and handed him the folder. "Tell me what you think of them."

Cornered, he frowned, riffled through the neat manuscript pages; he started to say something, thought better of it, sighed, and chose one out of the middle of the sheaf and began to scan the lines. It was one of the lighter pieces, an affectionate cameo of her self-appointed *cavaliere-servente,* the ebullient old Comte de la Garde; an inauspicious start, but there was no help for it. She forced herself to examine various objects in the office. The editor's expression changed as he read on, his irritation faded. A smile appeared, vanished, returned; he began tapping his blue pencil lightly on the desk's edge. He read another, a third. When he was finished he stacked the little block of sheets neatly and squared them against his blotter.

"They're good," he said finally; he shot her an odd glance, almost diffident. "They're very good indeed."

"Thank you."

"Frankly, I'm surprised. Oh, there are a few rough spots, a few places that need polishing here and there. But we can certainly use these, and if the others measure up . . ."

"Splendid," she said. "Then you wouldn't mind writing me a draft for them while I'm here?"

Robert Bonner stared at her—and burst out laughing again. "I don't see why on earth not, Mrs. Frémont. You've no idea how I have to horsewhip half my writers into producing one story over a month's time. You ought to get a medal for sheer grit!"

She smiled. "The check will be sufficient."

He sobered then. "Mrs. Frémont, I realize this has been a difficult time for you both. I'm really most impressed. Most women would have"—he shrugged eloquently—"well, thrown up their hands and gone under."

"I am not like most women, Mr. Bonner."

"I've just become aware of that!"

"You see—I'm like a deeply built ship. I drive best under a stormy wind."

Outside, on Fourth Avenue, it was snowing hard, whipping under the gaslights, swirling over the bluestone flags like salt; but the slip of paper deep in her purse warmed her to the very tips of her toes. Like Charles on the high plains long ago, sleepless and wary, dogged by doubts, she had hung on and found out what she could do. What she had to do. Not that her talent matched Charles'; she knew her limits. She was not truly creative. Already she realized that everything she wrote had to come from her own experience: she would have to snip the fabric of her life with consummate artistry, to realize its full complement of tales; and if her memory faltered, Charles would be there to bring his own rich perceptions to her aid. . . .

She turned, holding the brim of her hat, and waved to a passing hansom. No, nothing she could do would restore their lost position. The success of a Dickens or a Scott was beyond her. They would continue to live on that muddy street above the ferry. But never again would she have to ask Mr. Chaffee to wait for the rent; and that made all the difference in the world.

To the north and west the desert rilled away for miles on miles to where the Hualpais rose blue and hard, as if cut out of steel against the white of the sky. And on the trail out of Prescott rose the dust plume of a solitary horseman, fixed in the vast distances. Without raising his glasses Frémont smiled.

"It's Lily," he said.

Reined up beside him, Lieutenant Harmon laughed. "Your own private welcoming committee, General. I've never seen a lady who can ride the way your daughter can. Why, she'd rather ride than eat!"

"That's about the size of it." Frémont nudged the buckskin into motion and let it settle into an easy lope, pleased by the hot wind in his face, half-intoxicated on the thin dry air, the tart, remembered odors of leather and horseflesh and sage. Back in harness; he was back in harness. Finally, finally, after he'd given up all hope, they'd handed him the governorship of the Arizona Territory. It had been Zach Chandler's doing.

"High time, high time, Charlie—I know." His shrewd politician's eyes narrowed to slits. "The mills of politics grind slow, but they grind exceedingly fine. Some of us haven't forgotten what you did for the Party in '64."

That had angered him in spite of his elation. "That shouldn't have a damn thing to do with it," he'd said.

"Well, it does. You won't ever understand. But Jessie will."

Anyway, Grant was gone, Rutherford B. Hayes was in; he was no longer out of favor at court. The gods has smiled—at least they'd decided to stop frowning for a while. The post was considered a part-time job—apparently territorial governors were expected to be men of means and varied interests—and it paid a meager $2,000 a year, not much more than he'd drawn from the Texas Pacific. The figure meant scrimping in this country, where their rent was $90 a month and food cost three times as much as in the East. They did no entertaining, which put a few noses out of joint in the Territory, and the household help he'd hoped to hire for Jessie was out of the question. It hadn't been easy for her, contending with dust and scorpions and the awesome desert heat.

But for him the past year had been life itself; he'd been astonished at his own stamina and resilience, at sixty-six. He was up before dawn, full of flapjacks and coffee, riding out with his escort. He couldn't afford to keep horses, with hay at $50 a ton, but the Army gave him his pick of their mounts, which was almost as good. It all came back—he delighted in the trail, thought nothing of spending twelve hours in the saddle. The soldiers called him General and treated him with a shy deference that moved him strangely. He was old enough to be grandfather to the younger ones—a kind of frontier legend, warning and paragon both. Like old Provost, he thought, surprised and pleased; like Reddy Walker or sour Gabe Bridger. The sere seniority of the West . . .

Of course the post was largely ceremonial. There wasn't an awful lot to govern, and no Indians to fight, thank God—he knew he could never have carried out the campaigns of harassment and dislocation Sherman and Dodge and his old nemesis Pope had waged in the Powder River country and the Black Hills. But there were problems enough: the Territorial legislature was *for* the new mining tax—a shortsighted view at the very least—and pigheadedly *opposed* to his recommended appropriation for the Hopi and Yavapai—an even more stupid attitude. Down at Fort Yuma, Lord was screaming for two more cavalry troops. The Indian agents were up in arms over the latest ruling by the Bureau, which was run by Georgetown armchair dandies who had about as much knowledge of the West as Mrs. William Vanderbilt.

But the possibilities! It wasn't the lush Garden of Eden he'd staggered into out of the frozen Sierra that winter of '44, but it was an empire in its own right. There were mountains of copper and silver here that no one had begun to tap; the irrigation potential was fascinating—the whole Salton Sink could be turned into a rich valley with a daring, massive damming of the Colorado. . . .

Lily was plainly visible now, looming larger in that magical, mesmeric way only the desert air could produce. They galloped together; she swung close and kissed him, her full face ruddy under her sombrero. Out West again she'd gone back to wearing divided skirts and riding astride, which outraged some of the more staid citizens of Prescott, and delighted her father.

"Calamity Lil," he said. "What's the news?"

She tilted her head prettily. "There was a shooting down on Whiskey Row—one man was wounded. Sister Monica killed a rattler with her manzanita cane. Charley wrote us—from *Samoa*!"

"Good. How's your mother?"

"Writing away. Or was when I left."

He nodded, riding beside his daughter. He'd been disconcerted when Jessie had first told him about the thousand dollars. Watching her face he'd been happy for her, deeply relieved for Frank, but—disoriented. Supported by his wife, then; was that how it was to be? And the thought had stung him. She had shaken her head at him in amused disapproval—they could always read each other's hearts without effort. Look, now: he'd mapped half a continent, laid track, mined gold. Didn't he see?—she was only engaged in another kind of mining—the raw ore of their travels and triumphs and tribulations, their life together. She couldn't run a stamp mill or build a sluice, but this *was* something she could do; and after all, it was only until fortune smiled on them again, the good times returned. . . .

Frank had gone off to Arizona, and had come back in six months tanned and healthy. The stories kept pouring out. Jessie was tireless; she sold more pieces, moved on to *Harper's* and *Wide Awake.* Now and then she would query him about some particular person or occasion and, secretly pleased, he would summon up all he could: Charley and his fellow middies awe-struck before Napoleon's Tomb, Kit Carson and the Ute chieftain in the camp at Muddy River swapping crazy insults, the red-bearded Californio officer at Hawk's Peak, riding stiffly toward that gray boulder . . . Just before they left she'd published her first collection, *A Year of American Travel,* which had been well received.

She'd told him going West would make no difference, it was simply a matter of mailing manuscripts back to New York. But he knew better: she was leaving for his sake. For the past several weeks she'd seemed preoccupied, and curiously abstracted—she'd had a dizzy spell once and had to lie down. She was working too hard. Well, they'd take a week or two off, ride up to the Grand Canyon. She'd never seen those awesome rose and purple towers standing like a deathless temple to all the mountain gods.

The house was of weathered clapboard, the shutters drawn against the heat; an olla dripped soddenly outside the bedroom window where Jessie worked, its crude evaporation trying vainly to cool the furnace vapor creeping in through the shutters.

He stepped into the dim cool, swung off his broad-brimmed hat and slapped it against his boot and sang out: "Hail to the chief who in triumph advances!"

There was no answer. She was not in the parlor or the bedroom.

"Maybe she's gone over to the Mojave school," Lily said. "But it's too late for that. . . ."

Suddenly uneasy, he moved down the narrow hallway to the kitchen. A foot protruded from behind the table. His heart gave a great leap of fear. She was lying face down, motionless, her skirts rucked up on one side, one arm pinned under her.

No. He crouched over her, eased her gently over on her back. Her eyes rolled back, white under their lids. Her throat was warm. There was a pulse—ah, thank God!—but so feeble, so faint . . .

"What's happened? What's happened? *Papa—*"

He looked up at his daughter's strained face. "Get Dr. Rogers. Quick as you can. It'll be all right. Ride hard, now!"

"Then they weren't just dizzy spells."

"No," Major Homer Rogers said. He was a quiet, slope-shouldered Ohioan with thinning hair and a mild, deliberate manner. He'd served as a fledgling doctor under Lyon's old chief of staff Schofield in the Army of the Tennessee. "This country is killing her."

"I know—it's this blasted heat. She can't—"

"This has nothing to do with heat. I meant what I said quite literally, General." Frémont looked at him sharply, and he nodded. "It's the altitude. Her body craves oxygen, her heart is overtaxed trying to deliver it. It's that simple." He paused, said even more deliberately: "If she stays out here much longer, I cannot accept the responsibility for her life."

"I see." Frémont stared at the studious, inoffensive eyes, the tarnished caducei on the choke collar. The most strenuous of all the old Army warnings—protest and ultimatum both. The doctor clearly meant it. Frémont had caught her once with her hand pressed to her ribs. A stitch in her side, she'd told him, dismissing it blithely. But it wasn't a stitch at all . . .

"You've known about this for some time," he said aloud.

"Yes."

"Then why in God's name didn't you *tell* me?" he flared hotly.

Rogers looked back at him unruffled. "I wasn't too alarmed at first. The condition has worsened significantly over the past month. And as you know, your wife can be very persuasive."

"I know." The shock of discovery still held him—a huge, gaping tear like an arrow wound.

"And she has a will of iron."

"Yes. Well, so do I. She will have to be taken back East." The implications had only just begun to bite into him. "That's it, then. Thank you, Homer—I'm very grateful to you."

"Nothing at all, General."

She awoke slowly, rising through fantastic and discordant dreams. Morning sunlight was beating on the shutters, but the night's cool lay in the room. Indolently she turned toward Charles, saw his side of the bed was untouched—and then it all came back and she started to thrust herself up.

"Good morning, darling." Charles was sitting at the foot of the bed, holding a mug in one hand.

"You're back," she said. How he'd revived in this fearsome climate! The grayed acquiescence of Staten Island was gone. His face was burned to a deep walnut; his beard was silver, but his eyes flashed with that piercing blue intensity. Weak as she was, troubled and uncertain, she wanted him with the old burning need.

"My desert hawk," she said dreamily, smiling. "You look the way you did the first day I saw you in St. Louis."

"You're shameless." Then he stopped smiling. "Jessie—"

"Tell me about your trip," she broke in, bullying him a bit, fending it off. "What did you find?"

"Oh, there are lots of veins, all right. Copper. And strong silver traces in half a dozen seams—the best one's about ten miles from that bend where the Bill Williams River empties into the Colorado." He shook his head. "Isn't it fantastic that I should find myself making surveys near a river named for that crazy old fool?"

"Yes. It is."

"But it's there, all right." His eyes were snapping with the old ardor. "It's completely untouched—its potential is almost unlimited."

"Are we to be rich again, then?" she asked softly.

He caught himself up, and smiled a still, sad smile. "No. Nothing like that. There's plenty of color, but it'll take millions in seed capital and years of labor to get it out. It'll make Judge Silent rich, though; and several others. I seem to be good at that, don't I? Well, they're paying me five hundred dollars for my survey; but it's not that. One day it'll mean more people, more jobs for everybody—that falls within my duties, certainly."

Duty. Absently she listened to him, watching the fine, lean features, the restless eyes, loving him with each labored heartbeat. All John C. Frémont had ever wanted to do was his duty. Maybe that was why all that boundless wealth had slipped through his fingers—it had never been really important to him: all he'd wanted was to serve the Republic, in fair weather and foul. What a priceless irony that he, who times without number had been called braggart and charlatan, congenital mutineer and self-seeking schemer, should turn out to have possessed a more abiding sense of duty than most of his peers . . .

"You gave us quite a scare, honey." He was looking at her directly now, his face grave. "A bad scare."

"I feel fine," she answered. "Yes, really! All I needed was a—"

"That's the injection Homer Rogers gave you."

"I need to get up," she said, stirring. "I've got to—"

He put his hand on her arm, firmly. "You've got to do nothing."

"Where's Lily?"

He said quietly: "She's gone marketing."

She looked at him warily then. "I see."

"Jessie, you are a sick young lady."

"Nonsense! Not young, not sick."

"No. No 'nonsense' talk today." He leaned toward her. "Homer says you must leave here at once. You'll have to live at sea level, preferably on the ocean."

She chewed at her lip. "Well. Perhaps I should go back for a few weeks. I need to see the magazine people—"

"No. You're going back for good. We all are."

Her head came up. "That's silly. You *can't* leave, the legislature's meeting, it's no time to—"

"I'm taking you back. I've written out my resignation, I'm mailing it off this afternoon."

"*What?* But you can't—!" She was filled with consternation. "I won't let you do this!"

"I've done it." He looked away, said: "I can't be away from you, Jessie."

"But that's ridiculous—we've been separated before . . ."

"It was different, before. We weren't . . . the age we are now."

"We were younger, but we didn't know the things we know now. Don't you see—"

"No," he interrupted. "We are going East, Jessie. And that is all there is to it." She saw his jaw set; he was not going to change his mind on this.

"Charles, please . . ."

"No."

"Then I won't go. I mean it, Charles. You know I mean it."

He made himself grin, fell into Kit's bemused drawl. "I trust you won't provoke me into the use of force, ma'am."

"Charles, please. Listen to me, just hear me out—"

"No. You always could talk rings around me. But it won't work this time."

"Oh, Charles . . ." Gazing at him, loving and fearing for him, her eyes filled with tears. "You can't put this burden on me, not now—I couldn't bear it . . ."

He stared at her blankly. "Burden?"

"Of course, a burden. What would you call it? Look, you've found your trail again—don't throw it all away now. You can't." In her weakness and agitation she'd begun to weep and it enraged her—it smacked of women's wiles, something she'd always detested; it was the last thing she wanted to sound like now. "After all that gold and railroad will-o'-the-wisp lunacy, you've got back to what you can do better than anyone else in the world . . . Don't throw it all up just because height makes me a bit ill—"

"A bit ill—you could have died, Jessie!" he cried, and she could hear the naked fear in his voice.

"All right, then, we'll die one day, like everyone else. It's how we *live* that matters. All those years on Staten Island, watching you get grayer and more fearful, fading away . . . what do you think that did to *me?*"

He shook his head stubbornly. "My first duty is to you. I failed you once, you remember—I'm not going to fail you again."

"Good—then let me go alone!" She gripped him by the shoulders. "Charles, don't you understand? This has given you back your life! And therefore mine. It's given me back the man I married."

Very troubled, he nodded. "Yes. That's true. But your heart is more important than that."

"My heart . . ." She was weeping again, she couldn't help it. "You will break my heart if you give up this post," she said.

He searched her face in loving wonder. "You'd do this for me," he murmured, and tenderly traced the line of her cheek with his thumb.

"No. For us both."

He sighed, and she saw his longing in his eyes. "It's too great a gift," he said. "I'm not that selfish—I can't be."

"All right, then. Call it a gift, if you like. It's easy to give. Accepting is what's hard, especially for people like us. People with pride. That's what demands the real generosity of spirit. Please, darling. Do this for me. Stay here and reclaim your life, and save us both. Be generous, my love. . . ."

He sat for a moment looking down at his hands, then reached out and drew her to him powerfully. She felt a terrible grief, and below it the stoic fortitude that had sustained her since she'd sat in the captain's chair beside her father's desk on C Street. She clung to her husband with all her might.

"Such a gallant lady." His voice was muffled in her hair. "I don't know what I'm going to do with you."

"For now, just hold me," she said. "Just hold me like this. . . ."

EVENING STAR

THE WAR DEPARTMENT was housed in a vulgar new structure, overblown and confusing; the old building where Frémont had gone that desperate spring of '61 to plead with choleric old Scott for weapons had disappeared. A major with a small box mustache stared at him in disbelief when he explained the purpose of his visit. Topographical Engineers? *Topographical. . . ? Before* the war?

"Try Archives," he told Frémont irritably, disclaiming all knowledge, disowning any responsibility. "I've no idea where you'll track down any such material as that. Try Archives."

The wind off the Potomac was raw; there'd been a snowstorm three days earlier, which made for tricky footing. Frémont moved cautiously down Pennsylvania Avenue, grateful for his cane, bombarded by memories. The cough he kept suppressing broke again, flat and shallow; it was always there now—the sound of it made him think of Papa Joe. And here he was—my God, he was fifteen years older than Nicollet had been then . . .

He'd stayed on in Arizona for three more years, with Lily's companionship as solace; then, at seventy, tiring in the saddle, unable to cover the Territory as he had, and missing Jessie—an ache beyond all imagining—he'd resigned and come back to New York.

Hard years. Lily had again gone to work as a legal secretary, and now and then he'd picked up a small commission from Judge Silent or some other western financier on a mining or irrigation project; but they were living on Jessie's earnings, and those were dwindling. She had finished her autobiographical series, *Souvenirs of My Time,* selling each piece first to magazines, and the book had done rather well. But the writing came harder, it was forced now. They didn't discuss it, but the grim truth was that after twelve years of unremitting effort Jessie was approaching the end of that rich tapestry; she worked more and more slowly, anxiously threading it out ever thinner to put off the evil day. Friends in Congress pressed for compensation for Black Point—that $42,000 that was rightfully theirs and that would have rescued them in a twinkling from all their troubles—but entrenched behind a web of title technicalities and abstruse points of law, the Government stalled and evaded.

And then Grant's *Personal Memoirs* had come out, to resounding popular acclaim. Frémont had read them, admiring their rude, uncomplicated strength—and the idea had struck him like a thunderbolt. Why not? Why on earth not? Who had a more adventurous, compelling story to tell? A whole new generation had come of age that knew nothing about him—or for that matter about the gold rush, or the Bear Flag days. In his emphasis on the war years Grant had thrust forward a self-portrait that would comprise the most definitive statement on his character; why couldn't John C. Frémont forge a more durable defense of *his* life than was contained in yellowing War Department reports and court-martial minutes?

Most important, though, Grant had offered up his memories on the altar of his family's security. Almost broke, dying of cancer, old Unconditional Surrender had written with the same dogged tenacity that had finally taken Petersburg and broken that gallant Confederate Army; he had finished the book and even revised it, a prodigy of sheer courage. Surely Frémont could do as much for Jessie.

He became obsessed with the idea, persuaded Jessie to work with him each morning while he paced back and forth in the pinched living room on West 11th Street to shouts of children playing stickball outside the window; researching back into his childhood days, roaming the Charleston savannas, studying the stars. . . . When they reached the first expeditions he'd talked his wife and daughter into moving down to Washington: it was the only way to refresh themselves on the accurate details of those years. Lily had objected strenuously, maintaining it was putting all their eggs in one risky basket, and even Jessie's eyes had narrowed in remembrance of Capital vendettas; but in the end they'd both consented. They'd taken a furnished flat on Dupont Circle and settled in as best they could. But their Washington had disappeared—the courtly grace of prewar days had been swallowed up in a brash Yankee bureaucracy that was as offensive as it was arrogant. Frémont was already beginning to doubt the wisdom of the move. . . .

At Archives a bored, indifferent young captain looked at him with distaste. After a moment he indolently pulled down a huge leather-bound tome, consulted several pages, and led Frémont through room after room filled with blue and dun boxes on dusty shelves.

"There you are." The captain pointed to a nearly empty stack just beneath the ceiling. So few, Frémont thought in dismay, gazing upward. Was that all that remained of the arduous years of mapping all those millions of square miles, prairie and river and mountain? That handful of cases?

"Help yourself." The captain made a brief, contemptuous gesture toward a ladder stacked in a corner and turned away.

"Captain," Frémont said in an echo of the voice that had brought frightened, exhausted men to their feet in seconds, "I would be obliged if you would fetch that ladder and take down those boxes—for a retired major general of the Grand Army of the Republic. Then you may go."

The captain's eyes rolled up at him. "Yes, sir," he said, and got the ladder.

Frémont hooked his cane over the edge of the worktable and sat down heavily, ran his fingers over the case fronts. FRÉMONT, J. C., CAPT. Well, that was surely early enough. His life as a young soldier, engineer, astronomer, explorer, compressed into a single pasteboard box. He took a deep breath and opened it.

The box was empty.

He shut his eyes. Steady, he admonished himself; steady, now. Records could be mislaid, misfiled—it happened all the time. There were other boxes here. He unearthed Colonel Abert's correspondence book, which held copies of several querulous letters to Lieutenant Freemount, or Fremount, or Friemount—Abert never could get the names of subalterns right—complaining about lost equipment, overdrafts or supplies. Other names cropped up continually: Emory, Roper, Campbell. Not his. There were records of dam and levee projects, records on all five of the railroad surveys Jefferson Davis had commissioned in '52. But on his expeditions to South Pass and California, a handful of vouchers, pay records, lists of supplies—trivia, nothing more.

He sat there in the dim, silent corridor, gripping his hands together, beating down the nightmare sensation that he'd never existed, that all those arduous treks and careful starsights were no more than products of a fevered imagination. The cough erupted again, shaking him. A line from his childhood, from the Bible or maybe the Reverend Jasper Adams, rang in his head: *An enemy hath done this.* An enemy. . . . Of course they could have been released for the court-martial, and then mislaid—they might even have been lost by the printers; but he knew better.

Outside, the weather had shut down again; a needle-point sleet that stung his cheeks. Trudging up 10th Street, coughing compulsively, his free hand pressed against his chest, he thought, Thank God Jessie wasn't there—she'd have flayed every soldier within an inch of his life, demanded a congressional investigation. Old Toller Tom's girl, her eyes flashing in high indignation—

A carriage swung close to the curb, sprayed his trousers with gray slush. He bent over to brush them clean, was seized with vertigo, moved back and leaned gratefully against a building. Too far. He'd ridden too many miles in too many storms, plodded too long in deep snow, slept too often on wet ground under wet blankets; he'd climbed too high, strained too hard, carried his command burden too long, fighting down fear, checking guards, enforcing discipline—and for what? For *what,* in God's sweet name? So that some vengeful toady of Abert's, or Kearny's, or Hunter's, or Grant's could walk casually into Archives, quietly remove those papers and lose them in the deep six. . . .

Across the street was the white marquee of Ford's Theater. They had carried Lincoln across the street to where he now stood, brought him in here to die. Terrible, terrible. Still, that was the way to take your departure—swiftly and silently, at the cresting moment of high triumph . . .

Leaning against the gray stone he gave a groan that was like a prayer. He should have died like Kit, like Louie—even like Raffie Proue—

No. He thrust himself away from the building and tramped west on F Street, coughing dryly, heading toward the White House. No. Not like Proue. He would not lie down on the trail. No matter what.

She could not put it off any longer. She had brought Charles his lunch, done the dishes, put a pot roast in the oven; and all the while the business envelope lay on the edge of the table, a slender white threat. Intuition and long experience told her it contained no money. Deliberately she made herself a cup of tea, sipped at it, set it down—finally snatched up the envelope and tore it open.

My Dear General and Mrs. Frémont:

In answer to your queries, it grieves me to inform you that the sale for Volume I of the Memoirs *has been disappointing. Their excessive detail (particularly in regard to the expeditions) has clearly proven, as we feared, unpalatable to a general readership.*

Under the circumstances we feel that we cannot proceed, and therefore must terminate our agreement. Quite naturally we regret—

She went over to the window and stared down at Dupont Circle where carriages glided in smart parade, their wheels flashing in the low autumn sunlight. So there it was; what she'd dreaded, lying awake in the small hours. They were washing their hands of it: there would be no Volume II, no royalty income, no quiet vindication of a lifetime of service and controversy. It was all over.

It hadn't gone well from the beginning—it was as if the vanished files at Archives had been a warning. They'd returned to their old pattern of dictation and query, but none of it came easily; the silences grew longer and oppressive. It seemed like someone else's experience, Charles kept saying, like primitive daguerreotypes—frozen moments that didn't have anything to do with each other.

"We'll talk it out," she said. "We'll remember it together."

"You can't—you weren't there."

He wore down quickly; he was troubled with migraine headaches, bouts of nausea. He pushed himself, struggled on late into the night, reading and rereading the Reports, stifling the racking cough, pacing the floor, trying to summon up those years of audacity and triumph . . . and they would not come now. Fearing for him she had found him standing by the window at three o'clock one morning, holding the Wind River Peak flag against his chest, his hands shaking, his eyes hollow and wild.

"—I can't do it, Jessie," he cried. "I'm tired, I'm sick—I'm too old! I'm all played out. Body and mind both. I can't call it up anymore!"

"Hush, now," she said, holding him in her arms, rocking him gently. "It's all right, darling. Hush, now. And come and rest."

Defeated, they had incorporated the old Reports almost verbatim, held together by stitched-in passages. It made the book overlong, and curiously dated. It was an old man's measured view of his youth and Mexican exploits that had given Grant's memoirs a poignant and compelling perspective, she knew—but she lacked the energy to contend with Charles, face him down on it. He clung to the Reports like a drowning man, he wouldn't hear of altering them. Saddened, she acquiesced. Reality for him had always been rooted in action, precision. The only proof of his life lay in the Reports: they were his talisman.

He was coughing again. That spring his fever had soared, he'd collapsed. Dr. Harris came; she'd rigged a steam tent, and the small rooms stank of asafetida. Jessie understood pneumonia. It was dangerous, but if you were careful, if you rested adequately, it passed. Charles got better; he managed on sunny days to go out and sit in the circle and watch the traffic. He'd been impatient—he'd been eager then to get back to work on the memoirs.

But how would he react now? How would he take this final, irretrievable defeat?

Well, she had never lied to him before; she would not begin now.

She went up to the door to his study, paused a moment and composed herself, then knocked twice, shortly.

Dr. Harris closed the bedroom door with exaggerated care and came toward her. He had the mannerism of a village undertaker—small soft steps, hands frequently clasped, an unctuous deference.

"It is acute bronchitis," he said, with the tone of someone revealing a priceless vase. "The General's lungs are chronically weak, you see."

"Yes, I know."

He added in a disapproving tone: "I daresay *that's* the result of unduly hard living."

She started to reply, then glanced at him sharply. He meant . . . dear God, he meant it was the result of high living—drinking, wenching, debauchery! She could have laughed in his face if she hadn't been sick with worry. City practitioner, minister to the menial in this capital of power and affluence, how could he possibly conceive of riding all day through a blizzard, sleeping in deep snow, climbing where men had never dared to climb before?

He must have caught something in her expression. His mouth turned prim and forbidding; he said: "He *must* go to a warm climate, and at once."

"A warm climate."

"Without delay. It's October. With the cold weather, pneumonia will be a certain visitor."

The phrase enraged her—she wanted to snarl something scathing at this pompous little prig. Before she could decide what to say or do he added:

"My best opinion is that the General will not survive another winter in this climate." He cleared his throat. "I'm awfully sorry to have to tell you this."

"It's quite all right. Thank you, Doctor."

She sat at the kitchen table, conscious of the rosewood clock she'd rescued from Pocaho, conscious of hurrying time. Medical ultimatums. Seven years ago a doctor had passed sentence on her; now it was Charles . . .

A warm climate. They must get away, and quickly: somewhere warm—

the South, the desert, California . . . But he would never go South again—his homeland had slandered and reviled him, there would be no peace for him there; and the desert would destroy *her* and then she could not care for him. It would have to be California. Los Angeles—sunny, warm, indolent. Home. Near home.

But the *expense.* The rail tickets alone would eat up more than half their savings—they couldn't risk it, not with the failure of the *Mémoirs.* Their situation was more perilous than when she'd had to leave Charles in Prescott. She couldn't earn money as she had then—the editors were younger now, they looked at her with wary reluctance, even attempted to patronize her. The work came much harder, she was rejected more often; that dreaded day when she could no longer dredge up still another fresh incident from her life was coming swiftly.

Where, then? Where could she turn? They were near the end of a rope too long frayed thin; it certainly looked as if they were near—

She began to weep, silently, hopelessly; stifling the sound, her head bowed. Was he to die then, this man she loved more than life itself? Coughing out his lungs, faint with fever—because now, at the bleak, bitter end of his life they couldn't muster the price of train tickets? What a preposterous, macabre joke, for her to sit weeping in a cramped rented apartment in Washington, of all cities! Tom Benton's daughter, who had faced down Lincoln, dined with Polk, and amused Jackson. . . . Was it a very special kind of joke played solely on those fools who believed in brave and bold deeds, the rush of great events? But of course it wasn't the old Washington, her Washington, any longer—or maybe it never had been, and she simply hadn't seen it before; but now it was only a citadel of procurement and subvention, of lobbyists with suitcases crammed with greenbacks and plans for plunder—

She sat up then, suddenly, and dried her eyes. She could feel her jaw set, her eyes tighten subtly; her fighting face, Eliza used to call it. All right. So be it, then. It would be a kind of battle.

Moving very quietly she washed her face, put on her last good wool dress, and began carefully to rebraid her hair.

The doorbell gave its shrill, silvery cry. Jessie got to her feet and said: "That will be Collis Huntington."

"Collis?" Charles was sitting in his easy chair with a blanket over his lap and legs. "Are you sure?"

"Yes, I'm sure. He said he would call on us this evening."

He looked at her suspiciously then. He'd lost more weight; his face was white and very drawn. "For what reason?" he demanded.

"Because I asked him to."

"And why is that?"

"Can't an old friend drop in to see you?"

He glared at her. "I don't want to see him."

"Charles, you wouldn't be so rude!"

"I don't like this," he muttered as she went to the door.

Collis Huntington embraced her and came in with a rush of vigor. He was wearing an overcoat with a fur collar; an odor of expensive cologne clung to him. He'd grown heavier with the years and turned bald; his beard was beautifully trimmed and an emerald stickpin was centered on his silk tie. He'd come a very long way since he'd turned up at the Mariposa driving a wagon full of mining tools. He threw her a quick, sharp glance and then hurried across the room to shake hands with Charles, who had flung the blanket aside and got to his feet.

"Grand to see you again!" The note of exuberance in Collis' voice was forced. "How the years have whipped by, eh? Not an awful lot of us left from the old days."

Charles said icily: "You came here to inform me that we are aging?"

Collis stared at him a moment. "No, General," he answered in a different tone. "I came here to tell you that old friends ought to stick together. Jessie tells me you've been ill. I'm most sorry to hear that."

"It's nothing. Touch of grippe, that's all."

Collis shot that hard, sardonic glance at Jessie again, said: "Come on now, you know it's more than that. I can't tell you how glad I am I happened to be here in Washington. Jessie looked me up at the Willard—"

"She shouldn't have intruded on you," Charles snapped hotly.

His attitude—speaking directly to Huntington, acting as though she wasn't even in the room—angered her. "Charles, you know perfectly well you cannot stay here in the East any longer. Dr. Harris—"

"She should never have imposed on you," Charles repeated doggedly.

"Of course she should," Collis retorted pleasantly. "I'd never have forgiven her if she hadn't. Now, what you need is to head for California, muy pronto."

"California—!"

"Never heard of it? Land of perpetual sunshine—except when it rains. Or snows . . . Takes five locomotives to push one snowplow through Donner Pass. Forty-foot drifts! Thought of you when the first train went over—wish you could have been with us for that ride." He stopped grinning. "No, California's the place for you, and you know it. Everything's all arranged. Start late Thursday afternoon and then straight through to the coast! You ought to have my private car, but it's already lent." He turned and handed Jessie a handsome calfskin wallet. "I thought two compartments would be appropriate. And there are a couple of letters that'll help smooth the way."

She opened the wallet. There were tickets, letters—and a sheaf of bills. Hundred-dollar bills, a whole packet of them. She stared at him; she hadn't expected this.

"And there'll be expenses," he said in his bluff, hearty manner.

"Let me see that if I may," Charles demanded. He was woefully weak, but there was iron in his voice still; she had no choice. His face went cold as ice when he saw the money.

"This is uncommonly kind of you, Collis," he said with that exaggerated politeness that she knew concealed his deepest anger, "but it is entirely inappropriate. The fault is of course Jessie's. I would *never* have let her—"

"That's precisely why I didn't tell you!" she cried. "I knew you'd only make a fuss . . ." She glared back at him, furious, very near tears. Did he by any chance think it had been easy for her to knock on the door of that suite. She had never begged anyone's favor, friend or acquaintance, in her whole life—it had been all she could do to raise her hand and knock on that door. Couldn't he see that it was only the measure of her desperation, her despair?

"We can't possibly accept this," Charles said; he was still ignoring her. "You mean well, I know. But frankly, I find this insulting. I must ask you to take it back immediately."

Without hesitation Collis stepped forward and took the wallet from Charles' hand. Oh, sweet God, Jessie thought. Now he'll turn away and leave—and what will be gained?

But Collis stood there in the middle of the room, slapping the wallet reflectively against his palm.

"Charlie," he said, reverting to his old hardware merchant's manner, "I've known you for—what? twenty-five years. Give or take. Always admired you, more than you can guess. You've got about as much fiber as anyone I've ever known—and that's a quality I count high. There isn't a man on this globe who could have done the things *you* did . . . But you still don't know one damn thing about business. You never did. You mind my telling you that?"

"I should imagine that was dramatically evident by now," Charles answered tartly; though he seemed somewhat mollified.

"Well, I'm going to tell you the cardinal rule of good business: you make sure you get every penny that's due you—and you pay every penny you owe."

"I've honored the last part of that, all right."

"Yes, you have." Collis was not smiling. "And with interest . . . But you never cared about the first part. Your mistake is thinking I'm trying to give you something here. I'm not. I don't give away one hell of a lot. *That's* bad business, too. But I always pay my debts." His eyes rested on the other man with a steady, shrewd interest. "That railroad is my pride and joy, Charlie. We couldn't have driven that golden spike if it wasn't for you. You forget our road goes over your buried campfires—and climbs many a grade you jogged over on a mule." He set the wallet on the table gently. "I think we rather owe you this."

It was the last journey. He knew it deep in his belly. A last glimpse of the Capitol dome, with its burning memories of Toller Tom Benton, and the court-martial, and Bancroft's bland, veiled eyes . . . and now they were running up along the Potomac in one of George Pullman's fancy cars; past Manassas Junction, and Ball's Bluff, through the gap to Harpers Ferry where mad old Osawatomie Brown had started it all, and where Nat Banks had fled in wild disorder from the incomparable Stonewall Jackson. And then Frémont could look down the long Valley where those ragged, unconquerable rebel boys had humbled them all. Shenandoah. . . . At its far end was White Oak Ridge, and the Mill Creek at Cross Keys, where he'd sat his horse at the edge of the woods and drawn his pistol—always his weapon—and waited again for the pale rider, who had swept near him—and again passed him by . . .

He turned and took Jessie's hand. "You were right to come, honey. I feel better already."

"Oh, Charles." Gazing at him she all at once burst into tears. A young conductor came out of nowhere.

"What is it, madam? Is there anything at all I can do?"

"No, no," she protested, laughing and crying at the same time. "The General says he feels better. And you see, that's all that matters right now . . ."

The Mississippi swept its broad, majestic course south to the Gulf, burnished gold in the afternoon sun. Jessie leaned forward, thinking of that torrid July morning with all river traffic stilled, the Confederate flag flying from Judge Berthold's home, and young Gaines' voice guarded and fearful. Such a dark hour . . . Now barges and stern-wheelers plied its gleaming expanse, and smoke billowed from a forest of tall stacks. St. Louis was a great city. She'd known it when her father and Pierre Chouteau had been its two most important citizens; now they said it took a matched pair half an hour merely to drive the length of Rue Royale . . . Their car entered a web of rail lines, tracks crossing and recrossing in a glitter of steel. How Mr. T would laugh and wag his shaggy head at such teeming vindication! Twenty years ago she'd stood here in Lafayette Park and pulled the silken cord; the white drapery had fallen away and there was Papa, in gleaming bronze, looking like the grand old Roman he was, facing west, as he'd have wanted. The band had played "Hail, Columbia!" 40,000 people had roared their approval, and an outgoing train to San Francisco had saluted him three times, its whistle echoes drifting west; and in spite of her good intentions her eyes had filled with joyful tears . . .

Across the wide Missouri then, past towns as familiar as her childhood—Gasconade, Mokane; at Franklin—now New Franklin, rebuilt—Charles pointed toward the levee and said:

"Right there. Where I first saw Kit, coming on board. And wasn't he mad when I told him I'd never heard of him! I knew right then he was the man for me."

On to Council Bluffs and out along the Platte, "a mile wide and an inch deep," the wheels clicking their insistent, staccato rhythm: *Hurrying west, galloping free,* the vast prairie sky opening up like a brand new world aborning, everything unfettered and possible. She could feel her spirits rise, the last cold grip of the East slipping away. Charles was talking more now, remembering Tom Fitzpatrick cussing at him: "There is only *two* kinds of mules, Cap'n—them as is beat out and them as is balky!" Remembering the awful time the barometer had broken and he'd taken a powder horn, boiled and stretched it and scraped it thin as glass, secured it to the tube with glue rendered from buffalo tendons, and bailed out the expedition. Remembering lying huddled close with Louie around a fire, with ten thousand buffalo grazing and snorting all around them, remembering the lordly Wahanatan placing his hands on his shoulders, offering to make him a Sioux warrior. . . .

Here, in the open country, people began to recognize him. At Grand Island a heavyset man with a checkered vest stopped to shake his hand. "Hope you don't mind the intrusion, General. Name's Lindstrom, farming tools. Real pleasure, sir." Word ran ahead of them. At a town named Kearney where they'd stopped to take on water, a little crowd had gathered; the mayor gave Jessie an armful of her favorite white roses and made a speech which Charles gracefully acknowledged.

"Spelled his name wrong," he said later, with a trace of his quick, mischievous grin. "Wouldn't that have made the old tyrant furious, though? Can't you hear him?"

Climbing now, through red rock spires and tables, the Medicine Bow Mountains looming up ahead like harsh white waves cresting. At Laramie she was confused. "But—this isn't what we wrote about. Where's the fort?"

He shook his head. "That's the *old* Laramie—up on the North Platte. Long abandoned. It'll be gone by now. Melted away in the snow and rain."

"But why? Why let it go like that?"

"It was a trapper's fort, Jessie. It died with the trade. Things change."

A courier came on board saying that if they would disembark and make a short detour, the leading citizens of Denver would be happy to give them a grand testimonial dinner. Courteously Charles refused, and they sat in silence for a time, thinking their own thoughts. Catching her eye he said:

"Things change, Jessie. That's not for me now. . . . You didn't really want to accept, did you?"

"No," she answered honestly, and stuck out her lower lip. "But I'd much rather be invited than not!" She laughed when he smiled.

Sometime late in the night she awakened, her heart thumping and her mouth dry. Mountains. The train was moving more slowly now, laboring; the air had that thin, elusive feel to it, as though there weren't enough of it to inhale. Mountains: her enemy now. Charles' glory. She forced herself to breathe slowly and deeply, thinking of Prescott and the oven wind slipping through the shutters, and the way her writing swam and trembled on the page. . . . Well, this was her last crossing of the Great Divide; she'd be back to sea level and her beloved deep blue Pacific in a few days. . . .

The train was running faster now, they had cleared the pass; a moment later she heard the brakes go on, felt the oddly sexual, pulsing motion under her recumbent body. She fell asleep thinking about trains and railroads, loving and hating them.

Frémont had become aware of the man for several minutes; spare, like himself, with a drooping silver mustache, a high-crowned plains hat and a string tie; about his age, give or take a few years. The farmer had a child in each hand. One of the boys reminded him of Charley—a certain alert turn of his head. They were walking on the hardpan in front of the station at Provo, stretching their legs.

"Named for old Provost," he said to Jessie. "He'd have liked that." The fall air held that tart, winy bite that always excited him, made him want to saddle up and ride for miles drinking in the peppery odors of yarrow and sage. "When I came through here in '43 there was nothing, Jessie." He pointed his cane at the row of storefronts, the houses stretching off toward the hills. "Can you imagine that? Nothing at all. If you had told me—"

"Colonel Frémont?"

He turned. The farmer had come up to him, still holding the little boys. "Yes," he said.

"I recognized you right away—from the posters, back when you were running for high office. Heard you were coming through." He extended a hand. "My name's James Harbiston." He raised his hat to Jessie and murmured: "Ma'am," then turned to the children. "These are my two grandsons, James and Andrew. Boys, I want you to say hello to Colonel John C. Frémont. You're going to be proud of this moment for the rest of your lives, hear?"

Frémont took the small, eager hands in his, smiled down at the awestruck, innocent eyes. "How do you do," he said.

"I want you to know, sir: you turned my life around," Harbiston said. "And all for the better. Came out with a small party in '54. Martha carried your Report on her lap the whole way, treated it like the family Bible—which it was, in a way." He glanced at Jessie. "I don't mean that disrespectfully, ma'am. Martha—she's dead now eight years, but never was anyone more alive when she was with us. Nothing fazed her! Not like me—I've always been one for studying the lay of the land first." He paused, embarrassed, struggling for the words, marshaling them. "I'm a hard worker, Colonel. I came out here to work, and that's what I did. Ones that won't work don't last long. But I've never been a specially *courageous* feller. Doing what you did—shoot, I wouldn't have lasted three weeks! But your Report—that's what gave *me* all the courage I needed: told me how to get where I was going, and what I'd find when I got there."

He drew on the end of his mustache, squinting off toward the Wasatches. "I've raised a fine family over there near Salem. Got a thousand acres in wheat and more than three hundred head of cattle. My sons are working it—one of 'em's named for you, Colonel: John Charles Harbiston."

"I'm honored, sir," Frémont said.

"Thought you'd like to hear that. I just take it easy now; hurt my back a few years ago. Do a few odd jobs, read the paper. Bring my grandsons in to town, maybe spoil 'em a little. . . ."

"I'm pleased it worked out so well, Mr. Harbiston," Frémont said.

"It did. It's been a good life, for all the hard times. . . . And I saw you and Mrs. Frémont walking up and down, and I decided I'd never get another chance . . . so I just come up to say thank you for all you done for me and my neighbors here in the valley. All those years ago."

"I'm glad you did." Frémont took the hard hand again. "There's nothing I'd rather hear than what you've just said." He saw Harbiston turn in sudden consternation, glanced at Jessie. She was standing perfectly straight and smiling broadly—and tears were coursing down her cheeks.

She came wide awake all at once, as if someone had shaken her, and pushed back the curtain. A rectangle of light flared in the huge black expanse of land: barn doors flung open, lanterns placed low, crouching figures: cow birthing. Farther on a campfire burned red, sparks swirling on the wind, and two cowboy faces stared out at the train's passing, eyes glinting like the eyes of wild animals.

She drew on her dressing gown and moved across to Charles' section—saw his berth was empty. He was sitting by the window, fully dressed, chin on his hand, gazing out. For a long moment she watched him, the shifting play of expression on his fine, handsome features, tracing the course of his life on this last somber journey west. Once his fist clenched and his face set in an anger that deepened into the most intense despair; then the barest trace of a smile drew up the corners of his lips—then they parted in gentle, almost childlike wonder . . . and still she hung there motionless, gazing at this man she loved without lesion or reservation, who lay as close to her as the beating of her own heart.

Slowly his head turned, his eyes met hers: a long, steady gaze, the most naked, vulnerable look they had ever exchanged. Then she came over and sat beside him, took his hand.

"You should try to sleep," she said finally. "For a little."

"No. Not tonight." He shook his head vigorously. "Have to see it all . . . We brought the gun up through here," he said. "Took us two days to snake it up on hand lines, slipping and skidding and falling all the way. . . . Look how they've done it: started the grade two miles back there, snugged right into the curve of the river. . . . That damned brass cannon."

His voice had fallen, she had to strain to hear him. "I made a lot of mistakes, didn't I? Got into rapids I never should have tried. . . . It was a matter of judgment. I could always pick men for the field. Oh, a few wrong 'uns; not many. Louie, Kit, Alex—they never let me down. It was the politicians that betrayed me; and the money men. I never understood them, they never thought the way I did. They led me down into a box canyon every time. . . . And I didn't learn from it. I kept thinking the next project would turn out differently. I let the wrong things turn me off the trail."

"No," she said. "It was the pressure of all those demands."

"No. I let them tempt me. And then I wouldn't admit the situation. Face up to it." He sighed. "I guess in the end I've just been too proud."

"Yes," she said. "It was our biggest fault, yours and mine. Yet it served us, too. Don't forget that."

"Sometimes I think I could have led this country, led it well. But maybe not. Maybe the politicians would always have used me, trapped me, led me astray . . ."

"You still did," she said.

"Did what?"

"Led the country. It's yours." She gripped his worn hand in both of hers, cradling it. "You charted it, you defended it. You gave them the banner they needed for the war—even though they didn't have the courage or the wisdom to recognize that—and you gave them the general who could hammer it through . . . and then you withdrew, to heal the country—and only I know how much you did heal it, and what you suffered in the doing. . . . You didn't have to be President, or General of the Army either. It's true, you know. What they chanted: *Free-men, Free-mont!* . . . You led the country, anyway. It's yours."

His eyes seemed to seek to pierce the dark like an arrow as they watched a star, a distant campfire. "I had such visions, Jessie!" he cried softly. "What could be done—the limitless horizon . . ."

"It's still there," she said. "You gave it to them. That's why they're out there, Charles—all those people: you made it possible for them to live their dream. They're all here because of you. No one can do any more than that."

"Perhaps," he said after a moment. "Anyhow, it was worth it." He looked away, out of the window again. "First light," he murmured. "And there's old Arcturus, flashing away up there. . . . I hope that's the last thing I see—the stars. I'd like that."

They sat side by side, their hands entwined, swaying to the jolting roll of the train, while around them the new day lightened to slate, to soft pearl and saffron hues; and far ahead rose the towering alabaster wall of the high Sierra, their summits stained rose from the sun's first rays.

"California," he said, and his eyes flashed like swords.

"Yes." She drew him to her gently. "Oh, Charles—we're going home. . . ."